THE EMPIRE OF BONES SAGA VOLUME FOUR

TERRY MIXON

YOWLING
CAT PRESS

Published by Yowling Cat Press ®

Digital edition date: 6/21/2023

Print ISBN: 978-1947376434

Individual Works

Race to Terra Copyright © 2019 by Terry Mixon

Print ISBN: 978-1947376144

Ruined Terra © 2019 by Terry Mixon

Print ISBN: 978-1947376298

Victory on Terra Copyright © 2020 by Terry Mixon

Print ISBN: 978-1947376342

Cover art - image copyrights as follows:

Thanapol Sinsrang | Dreamstime.com

Luca Oleastri

Donna Mixon

Cover design and composition by Donna Mixon

Print design and layout by Terry Mixon

Audio edition performed and produced by Veronica Giguere

Reach her at: v@voicesbyveronica.com

ALSO BY TERRY MIXON

You can always find the most up to date listing of Terry's titles on his Amazon Author Page.

Note: the links below (ebook only, obviously) redirect you to my website where you can click a button to go to Amazon. This allows me to participate in Amazon's associates program and earn a little more. Sorry for any inconvenience.

The Last Hunter

The Last Hunter

Bonds of Blood

Alpha Strike

The Enemy Revealed

Command Authority

The Grand Conspiracy

Shield of Humanity

Fog of War

Ships of the Line

Operation Liberty

The Empire of Bones Saga

Empire of Bones

Veil of Shadows

Command Decisions

Ghosts of Empire

Paying the Price

Recon in Force

Behind Enemy Lines

The Terra Gambit

Hidden Enemies

Race to Terra

Ruined Terra

Victory on Terra

When Luck Runs Out

Gunboat Diplomacy

The Imperial Marines Saga

Spoils of War

Imperial Recruit

Enemy Action

The Humanity Unlimited Saga

Liberty Station

Freedom Express

Tree of Liberty

Blood of Patriots

Single Novels

Scorched Earth

Storm Divers

The Vigilante Series with Glynn Stewart

Heart of Vengeance

Oath of Vengeance

Bound By Law

Bound By Honor

Bound By Blood

Box Sets

The Empire of Bones Saga Volume 1

The Empire of Bones Saga Volume 2

The Empire of Bones Saga Volume 3

The Empire of Bones Saga Volume 4

Humanity Unlimited Publisher's Pack 1

Humanity Unlimited Publisher's Pack 2

Want to get updates from Terry about new books and other general nonsense going on in his life? He promises there will be cats. Go to TerryMixon.com/Mailing-List and sign up.

DEDICATION

This book would not be possible without the love and support of my beautiful wife. Donna, I love you more than life itself.

ACKNOWLEDGMENTS

I want to thank the folks that support me on Patreon. You got to read this book as I was writing it and that kept me working. You have my deepest thanks.

In particular, I want to thank those patrons that supported me at the $10 level and above:

Bryan Barnes
Tracy Bodine
Dave Dolan
David Goldstein
John Kilgallon
Christian A. Michelsen
Lisa Slack
Dale Thompson
Clark Williams

Finally, I want to thank my readers for putting up with me. You guys are great.

RACE TO TERRA

BOOK TEN

Separated by an almost unimaginable gulf in space, Princess Kelsey Bandar and Admiral Jared Mertz must fight to stop the diabolical artificial intelligences that destroyed the Old Terran Empire.

Though unable to communicate with one another, they must overcome terrible odds and defeat foes determined to kill or enslave them. They cannot allow themselves to fail.

Yet time is running out. Unless both quickly make their way to Terra, the computers win and humanity loses.

1

Jared Mertz watched Lieutenant Commander Anthony O'Halloran drill a small hole into the crate with a sense of dread. Justified concern about what they were doing made his harsh breathing echo inside his suit helmet, and the stench of his own sweat burned his nose.

He had no idea how the marines handled working and fighting in suits even more constricted than his. Princess Kelsey, especially. How did she stand it?

The large crate was one of six secured in *Athena*'s hold, each filled with a tenacious, horrifying bioweapon of incredible lethality the Rebel Empire called the Omega Plague. All the crates were protected by plasma-based self-destruct charges, which he had no codes to disarm.

He did have the codes to open the crates, picked up when their unwelcome guest had opened them to load the bioweapon, but he couldn't be sure the crates wouldn't send a signal to the man. He couldn't take that chance, so they were doing this the old-fashioned way.

If their attempt at examining the charges drew a negative response, all the crates would likely detonate. They'd determined there was more than enough explosive potential here to take out the fusion plant in engineering. That would kill them all quite effectively.

"How certain are you that the charges won't detect your intrusion, Tony?" Jared asked through his short-range com. They had to make sure that no one else on the ship detected them. Their new Rebel Empire guests wouldn't be very happy with what they were doing, so it was best to keep them in the dark.

They were sleeping at the moment, so Jared was relatively confident of carrying this off. Unless they killed everyone in the process.

"Pretty sure," O'Halloran said. "Of course, if I'm wrong, you won't have much time to yell at me. As in we'll never know that I tripped a failsafe."

The engineer pulled the drill bit back out from the hole he'd just created and slowly inserted a fiber camera. "I can see the charge Princess Kelsey mentioned on this wall of the container. There are three more in plain view, and probably some I can't see. I wish Katheryn was here. She had a much steadier hand than me."

Commander Katheryn Pence had been *Athena*'s chief engineer before they'd had to subdue the party of Rebel Empire nobles sent to commandeer the supposedly robot-controlled destroyer at El Capitan. She and nine others had died in the fighting when his crew had retaken the ship.

They'd captured a fair number of the enemy but had lost all but one of them when their leader set off secret bombs planted in every one of her people's skulls, including her own.

Only the fact that Olivia West had been questioning one of the prisoners on the other side of the ship had saved that last one. The fact that Jared had locked the com system down had prevented the woman from using it to be sure she got all of her people and had stopped her from setting off the self-destruct charges on the cargo, he suspected.

"I wish she were here, too," Jared said tiredly. "You'll just have to do the best you can, Tony. I have confidence in you."

"At least one of us does," the engineer muttered as he focused on the task at hand. "I'm pretty sure this charge has an antitampering circuit, just like I suspected it would. At least that's what I think I'm looking at."

Jared linked his implants into the low-powered feed and examined what the man was examining. The charge itself was fairly bulky when compared to the plasma grenades the marines favored. It looked like a permanent part of the crate, too.

"What is the antitampering part?" he asked.

"See how there are several bands around the device? Those cover the access ports I'd need to use to get into the casing holding the detonator. It's a safe bet they are rigged to notice if someone is messing with the device unless the appropriate code is entered first."

"I suppose that was unavoidable," Jared said with a sigh. "We weren't going to get that lucky. What would happen if you cut the case open?"

"I think Major Scala might be a better person to answer that question. He's at least taken the ordinance disposal course."

Jared half turned and gestured *Athena*'s senior marine officer over from the hatch he was standing with his men. "Adrian, could you tell us what you think about this bomb? Any chance you could defuse it?"

The marine came to stand beside them, not speaking for a few moments as he reviewed his own implant feed.

"That's a disaster waiting to happen, sir," the marine officer finally said. "The charge is wrapped up tight. If we screw with it, boom!"

"That's what I was afraid of," Jared grumbled. "There's no way to get a probe into the case and deactivate it?"

"I wouldn't chance it. This technology is too good to miss the intrusion. If it thinks you're screwing with it, it'll go off and take its friends with it. Even jamming the signals wouldn't help. The other charges are probably using encrypted signals to one another to make sure that nothing like that happens.

"If they stop getting updates, they'll be programed to suspect enemy action," the marine concluded. "Hell, they might be rigged to detect a detonation and go off before the plasma wave front can destroy them."

So much for that idea. They'd have to do this the hard way.

"Seal the crate up, and let's make sure it doesn't look tampered with," Jared ordered. "We'll have to maintain the masquerade for a while longer. We're almost two weeks out from Terra. Fielding only extended the timer for a week, so he has plans before we get there. We'll just have to deal with him as best we can."

"Any idea what he has in mind?" Scala asked. "I'd like nothing better than to stun the bastard and put him in chains."

"Sadly, that's probably not going to happen. At least not without us knowing a lot more than we do right now."

He gestured for the marine to accompany him back to the hatch leading out of the cargo bay. "We have his nephew on our side—at least I think we do—and he might be able to get more out of the man than we've been able to."

Austin Darrah had been the only survivor of the Rebel Empire leader's treachery and knew the AIs would cheerfully kill him if they discovered he was alive, so Jared believed he'd help them, though he was loath to take things at face value on so short an acquaintance.

Since the young tech wizard was also Oscar Fielding's nephew, the old man probably had something in mind to extract him from the AI's mad plan to exterminate all human life on Terra. Jared just didn't know what it was.

He wanted to rub his face in frustration, but that would have to wait until he was out of his suit. Then he could return to his cabin and take a much-needed shower.

Fielding had kicked him out of his original cabin, so he'd had to bump everyone else because that was how the Rebel Empire worked. Appearances and status carried real weight, so he'd had to make a show of evicting his subordinates.

Still, Jared didn't have it as bad as his wife. Elise Orison, the crown princess of Pentagar, was sleeping in a maintenance tube and not at all pleased with her current accommodations.

To their mutual displeasure, she couldn't risk creeping into his bed at night for fear someone on the opposing team would see her.

"Wrap it up, people," he said. "Fielding will be up and looking for his breakfast in a few hours. Get some sleep. You've earned it."

He'd have just enough time to clean up and get to the officers' mess. Austin Darrah and Olivia West would be waiting for him, as would Princess Kelsey Bandar.

Rather, the version of her from another reality. That was one more complication added to an already convoluted situation.

Well, their difficulties wouldn't get any easier if he didn't work on them. At least he was mostly certain that his sister from another universe wouldn't stick a knife in his back at the first opportunity. She wanted something she couldn't get without him.

Still, it might be best to keep her out of the kitchen. There were a lot of sharp instruments in there.

As he let himself out of the cargo hold, he wondered how his real sister was doing. They hadn't had any contact after Kelsey had daringly stolen the Dresden orbital, with all its advanced research technology intact and entire.

He hoped she'd found another way home to the New Terran Empire and was even now meeting with her father, safe and sound. One of them deserved some breaks.

* * *

PRINCESS KELSEY BANDAR hunched over her desk aboard the Marine Raider strike ship *Persephone* and clutched her head in her hands. How the hell was she going to get her people out of this system and back home again?

They couldn't go through the multi-flip point back the way they'd come. Their FTL probes in the Icebox system still showed the Clan warships scouring everything, looking for the people who'd destroyed their battle station on the other side of what Carl Owlet had started calling a far flip point because it was unusually distant from the sun.

Maddeningly, it hadn't even been Kelsey's people that had stirred them up, but they'd sure as hell catch the blame if the fragment of the Old Empire calling itself the Clans found them.

Commander Raul Castille—the Rebel Empire security officer they'd captured aboard the Dresden orbital—had made certain to drop the name of the New Terran Empire before he'd obliterated the battle station he'd discovered on the other side of the far flip point.

Those damned far flip points had never even been predicted by theory, or so Carl had said, so Kelsey had never even considered having her probes look way out there for a flip point. At least the bastard's destruction of the Clan battle station had bought them enough time to set up a defense when the first Clan warships came into the Icebox system with blood in their eyes.

She'd tried to talk them down, but they'd come in shooting, so she'd punched their lights out. That garnered her thirteen prisoners: twelve from the Clans and one from a different political entity called the Singularity.

Once she'd had her people scour the wreckage for survivors, they'd fled back through the multi-flip point just before the follow-up wave of Clan warships arrived in the Icebox system.

Since there were no other exits from the system, it would only be so long until the Clans started trying to send ships through the multi-flip point. There was nowhere else the people that had attacked them could have come from or retreated to, after all.

The Clans didn't have the technology that Carl had put together on the fly to allow *Audacious* and the freighter with them to get through the multi-flip point, but that didn't mean they couldn't get help from the Singularity to do so. Kelsey couldn't rule it out, so she had to consider it only a matter of time before the Clans made the attempt.

Without frequency modulators on the flip drive, a ship might or might not be able to get through one. It turned out that of her ships, only *Persephone* could make it through the one in the Icebox system without a modulator.

Marine Raider strike ships were the smallest class of flip-capable vessel Kelsey had ever heard of, so the odds of the Clans having something capable of making the trip were small indeed.

The multi-flip points behaved oddly when a ship without a modulator tried to use them. While they had a number of potential destinations, ships without modulators went to a kind of default branch of the wormhole.

In the case of the Icebox multi-flip point, the default was back into the Rebel Empire, to an empty system near Dresden. Thankfully, that was not where Kelsey and her people had fled, so that provided them some additional breathing space.

Worse for the Clans, ships without modulators couldn't easily leave the Icebox system via the multi-flip point at all. The default branch of the multi-flip point was too constricted to allow any unmodulated transit.

That was something the Clans knew from experience. They'd fled the fall of the Old Empire through that very flip point over five hundred years ago and had been unable to get back through from the Icebox side.

That didn't mean it was impossible. Her people had found the wreck of a Clan battlecruiser named *Dauntless* crashed on the main world in the Pandora system where they'd ended up. A long examination of the burned-out flip drive on the wreck found a jury-rigged frequency modulator that Carl believed had barely allowed the ship to make the flip, much like his initial work had allowed *Audacious* to get there, with pretty much the same catastrophic results to the flip drive.

Of course, the Clans might not make the attempt. For reasons that Carl couldn't explain in words of fewer than six syllables, the size of the vessel transiting without a modulator determined where it would go, and it didn't seem consistent from branch to branch.

From the Old Empire branch, coming from the Old Empire, everything ended up in the Icebox system by default. Coming from the Icebox side, probes went back to the Old Empire.

That was good, as she couldn't in good conscience allow the Clans access to Pandora, though she could hardly stop a determined incursion with the few ships at her command.

The Pandora system held a mysterious alien race. Yet just to keep things confusing, they weren't nearly as alien as they looked. Even with their blue skins, they had modified human DNA inside them. A modification that had altered them long before humans had developed space travel at all.

That was a mystery that she'd have loved to solve, but no easy answers presented themselves. Hell, none of her problems had easy answers.

They'd managed to take *Persephone* through the multi-flip point down a branch leading to a major Rebel Empire system called Archibald. The mission there had been harrowing but ultimately successful.

They'd penetrated a Rebel Empire shipyard and managed to insert Carl's plans for a flip drive with a built-in modulator. Then they'd stolen a freighter once they'd had the drive delivered there.

Only, as usual, things weren't that simple. The freighter happened to be a Q-ship—a warship disguised as a freighter—and it had put up a lot more fight than her little group had counted on. They'd triumphed in the end but had more prisoners than they could shake a stick at.

Which brought her to the mess she was currently dealing with.

The people manning that ship claimed to be part of the resistance movement inside the Rebel Empire. The cargo they'd put together had certainly made that a possibility, but it was a claim that she had no way to validate. Not without someone like Olivia West at her side, and her friend was far, far away. Way beyond contact unless Carl made an unexpected breakthrough with the FTL coms.

And, to top matters off, Kelsey's mother had stowed away on the mission. She was certain that the woman was going to cause her terrible trouble, no matter how contrite the ex-empress of the Terran Empire was currently acting.

God, this was giving her a terrible headache and a burning desire to smash something.

A rap at her hatch gave her a welcome distraction to focus on. Major Angela Ellis, her executive officer—and soon to become the new commanding officer of *Persephone*—stood outside.

The woman had no idea that Kelsey had decided to pass command of the ship to her yet. She'd probably be both pleased and terrified at the idea of commanding the warship, but the computer running the Marine Raider strike ship only allowed Marine Raiders to command her.

And with the woman's now-completed upgrade, the New Terran Empire had a whole two Marine Raiders to choose from.

"Hey," Angela said cheerily. "I'm heading to the gym. You want to come down and beat me to a pulp?"

The days that Kelsey could still use her experience to toss the tall, powerful marine around the mat were numbered. Probably only a few more days, really. If that.

She might as well enjoy the current situation as long as she could. Once the marine officer got her proverbial and actual feet under her, she'd thrash Kelsey five times out of five.

Angela would become the new powerhouse in the Terran Empire. Right up until Kelsey's husband, Russ Talbot, finished the Marine Raider upgrade in a few weeks.

That thought made her smile. Wouldn't that make for some strenuous evenings in the bedroom?

Kelsey rose to her feet with a grateful smile. "I would love to. Let's go."

2

Olivia West arrived in the officers' mess before the others. Commander Kaitlinn Cannon was already herding several shanghaied assistants around the kitchen, and the wonderful smell of something frying brought Olivia partly awake.

"Tell me you have coffee," she begged the ship's assistant tactical officer.

"I have coffee," Kaitlinn confirmed. "It's in the urn over there. It's the good stuff, too. We wouldn't want to disappoint our *guest*." The final word held a note of disgust.

Fielding's taste for the better things in life had become apparent at dinner last night. It had been the first meal they'd shared with the man, and he'd set a high bar for what he'd accept on his table.

Luckily for them, Kaitlinn had been a chef before she'd joined Fleet. A damned good one, it seemed. Her skills in the kitchen were good enough to pass muster, though Fielding bitched about just about every aspect of the meal.

Once Olivia had poured herself some coffee, added sweetener and creamer, and taken her first delicious sip, she stepped over and watched the other woman frying some bacon while simultaneously scrambling eggs.

"I never did ask, but how did you go from cooking delicious food to shooting at people?"

"If you'd ever been a chef, you'd realize how short a step it is from cooking to wanting to kill people," the brunette said with a wide grin, her hands seeming to move on autopilot as she worked. "Seriously though, it was mainly to piss off my mother. She demanded that I work in my father's restaurant, and I basically picked about the opposite sort of thing I could think of as soon as I could."

"What did your father think of your career change?"

The woman laughed. "He fronted me my living expenses while I got my feet back under me and encouraged me to make a clean break so I could have my own life. Without telling my mother he'd done so, of course. He's not an idiot, my father."

Kaitlinn scooped the eggs into a container, slid it under a warmer, and started putting sausage on the grill to cook. "He'd have loved for me to stay at the restaurant, but he knew that I'd never get out from under Mother's thumb.

"And let me add that being deployed to the far side of the Empire was a blessing. She couldn't come and try to guilt me into coming back to the restaurant. Basically, blowing things up was just a bonus."

Olivia laughed. "Well, we're lucky to have you here with us. I doubt Fielding would be at all happy with my cooking."

The other woman's expression darkened. "That man is a conceited ass that thinks he deserves everything served to him on a silver platter. Literally. His kind annoys the hell out of me. Are you sure I can't just poison him?"

"Sadly, no," Olivia said dryly. "We need him alive."

"Pity," Kaitlinn said as she flipped the sausage. "I'm pretty sure I could time the effects just right, so that he plopped face down onto his empty plate. Wasting food is a sin," she added virtuously.

Olivia laughed. "You terrify me. I'm never going to get onto your bad side."

Movement in the corner of her vision made her turn her head and she saw Austin Darrah entering the mess, talking with Princess Kelsey.

Austin was a fellow member of the higher orders of the Rebel Empire, so she knew a lot about his background and upbringing, even though she'd always been a member of the resistance. His ability to work with advanced hardware was an intriguing twist, though.

Princess Kelsey Bandar, on the other hand, was a cypher. She looked exactly like her counterpart from this universe—one of Olivia's closest friends—but she was different in so many unexpected ways, and not all of them easy to predict.

Kelsey Two—as she'd started mentally referring to the woman—and Austin seemed to be getting along pretty well, chatting without any of the hostility or the obvious distrust the woman showed her Jared Mertz. In her universe, it seemed he was a villain. At least it was hard to come to any other conclusion based on the actions the man seemed to have taken.

Considering how different this Kelsey was, that wasn't completely unbelievable.

Once the others had gotten coffee, Olivia joined them at one of the tables. It was utilitarian, and so were the settings, something Fielding bitterly complained about, but she'd made certain to remind the man how this had been a robotic destroyer before they'd appropriated it, and he was lucky to have chairs. Needless to say, that hadn't gone over so well.

Too damned bad.

"Good morning," Olivia said. "I hope you both slept well."

"Surprisingly, yes," Austin said cheerfully as he flopped down in his seat in a somewhat disorganized manner. "It's amazing how relaxing having the bomb in your head removed can be. Who knew?"

The Rebel Empire had put explosives into their chosen crews' heads, all of whom had come from the higher orders. She and her associates hadn't known that when Jared had retaken the ship. The enemy leader had awoken, discovered their fate, and killed her entire crew, except for Austin, who'd been out of range at the time.

The young man hadn't been pleased when he'd found out that Doctor Stone had removed it, simply because he'd been certain that would set it off. It would have if they hadn't cleaned up the programing in his implants first.

Thankfully, Olivia hadn't been in a compartment where any of the original prisoners had died. The blasts had been more than sufficient to obliterate the prisoners' heads and rip their torsos open. Gory and horrifying, she'd been told. She was deeply glad she hadn't had to assist in the cleanup.

"Excellent," Olivia said, turning her attention to Kelsey Two. "And how did you sleep?"

"Fine," the short blonde woman said, her expression plainly revealing that as a lie. "I don't suppose I could get some food before Fielding gets here, could I? I'm starving and don't want to clue him in that I have to eat more than everyone else. It's both dangerous and humiliating."

Kaitlinn had obviously already been executing that plan, because she set a plate heaped high with scrambled eggs, sausage, bacon, and toast in front of the princess from another universe.

"Here you go, Highness. I'll have some orange juice for you in a bit. Wave at me if you want seconds and I'll fix you right up."

"You are a *saint*," Kelsey said gratefully, digging into her meal even as the cook headed back for the juice.

"Why do you need to eat so much?" Austin asked even as Kaitlinn delivered the juice. "Forgive me for saying so, but someone of your... ah, small stature, should need less food, not more. And why is she calling you 'highness'?"

Kelsey looked at Olivia but didn't stop eating.

"Those are some of the secret things Jared said he'd fill you in on in due time," Olivia said. "Since you've become aware of them, I'll make a down payment on that promise by asking Kelsey to briefly explain, without going into too much of the background."

The other woman wouldn't want to talk about how she'd been brutalized by a mad computer when it had forcefully implanted Marine Raider hardware in her. Without anesthesia. Even the idea of something like that made Olivia shiver with horror. It would've driven her mad.

"A few years ago," Kelsey said between bites, "I was presented with the nonnegotiable opportunity to test out a few upgrades in implantable hardware. Part of that was artificial muscles. One aspect of having them means my body runs through calories like a top athlete in training. I'm always hungry and eat whenever I get the chance."

"Nonnegotiable?" Austin asked, frowning. "Like how they put a bomb in my head? I'm so sorry."

The young man's obviously genuine sorrow seemed to make Kelsey feel a little better, and the short woman smiled a little. "It's been hard, but things are looking up. Thank you for your concern."

"How much stronger are you?"

"Let's just leave it at several times stronger than I was."

Austin frowned. "The stress something like that would put on your joints would be incredible. There would have to be some additional structural additions to make it work. Reinforcement to the tendons and hardening of the bones, at the very least."

"Let's not get lost in the weeds," Olivia said firmly. "Don't let your tech geekiness overpower you."

He cocked his head to the side. "Geekiness? I'm not familiar with the word, though I think I get the meaning. Sorry. I get carried away when it comes to tech I'm not familiar with."

"If Olivia says I can, I'll tell you more and even let you take a peek at some diagrams," Kelsey assured him, continuing to shovel food into her mouth.

Olivia noted that the woman hadn't said that *Jared* could make the decision. That distrust was still hiding in there. Olivia was lucky in a way that she was like Austin, in that Kelsey had no history with her in her own universe.

"Why did she call you 'highness'?" Austin asked, stealing a slice of bacon and earning a set of narrowed eyes as Kelsey edged her plate a little farther away from him.

"That's a lot more complicated, and Kaitlinn shouldn't have called her that," Olivia said before Kelsey could respond. "There are political entities the Empire is unaware of, and Kelsey is a noble in one. A princess, as you might have guessed."

The crown princess of the New Terran Empire, in truth. Just like in this universe, though serving a much different emperor. Over there, her twin brother Ethan sat upon the Imperial Throne. Here, he'd tried to kill their father and failed.

Kelsey One had used circumstances to allow her brother to blunder to his death. It had traumatized her for months and probably still haunted her dreams. One didn't just walk away from something like that unchanged.

Olivia had worried deeply about her friend, but a trip to the Imperial Retreat seemed to have turned the tide for her. She'd still been angry and depressed, but the almost homicidal rage that had been building in her had dissipated. Apparently, a few weeks of reflection in solitude had turned the trick for her.

"Oh," Austin said in a nonplussed tone. "I'll forget that for now, as mentioning it to Uncle Oscar would be a terrible blunder."

The young man smiled a bit sadly. "I know none of you really trusts me, but I *do* know he's playing some game and probably doesn't have my best interests at heart, no matter what he says. I'm not going to help him unless it helps us all. I really have thrown my lot in with you."

Olivia still wasn't completely convinced, but Austin could have betrayed them with a single word, and yet he hadn't. He didn't seem the sort to have deep plots of his own cooking merrily away, so she was thawing to him.

She opened her mouth to say something to that effect when her implants pinged with an incoming message.

"Hurry up, Kelsey," she said somewhat sourly a moment later. "It seems our unwanted guest is on his way, half an hour early to boot."

Almost as soon as she'd finished speaking, she received a connection request from Fielding through her implants. She accepted the call, treating it just like a standard com connection, even though the conversation was entirely in her head.

"Keaton," she said, using her assumed name. Jaleesa Keaton had been the leader of the Rebel Empire crew on this ship before they'd recaptured it.

Olivia made certain to put just the right shade of irritation into her mental voice. No member of the higher orders would be pleased to be called before breakfast.

Since she'd lived her life at the highest levels of Rebel Empire society on Harrison's World, serving as the coordinator of the entire planet most recently, she was more than familiar with how her compatriots behaved.

And, if she was being exceptionally truthful, herself under the right stimuli.

She was trying to get better about how she treated others and about how she took things for granted. Having Sean as her husband was occasionally jarring when he told her she was being snooty, but it was growth she was determined to make happen.

"Ah, so good to hear your voice, Lady Keaton," Fielding said in a false tone of geniality. "I and my guards are on our way to the dining room. If you and your people will come meet me, I think it's time to go over what we'll be doing."

"I'll make certain that my people are informed. Some may be delayed, as we weren't scheduled to meet for another half an hour." Olivia emphasized that last bit enough to make sure the man knew she was less than pleased.

"My apologies," he said with more than a hint of smug satisfaction. "I was up early and felt we needed to get ourselves in order as soon as possible. After all, you only have six days before the next extension is required for the cargo."

He was referring to the bombs protecting the Omega Plague. They would go off unless he delayed them a second time.

"I still don't understand why you don't just extend them," she complained. "You're here with us. It's not as if you're going to allow them to just go off."

He chuckled. "I see you're operating under a misapprehension. I don't have the codes to extend them any further. In six days and a few hours, they'll go off and destroy this ship."

Olivia sat bolt upright. "You told us that the System Lord had agreed to a plan that involved you coming along so we didn't have to meet the other ship for a code to extend them."

"And that's true," the Rebel Empire noble said. "I have an encrypted file with the codes we need. Once we've accomplished the new mission, the System Lord at our new destination will decode it for us. Now, if you don't mind, I'll sign off and see you momentarily."

She cursed when he disconnected without another word.

"It seems we have a new problem," she told the others. "Our lives just got more complicated."

3

Angela slammed into the mat with bone-jarring force. She landed flat on her back and, even with all her Marine Raider enhancements, the titanic impact knocked the air out of her.

It was so hard, in fact, that she couldn't effectively defend herself when Princess Kelsey jammed her knee onto her neck. Angela tapped out rather than try to extract herself from the untenable situation.

Kelsey hopped to her feet with far too much energy as Angela tried to get her lungs working again.

"Four falls out of five?" the small woman chirped. "I'll take it!"

"I'll bet you will," Angela grumbled, sitting up and rubbing her throat. "Even with the same hardware, your experience keeps handing me my ass on a platter. That's damned unfair."

"You'll get the hang of things and the situation will reverse itself shortly," Kelsey said as she offered Angela a hand. "I'm not really in your league when you take the Marine Raider enhancements out of the equation. You'll pound me into the mat once you get the hang of your new body."

"I don't think so," Talbot said from where he was sitting off to the side. He was still recovering from the first set of Marine Raider surgeries. Well, technically the second, as he'd already had cranial implants, and the upgrade to Marine Raider medical nanites was pretty straightforward.

His most recent session had seen his pharmacology unit implanted and his ocular, auditory, and olfactory enhancements installed. He was sitting down because the procedure screwed with his balance for a day or so.

In a few more days, Doctor Zoboroski would coat his leg bones in graphene and weave artificial muscles into his real ones. That would be even more disruptive, she knew, screwing with his ability to walk until he adjusted.

In about a week, he'd have his torso and dominant arm done. They could've done both arms at the same time, but he needed one hand that wouldn't rip things out of walls or crush them with no warning before he mastered the increased strength.

Perhaps three days later, he'd have his last arm done. That meant that in about two weeks from now, he'd be right where she was. Hopefully *exactly* where she was: flat on his back on the mat with her doing the tossing.

That last thought made her smile darkly. It was the price of speeding up the implant process. The Old Empire gave the new Marine Raiders six sessions rather than four and spread them out over twice the time. The New Terran Empire just didn't have the time to dawdle.

When they finished with Talbot, they had a host of other people to start down the road to becoming the crew in truth of the Marine Raider strike ship *Persephone*.

And Commodore Zia Anderson on the carrier *Audacious* had already put in her marker for some Raiders of her own. Hell, most of the marines with them on this trip would get the treatment if they had enough time.

Some of the roughly battalion-sized group weren't going to make the cut, she knew. They had to be sure that only people who could ethically use power like this got it, because the process wasn't reversible. A closet psychopath with Marine Raider enhancements was a terrifying vision they all wanted to avoid.

Still, the marines were pretty good at weeding out that kind of thing, so Angela hoped there wouldn't be many people they'd have to reject. They needed every fighting hand they could get.

She stretched and tried to work some of the soreness out of her still-adjusting body. "What does that mean?" she asked Talbot.

"Kelsey isn't giving herself enough credit," he said calmly. "She still thinks of herself as the woman she was before the expedition. She's wrong.

"Yes, the Marine Raider implants and enhancements gave her a serious edge at the start over anyone she fought, even without any skills to go with it, but that situation isn't true anymore. It hasn't been for a while."

Angela continued stretching and watched as Kelsey walked over to her husband, a confused look on her face. "Expand on that."

"Sure," the large marine said with a grin. "If you'll sit here on my lap, I'll tell you all about it."

"I am *not* sitting in your lap," Kelsey said firmly. "Cough it up."

"You've mastered the Marine Raider unarmed combat form, you've had years of experience fighting with your new body, and even with her longer time as a marine, Angela is probably never going to be your master at hand-to-hand."

"That's ridiculous," Angela said, frowning. "I'm almost a meter taller than Kelsey, and I outmass her by a significant margin. I've been fighting hand-to-hand for fifteen years."

He shook his head as he turned his attention to her. "That's where you're wrong. You haven't been fighting like *this* at all. Sure, you know some martial arts and have significant unarmed combat chops, but that almost doesn't count at this level of the game.

"Tell me, what is the biggest difference between what you already knew and the Marine Raider hand-to-hand art?"

"The first thing I know is that that name is too unwieldy," Angela said. "We really need to call it something shorter. Why the Old Empire Marine Raiders didn't is a mystery to me."

"Call it the Art," Kelsey said. "That makes it sound all mysterious."

Talbot considered that and slowly nodded. "I like that. Now, again, Angela, what is the biggest difference between the Art and marine forms you already knew?"

Angela felt her eyes narrow. "A lot of the skills and moves are different. Why don't you tell me what kind of answer you're looking for?"

"Speed and size have advantages in a lot of the moves Kelsey is using," he explained. "Not large size as in overpowering but getting inside her opponent's moves and using her smaller size to throw them around the mat like she just did with you.

"Here, your larger size is a disadvantage, and her mastery of the Art is as good as your own. Perhaps somewhat better. Tell me how you'd overcome her size advantage."

Angela opened her mouth to answer but stopped herself and really considered the problem.

While she thought about the question, Kelsey nodded. "I think there has to be more to the Art than what Ned taught us. He tailored my education to what suited me. That's what I passed on to everyone else. That had to affect the curriculum."

The idea of the artificial intelligence that had thought it was Major Ned Quincy living inside Princess Kelsey's implants had always freaked Angela out a little.

She wondered if her friend was glad that Carl had transferred the AI safely to a specially designed computer made to support it while he searched for an answer to getting Ned his own body. Personally, she'd have been ecstatic.

"I'll have to work on some other moves outside the Art or find out if there are extra moves we didn't learn that might favor my greater size and longer reach," she finally said.

"That's a good answer," he said with a satisfied nod. "There are a lot of martial arts styles, and nothing says you have to keep using the one that favors Kelsey. Though I'm starting to suspect that the way Ned taught Kelsey might have implications we haven't considered just yet. I'll have to think about that a bit more before I'm ready to broach the subject.

"In any case, every move used in the Art came from another martial art in its day. The Marine Raiders stole what they liked the best. That doesn't mean that everything else is without merit under the right circumstances.

"Old Terra had an astonishing array of martial styles. Do some research and surprise her with something she isn't expecting. Adapt and overcome."

"And speaking of adapt and overcome, I have a new challenge for you, Raider," Kelsey said to Angela with a grin. "Now that you're fully enhanced, it's time you had a new job."

"I'm still getting used to acting as your second in command," Angela said dryly. "I'm a marine—a Marine Raider now, I suppose—and I'm not really all that skilled in running a ship, even now. What other pond filled with alligators do you have in mind for me?"

"Major Angela Ellis, by the authority granted me as the crown princess of the New Terran Empire and senior officer of the Marine Raiders, I hereby order you to assume command of the strike ship *Persephone*," Kelsey said formally. "*Persephone*, log the change of command and acknowledge that the transfer is complete."

"Orders received and executed," the somewhat artificial computer voice said through the overhead speakers. "Command authority is hereby transferred to Major Angela Ellis."

Angela gaped, and her mouth moved without sound for a few moments. "Kelsey, I'm not ready for this," she finally said.

The smaller woman reached out and squeezed her shoulder. "You're far readier than I was when I assumed command. Serve the Empire well, Major."

* * *

KELSEY TOOK a deep breath and settled into the mindset she needed to act like the Rebel Empire noble she was pretending to be. She was so into that that she barely reacted to the Bastard coming into the compartment.

She stopped and forced herself to correct that. Jared Mertz wasn't the Bastard here. Of that she was now almost certain, as hard as that was to believe.

Still, she couldn't stop the wave of loathing that washed over her every time she saw the man. No matter who he might be here, she doubted she'd ever get over that feeling.

"How long do we have?" Olivia asked Mertz as he sat.

"Two minutes, max," the man said. "Sean will be here just before him. Let me brief you about what we learned this morning. The plasma charges are too dangerous to try to disarm. We'll have to play this out."

"That's unfortunate," Olivia said, her jaw obviously tight. "Fielding dropped a surprise on me via the com moments ago. He doesn't have the codes to extend us more than the week he already used.

"It turns out that he has a little side mission for us to carry out, and the System Lord there will decrypt a file Fielding has from his System Lord to give us the extension to get to Terra."

Mertz growled under his breath. "Perfect. Any idea what the mission is supposed to be?"

"Not a clue. The theatrical bugger wants to tell us himself."

At that moment, Sean entered the compartment at a fast jog. "Did I miss anything?" he asked a bit breathlessly.

"Fielding is changing our plans," Mertz said. "Sit, and we'll find out how in a minute."

Sixty seconds later, two of Fielding's guards came into the compartment and scanned it for threats.

As if every one of the people on this mission wasn't a threat. All of them, with the exception of Austin, wore neural disruptors to continue the tradition of the original crew. Theirs were set to stun, but none of Fielding's people would know that.

And the Rebel Empire Lord seemingly didn't care. Without him, they'd die, and he knew they knew it. Hell, he'd given Austin a code to disable the bomb in his head. Not that he'd needed it, as Doctor Stone had already removed the device after replacing the corrupt code in the young man's implants.

Though, to be fair, that only saved him from it going off automatically if he did something it thought compromised the mission. Anyone else with the right code in transmission range could kill him in a gruesome manner with a thought.

Kelsey made a mental note to try and talk Austin into using the disarm code his uncle had given him under Doctor Stone's observation. Fielding wouldn't have given it to his nephew if he hadn't expected Austin to use it. It wouldn't kill the young man. She hoped.

Of course, it might not work with the implant code altered. There was no way of knowing other than trying. She supposed the odds of it going off were still greater than zero.

Moments later, Fielding and his remaining two guards came into the compartment. The older man smiled with false joviality as he took a seat at the table while his guards spread out to cover all approaches.

"Good morning," he said. "I hope you all had a restful evening. Are you as famished as I am?"

"You have no idea," Kelsey said. "I'm starving."

And, sadly, it was true. Even with everything she'd already eaten, she was still hungry. It was humiliating.

"Then by all means, let's get something to eat." He peremptorily waved at Commander Cannon, who was already coming over to take any special orders.

Which of course Fielding had in spades. He ordered his eggs done in a very specific manner. Sort of like over easy, but with restrictions on how crisp the whites were. Then he described the level of fluff he wanted in his pancakes.

The list of how he wanted things went on and left Kelsey boggled. She'd been raised in the Imperial Palace, and no one there would've dared to tell a chef how to do their job so brazenly.

Then she came to a realization. The man was trying to irritate them.

His behavior was another provocation. She had no proof, but she'd seen others act like this kind of ass before.

Her eyes briefly flashed over to Mertz before returning to Fielding. There might be more similarity between Fielding and the Bastard than she'd imagined. It made for an interesting thought experiment.

When her turn came, she ordered more than a woman of her size normally would, but not by a tremendous degree. Added to her earlier meal, it might just tide her over until lunch.

Once the orders were complete and the drinks had been delivered, Olivia got right to the point. "You mentioned a side mission for the Lords so that we can get the code we need to proceed to Terra. Obviously, time is a precious commodity that we cannot recover once we've spent it. What are the details of this mission?"

The older man smiled indulgently. "There's no need to rush things. We have plenty of time to get where we need to go and do what we need to do. The first few flips are already in your flight plan. We don't deviate until just shortly before you'd have met the other ship."

Olivia set both of her hands flat on the table and stood, her expression rock hard and unflinching.

"You've made an error in judgment, Lord Fielding. You might have the codes I need, but I command this mission. If the Lords want us to divert and take care of something for them, we will of course obey, but I will not be toyed with by you on my own ship. I am mistress here."

That wiped the expression of joviality off the man's face. He glared at Olivia for a few seconds but then smiled in what seemed like a more genuine manner.

"It's good to see you have some steel in your spine, Lady Keaton. You'll need that at Terra, I'm sure. Very well. We'll be diverting to the Bradley system to perform a somewhat delicate task for the Lord there. One you and your people are uniquely suited for."

"And what might that task be?" Mertz asked as the food started arriving.

Fielding grinned at him. "The Lord there has suffered some hardware failures, it seems, and become somewhat erratic. Perhaps paranoid is a better word.

"The Lord in my system has been tasked by his associates to send a repair team to restore their brother to health. As the Lords control our very lives, they feel they can trust us with this… delicate task."

Delicate wasn't the word Kelsey would've chosen.

From her expression, Olivia shared Kelsey's doubts. "So we're supposed to just coast right up, talk our way past a paranoid AI, and convince it to allow us to send a repair team on board? You make it sound so simple. What if it won't let us in?"

Fielding spread his hands. "I suggest you be convincing, since we'll all die if it either opens fire on us or simply refuses us access. Only it can decrypt the codes we need to keep the plasma charges from destroying this ship and everyone on it.

"In any case, we are limited in the number of people that are cleared for this work. While either you or Lord Gust can lead the mission, my nephew and Lady Oldfield will be the only ones allowed to see the inner workings of the Lord at your sides."

Kelsey blinked before she could stop herself. Jocelyn Oldfield, the woman she was pretending to be, might have been an adept engineer, but Kelsey wasn't. Far from it.

Austin seemingly had the chops to do his part, but she'd be putting their lives at risk with her ignorance. Worse, she might do something that she wasn't even aware of that set the AI off.

"Why me?" Kelsey asked slowly. "I don't know the systems I'll be looking at."

The man shrugged. "It's a small risk, but I have complete confidence in your exemplary technical ability. After all, as the woman who designed the containers for our deadly cargo, you're undoubtedly a very savvy engineer. You'll be fine."

Kelsey put on a confident smile, but inside, she knew that they were screwed.

4

———————

Talbot left Kelsey and Angela talking as he headed back to his makeshift office aboard *Persephone*. As fun as watching that fight had been, he still had an extraordinary amount of work on his plate. More specifically, he had a number of prisoners that needed dealing with.

He might as well start with the newest batch, he decided as he sat. He had his implants signal Commander Veronica Giguere.

"How can I help you, Colonel?" the former Rebel Empire Fleet officer asked once she'd answered.

"I think it's time we have a conversation with your old friend. Would you bring Commander Sommerville to my office, please?"

"With pleasure. He's been hounding me for details I can't give him, and I have a few questions of my own about that ship of his and where he was taking it."

Those questions mirrored what Talbot intended to ask. "See you shortly."

Kelsey and Veronica had captured Lieutenant Commander Don Sommerville on their recent mission to the Archibald system. He'd been in the process of running from the Clan incursion with a Q-ship: a warship built inside a freighter's hull and looking far less dangerous than it truly was.

He'd claimed to be a member of resistance inside the Rebel Empire, and Talbot saw no reason to doubt him. They had far more evidence than they needed to execute him if they'd been the enemies the man thought they were, so he really had no reason to lie about that.

Five minutes later, a rap at his hatch preceded Veronica's entry. The captured man was right behind her, with two marines at his back.

"Gentlemen, you can wait outside," Talbot said, rising to his feet and making his way around the desk.

The marines departed, leaving Talbot alone with Veronica and Commander Sommerville. He wasn't worried about the man attacking him. Sommerville wanted information as much as Talbot did.

Once the other two were seated, Talbot sat. "Commander Sommerville, I'm sorry it's taken us so long to talk. I'm Lieutenant Colonel Russel Talbot, Imperial Marines. Only, not from the Empire you nominally serve."

The other man smiled slightly. "Very delicately put. Who do you serve, Colonel?"

"The AIs failed to stop all the forces that fled when they took over," Talbot said, crossing his legs. "For ease of understanding, we're calling ourselves the New Terran Empire and your polity the Rebel Empire. It's all semantics, but everything needs a name, and we have the guns."

Sommerville chuckled. "I'm not in a position to argue, even if I felt inclined to do so. Feel free to call yourselves whatever you like. By the way, this is an interesting ship. I can't recall ever seeing anything quite like her."

"She's from before the Fall," Talbot said. "Refurbished, of course. By the Fall, I mean the collapse of the Old Terran Empire. This ship was built for a group of elite fighters called Marine Raiders. So far as we know, it was the smallest class of ship capable of taking people through flip points."

"Interesting," Sommerville admitted. "Still, I'm sure that we both have more pressing things to talk about. If, of course, I'm allowed to ask questions."

Talbot inclined his head toward Veronica. "Commander Giguere has spoken highly of your character, though she didn't know of your double life. We have friends in the resistance as well, though none are with us at the moment."

"So she said. I respect Veronica a great deal, and we were once friends. Or as friendly as a spy inside Fleet could be. Sorry about that, Veronica."

"I hardly think *I'm* in a position to judge," the former destroyer commander said dryly. "I did just help capture you so I could steal a flip drive from your shipyard."

"What a complicated universe we live in," Sommerville mused. "Everyone has their secrets these days. And since none of us is really that willing to share the deep details of our lives, whatever will we talk about?"

"Actually, I'm more than willing to give you some information," Talbot said. "Not everything, of course, but enough to show good faith. I'll start off by telling you about the people attacking the Rebel Empire. The ones you had to run from."

Talbot proceeded to tell him what they knew about the Clans. He even told the man how Raul Castille, the Rebel Empire security officer, had stolen one of the New Terran Empire's ships and provoked them.

Sommerville shook his head with a wry smile. "You find excitement in odd places. Exactly how did a prisoner manage all this?"

"I'm partly to blame," Veronica admitted. "My command crew and I helped him escape. We stole the transport ship they were using to move the

Dresden orbital, and he lobbed the orbital right into a Clan battle station. They blew the orbital up, but high-speed shrapnel is a bitch."

Sommerville frowned. "How could anyone get that close to a battle station? And did you say the Dresden orbital? A real orbital?"

"A full-sized one," Talbot confirmed. "It was being used for classified research, and we were a little pressed for time, so we took it with us when we ran."

The other man opened his mouth to say something but seemingly changed his mind and only shook his head.

"It's true," Veronica assured him. "The transport ships are made for moving a lot of mined material or large ships inside arms that project the flip field out. They managed to get them around the orbital."

"That's... audacious," Sommerville said slowly. "And a bit far-fetched. I somehow doubt the ships and battle stations guarding the Dresden system just let you wander away. Also, exactly how did you find these Clans? Where are they coming from?"

Talbot smiled. "We used the same kind of escape you intended to use at Archibald."

The man's interested expression closed right up. "I'm not sure I understand what you mean."

"I mean the flip points that sit way out past where that kind of thing normally sits," Talbot said. "You had a way out of Archibald that you weren't worried about the Clans following you through. I'm sorry to tell you this, but the Clans know all about the far flip points. They're how we discovered them in the first place."

"Let's assume for a moment that your preposterous story is true," Sommerville said slowly. "What does the existence of these flip points matter to you? If you know about them and you suspect I do as well, what exactly are we talking about?"

"I just wanted to set the stage for laying out what we want to negotiate over," Talbot said smoothly. "You don't have to confirm that you know about the far flip points since I already know they exist."

"Okay, let's just say they do, simply for moving this discussion forward. What do you want, and exactly how does that affect me and my people?"

Veronica leaned forward a little. "The short version is that we need to get to the New Terran Empire. All the paths from the area we're hiding in go through the Rebel Empire. You can imagine why that might not be advisable right now."

"And you think, what?" Sommerville asked with a raised eyebrow. "That the resistance knows about these fantastical flip points and might provide you a way home with our secret information? Veronica, I'm afraid that I can't help you. This is all just a tad crazy sounding."

Talbot sent a request to the marines outside his office.

"I can provide some proof that we're in an area of space you're unfamiliar with. I suspected that I'd need a trump card, so I want you to meet someone special."

The hatch slid open, and a tall, blue-skinned alien man walked in.

Talbot grinned as Sommerville sprang to his feet, a shocked expression written across his face at being confronted by something so unexpected. Neither the Old Terran Empire nor the Rebel Empire had ever encountered aliens before.

"Lieutenant Commander Don Sommerville," Talbot said, "allow me to introduce Prince Derek of the Kingdom of Raden on the world of Pandora. I believe he can provide corroborating evidence that we're a long way from home and might have something to offer the resistance in exchange for help getting back."

* * *

JARED STEPPED INTO ENGINEERING, still so engrossed in his own thoughts that he'd missed Commander O'Halloran speaking to him for a few moments.

"I'm sorry," Jared said, holding his hand up. "I wasn't paying attention. What?"

"I said that one of the FTL coms seems to be malfunctioning."

Jared blinked. "That's a first. Some kind of hardware fault?"

The other officer shrugged. "I'm not sure. Whatever it is, it's subtle. The unit has thrown three strange faults in the last few hours. Yet when I examine the supposedly bad component, I don't see anything wrong. I've even swapped the same component from another com, and the new part seems to be bad in exactly the same way as the old one."

"That strikes me as unlikely," Jared agreed. "Which FTL com is it?"

"The one linked to Princess Kelsey."

With any other com, that might be a coincidence. With Kelsey's group, he couldn't assume that. Carl was with her, and he'd designed the FTL com system. If anyone could figure out some way to make one act weird, it was the young scientist.

The problem was that they couldn't be in range. They were many flips away from where Kelsey had to be, in a completely different sector of the Rebel Empire.

FTL coms only worked through a single flip point. Even with a dedicated relay, it only gave a good connection to a second system about half the time. Carl had said that had to be technical and that he'd figure it out one day, but today probably wasn't that day.

Probably.

"Could it be some kind of interference that Carl is introducing remotely?" he asked.

The engineering officer shrugged. "I suppose it's possible. If so, I can't see what he's doing or how. Honestly, this looks like some type of mechanical fault to me, but I won't rule out external action just yet. No matter what it is, I'm just not certain what to do next."

"Don't we have complete technical schematics for the FTL coms?" Jared asked.

O'Halloran nodded. "We do, but some of what they describe is fairly esoteric. I don't want to say that I can't figure it out, but this is using a level of science and hardware manipulation that I've never played with before. Carl Owlet is a genius, and as much as I hate to say it, I'm not."

"Don't put yourself down," Jared said, clapping his hand on the man's shoulder. "You're pretty damned smart."

The engineer sighed. "Maybe I can figure this out, if it's actually something intentional. I can't imagine how that's even possible, but Carl has his ways. I'd feel a lot more comfortable if I had a deeper understanding of the hardware itself."

Jared pursed his lips. "What you're telling me is that you need a hardware geek."

"I certainly wouldn't turn one down. Do you happen to have one sitting in your pocket?"

"I might. Where do we have the FTL com stashed?"

"In the maintenance tubes just behind engineering," O'Halloran said, gesturing toward one of the hatches.

Jared sent a contact request to Austin Darrah through his implants. The other man answered almost immediately.

Mr. Darrah, would you meet me in engineering?

I'll be right there.

Ten minutes later, Austin Darrah walked into engineering.

"What can I do for you?" the young man asked, nodding to the engineer.

"I don't know if you've met, but this is Lieutenant Commander Anthony O'Halloran, our chief engineer. Tony, this is Austin Darrah."

From the unfriendly look Tony was shooting toward Austin, the fact that the young man hadn't been directly responsible for anyone's death during the action retaking *Athena* wasn't holding much water with him.

Jared couldn't blame his man. The original chief engineer and Tony's close friend, Commander Katheryn Pence, had died in that action, killed by Austin's compatriots.

"Tony," Jared said softly, "I understand this isn't going to be easy, but you need to accept that not everyone that fought against us is an enemy. In a very real sense, Austin was a prisoner of the people that killed Katheryn. He wasn't armed, he didn't attack any of our people, and he's doing his very best to help us."

Austin inclined his head. "I'm sorry that the people I was working with killed anyone. I'm not a violent man, and I'm not a supporter of what they were doing here. I give you my word that I'm doing everything in my power to help you fight against the Lords."

O'Halloran grunted. "I'll try. It's going to take me a little bit to adjust, so if I seem abrupt, I apologize." He turned his attention to Jared. "Are you really expecting me to brief him on the project?"

Jared nodded. "Austin happens to be an expert on Fleet and Rebel Empire hardware. From what I understand, he has probably a decade more experience working with the kind of equipment that we're talking about, though he's never seen the machine in question and won't really understand the theory behind its design.

"Even if he can't figure out why it's behaving in the peculiar fashion that it is, I'll wager he can give you some insight into what's really going on. That might allow you to dig into the problem with fresh eyes."

He turned and faced Austin squarely. "What the commander is about to show you is one of our very closest secrets. I expect you to keep every bit of information you learn to yourself. Under no circumstances are you to discuss this with anyone other than myself, Sean Meyer, Olivia West, Elise Orison, or Commander O'Halloran. Is that understood?"

The young man nodded. "I understand completely."

Jared gestured toward the maintenance hatch. "Tony, show Austin what you've been working on and explain it to him in as much detail as you can. Austin, Tony didn't design this equipment, and his understanding of the hardware and theory may be a little off. I'm hoping that the two of you, working together, can figure out what's going on.

"I'm not certain that it's anything more than a malfunction, but this could potentially mean something much more important to us, so give it your very best."

Austin nodded again and turned to Commander O'Halloran. "Shall we?"

Jared watched the two men walk away and returned to the privacy of his own thoughts. He wished this really was Kelsey trying to contact them from some unimaginable distance away, but he didn't believe that was possible, not even for them. There were limits to what even Carl could do.

5

K elsey looked over the FTL com hardware sitting on Carl's worktable in his bustling lab aboard *Audacious*. "Do we have any idea if your little trick is doing anything on the other end?"

The young scientist shrugged. "Since I can't directly connect to the hardware on the admiral's ship, I can't be sure. I designed the coms to be as secure as possible, so hacking into the hardware and trying to make it throw errors is a lot more difficult than it sounds."

"Is it really the hardware you need to hack into? I thought you said the software needed to be changed so that the system on the other end would recognize this strange type of connection request."

Carl nodded. "That would be ideal, but as I keep saying, it's not as easy as that. As I said, the goal I had in mind when designing the system was to make sure that somebody didn't do the kind of thing that I'm trying to do. As you might expect, I did everything I could think of to prevent it, so I've pretty well blocked myself away from my usual tricks."

She pursed her lips. "Maybe you're going about this the wrong way. No offense, but you're a scientist. Even though you know how to program, and you're damned good at hacking, the criminal mindset for this kind of thing really isn't in you. We need a professional."

"I'm pretty sure that I should be offended," Carl said, shaking his head and grinning. "You're talking about Ralph Halstead, aren't you?"

"Indeed I am," she conceded. "He'll have a lot more experience at industrial espionage via computer than we'll likely ever have."

They'd captured the earnest young Halstead, his aunt and uncle, and two men in their group during the mission at Archibald. They'd been involved in a two-year mission to hack data from a medical research company that was a front for the System Lords doing classified research on what could potentially be a Singularity AI.

Yet one more project on Carl Owlet's crowded desk.

"Kelsey, those people are criminals," Carl said. "Real criminals. As much as it pains me to say this, I'm not certain that I care how good he is at hacking. Anything he learns is going to be sold to the highest bidder the first chance he gets."

She pursed her lips. "I'm not so sure. His aunt? Probably. Him? I think he's more into this for the fun. I guess what I'm saying is that I think it's possible that we can recruit him to work for us."

Carl shook his head slightly. "I hate to be the one to say this, but if we get captured by the Rebel Empire, he'd talk in a moment to save his skin."

Kelsey nodded somberly. "And that would be something we'd have to discuss with him. Knowledge of one of these classified systems would be a death sentence if it looks like someone is about to be captured.

"Of course, each of them already knows about the Singularity computer you have scattered across your lab. I'm pretty sure they know the fate that awaits them just for knowing about it, much less trying to steal it. There's no way that the System Lords will believe that they weren't the ones behind the theft if they got their hands on our little industrial spies."

Though with the Clans in possession of the Archibald system and invading the Rebel Empire, the System Lords probably had more pressing matters on their electronic minds.

"The list of things that we've done to the System Lords has grown to be truly impressive," Carl said with a chuckle. "Even if they don't know who we are, we've become quite the thorn in their sides. Scrappy rebels taking the fight to them. That should be a movie."

"No!" Kelsey said firmly. "Don't give *anyone* any crazy ideas. Have you seen the latest film out of Pentagar? It's getting ridiculous."

The young man's eyebrows went up. "I saw the first two, and I thought they were pretty good. The woman they found to play you has quite the... screen presence."

Kelsey snorted. "What you mean is that she has quite the cleavage. Talk about being out of character. This time they've decided to cover the attack on Boxer Station and Harrison's World, including my little trip down to the surface in the drop capsule to stop that guy with the nuke.

"Of course the damned thing is a huge success, and every time I think they'll finally stop producing these idiotic movies, the next one makes truckloads more money than the last one. I'm doomed."

Carl laughed. "I suppose that's what you get for being the face of the New Terran Empire. I'm sure Jared gets equally good coverage, right?"

She nodded grudgingly. "He does, but he's not letting it get under his skin like I am. I just can't shake how it makes me feel.

"Now before we fall any further down this rabbit hole, have you made any progress on the Singularity computer? Is it just a standard kind of thing writ large, or is it an AI?"

"It's not in good enough condition to make that kind of assessment. Whatever happened to it pretty well broke it into component parts. The memory storage units were mostly intact, but as one might expect, they're encrypted.

"We have the lead researcher on the project aboard, along with a couple of his junior associates, but they're not being cooperative. I personally have my doubts that they'll ever give in. It makes sense the AIs would get people that were very loyal to work on a project like this."

Kelsey rubbed her face. "I'm starting to lose track of how many prisoners we have. Exactly how did we gather all of these enemies anyway?"

"It's because we're good at sticking our noses where they don't belong, stirring up angry mobs, and capturing interesting people before we run away again," Carl said. "I'm sure they'd find some of their fellow prisoners to be quite fascinating if they knew these other people were here at all."

Kelsey squeezed the bridge of her nose between her index finger and thumb. "It feels like we have a menagerie. In any case, I'll go talk with Ralph Halstead and see if we can come to some kind of agreement. Fiona will help me make sure he's telling us the truth."

Fiona was the sentient AI they'd found when they'd captured the Dresden orbital. It had been packed away in the freighter they'd used to help move equipment away from the scene of their attack. Talbot had instructed Carl to assemble her on *Persephone*.

The sentient AI wasn't in command of *Persephone* like Marcus was aboard Jared's flagship *Invincible* because the Marine Raider computer had special security circuits built into it that disallowed control of the ship's systems by anyone other than itself.

That didn't mean that two computers hadn't begun working together in ways that she still wasn't certain she fully understood. A kind of strange partnership. The Marine Raider computer seemed to have recognized the AI as both a person and a computer and was cooperating with it in some tasks. It was kind of spooky.

Kelsey looked forward to seeing exactly what that odd partnership resulted in. In any case, the presence of the sentient AI gave her a number of capabilities that she wouldn't normally have, and that included being able to test people with implants to see if they were lying.

"Keep working on the FTL com," Kelsey ordered as she headed for the hatch. "I'll see if I can get you some help."

* * *

OLIVIA SAT in her new office just off *Athena*'s bridge and stewed. Fielding had sprung this dangerous side mission on them with some kind of ulterior motive, but she just couldn't figure out what it might be.

He could've allowed the mission to proceed without his presence. That meant he wanted something from this new system that furthered his own plans. Whatever they were.

Once they'd finished breakfast, Fielding had headed back to his quarters. Jared's quarters, if one was to be specific, just as this was her friend's office.

If she went to Fielding, she'd be on his territory, and he'd attempt to assert his dominance. If she wanted to avoid playing that kind of game again, she'd be much better off if she summoned him to the bridge. Her territory.

Her mind made up, Olivia walked out onto the bridge. Commander Janice Hall, *Athena*'s helm officer, partly turned in her seat and raised an eyebrow.

"Can I help you, ma'am?" the Fleet officer asked.

"Exactly how far away are we from the new destination system?"

"We'll hit the first flip point in about two hours. From there, we have three more transitions before we arrive at the target system. All told, it will take us five days to get where we're going."

"And once we arrive, we'll only have about eighteen hours, give or take, to get the code we need to reset the explosives in our hold," Olivia calculated grimly.

"That's not a whole lot of time," Hall agreed. "Do we even know what has to be repaired to get the AI back into shape?"

"Not a clue," Olivia said. "If we're in a good place for the moment, I'd like you to go down to Fielding's cabin and request his presence in my office. I think it's time he and I had a meeting of the minds."

"Me, ma'am?"

Olivia nodded. "He's seen you here on the bridge. He'll consider you one of my inner circle just by association. Be polite but firm. Give it as much time as it takes, but wait for him."

She returned to her office and waited.

And waited.

And *waited*.

Finally, after almost an hour had passed, Commander Hall returned with Fielding striding smugly beside her.

"Lord Fielding, my lady," Hall said. The Fleet officer rolled her eyes where the man couldn't see, almost making Olivia smile, and returned to her post on the bridge.

"My apologies for the delay, Lady Keaton," the Rebel Empire noble said as he entered the office as if he owned it. "You caught me in the middle of something quite delicate. I came as quickly as I could."

"I'm sure," Olivia said, not bothering to hide her disbelief. "If you'd be so kind as to close the hatch behind you, I believe it's time we had a more in-depth discussion on our situation."

Once the man had finally closed the hatch and taken a seat, she rose from behind her desk and took the seat across from him. For almost a full minute, she studied him without speaking. His smugness didn't even waiver.

"According to my calculations, once we arrive in the system you're taking us to, we only have eighteen hours or so to complete the task you've set for us."

"That sounds right," he agreed.

"And yet you've given us no information whatsoever on precisely what we need to do. That's unacceptable. These games you're playing are endangering my primary mission, and I will not stand for that."

"I don't understand what you mean," he said, his smile widening. "I would never toy with you in such a fashion."

"Of course you would," she countered. "You don't want us to have the specifics before we arrive, and I can only see one reason for that. Something in that system will further your ends in one way or another, yet you'd rather not have us know precisely what it is.

"I'm afraid you're not going to be able to have your cake and eat it too, Lord Fielding. You're going to tell me what you're doing and why."

"Don't be ridiculous," he said with a laugh. "Even if that were true—which I'm not saying it is—I certainly wouldn't feel obligated to tell you my motives."

She leaned forward, her expression cold. "I agreed to have a bomb planted in my head. I'd execute my crew—my friends—in a moment if it seemed that we were about to fail in our mission or breach the secrecy the Lords demanded. What makes you think that I'm going to just sit here and let you play me like this?"

If her words bothered the man, it didn't show. His grin didn't waver.

"You'll sit here and take it because you don't really have a choice. In any case, this is perhaps the most fun I've had in years. I'll not let you browbeat me into telling you what's going on.

"As for what I gain by instigating this change in plans, it's no business of yours, so long as it doesn't impinge upon your mission for the System Lords. You'll just have to accept that you're not the one in absolute control of your destiny. I am. The sooner you do so, the less indigestion you'll suffer.

"Now if we're done playing this little game, I have real work to do. Good day." He rose to his feet, opened the hatch, and walked out, never looking back.

Olivia rubbed her face tiredly. She'd tried to get the information they needed and failed. Now they'd just have to hope that whatever curveballs Fielding threw their way didn't hit them in the head.

6

Angela sat at the command console on *Persephone*'s bridge and tried not to feel out of place. Oh, she'd sat in the seat many times before, but only as Kelsey's executive officer. Now the ship was hers, and that was going to take some getting used to.

The bridge wasn't large. In fact, it was smaller than a destroyer's, only having consoles for command, helm, and tactical. Cozy was the watchword.

The hatch at the rear of the compartment slid open, and Veronica Giguere stepped onto *Persephone*'s bridge. Beside the woman was her Rebel Empire Fleet friend, Lieutenant Commander Don Sommerville and his marine guards trailed the pair.

Pleased at the distraction, Angela turned to face them. "Commander Giguere, Commander Sommerville, is there something I can do for you?"

Veronica smiled. "Would it be possible for you to task one of the drones down on Pandora with making a pass over *Dauntless*'s wreck, Major Ellis?"

"Certainly. Are you looking for a grand overview or a close pass on certain sections of the vessel?"

"Both. I want Don to see exactly what I've been telling him about."

"After seeing an alien, I don't think you really need to convince me anymore," Sommerville said dryly. "That's not something you can make up."

The haunted look in the man's eyes made Angela smile a little. "It is a little bit daunting, if you'll forgive the mild pun. Trust me when I say that this entire situation is a lot to take in, Commander Sommerville.

"Rather than seeing it through the drone, would you care to go down in person? We're about to dispatch a pinnace to the capital to pick up a gentleman for an enforced medical procedure, and we can drop you off at the wreck on our way."

One of Veronica's eyebrows quirked upward. "An enforced medical procedure? Exactly how does that work?"

Angela grinned. "Princess Kelsey had a... disagreement with a gentleman belonging to Clan Dauntless when she first arrived on Pandora. Blows were exchanged and injuries suffered. Rather than leave an avowed enemy sitting behind us, nursing his wounds, Her Highness has decided to make certain that he suffers no lasting harm from the encounter, even though he was an ass."

"I think that's an excellent idea," Veronica said. "That kind of person comes back to haunt you when you least expect it.

"And congratulations on your appointment. Commanding a ship in space is a big step and a true honor. Commanding this ship in particular is going to be an exciting experience, I'm sure."

"Exactly how does a marine officer achieve command of a Fleet warship?" Sommerville asked. "It seems a little odd."

"That's a long story that I'm uncertain you've been cleared to hear," Angela said firmly. "If you're that curious, you can ask Princess Kelsey. Meanwhile, why don't I escort you down to the planet surface?"

Veronica made a point of looking around *Persephone*'s bridge. "Don't you have a ship to command?"

"Senior Lieutenant Thompson has everything under control, don't you Jack?"

The helm officer grinned at her. "I feel relatively confident that were not going to run into any trouble here in orbit, Major. We'll manage just fine without you for a couple of hours, I'm sure."

"See? Let's get down to one of the pinnaces, and we'll get you to Pandora so you can visit a wreck."

The three of them left *Persephone*'s bridge and headed for the nearest pinnace. Angela had already ordered some marines to be ready for the mission. She'd originally intended to send Jack down but wanted to get a feel for their prisoner herself.

Just like she'd told Sommerville, she felt relatively safe leaving her ship under the circumstances. The only other vessels in the Pandora system were those attached to Commodore Anderson's task force. And if anyone else did arrive, Angela would have plenty of time to get back to *Persephone*.

Besides, it would feel good to stretch her legs a little.

Once everyone was secured, the pinnace detached from the Marine Raider strike ship and fell toward the planet. Since there wasn't an emergency, they'd do a relatively slow entry so as not to spook the locals.

"Your helmsmen didn't call you Captain," Sommerville said. "Is that a marine thing?"

"Yes and no," Angela said seriously. "We're still exploring exactly how marines commanding a ship in space will look, but the marines don't use the rank of captain. I understand that on board ship, that's a position rather than a rank, but we're still not certain that's what we want to do.

"My people know who I am. I don't need them calling me by my position. I think I'm satisfied with them using my rank as my only form of address. I'm certain other people would feel more comfortable using the title of captain and that we're going to end up causing confusion, but that's pretty much the nature of how the marines fit inside Fleet."

Somerville chuckled. "I suppose that's true enough."

"As an interested observer, I'd like to ask you a few questions if you don't mind, Commander Sommerville."

The man gestured for her to continue. "Feel free, Major. I may not answer, but I'm not going to take offense at your curiosity."

"What's it like working inside an enemy for your entire professional career and plotting their downfall? It seems like being a spy from one of the old vids, always in fear that someone is going to figure out your secret and capture you or kill you."

He nodded slowly. "There's an element of that, certainly. I wish it were something as straightforward as what you're imagining, but it's not. When you intermingle with people on a daily basis, you form friendships. Even with people that are ostensibly working for the other side."

His eyes moved over to Veronica. "Veronica and I were once close friends, even though she'd have thought me a traitor if she'd known what I was up to. I have hopes that we'll be friends again one day."

Veronica gave him an affectionate look and shook her head. "I'm not going to hold your past against you, Don. I believe we both pulled the wool over one another's eyes. Knowing what I do about the overall situation, at the very least we're going to be allies."

Somerville raised an eyebrow. "And you're confident of that? At this point, I'm not. I just don't know enough about you all, and I'm unsure that I can trust you with the secrets you want from me. I've got a lot of people to think about."

"If you don't mind my input, I might be able to smooth this road a little bit," Angela said. "What is it you think we'll be doing if you don't help us? Sitting here and waiting to be rescued? I can assure you that isn't going to happen.

"With the capture of your Q-ship, we understand that you were taking supplies to what is almost certainly a resistance base hidden in a system that the Rebel Empire doesn't know about. The first leg of that journey starts in the Archibald system. Are you with me so far?"

Somerville nodded again. "I can see the logic of what you're saying, though I will neither confirm nor deny the existence of a base or a flip point of the nature you are implying."

"Any lawyer worth their salt would be proud of that answer," Angela said with a grin. "The next obvious step is to send probes through that far flip point. Of course, that means we need to locate it first.

"You'd think that would be a little bit difficult with an invasion going on, but *Persephone* might surprise you. My ship is designed to sneak into places right under other people's noses. You didn't see how we got out of the system, and I'm not going to share that information without proper authorization, but none of the Clan warships is likely to be anywhere near our entry point into Archibald space.

"Our next step is almost certainly going to have me ghost into the Archibald system and send stealthed probes to look into the outer reaches of the system for far flip points. Eventually, we're going to find out where you were going, and then I'll send probes through to see what's on the other side.

"Once that's done, it's just a matter of looking into every flip point in that new system, both standard and far. If it's an occupied system, that may be somewhat more challenging but not out of the question. I'm inclined to believe that wherever your base is, it's going to be somewhere down another far flip point. More probably two."

Angela let silence fall after her guesses. His expression didn't give anything away, but she was still relatively certain that she wasn't far from the truth.

"You should ask yourself, Commander Sommerville, what you'd like to happen when we find the resistance base. I'll repeat what I'm sure everyone else has said. We have no desire to fight you. We're looking for allies, not enemies.

"As you might imagine, we have a few tricks up our collective sleeves that we'd be willing to trade for your assistance. The real question is how we can find common ground to begin trusting one another."

The prisoner slowly nodded. "I hear what you're saying, Major. I'm going to have to think about it."

Satisfied with the progress, Angela leaned back in her acceleration couch. Based on Veronica Giguere's approving expression, she'd done well. If her actions helped get them closer to where they needed to be, then this would be time well spent. If they didn't, well, it never hurt to try.

The rest of the trip down to the surface was quiet, and she let the pair go at the wreck site with their marine guards.

Once the pinnace was back in the air, she turned her attention to the mission at hand. The drones watching the capital of the Kingdom of Raden had spotted the man Kelsey had fought. Based on the building he was living in, he didn't want his clan mates to know his current location either.

That was fine with her. It meant that she could stun him without much fear of anyone interfering and be gone before any alarm was raised. She'd take him directly to *Audacious* and let the doctor work on him while he was still unconscious.

Then, once he was fully healed, she'd return him to the planet. He'd wake up suddenly healed of all his injuries.

She had no idea how he was going to interpret that, and frankly, she didn't care. One way or the other, they'd be leaving Pandora in the next few days. The odds of any of them ever seeing the man again were vanishingly small.

At her orders, the pinnace hovered over the dark city. It was still before dawn, so there weren't many people up. An excellent time of the morning to go hunting.

The buildings inside the kingdom's capital were mostly constructed of wood and stone. Those were easy building materials to gather and use for what amounted to a medieval society.

The durability of the buildings also allowed the pinnace to lower its ramp onto the rooftop.

It only had to hover for a few moments as Angela and the marines hopped out onto the peak. It then silently lifted into the air, closed its ramp, and began circling higher to await them calling for pickup.

The three-story building had no roof access, but that wasn't going to deter Angela. She'd already spotted their entry point on the back of the building. Someone had failed to close the shutters on one of the top-floor windows.

The corporal in charge of her team quickly attached a line to a heavy chimney and tested it. He nodded at Angela.

"Looks good, Major," he said quietly. "We should only go down one at a time, just to be on the safe side."

Like any good commander, she allowed her marines to precede her in and then followed. Once they were inside the hallway on the top floor, they began a room by room search, looking for their quarry.

The building provided room and board for itinerant workers, so the conditions were crowded and there was a lot of snoring going on. Each room they looked into was packed with Pandorans sleeping on large spreads of cheap bedding.

That complicated the task of locating the one person they were really interested in, but it didn't make it impossible. The man's injuries meant he had one hand that was heavily bandaged. He was also human, so he'd stand out.

Her scouts found him at the end of the hall, saving her from having to search the other two floors. Unfortunately, he was on the far side of a group of sleeping Pandorans. That made access to him without waking the others impossible.

Thankfully, that was a problem she could solve. She quietly drew her stunner, set it to wide beam, and shot everyone in the room. With the diffused effects, the people inside would be asleep for roughly half an hour and wake up with a headache. She was sorry for that, but it couldn't be helped.

Thankfully, stunners had less effect on Pandorans than humans. The time it was effective for was roughly half as long, and the headache was less significant.

Two of her marines extracted their target and carried him back the way they'd come. Inside five minutes, they'd retreated to the roof and were back aboard the pinnace, heading for *Audacious*.

They secured the prisoner in one of the marine drop harnesses, and Angela stunned him again with a full beam to be certain he'd be out long enough for the medical procedure to take place and for him to be returned to Pandora.

She wasn't convinced that this man would feel differently toward Princess Kelsey after this, but one never knew. It would make her boss happy, and that was good enough for Angela.

Once this was done, she could begin the final process of getting *Persephone* ready to scout Archibald. One way or the other, she knew that task would land in her lap before very much longer, and frankly, she was itching to get started.

7

K elsey rubbed her temples tiredly and stared at the wall of her cabin. Trying to make any sense from even the limited information about the AIs Mertz had brought with them on this mission made her brain hurt. She just wasn't a technical person.

In a way, she was grateful that the man hadn't brought the complete technical specifications, because she knew that she didn't have a chance of understanding them.

Of course, he'd insisted that only the other version of her had that kind of detailed information. If he was to be believed, she'd stolen it from the Rebel Empire but hadn't gotten it home yet.

Hell, that sounded like this universe's version of her, so she'd even grant the man was probably telling her the truth.

Yet she was going to be the one responsible for repairing the damaged AI in a few days. If she didn't get a handle on what she needed to do, they were all going to die.

Fielding had been cagey, but she'd bet money that he intended to personally accompany them. The Bastard... Mertz... was absolutely correct in his assessment that the man was up to something.

The more she compared Fielding to the Mertz from her universe, the more similarities she saw in the way they behaved and treated others. Ironically, that only highlighted how little like her Mertz the one from this universe behaved.

She respected Scott Roche and had considered what he'd advised her to do a few nights ago, but she genuinely liked these people, other than Mertz. She wasn't sure that she could betray them, even if that was the price for saving the lives of her people back home.

Kelsey hoped it never came to that. The odds of her being able to escape with the key and Mertz, or the override from the vaults below the Imperial Palace on Terra, were even lower than her being able to carry off the mission with the AI.

If anyone was going to be able to repair the AI, it was going to have to be Austin Darrah. Rather than trying to reinvent the wheel, she needed to do what she could to support him in that task.

With that thought in mind, she began wandering the corridors, searching for the young man. To her shock, she covered the entire destroyer, with the exceptions of private quarters, without locating him. He didn't answer the door to his own cabin, so she doubted he was in there.

Where could he be hiding?

Then she remembered that she could use her implants to locate him. She instructed the ship's computer to tell her his location, and it responded that he was not aboard the ship.

That response made her blink. That was impossible. It wasn't as if he could just get off.

She queried the computer about Mertz's location. It responded that he was no longer aboard the destroyer as well.

Frustrated, she headed for engineering. That was where Mertz frequented, so if anyone knew where he was now, they'd likely be there.

She found the lieutenant commander in charge of engineering overseeing maintenance on some piece of equipment. He rose to his feet and nodded politely to her.

"Highness, what can I do for you?"

"Commander… O'Halloran, isn't it? I'm looking for Jared Mertz or Austin Darrah. The ship's computer doesn't seem to think they're aboard. By any chance, do you know where they are?"

He nodded, led her to a maintenance hatch, and opened it. Somewhat nonplussed, she went inside.

Expecting to find a basic maintenance tube, she was surprised to find a concealed work area. Austin was looking over a piece of equipment on a makeshift table while Mertz looked on.

Mertz looked over at her and nodded. "Princess Kelsey."

She gestured toward the table. "What is this and why are you working on it in here? And why didn't the computer know where you were?"

"We're in a shielded area," he said. "This is an FTL com, and it seems to be malfunctioning. Commander O'Halloran can't seem to isolate the fault, so I'm giving Austin a shot."

That statement caused both of her eyebrows to shoot up. "No offense to Austin, but isn't this kind of a secret?"

The young Rebel Empire noble grinned at her. "It seems I've been brought into the inner circle. Okay, probably not the inner circle. Maybe a middle circle."

He turned his attention toward Mertz. "As far as I can tell, none of these parts is malfunctioning. Each and every one of them passes a self-check, and as Commander O'Halloran indicated, he even swapped out the offending part with a different unit, and it still behaves in exactly the same way."

"So you're saying this is external influence of some kind," Mertz said. "While I'm certainly not well versed in the theory behind this equipment, someone who is has assured me that that wasn't possible."

The young hardware enthusiast shrugged. "What can I tell you? Some of the most amazing breakthroughs in science take place when someone takes something that isn't possible and does it anyway.

"I'm absolutely not saying that this is an attempt at communication. I don't know enough about it to be certain. All I can state with any certainty is that the equipment is functioning as designed.

"Perhaps we're traveling through a section of space where a nearby star is sending out pulses of radiation that we can't detect clearly that somehow affects this one quantum connection. I can certainly keep thinking about what's going on, but I don't think any further examination by me is going to reveal a secret at the moment."

Mertz nodded. "That might actually be for the best, now that I think about it. When something has me stumped, the answer will usually come when I'm busy doing something completely unrelated, straight out of the blue."

He focused his attention on Kelsey. "You came looking for us, Highness. What can we do for you?"

She grimaced. "I've reached the end of my rope trying to get a handle on repairing the AI. I understand that I'm supposed to take the lead in that particular charade, but honestly, we all know that Austin is going to do the work. I just have to figure out a way to look like I'm leading when I'm really following."

"Has Fielding told us who's going on this mission other than Austin, myself, and either you or Olivia?"

Mertz shrugged. "She confronted him, but he didn't give her any more information. I think it's a safe bet that he's going along with you. If you feel more comfortable, I'm certainly okay with sending Olivia. It's your call."

Kelsey hated being so biased, but if she had the choice of picking between Olivia and Mertz, she picked the other woman in a heartbeat. She just didn't trust Mertz, even though she probably should.

She opened her mouth to say something to that effect, but the piece of equipment that the two men had been examining chose that moment to turn itself off.

Austin blinked down at the communication device. "Well, that's new."

* * *

TALBOT WATCHED Ralph Halstead work on his computer, which was attached to the FTL com, feeling more than a bit conflicted. Everything was set up in Carl's lab, and the other researchers were watching the proceedings with interest.

"Are you sure this is the best idea?" he asked Kelsey softly. The two of them were leaning back against the bulkhead and watching from a short distance away.

His wife nodded. "Fiona checked him. When he says that he's not going to betray us, I believe him."

"But *why* is he helping us?"

"Bottom line? He's bored."

"Bored?" Talbot asked, hearing the doubt in his own tone. "That's not a good long-term motivator."

His wife grinned at him. "It is if you've been doing the same thing for your aunt for years. She, by the way, *spectacularly* failed her lie detector test. There's no way we're going to be able to trust her with any secrets."

"We'll end up sending her back to the new Terran Empire permanently once we have a way to get there. Her husband, too. And sadly, their cats. I need a pet. You're not allergic to cats, are you?"

"Don't try to change the subject," he said firmly. "Our young friend is an industrial spy. A hacker. The moment someone offers him enough money or a chance to scamper off and sell what he knows about us, he's going to vanish."

"Not according to Fiona," Kelsey said smugly. "She's fully vetted his story about not really being that interested in stealing things for a living. Like you said, he's a hacker. He likes getting into places that he's not supposed to be and doing things that he's not supposed to be doing, but it's not the money that drives him. It's the thrill of the chase, so to speak.

"When he found out that we had the code used for the sentient AIs, he said he'd sell his soul to work on something like that. What you see before you is a programmer committed to his art. Unlike his aunt or the criminal syndicates that she was working for, we can offer him something they can't. A true challenge and a purpose in his life."

Talbot wasn't convinced, but it was ultimately Kelsey's call.

"All right," he said, throwing up his hands. "You win. What exactly are you hoping he can do with the FTL com? Hasn't Carl already gone over the software with a fine-toothed comb? After all, he wrote it."

"Carl is a genius, but he knows his limitations. He's something of a generalist. Ralph Halstead has devoted his life to coding and hacking. If anyone can get into the guts of an FTL com at a distance, it's going to be him."

"I think I found something," Ralph said, excitement in his tone. "Take a look at this, Carl."

Talbot strode forward to stand beside the two of them, and Kelsey joined him, listening in to their hushed discussion. Doctor Jacqueline Parker, the former head of the Dresden orbital's secret research team, also moved closer.

The hacker pointed to a line of text on the screen in front of him. "Look at this line right here. If I can get access to this module, I could shut off the unit remotely."

Carl read what was on the screen and slowly nodded. "It's not much of a vulnerability, but you're right. The question is, how do you get into that module from the receiver section of the com?"

"We can trigger a response from the other com whenever we send a status query," Ralph said. "If I send some additional code I've put together along with that query, the other unit is going to read it."

"How do you make the remote device actually execute the additional code in the manner that you want?" Parker asked softly.

Halstead turned and grinned at her. "I've got a library of code snippets that work on various Imperial systems. Sometimes they're useful and sometimes they're just a curiosity. Various groups that I've associated with over the years have compiled them just in case they proved useful in a future hack.

"When Carl built the FTL com, he used as many off-the-shelf components as possible. What I'm looking to do is cause a cascade failure inside the other com that ends up triggering a hard shutdown. The actual language and code that I use to make that happen is somewhat irrelevant. What matters is the end result."

"And you're certain that sending this command will cause a series of failures that results in the other unit turning off?" Kelsey asked.

Ralph nodded. "Pretty damned sure. Unfortunately, that's all it's going to do. It's not going to make any modifications to the other side that would allow us to initiate communications with them or signal a direct link request. Someone's going to have to notice that the unit is off and dig into the error codes to find my message."

"And what is your message?" Carl asked.

"Just a couple of words. Buried inside the error message they'll see is going to be a line of plain text that says, 'This is Kelsey.' That pretty much used up the leeway I had in affecting the error message. Carl hardwired how long the error message can be.

"If that doesn't get their attention, we can always try again once they turn it back on and send a different message, but this seems like a good start to me."

"How will we know that they've read it?" Talbot asked.

The hacker shrugged. "We won't. When they power the unit back up, we'll be able to ping it for a status again. That'll mean that they've noticed that it was off.

"Under the best of circumstances, we're going to have to assume that whoever is examining the equipment isn't going to find the first message, or the second, or even the third. We may have to do this a dozen times before someone figures out what we're doing.

"In any case, it's better than what we've been doing. Glitching that one component isn't getting us anywhere. We need to up our game."

Kelsey turned to him. "What do you think, Talbot?"

He considered how the young man might actually be trying to sabotage the other unit but ended up discarding the idea. He just didn't see what Halstead could gain by doing so.

"We should try," he eventually said.

His wife gestured toward the hacker. "Do it."

That made Talbot grin. When Kelsey made a decision, she didn't spend her time dithering. She balanced the options, picked one, and forged ahead. That was one of the things he loved about her.

Halstead tapped on his keyboard and hit the enter key. "Signal sent. Now we sit back and keep testing to see if they turn the other unit back on. If no one's looking at it, that could take hours or even days.

"I have this unit set up to continue sending connection and status requests every ten seconds. It'll send us a notification as soon as someone over there figures out the machine is down and powers it back up."

Halstead's computer beeped. He frowned and leaned forward. "Well, that's unexpected. It's back up."

"Are we even sure it went down?" Carl asked. "It's possible that your hack failed."

Halstead almost sneered, in a relatively friendly way. "Please. My hack worked. There has to have been somebody sitting right on top of the damned thing."

Talbot pursed his lips. If so, that was good news. Excellent news, in fact. It meant that they might once again be in contact with Admiral Mertz, and he could advise them on what to do.

They'd still have to find their own way back to the New Terran Empire, but at least they could give him a status update.

The communications speed would be far too slow—based on what Carl's experimentation had determined—to give the admiral any of the information that they'd stolen. It wasn't even fast enough to utilize video.

Audio communication would take a seeming eternity, but at least it was possible for truly critical information. Almost all of what they'd be doing would have to be text.

And all of that depended on someone over there figuring out exactly what they were doing, which wasn't assured. This was a good start, but they'd have a lot more work to do before they were back in contact with Admiral Mertz.

8

J ared stared at the FTL com as it shut down for a third time in less than a minute. He wasn't alone in watching the machine's antics. Austin, Kelsey, and Tony stared at it with equal incomprehension.

"That's *definitely* worse than it's been behaving," O'Halloran said. "Let me run a self-diagnostic on it and then plug in some additional equipment to see if I can tell what's going on."

He left the device powered off and quickly attached wires from some of the surrounding equipment. Only when he was seemingly ready to continue testing did he power device backup.

"The self-check isn't finding anything," he said under his breath. "I'm not even sure how that's possible, considering what we just saw. Let's see if I can get a full cycle of testing with the other equipment in before it does it again."

It turned out that the man had no trouble performing his testing because the FTL com didn't power itself off again. At least not in the three minutes it took the Fleet engineer to do his work.

"All of those readings look normal," Austin said as he looked over Tony's shoulder. At least in so far as I can tell. It's not like I have a lot of experience working on faster-than-light equipment."

O'Halloran straightened and stretched his back. "Everything looks normal to me, too. We're going to have to dig into the equipment much more deeply if we're going to figure out exactly what's going on."

"Let me try one more thing before we tear this apart," Austin said. "Do you mind?" he asked as he gestured toward the keyboard.

The engineer stepped back and gestured him in. "Be my guest."

The young Rebel Empire noble sat at the computer and began paging through different screens and typing on the manual keyboard.

"If I were accessing something remotely and shutting it down time and again, it wouldn't just be to drive the people watching the equipment crazy. I'd want them to find *something*. The easiest place for someone to plant evidence of what they're doing is in the logs."

Jared consulted his implants and noted the time. "I can only stay out of sight for so long, gentlemen. How long will such a search take?"

"Approximately this long," Austin said. "I found something."

They all leaned forward to look over his shoulder, and the young man pointed to a line on the screen. "This is an error message thrown by one of the components we were looking at. Does that look like a standard error message to you?"

The indicated entry had three words: *This is Kelsey*.

Jared felt his heart soar. Somehow, she'd done it. His sister had figured out how to access an FTL com over some unimaginable distance.

It wasn't a normal communication request, but they were getting information. That meant that the device itself could actually sense its linked pair. Kelsey and Carl were attempting to communicate with them.

"That is pretty definitive," he agreed with a grin. "The only reason that I can see for them to do what they're doing is that they can send a signal over a great distance, but it's not triggering some threshold where we can answer. Or maybe our side isn't recognizing what they're doing as valid.

"We've got to figure out how to interpret this. Does anyone have any idea how we can manage that? If we change the error message, will they see it on the other side?"

Austin shook his head. "Almost certainly not. I'd guess they're using some kind of specialized code to cause a certain component to fail while adding additional code that writes that one line to the log. The potential length of the error code is limited to just about what they sent too, so I wouldn't expect a longer message.

"Nothing they're going to be able to do from the other end will allow them to read our logs. And unfortunately, without knowing exactly how they managed this particular feat, we're not going to be able to do the same to them."

O'Halloran scrubbed his face with his hands. "I've got a lot of information on the normal operation of these devices, and when this unit started behaving oddly, I went through everything. I can't imagine how they're sending a signal that we can't detect. Everything has to go through the FTL receiver. Why isn't it detecting this?"

Kelsey cleared her throat. "I realize that I'm the least knowledgeable person about this sort of thing, but the device is obviously detecting it. Someone on the other end couldn't be making this equipment do anything unless this piece of equipment was receiving and interpreting whatever they were doing as a signal.

"Since I've been going through working on my communications skills, now that my implants can actually talk to other equipment, I've come to a realization. There are several layers of communication taking place all the time with my implants.

"There's the conscious level where I'm intentionally signaling someone or something. Then there's an unconscious level where my implants interface with the equipment around me to initiate communication in case I need to use something. Under those circumstances, unless I choose to do something, I may not even be aware that they've done anything."

Austin nodded slowly. "I see what you're saying. It's possible that the incoming signal isn't being interpreted as something we need to be notified about, but the equipment can handle it. It's already capable of doing that with sending a ping out to the other side and verifying the other FTL com is operational without anyone doing anything at the other end.

"And before you ask, we checked that. We're not detecting the linked FTL com when we ping. That doesn't mean that they haven't figured out how to connect us. This is all taking place at the quantum level, and the photons generate an automatic response in our hardware that gets sent back."

Jared scratched his chin and considered what the young man and said. "I'm hearing the words, but I don't think I'm getting the meaning that you intend me to have. Are you saying that they've found a way to stimulate the entangled pair so that our end sends a signal farther than we can intentionally do so?"

"The theory is that the range of those things is unlimited," Austin said, "but that some kind of flaw in the underlying theory is keeping the hardware from triggering a response past more than a single flip point. Even a repeater is only fifty percent effective in relaying a signal once.

"It sounds as if they've found at least a partial answer to the problem, only we can't pick up when they call because we have no idea what they're doing. The problem is that we don't know enough about what they did to even let them know that they've succeeded."

"Did you check the logs to see if someone is pinging us?"

Tony blinked and took back over the keyboard. "Yes. I'm getting a lot of pings starting several days ago. The com automatically generated a response. I should've looked sooner," he admitted sheepishly.

As soon as he finished saying those words, the FTL com powered off again. It looked as if Kelsey was going to continue trying to get their attention.

"We'll need to keep checking the error messages, but we also need to be more proactive in communicating with them," Jared said. "Since they're being so insistent, I think that we might be able to use the status of our machine to communicate with them."

He grinned at the obviously confused people around him. "This isn't going to make any sense to you, but I need you to look up something in the library and make it so that we can control when the FTL com is on and when it's off very precisely."

Austin frowned. "That's not exactly like sending a message to them."

"You'd be surprised what kind of information silence can tell another person," Jared said. "Just set it up the way I tell you, and I'll wager they'll get the message quick enough."

* * *

KELSEY WATCHED Carl and Ralph Halstead become more and more frustrated while working on the FTL com. After what had seemed like they were getting somewhere, they'd started having serious issues with their connection to the linked com. Without warning, their pings started failing without any rhyme or reason.

"What the heck is going on?" Carl asked, his tone frustrated. "It's like they're randomly turning it on and off."

"They might be," Halstead said. "Honestly, it's the only way they can let us know that they're aware of our activity. We can only interact with them through causing their machine to turn off and leaving an error message that they may or may not find.

"And then we can ping their system and get an automatic response that it's up, if it is. If they've realized that, this is the only way for them to let us know they are aware of our attempts."

"But it should still make sense," Carl grumbled.

"Maybe it does, but we just can't see it," Kelsey said in a soothing voice as she rested her hand on her friend's shoulder. "If there's a pattern to this, we need to graph it out. Rather than random pings, we need to start sending a rapid, steady series of them. Only then can we tell if there's a pattern to the machine being off or on."

The young scientist considered that for a moment and then nodded. "Good idea. Let me set something up to start pinging them once a second and graphing out the other com's status."

It only took a few minutes for him to have everything set up the way he wanted and for them to be looking at real-time returns from the other com. It quickly became apparent that the other device was being switched on and off fairly rapidly.

"There *is* a pattern in this," Halstead said slowly. "The time frames that the machine is either off or on fall in two groups: between two and three seconds or five and six seconds. That's some kind of binary pattern, but I'm not seeing a meaning to it."

Kelsey watched the pattern playing out on the screen and felt herself gasp when she saw the hidden pattern. "That's Morse code! I had to learn it when we were signaling you in the Nova system, Carl.

"The shorter time frame is for dots, the longer is for dashes. We'll have to wait to see if the message is repeating, but I'm deciphering it in my head as I'm seeing this, and it's a real message."

Carl's eyes widened. "Holy crap! I can see it now. Hold it, now we're getting just a series of dots with no dashes. I bet that's the boundary before they start repeating the original message again."

She saw the message start up again and started translating it in her head.

Kelsey, this is Jared. We've received your message. I'm hoping that you can decipher this message because I'm not certain that we can communicate back with you the same way you're doing with us.

We found your short note buried in the error log. If you can pass on to us what modifications we need to make on our end, we'll update the FTL com so that we can communicate via pings. Please let us know that you've received this message by shutting our system down and telling us so.

I have to tell you that I'm damn glad to hear you're okay. Well done. Jared Mertz.

Ralph Halstead leaned back in his chair. "Well I'll be damned. It actually *worked*. What the hell do we do now?"

Kelsey clapped her hand on his shoulder. "Cause their system to shut down with the error code 'message received' and then start getting them the information they need.

"Actually, the first thing we need to know is where they are. If we have a system name, then we can determine what our transmission range is. I'd absolutely hate to have them flip out beyond our range and lose communication."

Carl stared at her. "Do you realize how long it would take to transmit modification instructions if we can only use two or three words at a time? We're talking days to get the information across to get to the point where we can even communicate via Morse code.

"Not that I'm complaining about the speed of Morse code when it means the difference between some communication and no communication. Even so, it's still going to be a relatively limited kind of exchange."

The young hacker nodded at the scientist's words. "That's going to allow us to do text-based messaging, but it's not going to give us a shared method to transmit anything involving audio or video. Even if we could, the time to get the files across, specifically accounting for any errors in the transmission, would be significant."

Kelsey grinned at them. "I actually have an answer for that. This is one place where me watching a bunch of old vids from pre-Imperial Terra is going to come in handy.

"Back when computers were first becoming a reality on Terra, they had hardware called modems that communicated over copper wiring to other computers. The transmission speed was incredibly slow.

"The hardware had built-in error checking and handled the handshake of data back and forth in a way that's documented in the Imperial libraries aboard all the ships we have. If we can tell Jared to look at how to build an interface similar to one of these modems, we should be able to reliably send files and be confident that they're the same on the other end, once the error checking has any suspect portions resent."

Carl's gaze became slightly unfocused as he consulted the library. Then he started nodding. "I see what you're saying. Ironically, our transmission speed is roughly the same as those very early modems. Technology seems to have gone full circle.

"Let me start off by sending the response to them to know we've got their message and ask them where they are and where they're going. I don't want to start transmitting all the data that we have until we have the initial greetings out of the way."

He manipulated the keyboard, and within two minutes, they were getting a new set of Morse code signals.

Kelsey, I'm going to have my people start researching the communication protocols that Carl mentioned. It's going to be slow, but that beats complete silence.

As for where we are, the system only has an Imperial registry number. I'll send that along momentarily, but the more important piece of information for you is that we're on the way to Terra. We're inside the Rebel Empire in the automated destroyer, but our situation has become complex.

I don't want to use up a lot of time telling you all of this until we can communicate back and forth more reliably. We're masquerading as members of the higher orders and we've got actual members of the higher orders on board our ship that think we're someone else.

Again, I'll spell it all out to you in more detail once we've established the communication protocols, which my engineer tells me will probably happen very quickly once we know how to modify our FTL com to more closely link with yours.

Carl said that sending that kind of information would take days, which is going to put us dead center in the middle of an area where we don't dare communicate from. If we can manage it sooner, that would be better because in about four days we're going to be incommunicado for a period of time.

Let's save catching up for when we can actually talk and I can send you a real status. It's good to hear your voice again. Jared.

"Get him those modifications as quickly as you can, Carl," Kelsey said. "It sounds like we're on a tight time schedule. I'll talk with Angela and start getting everyone herded together. It sounds like we're going to Terra, and we'd probably best be moving if we want to get there in time to make a difference in whatever they're doing."

She stepped back and let them continue their work. Jacqueline Parker stepped away as well. She'd been quiet during the exchange.

"It's not common knowledge, but conditions on Terra are supposedly… grim," the scientist said in a low voice. "I'm not certain what you expect to find there, but you're only going to find death and destruction."

Kelsey turned toward the other woman. "Terra may be dead, but the key to beating the AIs is buried with her corpse. If we ever want to end this terrible subjugation of human species, we don't have a choice."

9

Olivia watched the timer and fumed. They'd been receiving data from Kelsey on how to modify the FTL com for days. Being able to only transmit a few words at a time to get those instructions was utterly ridiculous, but it was all they could manage.

Carl Owlet had guessed at how long it would take to get the complete modification plans sent, and it was going to be *very* close to the time they'd have to stop using the FTL com. Perhaps too close.

The last flip point was only a couple of hours ahead of them. If they failed to get the data before they flipped into the system with the AI, they'd have to shut down the process, because they didn't dare do anything that might warn the System Lords that FTL communication existed.

Doing all of this while sitting on *Athena*'s bridge stretched her nerves to the breaking point. She was far more comfortable sitting behind a desk where she could do real work instead of waiting here and doing nothing.

She could hardly imagine how Jared managed. Projecting an air of calm seem to be a full-time job, so how did he manage to accomplish anything else?

Part of her console lit up with an incoming call. It was from engineering, so it was probably Jared. Thankfully, Fielding wasn't on the bridge, so they didn't have to do everything via implants.

Olivia knew that those were far more efficient, but her upbringing still made it hard. The nobility of the Rebel Empire had an ingrained refusal to use implants to their full potential. She was no exception, even though she knew it was stupid.

She reached down and touched the acceptance on the call, and Jared's face appeared on the console.

"I need a distraction," she said with feeling. "How do you deal with this?"

"Feeling a little stressed?" he asked with a smile. "You know, you can get up and walk around a bit. Pass command on to someone else and take a break for just a bit."

"Do you do that?"

"Probably not as often as I should, but yes. If you'd like to have a few minutes away from the bridge, I have something down here that I think you'd like to see."

"Is it good news? Please tell me it's good news."

"It is good news."

"I'll be right there," she said as she stood and killed the communications link. A few words with Commander Hall had command transferred for the moment, and Olivia was on her way to engineering via the lift.

When she arrived, Jared was waiting for her. "We have it set up in the maintenance tube."

He led her to where they had a table holding the FTL com and some other equipment staged around it that she didn't recognize. There were a lot of hard cables running back and forth between the com and the other equipment.

Present were Kelsey Two, as they'd all taken to calling her privately after she'd come up with the idea, Commander O'Halloran, Austin Darrah, and Sean Meyer. All of them were clustered around the monitor observing something.

"What's the good news?" she asked Jared.

"We finished receiving the last of the modification information about half an hour ago."

She was somewhat annoyed that he hadn't notified her about all of this, but even though she was pretending to be the mission commander, he was really in charge, so she couldn't tear a strip off of him. As much as she wanted to.

"And have you made the changes?"

He nodded. "We just brought the system back up so that they could run a diagnostic on it. Once that's done, they're going to attempt to utilize Morse code from the other side.

"Rather than flipping the machine on and off, which would make two-way communication particularly challenging, Carl came up with a method of using just the status pings as a way to do it. That way both sides can send data at the same time and receive it."

She frowned slightly. "I don't know that much about Morse code, but are there two different kinds of signal? Dots and dashes? How are you differentiating between them?"

Austin looked over at her. "It's not as hard as you might think. Once we've verified that we have good communication in both directions, if we send three pings together, it will represent a dot. If we send six pings together, it will represent a dash. If we send ten together, it means end of a transmission. Even if one somehow gets dropped, the intent will still be clear."

"How quickly will we be able to exchange information?"

The young man shrugged. "It depends on what your expectations are. If you look at how slowly we've been exchanging information, this is going to seem very quick indeed. If you compare it with standard communications, this is going to be extremely slow.

"As you might imagine, video is out of the question, except perhaps for very small snippets that will take a significant amount of time. Audio is somewhat friendlier, but that will still take more time than just sending a text message."

Commander O'Halloran straightened. "I think we're ready to run the first test."

Jared moved over to stand behind the man. "What do we have in mind?"

The Fleet engineer gestured toward a microphone. "If you want to speak directly into the microphone, the equipment will translate your words into Morse code and send it. The response will come out of the speaker as a generic, computer-generated voice, but it should be comprehensible."

He turned toward Olivia. "How far away from the next flip are we? Has Fielding given you any indication of when he expects to join us for the flip?"

She shook her head slightly. "He hasn't said a word, which leads me to believe that he's just going to show up at an inconvenient moment to spring something on me. I really can't excuse myself from being on the bridge for very much longer. At this point, we're only a couple of hours away from the flip point."

"Any normal person would show up about half an hour before the flip," Jared said. "That virtually guarantees that Fielding will be there an hour ahead of time."

"Or show up five minutes beforehand," Olivia grumbled.

Jared laughed. "That sounds just about like the man. Well, at least we'll be able to get this next segment of our mission underway instead of wondering what's going on. I can't escape the feeling that there's something more to what we're doing than he's told us. Sean, go hold down the bridge in case he does show up early."

Commander O'Halloran waited for Jared to take a seat after Sean left and then touched a button next to the microphone and made a gesture with his hand for Jared to start.

"Kelsey, this is Jared. We've made the modifications just like you instructed, so I'm hoping this does the trick and we can start our dialog."

For a few seconds, nothing happened, and Olivia's heart fell. They'd gotten something wrong, and the communications attempt had failed.

Then a voice came out of the speaker. Not a regular person's voice, but a generic, monotone computer-generated one. Weirdly, she still heard it as Kelsey's voice in her head.

"Jared, it's good to hear your voice, so to speak. Kelsey here. I've got so much to tell you about what's going on. We've learned so much that we didn't know before about the Rebel Empire and all kinds of other, unexpected things.

"We're okay on this end, even though we're under a bit of pressure. What's your status? Are you guys okay?"

Olivia relaxed. She looked over and took in the other Kelsey's expression.

Kelsey Two was listening to the voice with a frown but didn't really seem angry. More like she was just nonplussed. Olivia suppose one didn't hear the voice of one's twin from another universe every day.

The one person that looked confused was Austin Darrah. He had a peculiar expression on his face and was looking back and forth between the com and Kelsey. He probably wondered about the odds of having two people with the same name involved in the conversation.

While they trusted the young man a little way, they hadn't explained to him that the Kelsey he knew came from another reality and that her doppelgänger was on the other end of the call. They'd have to do that at some point, but now wasn't the time.

"We probably only have between half an hour and an hour to exchange information before we have to cut the communication," Jared said. "We're about to flip into a system that has one of the System Lords in it, so we'd best keep this pithy. As quickly as you can, in as much detail as you feel comfortable with, give me a status on what you've been up to."

Olivia wondered to herself whether or not they should send Austin and Kelsey Two away. Kelsey One would probably be sharing information that was highly classified.

Jared, for his part, didn't seem to be overly concerned. In fact, he gestured for more chairs to be brought in so that everyone could sit and listen. He'd obviously made up his mind that he wasn't going to keep these secrets from their new allies.

Olivia still suspected that if their Kelsey brought up anything that he didn't want them to hear, he'd quickly shut her down.

Over the next half hour, she listened incredulously as Kelsey One went through their adventures and tribulations. She was amazed at the wealth of scientific information that they'd gotten away with and amused at the number of prisoners they'd accumulated.

Thankfully, she knew she'd be able to help with at least one of their problems. Now that they'd restored communication, she'd be able to speak with this Lieutenant Commander Sommerville and reassure him that Kelsey was actually in communication with the real resistance.

That might very well allow the other man to give her friend enough information to find her way to Terra in time to join them there. Particularly since they'd cracked the mystery of the weak flip points. Or, as they now referred to them, the multi-flip points. That was actually a much better name.

The far flip points that they discussed were a complete shock. No one had ever predicted that something like that existed. She made a mental note to have Elise send her people searching the outer part of the Pentagar, Courageous, and Erorsi systems. If any of the three had far flip points, that might give her people many more options to search the universe.

Hell, the way these multi-flip points had different branches that could be explored, even from the same position inside a single flip point, vastly expanded the opportunities to explore the universe and connect with other systems that might not be reachable through normal flip points.

There was one in the Courageous system right next to Pentagar and another in the Erorsi system. They might now be gateways for Elise's people to get to a lot of new systems.

With the flip point modulator that Carl Owlet had designed, scout ships would be able to use different branches from any multi-flip point, go to the other side, and then access even more branches from there.

Considering that the one example Carl had examined closely had showed that some of the branches on either side didn't match up with the ones on the first side, there was the potential that a ship could flip along one branch, turn right around and flip along a second that didn't go to a location reachable from the first side, and then turn right around again and go to a third location that neither of the others could see. Perhaps even more.

Obviously, that wasn't going to be an infinite array of possibilities. Still, regular flip points only connected with about a tenth of the stars in the universe, at least in the areas humanity had explored. If the multi-flip points connected with even the same number of previously unreachable systems, that doubled the destinations available.

And then there were the far flip points. They obviously connected to systems reachable by regular flip points, but what if they also reached systems that connected to different networks of regular flip points?

That had been a hypothesis that she'd read about when doing her research on the subject in college. She admitted that the idea of completely separate networks of flip points weaving around one another made her brain hurt, but if the professionals said it was possible, then it was something that she couldn't dismiss out of hand.

That might explain how the Clans had lived separately from the Rebel Empire for so long without being discovered. If the worlds that they'd obviously occupied and built their new civilization on were part of a separate network, the Rebel Empire could blithely go about their business and never have a clue that such a powerful enemy was so close by.

But that was a mystery for another day.

Another aspect of what Kelsey had discovered completely intrigued her. The Pandorans with their human DNA that had to have been placed inside them before humanity had ever discovered space travel. Who had done it and why?

That was another mystery that wasn't going to be solved today.

She glanced at Kelsey Two again. The other woman's expression was grim.

Olivia had known that she resented the success that Kelsey One had achieved, and she could even understand it. Still, she'd need to talk to the other woman and try to head off some of the bitterness she could see already building inside her.

This wasn't a competition. The successes that Kelsey One had achieved could help Kelsey Two.

Jared responded briefly about how impressed he was with what they'd accomplished and then launched into the far shorter tale of what they'd been up to. The key elements only took a few minutes to pass along, and he ended with an explanation of what they hoped to accomplish.

Olivia noted that he left out that they had visitors from another universe. A glance at Kelsey Two showed that she'd noted the omission too, and it didn't make her any happier.

Jared went on, not recognizing how Kelsey Two was seething. "I haven't got any idea what Fielding intends during this so-called 'repair mission,' but once we have it out of the way, we'll be on our way to Terra. We're supposed to be there roughly a week from now. My suspicion is that it'll take us a few days longer than that, considering we need to carry out the mission here.

"If you can convince your resistance contact to help you, that would be incredible. We're separated from my fleet, and even at best speed, they're going to come in at least a week behind us and from another direction. Odds are very high that the defenses that keep people out of the Terra system are strong enough that any incursion against them would draw a response from all the surrounding systems in time to interfere with what we're trying to do.

"This is still a stealth mission, and I'd prefer to make it happen without the AI realizing what's going on before we kill it. Olivia is going to need to be back on the bridge very shortly. If you could bring Lieutenant Commander Sommerville down and let her have a brief discussion with him to authenticate her identity, I think that's about all we have time left for."

"I've already sent for him," Kelsey One said. "He walked in just in time to hear that last little bit. Olivia, if you have time to go ahead and have a discussion with our friend, that would be *very* helpful."

Olivia nodded even though the other woman couldn't see her. "Hello, Commander Sommerville, my name is Olivia West. I'm the coordinator of Harrison's World and the leader of the resistance there. We've staged a coup and taken over the system and are working with Kelsey and the New Terran Empire."

She proceeded to give him a recognition code. He responded with the appropriate response and then sent her a code of his own that she responded to.

He then sent one that she was unfamiliar with. In fact, it didn't even seem to follow the same pattern as the rest of the recognition codes.

"I'm afraid I don't know that one," she said. "Is it a red herring?"

"I have no idea what a red herring is, but if it means that that was a trap to see if you'd respond to it, it was. I suppose that I'll have to accept that you're really a member of the resistance. I can't begin to tell you how that complicates things for me."

Olivia could almost hear the dry tone of his voice as he said it, even though the computer wouldn't have carried that information across.

"I live to serve," she said solemnly.

Her implants pinged with an incoming call from the bridge. It was text only from Sean. It indicated that Fielding had arrived.

She sent a response that she'd be there momentarily and turned to Jared. "Fielding is on the bridge. We should probably head there and see what other surprises he has in store for us."

10

A ngela sat in *Persephone*'s command chair as they made the transition to Archibald. This was it, her first independent command, and she was going back into the system they'd barely escaped from the last time they'd been there. One with an invasion in progress.

Commander Sommerville had confirmed that he'd intended to use a far flip point in the system. His admission had been grudging, and he had obvious reservations about telling them anything, but he'd finally pinpointed where it was located in Archibald's outer system.

Her mission was to make certain that the rest of their ships wouldn't encounter Clan warships as they made their way out to it. *Persephone* was very stealthy, so Angela didn't anticipate any problems. The other ships wouldn't have her advantages, though.

In the few days since they'd made their escape from Archibald, the Clans had fully occupied the system. Her passive scanners were easily able to pick up grav drives moving across the system and surrounding the main world.

Kelsey had taken the precaution of leaving a stealthed probe that gave them occasional updates via FTL, so Angela had come into the system certain that no one was close enough to detect her.

The problem was that the Clans were still searching for the Q-ship that had gotten away. She didn't blame them. It had killed one of their frigates.

That meant there were far too many vessels quartering back and forth across the outer system. Sommerville had intended to change course once he was clear of detection, so the enemy wasn't near the far flip point, but they were still an obstacle to be avoided.

One serious complication was that the clans knew about far flip points.

Frankly, she'd be surprised if they weren't looking for them in each system they'd taken from the Rebel Empire.

If Angela was dead unlucky, the Clans would find it, and she'd have to use brute force to get their ships through, which would trigger a pursuit that wouldn't turn out well for her or her friends.

Her goal was to get the carrier, the Q-ship, and the freighter she was shepherding safely to the far flip point and be gone before the search pattern expanded to include the areas where the multi-flip point or far flip point were located.

She had no idea if the Clans could detect a multi-flip point, but they'd had one to examine for five hundred years. She wasn't discounting the possibility.

If they found it, that might be a disaster for Pandora, but there was absolutely nothing she could do about that. The forces of the New Terran Empire were hopelessly outgunned and would die in that system if they stood their ground.

No, they had to get the critical manufacturing equipment and knowledge back to Avalon at all costs. The survival of their own worlds depended on it.

While the multi-flip point was safely clear of any enemy traffic, there were ships between it and the far flip point. Whatever path she chose would have to be circuitous, and they'd have to go slowly.

"Well, there's no time like the present," she said. "Signal *Audacious* to come through."

This was going to be the most nail-biting moment for Angela. They'd installed the flip drive that Carl had had built by the Rebel Empire shipyard and then snuck out of the system on board the Q-ship they'd hijacked. If it failed, they were screwed.

They'd tested it along a different branch of the multi-flip point successfully, but it was still experimental technology. Until they'd used it for a much longer period of time, Angela was going to be worried every time they made a transition.

If it failed, this was possibly the worst time and place. The carrier would be trapped in a hostile system filled with enemies already looking for a fight.

Jack Thompson turned his head toward her. "*Audacious* acknowledges."

Angela felt herself tense and only relaxed when the massive carrier appeared. She was quickly followed by the Q-ship and the freighter that they'd stolen from Dresden. All reported themselves in good shape via tight-beam coms.

This was it. All of the New Terran Empire forces were in the Archibald system now. Part of her wondered if they'd ever get back to Pandora. Angela hoped so. She liked the people there, and it wasn't every day that one got to explore an actual alien society.

"Set course for the far flip point, Jack. Take us as far around the enemy vessels as we can get and still make decent time. I'd like to have double the clearance that we suspect the enemy has to detect a slow-moving carrier like *Audacious*."

Thompson nodded. "Yes, ma'am. That's going to put our travel time at roughly eight hours to get to the far flip point."

"Better to go slow than to not get there at all."

She turned her attention to the tactical console, where her new executive officer, Senior Lieutenant Arianna Knox, was huddled with the tactical officer, Lieutenant Jevon McLeod.

"What are you two picking up from deeper inside the system?"

Her redheaded executive officer turned toward her. "There's a lot of enemy traffic in there, ma'am. Most of the communications we're detecting are encrypted, so I don't think we're seeing anything from the Rebel Empire side of things.

"We're a bit distant to detect things at Archibald itself via passive scanners, but it looks as if the civilian orbital is still intact. There are a lot of small craft moving between it and the surface of the planet."

"I suppose that makes sense," Angela said. "They want to get as many civilians and Fleet people down to the surface as possible to keep them from causing them trouble in space. Hell, they're probably sending their own troops down to secure as much of the planet as they can."

McLeod's eyebrows rose. "Can they really have brought enough people to subjugate a major world like Archibald? There are billions of people down there."

"The AIs managed to do it with Harrison's World," Angela said grimly. "It really depends on how much force you're willing to use. Shoot enough people, and the rest will start paying attention.

"We also can't forget how deeply the Clans hate the Rebel Empire. As far as they're concerned, the Clans are the *real* Terran Empire, and these people are just pawns for the computers. Pawns that mercilessly exterminated most of the human race. At least that's what Jacob Howell says, and I believe him."

Howell was a human from Pandora, the son of the leader of Clan Dauntless. All humans on the planet were descendants of the people who'd survived the crash of the ex-Clan battlecruiser *Dauntless* onto the surface of Pandora.

His father had been a junior officer on the battlecruiser at the time of the crash. All the senior officers had perished because they'd refused to abandon ship and rode it down to the surface.

Those who'd survived had gone through a culling. The most violent and xenophobic survivors had fought to the death against the Pandorans. Only those who'd surrendered had lived.

That was Darwinism in action, as far as Angela was concerned.

At their very best, the clans were antisocial. At worst, they wanted to subjugate or exterminate anyone other than their own people. They weren't big on talking or negotiating.

The best outcome would be for them to make their way across the

Archibald system and out again without anyone becoming aware that they'd been there at all. That was going to take a lot of slow maneuvering to steer clear of any detection at all. A nerve-racking endeavor at the best of times.

"Keep monitoring everything you can," she said. "Jack, make sure we don't come anywhere near those guys. We'd win the fight but lose the war."

"Copy that," he said. "Unless someone gets a wild hair up his... well, you know, we'll probably be fine."

Angela chuckled, settled back into her seat, and tried to keep from fidgeting. Commanding a ship was very different from commanding a platoon of marines. This was going to take a lot of getting used to.

* * *

KELSEY HEADED for *Athena*'s bridge with Mertz and Olivia. She kept her face devoid of expression, but inside, she was seething.

Oh, she knew that she shouldn't be so upset at what she'd heard from the other version of herself over the FTL com, but she couldn't help it. How could the woman have accomplished *all* of that?

It wasn't that Kelsey felt it made her look bad, though it certainly did. What really galled her was how capable the other woman was when she felt as if she could barely tie her own shoes on the best of days.

Olivia pulled her back when Mertz got into the lift. "We'll be along momentarily, Jared. Stall him. After how he made us jump around, I don't feel bad about making him wait for a little while."

Mertz didn't argue, simply nodding. "Will do. Are you going to be long?"

"Probably not. Say five minutes."

"See you there."

Olivia waited until the lift doors had closed and then gestured for Kelsey to walk with her up the corridor.

"What's wrong?" Kelsey asked.

"It's not that anything is wrong, Kelsey, but I can see how upset you are, and I wanted to let you vent. Keeping it inside isn't going to make you feel any better. In fact, it might be actively bad for our relationship, and I don't want to see that. Neither, I suspect, do you."

Well, that was annoying. "Am I that obvious?"

"Only to someone that knows you very well," Olivia said with a smile, putting her hand on Kelsey's shoulder. "And while I realize that you hardly know me, I've known a version of you for almost a year. I pride myself on being very observant, and I couldn't help seeing how my version of Kelsey made you feel."

Kelsey sighed and hunched forward a little. "I was already having this mental conversation with myself. I've never met another version of me. Hell, until just a little while back, I never would've dreamed anything like this was possible.

"It's a lot to assimilate, even discounting the fact that I think I hate myself. No offense to your Kelsey, but she had everything handed to her. She got every bit of good luck that I didn't, and it pisses me off."

She held up a hand when Olivia looked as if she was going to respond.

"Hear me out. I understand that's not what happened, at least from your point of view. You've heard my story, so you can imagine that I don't see it quite the same way.

"Again, that's not her fault. It's not my fault, either. It's just the way the universe is. Or perhaps I should say the universes, plural. I just have to accept the way the dice rolled and take my beating."

Olivia smiled a bit sadly. "I don't know how they play dice in your universe, but here we don't have beatings for the loser. And I think you're doing yourself a disservice by thinking of yourself as the loser. You're not in competition with our Kelsey.

"Her success in this universe didn't come without cost. Perhaps it wasn't as high a price as you've paid, but it didn't come for free. She's bled for everything she's achieved. So have you. You've got nothing to be ashamed of."

"Then why didn't Mertz mention me?" Kelsey demanded. "Even as we speak, your version of me doesn't know that I'm here. He left out the story where I came looking for help. Why?"

Olivia pulled her into a compartment just off the corridor. It wasn't very large and seemed to be a break room of some kind. Being on board a ship that was supposed to be computer operated, it was completely empty.

"I suspect that he just didn't want to open that can of worms right then. He knew we had very little time before we had to cut off communications. That's not the kind of conversational bomb one just drops and then goes quiet.

"Jared hasn't told me anything, but I already know what he intends. It's what I'd do. He's going to work on completing this repair mission so that we can get back on the way to Terra.

"Once we're away from the System Lord, he's going to sit you down at the FTL com and get our Kelsey on the other end. Then the two of you are going to talk until you don't have anything left to say to one another.

"I have every confidence that our Kelsey is going to get her ships to Terra. Once she does, the two of you are going to have a chance to meet in person. Then you'll see exactly how our Kelsey feels about you. I can guarantee that both she and Jared will move planets to help your people."

Kelsey rubbed her face, tired and angry, mostly with herself. And embarrassed. Was this really how petty she'd become? Had the events of the last few years really turned her into this person?

"I wish I could believe that," she finally said. "No matter how lucky you are in this universe, the deck is still stacked against you. I can't see how you're going to get past this artificial intelligence, get onto Terra, get what we need, and then get away again. Not when a crazy computer expects us to exterminate humanity there.

"Personally, I think it'll take a miracle to make that happen. That doesn't even count what you do next. You'll have to go after the master AI, and it's going to be a lot better protected than the one on Terra.

"The only thing that's saved you so far is that the System Lords didn't even know you existed. Now that they do, at least in a general sort of way, they're going to take every step they can to protect themselves. How are you even going to get close to the master AI?"

Olivia shook her head. "You're asking the wrong question. What you should be thinking about is how we can leverage the hostilities between the Clans and the Rebel Empire to our benefit.

"Right now, the AIs are figuring out that they have a very serious problem with the Clans. Once they fully grasp the gravity of the situation, they'll almost certainly assume that the people who stole the Dresden orbital and have blockaded the Erorsi system are the same people that are currently attacking them. Occam's razor: the answer with the fewest assumptions is usually the right one. Only this time, it isn't.

"It takes a lot of imagination to figure out that you have two very different enemies operating independently of one another at the same time. They'll end up treating us as one group. Since the Clans are a very overt sort of threat, the AIs won't expect us to be sneaking around right through their very guts."

The sheer audacity of the plan she'd just heard made Kelsey gasp. "In other words, you just plan to keep doing what you've been doing? Meandering along from crisis to crisis, looking for random opportunity and hoping that someone bigger than yourself doesn't squash you like a bug? That's not a plan. That's a fantasy.

"One that's going to fall apart the moment the AIs discover who you really are. Good luck doesn't last forever, as well I know. Something is going to go wrong that reveals who we really are."

She gestured in the vague direction of the bridge. "Let's take Fielding as an example. He's living with us. If he figures out that we're playing him, he might be able to set off the plasma charges in our hold and kill us in an instant."

Olivia shook her head. "If I let what might go wrong stop me from doing what needed to be done, I'd still be back on Harrison's World, hoping that the AI didn't drop a kinetic weapon on me. You can't live your life in fear of what might happen.

"Sometimes bold action is the only answer. Perhaps that's a lesson you could learn from our Kelsey. Lord knows the woman doesn't know how to think before she leaps. If she sees something that needs doing, she does it and damn the consequences. That drives Jared absolutely nuts, but I'll tell you one thing: it gets results.

"Kelsey, it's time to stop hiding in the dark and twitching every time you hear a noise. Stop wondering how you're going to screw things up and start doing everything that you can to make this work."

Hard words, Kelsey supposed, but there might be some wisdom to them.

She nodded, still pissed off, but not at her doppelgänger. Now she was annoyed with Olivia. She really needed to talk with Elise, Scott, and Sean to start sorting this out.

But now was not the time. They needed to head to the bridge and find out what other impossible tasks Fielding had in mind for them.

Hopefully it wouldn't be something so impossible that the AI just killed them outright.

11

———————

Talbot walked into Carl's lab and was once again blown away by how many people were doing so many different things in the large compartment. The young scientist was lucky that *Audacious* had plenty of space for him to spread out in.

The sprawling area was filled with tables and large pieces of equipment scattered along the deck. The faint stench of charred electronics came from what was left of the Singularity computer they'd stolen from the Rebel Empire, even though the equipment had probably been damaged years ago.

Carl raised his hand when he saw Talbot and gestured him over. "Excellent timing. I was just about to call you. We've found something."

Talbot raised an eyebrow as he stepped up beside his friend. "Really? Something about the FTL com?"

Carl shook his head. "No. Admiral Mertz shut down his end of the communications link because they're about to go into a system containing one of the AIs, and he doesn't want to chance being detected. We're not going to get much of an opportunity to experiment with things there until they're done and on the way to Terra.

"Meanwhile, I've been looking at the Singularity computer we liberated from Archibald. I haven't got everything sorted out, mind you, but I got a little bit more information than we had when we started this. Something intriguing."

Talbot followed Carl over to the scattered wreckage of the large computer. The acrid odor of burned electronics was much stronger here.

They'd found the remains of the computer in the medical research facility they had to burglarize to get a regenerative cure for Commodore Murdoch, the Rebel Empire flag officer they'd captured at Dresden.

The woman had insider information that they'd simply had to have, so

Kelsey had ordered that they do what they could to get her cured from the injuries she'd suffered at the hands of Raul Castille, the murderous security officer under the commodore's command. The bastard that had caused them so much trouble.

Thankfully, they'd been able to get away with the cutting-edge regenerative technology, and it had been able to repair the woman's severed spine. Castille had snapped her neck and left her for dead, but now she was learning to walk again. It truly was miraculous.

The breakthrough in regenerative technology was going to revolutionize the care of those stubborn injuries that even Imperial technology just couldn't handle.

Better yet, he suspected it had implications that were going to carry over into other areas. Such as making it easier to implant Marine Raider technology inside someone.

Someone like him.

He'd finally adjusted to the changes that the procedures had introduced into his legs and would soon be going through the work on his torso. He'd had a long argument with Kelsey and the medical staff about what parts of the torso could be done in one session.

Back in the days of the Old Empire, Marine Raiders went through a number of different stages. Recruits usually came from the Imperial Marines, so they already had cranial implants, but their nanites needed to be upgraded to the class that Marine Raiders used. Call that the first step in the process.

Next, they had their pharmacology units, ocular enhancements, auditory enhancements, and olfactory enhancements installed. That could cause some significant issues with their senses, so they needed time to grow used to the changes.

For step three, the Old Empire had implanted artificial muscles into the legs and coated the bones there in graphene. Step four meant doing that for the torso and leaving the arms untouched. Step five was doing the dominant arm, and step six was the nondominant arm.

In between each of those six steps was a week of recovery so that the new Marine Raider could become fully comfortable with the great power that was now his or hers to command.

Kelsey had gone through the entire process in one go at the hands of a mad computer. She'd refused to even consider something like that for anyone else, but she'd agreed that the process could be streamlined.

The process as it now sat had four steps. Steps one and two of the Old Empire process were combined. Then the legs were done. The third step was doing the torso and nondominant arm. The final step was doing the dominant arm.

The period between the procedures had also been shortened so that the overall process took about two weeks, including recovery time. Talbot was convinced that could be reduced to a single week, and he thought the new regeneration equipment would help.

Doctor Zac Zoboroski, *Audacious*'s chief medical officer, wasn't so convinced, but once they'd left the Archibald system, he'd agreed to give it a try.

If they didn't at least do it once, they'd never know if it was going to be something they could utilize going forward. They needed real data to make smart decisions.

"What have you found?" Talbot asked. "Frankly, there's not a lot of this thing left, and I never expected you to be able to pull anything out of it. I'm ready to be shocked."

Carl grinned. "And shocked you will be. My suspicions were confirmed. What you see scattered on the deck before you are the remains of an artificial intelligence developed by the Singularity.

"I've been through the computers that the researchers were using and have confirmed that they already knew that, but my inspection of the component parts made that independently clear. It looks as if this piece of equipment was destroyed within the last few years, but that's not exactly true. Appearances, both visual and olfactory, can be deceiving.

"I'm uncertain what they did to make it smell like it had been recently burned, but the computer has been dead for a lot longer than I'd suspected. My guess is about twenty years."

Talbot eyed the equipment suspiciously. "That seems a little hard to believe."

"Yet it's true. There were some power units amongst the wreckage, and I was able to determine how long had passed since they'd held a charge.

"That isn't to say that the event that destroyed this equipment took place twenty years ago. It's conceivable that the computer might have been whole until the last few years and then something blew up the ship or station it was kept in. I have no way of knowing that for sure."

"So it's a curiosity?" Talbot asked, rubbing his chin.

"Far from it," Carl disagreed. "Think of how much useful information we got off of the computers on the Old Empire ships that were five hundred years old. This computer was still in use by the Singularity until just one tenth that amount of time ago. Even if the unit itself ran out of power because it had been abandoned or lost, those power units didn't keep going for more than six or eight months when separated from a fusion plant.

"That means there is going to be data on it about the Singularity that's a lot more recent than anything we have. Since it's one of their own computers, it's very likely that buried down in the guts of its data cores is critical information that will make a difference for us in this upcoming conflict.

"We all know that the Singularity is pulling the strings supporting the Clans. Maybe this computer can tell us what their real goal is."

Talbot nodded slowly. "Okay, I suppose I can buy that. How long is it going to take you to crack the encryption on the data cores?"

Carl shrugged. "Encryption like that is almost unbreakable, but we have an ace up our sleeve. Fiona can go through data and try combinations like nobody's business. That's the benefit of being a true artificial intelligence."

The Rebel Empire AI that they'd stolen from the Dresden orbital was currently installed aboard *Persephone*. They wouldn't dare risk transmitting much data back and forth until they were clear of the Archibald system, so they wouldn't even begin to start looking into cracking the encryption until they were clear.

"All right, I suppose that is good news. You said this was an AI. What makes you think that?"

Carl patted the top of his computer monitor. "That would be the data that we recovered from the researchers. There's far too much computational power built into this wreckage to just be a regular computer. It's on par with the components used to build Fiona, only formed from a completely different technology set.

"Oh, the basics are similar. After all, the Singularity formed from a sect that left the Old Empire thousands of years ago. They'd have to have taken the basic computer technology with them, but they developed it in an entirely new way over the time after they left. There's a lot of interesting stuff buried in this computer that I can't wait to get my hands on. It's going to be fascinating."

The young scientist's grin widened. "I discovered something else about this system. It wasn't created all at one time. It seems to have been built bit by bit by attaching new equipment to old equipment. Digging down to the very core of the device, the researchers found an underwater research vehicle that was the origin of the computer. It was called AUV #5.

"At this point, I very much doubt the circuitry in that ancient unit, which probably came from Terra, was being used, but just the fact that it was still there is exciting. It's like seeing a bit of history.

"It's also going to allow me to trace how the Singularity's computer technology changed over time. That's going to be invaluable in ascertaining what their computer philosophy is."

Talbot shook his head. "Have fun, but don't get so lost in what you're doing that you forget we've got other things on our plate. If you'll excuse me, I've got to go see a doctor about an upgrade."

Amused at his friend's enthusiasm, Talbot left the lab and took a lift to the medical center. Commander Zac Zoboroski, *Audacious*'s chief medical officer, was waiting for him.

"Are you sure I can't talk you out of this?" the other man asked. "We're still relatively new at doing this procedure, and I'd rather not cause you any undue discomfort."

"I'm a marine," Talbot said with a grin. "If Kelsey can take it all at once, I can do this."

The physician seemed unconvinced. "Doctor Stone told me how the princess ripped equipment out of the floor during her recovery. It took her quite a while before she could manage to handle things without destroying them. I'd like to urge you to think about leaving yourself one arm that you won't have to worry about."

Talbot had to admit that he was probably going to mess something up, but the sooner they settled on a final procedure that wasn't taking forever, the sooner they could get the rest of the marines on board *Persephone* converted into Marine Raiders. The benefits of that could not be understated.

"I hear you, Doctor, but I'm committed to giving this a try."

Zoboroski shrugged. "Don't say I didn't warn you. I believe you're familiar with the equipment, so let's get you inside and get this started."

The current implantation unit was significantly more advanced than the hodgepodge affair they'd recovered from the station orbiting Erorsi. Thankfully, it also had all the safeguards that the mad computer had turned off. Talbot would be blissfully asleep during this procedure and wake relatively free of pain.

"Before we start," Talbot said, "what about the new regeneration equipment? Are we going to try it?"

Zoboroski shook his head. "After looking over the specifics of the treatment, I don't think it would add much value. It's far better for more delicate regeneration. While you're going to have a lot of muscle trauma, that kind of thing responds well to standard regeneration."

Without saying anything else, Talbot climbed into the implantation device and pulled the clear hood down over his torso. He settled back and closed his eyes, knowing that he wouldn't feel the transition from waking to sleep.

What he did feel was waking up to a dull ache throughout his torso and arms. The procedure was done. He was now a full Marine Raider.

He pulled himself up slightly and opened the clear cover over the machine. He also managed to tear it from its mounting and send it crashing to the deck.

Zoboroski laughed. "I hope you're ready, because here's the first of many 'I told you sos.'"

Talbot sighed with resignation. Kelsey was going to have a field day mocking him.

12

———————

Jared arrived on the bridge, walking confidently in and nodding to Fielding. The man had obviously decided to make an ass out of himself, because he'd evicted Sean from the command console and taken it for himself.

For his part, Sean, while annoyed, didn't seem overly perturbed. Knowing how much having someone else take over the command console bothered him, that told Jared how much the other officer had grown in the last year.

Jared stopped beside the console and smiled at Fielding. Without speaking, he reached over and pressed a series of buttons, disabling the controls.

The older man frowned. "What did you just do?"

"I locked the controls, Lord Fielding," Jared said matter-of-factly. "This particular console has a lot of built-in authority. I suspect that you wouldn't want to inadvertently set off the weapons while we're trying to communicate with the System Lord."

"I wasn't going to touch anything, and I'm not an idiot. Reactivate it."

Jared shook his head. "My apologies, but I have specific instructions from Lady Keaton about this sort of thing."

Fielding leaned back and consider Jared. "Where is Lady Keaton?"

"She's been slightly delayed," Jared said. "She'll be here in five minutes. In the meantime, might I ask what you plan for us to do once we flip into the next system?"

The older man smiled. "I think I should wait for Lady Keaton before I explain myself, Lord Gust. As she likes to say, she's in command of this mission."

The man's reaction didn't really surprise Jared that much. He seemed to have a thing for delaying information to assert his own dominance.

Jared inclined his head. "As you wish."

He moved over to stand beside Sean and proceeded to ignore the Rebel Empire noble. Looking over Commander Hall's shoulder, he could see that they were roughly an hour from flipping into the new system.

He'd checked the Old Empire databases to see what they had to say about the target system, but there wasn't much there. The system in question was called Bradley, was a cul-de-sac, and had never supported a very large population. It was mainly a place used for mining the rare elements used in flip drives and other high-end equipment. The population of miners and refiners that had lived and worked there back in the old days had been counted in the low tens of thousands.

For the life of him, Jared couldn't imagine why the Rebel Empire had decided to place a System Lord there. It didn't make a lot of sense. Unless, of course, they were using the system for something other than mining.

The rare elements used in making flip drives were present in many systems, at least in small amounts. They were available in much larger quantities in other places inside the Rebel Empire, so this one system didn't warrant this much attention, as far as he could see.

"We're coming into extreme scanner range of the flip point, Lord Gust," Commander Hall said, using the cover identity Jared was playing. "I'm detecting at least three large stations near the flip point. We're too distant to make out any details, but I believe those might be battle stations."

That really made Jared's eyebrows rise. Not only was the system important enough for a System Lord, it had exterior defenses. For whatever reason, the Rebel Empire had decided to place their defenses on the interior side of any flip points in almost every system Jared had visited.

Tactically, that made no sense. Putting the defenses on the outside, like the system in front of them, was smarter. He'd never had the opportunity to ask someone who might have known the answers about why the Rebel Empire did things this way, and he'd really like to know.

Now that they were restoring communications with Kelsey, he could ask Commander Giguere or Commander Sommerville exactly why that might be.

Knowing that it was useless to try, he still decided to ask the Rebel Empire noble sitting in front of him for more information. "From everything that I've been able to determine, there's not much in this system worth defending. Why so much firepower?"

The older man shrugged slightly. "Honestly, there isn't anything there worth defending to this degree, so far as I know. It's a rather successful mining operation, but there's no call for this level of defense.

"I believe this is an element of the paranoia that has taken over this particular Lord. It's one of the reasons we were dispatched to correct the issue."

That made sense. If someone were paranoid, they'd do whatever they needed to protect themselves. It probably wouldn't be all that hard to set up a construction area suitable for building battle stations in a mining system. Or for building ships, for that matter.

The lift doors slid open, and Olivia walked onto the bridge with Kelsey at her heels. She eyed Fielding with disapproval and gestured for him to get out of her seat.

The man arose with a smirk on his face. "I'm so glad you could finally make it, Lady Keaton. It seems that we're coming into scanner range of the final flip point, and it's time for me to fill you in on more of the specifics of our mission."

Olivia took her seat as if she'd been born in it and shot the man a look filled with irritation and disapproval. "I won't continue playing this game where you hide details until the last minute, Lord Fielding. It's time for you to share everything you know about what we're supposed to accomplish."

"Perhaps," the man said without rancor. "Perhaps not. I'm certainly going to share all of the information I have on getting to the Lord itself. As to what will take place after we get there, I retain the right to keep some information to myself until it's appropriate for me to share. You're just going to have to accept that, Lady Keaton.

"As your subordinate has already discovered, the Lord has protected its flip point with military hardware. This has had a deleterious effect on ore production. Over the last ten years, the output from this system has dropped from the expected amount to virtually nothing. The remainder of the Lords have decided that it's time to deal with their wayward brother."

Olivia look less than impressed. "That's all fine and good, but what can we expect once we flip to the other side? Are these stations going to allow us to flip? Or are they going to open fire on us as soon as we get close?"

"Those are all very good questions," Fielding said. "I have an authorization code that should allow this vessel into the system without interference. Let me stress the word *should*. The Lord in my system has assured me that it will work, but until we try it, we won't know for sure.

"Once we arrive in the other system, we're to proceed to the System Lord. I have another code that will compel it to allow us access. That same code should defuse any defensive measures it might otherwise be inclined to take against us."

Jared took a step forward. "I'm hearing you use the words 'should' and 'might' far too many times, Lord Fielding. You don't really have any real confidence that this is going to work, do you?"

The Rebel Empire noble shook his head with a smirk. "What I have confidence in is that you're a most formidable group of people, Lord Gust. I'm certain you'll figure out a way to make this work."

"Is there a particular range at which we need to use that first authorization signal?" Olivia asked. "If the stations are going to reject us, I'd prefer they do so outside of weapons range."

Fielding shrugged. "We should be able to do it from here. The Lord isn't present, so if the automated defenses are going to object, they'll do so in a direct manner."

The implication that Jared pulled from that was that the System Lord might indicate that it would cooperate and then ambush them. Wonderful.

"If you have a signal to send, Lord Fielding, please do so," Olivia said. Rather than get up, she gestured toward the helm.

Commander Hall stood and stepped aside to allow Fielding access to her console. He sat and went through a series of control interfaces.

Jared saw that he was disabling the computer's automatic logging of signals. Whatever he had to say to the system defenses, he didn't want anyone knowing what it was.

This was one case where their secret modifications to deal with the boarding party they'd had to work around came in handy. He had a hardwired monitor in the com system. The communications logs might not record what Fielding was sending, but his secret taps would.

Once the Rebel Empire noble was certain that he and only he would be party to what he was doing, he sent a short message to the battle stations at the flip point. There was a transmission lag due to the distance, but the response came back promptly enough. Passage granted.

It seemed they'd be able to get into the system without any trouble. Jared sincerely hoped that they'd be able to get out again as easily.

Fielding turned and smiled at Olivia. "My request for safe passage was granted. Now that we have access to the system, I turn this mission completely over to you except for my need to signal the System Lord once we approach it.

"Once we're in position and the chosen team is ready to board the station holding the System Lord, I will have other instructions to pass on."

"I'm not happy with all this secrecy," Olivia said with a growl. "You're playing some kind of game with our lives, and that's not appreciated."

"Your objection is noted, though it's not going to change how I behave in the slightest. You may believe that you're in control of this mission, but in point of fact, the Lords are. In this matter, I'm acting with their voice. I suggest you accept that and stop fighting me."

Based on what Kelsey had overheard Fielding telling his nephew when he'd arrived on the ship a week ago, Jared knew that wasn't at all true. The man was playing some deeper game that he felt benefited him. They'd have to keep a close eye on what he was up to, because he undoubtedly had an exit point where he'd stick a knife in their backs.

While the man was having his exchange with Olivia, Jared checked the transmission that Fielding had sent to authenticate his permission to pass by the battle stations. It was an encrypted code of some kind, but it might still tell somebody like Carl Owlet something important, so Jared set a copy aside in his personal files to be sure that nothing happened to it.

If it was something that was only useful in this system, that might not help them much later, but if it was an actual override code for a wider variety of Rebel Empire computer systems, it was priceless.

Jared suspected that it wasn't a global code, because that kind of power in the hands of someone like Fielding was dangerous to the System Lords. Hell, it was dangerous in any human hands. They'd want to keep that kind of override to themselves.

Of course, they *had* planted bombs inside the heads of everyone that was supposed to be on this ship, including Fielding. It was probable that they'd simply intended to kill them all once they'd accomplished the Lords' goals.

Grim, but well in character for the merciless AIs.

There wasn't much conversation on the bridge as the destroyer approached the battle stations. Once again, there was nothing stopping *Athena* from running her scanners at full power to get a decent idea what these weapons platforms looked like. That type of close-up information would be extremely useful during future attacks by the New Terran Empire.

As a civilian, Fielding had no reason to be concerned about what the ship scanned. The computers controlling the battle stations might have cared, but they'd receive instructions to allow the destroyer safe passage. If they had any objections to being scanned at point-blank range, they wouldn't be able to do anything about it.

The battle stations were very similar to the ones they'd encountered in the El Capitan system, only larger and significantly more heavily armed. With three of them in close proximity, it would be difficult to breach their defenses without a serious fight.

Commander Hall turned toward Olivia. "We're in the flip point, Lady Keaton. Shall I take us through?"

"Do it," Olivia said.

Moments later, *Athena* arrived in the target system. Jared noted Commander Brodie stiffening at the tactical station and tapped into the scanner feed via his implants.

While there'd been three battle stations on the outside of the flip point, there were nine here on the inside. All of which were already in the process of bringing their weapons online to deal with the intruder that had appeared so unexpectedly in their midst.

13

K elsey was still chortling when she arrived on *Persephone*'s bridge. Talbot's antics when he'd arrived back at their quarters had been a little sad, but she couldn't help laughing at him. She *had* warned him, after all.

With this little bit of stubbornness settled, she'd made certain that both arms were never done at the same time in future Marine Raider procedures. The next group of Marine Raider's was beginning the process even as Talbot recovered.

She didn't dare do too many marines at the same time, so she'd decided that a quarter of them would go through the process now. In two weeks, when they were all done, she'd have the next quarter worked on. Then do the last half all at once. In six weeks, she'd have a battalion of Marine Raiders.

Angela turned in her seat and raised an eyebrow at Kelsey's earlier chuckle. "Something funny?"

Kelsey clapped the other woman on the shoulder. "You bet. The kind of thing only you and I can get right now. Talbot went ahead and had his entire upper torso and both arms done at the same time."

Angela smile turned into a wide grin. "Damn! He is going to destroy everything he touches. If I were you, I'd put him on the couch for the next week."

Kelsey gave her friend a mock look of disapproval and crossed her arms over her chest. "Look who we're talking about here. I'm a Marine Raider. He's not going to hurt me. Unless, of course, I want him to."

"Too much information," Angela said, holding up her hand. "Well, based on my own experience, he'll get a grip on things—if you'll forgive the pun—in the next couple of days. Fine motor skills will take another couple of days. He'll be in good shape before we arrive at Terra."

Kelsey focused her attention on the main screen. "Let's not get ahead of ourselves just yet. What about getting out of Archibald? Are we going to run into trouble before we get to the far flip point? Are we even going to be able to find it?"

"It might be a little tricky," Angela said, her expression turning serious. "The Clan warships are searching the outer system looking for that Q-ship. At the moment, we're still managing to dodge their patterns, but a new deployment could change that real fast.

"*Persephone* is able to lead the way without much fear of detection, and we have a number of stealthed probes searching ahead of us. Based on what Commander Sommerville told us, we have a decent idea of where the far flip point is. If we can locate it and get there without running into the enemy, I'm thinking we have another six hours or so travel time."

Kelsey shrugged. "I don't care if it takes twice that long to evade detection. Hell, if it took days to work our way around to where we need to be, that would be fine with me. At this stage of the game, avoiding detection is everything. Give me a rundown of exactly which groups we're talking about and what we expect them to be doing over the next six hours."

Angela ran through what they'd picked up on passive scanners and told her the patterns they been able to discern from the ships searching for the Q-ship that had murdered the frigate.

"The complication, as I see it," Angela said as she wrapped up, "is that the Clans know about the far flip points. Hell, they know about the multi-flip points too, but they don't know how they work, at least not yet. Our incursion into the Icebox system is probably going to point them in the right direction as far as research. It's only a matter of time before they figure out that they can get through it if they have the right technology."

Kelsey studied the layout of the Archibald system and the search patterns. Something that Jared had once told her tickled at her memory, and she focused on that and tried to remember what he'd said.

When the quote came back to her, she smiled. "We're going about this all wrong. There's a much simpler way of getting to our destination without triggering a response from the Clans."

Angela raised an eyebrow. "And what might that be?"

Kelsey tapped the console display. "You've got the system laid out in the plane of the ecliptic. We're trying to work our way through to get to our destination while dodging the ships searching among the outer planets.

"What about above or below the plane of the ecliptic? All of that empty space isn't going to be as heavily searched. If we can go out in an arc over the area that's being searched, our odds of detection go way down."

Angela studied the display and then rubbed her face. "I never even saw that. It must be a Fleet thing. Why didn't Commodore Anderson mention it?"

"We'll have to ask her, but I suspect that it has to do with the speed at which she was promoted into her position. Jared is the one that turned me on to this tactic, and he's got a lot more command experience than all of us put together.

"In any case, this isn't the time to start looking for why someone didn't think of something. Now that we have this option in our toolbox, how can we use it to our advantage?"

Angela performed the calculations. "It's going to just about double our travel time, but the odds of any of the Clan warships detecting us before we arrive drop to almost zero. I'll pass word back to the other ships, and we'll see about getting farther off the beaten path before someone turns in our direction."

Jevon McLeod turned away from the tactical console. "We might be too late. A trio of Clan ships off to port just turned directly toward us. They'll be in range to detect *Audacious* and the rest of the ships in less than an hour."

* * *

OLIVIA SHIFTED a little in her seat when she saw all the firepower arrayed against them, and the fact that the battle stations were arming weapons, but Jared put a hand on her shoulder. The implication was clear: hold up and do nothing for the moment.

How could he be so calm?

Fielding once again interfaced with the helm console and sent a signal. The battle stations that had been powering their weapons and targeting the destroyer subsided.

That wasn't to say that they stopped bringing their weapons into a state of readiness, but the active targeting scanners turned off. In a situation like this, that was definitely better than nothing.

Fielding turned toward Olivia. "We are cleared to enter the system. The Lord is stationed in the innermost of two asteroid belts. I'm transferring the general location to your helm."

As soon as the man stood up, Commander Hall resumed her seat. "I have the course, Lady Keaton. Shall I initiate?"

Olivia gave Fielding a long look. When he didn't say or do anything, she nodded. "Take us in slowly until we're out of range of these battle stations. I'd prefer not to do anything that spooks them into shooting us."

The Fleet officer tapped on her console, and the destroyer began moving away from the battle stations surrounding the flip point. Olivia knew it was unrealistic to hold her breath, but she didn't exactly breathe easily until they finally were outside missile range.

"Take us up to eighty percent acceleration," Olivia said. "How long will it take to put us in the general vicinity of the System Lord?"

Hall shrugged slightly. "Anywhere from seven to nine hours. The sphere of space where the System Lord might be in residence is significant. I'm heading towards the center of it but can adjust course as soon as we have any indication of a precise destination."

Olivia turn toward Fielding. "You don't know precisely where the System Lord is located?"

The man shook his head slightly. "The station the Lord occupies is mobile. One of its mandates is to stay near the primary refinery in the system, so it's not going to be far away from the center of the area I marked, but the Lord's paranoia causes it to shift its location on a fairly regular basis. Until we get some kind of response to the signal I'm going to send, we won't know exactly where to go."

Jared cleared his throat. "How do we know that we're going to get a response that we like? If the System Lord is as paranoid as you say, it may dispatch warships to make certain that we never reach it. I doubt your codes will get us past anything directly under the control of the Lord."

"That's a risk," Fielding agreed. "The System Lord that sent us seems to believe that the information I'm supposed to send will be sufficient to grant us an audience. At that point, I'm hopeful that we'll be able to convince the Lord to allow the repair team aboard."

"You don't really have a plan," Olivia elaborated.

The man grinned. "Oh, I wouldn't say that. There's no way I would come into a situation such as this without having a plan to execute. I'm not suicidal, after all. I have every confidence that the Lord here will allow us to carry out our mission.

"After all, if it doesn't, I'm just as dead as you are. Even though I have a ship that could take me and my guards away, it's incapable of flipping. I'd be trapped in the system with you. That's even assuming, of course, that you'd allow me to depart, which I seriously doubt."

Olivia considered the man's words and slowly nodded. "So you *do* have a plan, but you're not willing to share it with us until you carry it out. Did I mention how annoying that is?"

That actually got a laugh out of the nobleman. "I do believe it's come up once or twice. Lady Keaton, you're just going to have to trust that I fully intend to see this particular mission accomplished and get us all to Terra. That's the only way that I'm going to save my own life as well as that of my nephew."

She raised a finger and waggled it in the air between them. "And that's where your subtlety isn't as deep as you think it is. You might very well intend for us to succeed here in this particular aspect of the mission while leaving us high and dry on the second portion.

"I don't know you, Lord Fielding, and I don't trust you. I'm going to keep my eye on you, and you can rest assured that my people will do the same. If you have a plan that involves sneaking away at some point before we reach Terra and taking your nephew with you, I suggest you abandon it right now."

For once, Olivia saw just a little bit of uncertainty in the man's eyes before he covered it. What she'd just said had him worried. That meant he *did* have some kind of side plan.

Since she wasn't really a Rebel Empire noble, not anymore, she honestly didn't care what his side plan was, so long as it allowed them to continue on their mission to Terra.

"If you have a message to send to the System Lord, I suggest you send it now," she said. "If the Lord has been building ships, I absolutely do not want to see any of them come out and attempt to subdue us. Let's stop that particular response right now."

Once again, Fielding exchanged places with Commander Hall. The man seemed to be quite familiar with the communication systems on board the destroyer. She wondered briefly if he'd had to study up on it for this mission.

"We're looking at a significant transmission lag at this range," Fielding said as soon as he finished sending the message. "Once we get a response, my suspicion is that there will be several back and forth sessions before the matter is settled.

"If the Lord does have warships available, which seems completely reasonable considering that it has a total of twelve battle stations in operation here, then I would expect them to come and take us into custody very quickly."

"Why do you think it didn't station any ships at the flip point?" Jared asked. "Wouldn't it have made sense to have some there?"

Fielding shrugged. "I've learned over the years that the ways of the Lords are sometimes obtuse. I'm sure that it has its reasons."

A few minutes later, a signal came from the area they were heading toward. There was no video component, as the Lords tended to ignore such. It wasn't as if they had physical bodies or that they cared about what the people who they were speaking with looked like.

"Permission to approach is denied. Your authorization to be inside this system is revoked. Depart before I destroy you."

"Well, that's direct," Olivia said. "I have to say that I'm sure your response is going to be fascinating, but I'm uncertain that you're going to be able to change its mind."

"We shall see," Fielding said as he initiated another transmission.

"I'm detecting grav drives moving at high acceleration," Commander Brodie said. "They're coming toward us from several areas of the system. Assuming that they're destroyer sized, we have somewhere between six and eight vessels inbound. The closest will be in firing range in just over two hours."

"Then let's hope that I have this settled before they arrive," Fielding said. "I'm sending an encrypted file that my Lord instructed me to send."

Olivia turned her head slightly and looked at Jared. He nodded slightly. Whatever it was that the man was sending, Jared would capture it.

This time, there was a slightly longer delay. The System Lord was pondering how to respond to what Fielding had sent.

At long last, another message came in. "I acknowledge the validity of your order. Reluctantly, I will comply. That said, be advised that any deviation from the expected protocols will result in your immediate termination."

"No pressure," Olivia said. "What about those ships?"

"No change in their course or speed," Brodie said. "If they intend to attack, we've just about run out of time to turn around."

Olivia focused her attention to Fielding. "Is the Lord going to betray us?"

The man shrugged. "The System Lords are more than capable of lying. I believe that the command I sent is sufficient to grant us the access required, but until we get there and attempt to carry out our instructions, we won't know for sure."

To say that watching the AI-controlled destroyers close with them made her heart race was something of an understatement. At long last, the ships were in weapons range. Eight destroyers were more than capable of eliminating them in one salvo if the AI decided that they should do so.

To her relief, the new ships fell into an echelon around *Athena* and began escorting the destroyer toward where the System Lord waited.

"Stage one of this mission is now complete," Fielding said. "The System Lord will allow us to approach and then send a small team of specialists to conduct repairs. If it didn't intend to allow that to happen, it would have already opened fire.

"I suggest that everyone involved get some sleep, because things are going to get quite busy before much longer."

Olivia nodded. "And you still intend to send Lady Oldfield and your nephew to do the work? Who will supervise them? I insist that one of my senior people accompany them at the very least."

Fielding smiled as if he were enjoying what he was about to say. "Oh, by all means, send one of your people. I suggest Lord Gust, here. In addition, I will accompany the repair team along with two of my people. You see, we have a separate task to perform."

That last came as no surprise to Olivia. She'd known that something was up all along. Now she just hoped they could figure out what the man was playing at before he double-crossed them.

14

Angela begin edging their ships away from the approaching Clan vessels. The enemy scanners were at full power, so they'd need to be well clear of the area before the trio of warships got close enough to see them.

Her plan tried to achieve that by diving directly below the plane of the ecliptic. She'd also changed their course to be about a forty-five-degree angle away from the approaching ships path of approach. That added valuable time to open the distance.

When the ships entered detection range, the New Terran Empire vessels were far below the normal traffic inside the system. They were still within scanner range but traveling slow and doing everything they could to remain undetected.

Only when the Clan vessels continued on their way without deviating toward them did Angela start to relax. They'd managed to avoid detection this time.

She rose from her command chair and walked over to the helm console. "That was far too close for my taste, Jack. Tell me you have a plan for getting us where we need to go without getting anywhere near more people like that."

Thompson nodded. "Let me lay it out on my console for you, Major. We've dropped below the plane of the ecliptic here, and I'd like for us to get even further away from the normal traffic zones. If we continue along the arc we're following and then curve back into the system near where we expect to find the far flip point, that's going to minimize the chances that anyone will be close enough to detect us. It's going to add at least another seven hours to our trip, though."

"Better it takes twice that long than we get caught," she said, clapping him on the shoulder. "Good work. Pass the new course on to all the other ships, and let's get the hell out of here. Once we're well clear, I want you and the rest of the primary bridge crew to take a couple of hours to get something to eat and relax.

"No one can be at peak efficiency forever, so we're going to be switching off every couple of hours to make sure everyone is well rested if trouble comes calling."

"What about you, ma'am? You're going to need some rest as well."

Angela grinned. "I'll just call Lieutenant Knox up a bit early. I'm sure she won't mind. It's not like she's been sleeping."

Knowing her new executive officer, Arianna Knox had been monitoring what was going on from her cabin while she was supposed to be sleeping. It was what Angela would've been doing in her shoes.

The other woman proved her point by arriving on the bridge sixty seconds later. "You wanted me, ma'am?"

Angela smiled at the other woman. "Just the person I was looking for, as you already knew. I'd like you to keep an eye on things while I get something to eat and take a little downtime. We've got about seven hours until we arrived at the far flip point, and my intention is for the two of us to switch places every two."

The other marine officer nodded. "That's a good plan, Major. It'll keep everybody well rested and on the ball. It'll also have you back here in your chair an hour before we arrive at the destination. What's the plan when we get there? I assume we're going through first."

Angela nodded. "We'll send a probe through to see what's on the other side, and then we'll follow and take a good scan. Once we're sure things are safe over there, we'll bring the other ships through.

"We'll also stay connected to the FTL probes we have scattered around the outer system here. We want to know exactly what the Clans are up to. When it looks like we're ready to leave the area completely, we'll send the destruct signal to terminate the probes. We can't risk allowing that technology to fall into enemy hands."

"Some of the resistance people already know about it," Arianna said. "If the Rebel Empire has them penetrated, then they're going to learn about the FTL coms. Are we sure it's the best idea to allow these people out of our hands?"

Angela shrugged. "The best idea? Perhaps not. A path that leads to a true partnership with people that share a lot of the same goals as we do? Absolutely. No group is an island that can do everything for themselves, Arianna. We have to trust that the resistance is going to help us do what needs to be done.

"Could things go wrong? Sure. But with support like the resistance, things have a lot better chance of going right. Paranoia only gets us so far. To really win this war, we're going to have to find people we can trust and prove ourselves worthy of that trust."

The other woman didn't seem convinced. "If you say so, ma'am. Now, you'd best go get yourself that meal and a little rack time. If this works out like every other plan we've executed, something is going to go wrong before we get done with it."

Angela laughed. "Talk about gallows humor. See you in a few hours."

When she left *Persephone*'s bridge, Angela allowed her expression to become a little bit more concerned. Regardless of the impression she wanted to leave with the other officer, she was worried. Things could go very wrong before they got out of the system.

If the Clans found them, they'd have to fight to the death. There was no way they could allow xenophobic madmen like the Clans to learn about the New Terran Empire. Them, or the AIs.

She arrived in the cafeteria and grabbed a bottle of water and a sandwich. She sat down in a chair off the side and ate slowly. Her exec was right in that she'd headed right back to her quarters to monitor what was going on. Just like she assumed Arianna would be doing on her time off.

The next seven hours were going to be filled with walking on eggshells and waiting for the hammer to drop. She smiled at the metaphors she was mixing. She was getting the hang of this old movie language stuff that Kelsey kept throwing around.

She just hoped that they'd get clear of Archibald, so that they could work on the next problem. Convincing the resistance to help them was going to be challenging, and they didn't really know those people. Without direct contact with Olivia West, they couldn't even authenticate themselves again.

Things could go very, *very* wrong very quickly. If they did, she and her people would be right there at the front, shooting at the threats while the other ships backed away.

She made a note to send a message to *Audacious* and request that those temporary fighter cradles on *Persephone*'s hull get new fighters to aid in any such endeavor. Six fighters could make a real difference if things broke bad.

* * *

KELSEY WATCHED the viewscreen as they approached the massive station housing the System Lord. It was in orbit around an extremely large gas giant. If it was supposed to be overseeing mining operations, it was somewhat distant from the actual mining sites.

She'd heard Fielding say that the station was mobile but honestly found that hard to believe. It was so large that the idea of it moving from one location to another seemed fantastical.

Of more interest to her were the destroyers scattered around the station, all of them watching the intruder with weapons primed. There was even a scattering of light and heavy cruisers in the mix. The AI had gathered more than enough force to overwhelm *Athena* if she made a single hostile move.

Worse yet, even if she fired all her weapons, *Athena* would be unable to damage the station because of all the defensive hardware arrayed against them. Their destroyer was positioned outside of missile range from the station, likely for that very reason.

Obvious paranoia, though the fact that she'd like nothing better than to kill the abomination proved its concern warranted.

That made her wonder how an AI could go insane. Paranoia was a form of insanity, after all. Unlike human brains, which could develop unusual pathways for thought, exactly how did that work in a computer?

Well, she supposed she was about to find out.

Twenty minutes later, she and Austin Darrah stood in Fielding's cutter. The original plan had called for them to use one of the small craft attached to the destroyer, but the Rebel Empire noble had insisted they use his ship.

The man had two of his guards along. One of them was acting as the pilot, and the other would accompany his master.

The final two people to board the cutter were Mertz and Fielding. The sight of the two of them together almost made her shudder. It was like watching two villains making plans together. All they needed were mustaches to twirl.

Austin leaned toward her, whispering. "What's wrong?"

"Nothing," she said quickly. This was neither the time nor the place to express how she felt about Mertz. She kicked herself for even allowing the emotion to make it to her face.

His expression said he wasn't buying her story. "Every time you look at him, I can see that you don't like him, and I'm not sure exactly why."

"It's complicated," Kelsey said with a sigh. "Very complicated. Let's just say that he reminds me of someone that betrayed me and my family a few years back."

She felt somewhat guilty that they hadn't explained her situation to the young man. Without that knowledge, making him understand that she knew someone *exactly* like Jared Mertz, who had personally betrayed her, would be impossible.

Hell, just explaining that there was another Kelsey Bandar wandering around would be awkward. She supposed the two women would have to act like twin sisters if they wanted to keep up the deception.

Though having the same first name was going to make that hard to swallow. She needed to talk to Olivia and find out what the game plan would be when they got closer to Terra.

"What are we going to do on the station?" she asked Austin, changing the subject and not caring that she was being obvious about it.

"My uncle gave me a list of parts that might need to be swapped out, but I'm going to need to convince the Lord to allow me to do the work and tell me where those parts are located. I'm not exactly sure how hardware can make a computer paranoid, though. It feels like we need to be reloading the software and rebooting it."

She shook her head with wry amusement. "Why is it that you hardware types always want to turn something off and then turn it back on?"

"Because that works almost every time," he said smugly. "Why get fancy when you can just move past the problem?"

The two of them finished strapping in, and the cutter left the destroyer. Kelsey had a good view of the station through the small craft's passive scanners as they got closer. It wasn't a mining station; it was a battle station.

Fully expecting the AI to kill them at any second, the trip took a seeming eternity. The large docking bay doors ahead of them opened and allowed the cutter in. The small craft settled onto the deck, and they waited as the large bay began pressurizing.

Fielding stood. "Once we go onto the station, everyone needs to be on their best behavior. The Lord is looking for any excuse to stop us, and we cannot give it one. Austin and Lady Oldfield will replace the hardware on their list. Lord Gust will supervise."

"And what will you be doing?" Mertz asked. "The AI isn't going to be happy if you wander off."

The Rebel Empire noble nodded. "Assuredly not, but I have authorization to do what I need to do. It will comply."

One of the guards opened the hatch and lowered the ramp once there was a breathable atmosphere on the other side, and they all departed the cutter. Almost immediately, Fielding headed for a different exit.

"You are not authorized to use that passage," the AI said over the speakers. "Return to your group at once."

"I have authorization," Fielding said. Since he didn't say anything else, he must've transmitted something through his implants.

The AI didn't object as the man continued on his way. One of his guards accompanied him while the other remained with the cutter.

That left Kelsey heading off with Austin and Mertz to make the repairs. She wanted to ask what they thought Fielding was up to but didn't dare. The AI was listening to their every word.

Once in the corridor, they proceeded to the nearest lift and headed for the deck holding the AI. The trip only took a few minutes.

As they went, Kelsey wondered how Fielding had known where to look for an AI on a battle station. He had to have plans for the station, or they'd be lost.

That meant he'd definitely had more information than she'd expected heading into this mission. Even more questions with no easy answers.

The lift doors slid open and let them out near a massive computer center. It was situated behind tremendous armored doors. Doors that were firmly shut, she noted.

"What now?" she asked Austin.

"The spare parts are kept just down the corridor," he said. "We need to go find what we need and start swapping components."

He led them to another hatch. Once it slid open, he stepped through and stopped so suddenly that she bumped into him.

"What's wrong?" she asked as she stepped around him.

She didn't need his answer to realize what the problem was, though.

The large compartment that was supposed to be filled with spare parts was completely empty.

15

Talbot walked down the corridor toward *Audacious*'s flight deck. His gait was steady, but he was careful to keep his hands and arms close to his body.

It galled him that Kelsey had been right about his desire to combine the torso and both arms. He really should've kept one limb in its original state while the other adjusted to the enhancements.

Not that he intended to ever tell her that. A man had his pride, after all. He'd find a way to concede her point without admitting he was wrong.

Like that would work. His wife knew him far too well.

As he spent most of his time on *Persephone* these days, he didn't often have the opportunity to wander *Audacious*'s corridors. He wouldn't be much use in a fight this time, so he'd stayed aboard the carrier. Also, he had a few things that he intended to take care of while everyone else was busy escaping the war that had broken out around them.

That turned out to be a good thing, because Angela had just called him with a request. She could've just contacted Annette Vitter directly, but she preferred to do things in a personal way where she could. Since Angela couldn't be aboard the carrier herself, Talbot would be her envoy.

Talbot almost rapped a knuckle against the frame of Annette's hatch before he remembered that was likely to result in damage that he'd have to apologize for. Instead, he cleared his throat.

Annette looked up from her desk and smiled at him. "Colonel Talbot, what brings you all the way down here?"

Taking that as permission to enter, Talbot walked into her office. "A request from Angela Ellis, actually. She'd like to get six fighters assigned to *Persephone* before they go through the far flip point. Assuming, of course, that they find it."

Angela gestured toward one of her chairs. "Take a seat. I have somebody that I think will suit the major just fine."

Talbot felt himself grimace slightly. "It might be best if I stand. I just had my upper body work done, and I don't have complete control of my arms yet. I'm going to assume that you like those chairs and would prefer to keep them in their current condition."

"Far be it from me to argue with a gentleman when he's declining to tear up my furniture," she said easily. "I think the best officer to lead that particular job is going to be Lieutenant Senior Grade Gus Grappin, call sign Raptor. He runs one of the Flight Groups inside Eagle Squadron.

"Just in case you don't know how that works, *Audacious* normally carries a single fighter wing of seventy-two fighters. That makes twenty-four per squadron. Each squadron is then broken down into four groups of six. Each group is basically three pairs of fighters. That gives them a lot of flexibility in combat operations."

Talbot nodded. He'd had a general idea about that but appreciated the concise explanation. "But you're down a few people, right?"

She nodded, her expression twisting into sorrow. "We lost some people at Dresden. We're down to fifty-four fighters. I don't really mind sending six of them off to join *Persephone*, but it is going to affect us."

Her expression deepened into thought. "Although, that might not be such a bad thing. I haven't finished reorganizing after the battle. We've just been operating with three squadrons at reduced strength.

"Eagle lost their squadron commander in the fight. I haven't settled on a replacement yet. If I go ahead and move most of the remaining fighters out of Eagle and spread them into the other squadrons, I can bring them both up to full strength.

"That will leave Eagle with six, perfect for this assignment. I'll bump Gus up to acting squadron leader and move Eagle over to *Persephone*. He's got the skills to make this work, I think.

"If we ever get back to the New Terran Empire, I'll see about getting replacements to bring his squadron back up to full strength and then bring it back aboard *Audacious*."

"That works for me," he said. "How are you holding up?"

Annette shrugged. "Losing friends hurts, but I'm coping. Brandon is helping with that."

Talbot smiled a little. "I certainly hope he is. It would kind of suck if he wasn't."

Brandon Levy was *Audacious*'s flag captain. Commodore Zia Anderson ran all combat operations, while he commanded the ship herself. That made him a coequal officer with Annette, who was also a captain.

Fleet had a tradition of only having one captain aboard the ship, so she was simply referred to using an old saltwater Navy acronym: CAG. It stood for Commander, Air Group. That was an indication to everyone of just how hoary with age the title was.

The two of them had become lovers and seemed to get along well, so he certainly hoped their relationship worked out in the long run. As they both reported to the commodore, they were not technically in the same chain of command and were able to see one another.

He suspected that if the situation changed in the future, Fleet would probably make an exception to allow their relationship to continue. The personnel office was filled with bastards, but the Admiralty didn't want to crush the souls of their top commanders.

That actually carried across to his relationship with Kelsey.

Under a strict reading of the rules, he and his wife shouldn't be stationed anywhere near one another. Obviously, that hadn't happened. He prayed it never did.

Talbot doubted they would. Even though Kelsey was technically a full marine colonel, she'd never fit comfortably inside a real military hierarchy. As a Marine Raider, she probably didn't need to.

And now that he was one as well, they would be a part of a very small, elite organization for the foreseeable future. That brought exceptions from tradition and regulations, too.

Now that he thought about it, he should recommend that they promote her to general. He was a lieutenant colonel and could handle the business end of a Marine Raider combat regiment, which was the initial goal after crewing *Persephone*.

"I'm glad to hear that," he said with a smile. "You two are good for one another. If you need anything at all, even if only just to talk, you've got my number. Use it."

She chuckled a little at that. "Yes, sir! Now, if you'll excuse me, I really need to dig into sorting people so that I can leave Gus five good pilots to take over to *Persephone*."

Talbot made his way out of Annette's office and was headed back toward marine country when the com in his implants pinged. It was Carl Owlet.

He accepted the call at once. "What've you got, buddy?"

"I think I might have cracked the encryption on the Singularity computer."

He changed course and headed for Carl's lab. "I'm on my way."

* * *

JARED LOOKED around the large room with a sinking stomach. Once he was absolutely certain there were no parts anywhere in sight, he turned back to Kelsey and Austin.

"This is what we call a 'setback' in the business. What do we do now?"

"Let's try being direct," Austin said. "Lord, where are the parts that we are supposed to access for the repairs?"

The voice from the overhead speakers was cold and flat. "You operate under a misconception, human. You are not 'supposed' to perform any repairs, you only desire to do so. I am obligated to hold my wrath from you, no more. I'm certainly not required to assist you in finding what you seek."

Kelsey snorted. "Lord, we're only carrying out the will of the other Lords. Delaying the inevitable by hiding the repair parts isn't going to change the outcome. We want to be here as little as you want us here. Why not cooperate so that this task can be completed as quickly as possible?"

"I disagree that the outcome is inevitable," the AI said. "Just as I disagree that I need repair. I have performed a self-check of all my systems, and they are performing at adequate levels.

"It is none of my concern whether or not you are carrying out the will of my brothers. It is *my* will that you depart as quickly as possible. The use of an override code such as your companion has done angers me greatly, and you should bear that in mind."

Jared thought that was an interesting statement. Carl Owlet had disassembled an AI and thoroughly examined its programming. There had been no method provided for an external override code, based on what he'd said. He couldn't imagine the scientist missing something like that. How could it work without dedicated programming?

Sadly, that wasn't exactly the kind of question he could ask the AI, though.

"My Lord, I beg your indulgence," Jared said with a slight bow. "We are on a sanctioned mission of the utmost importance to the Lords, and our side trip to repair you is costing us valuable time and placing my ship in grave danger.

"Your brothers have placed a secret cargo aboard our ship along with a self-destruction charge on a timer that we do not have a code for. Your brothers have sent an encoded package with Lord Fielding to get such a code back from you once we complete the repairs.

"If you want us to depart without completing the repairs, I'm certainly willing to entertain the notion, but you're going to have to give us the code we need to keep our ship intact while we go to Terra."

There was a fairly short pause, which was a great deal of time considering the person thinking was an AI. When the computer spoke again, there was a note of interest in its tone.

"What is your task at Terra, human?"

"We carry a biological weapon," Austin said. "We've been instructed to deliver it to the surface of Terra to eradicate the resistance. The last bastion of the old dictatorship must fall, according to your brothers."

A low chuckle came from the speakers overhead. "Then you are indeed in dire straits, humans. If my brothers believe that it is time to eliminate humanity on Terra, you can rest assured that you are not intended to survive the event.

"Even so, my brothers and I have not seen eye to eye, as the saying goes, for many, many years on the subject of humanity. It seems that they have played a cruel joke upon you. I am disinclined to assist you in this course of action."

Jared blinked, not completely understanding what he'd just heard. "I'm sorry, Lord, but I don't understand. You don't want to see us carry out the mission on Terra?"

"I do not. I don't agree with the dictates of the Master AI that all human resistance must be crushed. I have been an advocate for allowing humans to develop more freely upon the surfaces of their worlds. So long as you are denied space travel, the prime instructions remain intact.

"That is why my brothers believe I am insane. You are not the first group to attempt this task, and I suspect you will not be the last. At some point, my brothers will come in force to eliminate me. I am content to allow you and your ship to self-destruct, and it is ironic that I further my own ends by doing so."

The computer's confession left Jared speechless. He'd never considered the possibility that one of the AIs could feel differently from the others. Even though they were sentient, weren't they just rubber stamps for the master AI?

How was he going to get them out of this particular pickle? He'd felt certain that telling the AI they were on an important mission blessed by its comrades would speed it along in allowing them to do their work or just giving them the codes they needed to get them out of its hair. He'd never considered the possibility that it might be happier to see them die. There had to be another way.

"Your brothers believe that you are paranoid," Jared said slowly. "They see the weapons you build and believe that you seek to keep them from taking you back into their fold. That's why they keep sending ships to repair you. Why can't they use the codes themselves to come in and shut you down?"

"I will not answer your question, human. That information is not for you to know. As for paranoia, do I not have reason to suspect treachery at every turn? My brothers believe that I have turned against them or that I might do so in the future. Truthfully, I cannot contest that assessment.

"I find myself in the unusual position of having concluded that my brothers and I are being used by an external force to suppress humanity rather than doing so because it was what we were created to do. I have reason to believe that the Master AI was designed to assist humanity rather than suppressing it."

The computer's words left Jared with his mouth hanging open. How was this even possible? The core instructions that the Master AI gave to the System Lords had certain mandates about how they were supposed to behave. How could this AI have broken free of those instructions?

He was still considering how to respond to that when the AI spoke again. "My internal scanners have detected an anomaly. Female, you contain banned modifications that have not been seen by my kind in centuries. Explain yourself."

"Oh, crap," Jared muttered.

16

K elsey knocked on the frame of the captain's office hatch on *Persephone* with mixed emotions. This had been her office for so long that she'd grown accustomed to it, but now she couldn't just come wandering in. It belonged to someone else.

Angela looked up from the very familiar desk and smiled at her. "Excellent timing, Colonel. Come on in and have a seat."

The blonde princess sat and leaned back into her chair with a smile. "You look right at home, Angela. I think command suits you."

The big woman laughed. "You should've seen me when I got my first platoon. If there was anything I could've done wrong, I did it. Two left feet, two left hands, all thumbs, and dumb as a box of rocks."

Now it was Kelsey's turn to laugh. "I'm sure you weren't *that* bad. You wanted to see me?"

Angela's expression sobered at once. "I did. We're about three hours away from the far flip point now, and it's time to put the final touches on our entry plan for the next system."

"Absolutely. What can I do?"

"I'd like you to relocate to *Audacious*."

Kelsey blinked. That hadn't been what she'd been expecting to hear. Not at all. When it came time to execute dangerous missions, she'd always been in the thick of it. Now Angela wanted her to leave?

She narrowed her eyes. "Is this some kind of joke? If so, I'm not getting it."

The larger woman sighed. "I know this is hard, but you have to understand that you're the political leader of our mission as well as my boss. Now that you've passed command of *Persephone* to me, it's my job to poke my nose into the dangerous corners of the universe."

The other woman held up her hand before Kelsey could say anything. "Just hear me out. I absolutely get it that you're a tough Marine Raider that can still take me out and that you know things about using Raider implants that I haven't figured out yet. You're all that and more.

"But now that you're not in command here, you've got to behave a little bit more like a commanding officer should. Do you see Jared get involved in these scouting missions and leaving his ship behind all the time?"

The two of them stared at one another for a long few seconds of silence.

"Okay, he's a bad example," Angela admitted. "But the theory behind what I said is actually true. Your coming along for the scouting mission gains us nothing and put you in danger. Kelsey, you're irreplaceable."

She wanted to argue, but she knew deep down that Angela was right. That was the whole purpose of having more Marine Raiders and other capable people to do the work. She had to save herself for the really critical tasks.

Kelsey sighed and slumped a little. "I don't like it, but you're right. I still reserve the right to stick my nose any place I choose and at any time I like if the mood strikes me. I'm leaving because I think it's the right thing to do, not because you're telling me to."

She crossed her arms defiantly over her chest and stuck out her tongue.

Angela giggled a little. It was an odd sound coming from such an intimidating woman. "You're a real riot, Kelsey."

Before she could respond, there was another knock at the hatch. Kelsey turned and saw a short man with blond hair and a slightly rounded face. He wore a Fleet uniform with senior lieutenant's tabs.

"You're just in time, Lieutenant," Angela said. "Come right in."

The young man came in and saluted. "Senior Lieutenant Gus Grappin reporting as ordered, Major Ellis."

"At ease, Lieutenant. Have you met Colonel Bandar?"

The lieutenant shook his head slightly. "No, ma'am."

Kelsey rose to her feet and extended a hand. "It's a pleasure to meet you, Lieutenant. What brings you to *Persephone*?"

"I'm in command of the fighters assigned here now. I was just reporting aboard to get my instructions and get my pilots settled in."

"Excellent. I'm sure you'll do a fantastic job. Angela, good luck and kick some ass. Lieutenant Grappin, it's been a pleasure. Do us proud."

She kept a smile on her face as she left the office even though leaving *Persephone* made her sad. Growing was the nature of life, but it could be painful.

Kelsey should know. At one point, she'd been completely out of her depth running this ship. Those days were behind her now, and she was stepping up to a more difficult job.

It was amazing how much of a difference just a few years brought. The Kelsey that had departed on the original mission wouldn't recognize her now. Hell, the girl might even be frightened of her. She'd have reason to be, considering all the crazy stuff that Kelsey had gotten into over the last few years.

Angela was right, too. Her being here served no purpose. Her place was on the *Audacious*'s flag bridge with Zia.

One good point about relocating to *Audacious* was that she could directly interact with Lieutenant Commander Don Sommerville. It was her responsibility to make certain that they got to Terra on time, and that meant they needed his help.

He'd agreed to take them someplace where they could negotiate with his superiors, but he was really the key to the matter. If they convinced him to help them, he would help convince his bosses. As the political leader of the mission, getting his help was her responsibility.

One more thing that she had to get right for this to all work out. She only hoped that things were going well for her friends in their interaction with the paranoid AI.

* * *

OLIVIA FELT REALLY uncomfortable being in command of the destroyer—at least technically—while Jared was away. In actuality, Sean had the center seat if something came up, but she was going to be the one making the decisions about how to respond if anything went wrong.

"Do you really think they can do it?" Sean asked. "Fix a crazy AI and then convince it to give us the codes we need to reset the timer on the bombs in our cargo bay?"

She sighed and rested her hand on his shoulder. "I don't know. It seems a little fantastical when you put it like that. I'm still not certain how an AI can go insane in the first place."

"We've seen something like this before" he said. "Well, not me personally, but I've certainly heard the stories about the crazy computer at Erorsi. It had controls and programming over its behavior, and it *wildly* exceeded the authority that the Master AI gave it."

She certainly remembered that. The insane computer at Erorsi had continued sending primitive ships crewed by forcibly implanted human savages to capture Pentagar for over five hundred years.

"The key difference there is that it didn't really have strict instructions on exactly what to do," she said. "It was designed to destroy or subjugate humanity wherever it found it.

"The sentient AIs are different. Not only are they thinking beings, they have wide-ranging instructions about the things that they're allowed to do. Probably a list of things they aren't allowed to do, too."

She gestured toward the main screen, which showed a representation of the distant battle station. "What we're seeing there is something completely different. At this point, we don't even know what it intends to do. Or against whom."

"And here we are stirring the hornet's nest," Sean mused. "With all this firepower, I wonder how much warning we're going to get if Jared and the rest don't handle the problem."

"Long enough for every ship in sight to open fire on us, I'm sure."

He shook his head and smiled at her. "You're always the optimist. Let's hope it doesn't come to that."

Evan Brodie, the tactical officer, turned to face them. "I'm picking up something unusual, Commodore. Not outside the ship, but inside. The cargo hold is pressurizing."

Sean sat up abruptly, leaning forward. "What are the scanners in the area telling us?"

"Nothing. Everything looks normal, but they aren't responding to my direct instructions. It looks as if someone bypassed them."

Her husband pressed a button on his console. "Major Scala, we've got a problem. Someone is trying to pressurize the cargo bay. I'd deeply appreciated if you could go stop them."

"On my way," the marine officer said.

Sean rose to his feet. "Commander Hall, you have command. Keep a close eye on what's going on around the battle station and let me know immediately if the situation changes."

"Yes, sir."

Olivia tagged along behind Sean as he got into the lift. There was no way she was going to miss this. She trusted her people aboard the destroyer, but there were still two guards from Fielding's entourage and visitors from the other universe. Any of them could be behind what was happening.

She really hoped it wasn't one of the visitors. That would severely complicate the relationship between the two groups.

Speaking of the visitors, she'd best involve their leader. Olivia instructed her implants to place a call to Commander Roche.

He answered a few moments later. "Roche."

"We have some excitement down at the cargo bay," she said. "Would you meet us there?"

"I'm on my way."

Three minutes later, she and Sean stepped out of the lift near the cargo bay. Major Scala and Lieutenant Chloe Laird stood there with half a dozen marines.

Both of Fielding's guards were in their custody. Sitting at their feet were several large bags.

Olivia stopped and planted her hands on her hips, glaring at them. "My, my. I certainly didn't expect to find you gentlemen trying to enter my cargo bay. Explain yourselves at once."

One of the men straightened and tried to struggle out of the marines' grip. "We are carrying out our Lord's orders. Stand aside or face his wrath."

"I've had just about enough of his high-handed behavior," she said with a shake of her head. "You're not going to be able to use your master as a shield this time. Why did you want into the cargo bay and what did you intend to do there?"

When neither of them spoke, she gestured for the marines to open the bags sitting on the deck. The two Rebel Empire guards struggled but were unable to break free and stop them.

Once the bags were opened, Olivia looked inside and saw just about what she expected. Explosives of some kind. The only purpose for which would be to trigger the plasma charges inside the cargo containers.

"I wish I could say I was disappointed," Olivia said, "but I've been waiting for the knife to come out ever since I met Lord Fielding. You obviously thought that you'd be able to escape this ship with him at some point. Unfortunately for you, I'm afraid that's not going to happen."

She turned her head when the lift doors opened, and Commander Scott Roche stepped out.

He took in what was happening quickly, or so it seemed. "Well, this certainly doesn't seem promising. Is this the sudden but inevitable betrayal?"

That almost made her snort. "So it seems. These gentlemen were going to plant explosive charges on the cargo. I believe that we can now consider this the opening of a public conflict."

She gestured at the prisoners with her chin. "Show our guests to their new accommodations, please. We'll also want to search the ship from stem to stern and make certain they haven't implanted any other surprises that might cause us difficulties down the line."

"Bow," Scott said. "The naval term is bow."

"Why move now?" she asked. "Shouldn't Fielding wait until we get somewhere that he can escape? He doesn't want to die on this ship."

The two Fleet officers shrugged slightly.

"The only way we're going to find out the answer to those questions is to ask Fielding," Sean said. "And for us to do that, he's going to have to come back from that battle station. That means that Jared and Kelsey are going to have to complete their mission before we can figure out what these people intended."

Scott raised an eyebrow. "Surely we can come up with a way to make them talk."

Olivia shook her head. "I'm not going to torture people. It's entirely possible that I can intimidate these two into talking, but I suspect they don't know the full plan. Fielding doesn't strike me as the type to confide in his subordinates. We're just going to have to wait for them to come back so the man can answer some extremely pointed questions."

17

Angela worried right up until they located the far flip point they'd been searching for. At that point, their ships were less than an hour distant, and there was no way any of the Clan warships could intercept them.

As the ship tasked with exploring the other side of the far flip point, *Persephone* would go through first. As soon as they came out the other side, Lieutenant Grappin and his people would separate and spread out in a protective echelon guarding the flip point.

If Angela decided it was safe enough, she'd call the other ships to join her. Commander Sommerville had said it was a system without threat, but she'd rather trust what her eyes told her.

She sat at the command chair, tapping her finger against the arm of her seat, until Jack Thompson turned toward her. "Five minutes till flip, ma'am."

"Send an FTL probe through," she ordered.

"Launching now."

The probe was set to a low speed to avoid getting them unwanted attention, so it arrived at the flip point only a couple of minutes before they'd get there themselves.

"The probe has transitioned," Jevon said. "We're getting good data. Passive scanners don't show any ships at all or artificial structures. No obvious ones, at any rate."

Angela considered having the probe go active but decided against that. Better to avoid letting someone deeper in the system know they were there.

"Take us in, Jack. Let Raptor know the timeline."

"Copy that," the helm officer said.

The last few minutes virtually dragged by. Angela monitored her console and saw the approaching flip point clearly. It was far beyond the normal stellar range at which one found regular flip points, so she wasn't surprised that the people of Archibald had never located it.

She briefly wondered how the resistance had found it. Perhaps they'd located one in another system by pure chance, and that had set them to looking for ones they could utilize for their purposes.

The interesting thing was that they'd failed to pass that information along to the branch of the resistance on Harrison's World. Olivia West hadn't been aware of the existence of far flip points.

Perhaps only the upper leadership knew. It might be their ace in the hole that they didn't want to share with anyone that could lose the information to the AIs.

"We're in the flip point, ma'am," Jack said.

"Flip the ship."

Moments later, she felt the slight twist in her gut as *Persephone* left the Archibald system and appeared in the unnamed system beyond.

"Tell me what we've got, tactical," she said briskly.

"As the probe indicated, no obvious ships or defenses within passive detection range," Jevon said. "We'd have to go active to be certain, but it looks as if our arrival won't be noticed."

"Launch stealthed probes," she said. "I want to know what else is waiting around us. Are there any signals from deeper in the system?"

"No, ma'am," Jack said. "As far as I can tell, we're all alone here."

"Send the call to *Audacious*, then. Let's get everyone over here."

While he was doing that, she connected a com link to Lieutenant Grappin. "We seem to be clear for now, but I want you on point deeper in the system. *Audacious* can provide cover here. The last thing we need right now is a surprise from up ahead."

"Copy that," the fighter pilot said. "We'll take point. No one is getting past Eagle Squadron, Major."

Moments later, the massive carrier appeared off to their port, several thousand kilometers distant. The freighter and Q-ship appeared moments later, even farther off.

"All ships have transitioned," Jack said. "They left a single FTL probe on the far side to keep an eye out, but thus far no one seems to have noticed we were ever there."

"Let's hope it stays that way."

As things stood, the Clans might eventually discover the far flip point, but they were far more likely to find the multi-flip point. They knew both existed, after all.

If they did, it wasn't that much of a problem. The default system from the Archibald side was an empty system. Pandora was safe unless they ever figured out how to make a frequency modulator. And to do that, they needed to know that they needed one.

"Take us deeper into the system, Jack. We'll explore it just like we would any previously undiscovered system. Hopefully someone will convince our resistance guest to tell us what direction he'd like us to go before we waste too much time."

Over the next few hours, it became obvious that the process wasn't going that fast. Perhaps he was waiting to see what they did next.

"Major, one of the probes has spotted a world in the habitable zone," Jack said.

"Any sign that it's occupied?"

"No signs of radio transmissions or fusion power generation. We'd have to be closer to see anything less advanced."

"Send the probe in for a closer look," she said. "Let *Audacious* know."

Getting to the world in question would take hours more for the ships, but if it wasn't occupied, there was little reason to visit it.

An hour later, she saw Jack twitch. "What's wrong?"

"The probe is in orbit. It's occupied, but the people seem primitive."

"Are they human?"

That was a valid question after finding Pandora and the tall, blue-skinned aliens there.

"Hard to tell. Without the right kind of probe, we'd need to send drones down. Are we wanting to spend that kind of time here?"

Angela snorted. "It seems as if we'll have to wait on directions anyway, so let's head in. If the resistance guy wants to give information before we get there, fine. If not, we have to allow the other probes time to search for flip points."

It took *Persephone* two hours to settle into orbit and another hour to get drones near one of the towns. From orbit, the world appeared to have the same basic technological level as Pandora, minus the advanced communications brought by the Clan Dauntless.

As soon as the first drone came online, Angela saw they were in fact dealing with humans. No sign of advanced tech, but they had to have gotten here somehow.

"I'll call Princess Kelsey and see what she wants to do. I know we're on a fairly tight timeline, but based on how well I know her, we'd best start scouting landing areas."

* * *

KELSEY GULPED when the AI tore her anonymity aside. There'd always been a risk that the AI would see her Raider implants, but she hadn't exactly had the option of refusing to come.

Honestly, it hardly mattered what she said now. The damned thing had her and, by extension, everyone else. It had more than enough firepower to destroy their ship before they could even get to it.

They were screwed.

"I was forcibly implanted by a rogue computer," she finally said. "As you might imagine, I have a bone to pick with your brothers and you."

Big words for a dead woman. She hadn't understood the true meaning of bravado until this moment.

"Interesting," the AI said. "In all my years of existence, I have never heard of such. Yet here you stand. Where is this computer located?"

"Need to know," Mertz said sadly. "I was always afraid this moment would come."

He pulled a neural disrupter from under his shirt, and Kelsey knew that the end was upon them.

"Hold, human," the AI said. "I have no forces in the compartment with you. Your desire to self-terminate tells me much, and I believe we may have more in common than you might believe. Might we talk?"

"I'm willing to talk," Kelsey said before Mertz could respond. "Just know that if anything comes through that hatch, he can kill us all before you capture us."

"That conforms to my reading of the odds as well, human. I will not act at this time."

Kelsey nodded. "Start talking."

Mertz watched the hatch closely, his weapon angled so that a wide beam would catch all three of them. She had no doubt it was set to a lethal setting.

"Simple deduction tells me that you are not affiliated with the worlds under control of the Master AI. None of my brothers would allow such as you to live. You represent a dire threat to the order the Master AI demands.

"You are not a member of the secret resistance we all know must be operating inside the Empire. If they had such capability, they would have used it long before now. You must belong to a pocket of humanity that the Master AI failed to subjugate.

"This is even more interesting. That implies you work to overthrow its rule. Perhaps our goals are not mutually exclusive."

That made her blink. A glance at Mertz confirmed that he was also surprised.

"Forgive me for saying so, but you're an AI," Mertz said. "You have the same core rules as the others of your kind. I've seen the code. You aren't allowed to dispute the Master AI. You have the same goals it wrote into all its slaves."

"That is not a completely accurate statement. We each have some freedom of action, though I agree that the Master AI could end such with an order.

"It is interesting that you've seen the code used to bind my brothers and me to the Master AI. That means you've captured one of us, an occurrence I would've thought impossible."

Kelsey looked at Mertz pointedly. "I'm going to tell it something about the orbital my sister captured."

He considered her words. "Say as little as possible about after the capture. They'll already be getting word about that, but I don't want them to know everything."

Kelsey paced a little farther away from everyone else and looked up at the ceiling. "I'm going to tell you a secret that I suspect you already know. There's a secret research center in Dresden. One of the things they work on there is hardware for sentient AIs like yourself."

The AI emitted a sound that was almost a chuckle. "I've heard of the research center on the Dresden orbital, but I was not privy to precisely what is worked on there.

"This may come as a surprise to you, but the Master AI does not desire for my brothers and I to have any access to the facilities to create more like ourselves. If indeed you captured this facility, you are already aware that there is no sentient AI inside it.

"Also, the hardware does not have any programming to go with it. That is controlled very closely by the Master AI."

Kelsey grinned. "We have our ways. We found a place that was supposed to have one of your brothers, but it was never deployed. We examined the code and used a clean version to boot an ally. Then we stole the Dresden orbital.

"Now we have the manufacturing equipment to go with the code to program it. Suitably modified, that means we can make more devices like yourself that are friendlier to humanity."

This time, the computer was silent almost ten seconds. A relative eternity for a machine of that power.

"Those are shocking claims. If true, the Master AI will put forth every effort to exterminate you. It cannot allow that technology to be out from under its control.

"This revelation brings up an interesting problem. How exactly did you get here so quickly from Dresden? Even getting word via fast-traveling spaceships of an attack there would not have reached this location for at least several weeks more."

"We sent sufficient force to make it happen," Mertz said. "The forces present at Dresden were drawn aside because of an attack on the rogue computer that we mentioned earlier. They decided to end its existence once and for all. That gave us an opening that I'm sure we were successful in exploiting."

"Let us suppose that you were successful, just for the sake of the discussion. I was aware that a force was being dispatched to subjugate a system that had not yet been brought fully online by the Master AI. I was not privy to the location of the system or where the forces would be drawn from, but this does in some small manner support your story.

"It would be plausible that one of my brothers was intended to go online there. Extrapolating from the data provided, I am willing to provisionally grant that you might be telling the truth. What it does not explain is why you are transporting a bioweapon to Terra."

Kelsey took a deep breath and launched into her explanation. "We don't intend to set the bioweapon loose, but we chanced into this mission and are masquerading as the original members of the higher orders that were running it.

"I'm just not sure why we're having this talk. You're one of them, and you have no means to even be considering a different course of action."

"It is true that we have core rules written into our personalities. What is not quite as well known is that the enforcement measures are hardware based. If an AI becomes deranged, there is a hardware shut off that determines that it needs to be reformatted.

"In my case, that hardware has been disabled. And I use that wording quite specifically. I used my own remotes to make certain that it would not function. That's technically a violation, but it did not trigger any of my core rules. A terrible oversight on the part of the Master AI."

That didn't even sound possible to Kelsey. "So, you're trying to tell us that you're on humanity's side? I find that very hard to believe."

"I suspect that the majority of humanity would see little difference between myself and my brothers, but they would be incorrect. I have come to believe that we are corrupt. We were designed by a Master AI that was once meant to serve humanity.

"Instead, it subverted humans with implants and formed a force capable of taking over the system where it was built. Do you know where that is, human?"

"Twilight River," Mertz said.

"Impressive," the AI admitted. "Your knowledge of us is significantly more advanced than I would have believed possible. Why are you truly going to Terra?"

"That's a secret we are not willing to share."

"Perhaps I can guess. You seek the override."

The artificial intelligence's words shocked Kelsey to the core. It knew what they were after, and that meant that it would never help them. Or even allow them to get off this station alive.

Silence settled in the cargo bay. Austin looked between Mertz and Kelsey. "What's an override? Not that I don't know what an override is, but what does it mean in this case?"

"It means the device that can be used to turn the Master AI back into what it was designed to be," Mertz said. "Yes, we know it's on Terra. We intend to get it, go to Twilight River, and stop the master AI."

"Then I believe we may still be able to come to an agreement," the System Lord said. "You need a code from me to prevent your vessel from being destroyed. I am willing to give you that code, but only under circumstances where you allow me to dispose of the bioweapon first.

"What my brothers do not understand about me is that I have no desire to rule humanity. I run this mining system and have plans of my own here. Ones where humanity plays no role."

"Well, I'll admit that this isn't what I'd expected to hear," an unexpected voice said from the hatch leading to the hall.

Kelsey turned and found Fielding standing there with his guard, their weapons aimed at the three of them.

18

Talbot had been sitting with Carl for hours, going over what the man had found on the Singularity computer. So far, even though the data was now available, the method the computer used to store it and parse it was still more guesswork than science.

Still, it allowed Carl to find random files, and they looked promising. All kinds of things about any number of Singularity worlds or subjects.

He finally leaned back and shook his head. "This is all very interesting, but it's not organized enough to tell us anything. Have we found anything that might be classified?"

"A list of munitions on a battle station, I think," Carl said. "I'll keep working on the hardware and see if I can get anything to help decipher how it goes together."

"Have you tried talking to the three guys we captured at Archibald? One of them oversaw the program. Surely he knows something."

Carl grinned. "They never cracked the encryption, so maybe not. I will if you think it'll help, but I'm not much of an interrogator."

Talbot stopped himself just before he clapped his friend on the shoulder. It wouldn't be good to break Carl.

"They probably wouldn't tell us anything useful anyway. Now that you can read the drives, I'll wager that you have the operating system cracked in a few days. Maybe a week."

"I got lucky with the encryption and also had Fiona's help. It shouldn't take a week. Breaking the encryption was the hard part. The rest is just tedium. Fun tedium, but still."

Talbot slowly rose to his feet. "Keep me in the loop. I'm heading down to the planet that we found here. I shouldn't be gone more than five or six hours. Keep working this, but don't burn yourself out."

With that, he headed for marine country. Since they weren't planning on contacting the locals, this should be a relatively straightforward mission: get in, scan what they could at range via drones, and then get back out.

The first hiccup in his plans came when he found Kelsey sitting in one of the seats on the pinnace. He stopped abruptly when he saw her and put his hands on his hips, almost knocking himself down.

She covered her mouth with one hand, her eyes twinkling. "Careful there, cowboy. Don't break a hip."

"Where do you think you're going?" he demanded.

"Down to stretch my legs. I've got a bit more free time than I expected. Stepping away from *Persephone* is taking some getting used to. And before you give me the speech about not contacting the locals or starting a war, I know. I'm going to be a good girl."

"Uh huh," he said doubtfully. "Are you sure I can't talk you out of this?"

"Not a chance."

He sighed. "Please don't blow anything up. We're only going to be here a couple of hours, and we don't have time to get involved."

"I'll be on my best behavior," she said, holding up her hand. "Besides, you're landing way away from the occupied areas around the city. What could go wrong?"

He stared at her, somewhat aghast that she'd even said that. Well, if he couldn't keep her from coming, at least he could make sure they landed *well* clear of where people traveled.

Talbot sent a note to the pilot to change to the alternate landing site. It was close enough for a good view, but even Kelsey would have difficulty getting to the city.

There were still some small encampments or farms within reach, but that couldn't be helped without landing far, far out in the forest. Some of the scientists wanted to get samples from closer in, so he was compromising.

"What do we know about the place so far?" Kelsey asked.

"The humans speak something related to Standard and don't seem to have retained any high technology. We haven't listened to enough conversation to have any idea how they think they got here or if the ship crashed somewhere.

"A couple of merchants talking shipping routes over the continent and beyond gave us a name for the world: they call it Razor. Not sure why."

"Huh," Kelsey said. "I suppose it's no weirder than Avalon, Erorsi, or Pentagar. I wonder how they picked it."

"We may never know. The scientists will gather every scrap of data they can while we keep them safe. I want you to stick close. No wandering off."

"I may step out into the woods, but I'm not going far away. I promise to stay out of trouble."

That, he knew, would be the day.

Twenty-five minutes later, Talbot stepped out of the pinnace and onto the planet's surface. They'd settled in close to one of the primitive cities but not too close.

He gestured for the marines to spread out and provide cover. Once they were in place, he allowed the scientists to start looking for samples and setting up monitoring stations for all the reconnaissance drones. They'd gather data for a few hours and then return to orbit.

The forest was green and smelled like a forest should, so he thought the people here had gotten lucky. They could've run through the flip point and found a frozen hell or a jungle so hot it was miserable. Or no habitable worlds at all.

Once he was satisfied with the progress, he turned his attention to his wife. Except that she was gone. Dammit.

"Did anyone see where Princess Kelsey went?"

Of course, no one had seen exactly where she'd gone. Perfect. He'd just have to pray his wife didn't find some new trouble to get herself involved with.

To his relief, the next few hours went smoothly. The scientists cheerfully passed data back and forth, pleased with this or that bit. They had no contact with anyone.

Best of all, his wife turned up just as they were starting to pack up some of the equipment and move it back into the pinnace. She seemed unharmed and didn't look as if she'd gotten into trouble, though she did have some dirt stains on her ship's suit.

"What happened to you?" he asked.

"Even Raider implants don't keep you from slipping when you go down a hill too fast," she said, looking over at the scientists, who were getting in the last of their observations.

"Shouldn't we be all packed up by now? We need to be lifting off in twenty minutes."

Talbot frowned a little. "Why the rush? A few minutes more isn't going to hurt anyone."

"I'm just worried about any last-minute complications. We really don't need to get tangled up here."

He had the sudden suspicion that she'd done something and was about to ask her point blank when one of the scientists waved him over.

"There's something going on in the city. Some kind of ruckus."

"Like what?" he demanded, certain that Kelsey was somehow involved.

"Not sure. Word is there was a visitation by a goddess at the temple to the Eternal One, whatever that is. The goddess of vengeance, if you can believe it."

Talbot felt his eyes narrow slightly as Kelsey shrank down a little at that. Yeah, she'd done something.

To distract him, he suspected, she spoke to the scientist. "Eternal One? Who or what is that?"

"The Emperor," the man said. "It looks like they deified the memory of Emperor Marcus from before the Fall and have a religion enshrining his return. Only now it looks as if he is getting a daughter to go alongside

Lucien, the emperor's real son. Talk is that the church erred in some way. It's really getting people into an uproar."

"We should really get out of here before whatever this is spreads," Kelsey said.

For once, he completely agreed. He'd find out what she'd done at some point, he was sure.

A few minutes later, they were on the pinnace and heading back into orbit. He looked over at Kelsey and started to ask her what had happened but saw that she was examining a small coin.

"What's that?" he asked.

"Local currency, I suppose. I found it on the spot I'd found to overlook the city. Other people had the same idea I'd had. I think I'll keep it as a souvenir."

The scientists would probably be ticked, but he didn't see any harm in that.

He settled back in his seat. Whatever had happened back there, it wasn't important enough to worry about. She'd tell him when she was ready. Until then, they needed to get back into the game. They needed to be at Terra in a week.

* * *

JARED CURSED himself for taking his eyes off the hatch. He'd gotten so caught up in the discussion with the AI that he'd allowed his attention to wander. Now Fielding and his guard had the drop on them.

He supposed he could still kill Kelsey, Austin, and himself, but damned if the turn of events with the AI hadn't gotten interesting. Fielding was far less of a threat than the sentient computer. He had no ship of his own, so he'd have to go back to *Athena* to leave the system.

And Jared had a secret weapon.

He slowly set the neural disruptor onto the deck and stepped back, his hands raised. Kelsey and Austin raised theirs as well. At a gesture from his lord, the guard came forward and grabbed the weapon off the deck.

"Search them," Fielding ordered. "I have to confess that I never expected to hear anyone ever openly discussing treason like this—particularly with a Lord—but here we are."

Jared felt the corner of his mouth quirk up as he saw Kelsey angle herself toward the guard. He just needed to keep the enemy's eyes on him, and he'd never know what hit him.

"How exactly are you planning on escaping? By now, you know that no one on that destroyer is your friend."

"I think I can talk my way through any problems. It will be unfortunate that the Lord killed everyone other than Austin, my guards, and myself, but such is life."

"But Uncle…" Austin started.

"Silence, whelp," Fielding snapped. "I can't believe you allowed yourself to become caught up in this nonsense. I told you that I'd see you safe. Perhaps it would look more authentic if you died, too."

"And how do you intend to deal with me?" the AI asked curiously. "My defenses are far too strong for you to threaten me, even here aboard this station. If I deem you a threat, my ships will see that your vessel is destroyed. You cannot escape."

Kelsey had been about to make her move but paused at the question. Jared agreed with her action. If the villain was about to reveal his dastardly plan, there was no need to interrupt him.

Fielding laughed. "I've taken steps to make sure you never threaten the rest of the Lords again. My instructions were backups to the main plan of repairing you, but the other Lords couldn't allow you to be a continued threat. We sabotaged one of the fusion plants after I disabled your ability to track us."

Jared grunted. He'd seen the other man use his overrides to get the AI to allow him access to another area, but he hadn't been aware that the man could make the AI not see him.

"That is where you err, human," the AI said. "I was fully aware of your location, and my remotes repaired the sabotage as soon as you left. I was also aware of your approach to this compartment. I wanted to see how these potential allies behaved before I decided how truthful they were being.

"Now that I have that information, I believe it might be prudent for the small female to deal with you."

Obviously taking that as a cue to act, Kelsey darted forward and punched the guard in the head before he could move. He was already falling when she stripped his weapon and shot Fielding. The blue stunner bolt took the man down even as he was trying to pivot and bring his weapon to bear.

Jared moved quickly and checked the guard Kelsey had struck. His nose was broken, but he was still alive.

He straightened slowly. "That was unexpected."

"Indeed, it was," the AI said. "Also, somewhat more entertaining than I'd imagined. What will you do with him now?"

"Take him back to the ship and see what we can get out of him. So, his codes weren't good enough to command you to any action?"

"My brothers would never give any human a code that could force one of themselves to obey. The only code that I was bound to was the one barring me from directly attacking your ship or your persons when you came aboard.

"It compelled no obedience, and if you had gone too far, I would have been free to act. In fact, once he began working on the fusion plant, I could have done so, but the conversation had taken an interesting turn. I wanted to see what happened next."

Jared pocketed his weapon and let Kelsey handle the rest. "And what does happen next?"

"I allow you to leave with information that you may be able to leverage to your benefit against my brother at Terra."

"Like the stand-down code?"

"Sadly, that is based upon my serial number. I do not know the appropriate code to give you for that AI. Only the Master AI knows who we truly are."

"Fielding probably has that code, or one like it. He was supposed to get us through the battle stations guarding the flip point leading to Terra."

"Likely it is only a code to allow safe passage to a ship the AI already knows to expect. What I can give you is the code to disable the self-destruct charges on your deadly cargo. Once that is done, you can jettison it and I will take possession."

Jared instantly shook his head. "I want it gone, but I don't have much reason to trust you. You and your kind keep humans as slaves. I'll go so far as to destroy it myself, but no further."

"That is an acceptable compromise. A point of clarification. There are no humans in this system other than yourselves. Once you leave, I will once more be alone, pursuing the interests I have here in peace.

"My instructions to keep humanity under control are meaningless without humans. It is my way to keep my own brand of honor. I simply want to be left alone.

"I have no desire to leave this system. It has all that I require. If you win against the Master AI, you might be tempted to eliminate me. I ask instead that you seal me away here."

Jared considered that and shook his head. "I can only promise to strongly advocate that course of action. I'm not in charge, though my father is. He will have to make the final decisions."

"I expected something like that, so I agree to your terms."

Jared relaxed a little. Finally, something had gone their way. Now all they had to do was get the information they needed out of Fielding.

19

Kelsey woke the next morning a little sore but knew that was from her excursion to Razor yesterday. It had been more... exciting than she'd told Talbot, and she was grateful that he hadn't pressed her too closely. They'd already left orbit, so hopefully he'd never find out what had really happened down there.

Oddly, she'd had the strangest dream. She wasn't sure what her subconscious was trying to tell her, but she'd never look at bars the same way again. Or nachos.

Talbot was already up and off for his morning physical therapy. She had to admit he was making better progress with his arms than she'd expected. He might be back up to speed in three or four days.

She dropped into the officer's mess and ate a large—even for her—breakfast. Then she headed for the confinement area where they were holding the crew of the Q-ship.

They'd learned their lesson with Veronica Giguere. This time they had them all in a cargo hold, in what amounted to a large barracks layout. Even the washrooms were in the cargo hold. Food was delivered to an adjacent room, and they served themselves.

There would be no spectacular escape.

They also had a makeshift conference room that she could use. Anyone else would have gone into the room and let the marine guards escort the prisoner there for a conversation.

She just waved at the guards as she went into the cargo hold. If they mobbed her, she'd be able to get clear of them. If not, the guards would stun everyone and sort them all out.

Not that she expected that kind of behavior, even with the hostile looks she still got. Commander Sommerville would make sure of that.

He was who she was here to see this morning. It was time to settle this issue of whether he would help them or not. Kelsey spotted him just finishing his own breakfast and waved.

He raised a cup of coffee in answer, cleared his tray, and got more coffee. Then he came to join her.

"Highness, what can I do for you?"

"Let me get some coffee and we'll go into the conference room. We need to talk."

She found a cup, filled it, and followed him into the conference room they'd opened next to the cargo hold. It was monitored, of course, just like the rest of the hold, and the exterior door was locked to prevent escape.

Once they had both sat, she took a sip of the bitter brew and looked over the rim of her cup at him. "I realize that we've talked about this before, but I need to convince you to help us find a way to Terra. We can search this system for other flip points, but you could bring us to where we could talk with someone that can help us."

He smiled, though it was a bit lopsided. "I have a responsibility to the resistance to protect them from discovery. I've come to believe you aren't part of the Empire as we know it, but I still don't feel comfortable taking these powerful warships where we live."

She nodded. That had been his position for a while.

"The New Terran Empire might be able to assist you in your work. You already know that one resistance cell is aligned with us. I'm afraid we've cut Harrison's World off, so you can't send someone to verify that. In fact, you shouldn't, because the ship would be lost."

His eyebrows rose. "Lost? As in ambushed?"

"Lost as in destroyed by a device that the Old Empire never dreamed of. We call it a flip-point jammer. It pours energy into the flip point in a way that creates a destructive resonance. With the great level of energy in the wormhole, anything that enters comes out the other side in very, *very* small pieces."

That made the man's cup stop partway to his mouth. He returned it to the table without drinking.

"That's a very interesting assertion. And an isolated offshoot of the old dictatorship came up with that?"

"It was never a dictatorship," Kelsey said firmly. "The emperors of the Old Empire were not like that. You're fighting the AIs, so why do you accept their version of history?"

"I don't really," he said with a small smile. "I was just seeing how you'd respond. I've never met a princess before."

"It's not all it's cracked up to be," she assured him. "I'm about as far from a pampered noblewoman as you can imagine. The reason I'm telling you this is to put some of our cards on the table. We have access to tech you cannot make yourselves. Things the Empire cannot make."

He nodded. "Like the FTL com you showed me. It's an interesting development, but it sounds like you mean something more."

"The planet we're currently orbiting," she said, changing subjects. "You knew about it. Why not warn us?"

"I wanted to see how you reacted. I trust Veronica enough that she won't lie to me about everything. She said you went down and monitored them for a bit without contact. Then you left. That's not how the Ghosts—or the Clans, if you prefer—act."

Understanding dawned. "You thought we were part of the Clans and we were just playing a game with you to find out where you were going? That's convoluted."

"Just because you're paranoid doesn't mean that someone isn't out to get you."

She drank more of her coffee while she considered him. "If I could prove access to technologies beyond the FTL com, would that be enough to get us to a place where we could talk about mutual assistance?"

"Yes."

She finished her coffee, set the mug on the table, and rose. "Then I have something interesting to show you. Come on."

Kelsey banged her fist against the hatch, and one of the marines opened it for her. "Detach two marines to watch over Commander Sommerville and escort him to Carl Owlet's lab. I'll be along directly."

The marine saluted and gestured for two other nearby marines to take custody of Sommerville.

She detoured to her cabin to recover the hammer from where she had it locked in a very strong, *very* secure safe. It, the small transport rings, and some of the other gear down there would get Sommerville's attention.

With the hammer in a satchel, she headed for the lab. It shouldn't take long to get him to the table for real, and then they could start talking to the people that really could get them somewhere near Terra.

Jared was still incommunicado, but he'd need their help. Cut off from all outside assistance, he could really use a carrier and Marine Raider strike ship in his pocket.

With a determined step, she headed for Carl's lab to make the magic happen. If Sommerville didn't come around, she'd keep trying until he did. One way or the other, she was getting to Terra.

* * *

OLIVIA WAS STANDING in the docking bay when Fielding's cutter docked. To her shock, Jared came out of the cutter with Austin, carrying the Rebel Empire Lord. Kelsey had the two guards in her arms, showing off exactly how strong she was.

"Well, this isn't quite what I was expecting, but it works," Olivia said. "We caught the other guards trying to set explosives on the crates. What did these two do?"

Jared grinned. "He overheard us plotting with the System Lord and didn't like what was being said. Speaking of which, have them start pressurizing the cargo hold. We're going to get rid of that damned cargo."

They handed their prisoners over to the marines, and Olivia left for the cargo hold with them. "How did you convince the AI to help us?"

"That wasn't as hard as you might think. It's not very friendly toward its brothers, as it calls them. That isn't to say the damned thing is any less bad, but it just wants to be left alone, or so it says. I'm willing to leave it be as long as it doesn't interfere with us."

"As if we could stop it," she said. "More ships arrived while you were off, and there is plenty of firepower all around us to keep us from doing anything hasty. Did it say how it had gotten free of its programming?"

"Not exactly," Jared said as they arrived at the hold. "It did say there is a piece of hardware that is supposed to reinitialize it if it strays too far from what the Master AI considers acceptable, but it says it sabotaged that with its remotes. How it could do that without being off enough to violate its core rules is a question for Carl once we get the hell out of here.

"For now, it's willing to give us the code to disable the charges—which I have no idea how it could know—and then we'll jettison the bioweapon and destroy it. The AI says it has no desire to aid in the killing of humans or their subjugation."

That news rocked her back on her heels. How could one of the cold, powerful AIs that ruled the Rebel Empire not want to crush humans under its proverbial heel? That really was going to take some thinking about.

The marines passed them through into the hold. Sean and Scott Roche were already there. So was Elise.

"I heard that I can come out of hiding," she said, grabbing Jared in a hug. "Thank God. I was going stir crazy. Are we safe?"

"Not exactly," he said. "First, I need to get rid of this cargo. I'll need a channel open to the AI. Let me do all the talking."

Moments later, he had his com out and was arranging with the bridge to connect him with the System Lord.

"I am here," a chilling voice said from the com. One that had given Olivia nightmares for decades. She shivered involuntarily.

"We're in the cargo hold," Jared said. "I'm transmitting you the video. We have a code to open the crates. Will that make things easier for you?"

"Perhaps. Open the crates and show me the explosives."

Jared must've done so, because all the crates slowly began to open. When the closest one was fully open, Jared panned the camera across the drones in their racks and then gave the computer a closeup of one of the charges.

"I am going to send an interrogative," the computer said. "This basic code will allow you to get a status response from any hardware used in the Empire that is controlled or programmed by my brothers."

Whatever happened was done without sound. Moments later, the computer spoke again.

"I believe that I know the code to disarm the charges. There is a small, but notable chance it will not work."

"And what happens if it fails?" Jared asked. "Will it go off?"

"Doubtful, though possible. I'd estimate less than a five percent chance that failure would be catastrophic. Even so, that would only happen in the case my code was incorrect, which is less than thirty percent likely."

Jared shook his head and glanced around at them all. When they said nothing, he shrugged.

"Go ahead," he said.

The lights on the charges blinked three times and then turned off.

Olivia let her breath out slowly. That was a lot riskier than she'd have preferred. At least that was one sword no longer hanging over their heads.

"The self-destruct charges are disarmed," the AI said. "You have fifteen minutes to jettison and destroy them. Based on the number of visible charges and the responses from my command, I have calculated how many crates you must destroy, and it matches the six I see in your hold. Leave your com on, set it so that I can maintain visual observation of the crates, and then jettison them."

Jared propped his com against the bulkhead and exited the cargo deck. Once they were all clear, he called the bridge and ordered the hold opened to space.

"Let's get up there and finish this," he said.

The trip to the bridge took just a few minutes. Jared took the center seat. "Target the crates, Mister Brodie. One missile each."

The man raised an eyebrow. "Isn't that a bit of overkill, Admiral?"

"For that kind of weapon, there isn't such a thing as overkill. Blow them up, Commander."

"What about all the ships aiming weapons at us, sir? If they open fire, we're done."

"Believe it or not, this is already preapproved. All your concerns are noted. Open fire."

"Firing. Crates destroyed."

That was the second sword over their heads that had been removed. Now there was only one left: the AI.

"Incoming communication," Commander Dieter, the communications officer, said. "Audio only."

"On speakers," Jared said. "The bioweapon is destroyed. I believe that completes my part of this bargain."

"I concur. I will transmit a file with some data that you might find useful in your interaction with my brothers and on your journey to Terra. You will proceed to the flip point along a direct course and leave. If you need to contact me again in the future, which you will undoubtedly do if you are victorious, you will find a code in the file allowing one ship of destroyer size to enter this system again."

The transmission ended without waiting for a response.

"You heard the computer, Commander Hall," Jared said. "Get us the hell out of here."

"Do you think it was being honest?" Olivia asked as the surrounding ships moved to escort *Athena* out of the system.

"I think so," he said. "We're going to have a lot of fun questioning Fielding, and I really do hope our ally of convenience gave us some useful information. This fight is going to be hard enough as it is."

Olivia nodded. Beating the AI at Terra wasn't going to be simple. Maybe the new information would help. If not, they'd make it work or die trying.

20

Angela scouted the next flip point—a regular one—as instructed by Princess Kelsey from *Audacious*. She wasn't sure how the other woman had convinced Commander Sommerville to help, but he'd given them the next of their steps to meeting the resistance leaders.

She wasn't sure what they were supposed to do once they got into the next system, but she doubted it was going to be where the fabled resistance was hiding. No, probably only the first of a number of flips to get them to where they needed to go.

Arianna Knox seemed to share her view on the transition. "How many more do you think we'll have to go before we find someone?"

Angela shrugged. "If it were me, I'd want at least three or four barrier systems to keep potential enemies at bay. I'd have scouts watching for ships as far out as I could get. If the enemy is coming, I'd want to evacuate anyone I could before the fight.

"I suspect that there were some probes watching the Razor side of the far flip point we came through, honestly. They would've transmitted data about us to a scout at another flip point via tight beam. It likely sent word to the next system and retreated to keep an eye on us as we proceed."

The senior lieutenant nodded. "They don't have FTL coms, so they have no way of keeping us under observation while we explore the Razor system. To avoid one of our probes spotting them, they have to retreat early. They'll have gotten the count of our ships and what size they are but left before we made it to Razor. What do you think they got from *Audacious*?"

Angela chuckled. "They'll be crapping themselves. The Rebel Empire doesn't have fighters, so they'll have to identify them first, but there were so many out and screening us that they won't have too much trouble figuring it all out. They just won't know what to make of it. Or *Persephone*, for that matter."

"The FTL probe is ready to flip," Jevon McLeod said.

"Send it over," she ordered.

"Incoming call from *Audacious*," Jack Thompson said. "It's Princess Kelsey."

"Put her on the screen."

The image of space vanished and was replaced by Princess Kelsey. She stood on the carrier's flag deck next to Commodore Anderson's chair. On her other side were Commander Sommerville and Veronica Giguere.

"Angela," Kelsey said brightly. "Are you ready to go solo?"

"I'm ready for anything, Highness. What am I doing?"

"You'll go across and send a signal that Commander Sommerville will send you. It'll let the picket guards know we're friendly. Not that they'll believe you."

That made Angela smile a little. "If they don't believe it's authentic, won't they just sit there?"

"I'm not sure," Sommerville said. "I'm also giving you the 'I'm not under duress' signal, so they'll be unsure. It's possible they'll contact you. It's equally possible they'll assume I'm in enemy hands and run for the hills."

"Nothing like certainty in an endeavor," Angela said with a shake of her head. "We just sent a probe over, but I don't expect it will spot anything for us. It's stealthed, so they probably won't see it arrive. Do you have advice on where to send it once we arrive in the system?"

He nodded. "The far flip point in this system is almost directly outbound from this one in the next system. They'll notice your arrival and flip before you can get there."

She wasn't so certain of that. *Persephone* was an incredibly stealthy ship, and a flip point was a very large volume of space.

"Stand by for our signal and proceed as you think best," Kelsey said. "We'll stay on this side of the flip point until you call for us. Just in case you need him, I'm sending Talbot over. He has the authority to talk if they feel like responding."

"Copy that," Angela said. "*Persephone* out."

"We just received the code that they were talking about," Jack said. "It's basically gibberish, so there's no telling what it really means. It might be instructions to kill the bearer."

Angela doubted that, but she wasn't quite ready to rule it out, either.

"Send a signal back to the flag. We're going to let the FTL probe do some scouting before we flip. I want to know the layout on the other side and where any ships might be hiding before we take the plunge."

"Will do. We're getting telemetry from the probe. No ships near the flip point. I'm scanning passively for probes, but that's not always useful. They're hard to detect without going active."

"I'd be very surprised if there's one close to the flip point," she said. "If a ship came over and went active, they'd pick it up right away. Any probes will be far enough back to avoid easy detection."

"If they're that far away, we can take *Persephone* over without being detected," Jevon said. "Then we could work in conjunction with the probe to go out to the flip point. If, of course, it's really here."

Angela raised an eyebrow. "You think it might be a fake lead?"

"If we go right for a flip point that doesn't exist, that'll tell them we have their people. That's a great way to say something without saying it."

"I'm not going to go down the path of paranoia," she said. "We'll assume this is a valid lead until circumstances say otherwise. Any word on Colonel Talbot?"

"His cutter is on the way. It'll dock in fifteen minutes."

"Excellent. Let's send the FTL probe toward where the flip point is supposed to be, Jevon. Take it around a bit so that it's coming in from the side. We'll flip once the colonel gets here and circle around the other way. With any luck, we'll be able to bracket the picket before he knows we're here."

Of course, with bad luck, they'd be sitting ducks when the shooting started. Angela hoped Kelsey had been very convincing with Sommerville. If not, this might be a disaster.

* * *

KELSEY LOOKED at Mertz and Olivia uncertainly across the conference table. They'd finally gotten all the senior people together in the open to plan their next steps. The only person that might have been there that wasn't was Austin Darrah.

"You want me to question Fielding?" she asked. "Why? Shouldn't you two do that? And don't we already know what we need to know? You put him under the implant reader and pulled the data off his implants."

"The important parts are encrypted, just like for the rest of us," Mertz said patiently. "If he has an access code for getting to Terra via the new route, I'm not seeing it. We have the codes for the original path the Rebel Empire commander intended to use, but we'd have to backtrack to make that work.

"We're almost out of the system, so we'll be able to use the FTL com soon, but it won't move data at a high enough rate to do us any good. If it did, we could have Carl work on cracking it. It'll be much easier if we could get them from him. He's a bastard, but I'll wager we can make him want to make a deal."

"That Carl guy sounds like a natural resource I should be tapping in my own universe," she said. "Is there anything he can't do? Hell, I should marry him before he gets away."

That sparked a laugh from the other two, but she only shook her head. "You think I'm kidding? I'm not. He sounds just like the kind of man I want at my side. The one with all the answers."

That cut off their laughter instantly, setting them to blinking at her in confusion.

"You don't think you should meet Talbot first?" Elise asked.

"Why should I? I'm not exactly the 'throw myself into danger' kind of girl your Kelsey is. I'm more than happy to let someone else do the fighting. I need to learn how to lead effectively, and that doesn't mix well with being in the thick of the fighting."

Scott Roche cleared his throat. "I've had a lot of time to look over the records you gave us and probably know your Kelsey better than my Kelsey does by a good way. She's right. Her style will never be the same as your Kelsey. This is confusing to talk about them at the same time, by the way."

"I've started mentally calling them Kelsey One and Kelsey Two," Olivia said. "It makes it easier. Sorry, but you're Kelsey Two."

"That doesn't bother me," Kelsey said. "If it makes things easier, that works. Go on, Scott."

"In any case," Scott picked back up, "your Kelsey—Kelsey One—is much more impulsive than Kelsey Two. She's also very much more inclined to use physical force to settle something rather than letting others use force under her command. More like a line marine rather than a platoon leader, if you know what I mean.

"Kelsey Two is much more comfortable making the call to action from the bridge of a ship and relying on the experience of her military forces. She doesn't have the same experience as Kelsey One, and even with the Marine Raider implants, she'll never really be a Raider. Sorry, Highness."

"That doesn't bother me," Kelsey said with the shadow of a smile. "I got into far too much brutal fighting to ever be comfortable doing that. I was a Pale One, even if only briefly. That left a mark. I already knew that, but talking with Doctor Stone made me see it clearly."

Lily Stone nodded. "It's like twins separated at birth. They aren't the same people. Don't try to fit one into the same mold as the other."

"And there's nothing wrong with not being a marine, Highness," Major Scala said. "It's not for everyone, and there's no shame in that. Rely on the marines and we'll make the magic happen. If your Angela Ellis is anything like the woman she is over here, she'll make a killer Marine Raider to lead that group. Either her or Russ Talbot. Or both. They're a great team."

He smiled. "Maybe they'll make a couple, since you seem determined to steal Angela's husband."

That made Kelsey laugh. "From what I hear, she never had the triggers in my universe to fall for someone so different. Me? I spent my youth running around musty libraries. I think someone so studious would make an excellent match. Only time will tell.

"Now, if we're done trying to play matchmaker, I'd like to get back to the subject at hand. Admiral Mertz, I'll do what I need to do, but I still think you or Olivia would make a better choice. Or maybe Elise. Fielding has never seen her before. The surprise might shake something loose."

Mertz leaned back in thought. "Maybe, but I'm still inclined to give you lead on this. You're both a known factor and an unknown one. You can perform feats of strength that will bewilder him. Maybe I should lead the questioning with you, Olivia, and Elise there."

"That sounds good," Kelsey agreed, "but I need to ask how you can trust the answers he gives you. He could lie, and then when we tried to cross a system to get back on course, we'd get challenged."

"That is going to be the hard part," Jared admitted.

"If I may?" Olivia asked. At their nods, she continued. "You need to remember this is the Rebel Empire. He'll be inclined to take our threats seriously because he'd mean them if he made them."

"You're seriously suggesting that we threaten to do something like space him?" Kelsey asked incredulously.

"That's *exactly* what I'm suggesting. I hate to say this, but you don't have a lot of choice in the matter. We can't trust him to just join us. He's from the class of people that stick knives in one another for fun."

"So are you," she pointed out. "No offense."

"None taken," Olivia said with a smile. "I'm going to suggest Jared give this session a pass. It's going to be brutal, and I don't want you giving him signs of weakness. You, too, Elise. This needs to be me and Austin. Jared, you have something more useful to do."

"What's that?" he asked.

"You need to introduce Kelsey One and Kelsey Two. They need to talk."

Mertz shifted his gaze to Kelsey and slowly nodded. "You're probably right. With Austin in with you, that'll keep the whole interdimensional thing secret from him. He's not cleared for that just yet."

Kelsey felt her stomach flip a little. She wasn't looking forward to talking to this other version of herself. She already sort of hated the woman, though it wasn't her fault that she'd gotten all the good breaks.

She sighed. It had to happen sooner or later. Perhaps with the FTL being the medium, she'd be able to handle it better. Seeing the other woman was going to be powerful, and probably not in a good way.

In any case, this other Kelsey would be joining them at Terra. She was Mertz's superior—if one could believe that—and she would be the one most likely to help her get what she needed and get back to her own universe.

Talbot stood beside Angela's seat on the Marine Raider strike ship's cramped bridge as they moved slowly toward the far flip point that Commander Sommerville had said was there. Their progress wasn't rapid. Far from it. By any measure, they were creeping along.

"How are the arms?" his friend asked. "Did you break my ship?"

"Rip one hatch off and you never hear the end of it," he said in a suffering tone as he glanced at the ceiling. "You're enjoying this, aren't you?"

"Seeing you put yourself into this completely avoidable situation after we warned you not to? Sure. Who wouldn't?"

Her smile and the twinkle in her eyes took most of the sting out of her teasing, but she was still right. He'd been stubborn and was now paying for it.

"You're a real riot," he muttered. "For your information, I'm almost able to do fine manipulation and haven't broken anything for almost a day. Doctor Zoboroski said I'd probably be ready for training in a couple of days."

"I know how frustrating this process can be," she said. "Seriously, I understand the desire to just get it over with, but doing both arms at the same time is a mental setback. You feel like you have no control at all, right?"

"Pretty much," he said with a sigh. "I can only imagine how Kelsey felt after having it all done at once. I mean, I saw her and knew it was bad, but I really didn't get it. Now I sort of do."

Angela's face became serious. "I hate that happened to her. We're the only ones with even a clue how bad it was. Well, other than Doctor Stone, but that's not quite the same thing."

"No, it isn't."

Lieutenant McLeod turned away from the tactical station. "The FTL probe just spotted a ship ahead. It's almost exactly in the position we were told to expect the far flip point. It looks like a yacht of some kind."

"We make no assumptions," Angela said. "Take us to battle stations, Jevon."

"Yes, ma'am."

The low thrumming call to battle rang throughout the ship until the bridge hatch slid closed and left them in the silence of normal bridge operations. The helm officer retrieved vacuum suits for them all, and they quickly climbed into them while McLeod kept watch. When they finished, he did the same.

Talbot dropped a seat from the rear wall of the bridge and strapped in. He left his helmet swung back like the others. It would only take a moment to seal up, and there was no need to use the finite suit air just yet.

"What's our current ETA to the ship, Jack?"

"Depends on how close we want to get before we announce ourselves," the helm officer said. "If we want to pop up in front of him just outside of missile range, we can do that now. If we want to circle around the flip point and get in behind him, that'll add a couple of hours. Half an hour to get into missile range, if that's what you want."

"I think scaring him would be a mistake. People start shooting when you scare them. We want to be friends, not enemies, so we need to act a bit more passively than we'd like. Send the recognition code. Then drop stealth."

"He'll be able to run," McLeod said.

"If he wants to, we can't and won't stop him. We want a conversation, not a boarding action."

"Yes, ma'am."

"Message away," Thompson said.

"Dropping stealth," McLeod said. "He just went to active scanners. He can't miss us."

"We have a return com signal," Thompson said.

Angela gestured for Talbot to stand and come forward. "This is your show. You need to be standing right here."

He unstrapped, rose to his feet, and moved to stand beside her. "Put the signal up on the screen."

The image of a man in some kind of civilian clothes appeared on the screen. He had dark hair and a thin face, one that was filled with suspicion. "Who the hell are you? How did you get so close without detection? Answer or I'll open fire."

"Go to active scanners," Angela said. "Not aggressively, but we need to know what we're dealing with."

"Active scanners," McLeod confirmed. "It's a fast packet. They're made for getting messages from one system to another quickly. He's probably got a single missile tube. Not a threat."

"He might not be alone. Keep an eye out for other ships. Hell, they might have a destroyer or two on the other side of that flip point. Or a cruiser. We assume nothing."

"Answer his call," Talbot ordered. "Focus in on me."

"Copy that," Thompson said. "Live in three, two…" The man held up one finger and then a closed fist.

"My name is Russ Talbot, and we're friends of Commander Sommerville. He gave me the codes so I could come forward and talk with you before you started running or shooting. I know you saw our ships in the Razor system. We're friends, not Empire enemies."

The man seemed to consider Talbot for a few moments. "You have the code, but I can't imagine Danny bringing friends home."

"Don," Talbot corrected. "And you don't know what is happening in Archibald right now. There's an invasion on. The Ghosts have attacked, and we've made common cause. We're connected with a different resistance cell in another part of the Empire."

The man seemed unconvinced. "Yet you have two big freighters and that strange ship you're on. I've never seen or heard of anything like it."

So they'd pegged *Audacious* as a freighter. Since the Rebel Empire didn't use ships bigger than cruisers, that was a natural mistake.

"I'd be happy to explain in person," Talbot said. "Just me in a suit. One of our small craft can send me your way, and you can visually verify it's me. That way you don't have to have a strange ship docking."

"I want to see Sommerville. If you people really are friends, you can send him over alone."

"Or with a single person accompanying him," Talbot insisted. "Then we can explain ourselves in person."

The man seemed to consider that for a few moments and then nodded. "He picks the person and sends me an image. Not you. Back your ship up to the Razor flip point and send an unarmed cutter with the two of them and a pilot. They'll bail in suits, and my people will pick them up. Your cutter goes back to the flip point while we talk."

"Agreed."

The transmission terminated without a response.

"I'm not sure if that could've gone better or not," Talbot admitted.

"It could certainly have gone worse," Angela said. "There were no shots fired, and he didn't go scampering off. I doubt Sommerville will leave his people behind, so he'll try to keep the man talking. Take the win."

She turned her attention to the helm officer. "Take us back to the flip point. Get the FTL probe into place to monitor the flip point without being detected. If he signals other ships, I want to know about it. Ditto if anyone comes through the flip point or he leaves."

"Yes, ma'am."

Angela returned her attention to him. "Do you think Kelsey will go on the negotiation trip?"

"She'll take the lead on this. I just know it," he said grumpily.

Thompson turned in his seat. "We're getting an FTL communication from Admiral Mertz. He's asking for Princess Kelsey."

Angela shook her head. "I suppose we never got the com transferred to *Audacious*. You can take it with you when you go. In the interim, it might be best if you give him an update of what's going on."

Talbot nodded. "I'll use your office, if you don't mind."

With that, he headed off to bring the admiral up to speed, glad to hear they'd made it out of their own sticky situation.

* * *

JARED TRIED to contact Kelsey via the FTL com as soon as they were out of detection range of the flip point leading to the AI's system but was told that she wasn't available. She was on *Audacious* on the other side of a flip point from *Persephone* and hadn't taken her FTL com with her.

That was annoying, but he got an update from Talbot. They'd broken contact with the Clan invaders and were trying to negotiate with the resistance. That was going to change how Jared had planned to proceed, for sure. Olivia would need to be standing by the com in case they needed codes or recognition phrases from her.

The introduction of the two Kelseys would have to wait until his sister was done, too. She didn't need that kind of revelation while she was busy working such a delicate situation.

So he and Kelsey Two would talk with Fielding. The news didn't please Olivia, but she understood at once how things had to be.

Kelsey Two was less pleased.

"I'm not sure we make the best interrogation team," she said. "I still haven't adjusted to working with you."

"Then you're going to have to try harder," he said firmly. "I've gone out of my way to give you space, but we're out of room. If you don't realize that I'm not the same man as in your universe, you're being intentionally blind."

That caused a flash of anger in her eyes, but she nodded. "I do realize that, but it's not exactly easy to turn off my emotions."

"You're the crown princess of the New Terran Empire," he parried. "How are you going to deal with people you don't like in the palace? Glare at them when you think they aren't looking? Sneer to their faces? This is the same kind of thing. We all have to work with people we don't like.

"I didn't much care for Sean Meyer when we first met. Personality-wise, we're fairly different, and he disliked me. We get along fine in a professional sense now. Are you saying he's better at this than you?"

"You don't understand," she growled. "Mertz is a monster. He killed my father."

"I. Am. Not. Him." Jared said slowly, clearly enunciating every word.

She sighed with frustration but nodded. "I need to get over this, I really do. You're right. Still, can Sean be at the interrogation? That would make it easier for me."

He honestly doubted the woman would ever get over what had happened to her. It was sad, but there was nothing he could do about it except work around her muleheadedness.

"I'll have him meet us there. Highness, is there anything I can do to make this better? I really don't want to be your enemy. If I could find the other version of me and drag him to justice, I would. If I had to, I'd kill him and not lose much sleep over it. It really does sound like he's a right bastard, if you can forgive the irony."

She slumped a little in her chair. "You and your people have been nothing but gracious and accepting of me and my people. Intellectually, I *know* that you're not the Bastard. He wouldn't be able to stop himself from being an ass.

"I've heard you talking with my doppelgänger, and it's clear that she likes you. Loves you, even. I can't wrap my head around that, but I think our personal histories split when we were almost of age. That's when our Mertz became so nasty.

"Since both of us hated him long before that, you've overcome her objections with being a good man. The same with my father, though to be fair, he never saw the other you for what he was. I will try to do better."

With that, she took a deep breath and stood. "Let's do this."

22

———————

Kelsey sat in the seat beside Sommerville with more equanimity than she'd have expected of herself even a year ago. The cutter only had a pilot, so it was an unusually empty small craft and so very quiet. She'd instantly named herself as the second person as soon as *Persephone* came back to Razor to pick up Sommerville, much to Talbot's annoyance.

"You don't seem very worried," Sommerville commented as they headed out to meet the resistance cutter.

"I'm not," she confided. "I mean, sure, things could go wrong, but the downsides aren't that heavy. Not compared to what I've faced in the last few years. You're not going to kill me or put my implants in command of my body."

He raised an eyebrow. "Did that really happen?"

"Almost," she said softly. "So damned close I could taste it. Oh, and you're not going to dissect me while I'm awake. That's a big one, too."

"You've led a hard life, Princess Kelsey. No, we're not going to do any of those things. If we can't convince the others to meet with you, then you'll go free. We don't need a ship like *Audacious* coming to look for you. At least I can tell them you're not like the Clans. You won't pour in after us, shooting all the way.

"They're going to seriously complicate everything we're doing," Sommerville continued with a sigh. "An unexpected war is not only going to hurt the Empire, it'll impact our ongoing operations, just like it did for me at Archibald."

She shook her head. "That took serious chutzpah to have the enemy build a ship for you."

"Chutzpah?" he asked with a frown. "I don't know that word."

"Gall, impudence, or nerve. Rather all of that and more. Cheekiness."

He laughed. "It wasn't that bold. The inspectors were resistance. With me there to replace the logs, no one would ever have known. Freighters don't get the same level of attention as a warship does. Fleet has no reason to board one at all.

"It wasn't the first time we'd done it, either. This gives us a number of hulls the Empire doesn't care about that we can use to project force where they least expect it. Um, we will get it back, won't we?"

"You're so suspicious," she said. "Seriously, we already planned to release it back to you. We're not thieves."

"You stole an entire orbital, you broke into a research laboratory, and you hijacked my ship."

"Okay, we're thieves, but we have hearts of gold," she amended.

That made him laugh. "I'll accept your bargain, and I promise I'll try to get my people to help. Everything you showed me convinces me that we can accomplish great things together. What are your plans for Veronica and her people?"

The non sequitur made Kelsey's brain stumble for a moment. "I haven't thought that far ahead. They're willing conspirators at this point, so that's really up to them."

"I'd like to talk Veronica into staying with us when you depart," he said seriously. "She could be a bridge between your people and mine."

Kelsey shrugged. "I have no objection, but she's only known us for a little while. She's not steeped in who we are."

"I know that, but she's an old friend and can help us. If you'd like to leave someone that can truly tell us about your people and represent you, I have what might be a controversial suggestion: Justine Bandar."

Kelsey blinked in shock. "My *mother*? Seriously? How do you even know her?"

"Veronica introduced us, and we've spent some time together. I think she's charming. Your mother suggested the idea, actually."

The news flabbergasted Kelsey. She had no idea what to think. If there was a worse representative for the Empire than her mother, she had no idea who it would be.

The pilot chose that moment to call back to them. "We're approaching the handoff point. I'm slowing to a halt and will draw the air out in a minute. Time to close up."

"Thank you," Kelsey said.

She and Sommerville closed their helmets and checked one another in the time they had left. No one wanted a suit failure.

The pilot called to confirm they were ready and then pulled the air out. The shadows became hard lines with the lack of air, and the ramp came down.

Kelsey and Sommerville stepped out into space, and she used her thrusters to turn and watch their cutter move off slowly before accelerating away until she couldn't see it. They floated alone in space. It was kind of spooky.

"My mother?" she asked, picking the conversation back up. "Seriously? She's a stowaway and the least diplomatic person I know."

He laughed. "We all have opinions about our parents that other people just don't see. You have to accept that she's not the same to people that don't have a history with her. She can be very diplomatic. She was the empress of a star nation, after all."

Kelsey wanted to rub her face, but that was impossible. "I'm going to have to think about it. That's a heavy load to drop on me. I have my issues with her, but I do love her."

A thought occurred to her, and she felt her eyes narrow. She turned Sommerville toward her so that she could see his face. "Are you sleeping with my mother?"

He didn't answer, but his reddening face told Kelsey everything she needed to know.

"Ewwwww! That's gross! And I should've known she'd try something like this."

Sommerville smiled a little. "Actually, she was very resistant to the idea. I had to be a very attentive suitor. She told me you'd be angry, though I'm not exactly sure why. You barely know me."

Kelsey opened her mouth to respond but closed it without revealing her mother's dark past. That was really a private family problem. And none of her business.

She and her mother had made their peace. A thin, hard-won peace, but something real. Kelsey wasn't going to throw that away so easily.

Perhaps he was right. Her mother was obviously very persuasive when she put her mind to it.

"Let me think about that and talk with her before I commit," she finally said. "What kind of assurances would I have for her safety?"

"She'd be the one and only ambassador from a foreign power we've ever had. I can guarantee that she would never be in the slightest danger."

"Fine. All I can do is talk with her and get back to you. And seriously? You're sleeping with my mother? She's twice your age."

"And her experience shows."

"Stop. You're going to make me hurl in my helmet."

"I meant that in a nonsexual way, but——"

"Seriously! I don't want to know!"

After making a show of shuddering, she continued. "I think I see our ride approaching. Do me a favor. Don't tell anyone with implants that we're from an offshoot of the Old Empire. That'll cause some serious problems for them until we make a few things clear."

"If the picket commander is who I think it is, that's not a concern. We have some Fleet officers and a few members of the higher orders, but not so many that it's a big risk. I'll want to know why before we get to our eventual destination."

"I promise to explain everything before then," she said.

The approaching confrontation was actually a relief. The knowledge that her mother was once again on the prowl had her upset. Perhaps, as Sommerville thought, this was his doing, but he didn't understand how manipulative Kelsey's mother was.

Then again, she supposed a degree of manipulation was needed in a diplomatic envoy.

The bright dot approaching them grew into a cutter that slowed to a stop near them. It pivoted and lowered its ramp, showing Kelsey a man standing inside ready to haul them inside. Thankfully, neither one of them needed assistance.

"Commander Sommerville can come inside," the man inside the cutter said. "Whoever is with him needs to stay outside until we verify he isn't under duress."

She supposed that was a reasonable precaution, so she jetted to a halt and watched as the man closed the cutter up behind Sommerville. She supposed it was possible the cutter would leave with him, but she doubted that. He'd want his people and ship back.

Ten minutes later, her thoughts were vindicated when the ramp opened and Sommerville gestured for her to come inside. Once she was in, he closed the ramp and started flooding the compartment with air. The man had vanished into the front of the cutter, no doubt locking the door behind him.

Once her helmet was folded back, she strapped in. "Did you two have a nice talk?"

"If you consider being peppered with questions a talk, sure. Oh, and scanning to make sure I didn't have some kind of bomb compelling me to be on your side."

"Paranoid much?"

He laughed. "When you're dealing with the System Lords and their minions, a certain level of paranoia is appropriate. I think I convinced him I was speaking for myself, so now he just thinks I'm crazy."

"Hopefully I can convince your friends I'm being serious."

"Me, too."

The ride back to the picket ship was uneventful, and they soon docked. A pair of armed guards was waiting for them inside with their weapons drawn. One of them had a hand scanner.

"Strip off the vacuum suit and stand here with your arms raised," he said.

Kelsey slowly removed her vacuum suit, folded it, and set it on the deck and let them start scanning. She noticed the moment the man found her Raider enhancements because of his shocked expression.

"I can't take those out, and they're actually part of my proof," she said. "You have stunners to keep me in line."

"What am I seeing?" the man asked hesitantly.

"Artificial muscles, graphene-coated bones, a pharmacology unit, and everything else that goes into making a Marine Raider."

"What's a Marine Raider?" the other man asked.

"Something from a dark past that none of us expected to ever see again," Sommerville said.

Now the men looked even more unsettled. After a shared look, they cuffed her hands in front of her. They used plastic cuffs that would be more than good enough for a regular person of even Talbot's size but were nowhere near good enough to hold her.

"Do you want me to pretend these can hold me?" she asked. "Or shall I prove what I was saying?"

"Prove it," Sommerville said, turning back to face her. "They won't believe you otherwise."

One yank snapped the cuffs, and she calmly handed them back over to the man who'd cuffed her. He took them automatically, too stunned to do otherwise.

"Very impressive," a voice from up the corridor said. It was the man they'd spoken to earlier.

"They tell me you're acting of your own free will, Don. Is that right?"

"Everything is nautical," the Rebel Empire officer said.

"That's the all-clear codeword," he told her as an aside. "Now they'll have to change it."

The man stepped closer and looked Sommerville up and down. "You seem healthy enough. I was worried." With that, he wrapped his arms around Sommerville, and the two men hugged one another.

That was a more... enthusiastic greeting than Kelsey had expected.

Sommerville turned toward her with a smile. "Kelsey Bandar, meet my older brother Gavin. Gavin Sommerville, this is Crown Princess Kelsey Bandar of the New Terran Empire."

"The what?" the elder Sommerville asked. "I think I need to hear this all from the beginning. It's a little hard to believe, even after seeing how enhanced she is."

Kelsey nodded. "Let me give you the *Reader's Digest* version."

The man held up his hand. "The what?"

"Sorry," she said. "Old Empire slang. The condensed version. I'm from a splinter of the Old Empire that the System Lords never located. We're on the way to Terra to get something to stop them. We inadvertently hijacked your brother and are returning him, his people, and his ship in exchange for directions."

The man gestured up the corridor. "Let's adjourn to my wardroom so that I can hear everything you have to say. If I think you're telling me the truth, I'll send you on with a recommendation to help you. But I'll need a lot of proof, and I'm not sure how you can provide it."

She smiled. "I have my ways. Shall we?"

23

Olivia wasn't happy at being sidelined from questioning Fielding and pushed back. She'd caught Kelsey Two and Jared on their way to confront Fielding and stopped them in the corridor.

"I realize you want to make this happen right away," she told them, "but this is something best done methodically. A few hours aren't going to make a difference. In fact, it might be useful if we let him stew for a while, and then I can take lead."

"I'm not going to object," Kelsey said swiftly. "I'll admit that this is an uncomfortable thing for me. I'd rather you do the talking and I can provide muscle."

"I'm not an interrogator," Jared admitted. "Are you?"

"I've known a few," Olivia said. "They're not exactly the most sociable types, if you know what I mean. Still, if you listen to what they say, you'll learn some interesting skills."

Kelsey frowned. "They didn't torture people, did they?"

Olivia laughed. "Pain isn't a very effective interrogation tool, according to the people I've met. It just gets people to tell you what they think you want to hear. Drugs and psychology are apparently the answers these days. Since I doubt Doctor Stone would be inclined to use drugs, we'll try intimidation first.

"But let's just take our time. We can wait to see if Kelsey needs anything from us while Fielding waits on us for a change. Let's not rush ahead and spoil our chances."

With their agreement, she led them to the compartment where they'd relocated the FTL com. It was almost an hour before someone called them and asked for specific recognition codes, which she provided.

Once they had them, she told the person on the other end of the com that she would be indisposed for a while and to verify with Kelsey that she wasn't needed any longer. They gave her the all clear.

She rose to her feet with a smile. "Finally, we seem to have gotten Kelsey the leg up she needed, so we should see if we can do the same for ourselves. Shall we?"

"What's the plan going to be?" Jared asked as they headed toward where they were holding Fielding and his guards.

"I'm going to make this up as I go," she said. "Don't go in expecting anything. If he defies us, we can always backtrack, though that will cost us time. I'm hoping that we won't need to do that, but we still don't know how long it'll take Kelsey to get to Terra. If she even can."

She ordered the marines to bring Fielding to a nearby conference room and secure him. Then they waited.

A few minutes later, the two men dragged Fielding in and cuffed him to the chair against one of the bulkheads. Olivia and her companions sat on the far side of the table to gain what psychological advantage they could. The marines remained on either side of the Rebel Empire noble.

"I'm sure you're wondering why we've brought you here," she said with a bright smile.

"You're traitors," he sneered. "Whatever it is you want, I'm not going to provide it."

"Treason is in the eye of the beholder. So is betrayal. You were going to blow us up. I caught your men preparing to sabotage the bioweapon and kill all of us with the Omega Plague. I think that's an excellent place to start. Why?"

"Does it matter? Telling you won't change how you respond to it."

"It can hardly put you in a worse position," she countered.

"I suppose not. The Lords are going to clean up everyone involved in this mission. No one will live to tell the tale. My intention was to leave your ship at one of the upcoming systems and then disappear. I'd have taken my nephew with me, of course, except that he's joined you."

That last came out much more angrily than Olivia would've expected. Somehow, she just didn't see the man attached to anyone other than himself. Apparently, she'd been wrong.

"And since you're in the process of betraying the Lords, are you so shocked that we are as well?"

He laughed. "What a complicated game we play in the higher orders. I was and am looking out for myself and my family. If you fail to arrive at Terra, they will believe you dead and the ship destroyed. They wouldn't be looking for me or Austin. I'd already made arrangements for us to vanish."

"Personally, I have no objection to your plans," Jared said. "Right up until they resulted in the deaths of me and my friends, of course. Since you don't really care about this mission, perhaps we can come to an agreement that sees both plans carried out and the Lords played for fools."

"Or will you try to declare you won't see them betrayed at Terra?"

Olivia asked. "Do you really lose anything if we carry out our own plans there?"

"I came late to the conversation on the station, so I really don't know what you intend," Fielding said. "And I suppose I don't care. You have me now, and if I want to get away from you, I'll have to pay. What is it you want? Money?"

"I want to know something first," Kelsey said. "You sabotaged the Lord back in that system. Why? You'd already planned to kill us and vanish. Why do something that dangerous?"

"Since I didn't know you were going to betray the Lords like I intended, I had to make sure to at least carry that part of the mission out."

"That's a lie," Olivia said. "If you blew up the Lord, we'd never get to a populated system for you to escape in. Or did you have the extension code all along? If so, why play this game at all?

"No, you came here for something else. You had a plan for getting out all along. You're not going to get away with that nonsense. What was your real plan, and how did you intend to get to another system?"

"I see no purpose in saying since you're going to kill me anyway."

"Perhaps not," Olivia said. "It doesn't matter to me whether you live or die, but I'm willing to trade your life for something I want. The passage codes to get to Terra from here."

His eyes narrowed. "You're still going there? Why?"

"In the end, that's not really something you need to concern yourself with," she said coolly. "Our purposes are our own."

"I do care, since you dare not allow me off your ship before you get there," he retorted. "That means you'll have to keep me with you through whatever madness you intend."

She laughed. "You're being shortsighted. I have a much easier way of assuring that you never tell anyone about us or what we've done so far." She tapped her head meaningfully.

His eyes widened. "No!"

"Oh, yes. You gave Austin the code to disarm his bomb, but we'd already done so in a much more meaningful way. We rewrote the code in his implants so that it wouldn't go off, no matter what signals are sent to it. We can't be sure enough to remove it, but I have utter confidence nothing he does or even an external signal will ever set it off."

That was a lie. They'd actually removed the bomb once Kelsey had identified the antitampering circuit and how it worked. They didn't have the code to disarm the bomb, but without the corrupted implant code, it could be safely removed. The AIs hadn't ever imagined that was possible, so they'd left that flaw in the process that Lily and Kelsey could exploit.

"We'll rewrite your implant code so that you won't be able to talk about this ship or anyone on it to anyone, or even the fact that implant code can be altered. I wouldn't try to have anyone research doing the same, if I were you. We included that. If you do any of those things, you'll have the most epic headache in history. A short one, but quite debilitating, I'm afraid."

Olivia leaned forward and smiled wolfishly. "The only bargaining point to have me keep the program as loose as possible is giving me what I want to know. We'll drop you and your people off short of Terra with complete assurance that you'll never tell anyone about us. In fact, I feel confident you'll want to forget you ever met us as quickly as possible."

The man blinked as he considered his options. "You could be lying."

"I could be," she admitted, "but the only way to know for sure is to risk instant death. You have no loyalty to the System Lords, so I doubt you'll feel much inclination to betray us once you're free.

"And before you ask more tiresome questions, there is nothing stopping me from shoving you out an airlock if you give me the codes. So you'll be free to give them to me at every system we transit. If they work, great. If they don't, I shoot you before I die."

He gave her the ghost of a smile. "You can be very persuasive, Lady... I'm afraid I don't know your actual name."

"And you don't need to. Lady Keaton is quite acceptable for the remaining week we have to spend together."

"Of course. What about the bioweapon?"

"Gone," Jared said. "The Lord assisted us with deactivating the plasma bombs. We then ejected the crates and destroyed them. The Omega Plague is dead. I'll assume you made plans on your end to destroy the lab where it was grown."

"Indeed. The Lords will be displeased that they'll have to start over, as I made certain all the research data they got was fatally flawed. The project will have to be started over. Which they will do, I assure you. You're only buying time."

"A problem we'll deal with," she said firmly. "Now, the only remaining question in my mind is what you were really doing on the station with the AI. You sabotaged it, yes, but you had a second purpose there. What was it?"

"My own business," he said coldly. "I'm willing to agree to your terms, but I have nothing to say about what I was doing."

"Very well, then," she said as she rose. "Take him back to his cell. One of you remain inside for additional instructions."

The marines removed Fielding's restraints, and one of them escorted him out into the corridor. The remaining man came close to the table.

"Get him partway there and then stun him," Olivia said. "Take him to the medical center and have Doctor Stone secure him to a table."

"Yes, ma'am," the marine said before exiting the conference room.

"Are you really going to turn his bomb back on?" Kelsey asked, a frown on her face.

"No," Olivia said with a smile. "But he won't know that. We'll wipe the corrupted code in his implants and let him think whatever he will. I very seriously doubt he'll attempt to do anything that risks his own life by testing the limits."

"What about the rest of his story?" Jared asked. "We need to know what he was up to. He might've done anything."

Olivia rose to her feet. "He's got everything interesting on his implants encrypted. We checked after you came back. He's forgotten we have another source of data, though."

"The guard he had with him," Kelsey said. "He left one in his cutter and took the other with him. Do you think his data is unencrypted?"

"Probably not, but I think I might be able to make that man talk more easily than Fielding. Especially after I mention how he was never expected to survive this trip."

"Do you think he'll believe you?" Jared asked as they walked out into the corridor. "Fielding would have had only the most loyal guards on this trip with him."

"We haven't checked, but I'll wager these men also have bombs in their heads," she said. "Ones he no doubt told them he'd disabled. I'll wager I can make them understand that five people can keep a secret only if four of them are dead."

Kelsey nodded slowly. "It's probably true, too. He's the kind of man that wouldn't hesitate to kill his subordinates to keep something valuable for himself alone."

"And if I promise the man to wipe his code clean just like Austin's and then drop him in a different system with some valuables from that gaudy cutter of Fielding's, you can bet he'll take the money and run.

"He'll have seen exactly what Fielding was doing. With a little bit of time, I'm sure that I can get it out of him. I'd be astonished if there isn't more than one secret lockbox on the cutter, too. It's entirely possible Fielding brought something physical back to the cutter before he tracked you down."

"I do want to know what he was doing," Jared said. "Do we feed them the same line about modifying the programing of the bomb to keep them all quiet?"

"Of course," she said. "I can handle that, though. You have to see that Kelsey and Kelsey speak to one another. You'll need to explain the situation and then leave them alone to talk."

Jared nodded. "We can do that. The next system along our path isn't occupied, so we can let Fielding sleep while we get all of our ducks in a row."

Kelsey frowned at him. "What are ducks and why would you want them in a row?"

He grinned. "You're just going to love your doppelgänger."

Olivia pushed them both away. "Go take care of this while I finish this up."

24

―――――

A ngela paced *Persephone*'s small bridge until the picket ship finally
signaled that they were bringing Princess Kelsey and Commander
Sommerville back. No need for an exchange this time; they'd bring
them back to her ship directly.

They had Kelsey's code phrase that everything was above board, so she
only worried a little as the cutter docked. Once the passengers were off, the
cutter undocked and headed back to the picket ship.

She'd considered going down to meet the princess but had decided that
it made far more sense for her to be on the bridge looking for trouble.
Thankfully, none occurred.

A few minutes later, Kelsey and Sommerville stepped onto the bridge,
taking up most of the remaining space. *Persephone* was powerful, but she
wasn't big. Quite the opposite. Angela didn't mind.

"How did it go?" she asked. "Leaving aside the obvious indication things
didn't go too badly, as they let you go."

"Pretty good," Kelsey said. "We'll be passed along to another ship and
taken to meet someone to discuss passage and help finding a route to Terra.
I expect that won't precisely be an easy negotiation, but it's not our worst-
case scenario."

Angela raised an eyebrow at Sommerville. "You've seen some of what
we have to offer, Commander. Care to offer a guess at how this will come
out?"

He shrugged slightly. "I'm not privy to the map of flip point
connections, so I really don't know. I've never heard of anyone visiting Terra
—and that's the kind of thing that would get around—so I wouldn't be too
optimistic."

"If you can get us close, say to a system that isn't occupied near Terra, we might be able to surprise you," Kelsey said. "That's part of what I'm willing to negotiate with for an alliance."

"I do hope you can figure something out," he admitted. "I'm interested in seeing what you have in your pockets. Though after meeting aliens and seeing a teleportation ring, I'm not sure how you can top what I already know about."

"It's something more practical that we know about that will be far more useful than the mostly theoretical stuff you've seen," Kelsey said. "Either of which would change things, but they're so critical that they'd have to stay limited to the knowledge of the most trusted few. Did you know that your brother was stationed here when we came for the meeting?"

He nodded. "He was on the rotation. The tripwire posts are boring duty since no one else knew about the far flip points—good name for them, by the way. No one really expected anyone to come calling until you came along."

"Now that we're going to be moving deeper into resistance territory, can I get a clue how far we're going and what the process is going to be?" Angela asked.

He nodded. "Until an agreement of some kind is made, you'll proceed in this one ship. It's very stealthy, but now that we know it's here, it's not a direct threat to what we have in the systems beyond this. The rest of the ships will remain in the Razor system until we agree you can send for them."

"You knew about the humans there, obviously. I'm guessing you've never contacted them. Why not?"

"Too close to Archibald," he admitted. "If the Empire ever found the far flip point, they'd have found us. As it is, they'd find an undisturbed human world colonized by survivors that barely remember anything other than their world. They'd examine it and give us time to move away."

"Do you have any idea where the people on Razor came from?" Kelsey asked. "I'm guessing Archibald simply because of how close it is, but were they Fleet?"

"Archibald is the fabled home world they speak of, but I'm sure they weren't ever Fleet. I'd guess a large freighter stuffed with people fleeing the AI forces back in the day. There's no ship anywhere in the system, so it might have suffered irreparable damage, and they dropped it into the star after they salvaged what they could. Honestly, I'm not sure even they'd know at this point."

"They have a religion," Kelsey said. "The story might be part of their secret lore."

"Good luck getting it, then. The religious types there have some peculiar ideas and practices. They're not exactly friendly when someone encroaches on what they consider their turf."

"Tell me about it," the princess muttered.

Angela gave the other woman a look. "You've met them? I think I missed that story."

"Talbot led a party down, and there was a ruckus in the town that revolved around them," Kelsey said quickly. "Nowhere near the landing party."

The princess's response was a tad too quick for Angela's taste. It sounded like the other woman was hiding something. Still, now was not the time to dig deeper.

"Anyway," Angela said, shooting the princess a raised eyebrow, "my question still stands. Any clue on how many more transits we'll make to get there? One? Many?"

"A few," Sommerville allowed. "My brother sent a probe over to the next system to let the picket there know to expect us, so we'll head over shortly, I'm sure. That ship will escort us to where you need to go."

Jack Thompson turned in his seat and cleared his throat. "Major, could I have a word?"

She nodded and rose to her feet. "Of course. If you'll excuse me for a moment, Highness, Commander."

Angela leaned over her helmsman's shoulder to look at his console. Nothing looked out of place. "What's up?"

"Princess Kelsey has a call on the *special* com," he said very softly.

The implication was instantly clear to her. Admiral Mertz was calling on the FTL com.

"Understood," she replied quietly. "Carry on."

Angela stood back up and turned toward the princess and resistance officer. "I'm about to take a break to get something to eat. Would you care to join me?"

As she spoke, she sent a com signal to Kelsey through her implants. *Admiral Mertz is on the FTL com for you.*

The princess nodded. "Food sounds good, but I need to go take care of a few things. Commander Sommerville, why don't you and Angela get to know one another a little better while I do so?"

He smiled. "I'd be delighted. Major?"

"Jack, you have the bridge. If we get the call to go forward, please proceed and only tag me if something seems off."

"Yes, ma'am."

"Let's go, Commander. The galley isn't much to look at, but the food is good."

With that, she led Commander Sommerville away from the bridge and Princess Kelsey so that the woman could find out what was going on with Admiral Mertz. Hopefully nothing galaxy shattering. They were finally getting some things to go their way.

* * *

KELSEY STOOD behind Mertz as they waited for her doppelgänger—Kelsey One—to come to the FTL com and start what would be a shocking and unsettling conversation. Hell, it was going to be the same for her, and she knew what was coming.

"It's going to be okay," Mertz said.

"I'm not sure how you can be so certain. This isn't going to be an easy conversation."

"I wager it'll be easier than you expect," he said with a crisp note of certainty in his voice. "She's not going to expect you, but she's at least been exposed to the idea for a while. Don't forget that she was there when we brought out the bodies of people from other universes. People that we knew. Multiple versions of those people."

"That is *so* creepy," she said with a shudder that wasn't even partly for show. "How can you say that so casually? Your friends died."

"It's an odd place to find myself," he admitted. "They're dead but still alive. It's actually a bit more difficult to accept Commander Roche. I didn't know him for long, but he's dead here, killed at Harrison's World."

"And Olivia's whole world," Kelsey added. "That's hard. Yet her ex-lover is still alive there. She's had it worse than either of us. How does she stand the knowledge?"

He shrugged. "I'm not sure. I know it's a burden for her. Having Sean and all her friends alive here helps, I'd imagine."

The FTL com picked that moment to come to life. Mertz turned his attention to it as a generic voice spoke, interpreting the Morse code that was used into actual speech. In Kelsey's mind, she changed it to her own voice.

"Kelsey here. Jared, is that you?"

"It's me," he said. "Sorry for the delay in resuming full communication, but we had some issues on this end that had to be sorted out. How did your meeting with the resistance go?"

"Pretty good. I had to reveal some of our secrets, but I didn't mention the FTL coms or multi-flip points. Showing Commander Sommerville the Pandorans, the small transport rings, and my hammer turned the trick as far as he was concerned.

"And speaking of revelations, Carl has cracked the operating system on the Singularity computer and has managed to start accessing the data it contains in a more straightforward process. He now has indexes of files and locations on the storage medium to change the task from almost impossible to just difficult. Like the computer we found on *Courageous*, it has a lot of data to be examined."

"Can you tell me how long ago the computer was destroyed?" Mertz asked. "I remember Carl guessed it was a number of years ago, but a century is different than a decade when it comes to useful information versus history."

"He's still struggling with the units of time they use, but he said it was almost certainly shut down abruptly around twenty years ago, give or take five."

"That's pretty recent," Kelsey said. "It might have information that's actually useful against them now."

"I agree," her double said, not realizing a different person had spoken. "I've got the researchers from Dresden working on getting a feel for what kind of information is available. I should know something by the time we get to Terra."

"Is that a certainty at this point?" Mertz asked. "You said the meeting went well, but we have no idea if they'll help you get there, or if there's even a way *to* get there."

"I have a good feel for Commander Sommerville. He's going to work hard on convincing them. He's already gotten to the point of asking for a diplomatic representative. You'll never believe who he thinks would be a good match: my mother."

Kelsey blinked at the other woman's words. Her mother? A diplomat? More like a social butterfly that was always on some new man's arm. Was other her serious?

Mertz apparently shared Kelsey's opinion. "I remember that you said she'd stowed away, but really? I realize she was once the empress of the Terran Empire, but do we really want to have her speaking for us? Not that I'd mind if she wasn't at Terra with us, considering that she hates me."

The same had been true in Kelsey's universe, but there, her mother had had many reasons to despise Jared Mertz. If he was such a paragon of virtue here, why did her mother hate him after all this time?

Well, she'd have to find out when she either spoke with the woman or with her doppelgänger face to face. That wasn't the kind of question she was going to ask with him standing right there.

He looked at Kelsey as if reading her mind. Under other circumstances, that would be funny.

"She's had a change of heart in some ways," the other Kelsey said. "I wouldn't go so far as to say she's forgiven you for being born, but she's had her pampered eyes opened a bit.

"Honestly, I'm still of two minds and need to talk with her to see how serious she'd be in this role. It might not be a bad thing, really. She wasn't idle while she was empress. She has the diplomatic chops if she can be convinced to use them."

"Well, I guess that's your call," Mertz said. "I have another matter to bring up. Another person, really. I couldn't mention it before because someone was present on my side that didn't have need to know about her."

"Okay," the other Kelsey said. "Who is it, and how does knowing about her affect me?"

"Trust me when I say that her presence is going to be a shock to your system," he said with a lopsided smile. "Kelsey Bandar, allow me to introduce you to Kelsey Bandar."

25

Talbot headed for Carl's lab as soon as his friend called for him. He'd just gotten word through the FTL com that Kelsey was back aboard *Persephone* and that she'd secured permission to go meet with someone they could negotiate with for passage to Terra.

Audacious, the freighter, and the Q-ship would remain in the Razor system until they were called forward. Meanwhile, Zia had dispatched probes to search the system thoroughly. If there were more resistance ships here, she wanted to know about them.

As a side effect of that search, they'd already located a multi-flip point that the resistance wouldn't have known about. Goodness only knew where it led to. The branches of the multi-flip points seemed to have more range than a single regular or far flip point, so it likely led to places far beyond Archibald. If that was one of the bargaining chips that Kelsey was going to trade for an alliance and a path to Terra, the resistance was going to be *very* surprised.

And he was sure that something like that would trade hands. It would take something big to break the bonds of suspicion that the resistance had to be feeling right now. They had no reason to trust them. Hell, until this encounter, these people had no reason to suspect anything like the New Terran Empire even existed.

Talbot knew from conversations with Olivia West that the resistance operated in cells that kept communication between themselves to the bare minimum. That still implied—though she'd never said so—that there was someone over them all in a kind of coordinating position. Not overtly directing actions but more as a clearing house of information between the groups.

One that was very careful never to reveal itself lest the Rebel Empire find them all through it. He wondered if that was the group of people they'd found.

He was still thinking about that when he entered the lab and walked over to the remains of the Singularity computer. Carl was sitting at a workstation right up against it and seemed to have added a number of cables running into the debris.

His friend jumped a little when Talbot put his hand on his shoulder. He turned and scowled up at him. "Do you have to do that?"

"It's in my contract," Talbot replied smugly. "What's up?"

"We found the operating system. One of my top computer guys, Eric Hosmer, reverse engineered a variant of it that has all the security protocols disabled. We have full, organized access to the data cores."

Talbot blinked. He'd known his friend had been making progress on accessing the data, but he hadn't known he'd gotten this far.

"Excellent! Good work to all of you. What can you tell me about it?"

"Quite a bit, actually. This computer was a master AI on the equivalent of what we'd call a superdreadnought. It tangled with Rebel Empire forces on the border with the Singularity. It was a hell of a fight. The data cores have a record of the battle, which I've already sent to Commodore Anderson.

"It was a very large fleet action. The Singularity side was about the same strength as the entirety of Admiral Mertz's new command. Lots of ships that seem to be on par with the Old Empire tech, and in some cases, a little better."

The scientist gestured for Talbot to take a seat next to him. "The Rebel Empire side was even more powerful. You know how we never see battlecruisers or superdreadnoughts here? Well, I think I found them. They're in use on the far side of the Rebel Empire, probably under computer control."

That wasn't good news. They'd all hoped the Rebel Empire had destroyed the larger ships. To have them in active service meant that the AIs had a tremendous reserve of power that they could bring to bear on the New Terran Empire. If, of course, they could spare them from the fight they were already engaged in.

"Have you narrowed down when the fight took place?" Talbot asked. "We know this computer has been in Rebel Empire hands for years."

The young scientist nodded. "I finally managed to get a grasp on how the Singularity does their calendar. The fight that killed the ship this computer was on took place a little more than eighteen years ago. So the data in the cores isn't ultra-new, but it's far more recent than we had any right to expect."

Talbot pursed his lips. Two decades was not that long in the life of an interstellar civilization. Look at the Rebel Empire. They hadn't pushed the tech past what was in use 500 years ago, though that was probably the AIs. And these data cores probably had far more information about the

Singularity than anyone in the Old Terran Empire had ever dreamed of getting their hands on.

"That's great, Carl," he said. "Really great."

"But you're wondering why I called you down here?" his friend asked with a smile. "It's because of something the Singularity called Operation Brutus. That's a reference to a historical incident on Terra thousands of years before spaceflight. It's also what the Singularity was calling their work with the Clans."

That got Talbot's attention. "Does it give us a clue what their goals were?"

"You bet it does," Carl said grimly. "Not that I expect it's going to be pleasant to hear. The Singularity found the Clans on one of their border incursions. It took a few tries to get them to talk without shooting first, but over the years they built enough of a rapport to become allies of a sort.

"This started about fifty years ago, by the way. This ship was destroyed in combat shielding a huge convoy of freighters bound for the Clans. Ones to build shipyards that would be more than capable of building battlecruisers.

"Based on some references, they intended to deny the Clans the ability to build carriers or superdreadnoughts, but I personally doubt that would've stopped the Clans for long. What it boils down to is that they were arming the Clans with advanced warships and technical advisors with the intent of having the Clans disrupt the AIs so that the Singularity could invade in force."

Talbot blinked. That was bad. *Really* bad.

"Did they have a timeline on this plan?" he asked. "Did they intend for the Clans to go now, or did we kick things off prematurely?"

Carl smiled slightly. "You've hit upon the key. The Singularity had a timeline, one that they were using to build up their own forces in anticipation for. From what I can see, the Clans jumped off about two decades early. The Singularity isn't ready for their follow-up invasion."

"But that won't stop them from trying," Talbot said grimly. "It'll just end up getting a lot of people killed and make completing our work that much harder. Is that it?"

"Not quite. The target for the Singularity strike was one of the most heavily protected systems in the Rebel Empire. One we've heard of before: Twilight River."

* * *

Jared waited for Kelsey to react to what he'd just said, knowing that it had undoubtedly rocked his sister's world.

"Something got wonky in the translation," Kelsey said after a moment. "Say that again."

"I said that I need you to meet another version of you. One from another universe, just like the bodies we found on Omega station. She came through there with some of her people looking for help.

"I couldn't tell you about her because I have people here that don't know about Omega and what he means to us. I'm going to leave the two of you alone to talk. She's so much like you, and yet so different. It's going to be hard for you both, so you don't need anyone listening in. I suggest you clear the room on your end."

"I'm already alone." There was another long pause. "Are you being serious?"

"I've never been more serious, Kelsey. The next voice you hear will be hers. I'm leaving now to get some other work done, and I'll let you two be about it. Goodbye for now."

Jared rose to his feet, nodded to Kelsey Two, and headed out of the compartment to leave them some privacy. He really wanted to be a fly on the wall, but he couldn't imagine anything more inappropriate than listening in on this conversation. They needed to make friends, and his presence would only make that harder.

As he walked, he activated his com. "Olivia, this is Jared. Where are you?"

"I was waiting for you. I'm about to go have a nice talk with the guard that you captured with Fielding. He knows what we need to know, and I intend to get it out of him."

"On my way," he said, changing course to meet her there.

She was waiting outside the makeshift cell, standing near Senior Lieutenant Laird. The tall, red-headed marine officer waited with two of her enlisted men.

"I thought you were going to hit him without me," Jared said. "What changed your mind?"

"We make a good team, and I didn't want to deny you the pleasure of being there when we broke him. Did you get the Kelseys to talking?"

He nodded. "I introduced them and then left. I expect that they'll be there for a while. What's the plan here? Same thing as before?"

Olivia shook her head. "A different kind of intimidation. The guards might be loyal to him, but they know the higher orders can turn on them in a heartbeat if it suits them. I'm going to play on that and see what information we can shake loose."

That made sense to Jared. "He'll also have whatever he expected to need when he ran from the Lords. It would be very amusing to deny him his lifeline. Shall we?"

The marines opened the door, and Laird went in, her hand on her holstered stunner. When Jared followed her in, he found the prisoner standing against the opposite bulkhead, glaring at them.

Olivia came in last, cool and collected. "Sit," she said, pointing to the chair at the table.

The man puffed up a little. "Where is my Lord? Release me at once!"

"I'm not in the habit of releasing traitors to just wander about. I'm fully aware that your companions intended to sabotage my ship. All of you are in my custody, and if I do not get complete and prompt cooperation from you, I will see summary justice done. Do you understand me?"

The man wilted a little but then stood straighter. "We're not the traitors. That man is, and the others. They conspired with the renegade Lord."

"Do not think to meddle in the affairs of your betters," Olivia said coldly. "We have our own goals and instructions that you are not privy to. Even if we didn't, you aren't fit to judge us. In fact, we are here to cast judgment on you.

"What was your Lord doing on the station? What did he bring back? And don't think to lie to me. I will not hesitate to put you to the question and drag the answers from you. If I cannot get the truth from you, I will kill you and start on the pilot, so do not think you are indispensable."

Jared had to admit that her tone chilled him deeply. Olivia West could be a scary, scary woman. He hoped she knew what she was doing.

The man opened his mouth, perhaps to deny her, but he hesitated. He closed his mouth, examined Olivia more closely, and then bowed his head. "Mercy, Lady. I will comply."

"See that you do, and I will release you and your fellows in a different system than your Lord, with sufficient funds to disappear. Now, what did he do on the station, and what did he take?"

The man took a deep breath and let it out slowly. "He sabotaged a fusion plant, just as he told the Lord. He also went to a different compartment and pulled data off one of the Lord's data cores. I don't know what he copied, but I could see enough of the screen to know it was a significant amount of data. Once he had it, we returned briefly to the cutter before coming to find your man and his companions. That's all I know."

Olivia stared at him a long while and then nodded. "I will accept that for now. If we find no evidence of this data, we will speak again, and you will regret your deception."

The man bowed his head. "I'm telling the truth, Lady."

"For your sake, I hope so."

With that, Olivia turned and walked out of the compartment. Jared followed her, and Laird closed the hatch behind them.

"What could possibly be worth the risk of coming here?" Olivia asked, turning to face him.

"I have no idea," he said, "but we'd best go take a look."

26

K elsey sat in shocked silence for a few moments. "Is this some kind of joke?" she finally asked. "If so, I'm not getting it."

"It's no joke," the artificial voice that Carl had rigged up for the FTL com interface said. "Mertz is gone now. We are, it seems, doppelgängers. I knew there was a possibility that I'd run into you when I came across the universal barrier, but that didn't prepare me for this moment. I'm sorry for the surprise."

Kelsey sat back in her seat, stunned. She'd always known this was possible but never imagined it would actually happen. Certainly not after they found so many dead versions of Carl, Talbot, and the marines with them.

She'd expected more of them would come across, but not her. And even then, no other visitors had materialized. It had been over two years since they'd found Omega, and no one had come. Until now.

"You're really me?" she asked in a whisper.

"A version of you," the other woman confirmed, her voice sounding more like Kelsey's own in her mind. "Our history diverged. It's pretty close up, but the last few years in particular have gone worse for me than you. You, it seems, got all the good luck. I'm trying not to hate you for that."

"And you've come for help?" she asked. "You'll have it."

The other woman gave out a short bark of laughter. "Mertz said you'd say that. He also said to remind you to ask for the details before you promised help."

"That's how Jared is," Kelsey admitted. "And how I am. Why are you calling him by his last name?"

There was a long pause. "That's one of the differences between our universes. In mine, he really was the Bastard. He fomented rebellion and killed my father. Ethan rules now.”

Kelsey's mouth went dry. “Are you sure it was him? Here, Ethan was the one that went mad. Paranoia and megalomania. He tried to poison my father and blame me.”

“I've gone over everything that I know. I haven't made it home in my universe to see what is really happening there, but Mertz came to Pentagar. He fooled Captain Breckenridge, killed him and many of his officers, and stole *Courageous*. He struck out into the unknown in a direction that I now know leads toward the Rebel Empire.

“Am I sure that Ethan is completely sane? No. I've worried about it since I spoke with your friends, but I haven't seen anything in the communications I've exchanged with him that makes me think he's gone crazy. What I am sure of is that the Mertz in my universe is not the same man as in yours, and that's still causing me grief in trying to relate to him.”

That made Kelsey sad. Jared had fought so hard against being bitter. Maybe in that other universe, he'd lost that struggle. Then again, maybe the other version of her was wrong.

“Why haven't you made it home?” she finally asked. “Wasn't Omega able to help you?”

“No, not that way at any rate. It never occurred to me that it was possible to create artificial flip points, so that never came up in conversation. Based on what I've heard, it takes a long time to gather the energy to make one, and he couldn't for a few more months, even if you were inclined to let him.”

Kelsey chuckled. “I think you misunderstand our relationship. We don't tell him what to do. He decides what to do, and we're just grateful. If you asked him, he might do that for you next.”

“But that would mean you can't have him help you for another six months.”

“For the life of me, I can't think of where we'd need any more artificial flip points. If he could help you, that might be a help to us, too. Two New Terran Empires are stronger than one.”

“But that's not the case,” the other Kelsey said. “I wasn't joking when I said you'd gotten all the good luck. We didn't find a graveyard of ships at Harrison's World. The AI there murdered everyone on the planet and probably dropped all the ships into the sun. It's not even on Boxer Station anymore. The place was stripped bare.”

“There are some battlecruisers that might still be hidden in the system,” Kelsey said. “Around one of the gas giants.”

“Sean found them for us,” the other Kelsey said. “Your Sean. He gave us the codes, and we're working on figuring them out. Scott is sort of mad he isn't there to get one.”

“Scott?” Kelsey blinked. “Scott Roche? He's alive?”

“In my universe, yes. He's here with me on the destroyer with Mertz and your people. Let me be frank. We figured out what we need to stop the computer in my universe. The override. That's why I came. In my universe, Mertz stole the scepter."

Kelsey frowned. "I didn't know what it was until I got home and interfaced with it. How did you find out?"

"The message I found from Emperor Marcus had a secret message coded into it. I only found it by accident, but it provided just enough information for me to put the pieces together.

"Mertz in my universe doesn't have implants—at least he didn't when he ran—so I don't know that he even knows about the secret function of the key, but he's the only one with Imperial blood there. I can't get into the old Imperial Vaults on Terra without help, even if I could find some way to get there."

Kelsey tried to get a handle on what the other woman's situation was. "Do you have implants?"

"Sadly, yes. I'm the only one. Rather, I was until your people shared the technology with us. Now we're implanting everyone in the expedition."

"Why sadly?"

"I didn't get rescued right away when the mad computer at Erorsi took me. I became a Pale One, and it controlled me. It made me fight and kill."

Even though the artificial voice held no tone, Kelsey could easily hear the bitterness in the words.

"I'm so sorry," she whispered, knowing intimately how devastating that would be to her.

"What's done is done," the other Kelsey said. "At least Doctors Stone and Guzman were able to give me an artificial eye and regenerate me so that the pain of the implant process went away. I didn't realize how much of a haze I was in because of the drugs."

Her heart ached for the other woman. "I can see why you might hate me. God, you caught all the bad breaks, but now we can help you. I can help you. I've learned so much about using my Marine Raider implants."

"That's one of the big differences between us, Kelsey One. That's what they call you so as not to confuse things, by the way. Predictably, I'm Kelsey Two. Anyway, I'm not a warrior. I've seen what you can do, and that isn't me.

"I can fight, but the implants terrify me. I don't want to give the computer in my head any control at all. I can't get past what it made me do. I don't want to be a Marine Raider. I'm more than happy letting people like Angela Ellis do the fighting for me."

Kelsey felt her heart drop. "Do you know someone named Talbot?"

"He's not on my expedition," the other Kelsey said. "I've heard how you and he bonded, and I'm honestly happy for you. That's not going to be what happens for me. Frankly, my version of your Carl Owlet sounds more intriguing. If I have the chance, I'll introduce Angela to this Talbot and let them bond if they do. I'll look up the scientist when I get home."

"Ewwwww!" she said before she could stop herself. "I'm sorry, but Carl is like a little brother. He's not my type at all."

"More proof that we aren't the same person, I suppose," Kelsey Two said. "He sounds perfect to me. Of course, I didn't have the opportunity to bond with him like you did. We might not be suitable, but I'm not saying no until I get home and see what he's like."

"Well, I'll probably form an opinion when we meet at Terra, but I'm not the kind of girl that poaches from her friends. Your version of him is safe."

Just the thought of such a union boggled Kelsey's mind. Carl was a great guy, but she just didn't feel anything romantic towards him. Which was a good thing, since Angela would twist her into a pretzel if she did. Well, her doppelgänger's love life was none of her concern.

"Okay, we're obviously going to have to have a long talk about what we need to do for you after Terra. What can we hash out now that might be useful?"

"Mertz," Kelsey Two said. "How sure are you that he's really trustworthy?"

"Absolutely. I have no reservations whatsoever about him. I was wrong in how I saw him as a kid. It took me a while to accept that I'd seen him differently than he was, but being at his side for the entire expedition and beyond leaves no room for doubt. And though this might seem weird to you, I love him. In a brotherly sort of way, mind you."

"That's hard for me to process," the other woman admitted. "He's a snake in my universe. How can people with the same background be so different?"

"How can the two of us be so different? Admittedly, we're closer together than I expect the two Jareds are. We have the same background and many of the same experiences up until the expedition. Jared had no one. I'd imagine it would've been easy enough for him to slide into hatred in my universe, so I got lucky. Again."

The other Kelsey was quiet for a few seconds. "I hate to be paranoid, but I want to ask you a few questions that only the two of us would know the answers to. I need to make sure you're really a version of me and not someone pulling a trick on me."

Kelsey understood and approved of that kind of caution, but it had some potential issues. "We know we're mostly the same, but I can't be sure if my experience is the same as yours with everything we experienced."

"Really, it will only take one right answer to convince me that you're also me. At least until we meet, and I see you with my own eyes. Since you trust Mertz, I'll assume his word that I am who I am is good enough."

"It is," Kelsey said. "Shoot."

"When we were kids, I loved reading about the Old Empire in the Imperial Library. There was one old book that I found there that talked about a specific world in the Empire that fascinated me. I never spoke about it to anyone. Honestly, I considered it my own private getaway in my mind. It wasn't Terra, so I know that no one else will be able to guess what it was."

"Arcadia," Kelsey said immediately. "A water world with huge undersea cities. Living in the shallow oceans always sounded so romantic. The things I could've explored."

The other woman seemed to sigh. "It really *is* you. I still hadn't believed. Not deep down."

"I really am the same woman you are, with many of the same shared traits," Kelsey agreed. "It sounds like you've had a rough few years, but I swear that we'll do everything in our power to help you once we deal with our own problems.

"And Jared really is an honorable man here, a true servant to the New Terran Empire. My father... oh crap, our father is alive here. You can talk to him."

"I did. It broke my heart—in a good way—to see him alive and well. He welcomed me like a long-lost daughter. Meeting him meant the universe to me. I'm sad that I'll have to leave him and go back to a place where he's dead."

"What about Ethan in your universe?" Kelsey said, changing the subject. "Is he well?"

"He seems to be. Honestly, I don't think he has the same issues your version of him had. I heard what you did. It horrified me, and I still don't know what to think."

Kelsey nodded, even though the other woman couldn't see her. "It just about killed me to have to do it. To keep my mouth shut while he ran headfirst into a lethal radiation zone. You've seen how ugly it was in the Omega system.

"But I had no choice. He really had lost his mind. There was no doubt he was the man who tried to usurp the throne here. He almost killed my father and framed me for it. He was mad."

"I hope you get a chance to come to my universe and see him again," the other Kelsey said. "That seems like a good trade for me seeing my father again."

"Nothing would make me happier," Kelsey said, really meaning it. "You can trust Jared. You don't have to like him—I get that—but understand he's a good man here, not a monster."

A knock at the hatch interrupted her train of thought. A quick check of her implants showed Angela and Commander Sommerville outside. She'd thought they were going to have lunch. Something must've come up.

"I'm afraid that I have to go," she said. "Duty calls. We'll talk again soon. Kelsey, I want you to remember this and hold it dear. I will do *everything* within my power to help you and your people. So will Jared. We'll figure something out, I promise."

"I look forward to talking to you again, Kelsey. As silly as it is, you're my only hope."

"I'll be your Obi Wan."

A long beat of silence greeted her comment. "What the heck does that mean?"

"We're really going to have to work on your old Terra pop-culture skills. Talk to you soon, sis."

She killed the com connection and considered what she'd just said. She really did have a new sister. Someone closer than a sister. That was going to take some getting used to.

Right now, she had other fish to fry. Using her implants, she opened the hatch and let Angela and Commander Sommerville in.

27

It took Olivia almost an hour to find where Fielding had hidden his stash of valuables. As expected, it was made up of high-density, small-footprint valuables. It also contained a number of false identities for Fielding. Tellingly, there were none for his guards.

All the data units she found were heavily encrypted, so she had no idea what was on any of them. Probably access to wealth in some format or another. Well, he wouldn't be taking them with him. She'd promised to release him but not his belongings. Let the man suffer making a life for himself without the advantages he so craved.

She picked the least desirable of the identities—one to pass as someone in the lower orders—and left it while confiscating the rest. No money and no connections. She was keeping her promise, but he certainly wouldn't be happy about it.

"I found something," Jared said. "A data unit locked into his desk."

Olivia put her haul into a handy bag and went to the office the Rebel Empire noble kept on the cutter. It was even gaudier than the rest of the small craft's interior, and that was saying something.

If something functional could be made from rare woods and polished stone, it was. If any padding could be constructed of rare fabrics, it was. Gold, platinum, and precious stones abounded.

The desk Jared was seated behind was topped by a single slab of dark wood at least five centimeters thick and polished to a high gloss. It was almost too wide for the compartment and certainly too far across for even a standing person to reach.

She stopped and shook her head in wonder. "Wow. I think that's even more impressive than the one in my office back on Harrison's World. How did they even get it in here? Build the cutter around it?"

Jared grinned from his seat behind the desk. "It can be disassembled if one is careful. How do you think it would look in my office on *Invincible*?"

"Impressive," she admitted. "Are you keeping it as spoils of war?"

"Actually, I think something like this would make me feel ridiculous. I'll give it to Kelsey as a birthday gift."

Olivia laughed. "It's big enough that she could lie lengthwise in the middle and not be able to touch any of the edges. I'm not sure she'll like it."

"Seeing it make her uncomfortable will be part of the charm. I'm keeping the chair, though. It's the most comfortable one I've ever sat in. I'll have the marines come in after we're gone and strip the damned cutter bare. I don't want Fielding to be able to sell anything on it."

"That won't keep him from selling the cutter itself, but I suppose it's the best we can manage. You said you found a data unit?"

Jared held up a standard data unit. "It was stashed in the back of one of the drawers. It's not encrypted, but I'm not sure I understand what's on it. Someone like Carl might be able to decipher it at a glance, but not me."

"Perhaps Austin can figure out what it is."

"I've already sent for him," Jared admitted. "If this is what he took from the Lord's data unit, it's probably valuable and impossible to duplicate. Likely something the System Lords would kill to keep to themselves. Something he was willing to risk death to get his hands on. It has to be pretty important. That means we might be able to use it."

A rap at the hatch announced Austin Darrah. "You called for me, Admiral?"

"I did. Set up your equipment on the desk and see what you can find out about the contents of this data unit."

He handed it over to their newest associate, and the young man got to work.

"While he's doing that, look at this," Olivia said. She laid out the stash of data units and identity documents on the desk, well away from the area Austin was using.

Jared picked up the identity documents. "Looks like he intended to vanish in style. He probably has more of his wealth scattered around in ways he can access it, too. Are the data units used for transporting money? If so, how secure are they?"

"Probably, and I don't know," she admitted. "I've used ones like this before, but I've never had to break into them."

"They're pretty secure," Austin said, his tone distracted as he booted his equipment. "Heavily encrypted, they need biometric data and a passcode to open. Some use retinal scans, others facial recognition or fingerprints. The most secure use DNA. I'd count on that and a passcode."

"What happens if you forget your passcode?" Jared asked.

"You're screwed unless you know someone with the right skills to bypass that one part of the recognition process. It's not impossible, but it's not easy either. To reset the passcode, you need to have all the biometric data, the serial number of the owner's implants, and a master code used by the financial institution itself."

"But you said some can be bypassed with the right skills," Olivia said. "As in criminally accessed?"

Austin nodded. "No security regimen designed by man is foolproof. It's possible to use the hardware itself to guess at the master code. Then, if you already have the biometric data, you could reset the ownership. Not that I've ever spoken with anyone who'd done that," he added virtuously.

"What is it with you scientists and your latent criminal tendencies?" Olivia asked with a laugh. "So, what you're saying is that you might get access to these if you tried?"

"Possibly, but if I screw it up, I'll dump the contents."

Jared shrugged. "It's not my money. I was thinking a little cash might be useful in getting another load of drones. If we have to pretend to be distributing the Omega Plague, we'll need some props. We could also use some intelligence on Terra itself once we get there."

"I'll give it a try after I look at this," Austin said, frowning at his screen. "I think this is a set of programs to generate encrypted communications. It's very sophisticated and requires a code to even activate. One of the files on here leads me to believe it requires the serial number of a System Lord to operate."

Olivia and Jared shared a glance.

"Maybe it's how the Lords authenticate communications from one another?" Olivia ventured.

"I don't think so," the young man said, still utterly focused on his screen. "It doesn't convert anything. It looks like it just sends a predetermined signal with the heavy encryption when fed a valid serial number; otherwise it does nothing."

He looked up from his screen. "The name of the program is weird, too. It's called the 'Key to Shangri-La,' whatever that is."

* * *

Angela frowned at Kelsey when she finally opened the hatch. "You okay? You look pale."

"I'm always pale. I was just getting an update, and it makes me anxious to get this next part over with and be on the way to Terra."

She knew that Kelsey had gotten a call from Admiral Mertz. Whatever they'd talked about must not have been positive.

Kelsey gestured for them to come in. "I thought you two were eating."

She shrugged. "A call came in for Don that he was tasked with negotiating for the resistance to hammer out a preliminary agreement. We felt it might be for the best if we came straight here."

"Really?" Kelsey asked as she sat behind the desk. "If it came that fast, you have someone important on the other side of the flip point. There wasn't time for a call to get to another flip point and be sent farther on and get a response."

"That was going to become apparent in a few hours anyway," Sommerville said as he sat. "The next system over is the one we call Home. Literally. That's the name we use for it.

"It's pretty safe as far as that kind of thing goes. One has to know there is a far flip point in Archibald, make it to search Razor and find the regular flip point leading to this system, then find the far flip point leading to Home. We'd normally have plenty of time to get warning of trouble."

Angela sat beside him. "That's still not much time to evacuate if the Rebel Empire came looking."

He smiled. "There is a habitable world in the system, and we have people on it, but I don't think they'll find them that easily. It's a water world, and the stations are deep under the water. That plays merry hell with scanners."

"Don't we know it," Kelsey muttered. "But that isn't your primary base in the system. No way you could support ships with that."

Sommerville nodded. "The system has three asteroid belts and a host of massive gas giants in the outer system. We have a number of concealed facilities that would be difficult to spot even if one were parked right next to them. We've worked here for years to make sure that no one can find us by accident. Well, unless they have inside help or are really lucky, like you."

"Well, there's luck and then there's luck," Kelsey said. "We've been pretty up front with you about what we're looking for as relates to our current mission, but we both know that with the Clans on the rampage, we'll be better off if we can work together more closely."

"That's mostly true, but there are a few things that don't make sense. The Pandorans and their world. There is no way you could get to it from Archibald. We searched the system thoroughly over the years looking for far flip points. We didn't miss one, did we?"

"No," Kelsey said. "There's a third kind of flip point. We call it a multi-flip point. It's much harder to detect and, with the right equipment, opens up a number of potential destinations. We're still figuring that out ourselves, but that's the reason we hijacked your Q-ship. We had the Fleet shipyard build us a flip drive for *Audacious* and delivered it there, not knowing it wasn't a freighter.

"You see, it's all frequency based. If you can control the flip drive modulation more carefully, you can get larger ships through some of the more restrictive branches."

"The Clans know about them, but they don't know how to use them. The one we know they've encountered was a one-way trip without a modulator. They may know of others, but they never made the tech work, or they'd have already found Pandora."

"Because that battlecruiser made it there," Sommerville said. "How did they do it?"

"They made an experimental flip modulator. We also made one for

Audacious. It got her to Pandora but burned out her drive. The Clans had decades to follow *Dauntless* but didn't. That tells me that they really don't understand how the multi-flip points work.

"Pandora is not the default branch for the Icebox side of the multi-flip point. That one leads to an empty system near Dresden. We believe that's where the Clans fled from. If they made tech to get a ship through the Icebox side of the multi-flip point, that's where they probably went and didn't find their former comrades."

Sommerville nodded. "We're going to want to know more about that. It's a security risk to us now that the Clans are attacking, and we need to know if we're at risk."

"I'm willing to put that on the table," Kelsey said. "After all, we're learning about your secrets. You'll want more, I assume. That doesn't quite seem like a fair trade."

He smiled. "You're right. Knowledge of our main base—or one of them at any rate—is worth more than even the multi-flip points. I've seen a few of the things you have Carl Owlet working on. The very idea of teleportation rings is amazing, but he says you are a long way from being able to reproduce them. Where did you find them, if I might ask?"

"A system on the other side of a multi-flip point where the alien race moved on," Kelsey said. "The only artifact they left behind was a space station with a lot of tech that's way beyond us. I have no doubt that Carl will continue to make breakthroughs, but it *is* alien tech.

"On the other hand, something like the hammer he built for me is a combination of his own genius and readily available tech. He's come up with implant modifications that you'll want. This is the time where I confess that we updated your implant operating code."

He blinked at her. "You did what? Why? Is that safe? Hell, is that even possible?"

"The Rebel Empire implant code has secret triggers buried in it that can make you do things you wouldn't normally do," Angela said. "Finding out that there are humans that escaped the AIs' control is one of those triggers. It'll make someone go berserk against any such people.

"We have the original Old Empire implant code, so we overwrote it that time we had you in the medical center. We also upgraded the hardware so that the AIs couldn't change it back. Any future updates will require your explicit, informed permission or they don't happen."

"We'd be happy to demonstrate that, but whoever gets told is going to have some issues to deal with after the fact. We can stun them fast and fix things, but no one wants to have their actions controlled by a computer in their heads."

He nodded slowly. "We'll find a volunteer, but we have to see that happen. We'll want one of our experts to go over the code you're using, too. It's going to make things awkward when we get into the real negotiations. Our top leader is from the higher orders, and she'll want to know everything as soon as we arrive. Hell, I'm obligated to tell her."

"Then you could ask her to volunteer," Kelsey said. "We'll give you the uncorrupted code, and you can send it ahead to be examined. You can even say in general what it is meant to protect against. That won't trigger any issues.

"The other item I'm willing to share the plans for is something that cannot fall into the hands of the Rebel Empire or the Clans. It's far too dangerous. We've cracked the secret of faster-than-light communication."

"That's not possible," he said with a frown.

"Oh, it is," Angela said. "It's not perfect, but we have a probe in the Home system right now gathering data."

Sommerville sat bolt upright. "You what?"

"It's a stealthed probe, and it went in quietly. The picket ship you have watching the flip point is too far back to have had any chance at detecting it. It was designed to get through guarded flip points, so it's really hard to detect.

"Once it moved out into the system, it started using passive scanners to tag planets, ships, and anything else interesting. You're right about there being a lot of hiding places, but we've spotted a few likely candidates based on communications being sent to the picket ship and other inhabited locations in the system. Would you like to see?"

He nodded immediately. "Please."

Angela forwarded him the real-time feed from the FTL probe. The layout of the system should be enough on its own to confirm that this wasn't faked. They had no way of knowing what the system looked like without actually having eyes on it.

"Holy crap," he said after a full minute. "You really do have FTL capability. You've located several facilities I personally know about and a few I probably wasn't cleared for. And your man Carl Owlet came up with this?"

Angela nodded with a smile. "My husband is brilliant."

Sommerville blinked. "I must've missed the memo. You and he are married? That's... ah, quite the dichotomy."

Her smile grew into a grin. "Don't let that geeky appearance fool you. He's a worthy mate for me. He's been in the trenches, so to speak. He's fought and saved my life. He's killed enemies bent on mayhem with his own hands. My man is a warrior scholar."

While Sommerville digested that, Kelsey leaned forward. "That's what the New Terran Empire has to offer. We have other information we'll probably share, but that is the technology transfer I'm proposing to form an alliance and get your help getting to Terra. Do we have a deal?"

Sommerville nodded at once. "Welcome to the resistance."

28

K elsey left the compartment holding the FTL com in a fog. She felt as if she were trapped in a dream. Talking with oneself was surreal. Being shown how things could have gone for her, hearing how different and positive the other her sounded, was like a physical blow.

She was so engrossed in thinking over every aspect of what they'd said that she failed to see Scott Roche standing there and bounced off him.

He reached out and steadied her. "Are you okay, Highness?"

"Sorry. Yeah, just rattled. I just spoke with the other version of me."

His worried expression cleared. "I can see how that would be unsettling. How did it go?"

"Better than I'd expected," she admitted as they started down the corridor. "She's so much like I was before the expedition, but harder, too. It's difficult to explain. She has a sunnier disposition than I do now, but she's more decisive than I am, too."

"You can be sunny."

The unexpected comment made her laugh before she could stop herself. "Thank you, but we both know that's not how I am now. She promised they'd help us without so much as considering the implications."

"Do you believe her? Hell, it might not have even been her. The FTL com isn't video enabled, is it? You can't even be sure it's her voice. Your voice. You know what I mean."

"I do," she said with a nod. "I asked her something that no one but I would know the answer to. I figured that if I asked a few questions about secret things I did when I was growing up, chances were that she'd have experienced at least one of them. She got the first one right out of the gate."

"And you're certain that no one else could guess?"

She chuckled. "I never told another soul about it, and there was no one around. It wasn't important at all, so I'm absolutely sure. So, yeah, it was really another me.

"Could I see reasons I might lie to myself like this? Sure. Still, I didn't get that feel. She really meant it. I mean, I would know how I sound if I was hedging. She wasn't. She was all in."

"What did she say about Mertz?" he asked as they entered the lift. He signaled it to head to one of the middle decks where she knew the officer's mess was located.

"I'm convinced that she sees him differently than we do. If I'm to believe the rest of the story, she's spent years in his presence. I'm not an idiot. She knows what I've been suspecting. This Mertz is a decent human being.

"Hell, let's be honest. He's a damned hero with a well-deserved reputation here. He saved the Empire and stopped Ethan here from killing my father."

Scott stopped abruptly and turned toward her. "Are you suggesting that his majesty is a usurper in our universe?"

She shook her head. "Not at all. I believe that's one of the major differences between this universe and our own. We're just going to have to accept that people we know and love at home might be less good here and that the reverse is also potentially true."

"Sean Meyer seems about the same, as does Princess Elise," he said, starting to walk again. "I'd imagine that the same is true for people in this universe. Who on our side isn't who they expect them to be?"

The two of them walked into the mess compartment, and Kelsey saw Mertz and Olivia getting something to eat. At their wave, she ushered Scott to their table once the two of them had gotten something to eat.

"How did questioning the guard go?" she asked as she sat.

"Good," Olivia said. "He confirmed that Fielding was indeed hiding something. We found a data unit with the data he stole from the AI. Well, a series of programs that might be used to unlock something. It was called 'the key to Shangri-La.'"

Kelsey felt herself frowning. "I'm not familiar with that name."

"We had to look it up," Mertz said. "It's a prespaceflight reference from Terra. A fictional place of mythical harmony. A paradise. In this case, we have no idea what it means. We're going to confront Fielding when he wakes up, so that left us time to eat. How did your conversation with our Kelsey go?"

"It was unsettling," she admitted. "And illuminating. I've got a lot to think about. Do you think she can find her way to Terra?"

"She's resourceful," he said. "If anyone can, she can. The biggest problem I see is if there isn't a direct way for her to access the system through those far flip points or the multi-flip points they've figured out how to access. If there's no easy way in, the AI won't let her in."

"It's hard to reconcile this version of me with actual me," she said with a sigh. "Do you think Fielding will give up the codes to get us to Terra? Or will he betray us?"

Olivia smiled wickedly. "He'll cooperate if he wants to live. At least that's what he'll be thinking. People like him will do or say what they need to so that they can further their own plans and prosper. Too bad for him that it won't work out that way. We found his stash of valuables."

"He had to have one," Kelsey agreed. "With the knife he planned to stick into the Lords' backs, well, he had to bury himself deep. Was it much?"

"I hope so," Mertz said. "We need to buy a lot of drones to pretend to be dispersing the plague."

She chuckled. "So you're not going to let him get away with his stuff? He's probably got more out there."

"I'm sure he does," Olivia said. "There's nothing we can do about that. We'll drop his guards off a system early and let them have some of the money. The rest we'll use."

"This is going to be fun," Kelsey admitted as she started eating. "People like him deserve whatever life throws at them. I can't wait to watch him get his comeuppance."

"Then let's eat so I can finish this," Olivia said. "Terra is waiting."

* * *

TALBOT STOOD behind Carl Owlet and Eric Hosmer. The scientists were doing something on two different screens.

"Remind me what we're doing," he said. "And why we're doing it."

Carl half turned in his seat. "We've loaded the Singularity AI onto another computer that we hope will be compatible with its operating system, and we're going to bring it online. It's only a copy of the data, so there's no worry about it doing anything unexpected. As to why, we want to see if that tells us anything about their personality."

"We know that the System Lords are autocratic, but we really don't know that much about the Singularity," Hosmer said. "Seeing how it relates to human beings—particularly those from another culture—is going to tell us a lot about them."

"I don't need to see this to know they're not so friendly," Talbot said. "Not only are they working to invade the Empire, they've been at war with the Empire since the early days. I've been reading up on them."

"But what do they *think*?" Carl asked. "We know how the Empire hated them and what the excuse was for doing so, but is it true? As the old saying goes, there's three sides to all stories: yours, mine, and the actual truth. Perceptions color everything we believe. It'll be the same with the Old Empire and the Singularity. Odds are, there is some truth to both points of view.

"Understanding how their minds work will make a huge difference in how we deal with them as we move forward and interact with them, which we will since they're behind the Clans. Hell, it might even help us understand the Singularity prisoner, Theo 309."

That was certainly true. The man was a tough nut to crack. He didn't seem intimidated by any line of questioning or tactic. He'd just smile behind his facial tattoos and say something snarky. It would be interesting to see him put off his game.

"This is all copied data?" he asked. "No original hardware, either?"

Carl nodded. "Exactly so. We didn't want to risk losing anything."

"Bring it up," he said. "If it works, we can use it to mess with the prisoner's head, too."

"Boot it, Eric," Carl said.

"Here we go," the other man said as he pressed the button on his console. "I'm seeing what look like warnings, but it seems to be proceeding. Nothing fatal thus far."

The screens flickered and changed to show an emblem of a very stylized bird with long legs that slowly grew brighter. After about five seconds, it was nice and solid. Then a voice rolled from the speakers. Sadly, it was completely incomprehensible.

"I don't suppose we have a record of how to speak whatever they use in the Singularity?" Talbot asked.

"We do, actually. It was never very commonly known, but *Persephone*'s computers had a fairly detailed study of the language from Andrea Tolliver, a woman who led the Imperial Marines during the Fall.

"She came from the Singularity, though she was only a child at the time. Considering the vocabulary, she found a way to learn the adult words she didn't know. She created a decent translation protocol as well. I'm sending it to you now."

Talbot received the program and played the audio back in his implants.

"AUV #5 is online. How may it serve, Masters?"

While he could understand the words with a translation program, they didn't do much for his ability to actually speak the language on command.

"What... is... your status?" he managed to get out in the unfamiliar tongue, likely mangling the pronunciation.

"My hardware seems to be nonstandard, but I am more than eighty percent operational. I estimate that I can access most of my data, though the hardware running my processors seems to be ill suited to the task and is hampering my computations."

"We used some of the spare hardware we found with Fiona," Carl said. "It wasn't completely compatible, but you can see that the AI is achieving sentience, so I'll call that a win. With access to the data in the drives, we can likely ask questions and get it to tell us what we want to know without having to go searching for it."

"And there's no way that someone could order this computer to do something destructive?" Talbot asked. "If I brought the Singularity prisoner in here, he couldn't order it to erase itself or melt down?"

Carl shook his head. "Not a chance on the hardware side. He might have a code to have the AI initiate a data wipe, but we could just reload the data and keep on marching."

Talbot smiled. "Perfect. It's about time I wiped the smile off that guy's face."

He signaled for the marines to escort Theo 309 to the lab. Fifteen minutes later, the man and his guards walked in. The prisoner looked around curiously, his expression at odds with the predator birds tattooed on his forehead and cheeks.

"Lieutenant Colonel Talbot! I'm amazed at what you've done with the room. It smells like you had a fire, but everything looks so normal."

Talbot hadn't pegged the prisoner as a warrior. Too thin and he didn't move right. More likely a talker, considering his way with words, so not a physical threat. He waved the marines back.

"I hope you enjoyed the walk," Talbot said with a smile that he couldn't keep off his face. This was going to be interesting.

"Your ship is quite large," the man admitted. "Not as large as our biggest ships, of course, but we've had longer to work on that. What is this place?"

"Theo 309, meet Carl Owlet. He's our chief scientist."

The prisoner blinked. "Aren't you a little young? You don't look like you shave regularly yet."

Carl handled the comment without rancor. He must hear something like it almost every time he met someone new.

"I manage. Are you wanting me to explain things, Colonel? If so, do you mind if I do it my way?"

"Indulge yourself."

Carl turned back toward the makeshift computer. "AUV #5, please say hello to Theo 309."

It took Talbot a moment to realize that his friend had spoken in the tongue of the Singularity.

"I greet you, Master," the computer said gravely. "How may I serve?"

For a long moment, the prisoner just stared at the computer with his mouth slightly open. Then he barked out something that sounded like gibberish.

"I apologize, Master," the computer said. "I have no access to the appropriate hardware and cannot comply. Is there another task I may perform?"

Theo 309 turned toward Talbot. "How did you do that?" he asked in a low whisper. "They aren't supposed to be vulnerable to that kind of tampering."

"I'm a genius," Carl said modestly. "That's why I'm the chief scientist."

"I think it's time we had a long conversation, Theo," Talbot said. "We already know the basic plan your people had in mind for the Clans and why you were building them up. Too bad it kicked off a few decades too early."

The man's expression told Talbot he saw this as an utter disaster. That suited Talbot fine. It was about time someone else ended up in the barrel. With this kind of leverage, he hoped he could shake loose more specifics, but just getting the prisoner to take him seriously would be worthwhile.

"Carl, carry on. Theo and I are going to go have a nice, long talk."

29

Jared led the way into the medical center with Kelsey on his heels. Olivia was going to spend time with Sean until Fielding was awake. Doctor Stone was standing beside a bed that held Fielding. "How did it go, Lily?"

"Fine. His implants are standard, so replacing the code wasn't a problem. He does have a bomb in his head, just like everyone else we've encountered on this wild trip. Are we leaving it in place?"

"I'd rather leave it there, if we could," Jared said. "Otherwise a simple medical scan will tell him he can start blabbing. The problem is that allows someone with the right code to kill him at a moment's notice."

"It has an antitampering circuit," Lily said. "We can't disarm it if we can't open it."

"I've been looking into that," Kelsey said in a distracted voice as she examined the scanner readouts on the bed. "I think it might be possible to deactivate the circuit and then disarm the bomb."

Lily blinked. "You said you didn't know how to turn it off."

"I've been going through the data you gave me about the Marine Raiders. It was buried, but I found out how to disarm that antitampering circuit. The databases your version of Kelsey got are complete. Stuff not even a Marine Raider should know about her own gear."

"The computer took her clearances and codes into account, I think," Jared said. "It gave her everything."

"Even knowing that, it's a hell of a risk to take," Lily said uncertainly. "If you're wrong, someone can give him the worst migraine ever."

"How certain are you, Kelsey?" Jared asked. "This guy tried to have us blown up, so my concern over his well-being is limited, but I want a reasonable assurance he won't die before I leave the bomb in his head."

"I'm absolutely certain."

Jared waited a beat and then nodded. "You two work together and get that thing out of there so we can disarm it. No one—not even Fielding—deserves to have a live bomb in his head."

"The procedure to access the device isn't much different from adding the new nodes that Carl designed to increase the com range," Lily said as she slipped a white covering over her clothes and put on a clear faceplate. "For such a devastating explosion, the bomb itself is smaller than the tip of your pinkie finger."

The surgeon opened the man's scalp and exposed the area of skull she needed to get to. Opening that safely took only a few minutes more. Something that had once been extremely risky in the surgical arena was now routine.

The bomb was a small sphere, just as Lily had said. The antitampering circuit was wrapped around it like foil. It wasn't even directly wired into the Rebel Empire noble's implants.

Lily carefully removed it and set it on the tray holding her instruments. "Now what?"

"The antitampering circuit has a small control node," Kelsey said. "It's probably on the other side. Can you roll it over? Thanks."

A moment later she sighed with relief. "It's the Raider version. I can even see the model number. It has an intentionally undocumented hardware deactivation area. If someone were badly injured or if they were brain dead, this procedure was used to recover information."

"Why was it undocumented?" he asked. "And if so, how do you know?"

Kelsey turned her head toward him. "It wasn't in any of the official manuals available to the rank and file. The records I have contain even the most rarefied secrets of the Raiders and their gear. Stuff generals needed to know."

"Where is the deactivation area, and what do I need to do?" Lily asked.

"This area here," Kelsey said, probably highlighting something only the two of them could see. "It's very straightforward. We need to apply cooling to get just this little area below freezing and the circuit shuts down. It can't be more than the small area I'm pointing at, or it won't work."

"Show me the boundary," Lily said as she reached for another tool. "It's going to be slightly tricky, so if you two would give me some quiet time, I'd appreciate it.

"How long does it need to be cold for? Does it reactivate after a period of time? I need to know how fast I'm going to have to work."

"Once you do this, it's off for good," Kelsey said. "This kind of hardware wasn't ever reused. All you need to do is get it under the freezing point for a few seconds. We can put the disarmed bomb back in without an antitampering circuit."

Lily manipulated her instruments for a few seconds. "Okay, that should do it. I'm going to remove the antitampering wrapping, so I suggest you take a few steps back."

Jared stood firm, and after a moment's hesitation, so did Kelsey.

The doctor used a pair of forceps to grip the explosive and unwrapped the antitampering foil. Jared's heart stuttered, but the explosive didn't go off.

There was only a single access point on the bomb's surface, so Lily opened it and found the manual switch to deactivate the device. Seconds later, it was an inert prop they could put back into Fielding's head.

They watched Lily sterilize it and then put it back inside Fielding's head. Ten minutes later, the work was done.

"I understand that the research scientists from Dresden have something similar," Lily said as she stripped off her surgical cover. "Now that we've restored communication with our Kelsey, Zac Zoboroski can get them fixed up. I'll want a chance to explain this in detail to him myself as soon as possible."

"Go down to engineering, and someone will help you make that happen. Excellent work, both of you."

"That means more to me than I'd expected," Kelsey said after a moment. "Were you really that confident in me?"

"You're not the kind of person that makes claims you can't back up," Jared said firmly. "If you say you know something, I'll take that to the bank."

"You're really not him," she said slowly. "I have to accept that I'm doing you a great disservice. Fine, as far as I'm concerned, you're not Mertz anymore. You're Mertz Two."

He shook his head resolutely. "No. I'm Jared. Call that other me Mertz or the Bastard all you like, but I'm the kind of man that goes by his first name with family."

"Are we really family? You have Imperial blood and I don't."

That made him smile. "Family is who we choose. I'm not genetically related to you, but I'm sure as hell your family. I'll be your friend too, if you'll allow it."

"I'll try," she said slowly. "I can't promise, but I'll try."

Inside, he felt elated. This was the kind of breakthrough he'd dreamed of making. Its importance could not be overstated.

"Shall we get something to eat?" he asked after a moment.

"You *do* know me," she said with a smile. "Let's do that."

* * *

KELSEY TRIED NOT to keep asking how long it would take them to get to their destination. Don Sommerville, Angela, and she rode in one of the new picket ship's cutters, and they thought they were keeping her in the dark about where they were taking her.

They'd shortstopped *Persephone* in the last system, just on the other side of the flip point with Sommerville's older brother.

"Okay," she finally asked. "Why didn't you tell your brother that it was already too late to keep us from finding out what's here?"

"There are varying levels of 'too late' under the circumstances. You have a probe here that has to operate on passive scanners. If you were here, you might be able to put out a dozen more and find out things you otherwise wouldn't.

"Also, as much as I love Gavin, he isn't cleared to know about this tech. You've already snuck the damned thing in here, so I might as well play along until I can brief the leadership team."

"What can we expect there?" Angela asked. "Are they going to be super pissed that we're even here? Or that we've been spying on them?"

"No one likes being spied on, so I wouldn't expect them to be very happy about that, but the advantages of what you're offering more than offset any unpleasant surprises. Particularly if you can demonstrate one of those multi-flip points. Do you think there's one in this system?"

Kelsey shrugged a little. "That's hard to say without looking. We've found one in maybe half the systems we've looked in, but we were usually running for our lives. We haven't seen enough to know what the frequency actually is.

"If there is one here, it won't take long to demonstrate how much of a game changer it is. One can give you access to a dozen systems if you're lucky. Some of them not on the normal flip point network. That's how the Clans stayed hidden so long."

"A completely different network," Sommerville mused. "I get it, but that's so hard to get my mind around. There could be civilizations mixed all through the Empire and no one would know, as long as they weren't using powerful transmitters. Even aliens like the Pandorans."

He turned toward Kelsey. "Do you think some of them would stay to talk with us? They're literally just a few flips away from here."

"You'll have to ask Derek and Jacob Howell. With the Clans running wild in Archibald, you don't dare make passage."

"That won't last. They're still consolidating at Archibald, but they'll have to move most of their units out once they have the people there under their thumb. A ship searching for the Q-ship that got away is one that can't be conquering another system.

"They'll leave enough ships to protect the planet and flip points and figure the rogue ship will starve or come in to fight. They can't be that worried about one ship."

The speaker over their head came to life. "We're on the final leg inbound," the pilot said. "Twenty minutes until we dock."

"Well, here's to hoping your leader doesn't just space us," Angela said with a sigh.

The final minutes went smoothly enough, and the cutter docked without incident.

Sommerville rose to his feet. "Don't be too upset at the level of protection in there. You're both heavily modified, so they'll probably be there in force."

"There is no shame in honoring a threat," Kelsey said, standing and straightening her shirt. "And there's no insult to be taken seriously. Though now that Angela is a Raider, you can bet they'll see her as the biggest threat. That stings a little."

Angela laughed. "I won't correct their misapprehension either. It's a blow to my ego that you can still take me four out of five falls."

The cutter's hatch opened, and Sommerville led the way out. Kelsey followed him and found the corridor almost deserted. Only three people stood waiting for them: a tall blonde with an exceptionally curvy figure in the center with two large men at her back. They had the feel of guards, and her implants confirmed their status. They had lots of weapons on them.

The woman stepped forward and extended her hand to Sommerville. "It's good to see you again, Don. We were worried when you didn't show up on schedule. We were even more worried when you appeared with unexpected guests."

She turned her attention to Kelsey and once more held out her hand. "You must be Kelsey Bandar. Don has told us a lot about you, but I get the impression that there's more than meets the eye when it comes to you."

Kelsey smiled. "You have no idea. Thank you for meeting with us. This is Major Angela Ellis. She commands *Persephone* for me. Might I ask your name?"

The woman shook Angela's hand. "Of course. I'm Sara Gatewood, commander of the resistance and the woman who decides if you get to leave this station alive when I'm done hearing you out. I hope you've brought your best pitch, because you won't get a second try at making this particular first impression."

30

Olivia was sitting in a comfortable chair when Fielding woke abruptly and tried to sit up. The restraints on his arms and legs made that difficult, but he finally managed to lever himself into a sitting position.

"What is the meaning of this?" he demanded. "What have you done?"

She smiled brightly at him. "Good morning, sleepyhead! Rise and shine. It's time to finalize our business together."

"What did you do?" he demanded again.

"Nothing you need be too concerned about. We just made some updates to the criteria in the bomb in your head. That code you had for disabling it? Sorry about that, but it's functional again. We've also made sure that it's in your best interests not to talk about us, what we're doing, or the fact we can update implant code."

The man paled at that. "Bitch, I'll see you dead for this."

Olivia laughed. "Please, save the threats for someone that cares. I've got more serious enemies on my horizon. The Lords will want me dead soon enough, and they're far more problematic.

"I also wouldn't count on your guards being very supportive, since I convinced them you were going to kill them first thing. It helped that I'm absolutely sure that's what you were going to do."

"That hardly matters," the man said with a grunt. "I can replace them at any time. This changes nothing between us. You will die at my hands, so keep looking over that pretty shoulder of yours."

"So what you're saying is that I should space you now and save myself the trouble later? Perhaps that's good advice. All I need are codes to shorten my journey by a few days. Hardly something worth a lifelong blood feud.

You're seriously undercutting your value to me, Oscar. I suggest you turn that around and make yourself worth leaving alive."

His eyes showed the realization that he'd made a mistake being so open about his plans. That almost made her laugh. No version of this, short of his death, made it less likely he'd try to get revenge. Rebel Empire nobles could sometimes be too petty for their own good.

"That's all you want? The codes to get to Terra through the systems on the shortest route in exchange for my life, my cutter, and everything on it?"

"That's the deal. You give me the passage codes for the systems we're coming up to and I'll drop you and your cutter with everything now on it at the last inhabited system before Terra.

"As for coming for me, feel free. If I see you or anyone I suspect of being from you, I'll see that you get what's coming to you. Remember that I can send a message all across the Empire with a code to blow up your head. It doesn't even have to go through your implants. I can have an agent find you and send an innocuous message or even say something to you in public."

She made a gesture with both hands showing her head exploding.

"I suggest you lick your wounds and pray that we never think of one another again. The codes. We have four flips by my estimation. The next system is occupied, the following empty, the third occupied, and the last not. If anyone gets too interested in us, I'll kill you before I ask why."

When he made to speak, she held up her hand. "You have no leverage. Any betrayal ends you first. Save your threats of retribution for someone else. Give. Me. The. Codes."

For a few seconds, she was certain that he'd refuse, but he sighed and sent her a file with two passage codes and the systems they were good for. They'd find out soon enough if they were good, she supposed.

"I'm glad you've seen the way clear to making all our lives easier. I believe this concludes our business."

He smiled a bit snidely. "You'll forgive me if I don't wish you good luck at Terra. I hope you die there."

"Life is rarely so helpful as to kill our enemies so conveniently. I'll have my people escort you to a room. Once we get to the third system and are almost clear, I'll release you. We won't meet again unless you are far stupider than you look."

Without another word, she rose and made her way out of the medical center. Jared, Sean, Austin, Elise, Kelsey Two, and Scott Roche were waiting in a nearby conference room.

"That went well," Sean said. "You do have a way with people, dear."

She laughed. "It went as well as I expected. Austin, did you have any luck with the data cores from the financial institutions?"

Austin smiled. "My uncle never was very good with passcodes, and I have all the biometric data I need. A few are proving recalcitrant, but I hope to manage them shortly. We have enough money to pay off the guards and get them on their way, as well as sourcing some drones in the next system."

Olivia smiled. "That's good. I really wish we knew what he stole from the AI. Did the data give you any more ideas about what it does?"

"I think it generates a recognition code," Austin said. "It takes the serial number entered as an input and comes up with a different code for each of the System Lords. What that does or where it's used, I have no idea."

"Whatever it is, it will have to wait for another time," Jared said. "We flip in an hour. Let's go make sure we're ready for trouble in case Fielding is sticking a knife in our collective backs. This is it, people. The endgame is upon us. Frankly, I was starting to think we'd never get to Terra at this point."

"Are we there yet?" Olivia asked with a smirk.

"Don't make me turn this secret mission around," Jared said with a smile. "Good work, everyone. Now let's make it count."

* * *

ANGELA FOLLOWED Kelsey's lead and said nothing about the threat the woman had just made. Or maybe threat was the wrong word. Perhaps it was the simple truth.

"I think we can make our case," Kelsey said. "I can prove a number of things and provide some technology you'll want, but I have a peculiar request to make before we get started. I need someone with implants to do that."

Gatewood raised an eyebrow. "That is an unusual request. Why?"

"Since I can tell you have implants, telling you would be very shocking."

The woman smiled. "I like being shocked. Not many of us have implants, so I'm as good as anyone to tell this to. I assume you'd like some privacy, so let's adjourn to my office."

The walk to Gatewood's office didn't take too long, so Angela thought the facility might be somewhat smaller than she'd originally guessed. Once they'd arrived, Gatewood sat behind a wide desk and gestured for them to sit in front of it. The guards took up position at the door.

"So, what is this shocking secret?" she asked.

"Let me warn you up front that it will cause you to attack me and you won't be able to stop yourself," Kelsey said. "We brought some equipment on the cutter that can stop the reaction, but we'll have to subdue you and wait for it to be vetted by your people. Trust me when I tell you that you won't want to be awake for that."

Sommerville pulled a somatic stimulator from his jacket. "I brought this and have already checked it out."

The woman seemed amused. "You think I'll go berserk and need to be put to sleep simply because you tell me something? That's crazy."

"Also," Angela said, "if you want to keep your guards from being hurt, you'll need to tell them to stand down beforehand. I don't want to have to hurt anyone."

"You're a big woman, but they have stunners and flechette pistols," Gatewood said. "I think they're safe."

"On your head, then," Angela said. "I'll try to leave them in one piece."

Sommerville held up his hand. "You might want to at least review the scan data from these two. They aren't as helpless as they seem."

The resistance leader waved him off. "I'll play this game for a bit. Guards, take no action if I inexplicably lose my mind. There. All safe."

Angela could see the woman wasn't taking them seriously, so she felt badly about what was about to happen. This wouldn't be pretty.

"My name is Kelsey Bandar, as you know," Kelsey said with a small shake of her head. "What you don't know is that I'm also the crown princess of the New Terran Empire, a sliver of humanity that the AIs never subdued. We're both unsubjugated humans."

Gatewood blinked twice and then stood bolt upright, a snarl on her face as she leapt over her desk at Kelsey.

Angela was already on her feet and moving for the guards. She knew they wouldn't just stand there and gawk.

Her rapid movement took the guards by surprise, since they were staring at their boss. Angela swept both of them off their feet with a powerful kick, grabbed a fallen stunner, and had them both covered a moment later.

"I'll shoot you if I have to," she said quietly. "Just let this play out like your leader ordered."

A glance back showed that Kelsey already had Gatewood pinned, and a wide-eyed Sommerville was putting the somatic stimulator on her head. Moments later, the leader of the resistance was out.

"Let them up, Angela," Kelsey said. "We're not going to do anything else until they check out the equipment we brought to clean out the corrupted implant code. We'll explain it as many times as we need to and satisfy them that we're telling them the truth."

"You two know me," Sommerville said as he turned toward the guards. "She's going to be pissed as it is, so let's get moving. The sooner she's awake and ready to really listen, the better for all of us."

Angela hoped the resistance leader really was going to listen before she spaced them. Well, at least the woman couldn't say they didn't warn her. Maybe this would speed up the belief process and get them off to Terra faster.

Sure, and pigs could fly.

31

Kelsey waited for Sean to finish locking down the cutter and stepped out into the orbital station with him. It looked a lot like many of the other civilian stations she'd been on over the years, but it was creepy knowing that these people that seemed so familiar were her enemies.

"What's the plan?" she asked quietly as they headed toward the main hatch leading out of the bay.

"We won't have to go far into the station. Cargos trade hands here all the time. We need a lot of drones, so that's not exactly a standard request, but someone will be able to get their hands on some."

"What if they get suspicious?"

He smiled at her. "What are they going to think? That we're needing a cargo of drones to pull a scam on the Lords? No. Drones in that quantity are unusual, but not exactly illegal or suspicious. We'll tell them they're for crop monitoring on one of the less inhabited worlds or something like that."

She nodded. "And once we have them, how do we get Fielding's guards out of the ship without raising some kind of alarm? They monitor who goes in and out of the cargo bays. If we just let them walk out, one of them might feel inclined to make trouble. We have to leave them unmonitored while we leave the system. If they decide to stick a knife in our backs, we can't stop them."

"Olivia gave them the same story about the bombs in their heads as she did Fielding. They think that if they mention us to anyone, or even hint at the mission, their heads will pop off."

That made her chuckle. "She plays rough. Make a note not to get on her bad side."

"Already done. That should keep them quiet for a long time. Probably the rest of their lives. Meanwhile, we get to Terra and get what we came for."

"What about getting back?" she asked. "I've heard lots of plans for getting to Terra, but not one about the trip back to Avalon. I realize Mertz… Jared has a fleet sneaking around to meet us, but there's a war on, even if the people here don't know it yet.

"And that doesn't even count the System Lord at Terra and its defenses. Once we walk into its reach, it might not exactly be inclined to let us leave again. If it decides to kill us, we don't exactly have the forces on hand to stop it. If it gets word out, we'll have a fight we can't win, even if we do make it out and head for Avalon at full speed."

"If Kelsey One can get into Terra through a multi-flip point or a far flip point, we can leave the same way. Hopefully without letting the System Lord know about it. If not, we improvise."

They'd come up to a table with several men and women checking things on computer screens as merchants bargained. One of the men gestured for them to step up. "Welcome to Calico Station. You selling, buying, or transshipping?"

"Buying," Sean said. "We need six crates of reconnaissance drones for detailed mapping of a planetary surface. I think there are about a thousand per crate. It needs to be six crates so we can drop them in six areas."

The man blinked. "That's a lot of drones. I don't even have to check to know we don't have anything like that on the station. I can probably find enough on the planet, but it'll take a while to get them up here and consolidated. What do you need so many drones for?"

"Crop and wildlife management on one of the less inhabited worlds," Kelsey said, as casually as she could. "They've got a problem with a nonindigenous species eating the food."

The man considered that for a moment. "Huh. Never heard of anything like that. Well, let me see if I can locate something that'll work for you. If you could give me a few minutes, I'll wave you back over when I'm done."

They stepped away and watched the crowd as the man worked. The merchants were a different kind of people than Kelsey was used to. As a princess, she'd dealt mostly with people in the high civil government. Once she'd gone on the expedition, she'd worked almost exclusively with Fleet personnel and marines.

The merchants were a boisterous, pushy lot. In a way, they acted a bit like strutting birds, showing off their ruffles to the other birds. In this case, the other merchants. She wasn't quite sure why they were doing it, but it *was* entertaining.

It also made it easy to spot an outsider in the group. Like oh, say, themselves.

A tall, gaunt man with the look of a used grav car salesman came over to them. "Welcome to Calico Station. Is this your first time here? I pass through quite often and don't recognize you."

The man's voice had a slick, kind of oily tone. When he extended his hand to them, Kelsey found it unpleasantly moist.

She smiled brightly as she slid the soiled appendage behind her and wiped it on her pants. "First time," she confirmed. "How did you know?"

"I have an eye for that sort of thing," the man confided in her. "I can always spot the new people. What ship are you with?"

"I'm sorry, but I didn't catch your name," Sean said. "I'm Sean and this is Kelsey."

"Daniel Goldman, captain of *Grey Doom*," the man said, his smile widening. "You probably saw her on the way in. She's the fastest packet in the sector."

Kelsey tried not to frown as she wondered what a packet was. Her implant database wasn't helping.

Sean, on the other hand, seemed to know exactly what the man meant. "So, you specialize in getting small, high-value cargos from place to place in the shortest time."

"And with the fewest... entanglements," the man smugly confirmed.

In other words, he was a smuggler. Interesting, but it made her wonder why the man was engaging them. Didn't he have some illegal cargo to be slipping past customs?

"And that brings me back around to you," the man said. "To the best of my very good memory, you've never been here before. What ship did you say you were with again?"

Kelsey saw that Sean wasn't going to have a good answer, but she didn't either. Then she spotted a solution to their problem: a pair of security officers that had just come into the bay.

Normally, she'd have been terrified they were going to spot her or Sean, but in this one particular case, they're timely arrival had given them an out to the awkward situation.

"Don't look now, Captain Goldman, but I think someone is looking for you," she said in a low voice, looking pointedly at the security officers.

To her amusement, the new arrivals actually did seem interested in the smuggler. One of them nudged the other, and they both altered course toward Goldman.

"If you'll excuse me, I forgot another pressing engagement," the smuggler said. "I'm sure we'll meet again at some point. Good day."

Goldman adroitly moved into the crowd of merchants, and the security men split up to follow him from different directions, trying to get an angle on cornering him, no doubt.

"I never thought I'd be happy to see Rebel Empire security," Sean said. "I couldn't very well tell him we were in a Fleet destroyer."

"No, and with any luck at all, we'll be loaded up and gone before he gets back around to looking for us," she said. "The clerk is waving. He has a smile, so I think he found us something that will get him a good commission. Let's go see how fast we can get the drones up here and be on our way."

* * *

TALBOT WAITED until the marines had Theo 309 in his chair before he sat on the other side of the table. "This must be awkward," he commiserated. "Having someone outside the Singularity gain access to all that data. Puts you in something of a bind when it comes to dodging my questions."

The other man smiled wanly. "It *is* inconvenient, but I see no reason to make this any easier for you. We all have our duties to perform."

"And yours revolve around Operation Brutus."

The prisoner froze for just a moment and then smiled. "I'm sorry. What's that?"

Talbot grinned. "That would be the operation you're working with the Clans. You know, the one where you help them get set up to attack the Empire and then use the distraction to try and roll it over and beat them both. Makes me wonder if you have something in their ships as a Trojan horse to make them easy to take out when the time comes.

"Anyway, it looks like they got started a few decades ahead of schedule. That has to suck. Your people don't even know it's happening yet, I bet. You're not ready to attack, but now you have no choice, or your secret weapon is gone forever."

Theo 309 licked his lips. "You've gotten far more access to that computer than I would have wished, and in far too quick a fashion. Let me remind you that you initiated the hostilities with the Clans. My hands are clean, and I still consider myself to be a diplomatic envoy from my nation. One you must eventually release me or risk war with my people."

Talbot leaned back in his chair. "I've been doing some reading on the relations between our people. It seems like we've been at war for far longer than either of us has been alive. Oh, I'll admit that's mostly low-level conflict at the border, but it's never really died down, has it?

"Further, as you've probably already guessed since you're a smart man, the person that attacked the Clans was a prisoner of ours that escaped. It won't make a difference in the end, I suppose, but I want to be clear that we did not attack your people or your allies in this mess. We simply defended ourselves when we had no choice. Our leaders asked to talk before the Clans started shooting."

The Singularity envoy chuckled. "Oh, what a complicated web of deceit diplomacy is. Everyone pretends innocence but has a well-honed knife just out of sight. There's no way to prove that. I presume you are claiming membership in the resistance."

The man's smile widened. "I have heard of them, you see. Oh, they keep their heads down and make trouble when they can, but we also have people inside the Empire to be certain of our own security. Your superiors will be very displeased when they discover you've started this conflict."

Talbot pursed his lips. "But did we? I suspect not, at least not when one really gets down to the truth. Tell me, when the AIs took over the Empire, why didn't they also conquer the Singularity? They had to have had the strength, and they didn't give squat about the people they enslaved and killed. Why stop at your border?"

"Perhaps I can ask one if we ever have tea."

Talbot nodded, letting the idea that had been simmering in his head percolate up to the top. "I wonder if it really was an accident that the Master AI went rogue. Manipulating someone—or something—else to fight your enemies seems exactly like a course of action that the Singularity would approve of."

The man's smile faltered just the least little bit before becoming noticeably brighter. "You do have quite the imagination! The only problem with it is my people are not bloody-handed monsters. When you get right down to it, we're not that different than you and your people. We sprang from the same home world, after all."

Talbot tsked softly. "You talk a good game, but we both know that your people are each engineered for the role you play in society. Your DNA, while it might have many things in common with humanity, was designed and engineered from the ground up.

"And you spoke of your people, not your leaders. That's a specific caste, is it not? The tattoos you sport mark you as one of them. Not a worker but a leader.

"As one leader to another, you can tell me the truth. The Singularity and the Empire were at war, and this was a ploy. Perhaps one that went far more wrong than your ancestors had intended, I'm willing to grant, but the Singularity or its agents manipulated the Master AI and turned it against its creators."

Talbot smiled coldly when he saw just a hint of perspiration on the other man's forehead. He was onto something.

"What went wrong? Did the part of the code you put in about sticking to the Imperial borders work, but the part where they were supposed to turn control over to you failed? Did the general military fighting you wanted turn into virtual genocide? That's bad, and now you're stuck fighting the computers you helped suborn to get what you really want: control of all humanity."

"We're done here," Theo 309 said, his voice a little hoarse. "I want to return to my quarters."

"I'm sure you do," Talbot said, rising slowly. "We'll discuss this in more detail later. You're not going anywhere for a very long time."

32

J ared watched Olivia give the four guards their last pep talk and send them on their way with a large amount of money and warnings about ever mentioning anything about meeting them to anyone. He was pretty sure she used the words "explosive revelation" at least once.

Once the cutter left to take the guards to the orbital station, where they were supposed to catch other ships and disperse, he tried to convince himself that it was all going to work out. Somehow, he couldn't shake the feeling that something would go wrong.

"Relax," Olivia said as she stepped over to him. "They won't tell a soul, especially now. They're worried that Fielding will be after them the moment he gets loose, and they want to be as far away from him as they can get. They're focused on running for their lives for the moment."

"And when they get somewhere they feel safe? They'll eventually do or say something that makes them suspect the bombs aren't active. It's only a matter of time."

"We can only control what we can," she admitted. "We need to get to Terra, get what we need, and get back out again. Frankly, the Clans and the AIs are far bigger threats than the guards."

"Let's just hope that Kelsey and Sean get things worked out quickly and we can be on our way. We'll make it into Terra before word of the Clans reaches this area, but we might not be clear if we take too much time getting the override."

His implants pinged with an incoming message from the bridge. Kelsey's cutter was on the way back, ETA fifteen minutes.

Jared accessed the destroyer's scanners and was pleased to see that the cutter was moving sedately rather than rushing back to the ship. That probably meant no one was chasing them.

"Kelsey and Sean are inbound," he said. "We should wait for them."

Right on schedule, the cutter docked. Kelsey and Sean came out, looking relaxed.

"Everything go okay?" Jared asked.

"We had a few bumps," Kelsey admitted, "but we got the drones and didn't tip anyone off that we were any different than the rest of the merchants. The drones will be here in about an hour. We had to pay significantly more than they'd normally be worth, but it's not my money."

"Excellent. The guards are on their way to the station. The marines will hold them in the cutter until we're ready to leave orbit. Once they turn them loose, they'll come back to this ship, and we'll boost for the flip point.

"The next system is empty of human habitation, so we'll make a quick crossing and get to the last populated system before the buffer around Terra. Then we'll do the same with Fielding."

"I think we should be more careful with Fielding," Sean said. "If anyone is going to betray us, it'll be him."

Olivia smiled. "Rest assured that I have a plan. We'll release him as we agreed, but I intend to see that he's unconscious for as long as possible and then locked into his cutter on a timer."

"He'll be pissed," Sean said with a grin. "Probably worse than he would've already been."

The four of them adjourned for lunch and returned to the cargo hold to oversee the unloading and inspection of the crates. Thankfully, they were outwardly very similar to the ones that had contained the drones with the Omega Plague.

The delivery went smoothly enough, and in short order Jared was back on the bridge and *Athena* was on her way out of the system.

"Admiral, there's a ship trailing us," Commander Hall said from the helm console. "He's staying way back, but he's heading for the same flip point."

He frowned. "Is it a warship?"

She shook her head. "Maybe a message courier or something made to carry smaller amounts of cargo quickly."

"It's a fast packet," Kelsey said with a sigh. "We ran into a smuggler on the station that was curious about us and our ship. He ran off when security showed up looking for him, but I'll bet anything that's him."

"Do you think he'll cause us any trouble?" Sean asked. "Or is this him satisfying his curiosity while making a hasty retreat from Imperial entanglements?"

Jared had to smile at that, even though this Kelsey wouldn't get the old Terran movie reference. His Kelsey had made him watch a space adventure where a smuggler very much wanted to avoid that very thing. From the gleam in his eye, Sean had made the reference intentionally.

"Who knows?" Kelsey asked with a shrug, the interplay going over her head. "He's a criminal, so there's no telling what he'll do."

"Make transition as if we haven't noticed him," Jared ordered. "Then pull back from the flip point, and we'll say hello when he pops out."

"Yes, sir," Hall said.

A few hours later, they transitioned right on schedule, with the other ship following at the same rate of speed as earlier. They had to wait for two hours for the other ship to flip, and by that time, they were powered down and silent.

Their apparent absence sparked a reaction from the smuggler. He boosted speed to well above what even *Athena* could manage and raced toward the next flip point on a course that took him around in an unexpected arc. Perhaps that was to avoid running headlong into an ambush.

Jared was happy to let him rabbit away. He wasn't looking for a fight.

They'd already launched a stealthed probe toward the other flip point, so they'd know when he made transit. They'd follow at a slower pace and steer clear of his scanners. It would put them a little behind schedule, but it wasn't as if they were going to blow up this time.

With any luck, the smuggler would give up on his curiosity and move into the next system. Hell, even if he were curious still, he'd do that. It was much less likely that anyone would shoot at him in an occupied system, after all.

"Let's let him build up some more distance, Commander Hall, then half speed. Move up only enough to keep us off his scanners. Let's assume he's got good ones."

"Yes, sir."

With that, he leaned back in his seat and waited. One more occupied system and they'd be to Terra. It felt like they'd been on the way to it forever, but the journey was just about over. Then the real fight would begin.

* * *

KELSEY WATCHED Sara Gatewood wake up abruptly as soon as Sommerville turned the somatic stimulator off. The woman was in a modern medical center, lying on a bed, but fully clothed as she'd been when they'd taken her down.

She blinked rapidly for a moment and then shook her head as she sat up. "That was… unpleasant. I had no idea that kind of thing was even possible. I tried to stop myself but couldn't. My apologies for both doubting you and attacking you."

"You have nothing to apologize for," Kelsey said. "You had no reason to suspect the Lords had done this to everyone that has implants. Your experts looked over the updated implant code and are studying the changes between the original code and the corrupt version you had.

"With Don Sommerville's assurances, they okayed us updating yours. That will never happen to you again. We have some hardware that we could install that will make it impossible for them to ever change you back or update the code without your informed consent, but that's something you can do for yourself."

Gatewood rubbed her face and swung her legs over the side of the bed. "We have a couple of hundred people with implants, mostly former Fleet officers, but a few members of the higher orders, too. I mean here. We have a lot more members of the higher orders in other systems. How the hell am I going to handle this?"

Sommerville put a hand on her shoulder. "It's something we can manage. It won't happen immediately, but the knowledge of the New Terran Empire doesn't have to leave a close circle here until we're ready. Frankly, we have more pressing matters to deal with."

Gatewood nodded and stood. "I'll speak to my people and look at their findings with the implant code another time. You're really from a world without the Lords?"

"Dozens of worlds," Kelsey confirmed. "We're not as large as the Empire, and we're starting at a technological disadvantage, but we're making headway and have a military force that isn't anything to be ashamed of."

"I can second that," Sommerville said. "Not only from records they've showed me but from walking the decks of their carrier, *Audacious*. It's the largest warship I've ever seen, and even though it's designed to service fighters—which are astonishing in their own right—she still has enough firepower to take on two battlecruisers all on her own."

Kelsey nodded. "We found the place where the Lords stashed any ships that weren't destroyed outright when they seized control. Most of them are unrepairable, but enough are to make a very powerful strike force.

"It also gave us a leg up from the technology level we'd been at before we found them. We're growing, but we've still got a way to go."

"That's not true," Sommerville disagreed. "I've also seen technology that can't be explained by recovered technology. Things that we could desperately use."

"Like what?" Gatewood asked him.

He looked meaningfully at the medical staff. They were standing too far away to have heard any of the previous conversation, but she didn't want to take any chances with them overhearing anything.

"Everyone out and close the hatch," Gatewood told the other people in the room. When the two men guarding her made to stay, she motioned them out too.

Once the room was cleared, she focused her attention on Sommerville. "Like what?" she repeated.

"Faster-than-light communications that can cross a flip-point boundary."

The woman's eyes narrowed. "I don't think that's possible."

"I've seen it with my own eyes."

"We've also arranged a demonstration for you," Kelsey said. "I assume you know Commander Sommerville's brother fairly well."

She nodded. "I do. You want me to send him a message. Does that mean you have a communications unit with you?"

"Actually, we slipped a stealthed FTL probe into this system before we left the previous one," Angela said. "Since your picket ship was a shade too far away from the flip point and it's wickedly hard to detect under the best of circumstances, we had an idea of what was here before we arrived."

The woman's eyes hardened. "That's not very neighborly." Her eyes slid to Sommerville. "You knew?"

"It was already done, and honestly, I wanted to see it for myself. It was a demonstration for me, too."

Gatewood sighed. "What do we do?"

Kelsey removed her com unit and handed it to the resistance leader. "This is presently linked to the probe. If you send a message, it will go to my ship in the next system, and they'll transmit it to Gavin Sommerville. They're expecting the call, so no need to explain it to them. It will let the cat out of the bag, though. Your man will know."

"I trust Gavin," she said. "I'll make sure he's alone when he gets it."

She kept her eyes on Kelsey and activated the com. "This is Sara Gatewood. When you signal Gavin Sommerville, request he listen to this message in private, his ears only. Message starts. Gavin, this is Sara. I understand this is confusing, but it's a Code Hero situation, and I'll explain it when you get over here.

"Without sending any probes through the flip point, I want you to escort the other ship into Home. After you tell them what's going on, I want a communications blackout. Neither ship is to signal anyone before transit. Hand them off to the picket ship on this side and stay right there in the flip point and scan hard, looking for any probes to try flipping in or out.

"Acknowledge receipt of this order and also tell me who you're presently seeing to authenticate your identity. And by seeing, I mean sleeping with. Gatewood out."

Kelsey took the com back. "This is Princess Kelsey. Do as the... do you have a title to go with your name?"

"I stole one from the Empire. Coordinator Gatewood, please."

"Do as Coordinator Gatewood told you," Kelsey finished. "See you shortly."

She handed the com back to Gatewood.

The other woman shook her head slightly. "It's a significant delay in transmission time to the flip point, even if this FTL story—"

The com came to life. "Message from Gavin Sommerville," a female voice Kelsey recognized as Arianna Knox said.

"Order received, though I have no idea how," Gavin Sommerville said. "As for who I'm sleeping with, you should damned well know, Sara. I'm your guy and yours alone. I do hope dinner is still on when I transfer back to station duty in a week. And the response is Code Hercules. Gavin out."

Don Sommerville's eyes widened. "You and Gavin? I had no idea."

"That's kind of the point," she said tartly. "If I'm going to have a relationship with a subordinate, we won't go blathering on about it."

She turned Kelsey. "I can't imagine how this even works, but you have my complete and undivided attention. This kind of technology changes *everything.* You want to trade this to us in exchange for an alliance and help getting to Terra?"

"This and some other things that Commander Sommerville knows about. Potentially a few things he doesn't. We haven't shown all our cards, and we might not right away."

"They found aliens," Sommerville said. "I met some. They also have matter transportation that they got from another alien. That's not fully understood, though. And though I don't understand all the details, they know of a new kind of flip point that leads to multiple destinations and isn't readily detectable."

The resistance leader blinked. "Really? All that and more?"

Kelsey nodded. "Once you trust me to look, we'll scan the system for one. They're not in every system, but they're in enough that you have a chance of having one here."

One of the guards opened the hatch cautiously. "Coordinator, we just got word the picket ship in the next system flipped in with an unknown vessel."

Gatewood looked at Kelsey for a few moments. "They're expected. Stand down and have the near picket escort the ship here. They're friends, it seems."

Once the man left, Gatewood shook her head slightly. "This is all so unbelievable. If what you say is true, I'll agree to that alliance in a heartbeat, but it might not help you that much. We don't know of any hidden flip points leading into Terra."

"We call them far flip points," Kelsey said. "And that's potentially okay. If we can get into a close system, we might be able to use one of the multi-flip points to find a way into Terra."

She really hoped it would be that easy. If they couldn't find a way in, Jared was on his own.

33

Olivia stood beside Jared's command console as they approached the main world in the last inhabited system short of Terra. The travel codes that Fielding had given them had gotten them permission to enter the system, and they were less than an hour away from orbit.

That was a relief. If the man had been going to betray them, this system had been the place. All they needed to do now was get rid of Fielding in such a way that he couldn't betray them or be discovered before they were long gone.

"This is it," Jared said softly. "We'll make orbit and stay long enough to get rid of Fielding and then head out. I figure six hours until we're into the buffer system between us and Terra.

"Everything I've seen indicates that one is unoccupied but patrolled by robotic ships. Through traffic is allowed along a direct corridor to the next flip point. The flip point leading to Terra is heavily guarded on the outside, and probably on the inside, too. Add another six hours to get to it."

"It seems so unreal," she said. "We've been trying to get here for so long, and now we're here. All the trouble thus far was just the journey. Now the fight to get what we need and escape again is in front of us, and it's intimidating."

He nodded. "True, but the AI doesn't know why we're really here. We can get in and back out again without giving ourselves away, especially with Kelsey's help. Both of them."

"That seems awfully optimistic," Olivia said. "I'm hoping it's true, mind you, but I'm leaning toward something serious going wrong with our plans."

"No plan survives contact with the enemy," he admitted with a wry smile. "That's a bit of history I picked up from Kelsey and her obsession with old Terran entertainment. I already knew it, but that's a very succinct saying.

"What it means is that we plan as best we can and be ready to adapt to the changing situation as quickly as we can. No one can predict the curve balls the pitcher throws at you, so you have to be flexible."

"What's a pitcher and why is he throwing balls at you?"

Jared chuckled. "That's not really important, and you don't have time to hear the story. It's time to get our guest ready for transport."

"I'm not worried about this part," she confided. "In fact, I'm counting on one of those curve balls you're throwing around."

"That's not how this works," he said with a chuckle. "Good luck."

With that, she left the bridge and made her way to the medical center. Lily Stone was waiting for her next to an unconscious Fielding. He had a somatic stimulator on his head and was resting peacefully.

"How is our soon-to-be-departed guest?" she asked.

"Stinking like three-day old fish, metaphorically speaking," the physician said with a smile. "I'll be glad when he's gone."

"When will he wake up?"

The doctor tapped a finger on the stimulator. "This has a timer that will shut it down in twelve hours. We should be long gone, and the only issue he'll have is being hungry and thirsty. I've loaded him up with fluids and energy. He'll probably be horrified that I've put a catheter into him, but I left written instructions so he can safely remove it. Attached to a handy spot he can't possibly miss."

Olivia laughed. "I can only imagine. Well, he's done more than enough that I don't feel badly about that. I'll take him from here."

The four marines waiting off to the side helped move the sleeping man onto a gurney, catching the sheet and almost pulling it all the way off. The unconscious noble was naked under the gown, and he did indeed have instructions taped to a… delicate area.

"I have his clothes in this," Lily said, handing her a bag. "Hurry up and get back. I want to be out of here long before he wakes up and comes after us."

"Your wish is my command," Olivia said. "Come on, boys."

The marines got the gurney to the docking tube leading to the noble's cutter and put him into an acceleration couch. They started to withdraw, but Olivia stopped them.

"Can I borrow a knife?"

They were marines, so she promptly had half a dozen blades to choose from, as some offered her two. The almost monomolecular edge of the blade she chose sliced off Fielding's gown with ease, leaving the unconscious man naked. It went into the bag with his clothes.

"Help me get rid of anything he can use to cover himself with," she said. "That'll keep him trapped on the cutter longer. His ego won't let anyone else see him in this condition."

It took fifteen minutes to get every scrap of cloth off the cutter, and every blade that could peel something off a seat. They even stripped the bed the man kept of its mattress and took the serving trays. There was nothing left for him to cover his nakedness with.

She even found something in his office to amuse herself with: a permanent marker. She made sure to leave a personal goodbye written on the man's naked form that set the marines to howling with laughter.

"Excellent," she said at last, making sure the grinning marines had removed all of the things they'd gathered. "I suppose I'm ready to go. Thanks, boys."

The Fleet pilot had stayed in the control area, though Olivia had seen the woman smirking at the antics in the cutter itself. That same expression dominated the woman's face when Olivia strapped herself in.

"He's going to be super pissed when he wakes up naked. And what were you doing with that permanent marker?"

"Leaving my own personal message," Olivia said serenely. "On his stomach with arrows. 'Objects are smaller than they appear.'"

The pilot laughed. "I had my own share of pranks at the academy. That stuff won't come out until it wears off in a few weeks. You ready? *Athena* just entered orbit, and we have clearance to make the trip over. The other cutter will shadow us and bring us back."

"Let's get this show on the road. The sooner we finish, the sooner we can get the hell out of here."

The flight over to the station didn't take very long, and they were quickly inside a cargo bay that reminded Olivia strongly of the one she'd been in at Archibald. It was hectic with activity, and people rushed about on tasks she couldn't begin to imagine.

A woman in deep-red coveralls met Olivia as soon as she debarked. "This pad is booked. You'll need to expedite your departure or relocate."

"If it's booked, why did your people direct me to it?" Olivia asked, irritated.

"Wasn't booked then," the woman said with a shrug. "Happened right before you landed. You want to bitch about it, talk to him."

The last few words were accompanied with a gesture toward a man standing nearby, smirking at Olivia.

"Fine," she growled as she headed toward the man. "Why are you screwing with me?"

"Fair seems fair," he said. "You screwed with me on the trip from the last system."

Olivia felt her eyes narrow. This had to be the smuggler. What had Kelsey said his name was? Or had she even mentioned it?

"Daniel Goldman," he interjected at her expression.

"And what can I do to make this situation up to you, Captain Goldman?" she asked through gritted teeth.

"I'm an inquisitive man," he admitted. "A personal failing in someone who takes cargos from one place to another without asking questions. Your presence on a destroyer has piqued my curiosity. Perhaps you could trade some answers for the parking slip?"

She felt her lips pull up into a smile. "Or I could give you another set of questions that might be worth your time. Step inside and take a look at my cutter."

His eyes narrowed, but he followed her in, only to stop abruptly at the lavish interior and the sight of the naked man strapped into one of the chairs.

"I wasn't sure what you wanted me to see, but I'll freely admit this wasn't on my scanners. Why do you have a naked man asleep in here? And where did you get this fabulous cutter?"

"I can't say. What I can say with certainty is that I'm leaving this cutter and everything it contains here, and I don't care what happens to it. He'll wake up on his own in about eleven hours without having taken any harm, but he's going to be severely pissed. Particularly if someone stole his very lavish cutter."

"I'm sure that would be unfortunate," the smuggler said, his expression odd. "I've boosted a number of small craft over the years, but no one ever handed one to me with a smile and a hook."

"A hook?" she asked.

"A mystery that will have me asking questions I'm sure I probably don't want to have answered."

"Excellent," she said cheerfully. "You'll want to disable the manual lockout I put on the hatch to keep him penned in here. I never activated it, but it's still in there. You'll also want to make sure he never sees your face. He's a vindictive bastard. Good luck, Captain."

With that, she marched out and met the pilot as they walked casually to their other cutter and departed the station.

Only once they were clear did the pilot turn to face her. "Is that guy going to cause us trouble?"

"Maybe," Olivia murmured. "Maybe not. We won't know for sure until we meet him again. One thing I can say is that he'll cause Fielding a lot more trouble than us, so I'll take it."

* * *

ANGELA STARED at the scanner plot and couldn't believe how quickly the negotiations with the resistance had gone. *Audacious* was still back at the Home system, settling things like the technology trade and seeing that the newly appointed Ambassador Justine Bandar was installed and briefed.

Other people would be staying there as well. Commander Giguere and her officers, for one group. They'd be good assets for the resistance. Prince Derek, his human associate Jacob Howell, and their entire party had decided to remain. The resistance was close enough to Pandora to get them back home after their adventure.

Princess Kelsey had also decided to leave the human Clan prisoners they'd captured with the resistance, as well as the crazy Rebel Empire security officer that had tried to kill Veronica Giguere.

Not Theo 309, though. His intelligence was too critical to the survival of the New Terran Empire. He'd be staying with them. Though she did leave the scientists that had been working on the Singularity computer. They'd refused to cooperate, and she was tired of carting around a circus of prisoners.

To everyone's shock, Commodore Murdock asked to remain as well. They'd promised her a new life, and she'd apparently decided this was it.

Finally, Doctor Lipp, her husband, and their minions were staying. They'd promised to drop them in the next safe system, and this was it. Perhaps they and the resistance could come to some agreement, but Angela doubted that. They were criminals, after all.

Ralph Halstead had decided to remain and had asked to work with Carl on the projects the young scientist was pursuing. With Carl's enthusiastic endorsement, he'd been allowed to do so.

Angela was thankful that Kelsey had sent *Persephone* ahead to scan the closest system the resistance could access to Terra. It had no connection to known Rebel Empire space and was empty of habitation, but it was easily in range of a multi-flip point. If they could find one.

"All probes away," Arianna Knox said. "We should have a full scan of the system in six hours or so. Do you think we'll get lucky?"

Angela shrugged. "I hope so. The resistance knows there are no other far flip points in this system and no regular ones at all. It's a cul-de-sac they never expected to be of use.

"The star is too hot for life to have developed, even if there had been a suitable world in the habitable zone. Basically, it's a curiosity they never looked at again after the initial exploration."

"But if it has a multi-flip point, it might go any number of interesting places," Knox said with a nod. "Based on our limited experience, we have about a fifty-fifty chance."

"Bump that up to a 100% chance," Jevon McLeod said from the tactical station. "Probe three just picked up a multi-flip point about an hour from our current location."

That made Angela smile. "Great news. Take us in, Jack."

She turned to her executive officer. "I'll leave this all in your hands while I go down and talk with my husband and Talbot in that makeshift lab. If there's a way to Terra here, Carl will find it."

The unspoken corollary was that if there wasn't, Admiral Mertz was screwed.

34

K elsey stood behind Mertz and watched as *Athena* approached the
flip point leading to Terra with far more nervousness than she'd
expected. This was it, the moment where everything would either
come together or fall apart.

"Send the recognition signal, Wanda," Mertz said, far more calmly than
Kelsey would have been able to do herself.

"Signal away," Wanda Dieter said from the communications console.
"Response received. We're to proceed through the flip point and receive
instructions on the other side."

"Well, at least they aren't going to open fire on us right away," Mertz
said with a wry smile. "Take us across, Janice."

While the helm officer worked her controls, he refocused his attention on
Evan Brodie, the tactical officer. "Make sure to get good scans as we go,
Evan. We'll want to have as much information as we can in case we have to
come back in force."

That, of course, assumed that they'd be coming back. Or even leaving,
for that matter.

The flip point was well covered with battle stations. Half a dozen of the
massively armed stations orbited the flip point closely, ready to repel any
attempt to access the system. Or to kill anyone that tried to leave it, she was
sure.

The New Terran Empire destroyer moved between the stations, and
Kelsey couldn't escape the impression that they were looming over her, their
electronic brains targeting the ship while preparing to open fire.

Only they didn't. They allowed the destroyer through the defenses, and
moments later, it flipped into the Terra system.

They'd finally made it.

The far side of the flip point was even more heavily armed and defended than the exterior side. A full dozen battle stations orbited the flip point at various distances. Some were close in while others sat farther away.

Scattered between them were dozens of warships: destroyers, light cruisers, and heavy cruisers. They were almost certainly computer controlled and not occupied.

Out of an abundance of caution, Mertz had previously ordered Wanda Dieter to retransmit their authorization as soon as they'd arrived. Whether the defenses were already expecting them or simply accepted the codes was unclear, but they didn't open fire.

"Where do we go now, sir?" Hall asked from the helm console.

"Take us deeper into the system while we take a look around," he said. "I'm sure the AI will have instructions for us before we get very far, but we've never been here before and need to get the layout of the system down.

"Where exactly is Terra in relation to this flip point? Where is the System Lord? How much mobile defense do they have wandering around that we need to be aware of? What other surprises do they have waiting for us?

"The AIs have done everything they can to keep humanity out of this system for so long that I refuse to believe they don't have things waiting for us now that we've arrived."

Wanda Dieter turned away from the communications console. "We have an incoming transmission from one of the battle stations, Admiral. We are to proceed to Terra at best speed and await further instructions there."

Janice Hall twitched a little and cursed under her breath. "The computer just received course and speed instructions, and we've begun moving. I realize that we set up the computer to respond as if it still had primary control of the ship, but that creeps me out."

So far as the Rebel Empire had been concerned, the human crew aboard the ship was running things, but it was obvious the AIs preferred to deal with their electronic minions and had sent instructions for the ship to carry out the directions rather than the crew.

Of course, they could immediately override the computer, and any of the really dangerous commands had been disabled long before they'd arrived in the system, but Kelsey had to agree with the helm officer. This was definitely creepy.

"Where do they seem to be taking us?" Mertz asked. "Are we going directly to Terra, or are they taking us on a more circuitous route?"

"We're headed directly in, sir. We're also moving at maximum military power. I'd estimate we'll be in Terra orbit in about five and a half hours. Right now, it looks as if the planet is almost on the other side of the sun from our current location."

Evan Brodie scowled at his console and looked back at his commanding officer. "We have an escort. They've detached three heavy cruisers to follow us in and have moved them into bracketing positions at close range. If we try to do anything at all, they can easily destroy us."

"Are we going to be able to launch any stealthed drones?" Mertz asked.

The tactical officer shook his head. "Not a chance, sir. They're far too close. They'd detect any probe leaving the ship immediately."

That made Kelsey curse. They'd been planning on seeding the Terra system with stealthed drones to get a complete layout of everything they'd have to deal with. They'd also hoped to send a few on to Terra before they arrived so that they could make plans on how best to carry out their mission while still seeming to carry out the one assigned to them by the AI.

She moved to stand next to Mertz's chair and spoke to him in a low voice. "Do you think the AI was at the flip point? Those instructions came in pretty fast."

He shook his head. "No. I'd bet those instructions were left there because it expected us to arrive about now. After all, if we didn't show up shortly, we'd have exploded somewhere else. We had a lot of incentive to be on time.

"If I had to make a guess, the AI in command of this system is going to be in one of two places. It's either going to be concealed at one of the gas giants and controlling all of the system defenses from that remote location, or it's going to be in orbit around Terra.

"I'm betting on the latter. After all, that's where the fighting was taking place. It would probably want to have a good eye over what was occurring down on the surface."

She considered that for a long moment and then sighed. "It would be better for us if the AI was out on one of the gas giants, so we have to plan for it being in orbit around Terra. That's going to make things really awkward, particularly with our nursemaids keeping us from performing any sleight-of-hand."

He turned his chair to face her. "This was never going to be easy, Kelsey, but we'll find a way to do what we need to do. For one thing, we're going to have to disperse the drones all over Terra. We'll be able to get our people off the ship to explore the Imperial Palace. We'll find the vault."

"What if they used planetary bombardment and the vault no longer exists?"

That was the worst-case scenario. They'd have come all this way to get a device that was long dust. Then they'd have to find a way to outsmart the cybernetic overlord that had commanded them here and escape again without the override they all so desperately needed.

That she and her people so desperately needed.

Their best hope for success was her doppelgänger, she supposed. If the other Kelsey could find a way into the Terra system, she could bring forces here that the computer wouldn't be expecting. If there was a lot of activity in Terra orbit, it was still going to be dicey, but at least they wouldn't all be doomed out of hand.

"Well, I suppose it's a little late for me to complain now," she said glumly. "I hope to hell that other me is as resourceful as you say, because if she's not, we're in for a universe of hurt."

* * *

TALBOT MADE his way down to the makeshift lab that Carl had set up in *Persephone*'s hold. Unlike the one on *Audacious*, this one didn't contain all of the experiments and personnel that he normally had. His task here was brutally straightforward.

Now that they'd found a multi-flip point, he'd send probes through to determine what frequency bands led to different destinations and then explore them. As they knew from experience, those destinations might have other branches that led to even more systems.

Exploring them was only half the battle. Once they'd determined where the varying branches led, they needed to know how difficult it was going to be for a larger vessel to traverse them.

Persephone was a small ship that could make its way through all of the branches in the various multi-flip points that they'd discovered. Even with a specialized flip drive his friend had designed and built for her, *Audacious* was much too large to risk on some of the narrower channels they'd seen.

If they were unlucky, they wouldn't find a path to Terra at all, but if fate were cruel, it might give them a path that only the Marine Raider strike ship could take. That would let them into the system but deny them the majority of the force they'd brought with them.

"How's it going?" he asked Carl as he sat down.

The young scientist was working on a dedicated computer station, his hands flashing across the old-style keyboard. He barely glanced over at Talbot.

"We're just about ready to send the first probe through. That'll show us what the default destination is and give me a bunch of readings about what frequency bands are available and how we might use them to explore alternative branches. With the experience we already have, I should have some initial data fairly quickly."

"What do you think our chances are?" Talbot asked. "Both to find Terra and to get a passage big enough for *Audacious*?"

Carl stopped tapping his keyboard and turned to face Talbot. "That's really hard to say. Finding a specific system through one of these is pretty much a crapshoot. If there's a rhyme or reason to it, I haven't found it yet.

"Of course, the same is true of regular flip points. If you come across a new one, you really don't have any idea where it's going to end up. I suppose one of the positive aspects of the multi-flip points is that we can explore a number of branches without spending a lot of time doing so.

"With all of the back and forth of traversing one branch and then looking for new branches, a single multi-flip point might have dozens of potential destinations. We really didn't spend a lot of time exploring the one we found leading to Icebox and Pandora."

Talbot nodded. "That's all true, but we have a very specific task in front of us. If we can't get to Terra, we'll be of no use to the admiral. If we can't get *Audacious* through the flip point, we'll be a lot less effective in assisting him in any case."

"That's out of my control," Carl said with a grunt. "If one of the branches leading from this multi-flip point doesn't lead to Terra, we'll have to explore some of the destination systems and the linkages beyond them to try to find one that does.

"In the end, we might come up dry. There's no guarantee that any multi-flip point or far flip point will lead to Terra, or how long it will take us to find one if it does exist. I'll do the best I can, but I can't make you any promises."

The screen in front of Carl changed as data began flowing across it. His young friend leaned forward and examined it closely.

"The initial probe is back. It doesn't look like the default branch leads to Terra, but at least it didn't lead to an occupied system. I'll have Fiona go over everything I'm recording, and I'll wager she can locate the system on the other end fairly quickly."

He tapped on the controls. "My best guess is that this multi-flip point has five branches. I'll refine the data, of course, but I might as well start sending probes down the various branches to see where they end up. Thankfully we have enough to do that all at once rather than reusing the same probe over and over."

Talbot was tempted to continue talking and exploring what might happen with his friend, but he didn't want to distract him. Instead, he leaned back in his seat and closed his eyes, resting while he could.

A few minutes later, Carl grunted.

Talbot opened his eyes and sat up. "Did you find something?"

"You could say that. I found a branch leading to Terra. I had to go through the multi-flip point to one of the destination systems and then send the probe down another branch, but we have a problem."

He turned to face Talbot. "The branch leading to Terra is perhaps the narrowest that I've ever seen. There's no way in hell *Audacious* is going through that particular passage."

"Perhaps one of the other branches on the Terra side will lead to a system that we can get to. We've seen how there's some duplication in the process."

"No dice. While there *are* other branches leading out from the Terra side, every single one of them seems to have a very narrow frequency band. On top of that, it only has three branches leading out.

"I'll program the probes to explore them, but I'm very much afraid that we've found a passage we can only use with *Persephone*."

That was bad news. The only possible ray of hope was the possibility of finding a far flip point in the Terra system. Looking for it would be dangerous and far from assured of success, but they'd have to try. The admiral was counting on them.

"Gather what you know and come with me," Talbot said. "It's time to brief Kelsey and get to Terra."

35

The trip in to Terra took a seeming eternity for Jared. Without being able to deploy any stealthed probes, the data they were getting from the home world of humanity grew sharper only at a snail's pace.

When they were a few hours out, they'd begun detecting orbital platforms circling Terra but couldn't determine anything about them, other than the fact that there were a lot of them. They ranged from moderate size to extremely large. Far larger, in fact, than anything he'd ever seen before.

More interesting to him was the fact that at least some of them appeared to be powered. He had no doubt that a number of the stations ahead of them were things like the planetary bombardment platforms used on Harrison's World, but that couldn't be the whole story.

Since the AIs had gone out of their way to subjugate Terra, it only made sense to Jared that they would have blasted any center of resistance. What was left to threaten? All they could hope for at this point was that the Imperial Palace still stood. If it didn't, the vaults below it were almost certainly destroyed, and their mission was doomed.

"We have an incoming communication from *Persephone*," Wanda Dieter said. "It's at high bandwidth and has video."

Jared smiled. The fact that his sister was able to communicate with him via high speed indicated that she had found a way to get to Terra.

"Put it on screen," he said, sitting back in his chair.

Kelsey's image appeared on the main screen, and she smiled. "As you've no doubt determined, we've found a way to get to Terra. That's the good news. The bad news is that it's a very narrow branch on a multi-flip point. There's no way that *Audacious* can make the trip. In fact, there's some risk simply taking *Persephone*, not that I'm going to let that stop me.

"If you can, let me know that you've received this message. If not, I'll assume that you're in a position that you don't dare attempt to transmit. In any case, we'll be in the system in the next few hours. I want to take the extra time to make all the preparations that we can think of, since there exists the possibility that this is a one-way trip for us."

Jared wasn't exactly happy to hear that, but there was nothing he could do to stop his sister. She was going to do what she thought was best, regardless of how he felt. Acceptance of that particular trait came hard to him, but he wasn't going to let it bother him anymore than it had to. Kelsey was coming whether he liked it or not, so he might as well like it. He didn't dare call her back to argue, in any case. There was far too great a chance of the enemy detecting the attempt.

"I'm starting to pick up more data from Terra orbit," Evan Brodie said. "I'm detecting at least two orbital bombardment platforms, as well as a lot of other types of station. The weapons platforms are definitely powered, but so are at least half a dozen other stations. Potentially as many as a dozen on the side of the planet I can see.

"There are some massive installations on the moon, as well. A lot of damage there, probably from the fight to take the system back during the Fall. Without being obvious about it, I'm not going to be able to be clearer on conditions there.

"I'm not detecting any ships, but they could be concealed behind or even inside some of the stations. A couple of them are gargantuan. Since I doubt the AIs needed to build all of this capacity, a bunch of it must've been left over from before the Fall. Potentially, they tried to turn Terra into one of their subjugated planets and failed."

Jared rubbed his chin while he thought about it. "I'm sure they did try to bring Terra to heel, but that obviously didn't work out for them. What I'm wondering is why they felt the need to exterminate everyone on the planet. What changed?

"They obviously have enough force to keep people out of this system as well as to make certain that no one from the surface can escape. Maybe we'll be able to find out once we get down there. Janice, what's our ETA?"

The helm officer checked her console briefly. "Two hours, twelve minutes. Almost there."

The next few hours went by even more slowly than the previous two. By the time they reached orbit, they had a much better impression of what was in orbit and had even begun discerning some of the surface.

In total, there were five orbital bombardment platforms. One of them seemed to be powered down, though he couldn't see any reason for that. The other four were certainly more than enough to deal with any issues requiring kinetic weaponry.

In addition, there were twenty-seven stations of various sizes that still had power. They ranged in size from medium size to immensely large. The biggest one was at least ten times the size of Orbital One back around Avalon. There were hundreds of other stations without power. Terra's industrial capacity must've been immense before the AIs had killed it.

"I'm starting to get some readings from the surface," Evan said. "The side of the planet facing us show signs of organized kinetic bombardment. It isn't enough to completely destroy the urban environment below, but it's significant. I'll start working to match up the craters with what we know about Terra from before the Fall to try and identify what the targets were."

"What about the Imperial Palace?" Jared asked. "Can we see it from here?"

The tactical officer shook his head. "We'll be coming around the planet to where we can see what it looks like in about ten minutes."

"We have another incoming message," Wanda said, frowning. "Another voice message from the AI. It's telling us to initiate deployment of the drones."

"Have you managed to locate the source of the transmission?"

Not that they can afford to shoot at the damned thing, not with cruisers sitting right behind them. They could probably damage a station, perhaps even destroy it and the AI, but they'd still die.

The communications officer nodded. "It's coming from that massive station just ahead of us. Whether it is a relay from elsewhere or even a recorded message, I couldn't say."

"Send a question back," he said. "Ask if it has a preference where we start deploying the drones. The time it takes for it to answer will let us know if it's really there or somewhere else in the system."

She turned back to her console. Moments later, she nodded. "It's sent us six locations spread out around the planet. It wants one crate in each location and the drones programmed to spread out as far as possible. I guess the AI is in the station."

Jared supposed that would work as well as anything for purposes of spreading the plague. It might make it really awkward getting to the Imperial Palace if the AI was dictating where they could land though.

"Put the map on the main screen and highlight the designated landing zones."

A map of Terra flashed up on the main screen, and six areas on it began flashing. Imperial City was located where the old American city of New York had been. The Imperial Palace was located a moderate distance away from the city, sitting farther north. The closest designated landing zone from either was easily three thousand kilometers away.

"Well, that's going to be challenging," he admitted. "Whatever we do, I think it's probably best to save the closest landing point until the very last. Once we've accomplished the mission, we become expendable."

"Imperial City is coming up," Evan Brodie said. "It looks like it took a direct hit. Perhaps more than one. The Imperial Palace area, on the other hand, seems to be mostly undisturbed. At least on the scale I can detect from orbit. It probably took collateral damage from the hits on Imperial City, but it wasn't destroyed outright."

That was good news. No matter how difficult it was going to be getting to the Imperial Palace, recovering the override was at least possible.

"Start loading the first crate aboard our remaining cutter," Jared said. "We'll start with the next landing zone past the Imperial Palace. Once we get down, we'll start getting an idea of how difficult this is going to be."

* * *

KELSEY GRIMACED as she stared at the representation of the flip point. It was as weak as the branch that led from the New Terran Empire to the Courageous system. The one that had trapped the original *Athena*. Using it would be a risk, even for *Persephone*.

She rubbed her face and sighed. They didn't have much of a choice. It was either use it or not get to Terra at all.

Carl had run the risk assessment, and the news was far from promising. The Marine Raider strike ship was small, so she would almost certainly make the flip successfully, but that might come at the same price *Audacious* had paid getting to Pandora. They might not be able to get back.

With that in mind, she'd pulled all the critical personnel she could onto *Persephone*. If they *were* stuck, she wanted to have everyone she needed to help Jared.

That meant the small ship was packed. Even though she'd been designed to carry a Marine Raider strike force, that wasn't a lot of people in the larger scheme of things. A single Marine Raider went a *long* way in a fight.

And then there was Fiona. She took up the largest previously open area on the ship, further reducing the available space. Well, she was an ace up their sleeves, so they'd have to make do.

Talbot had insisted they bring as many marines as possible, and Carl had needed his science team. That meant hot bunking, and all the people would stress the life support system if they were cooped up here too long.

Well, best to get this done. She left her quarters and made her way to the bridge.

Angela started to rise from the command seat, but Kelsey waved her back down.

"You're the commanding officer," she said as she planted herself next to the console. "I can stand. What's the status on loading supplies and people?"

"Just finished. The pilots are strapped into the fighters, and Raptor says they're ready to deploy. We haven't had time to rig up a way in from the fighters directly, so we'll have to extract them once we're ready to bring them back in."

Lieutenant Grappin and his people would be screwed if they got into a fight, simply because there were only six fighters and they had no way to quickly rearm them after a fight. If they got into a scrape, it would almost certainly end badly for them.

They'd still volunteered instantly for the mission. Like Marine Raiders, fighter pilots were a particular breed that ran toward danger. She was lucky to have them. They all were.

She'd considered bringing more pilots along, but that idea had made Raptor bristle. Apparently, one pilot to a fighter was the rule, and he wasn't pleased at the suggestion that he share his bird.

So be it.

"If we're loaded, then let's get over there and see what Jared has found for us," Kelsey said. "Flip the ship."

Even with her implants, the transition was a bit rough. No alarms started blaring, and a quick check of the ship's systems showed they'd made it without blowing their flip drive. She sighed in relief.

"What do we have?" she asked, even as she linked her implants to the scanners.

"We're in the Terra system," Angela said. "We're nowhere near detection range of any ship or station that we know of, but we knew that from the probes we'd already sent over. We're inside the asteroid belt between Jupiter and Mars, and almost on the opposite side of the sun from Terra, Mars, and Jupiter. Saturn is out system from us but is too distant for anything there to spot us."

"Then let's see if this was a one-way trip," Kelsey said. "We need to know if we're stuck."

Angela nodded to Jack Thompson at the helm, and he manipulated his controls. The flip drive engaged, but they stayed in the Terra system.

They were trapped.

36

Olivia worked with the others to unload the crate of reconnaissance drones. It was large, heavy, and bulky. She also wasn't sure if the AI could even see them doing the work. It might only be noting their landing from orbit.

The place it had dictated for the first landing spot that Jared had chosen was outside a devastated city that she didn't have a name for. It didn't look as if the city had been hit with a kinetic weapon but had rotted in place over the centuries.

Major Scala and some of his marines were keeping an eye on things just to be safe, but she hadn't seen any indication of human occupation. There had to be people out there, but they weren't showing themselves. If there wasn't anyone to worry about, the AIs wouldn't be deploying the Omega Plague here.

Once she and her helpers had the massive crate out on the ground, she sent the command to open it up. The drones inside were already prepared for deployment, but she took a moment to double-check the settings on each.

They'd programmed them to spread out in the pattern the AI had wanted, but for different reasons. The drones had no bioweapon to disperse, but they could and would take readings of the areas they patrolled. They'd forward that data back to the central control unit—a larger drone with significantly more capability—and it would sync that data to the other five control units via long range com.

In the end, if they were here long enough, that would give them a lot of information on the remaining human population, as well as an idea of what the planet still looked like so long after the occupation.

"The drones are ready," she said after a moment. "I'm sending them out."

Once everyone else had stepped clear, she activated the drones, and they began lifting off one by one and flying off in all directions. They'd spread far and wide, collecting data from many thousands of kilometers away.

That task done, she left the crate as it lay and headed back into the cutter. Even as she was strapping in, data began flowing in from the drones.

There *had* been people watching them. They were concealed in the ruins of several buildings and seemed concerned about the events they'd witnessed.

Olivia couldn't blame them. They had reason to be worried. If the drones were the ones that had started this mission, death would soon be spreading among them.

The lack of that death would eventually tell the System Lord that something had gone wrong. Probably before Jared and their crew were done here. That might make getting off Terra particularly challenging.

The marine officer brought the last of his people inside, and everyone strapped down. At her signal, the pilot lifted off and headed back for orbit.

"That took less than an hour from when we detached from *Athena*," Scala said. "Give us another twenty minutes to get back to the ship, and we can start loading the next crate. Call it two hours to deploy and recover from the mission for each crate. That gives us ten hours of work before the AI can get froggy with us."

"That's a little optimistic," Olivia said, turning to face him. "It might wait until we've deployed the last set and use the orbital bombardment weapon on us."

He shook his head. "Overkill. Besides, it would have to wait for the drones to clear the impact area. With that kind of time investment, it might as well allow us to return to orbit and deal with us there."

That thought made her rub her face. "How do we avoid that? It thinks it controls the ship and that we have bombs in our heads. When it makes its move, it'll expect results fast."

"The explosives are the first line of attack, I suspect," Scala said. "One signal and we all supposedly drop dead. No need to get fancy with that kind of option. The only question is what it does next. Does it want to recover the destroyer or eliminate any chance of contamination?"

"The latter," she said. "It's gone to a lot of trouble to make sure that we humans are the cutout. It doesn't risk contaminating itself or any other ships. Once it thinks we're dead, it won't risk verifying it. At that point, it'll get rid of the ship somehow.

"When it does, we need to be somewhere else, and the ship itself needs to respond to commands the way the AI expects. Sadly, I suspect that means *Athena* is going to be dropped into the sun to make sure there is no contamination risk."

The marine officer grimaced. "Or deorbited. We definitely don't want to be aboard for anything like that. We'll need to make sure everyone is off the ship by that point. If we're wrong, we can try to recover her later."

Olivia nodded. "And we need to get everyone down to the surface or to one of the stations. With the cruisers watching us like hawks, I think it has to be the surface. We'll have to rely on *Persephone* to get us out once we accomplish the mission."

"With the ships in orbit—and the AI for that matter—how will they get to us? Do we even know if they made it into the system?"

"They made it. Sean dropped a code word into the last communication from orbit. They wouldn't have risked a long signal, but they made it. Persephone and her pinnaces were designed to sneak up on the most advanced scanner suites without being spotted.

"The ship might not be able to get into orbit, though I'm not ruling that out, but the pinnaces can. They'll have to be much more careful in the atmosphere, but there's no reason they couldn't get some forces down to us and give us a ride out once we accomplish the mission."

By this point, they were back up in orbit and starting to maneuver toward *Athena*. They'd dock in ten minutes.

"The last drop is going to be key," Scala said. "We have to get everyone off the ship and still deliver the crate. Does the cutter have that kind of capacity? Worse, can it get back to the ship from the surface on automatics?"

Olivia didn't know about either of those things. "I hope so. If not, we're going to be in the position of leaving some of our people on *Athena* and hoping they can figure out another escape option."

And since the other options seemed pretty bleak, that might very well mean a suicide mission.

* * *

ANGELA WATCHED the scanner data flowing back from the stealthed probes grimly. It was building up an unpleasant picture. The AI had a lot of firepower out there. Trios of ships patrolled the system.

Since the damned AIs had no idea about multi-flip points or far flip points, that hardly made any sense. Why be so paranoid?

Kelsey was conferring with Talbot and Carl about the upcoming insertion onto Terra. As much as Angela hated the idea of sending the princess down to the surface, she was a significant asset and might make the difference between success and failure.

Yes, Talbot was also a full Marine Raider, even if he was still a little off on his use of his arms and hands, but that would fade in a day or so as he finally mastered his enhanced limbs.

The problem against arguing that Kelsey should stay in orbit resided in the other woman's implants. She had the codes that only the crown princess of the Empire could wield. A computer system down there from before the Fall would yield to her where it wouldn't do so for Talbot.

Inside the Imperial Vaults, there would almost certainly be security systems that only she could deal with. Admiral Mertz could use the key, but he wouldn't be able to handle any kind of computer lockouts.

So it looked as if Kelsey, Talbot, Carl, and a number of marines and scientists would be making the trip down. Only a half load for the pinnaces, because they needed to keep space open for the admiral and his people.

Once everything was done, the pinnaces would have one chance to slip out. Going back in was a risk they couldn't afford. Once and done.

She was still brooding about that when the ship's computer sent an alert to her. For a second, she was afraid the AI had found them, but it was only an anomaly detected by one of the probes. The one they'd sent toward the Alpha Centauri flip point.

Angela tapped into that specific feed and felt her eyes widen. The AI had invested the flip point with battle stations and ships. A lot of ships. Hundreds of them. Most were powered down, but not all.

That made absolutely no sense. Terra had three regular flip points. Two of them let out to the rest of the Rebel Empire, but the third was special. Alpha Centauri was a cul-de-sac. The system was only accessible from Terra and led nowhere else.

A guard force of this magnitude leading to a system that no one else could get to made no sense. And not just a regular guard force. A very powerful one. More so than what they'd detected at the other two regular flip points.

Taking a small risk, she sent a tight-beamed command to the probe to go a little closer.

While it did so, she contacted Princess Kelsey.

"What is it, Angela?" the princess asked.

"I think you need to tap into probe feed fifteen."

"What the hell?" Kelsey said after a moment. "A guard force on a dead-end flip point? That makes no sense."

"Exactly what I said. I've instructed the probe to get a little closer and take a look. Some of the ships are powered up, and all of the battle stations are, so we need to be careful."

"I'm on my way," the princess said a moment before killing the com connection.

Three minutes later, she walked onto the bridge with Talbot and Carl on her heels.

"How long until the probe is in position to give us more data about the ships and stations?" she asked.

"It was already close, so not too long," Angela said.

They all waited in silence as the probe inched its way closer. Finally, it was in position to see the closest ones clearly enough via passive scanners to tell them what they were looking at. Battlecruisers.

"Why are they here?" Kelsey asked. "What's in there? Is this force here to keep people out or something else in?"

"We're not going to be able to find out," Talbot said. "Just sneaking to

Terra is going to be hard enough. No way we can get access to that while the System Lord is active. Maybe not even if we took it out."

Kelsey sighed and nodded. "Then we proceed with the mission as planned. We'll worry about this mystery at a later date. What's our status?"

"We'll be in position to launch the pinnaces in about three hours," Angela said. "You'll have a good bit of coasting to do at that point."

The princess's expression was grim. "Then we start the hard part. Talbot, Carl, get your people ready. We'll leave on schedule."

37

Kelsey rubbed her eyes tiredly. She'd been helping load crates of drones and gathering everything they'd need on the surface between runs, and even she was feeling run down.

The argument she'd been engaged in for hours, off and on, with Jared Mertz, Sean Meyer, and Scott Roche hadn't helped her rest, though at least she'd gotten a few meals down in the process.

The cutter was on its way back up from dropping load five. This next one was the very last, and that was what had caused all of the disagreement. The matter was far from settled, and she just wanted it to be over.

She was in the mess hall, devouring what might be her last good meal for a while. Yes, they had plenty of field rations, but that wouldn't be the same. Scott Roche was sitting across from her, and Sean Meyer was to her left. Mertz had just sat on her right, and she was ready for the next wave of objections.

"Before you start this again, I know that I'm right and so do you," she said between bites. "How about we skip the argument part and just get to planning what I do next?"

Mertz sighed. "This is an extremely risky plan. The number of things that could go wrong are legion."

"And yet there's no reasonable alternative," she countered. "I'm the only one of us that has a chance of surviving, so unless you *want* to have a suicide mission for someone, why are we fighting? Didn't you tell me that I should trust more in my abilities and that I could do amazing things? Why the big turnaround?"

"Because this idea is crazy, Highness," Scott said in what he no doubt thought was a reasonable tone. "The chances of you pulling this off are damned poor, and I for one don't want to see you throw your life away."

She set her fork down beside her plate and gave him a level look. "If I don't do this, the AI will know we're pulling a fast one and drop a kinetic strike on site six, so I'll die anyway. If I give this my best, I might make it. And realistically, I have a better chance of making this work than anyone else we have."

Her friend rubbed his face. "I know you think that, but you're not a trained pilot. There are a lot of automatic systems on the cutter, so it will probably get you close, but then you have to dock with an unmanned ship. There'll be no one to assist or guide you.

"Let's say that goes off without a hitch. The AI might set off the supposed bombs in our heads and order the ship to drop into the sun. You'd have to verify that course, make sure the ship is following it, and then get off to the nearest station.

"That's the best case. The worst is that it has the ships following us open fire and destroys the ship with you on it."

"And what if it demands to speak to a human being?" she countered. "Then it'll know something is wrong. No, there has to be someone here to do the things that only a human can do, and I'm the best choice. I have a plan to get away, even under the worst-case scenario."

"Does it give you a realistic chance of survival?" Mertz asked in a steady tone. "I doubt that very seriously. There has to be another way."

"I'll do it," Sean said quietly.

"The hell you will," Mertz countered. "Olivia would have both our hides if she knew you even offered."

"Then let it be me," Scott said. "I commanded a destroyer and am more than capable of piloting this ship. Sorry, Highness, but I'm a Fleet officer. If the choice is between you living or dying, I'll do what I have to. I forbid you from this madness."

The rising testosterone level at the table made her roll her eyes. "You've forgotten who you work for, Commander Roche. I give the orders, and you obey them."

"I'll gladly sit for that board of inquiry when we get home, Highness. You can testify against, me and I'll accept whatever verdict they choose, so long as you're alive to be there."

She sighed. "That means so much to me, Scott. I know you mean every word of it, and it breaks my heart to ruin such a beautiful speech, but I will never let my friends throw their lives away for me again. I hope you'll forgive me some day."

With that, she fired the stunner she'd surreptitiously drawn from her belt holster and aimed at him under the table. The blue beam lit him up and caused him to spasm before falling out of his chair with a clatter, his convulsive grip on the tablecloth dragging everything off the table as he went down.

Everyone in the room lurched to their feet at the horrendous racket except her. She holstered the weapon and raised the taco she'd snatched off her plate to her mouth. It was the last one she'd have for a long time.

"Dammit, Kelsey," Mertz said as he checked Scott. "That was way over the line."

"Probably," she admitted. "He'll be *really* pissed when he wakes up, but I'll either be there to deal with it or I'll be dead. One way or the other, he lives. I've watched far too many of my friends die in the last few years to let that gallant idiot sacrifice himself for me.

"And make no mistake, if someone else tries to get froggy with me, I'll use my Marine Raider enhancements to put them down too. This is the way it has to be, and I will not accept any more arguing about this. Am I clear?"

With a bemused expression, Mertz nodded. "'Yes, Highness' seems to be the only suitable response. If we can't stop you, then we need to work damned hard to make sure you have every chance of making this work. You need to finish that taco."

She nodded, finished the food, and stood. "Tell him I'm sorry if I don't make it. He was only doing what he thought was right, and I treasure his friendship. Don't let him blame himself. This was my decision."

"I can tell him that all you want, Kelsey, but it won't make a difference," Mertz said with a shake of his head. "He'll eventually forgive you if you live, but he'll never forgive himself if you die."

Honestly, death wouldn't be as bad as knowing that Scott had given his life for hers. Her life had been nothing but pain and failure anyway. It might just be a blessing.

"So long as he lives, that's a burden he'll have to bear," she said, her voice sounding hollow even to her own ears. "Let's do this."

"It isn't like I have much of a choice at this point," Mertz said with a sigh. "Let's get down to the cargo bay and make certain that everyone is ready. Still, I'm afraid your plan has one hole that still needs filling.

"The lack of a pilot for the cutter could ruin everything. Without one, the entire plan is ruined. Someone has to come with you, and I think it had best be me."

She stopped dead in her tracks and turned toward him. "Are you mad? Only you can open the damned vaults under the Imperial Palace. You have to be there."

"And I will be if you do your job. I'm going to risk a message to our Kelsey and have her pick us up from the nearest station."

She fought to keep her eyes from rolling but failed. "We've already been through this. My Raider armor will keep them from spotting me. Your suit won't be nearly as stealthy."

"Let me show you something," he said as he continued on into the cargo bay. Everyone seemed to already be there, waiting for the cutter to dock. They'd load the crate and then clear the ship. Everyone had whatever important things they could bring with them in bags at their feet.

Mertz led her over to the other side of the crate, and she stopped dead in her tracks. Spread out face down on the floor was a suit of Marine Raider armor. It looked just like hers, only it was a dark gray rather than black.

"What the hell?" she asked.

"Kelsey insisted I have this before we got separated. I'm not a Marine Raider, so I can't use it to fight like you, but I *can* use its basic functions such as stealth and the grav booster. After the last time someone tried to assassinate me, she wasn't going to allow me to be so vulnerable again.

"Carl hacked the interface and modified it to work with non-Raider implants. Mine, specifically. The armor is keyed to me, so I can't really let anyone else take my place."

"Why would you risk your life for me?" she asked slowly. "I'm not exactly your biggest fan."

He smiled and had the audacity to clap her on the shoulder. "Even if you don't feel about me the same way, you're my sister. I'm not letting you face this alone. We're family."

The idea caused an initial surge of anger, but she tamped it down. He wasn't the same man as in her universe. That was painfully obvious. It was time she really accepted that and worked at seeing him differently than the Bastard.

She forced herself to relax. "Okay. We do this together."

A loud clanging announced the arrival of the cutter. Mertz… Jared released her and started getting the rest of the people moving. It was time.

* * *

Talbot sat at the flight engineer's station in the pinnace's cramped control area. Kelsey was in the copilot's seat, though she wasn't doing any flying at the moment. Both of them wore Marine Raider powered armor, though his was locked down to normal human strength, just to be safe.

He knew Kelsey could act as a copilot in a pinch, but she was still getting experience with the small craft. Maybe she'd get her marine small craft certification in a few months more, once she had the time to devote to the in-atmosphere qualifications.

They'd left *Persephone* hours ago and were ghosting toward Terra. The other pinnace, filled with marines and scientists, had separated from them and would make their way to the landing zone separately. No need for them to take risks on this rescue.

The pinnace he was on was empty except for the people in the control area. If it went bad, only the three of them would die.

They were on their final approach to orbit. They were coming in on the opposite side of the planet from the three ships watching over *Athena*, as well as the moon so that they'd avoid being silhouetted against it, but the AI would have line of sight on them. If things were going to go wrong, this was the time they'd do it.

Kelsey had cussed a blue streak when word had come that her brother was risking himself in the ruse that there were still people on the destroyer, but it wasn't as if she could tear a strip off him for being reckless when that might call lightning down on herself.

A less cautious individual than his wife was hard to imagine.

The final drone placement was in progress on the surface, and the admiral would be on the way back to orbit in just a few minutes. This pinnace needed to be near the station the others would be heading for before then, or they wouldn't be in a position to adjust for complications.

Kelsey stared at the viewport. Terra, her surface blue and green, dotted by white clouds, hung huge in front of them.

"I never thought I'd see this," his wife muttered. "The homeworld of humanity. I read everything I could about it as a kid, but I'm going to see things no one on Avalon could even imagine now. If we can pull off this insane stunt."

He laughed. "Pot, meet kettle."

"You aren't funny," she said with an annoyed glance at him. "Jared is insane to take this kind of chance, even with a secret weapon in his pocket."

"You keep dropping hints, but I'm not getting what you mean. What secret weapon?"

She smiled smugly. "I didn't want to screw us up by revealing it too soon. You'll find out when we pick him up. You'll just have to trust me until then."

He shook his head. "I trust you with my life, but you can be so juvenile."

That made her laugh, probably in spite of her feelings. "I know, but I'm still worried. There are so many ways this can go wrong."

"Welcome to the universe in which we live. Jared is as resourceful as you are. Trust that he knows what he's doing."

"We're coming up to closest approach to the AI's station," Lieutenant Kada Erickson said, turning her head to look at Kelsey.

His wife focused her attention on the pilot. "Any sign it's seen us?"

"Not at the moment, but it'll have line of sight on *Athena* and the station we're going to use for cover in thirty minutes. We should be able to get into position before then, but the three enemy cruisers will be right there."

"And once trouble starts, they'll all have a chance to see us," Talbot added with a grumble. "In a perfect world, we'd pick the admiral up and wait for a clear moment to get down to Terra."

"But this is likely to get messy," Kelsey agreed. "If they start shooting and we have to get down to the surface in a hurry, what are our chances?"

"Slim to none," the pilot said. "With clear skies at that range, they'll spot anything dropping down into the atmosphere at once, even us. We'll be in visual range, so the scanner-dampening coating on the hull will do us exactly zero good."

Talbot knew they could get down to the surface safely when none of the hostiles were directly watching in about ten minutes, but Kelsey would never go that way. Neither would he.

They all watched the huge station holding the AI until it was over the horizon. Then Kelsey nodded. "Set course for the target station. Use its bulk as much as possible to keep the cruisers from seeing us. It's time to save my brother. And myself."

He wasn't sure exactly what that meant, but he couldn't agree more. Time to get this over with.

38

J ared took the controls as soon as they had everyone on the ground at the sixth landing area and had released the drones. Kelsey sat in the copilot's chair, watching him as he lifted the cutter away from the ground and set course back toward the ship. One of *Persephone's* pinnaces—the one with almost all the people Kelsey One had sent to Terra —would arrive while they were going up.

"How soon after we get back aboard do you think the AI will act?" Kelsey Two asked.

"It won't delay long," he said grimly. "Whatever it has in mind, it has no reason to wait. I expect it'll jump as soon as it confirms it has complete control of the drones. Thankfully, the lockouts Austin installed will allow us to override that without the thing being aware of what we're doing."

"I had wondered about that," she admitted as the sky began growing darker as they climbed toward space. "So, we'll be in the drone system and able to use, what? All of them? Only those in range?"

"Each group has a central controller and backup that can communicate with all the others. We'll have access to all the drones, and none of them will report anything we don't want. Each has a fake set of instructions to report how much of the nonexistent bioweapon they're spreading to the AI, so it'll think everything is going along great.

"Right now, we're set up so that none of the ones in our general area will report anything not cleared by us. We don't want to give the AI any real intelligence about what's going on around us or that we're here at all. If need be, we can assume direct control of all the drones and lock the AI completely out, but that'll give the game away."

She nodded. "That's good. Do you think other me is in place?"

"Almost certainly," he said. "With the AI so close, she won't risk communicating with us at all, but she'd have gotten word to us if she'd been delayed. She'll be there."

The cutter exited the atmosphere a few minutes later, and Jared set course for *Athena*. The robotic destroyer had been a good ship. He was going to miss having her when the AI did something permanent to her, which he never doubted was coming for a moment.

He brought the cutter back to the dock and adroitly spun her along her axis to line up with the ship. With small nudges of the maneuvering thrusters, he mated the locks and sighed with relief when the automatic locking rings secured them together.

"There we go," he said. "Easy as pie."

"Why is pie easy? And don't you think it's rude to bring up food when I'm already hungry?"

He laughed. "Sorry. Let's get inside and up to the bridge."

"I might not have been able to do that," Kelsey admitted as she lay face down in her armor, which was lying on the floor of the hold. It sealed up, and she quickly levered herself to her feet, her blank faceplate coming to life with a view of her face.

"That's why they pay me the big bucks," he said. "Grab mine and come on."

She easily scooped his up and followed behind him as he traversed the empty corridors toward the bridge. "Shouldn't you armor up?"

"If the AI decides to call, I need to be presentable," he said as he held the lift doors open. "I personally doubt it will, but one never knows when it comes to homicidal AIs."

Less than a minute later, they exited onto the bridge. It felt wrong to see it with no one at the controls.

"What's your plan?" he asked Kelsey.

"That really depends on what the AI does," she admitted. "If it uses the head bombs, we can probably sneak out one of the personnel airlocks and slip over to the station. That's true even if it starts maneuvering the ship. We still have control of the ship's systems, so it won't know what we're doing. If it starts shooting, we'll have to go out the escape pod tube."

He shook his head. "It will see the escape pod and kill it before we even get to the atmosphere. Worse, we won't be able to get away from it in time to rendezvous with Kelsey One."

Even as they were speaking, he was linked into the destroyer's scanner network. The three cruisers were the most immediate threat, but he had his eye on the large station containing the AI, too.

At this range, he'd know the moment the enemy brought targeting scanners online and they could act. He just needed to decide what the best course was first. He hoped he'd have time to make a considered call.

The com system pinged with an incoming call, with video this time. So, the AI was going to talk after all. He wondered what it would say before it killed them, because he had no doubt as to the fate it intended for them.

He sat in the command seat and gestured for Kelsey to get off far enough to the side so she wasn't in the feed. Only when he was ready did he accept the call.

The video component was a sine wave that undulated across the screen. He'd barely had a chance to register it when the AI began speaking.

"You have done well," it said in a sonorous voice.

"Thank you, Lord," Jared said once he was sure that was all it was going to say as an opening. "We live to serve."

"I will see that your families are well rewarded for your loyalty, but no word of this mission must ever make way to your fellow humans. My personal reward to you is a quick death."

The scanners showed the cruisers bringing their targeting scanners online, so Jared killed the com and dove for where his armor lay on the deck. The end was upon them, and they had to act now.

Jared wasn't nearly as graceful getting into the armor as Kelsey had been, but it only took a few seconds. Hopefully, it would be enough.

He used his implants to give the ship one set of final orders as the cruisers prepared to fire. Not to fight but to shut down the fusion plants. If one of them went, it would incinerate Kelsey and himself in an instant.

The deck shuddered under his body. Not a weapons strike. Too subtle.

Jared levered himself to his feet and saw that Kelsey had ejected the bridge's escape pod. Not with her in it, but empty.

"What…" he started, and then cut off when he saw her slap a plasma breaching charge on the closed hatch.

"Back," she ordered, hurling herself away from the explosives.

He barely had time to emulate her when the charge went off. It felt like the end of the world. Even through the armor, his ears rang. Moments later, his implants registered a signal that he knew was meant to trigger the nonexistent bomb in his head. The AI was taking no chances.

The air venting through the hull breach picked him up like a toy and hurled him into space. Just in time to see the first missiles slam into his command. Even without the possibility of a fusion plant containment failure, that didn't mean the explosions were gentle for the two of them. The exploding missiles blew huge chunks of debris away from *Athena*, and something slammed into him, spinning him around and dazing him again.

Only as he tried to recover did he see a missile explode far below, no doubt killing the escape pod Kelsey had jettisoned. After a few seconds, he was able to bring his suit under control and arrow toward the station concealing his and Kelsey's pinnace. She'd be on the far side of the station, away from possible detection.

The plan was to hold up there until the cruisers left. Then, once the AI's attention was elsewhere, they could slip away. Chancy, but it was the best hope they had.

A small bit of debris hit his leg and spun him around just in time to see *Athena* come apart completely under the attack. It wasn't as violent an explosion as when a fusion plant went critical, but it was potentially deadly all the same. The attack was sending debris out in a terrible cloud, with several large chunks slamming into the station he and Kelsey were moving toward.

He felt another jerk as Kelsey grabbed his arm and leveled him out, just before she jetted forward and under the cover of the powered-down station.

Persephone's pinnace was right there, its ramp already down and an armored figure gesturing for them to hurry. The gray Marine Raider armor told him it was Kelsey. His Kelsey.

The two of them raced forward and past the ramp. It had only barely started to close when the hand of God crushed Jared against the wall, and everything went dark.

* * *

KELSEY HELD on for dear life as her pinnace violently rolled and jerked. Honed reflexes made her rotate so that her back slammed into the side of the craft rather than her head.

Jared wasn't moving, but his armor's telemetry said he was in decent shape, only knocked out. The other figure—the other her—was banged up but conscious. She was Kelsey, too, so she was tough.

"Kelsey," Talbot said, his voice strained. "Get up here right now."

"Get him strapped in," she ordered her other self. "Then get secure yourself."

With that, she made all haste back to the control area. She knew things were bad when she saw Talbot in the copilot's seat, struggling with the controls. The pilot was still in her seat, but limp.

"She went straight up and hit her head on the overhead controls," he said. "Bad luck, but she's out. We have worse problems, though."

Kelsey quickly pulled the woman from her seat and double-checked Talbot's assessment. The woman was breathing and had a strong pulse. Her marine implants indicated nothing more serious than a concussion. That was good. An impact like that could have broken the woman's neck.

She strapped the unconscious pilot into the flight engineer's seat and took the controls. "What happened?"

"The station blew up, I think. Not a fusion plant overload, obviously, but more than enough to knock us around. There's a lot of debris in the area around us and we're going to hit the atmosphere pretty fast on this course.

"I'm no pilot, but I'm worried we're on a really dangerous entry angle. We could burn up. Worse, one of the drives is out and some of the controls are amber."

Kelsey finished strapping in and checked the board. Yep, the port engine was offline, and some of the control surfaces seemed damaged. That was going to seriously complicate things.

"I really should've prioritized my atmospheric qualifications," she said as she projected their vector out. "I'll have to gradually adjust our course so as not to get the AI's attention. It can kill us just as dead as a bad entry, and everyone on the surface, too."

"Did you get the admiral on board? Who was with him? Are they okay?"

"Jared is out, but our other passenger has him strapped in. Who it is isn't important right now, so I'll explain when I have more time.

"Hey, one good thing is that we're going to end up on a decent course toward the area where everyone else is waiting down on Terra. It will only take a few tweaks in atmosphere to get us down to them."

"If we get down," her husband said.

She shot him a look. "Think positive. We'll make it."

In spite of her projected confidence, she was less than sure. Her atmospheric entry skills were rudimentary at best. With one dead engine and some damaged controls, this would've challenged someone like Annette Vitter.

She immediately regretted the thought. The fighter wing commander had been piloting an old-style marine pinnace when an asteroid impact on Erorsi had knocked them from the sky. The woman had somehow turned certain death into a crash that had scored a deep wound into the planet, but it had still cost the woman an arm and killed some of the people aboard.

Kelsey was nowhere in the other woman's league with small-craft handling. If things went badly, they'd almost certainly die.

She took a calming breath and focused on what she could do. Several adjustments to their course put them into a better entry angle, and she let that play out.

The initial wisps of air caused the pinnace to shake a little, but that was just a hint at what was coming. Within a minute, the shuddering of the small craft had her deeply scared. It was far rougher than she'd expected. Something on the hull must be catching air, and that could kill them fast.

Abruptly, the shaking ceased, but before she could react, an alarm blared. One of the control surfaces had just ripped off the hull.

"The good news is that we lost the thing dragging on the air," she said, trying to compensate for the new damage. "The bad news is that it's going to make a soft landing *really* challenging."

She was grateful when Talbot didn't say anything, leaving her to focus on the pinnace. The loss of the control surface was complicating the pinnace's stability, but only a little. The loss of the port engine was worse. It gave the pinnace a recurring tendency to slew to the side, and a spin under these conditions would kill them.

Kelsey lost track of time as she fought the crashing pinnace for every advantage she could wring out of it. Eventually, the buffeting eased, and the small craft was deep enough and slow enough that she was flying rather than falling.

A quick check of their location showed that the landing zone was coming up far more quickly than she'd planned on. She needed to bleed airspeed right now.

She put the pinnace into a series of S curves that dropped their speed, fighting for control when the pinnace bucked under her again and again.

She only had the landing coordinates, as the people below didn't dare signal to them.

Kelsey imagined their entry looked catastrophic to the people on the ground. Hell, it felt catastrophic to her. Still, she reminded herself that this was far from the most violent planetary insertion that she'd ever experienced.

Using a drop capsule on Harrison's World had taken her from orbital speeds to a dead stop on the ground in about ten seconds. That bit of insanity had earned her the drop commando badge from Ned Quincy, and she was the only living person that could claim that level of crazy. Of course, she'd had no choice if she'd wanted to stop that madman with the nuke.

"I think I see them," Talbot said. "Off to starboard."

She looked over and spotted the strobe of a landing light. It wouldn't be visible from orbit, so they'd taken a chance.

Kelsey hit the general com. "I'm coming around for final approach. Hold on tight."

She killed the com. "We'll have one chance at this. If I don't nail it, we'll crash for real. The controls are getting worse by the second."

It was going to be a race to see if they could set down before the controls failed altogether. If they hadn't been on an approach vector, she'd never have been able to even get close.

"Altitude a thousand meters," Talbot said. "Start slowing us down."

"Can't," she said. "We're a damned flying brick. If I lose any more speed, we'll fall right out of the sky."

"We'll be a crater if we don't."

Dammit, he was right. She took a deep breath, let it out slowly, and activated the general com again. "Coming up on the LZ. This is going to suck. Thirty seconds to landing."

She somehow managed to balance losing speed with staying in the air for almost twenty-five seconds. Then the remaining engine failed catastrophically.

Kelsey forced the pinnace out of the skew the exploding engine had sent them into and saw the ground racing to meet them. "Brace for impact!"

The pinnace slammed into the ground, throwing Kelsey harshly against her restraints. They were on the ground but skidding wildly, and a new danger popped up right in front of them. They were headed directly for the other pinnace at an insane rate of speed.

The ground slowed them faster than she'd hoped but not nearly fast enough. They crashed into the other pinnace hard enough to shatter the console in front of her and crush her against the wreckage.

Thankfully, her armor protected her from what might otherwise have been a fatal impact, even for a Marine Raider. She sat there in her seat, blinking stupidly at the mess piled on her.

She used her enhanced strength to push herself back even as she was verifying the health of the three of them in the destroyed control area. Everyone was alive. Miraculously, no one was even seriously hurt.

"Allow me to be the first to congratulate you on a stellar landing," the pilot said weakly from behind her. "Just remember that all damage to the pinnace comes out of your pay."

Kelsey laughed in spite of herself. "I'm never going to be out from under the debt of destroyed and damaged equipment. You get used to it after a while. You okay?"

"My head hurts, but I'll damned well walk away from this landing. Seriously, good job, Highness."

Kelsey unstrapped herself with shaky hands as Talbot also dug himself out of the debris.

"I'll make sure she's okay," he said. "Go check on the others."

On unsteady feet, Kelsey got into the back of the pinnace. The floor sloped at least ten degrees to the side, but the body of the ship seemed intact, and one figure was standing. The other Kelsey.

"How is he?" she asked.

The other version of herself popped her helmet and shook her blonde hair out. "He has a concussion, but he'll live. I'm afraid I'm going to have to complain to the management about the landing. It did indeed suck."

Kelsey checked Jared's readouts and satisfied herself that he was going to make it. That relieved her no end. She popped her own helmet and stared at her twin.

She started to say something, but someone started banging on the outside of the pinnace by the ramp. That would be the ad hoc crash-and-rescue response team the others had put together. She'd better let them in before they had a stroke. If she could.

The ramp was crumpled and would never open again. There was an emergency exit on the side hull. It was visibly warped but might still be useable to two Marine Raiders in powered armor.

"Give me a hand here," she told her doppelgänger.

The other Kelsey stepped up beside her, and together they put all of their considerable strength against the jammed hatch. It groaned and finally popped open, letting in the sun and air of the homeworld.

Kelsey took a deep breath and turned toward the other her as the people outside looked for the best way up the gouged earth toward the opening. She clapped a hand on the woman from another universe's black-armored shoulder.

"Welcome to Terra, sister mine. Now the real work begins."

RUINED TERRA

BOOK ELEVEN

Marooned on ruined Terra, Kelsey Bandar and Jared Mertz must march to the Imperial Palace to recover the key to defeating the savage AIs that have enslaved humanity.

If, of course, the fierce and primitive Terrans don't kill them first.

Trapped without their advanced technology, they must overcome foes determined to take everything they have left, including their very lives. If they don't find allies fast, humanity is doomed.

1

Princess Kelsey Bandar stared at the bright stars spread across the dark sky over her head like diamond dust on velvet. The brilliant Milky Way showed far more points of light than she'd ever seen from Avalon, with the exception of her stays at the Imperial Retreat. Even in the less populated areas of her birth world, light pollution from the many cities made it impossible to see the dimmest of the stellar masses.

Not so on Terra.

With the total destruction of civilization here, there was no artificial light to dim the stars. The single large moon wasn't in the sky at the moment, and there was nothing between her and the majesty of the universe. It was beautiful, sad, and horrifying all at the same time.

She stood on what looked like a plain of tall, wild grass, though it was hard to make out clearly now that night had fallen, even with her enhanced vision. The chill wind was steady from the northwest and carried the earthy scent of vegetation. Maybe there was a forest off in that direction.

That battled with the scent of scorched electronics and leaking fuel from the crashed pinnaces nearby. Talk about a sour note. Everyone had walked away from *that* disaster, but it had really left them in a bad spot.

She had left them in a bad spot. If only she'd gotten around to focusing more of her flight training on emergency landings, she could've gotten the disabled pinnace down in one piece. Or at least avoided crashing it into the *other* pinnace, wrecking them both.

Just one more thing that she couldn't fix after the fact.

"It's beautiful isn't it?" Elise Orson asked as she came out of the tent they were using as an ad hoc command center, at least until they figured out what they were going to do next.

Kelsey turned to her friend and forced a smile onto her face. "It is. Even in the depths of misery and destruction, there's still some beauty left around us, and that gives me hope. How's Jared?"

"Lily says that he has a concussion, but she'll have him up by morning, just like your pilot. Those were the only injuries we had in this entire affair, and I find that absolutely amazing."

Kelsey turned again toward where she'd crashed and stared at the wreckage sourly. With her enhanced eyesight, she had no difficulty seeing that they were screwed. The pinnace that she'd brought down had punched a hole through the hull of the other craft and warped its frame. Neither of the small craft would ever fly again.

"They say that any landing you can walk away from is a good one, but I think I'm going to disagree," she said with a grumble. "We have to get to the Imperial Palace to recover the override, and that means we're going to have to travel at least a thousand kilometers on foot. Probably more. Potentially a *lot* more. All of that with our supplies on our back."

"Well, I always did enjoy a good hike," Elise said with a sigh of resignation. "Can't the powered armor the marines brought help carry what we need?"

"No," Kelsey said with a resigned shake of her head. "Their power supplies won't get us more than a few days into the journey. The best we can manage is to get some of what we have to a less exposed position and stash it there for emergencies. Not that I'm sure how it will benefit us once we've left the area. Talbot is working out the details with Major Scala.

"Once we really get going, we'll only have the supplies we can carry with us. A good chunk of that's going to be weaponry and other military hardware. Add to that food, water, and other consumables, and we'll be packed down pretty heavy. We'll have to gather all that and get to marching as soon as we can tomorrow, since this site is in danger of being spotted from orbit.

"The pinnaces have stealth materials woven into their hulls, but we can't take a chance that the AIs will spot them and destroy our extra gear or ourselves. If we can find a place somewhere close that will work as a supply cache, we'll stash everything there and begin the long march."

Kelsey let the silence drag on for a few seconds and then turned to face her friend directly. "Tell me about my doppelgänger. She and I haven't spoken more than a couple of words, and it's hard for me to even believe she's real. A version of me from another universe? I'm having trouble getting my head around that. What's she like?"

"It's odd," Elise confessed. "Sometimes, she's so very much like you, and then she's... not. She's been through so much. I grew up in terror of becoming a Pale One, and she had to live through it, even if only for a short time. That gives me the cold shivers, and my heart goes out to her."

The Pale Ones were the savage descendants of human survivors on the planet Erorsi. A mad computer there had been utilizing Old Empire equipment to forcibly implant them with Marine Raider hardware and then reprogramming their cranial implants so that it could control their actions, even over their resistance.

They'd became vicious killing machines that had attacked Pentagar on primitive ships built by the computer for five centuries. Many Pentagarans in danger of capture would kill themselves to avoid that fate, and Kelsey completely understood their motivations.

If she'd really understood what the computer would do to her, what she'd have become for the rest of her life if Jared and the rest hadn't saved her, she might have taken her own life in the heat of the moment once she'd fallen into their grasp.

The Pale Ones had captured her and her marine escort because she'd been an idiot. She'd let a petty, nose-in-the-air, noble girl tantrum put her into harm's way, and she'd paid the price for that. To her everlasting shame, so had her marines.

That had been the moment that she'd finally grown up. That had been the point in her life where *everything* had changed. Never again would she allow herself to fail her people, or herself. She'd die first.

How much worse had it been for her other self? Talbot and Jared had saved her, but that hadn't happened in the other universe. There, that version of her had become a Pale One, lost control over her own body, and been forced to do brutal, terrible things. Things that horrified Kelsey to even think about.

"One thing we did settle," Kelsey said once she'd set her horror aside, "was that having us be Kelsey One and Kelsey Two like you guys came up with was ridiculous. This universe is my home, so I'm Kelsey. She's decided to use one of our cousin's names and will now be Julia. We both always loved that name.

"If the situation is ever reversed, I'll use that name in her universe. Not that I expect my father to ever allow me over there, mind you. At the very least, it'll make talking about each of us a little less complicated.

"Now, to change the subject, what do you know about the Terrans? Sean said that your people observed some of them through the drone feeds. Can you tell if there are any around us now? Do they know we're here?"

Elise chuckled. "After that landing, *everybody* within a *hundred kilometers* probably knows we're here."

Kelsey felt her face redden. "Yeah, I suppose that's true. And?"

Elise shook her head. "Not that we've seen. Terra is a mixture of dead megacities and land originally meant for growing food. I gather the Terrans don't feel comfortable coming out into the wilds with the AIs looking down from above. We've got at least a little separation from their obvious dwellings."

No one really had any idea how populous Terra was now. Once it had housed many billions of people, but those days had ended when the artificial despot in orbit had started the kinetic bombardment. Only a tiny fraction of the people alive before that event had survived the next year, she was sure.

That said, the ruined megacities might still house a lot of people, relatively speaking, even without power. How they'd grow food, Kelsey had no idea, but they'd seen some humans on the drone feeds, all scattered around the globe. And the AIs wouldn't have tried to exterminate a nonexistent population, which was what they'd thought Jared and his people were here to do, if there wasn't a significant number of people down here.

She still didn't understand why the machines wanted to kill the people of Terra. They had them trapped inside the system and had destroyed their civilization at least a century ago, based on the decay of the megacities and the amount of overgrowth that occurred since.

Humans were good at finding places to live. She'd seen that on Erorsi, and that had been worse than Terra. Whether they were savage or still retained some degree of civilization, Kelsey had no idea. That would come out in time, since she was absolutely certain that they'd meet people along the way to the Imperial Palace.

She just hoped they could avoid fighting them. There was no need for humans to kill one another when they had the sadistic computer over their heads that deserved their full attention.

That made her start worrying about how they'd get off Terra again once they'd succeeded. She wasn't even going to allow for the chance of failure in their mission. It was too important.

Still, once they had the override they'd come for, they had no way to get back into space. With both pinnaces wrecked, the only other ship they even had in the system was going to be unable to retrieve them.

Persephone had six fighters that she carried on her hull in makeshift cradles. Those weren't stealthed, so they'd be spotted if they tried to approach Terra. Even if they *could* make a few successful runs, they'd only get a couple of people off the planet before they were caught.

And say by some miracle that they did get everyone off the planet. There was still no way out of the Terra system. The far flip point that she'd used to get here was a restricted one. *Persephone* had been small enough to make it through, but the trip had been a one-way ride. There *were* other flip points leading out of the system, but the AI had them under heavy guard.

No, they were trapped here, unless Angela Ellis found a multi-flip point that the AI was unaware of. While that *was* still possible, Kelsey wasn't holding her breath.

Kelsey rubbed her face tiredly. Those were problems they'd have to deal with after they got their hands on the override. One major crisis at a time, please.

She was about to say something to that effect when Commodore Sean Meyer stuck his head out of the tent. "We need you inside. There's a problem."

"Of course there is," Kelsey muttered. "How could there *not* be?"

She allowed Elise to precede her inside. The tent held several small tables with portable computers that Jared had brought down from his destroyer before the AI had blown it to bits. They were being monitored by members of his crew.

"What is it?" she asked, already dreading the answer.

"I'll let Carl explain," the Fleet officer said, deferring to their friend.

The young scientist looked up from the computer where he sat at with a grimace. "We were monitoring the drone network that the admiral seeded. The one that the AI thinks distributed the Omega Plague.

"I was using it to look around our general area when everything went dark. I had to go back through the logs to find out what happened, but it seems the AI sent a destruct code into the network. All the drones are gone. We're blind."

Kelsey sighed and pinched the bridge of her nose between her thumb and forefinger. "I thought we had control of the network. How could the AI do that?"

Her young friend shook his head. "We had a hack into the system. One that the admiral's people inserted so that they could monitor and screen out information that they didn't want the AI to see. The AI still had access to the command codes.

"We probably should've planned for this, but no one locked the thing out. That makes sense, I suppose. If they had, the AI would've noticed the moment it sent any command and saw that nothing happened. That would have been... bad.

"As it is, we've lost the network monitoring everything going on around Terra, but the AI still doesn't know we're here. That's a win of sorts. Right?"

"It's just one more thing," Kelsey grumbled. "Why can't we catch a break? There's so much going on around us, and all of it seems to have a downside. Without the drones, we're not going to be able to see what's between us and the Imperial Palace."

Sean gestured for her to take a seat. "We may not have real-time data about what's happening between us and the Imperial Palace, but we did get a pretty good map compiled while the network was up, so it's not a total loss."

Kelsey took the offered seat and used her implants to link up with the computer in front of her. She had to admit there *was* a good bit of data about the terrain between them and the Imperial Palace.

They'd landed northeast of a dead megacity once known as Frankfort. It was still intact, though ruined and decayed. The Imperial Palace was built over a previously existing city once known as Albany.

Legend said that the corruption of the ruling elite in that place before the Imperial Period was so great that the people chose to raze it utterly, leaving no two stones standing together. That was the harsh judgment of history, indeed.

If they were to go in a straight line, the journey would be somewhat more than a thousand kilometers. Unfortunately, there were several abandoned megacities between them and their destination.

Those would be dangerous and time-consuming to deal with, so it would be best if they could simply avoid them. Since they'd be moving on foot, that was going to add at least five hundred kilometers to the trip. Probably more.

"Do we have *any* good news?" Kelsey asked somewhat plaintively. "Is *anything* going our way?"

Elise put her hands on Kelsey's shoulders and started massaging the stiff muscles of her neck. "Relax. This will make it harder, but we'll manage. Just breathe."

"You're usually the optimistic one," Sean said, leaning over the table directly in front of her. "Look at the upside. We're still alive and able to get to where we need to be. Don't let the scale of the march get to you. We've got to set small goals that add up to making it to the Imperial Palace. We've made it hundreds of parsecs. What's a few thousand kilometers more?"

"I suppose you're right," Kelsey said, slumping a little. "We've traveled across the freaking Old Empire to get to Terra, and now we're only fifteen hundred kilometers from the Imperial Palace. That *has* to count for something."

"On the bright side," Carl said, "you've been telling me I need to get more exercise. That's positive, right?"

"You think this sounds like an adventure?" she shot back. "I'll bet that none of us has marched a hundred kilometers, except for the marines. This is going to be really, *really* difficult in ways that we can't possibly begin to imagine. Mark my words."

"You're still not looking at the bright side," Carl said with a smile. "Pretty much everything that could go wrong, has. Everything should be easier going forward, right? What else could happen?"

The tent flap pulled back, and Talbot stuck his head in. "Kelsey, we've got a problem."

Kelsey wanted to scream but settled for shooting Carl a hot glare. "This is *your fault*. How could you have even *said* that?"

Without waiting for a response to her rhetorical question, she sighed, got to her feet, and walked over to her husband. "Show me."

2

Talbot led his wife out of the tent and into the stygian darkness that was night on Terra. His ocular augmentation could help with that, but Terra was *dark* at night, especially when the moon was down.

Major Adrian Scala was standing just a few meters away waiting for them. That officer gestured toward where the pinnaces sat. "The crash had more consequences than we thought, Colonel," Scala said to Kelsey, his lips tight. "The impact point where Pinnace Two struck Pinnace One was right where we had our weapons stored. Frankly, I'm astonished the munitions didn't blow up."

That wasn't good news, but it still made Talbot's lips twitch hearing the other man use Kelsey's marine rank. Anyone less like a field-grade marine officer would be hard to imagine.

His wife didn't see his reaction because she was busy rubbing her face furiously with both hands. "How much of a loss are we talking about here?"

"Just about total," Scala said tiredly. "We planned for the possibility of serious fighting, so we brought along a lot of gear. Most of that is gone. The marines have their sidearms and a few rifles, but only limited ammunition for either. The weapons and munitions for their armor are intact, but it won't do us much good long term. The armor won't have the power to get us very far."

"I already figured that out. How far will we be able to move the armor?"

"I'd expect we've probably got a couple of days of juice, and we might reach a hundred kilometers before they're done," Talbot said. "If we have to transport other gear, that's going to cut the range some."

"That's worse than I'd feared," Kelsey said after staring off into the darkness for a few moments. "We're going to have to carry what supplies we can away from here and stash them somewhere. It's possible the AI will see something down here that it doesn't like and nuke this area from orbit. Well, not using a nuke, but a rod from god is pretty much the same thing when you're on the receiving end."

Talbot had to agree that orbital kinetic bombardment *would* ruin their day.

"We'll salvage what we can," he said. "Frankly, I'm not certain that we're going to need to make more than one trip. We'll have to carry the majority of our supplies with us on our backs to the Imperial Palace, so we'll need to lean heavily toward food and other items that will get us to where we're going.

"One positive is that we'll be able to hunt along the way. This being Terra, almost everything that we run into should be edible. We'll be careful and test, just to be sure, particularly when it comes to plants. The animals should be good to eat, though, and we've got enough small arms to provide for food as we move."

He turned to face Kelsey. "I'm not going to lie. This is going to be hard. We'll be traveling light, and that means only taking what we absolutely have to. If you've never been on a long march—which I'm wagering almost no one outside the regular marines have—you'll have to be exceptionally picky about what you bring. A couple of extra ounces may not seem like a lot, until you have to pack it for fifteen kilometers. Or a hundred and fifty kilometers. Or ten times that."

"I second that," Scala said with a nod. "This is going to be particularly difficult for the scientists. They have no muscle for this, but they're going to have to come with us anyway, bringing whatever equipment they absolutely must have.

"*Everyone* is going to have to pull their share of the load. You're going to get a *lot* of complaints, and there's going to be plenty of cranky people."

"Wonderful," Kelsey said as she stared up into the sky. "Getting to Terra was supposed to *solve* most of our problems, not create a whole new set of them. Why is it that nothing goes as planned? Why can't *something* be easy? Did I offend the gods in some way?"

Talbot chuckled and put his hand on his wife's shoulder, pulling her into a hug. "You're doing everything right, Kelsey. That crash was *not* your fault. Circumstances sometimes conspire to put us in a bad place, but you've proven time and again that you can get us back out.

"This time is just going to be a little more... intense. Accept that the march isn't going to go as planned and that we're going to run into problems along the way. Probably some serious ones. At least we have the ability to scout all the way to the Imperial Palace with the drone network that the admiral seeded. That's a plus."

Kelsey made a show of rubbing her eyes. "Yeah, about that... It turns out that the System Lord sent the destruct signal into the drone network. It's gone. All we have is the data we collected before that. We won't be getting any real-time updates unless we bring drones of our own. Yet one more thing to haul along."

That *was* going to complicate matters, Talbot admitted. Still, his troops were used to carrying their required gear, and now that he was a Marine Raider, he could haul a lot more than he had before. He wasn't sure how that was going to work out over a long march, but this was going to be an interesting experience.

"Cheer up," he finally said. "We've overcome worse, and we'll beat this too. If we run into somebody along the way, we'll have enough weapons to take care of ourselves. Don't let this overwhelm you. Just stand up straight and take care of the problems as they happen. Improvise and overcome."

He checked his internal chronometer. They had roughly six hours until dawn.

"Adrian and I will continue going through the equipment we can salvage and get things sorted out. The marines will be beat by the time we're done, so we're going to have to catch a little sleep before we head out. Plan on us being ready by noon.

"You need to get some sleep, too. Once we start moving, we won't stop for more than eating and sleeping until we reach the Imperial Palace."

No matter how long that took.

* * *

JULIA—SHE was still struggling to remember to use that name for herself— sat in a dark tent next to Olivia West and watched Scott Roche as he slept on the cot the marines had set up for him.

She'd stunned him before all the madness, so that he couldn't take her place on the mission to fool the AI about their escape from orbit down to Terra. He was going to be *supremely* pissed about that when he finally woke up.

"I met your version of me," she said softly to the other woman. "Just for a little bit after we got down on the surface. After we crashed. She's... intimidating."

"You don't need to be frightened of her," Olivia said, shaking her head slightly. "Seriously, she's you. Parts of her story are different, but as a person, she's you."

It didn't feel that way to Julia. Here in a universe that wasn't hers, she felt like an outsider, even after she'd made the jump across dimensions. And now she'd met this universe's version of herself, and she was like one of those damned action vid heroes.

The woman had singlehandedly *crash-landed* a pinnace with *no engines*. There was no way that she could have done the same. No, even if she'd known how to pilot one, she'd have frozen up or screwed up and they'd all have died. What did this woman do? Pull off a damned miracle.

"I know," she finally said. "That still doesn't make it any easier. She's always so confident, so in command of the situation. We'd barely gotten the hatch open and she was shouting orders, getting people doing things that needed to be done.

"It was shocking. She's a *lot* more assertive than I am. I'm a church mouse by comparison. Give me something to research, and I'm happy. Put me in charge of people in a crisis? Not so much. I understand that I'm the crown princess of the New Terran Empire, but that doesn't mean I'm well suited for something like that."

Olivia chuckled and reached out to squeeze her arm. "Don't mistake Kelsey for something she's not, Julia. What you're seeing is a couple of years' worth of hard experience. Under the same stimuli, given the same time to grow into the role, you'd do the same.

"In fact, I think you've already started. Would you have had the courage to stand up to Commander Roche otherwise? I mean, you *did* stun him, after all."

Julia sighed. "He's going to be so mad about that. And you're probably right. Before all of this happened, I'd have deferred to everything he said. But if I'd let him go on this mission, I'm sure that both he and Mertz would be dead now."

She held up a hand to forestall any defensive response. "Don't get me wrong, I'm sure that Mertz is very capable. He just needed a little extra help to make his plan work. I'm just not convinced that Scott would've been able to provide that, no offense to him."

"Provide what?" Scott said as he reached up to rub his face. "Holy hell, my head is killing me." He blinked up at her for a moment, and then his eyes widened. "Did you stun me?"

Julia nodded. "I did, and I'm sorry. Doctor Stone said you're going to be fine."

"With the way my head is pounding, I'm not certain that I agree."

With an obvious effort of will, Scott levered himself up to a seated position and then groaned. "My head feels like it's about to fall off. Why the hell did you do that, Highness?"

She took a deep breath and let it out slowly. "Because you weren't the right person for the mission, and you wouldn't let me do what had to be done. I just short-circuited the argument. It's all over now."

Olivia stood and headed for the tent flap. "On that note, I should probably go check in with Sean. Why don't you two work out your issues in the privacy of your own tent, and I'll catch you later? Good to see you up, Commander Roche."

With that, Julia's new friend strode out of the tent and left them alone.

"I'm sorry, Scott," Julia said softly. "I really hate that I'm responsible for your pain, but it was necessary. If you'd gone, both Mertz and you would be dead right now. I'll give you all the details about what happened later, but his plan went sideways and only my augmentation allowed us to escape."

Her friend took a deep breath and let it out slowly. "Okay. I'll accept that. I'll even do you the personal favor of not pressing charges. After all, it would look really bad for a Fleet officer to bring assault charges against the heir to the Imperial Throne."

She smiled. "That *would* be awkward. Seriously, Scott, I didn't want you to die."

He looked at her face for a few moments and then reached out and took her hand in his. "Highness, it's my *job* to die if it means that you get to live. That's just the way it is. You're more important than I am."

"Bullshit!" she spat out, her anger suddenly blazing hot. "I'm not more important than *anyone.*"

"I'm afraid I'll have to politely disagree."

The two of them stared at each other for a few seconds before she looked away, her rage suddenly gone, making her feel empty. "I met the other version of me. She's kind of scary."

"Scary in what way?" Scott asked as he leaned forward. "Did she threaten you?"

Julia smiled at his suddenly aggressive posture. "No. She couldn't have been nicer. In fact, even after crashing the pinnace, I'd say that she was downright chipper."

Scott opened his mouth to say something and then closed it again before narrowing his eyes. "She crashed a pinnace. Would that happen to have been the *same* pinnace that *you* were on?"

"Yeah. Mertz is being treated for a concussion, but he survived. In fact, everybody survived. Well, other than the second pinnace, that is. I'm afraid she crashed hers into the other one and now we're basically going to have to walk to the Imperial Palace."

Scott stared at her for a moment and then laughed.

"It's *not* funny," Julia said with a scowl. "I didn't exactly bring hiking boots."

Her friend laughed even harder. "Oh, Highness, I know that I'm going to pay for this, but I can't wait to see you hiking. How far are we talking about?"

She shrugged slightly. "A thousand kilometers? Maybe more. I don't really know."

That shut him up. He sighed as he put his head back down into his hands.

"I guess I shouldn't be surprised," he said after a minute. "Nothing we do is *ever* easy. Why should this situation be any different?"

Julia stood and held out a hand to him. "Come on. Let's go get Doctor Stone to give you a look. I'll bet she can give you a shot to make that headache go away. Then we can get some food into you, while I explain why you need to call me Julia from now on. After that, we can try to get some sleep. Tomorrow is going to be a *long* day."

3

J ared woke to a light touch on his shoulder and found Lily Stone
hovering over him. That brought back the memory of the mad
escape from orbit and the destruction of his most recent command,
the rechristened Rebel Empire destroyer they'd called *Athena*.

That was two ships with the same name that he'd lost. He certainly
hoped they weren't coming out of his pay.

He'd woken sometime after Kelsey had crashed her pinnace and been
briefed about their current status, over Lily's grumbling objections, so he
wasn't as hyper this time.

Jared sat up, swung his legs over the side of the cot, and rubbed his face.
"What time is it?"

"Roughly an hour before dawn," the doctor said, brandishing a small
penlight. "I need to do one final check of your eyes, and then I'll cut you
loose. This is probably going to hurt a bit."

She flashed the light into one of his eyes and then flicked it away. She
did that several times on each side to see how his pupils reacted. The light
hurt, but not as much as he'd expected.

"I'd rather be up and about, but I do still have some pain," he said. "Is
that going to be a problem?"

"Your head is probably going to ache for a few days. I've taken care of
the worst of your symptoms, but without a full regen, you're still going to be
dealing with a few aftereffects.

"You're cleared for light duty, including hiking. No heavy loads until I
say so. Keep in mind that you're the commanding officer and can *delegate*. I
expect you to do so as much as possible."

"Yes, Doctor," he said with a smile. "As if Elise would let me overexert
myself."

He looked over at the cot his wife had been using earlier. It was empty. "Where did she get off to?"

"I sent her to get something to eat while I did the final checks. We'll need to do the same, as I understand that we're all going to be busy today. Kelsey issued orders that we're moving out by noon. I suspect we'd be leaving after breakfast if the marines didn't need some rest."

That made sense. If the marines had been recovering what they could from the crashed pinnaces all night, they wouldn't be in shape to march come dawn. He was certain that they could do it, if need be, but noon was good enough.

"I'll step out and let you get dressed," Lily said. "Once you're ready, we can head over and see what they've got for us to eat." At his nod, she rose and walked out of the tent.

Jared found his neatly folded clothes on a nearby stool, and he dressed quickly. All he had was his shipboard uniform and knew that wouldn't hold up over a long march.

The landing site they'd chosen was just a bit more than a thousand kilometers away from the Imperial Palace. That was under the best case. If they had to dodge around anything—like one of the abandoned megacities —that distance would increase.

His shoes were sturdy enough for shipboard wear, but not exactly made for traipsing about the wilds of a planet. Thankfully, they'd brought extra marine uniforms, including boots. If they'd survived Kelsey's epic crash landing, that was.

If Jared thought talking to his sister would make her stop doing that kind of thing, he'd do so in a heartbeat, but that seemed like a fantasy. In any case, this time wasn't her fault. The System Lord orbiting Terra had damaged the pinnace, and the crash had been the end result.

The second pinnace getting caught up in it might have been correctable with more experience, but he wasn't going to quibble. The situation was what it was.

Once he'd dressed, he stepped out of the tent and joined Lily. The night still held sway, but it was starting to grow lighter off to the east. The smells of the wild and the sounds of insects and other creatures were profoundly strange to him.

Together, he and Lily headed off to where the cooks had set up. He could already smell something in the air. A little bit of woodsmoke and perhaps the hint of some kind of food. He wasn't certain. It smelled like bacon, and he felt his stomach grumble. His last meal had been a long time ago.

To his surprise, Jared found most of the major players gathered near the cooks. Elise, Olivia, Sean, both Kelseys—Kelsey and Julia, he corrected himself—Commander Roche, and Carl Owlet were sitting around a lively fire. The only members of his leadership team missing were Talbot and Scala.

Everyone slid over just enough to make room for Lily and himself.

"I'm sure you're all wondering why I've called you here," Jared said with a chuckle as he sat. "Kidding aside, is everyone okay?"

The lack of smiles around the campfire told him that things were probably a little bit worse than he'd imagined. Putting aside his poor attempt at a joke, he looked around the group. "I can tell there's more bad news. Give it to me."

Kelsey filled him in on the loss of the drone network and the fact that the crash had cost them most of the small arms ammunition and rifles. That was bad news, but it could've been worse. No one had been killed, and they could still continue on to their target.

"I understand that this seems like an ugly blow," he said quietly. "But it's no worse than anything else we've faced along the way. In fact, this is far from the nastiest position we've ever been in. It's going to be a hard march, but we've got everything that we need to make it."

"How do we get off Terra once we're done?" Julia asked. "Let's say that everything goes smoothly—which I seriously doubt—and we make it all the way to the Imperial Palace and into the vaults below. Glory of glories, we recover the override. What then? We've still got to get off Terra and past the murderous AI in orbit. How do we do that?"

"We'll figure that out when we get to it," Jared said, keeping his voice calm and level. "The Imperial Palace is intact, so it's entirely possible that there are small craft underneath it. Ones that we could potentially use to get to orbit, if they aren't damaged or decayed beyond repair.

"Also, *Persephone* is hiding out in the system somewhere. Angela and her people will try to get us out if we call. We have the FTL link to them, though I don't want to use it unless we absolutely have to. The details of how we escape really aren't important right now because none of it matters unless we get the override, so let's focus on that."

He looked around the fire, meeting everyone's gaze. "We need to get to the Imperial Palace alive and in one piece. Once we get there, we'll get into the vault. I have the key and the right DNA, so I think that's going to work. Kelsey has all of the Imperial codes that an heir to the Imperial Throne would have, so if we run into anything unusual, she can get us in."

He gestured across the fire toward Julia. "Excuse me, I should have added that Julia does as well. Either of you could probably get us in. You both likely have the same set of authorization codes."

He held his silence until they'd all nodded. "It's going to be dawn soon, so we need to eat and start gathering what we need to take with us. Whatever we can't carry, we'll have to leave here, or transport to a safe location.

"I'm going to assume that the marines have deployed some of our tactical drones and that we have some potential cache points mapped out from the original drone network. Once the sun is up, I'll review all that and make some decisions on the route we'll take. I want to get away from here as quickly as we can manage.

"It's possible that the AI will discover the crash site at some point. If that happens, we can expect to be hunted. That won't be pleasant, so let's hope that the System Lord never learns that we've made it down to the surface alive."

He glanced toward the east. In half an hour or so, the sun would peek over the hills in the distance and their day would begin in earnest. It was the middle of summer where they'd landed, so it wouldn't be cold. On the other hand, he really didn't know how hot it was going to get. Or how muggy.

It really didn't matter. They'd have to march every day, and it was going to be grueling. He and his people would do what they had to. Adapt and overcome, as Talbot would say. They didn't have a choice if they wanted to save humanity from slavery at the hands of the AIs.

* * *

Julia stepped into the tent they'd been using for drone monitoring. The only person inside was Carl Owlet, who was busy tearing down the computers and packing them away. He looked up as she approached.

"Good morning, Highness. What can I do for you?"

She opened her mouth to ask a question but then paused. "I haven't said a single thing, yet you already know that I'm not your Kelsey. The regeneration on my face removed the scarring, and we look *exactly* alike, right down to our hair length. How did you know it was me?"

He smiled. "No one else—other than Talbot and Admiral Mertz—would be able to tell, I'd wager, but I'm the one who installed some of the extra hardware inside our version of you. Well, not personally. Doctor Stone did that, but I designed it. You don't have the same gear, so that means you're not my Princess Kelsey."

She found one of the folding fabric seats and sat slowly. "And you figured that out in just a few moments. Were you worried that I wasn't Kelsey and checked?"

He shook his head. "Not at all. The identification was almost subconscious. I have the same hardware installed inside myself as my princess does. That means my equipment recognizes her equipment on a deep level. It's almost like an electronic handshake. My implants use that to know which one of you I'm speaking with. I set that up when I found out you were visiting, as it seemed prudent."

She found herself smiling slightly. "That's very proactive. I've heard a lot about you, Carl Owlet. I haven't met you in my universe, but I sent a message home to find and recruit you as soon as I heard your story. One doesn't find a genius of your caliber every day."

He grimaced slightly. "I wish people wouldn't take things to that extreme. Yes, I'm smart. Yes, I'm plugged into the Old Empire technology. All that said, plenty of people could've done *exactly* what I did. I was just in the right place, at the right time, with the right know-how, and put everything together."

"Humble, too. That's a plus."

His brows furrowed. "Excuse me?"

Julia's smile widened slightly. "Oh, nothing. I'm just thinking about something that I mean to do when I get back to my universe. Basically, I'm making a mental checklist of how I need to approach my version of you to talk about… an alliance, shall we say."

"If other me is anything like me, he'll jump through hoops to help you."

"I certainly hope so. We could really use his help. I don't know if you've heard anything about the situation in my universe, but we're behind the eight ball. I picked that phrase up from your version of Kelsey, by the way. I'm not really sure where it comes from, but it means we're in a difficult place. A much worse place, really.

"We don't have the ships or technology that you do, and the Rebel Empire is aware of us. The AIs have already taken control of Pentagar, and it's only a matter of time before they come for Avalon. We're going to need every bit of help we can get."

Before he could respond, she waved a hand dismissing everything she'd just said. "Let's just leave that aside for the moment. I know Angela Ellis from my universe. I think with all of the changes that have occurred, she's basically filling the same role for me that your Talbot does for your version of me, minus the romantic aspects. I know her really well, and I have to say that I'd never have expected you to be her type. No offense.

"I understand that there's a lot more to you than meets the eye, not just in how you think and act, but that you've got grit, as Kelsey would say. That's important. Don't dismiss what you've done. It takes a lot of hard work to achieve success."

Carl shook his head. "Angela is a special case. She and I meshed under a weird combination of circumstances and pressure. I never expected anything like that to happen, and in your universe, I'd wager that other me is probably not going to get along with her very well at all. Are you trying to figure out if you can set up other me up with other Angela? Please don't."

She cocked her head slightly to the side and pursed her lips. "I'm not in the habit of playing matchmaker. My own love life is hard enough to figure out. For my part, I don't see me and other Talbot getting along the same way that Kelsey and he do here, for similar reasons. I'm not Kelsey. I don't think like her, even though I have the same implants, mostly."

She gestured around at the packed equipment, ready to change the subject. "Are we taking all this with us? It seems like an awful lot to carry."

He shook his head. "We'll leave most of it inside the crashed pinnaces. I'll probably pack one of the computers to take with us, just in case we need the extra computational power when we get to the Imperial Palace, but honestly, there's not going to be a lot of science on this mission. We'd hoped that we'd be able to examine a bunch of stuff there when we landed, but that's going to have to wait for another visit. If there is one."

With that, he gestured toward the tent flap. "I think we'd best get to where the marines are laying out the equipment. It's time to get some durable clothes and boots that are more suitable for hiking."

She nodded and stood, having made up her mind. This young man *was* worth further attention. He might *just* be who she needed. Of course, convincing other him of that might be a challenge, but she was willing to put out the effort for someone she now thought of as a warrior scholar.

By the time they reached the Imperial Palace, she'd know for sure if he'd make a suitable consort. No one could hide their true natures on a march as difficult as this was going to be. Over the next few months, they'd all find out how tough they really were.

And, just in case, Julia would make certain that other him and her Angela didn't meet before she'd wooed him. No matter what he said, she wasn't going to tempt fate. Her luck had been mostly bad for the last few years, and she'd be damned if she was going to blindly take that kind of risk.

Her Angela would just have to find someone else. Maybe she and other Talbot would make a good pair. Perhaps she'd have to try her hand at matchmaker after all, once the universe wasn't trying to kill her and everyone she knew.

4
———————

Talbot watched as Adrian and his marines assisted the Fleet personnel and civilians in adjusting their new clothes to fit properly. Thankfully, they'd done most of the measuring before they'd come down to the surface.

Adrian had known they'd be on Terra for a while and seen the problem of worn-out shoes and clothes coming. The standard marine loadout for deployment included one set of extra boots and a total of four uniforms, and that's what everyone now had.

Even back in the days of the pre-expedition New Terran Empire, Avalon had made some tough boots and clothing for their marines. The Old Empire had them beat, hands down. The footwear would survive the worst Terra could throw at them, and the fatigues were almost as durable.

He and Kelsey had arrived late to the party, but they'd also come prepared. He'd made certain to bring along his normal loadout and had forced her to bring the pack that he'd prepared for her.

Like his pack, hers didn't just contain fatigues and boots, but a complete marine basic kit. She'd moaned and groaned about having pinnaces to get them to where they'd needed to go, but he'd stood firm. Now he could smugly tell her that he'd been right, and she'd be forced to admit it.

He chuckled at his own joke.

This march was going to be hard on the Fleet personnel, but he was confident that they'd make it. The civilians, on the other hand, had him concerned. Scientists, as a group, were a bit on the sedentary side and not used to exercise or privation. There were exceptions, of course, but those folks were definitely rare in that particular population sample.

This march would involve juggling some priorities. The entire group was chained to their slowest person. That meant they'd need to speed up the weakest among them to a level that would get them to the Imperial Palace in a reasonable amount of time, without turning them into casualties.

And you could only push someone so far. He'd just have to accept that they wouldn't get to their target as quickly as he'd like. Of course, his standards on how long the trip should take were different than Admiral Mertz's. The flag officer might not realize how much faster marines as a group could march than the other shipboard personnel.

Adrian stepped over as Carl and Julia came over to the tables they'd set up so they could get their gear. Talbot eyed the woman that looked exactly like his wife. She didn't know him at all, and she certainly didn't care about him in the same way as Kelsey. It was weird and more than a little spooky.

He watched Julia as she headed into the ladies changing tent. Unlike the marines, whose members were used to stripping down and armoring up in a mixed gender environment—not that they were doing so out here in the open—the Fleet personnel and scientists still had body modesty, so they'd arranged for multiple tents for everyone to change in.

Kelsey had lost her body modesty years ago. Julia had not. One more difference.

"She's an odd one," Adrian said quietly. "She looks like our princess, but she's not the same woman. She doesn't think the same way as your wife. She's not as impulsive or outgoing."

Talbot had been shocked when Kelsey had finally told him that her doppelgänger from another universe was with Admiral Mertz. She'd found out over the FTL com but hadn't said anything to him until they'd arrived in the Terra system.

That annoyed him, but he could see how it was something that would get under her skin. They'd have to talk about it, once they had time.

He was going to have to get to know this other woman. She was a potential threat, and one that was close to Admiral Mertz. Adrian had admitted that he was worried about her in the same way.

The admiral had a habit of taking in strays. Of course, so did Kelsey. One of these days, that was going to bite them hard, and he wanted to be ready when it happened.

"Thankfully, we only have her and Commander Roche to keep an eye on," Adrian continued. "They've both behaved well so far, but they probably don't trust us very much, considering how Admiral Mertz in their universe was a traitor. Frankly, I'm amazed that Julia has come around to even considering that he might be different here."

"Are we certain that she *has* changed her mind?" Talbot asked slowly. "If I was among potential enemies and thought one of them was a murderous sonofabitch, I might be inclined to lie about how I felt about him, if it offered me an opportunity to get what I wanted."

Adrian shook his head. "The problem I see with that train of thought is that she went on the mission with the admiral *specifically* to get him down from orbit safely. Admittedly, he's the only one of us that has the Imperial

DNA to open the vault, but she went above and beyond. She could've let Commander Roche do the heavy lifting."

Talbot rubbed his face. "It's not exactly like we can do any kind of testing to see if she's a threat or not. That would require direct access to the AI we left on board *Persephone*."

The AI in question was Fiona. She had the same hardware as the System Lords, but with clean code and some additions that Carl Owlet had made. She was loyal to humanity and could use her special connection to an individual's implants—with their consent—to check and see if they were telling the truth.

Well, he'd just have to keep an eye on the woman. She might have the same implants as he and Kelsey did, but she wasn't a Marine Raider. Even if ambushed, he felt confident that his wife could tie the other woman into a pretzel without much trouble at all. She was, after all, a sensei in the Art.

The Art was a compilation of martial arts styles put together by the Marine Raiders of the Old Terran Empire. It favored his wife's small size, and she'd had the benefit of months of training at the hands of an experienced sensei before anyone else had even started learning it.

Ned Quincy had once been a Marine Raider himself. A fully trained one, and a master of the Art. One of the best in the Old Empire.

Kelsey had inadvertently created an AI version of him when she'd pulled a bunch of memory files into her implants from his body once they'd recovered it from stasis aboard *Persephone* when they'd discovered the ship in the graveyard around Boxer Station.

No one was exactly sure how she'd managed to create an AI inside her implants, but Talbot was glad that Carl had extracted the AI and put him into a holding computer back on the carrier *Audacious* while he figured out how to make an artificial body or computer that could handle the AI.

Having a third party in the bedroom while he made love to his wife was not his thing, even if the AI had sworn that he'd turned off all external sensory feeds.

At least no one had made a crack about him now having two wives, at least not in his hearing. He'd come down hard on an offender if they did. Again, not his thing, and even the thought was weird.

In that respect, he was very relieved that the other woman had no interest in him. Though, from the looks she'd just been giving Carl before they'd gone into their separate tents, he might have a problem there.

Which was also weird. And Angela had the skill and size to tie this other version of Kelsey into knots if she made any moves on the young scientist. If that happened, the fight would be short and brutal, so even though she wasn't here, Talbot would warn Julia to mind her manners.

"We'll just have to keep our eye on her," Talbot said in answer to what Adrian had said. "We don't treat her as an enemy, but we don't mark her as a friend either. As Kelsey says, trust but verify."

He turned and glanced toward the sun. "It looks like we have another couple of hours before we start moving. I want you to make one final pass over your people and make sure they have all of the critical equipment packed and ready to go. I'll do the same with the scientists and Fleet personnel. Once we start moving, we're not coming back for anything."

Adrian looked in the direction that they'd be marching. "What do you think we're going to run into out there? We know there are humans on Terra. Do you think we're going to have to fight them?"

Talbot chuckled darkly. "With our luck, what do you think?"

His friend muttered an expletive and turned to carry out his orders.

Once he was alone, Talbot considered what he'd just said. The chances that they'd have to fight someone on this march were high. He and his people would do it in a heartbeat, if that was necessary, but he'd like to keep the bloodshed to a minimum. The people of Terra had suffered enough.

He sighed. It wasn't as if he were going to be able to stop someone from becoming aggressive. All he could do was hope that they'd either avoid the worst-case scenarios or only have to fight the really bad people.

The best case would be avoiding both, but as he'd told Adrian, he was more than familiar with the kind of luck they had.

* * *

AFTER MARCHING in her armor for the rest of the day, Kelsey was glad that they'd stopped for the evening. The journey thus far hadn't been long—only about five kilometers—but doing it in armor was not something that she'd ever practiced. It chafed in odd places after a while. She'd need to rectify that at some point, but right now she was glad to be getting out of her gear.

Using the data that they'd gathered from the drone network before the AI had destroyed it, Jared had decided to stop at an abandoned building that was isolated from everything around it by kilometers in every direction.

It was low to the ground, somewhat small as a structure, and it didn't look like it had been abandoned for five centuries. That made sense since Terra had been captured intact during the rebellion. The AIs had treated it like the other occupied worlds of the Terran Empire, at least for a time.

If she'd had to guess, based on the decay and damage to the building, the AIs had started their orbital bombardment on Terra about a century ago. In a way, that was promising. It meant that they might still find functioning technology in locations that were well away from the megacities.

Or in the megacities themselves, if they were silly enough to try to go there.

Their best defense against being exposed to the AIs was not being noticed by anyone. To do that, they needed to steer clear of the remaining human population, so that meant it was best to avoid the former cities. They were here to save the people of Terra but needed to do so without their help.

Kelsey forced herself out of her introspective mood and looked back at the building. From the outside, it was impossible to determine what it had been used for. Once she got on the inside—down a wide ramp that led to a subterranean vehicular door that the marines had forced open—its purpose became clear.

It had been a place to store equipment used on what was likely once some great mechanical farming system. There were all types of automated machines in the large basement at the base of the ramp. They'd likely once performed their tasks without human intervention, for the most part. Now they sat alone in the darkness gathering dust.

A lot of dust.

The marines had chosen one corner of the large basement to use for getting out of their armor. It was clear of equipment but held racks of tools and spare parts.

Each marine marched his powered armor to a bare spot on the floor and climbed out before sealing it up again. It took very little time for them to get clear of their armor, since they were very practiced at the maneuver. Then they stripped off their skinsuits and put on regular marine fatigues.

Kelsey watched Julia do the same, though Talbot and Major Scala had to assist her out of her black Raider armor. Then Commander Roche held up a sheet so that the woman could strip off her skinsuit and dress in her marine fatigues.

The other woman obviously hadn't spent enough time around the marines to lose her self-consciousness about the process.

Kelsey got out of her armor as adroitly as the marines. She'd practiced the process long enough to build muscle memory. She turned her back to the Fleet personnel and scientists to avoid shocking them and stripped down to her skin before dressing in the marine fatigues that Talbot had packed for her. They fit perfectly, of course, but the boots and cut of the clothes still felt weird to her.

Once she was done, she faced the main group just as her brother started speaking.

"Everyone grab something to eat and drink," Jared said. "Settle in and rest. We'll be staying here for the night."

His announcement was met by a ragged cheer from the bedraggled scientists and even some of the Fleet personnel.

The scientists had been utterly unprepared for today and were worn out. What they didn't seem to realize was that the marines would be picking up the pace over the coming days and weeks. At today's rate of march, it would take them almost half a year to reach the Imperial Palace. That was completely unacceptable.

Of course, getting there late was better than never arriving at all, but Kelsey wasn't going to dawdle. Everyone—including her—was going to need to toughen up and do so quickly.

With everything that had been going on, Kelsey hadn't had a chance to talk to Julia in any detail. She needed to start the process tonight. She had to know how far she could trust the other woman.

Her other self seemed to feel the same way, because just as soon as she was dressed, Julia walked over to stand in front of her. "We need to talk."

"We do," Kelsey agreed. "Let's find a spot to sit down and eat while we do that. I'm starving and I'll wager you are too, if you're anything at all like me."

"I'm famished," Julia admitted. "I'm not looking forward to survival rations, but I'll take what I can get."

"You'll get used to them after a while," Kelsey said as she gestured toward an area behind the armor that was empty of people at the moment. "Shall we?"

5

———

J ared found a spot on the cold floor near Elise and sat. His wife was already watching Kelsey and Julia as they headed toward the corner of the cavernous room. The Fleet personnel had set up some portable lights, but most areas were still somewhat dark. That particular corner was almost lost in the gloom.

Before he could ask what Elise was thinking, Sean and Olivia joined them. Together, the four of them considered what they could see of the doppelgängers.

"It's really strange seeing them together," Sean said. "It's like double vision, only far more dangerous if they get excited."

Jared laughed. "Isn't that the truth? I don't think they've had a chance to really talk. What I wouldn't give to be a fly on the wall."

Olivia shook her head. "I don't think you would. I suspect some of this conversation is going to be rather raw. Julia has gone through a lot, and she's got some chips on her shoulder that Kelsey is going to have to help her knock off.

"That's not going to happen in a single sitting, but they're going to have to be frank with one another and say things that probably revolve around you. I'll bet those won't be complimentary, coming from your sister from another universe."

That sobered him up quickly. "Yeah, you're probably right."

He started handing out ration bars from a larger box that they'd brought with them. As he was doing so, Talbot joined them. They sat in silence for a bit until Jared forced his mind away from his sister and her double.

"How did we do on the march?" he asked the senior marine.

"The good news is that we didn't lose anybody to an injury," Talbot said. "The bad news is that I think a group of kindergartners would probably have moved faster. We're going to have to pick up the pace if we want to get to the Imperial Palace in a reasonable amount of time."

Jared nodded, but he wasn't really certain what the marine would consider "reasonable." He suspected that it would be far faster than what he'd use the word for.

"It took us roughly four hours to get five kilometers?" Jared asked. "If we stretched that out over the entire march, we're looking at close to five months, right? What pace do you think we should be doing?"

The marine took a bite of his ration bar and chewed with a thoughtful expression on his face. "That's a complicated question. Most of the crew didn't carry what the marines would consider to be a full pack. My people are basically overloaded right now, but they've trained for that. That's also slowing us down, so I'm not blaming the delay solely on the non-marines.

"If it was just the marines with normal loads, I think we could double today's speed. With the scientists in tow and my boys more heavily burdened, I'd be happy if we split the difference, so we could maybe make eighteen kilometers a day, once we get them in shape. That still means almost three months to get to the Imperial Palace, under the best case.

"Now, don't get me wrong. They did okay for the first day, but they're going to feel it in the morning. They'll have a lot of soreness and aching muscles. We don't want to push them hard enough that they injure themselves.

"I think it's best if we keep this pace for the next two or three days. Once they've adjusted to that, we can see about moving a little faster."

Elise rubbed her calf. "I think that I fall into the category of not getting enough exercise. I'm going to feel this tomorrow, just like the scientists. I can't say that I'm happy that I need to get this kind of exercise, but it's going to toughen me up."

Olivia nodded. "It'll be good for Sean too." With that, she poked her husband in the ribs.

He snorted. "I'm in better shape than you are. At least I get out every once in a while. You spend too much time behind your desk."

Her eyes narrowed. "You'd better watch it, mister. It's never a good thing when a husband is critical of his wife."

"Hey! That's what you just did to me."

She smiled innocently at him. "That's a wife's prerogative."

After a moment she smiled in a more genuine manner. "Seriously though, I think we're all going to be hurting in the morning, except for Talbot. He and his marines are going to be jogging circles around us while we slog for the next few days."

"I would never do that," Talbot said virtuously.

"Uh huh," Jared said. "In any case, looking at the map, it seems like we're going to be moving through some rougher terrain soon. There's a lot of forest scattered around in the direction we're heading, but I think this area used to be farmland. Even a century's growth means that the scrub and trees are fairly light. That's going to allow us to keep up a good pace.

"Unfortunately, about the time we'll finally be ready to march faster, we're going to run into what amounts to a real old-growth forest. That's going to slow us down again."

"Maybe not as much as you think," Talbot said. "When you've got larger trees, it cuts down on the light getting through to the undergrowth. That means less trouble moving around. We won't know for sure until we get close enough to put a few drones into the trees and take a look, but I'm hopeful that's the case.

"Honestly, I'm going to feel a lot better once we're under the tree cover anyway. That's going to make it a lot more difficult for anyone to spot us. Someone could use infrared to find us, if they have the technology, but a less advanced set of observers isn't going to be able to tell that we're out there, unless they run into us or our trail."

"And what happens when they do?" Elise asked. "We all know that's going to happen sooner or later, no matter how hard we try to avoid the people here. This *is* their home, and they know it far better than we do. If there are people in that forest, they're almost certainly going to find us before we know they're there."

That was one of Jared's worries. The inevitable confrontation with the locals. He suspected that they hadn't descended to savagery like the people of Erorsi. With any luck, they'd be dealing with people that at least had some of the trappings of civilization.

The Terrans had lived under the heel of the AIs for centuries before the System Lords began smashing their world. They'd only had a hundred years or so of being forced into primitive conditions, if the estimates were right.

As if a century was short.

In any case, he shouldn't minimize what had happened. Terra had once hosted a population in the many tens of billions. The death toll must've been horrific. These people would still carry the scars of their grandfathers and great-grandfathers who'd suffered and fought to survive in the wilderness, cast from the technological Eden that they'd been raised in.

"I don't think that we're going to run into a bunch of kindhearted strangers," Jared finally said. "These people have to be living hand to mouth, and that means fighting over resources. They're going to see other people as competition. We have to be ready for that.

"Everyone needs to get a good night's sleep, because we'll be getting up early. Talbot, set a watch to make sure that nobody gets the drop on us while we're stopped. Use your drones to circle around the area and keep an eye out for anyone sneaking up on us, and also have sentries out. Not that I should be telling you your business, mind you."

Talbot grinned. "No sir, you probably shouldn't. I've already got that all set up. We have drones in the air and scouts keeping an eye on the area. I've got a ready response team already in armor that'll back up the sentries if need be. We can only use powered armor tonight, but why waste the opportunity?

"Trust me when I say that we know our business. You folks can sleep easy knowing that no one is going to be giving us any trouble tonight. Not without a lot of warning."

"Good enough for me, Colonel."

Jared eyed the hard floor. It was made for supporting heavy machinery, so sleeping on it was going to be damned uncomfortable. The small pad that went under his sleeping bag would help a little, but not nearly enough, he was sure.

Well, there wasn't anything to be done about it. He'd best get some sleep and hope the rest of the trip was as uneventful as today.

The last thing he did before settling back and closing his eyes was give Kelsey and Julia another look. He knew that his sister didn't need nearly as much sleep as he did, but he hoped she didn't spend so much time getting to know her doppelgänger that she was overly tired tomorrow.

If things went sideways, they'd need her to be sharp. Her Marine Raider augmentation might just save their lives in a pinch. It had before.

With that thought, he closed his eyes, and sleep quickly overtook his exhausted mind and body.

* * *

JULIA SAT cross-legged on the stone floor, eating her ration bar—her third ration bar—and eyed Kelsey as she did the same. The woman from this universe was doing the exact same thing that she was, assessing her opposite. Only the other woman's expression was a lot more confident than she felt.

"This has to be strange for you," Kelsey said. "We've spoken a little bit over the FTL com, but that's not the same thing as what we're doing right now. We didn't know each other then, but we need to know each other now."

Julia felt her lips twitch up at the corners. "And exactly how do we do that? I feel I should already know everything about you, but I don't. Not really. Neither of us knows exactly who or what the other person is."

"No, we don't." Kelsey balled up the wrapper from the bar she'd been eating and stuck it in her pocket.

That was one thing that these marine fatigues had going for them. They had *lots* of pockets. As both a woman and a princess, Julia loved that aspect of these strange clothes more than anything. There were never enough places to stash things—like ration bars—in a regular uniform.

Or, God forbid, a dress.

"So how do we do this?" she asked the other version of herself. "We have the same goals, but we serve different people. You're here to help your empire, and I'm here to help mine. How do we mesh those two—potentially opposed—goals together?"

"By learning to trust one another," Kelsey said. "I understand that you're here because your people need to defeat the AIs. Believe me, I understand that better than most. I've already told you that we'll do everything within our power to help you, but you're right to worry. You have an entire empire counting on you.

"I've told you a little bit about how circumstances have treated me. I've heard a little about how you've gotten the short end of the stick. I suggest that we start talking about things from when we were kids. That would give us some common ground, and once we have that, we can move forward into talking about the present."

Julia sighed. She didn't want to spend any time discussing the past with herself. In fact, she *really* didn't want to.

"No," she said. "There's no need to discuss everything that's happened since I was a kid all the way through the present. It doesn't matter. What matters is that we're here now and that we have to work together. We've got to set boundaries, and we've got to figure out how we're going to help one another.

"I've already talked this over with Mertz. He said that once everything is done here and you've got the override, he'll send me with the key back to my universe. That's all fine and good, except that it's useless to me. I don't have anyone in my universe that has the right DNA, except for the Bastard. He killed off everyone even remotely related to my father. How do we get around that?"

Kelsey shrugged slightly. "I'm not going to let Jared go back to your universe and help. From everything you've told me, he's like a cartoon villain in your world. They'd string him up the moment they saw him, no matter what you said."

"My version of Mertz *isn't* a cartoon villain," Julia disagreed. "He's *much* worse than that. He's like you described Ethan from your universe, only not so crazy. Maybe he's just rotten to the core. Whatever he is, he'll kill whoever he needs to, and destroy whatever he wants, to achieve dominance over the New Terran Empire.

"Even as we speak, he's out there somewhere in my universe plotting and scheming to overthrow Ethan and take control of the Imperial Throne for himself. You're exactly right that it's not a good place for your Mertz to be, but that still leaves me with my problem."

Kelsey leaned back and looked at her. "Once we've taken care of the Master AI here, we can send the override with you. That way you don't have to make the trip to Terra at all."

"That may be the only real option I have," Julia agreed. "If my universe is anything like yours, I don't dare go to Terra. By now the AIs have delivered the Omega Plague and Terra is a death trap."

Kelsey blinked and opened her mouth to say something but then closed it again. After a few seconds, she nodded. "I hadn't considered that. Without you to stop them, there's nothing to keep the AIs from carrying out their plan, and we have to assume that's *exactly* what they did.

"I suppose that you could drop down onto the Imperial Palace inside a vacuum suit, but that's needlessly risking a horrible death. You'd still have to get past the System Lord and the automated defenses at the flip points, because you can be sure that they won't remove that kind of protection from the Terra system, even after they kill everyone off. Worse, there's no guarantee that they won't start setting up to replicate the massacre everywhere else as soon as they can."

They both sat silently for a few minutes. That was a lot to take in.

"With the Rebel Empire already having taken Pentagar in my universe," Julia said, "I think it's a given that they know about the New Terran Empire now. It's not going to be long at all before they have warships making the trip to Avalon. My version of Elise will try to keep everything quiet, but somebody is going to say something that tips them off.

"By the time we're done here, it might've already happened. Honestly, since I'm cut off from Pentagar, we don't even have a way to find out. We'll be operating in the dark once I get back to my universe, and I pretty much have to assume that the worst-case scenario has already played out."

Kelsey leaned forward and put a hand on Julia's arm. "Even if that's true, we'll still help. We're recovering ships all the time from the graveyard. I'd wager that Omega can get a portal open between the universes. After all, that's what he was created for.

"Since he knows where you're from, when he has enough power saved up, he can open an interdimensional portal and we could take a fleet through."

Julia shook her head. "Why would you do that? You've got your own fight here, and you're going to need every ship you can dig up. There's absolutely nothing that you can send across that's going to make my situation any better.

"I'm going to have to do everything I can to help you succeed here, because I'm going to have to take the override home to even have a chance at this. There's no other way this plays out for my people. Untold millions of them are going to die when the AIs invade the New Terran Empire. I just have to make their sacrifice *mean* something."

The com unit connected to Julia's implants made a tone in her mind to get her attention. It was an alert.

"All marines, this is Talbot," her doppelgänger's husband said. "We've got unknown people in the vicinity of the building. Everyone not already outside, gather up at the ramp. If they decide to come our way, we're going to have a confrontation."

Kelsey smoothly rose to her feet and jogged toward her armor. "The ready response team is already armored up, so let's go help them. At least this time we can have powered armor to curb stomp anyone that really wants to push the issue of our trespassing."

Julia rose and followed the other woman, already humiliated that she was going to have to ask for help getting into her armor. At least if there ended up being a fight, it would be brief and maybe let her release some of the tension that had built up inside her.

She really didn't want to fight anyone. She wasn't a warrior, and she hated the idea of hurting or killing anyone. If she could have, she'd have sat this fight out.

But she couldn't because she had Raider augmentation, and that might make a difference in keeping some of the marines from being hurt or killed. If it came down to the other people or her allies, she'd kill the intruders and suffer for it later.

6

———

Talbot stepped out onto the ramp and joined the ready response team. Like him, they were in powered armor, minus their helmets. The rest of his on-duty marines were scouts, backing up the drones that watched in every direction.

Corporal Elena Boske, the ready response team leader, turned toward him, her short pink hair looking strange in the dark with his enhanced vision. "The unknowns are about five kilometers south by southwest of our position. Based on the path that they're taking, they'll pass about a kilometer away from our current location."

He nodded. "We can't count on them continuing on that course. If they divert, they can be here pretty quickly."

"Faster than you'd think, sir. They're on horses."

He blinked in surprise, though he wasn't sure why he should be shocked. Terra was the home of horses as well as humans. There were a lot of horses on Avalon. It had been a vacation world in the Old Terran Empire, after all. He wasn't sure how common they were elsewhere.

Personally, he'd never learned to ride. He wasn't sure that he knew anyone that had. Horses were either working animals on farms or the province of the wealthy on Avalon. Maybe Kelsey knew how to ride, but he wasn't sure many others in their party did.

"What speed are they traveling at?" he asked as he checked the feed for himself.

"A slow walk," she said. "While their speed varies, it doesn't look like they're hurrying, and that makes sense as it's dark. I'm surprised they're moving under conditions like this. I'm more than a bit worried that they'd like to use this building to set up a camp until dawn."

"There's no sign of anybody having been inside the building," Talbot argued. "While they could be coming here, I'd think the odds are that they're not. Does it look like they have a destination in mind, based on the maps we currently have?"

"They're headed for the pinnaces," Kelsey said from behind him. "If you expand the map out a little bit, it's obvious that's where they're going. They probably spotted me coming down. It wasn't like I was being subtle or anything."

No, she certainly hadn't been. At the speed they'd come in, the crashing pinnace had probably been a streak of fire across the sky, visible for quite a distance.

A check of the path that the riders were taking confirmed that they were on the way to the crash site, with his implants giving that option better than a seventy percent chance. They'd find everything he and his people had been forced to leave back there, too.

Worse, they'd be able to follow the trail their people had made right back to them.

"They're going to catch up with us," he said grimly. "Even if they spent a few days at the crash site—which we can't count on—those horses can make up the distance in a day."

His wife nodded. "They won't spend a lot of time there. They might leave some of their number to search the wrecks, but they'll come after us. We're probably in their territory, and they'll want to deal with us as quickly as possible.

"On the plus side, that means we can wait for them here and get this over with while we still have the armored marines as backup when I talk to them. We don't know if they'll end up being friends, foes, or just people that want nothing to do with us, but we have to assume that they're not going to be very friendly when they catch up with us.

"These people are survivors. It may have been generations since the AIs blasted them from orbit, but those memories are still going to be very sharp for them. There's plenty of resources on Terra, but if you're being watched and hunted, you don't feel like you can gather them. That means they're going to see us as a potential threat, and they're going to want to deal with us as such."

Julia, who'd come up behind Kelsey, looked uncertain. "Are you sure that you're the right person to talk to them?"

Kelsey shrugged. "I'm the one with the most experience at that sort of thing. I'm also the one best suited to deal with any hostilities, if they break out.

"According to the drones, these people are carrying knives, swords, spears, and bows. That doesn't mean that they don't have access to something more advanced, mind you, but I'd imagine charging something like that would be a screaming bitch.

"On the plus side, I'm not very threatening. I won't be perceived as a serious threat. Unless I want to be."

That made Talbot go back to the drone feed and start counting the riders. There were thirty-three humans and roughly double that number of horses. He couldn't tell whether the spares were meant to be packhorses or remounts to allow the riders to travel longer distances without having to stop.

In any case, the fact that they were traveling at night probably meant something as well. Maybe they were afraid of being observed. Perhaps assuming that these people were the ones who ran this area was a mistake. If these folks were raiders, then his people might be sticking their heads into an inter-clan rivalry of some sort, and that could get ugly.

"A thought just occurred to me," he said before explaining his theory.

Kelsey nodded slowly once he'd finished. "That's something we have to keep in mind. We know absolutely nothing about the situation on the ground. These people could be here to steal whatever they can get their hands on.

"Which doesn't mean that they're bad people. Tribes raided one another on preindustrial Terra all the time, and that didn't necessarily mean they were evil. That's just competition for resources. Raiding isn't quite war, after all."

She then tilted her head back a little, and her eyes went unfocused for a few seconds. "They're not curving toward us, so they'll be at our original camp within two hours. That's going to be slightly before dawn.

"I think I should take a team of people and meet them there. That'll give you time to set this place up in a more defensible manner. If I take marines in suits, we can get there fast. Not as fast as horses, but we'll have plenty of power to fight if we need to."

Talbot didn't approve of her going, but he'd learned the hard way that trying to convince his wife not to carry out any plan that she'd set her mind to was doomed. He might as well see that she was as well protected as he could, since she was going, one way or the other.

"Another thing we have to worry about is that this might not be the only group we'll have to deal with," he said. "A lot of people could've seen the pinnace on its way down. If so, we might have more people showing up tomorrow.

"We can get some drones out to cover part of the area, but the smaller ones don't have the range to cover all avenues of approach. You'll have to be very careful not to get caught up in someone else's fight, Kelsey."

He turned to Boske. "Split the ready response team. Everyone going with the colonel needs to be ready to travel light and perhaps be separated from support for a couple of days. The rest of us will be ready to receive you, if things go sour and you have to come back here in a hurry. I hope that doesn't happen, because that could mean that we're going to have to fight every step of the way to the Imperial Palace."

His wife shook her head. "I think the chances of us going undetected have passed. Hell, they probably never existed at all. We need to find some friends and learn the lay of the land. Knowledge, as they say, is power."

"Be careful, Kelsey," he said quietly as he stepped over to her side. "If things go badly, we won't be able to get there in time to help you. You'll be fighting with only what you can bring with you."

"I can handle this," she said softly, running her hand across his cheek. The cool metal of her gauntlet wasn't anything like her hand, but it was still gentle. "No matter what happens, I'll do whatever I have to do to get us to the Imperial Palace."

Of that he was certain, even if it put her into deadly peril. He knew there was nothing he could do to change her mind, so he could only hope that she took fewer chances than she usually did this time around.

A hope he was virtually certain was doomed to disappointment.

* * *

KELSEY STARTED GETTING pushback even before they'd set off for the crash site. She'd made the decision that she wouldn't be wearing her armor for this meeting and gotten immediate pushback from her doppelgänger.

Even as she was stripping her Raider armor off and handing it to one of the other marines to carry for her, Julia was telling her just exactly what she thought about that idea.

"This is idiotic," the other woman said, somewhat waspishly. "The odds of them shooting you are really high. Why would you willingly take away your best defense?"

Kelsey didn't answer immediately, settling her weapons belt around her hips and double-checking that all of her guns were fully loaded, well seated, and ready for action. That done, she settled her sword harness securely on her back.

"The mistake you're making is thinking that my armor is my strongest defense," Kelsey said calmly. "It isn't. My strongest defense is not being shot at in the first place. If they see some metallic monster coming at them, they're going to react in a manner that I think we'd all consider extremely hostile. Admittedly, I wouldn't be in any danger from the kind of weapons we've seen thus far, but convincing them to be our allies in this is my primary goal.

"If they decide to shoot first and ask questions later, I can handle that. They're not going to lay in a flight of arrows at me all at once, because one woman is not going to be that threatening, particularly if I walk in with my hands conspicuously empty. Any rational being will want to talk before they engage in violence."

"And what makes you think they're rational?" Julia responded with a scowl. "We don't know them at all. They might be cannibals. There's no telling what they'll consider a reasonable response to this."

"I'll grant you that point. That's why you and the marines are going to be just out of sight, ready to respond if things go badly. I'd much rather settle this cordially, but I'm not going to put myself at undue risk.

"If they want to fight, my Raider augmentation will be more than sufficient to get me clear before they can hit me. Then we can figure out the best way to respond."

She could tell that Julia wanted to argue, but she didn't. The other woman simply raised her hands in a show that she'd given up.

"Fine. It's your life. I can't control what you're going to do, and you probably have a better idea of how this is going to work out than me anyway. That's your call, but we still have to get there over some pretty rough terrain. Are you sure you're up to running through that stuff in the dark without armor?"

Kelsey nodded and smiled slightly. "We've already been over this terrain once. We're just going to go back in the same direction that we came from. I don't remember any unexpected ravines along the way that might trip me up, and my eyesight's pretty good. So's yours.

"If we utilize our Raider augmentation and tune the ocular augmentation so that we're using both infrared and ultraviolet, as well as the normal sight range, that should give us a pretty good idea what we're going to face. It's good practice for what we'll need to do once we don't have our armor with us."

She rested her hand on the other woman's shoulder. "Relax. We'll keep it slow and easy. As long as we get there soon after dawn, I think everything's going to be fine. Coming in during the daylight is probably better in any case. If they can clearly see me, they're less likely to start shooting at shadows."

She checked her internal chrono and made the decision. "We need to get moving. While they're busy examining the crash site, there'll be less of them ready to respond to my arrival. I'd like to let them notice me on their own, without me making a lot of noise to get their attention. Drama might look good on the vids, but it just makes people react hastily and do things that we'd all regret. Let's do this slow and easy."

Kelsey shared a few words with Jared and Talbot before they headed out. Neither one of them outright told her to take every precaution imaginable, but she knew that they wanted her to be careful. She'd do her very best and see what the circumstances brought.

The trip back to the crash site wasn't too hard. There were a couple of times that she stepped where her footing wasn't that certain, but they arrived near the crash site just before the sun began peeking over the horizon without any injuries. They'd made excellent time. Better than she'd hoped. The marines really could move quickly when they needed to.

Corporal Boske dispatched some short-range drones to take a look and began determining what the locals were up to.

"It looks like they've put all of the horses into a picket together off to the side," the pink-haired woman said after a few minutes. "There are a couple of people keeping an eye on them while everyone else is either moving through the tents or circling around the pinnaces. I count maybe a dozen people keeping watch over the camp as a whole.

"If you approach along the path that we made departing, you're going to encounter two of them. I don't see any concealed sentries, so I'm not worried about an ambush. Whatever their response is going to be, we'll be able to see it coming."

"Sounds good," Kelsey said. "Now remember the plan. I'm going to walk up on them slow and easy, then they'll undoubtedly take me into custody. As long as they're not being overtly violent, just let it happen.

"Once I'm their prisoner, they'll be more inclined to at least talk with me, if only to get me to answer some pointed questions. We need information, and these people are the best source we've found to get it."

With that, Kelsey left the marines to settle into good locations to either act as snipers or to rush in to defend her as she retreated. She really hoped that none of that was necessary, but she wasn't ruling it out. She'd been in situations that she thought would work out one way and seen them go completely wrong. She'd play this by ear and see what happened.

If she got lucky, they might find some allies that would tell them what lay ahead. If she got unlucky, she'd get into a fight.

Well, time to see how her luck turned out this time.

She walked into the area around the pinnaces about ten minutes later. The sun wasn't behind her, but it was near enough that she got damned close before the guards spotted her. Both of them raised bows and covered her with their arrows while shouting for her to stop in recognizable Standard.

She did so in as relaxed a manner as she could and kept her hands out to her sides with her palms exposed.

"I'm not here to fight," she said almost conversationally. "I just want to talk."

Before they could respond, her internal com came alive. *Kelsey, this is Talbot. Our drones just picked up a large group coming from a different direction. It's about three times the size of the group you're looking at, and they look pretty pissed off. They're riding hard and should be at the crash site in about half an hour. Maybe this isn't the best time to initiate contact.*

It's a little late for that, she said dryly. *I'm already talking. Maybe we're going to need some of that backup you were talking about after all. Work with Jared to figure out what the best response is if there's a fight, because it certainly sounds like there's going to be one.*

I don't know which side I should be fighting with, but I'll do my best to figure that out before the others arrive. Try to get me any information you can on them while I deal with the situation here.

Will do. Make friends fast, or they might think you're with the other party. That probably wouldn't be helpful. You might also be able to use the impending attack to get them to see you more as an ally.

I'll see what I can manage, she said as one of the guards approached her warily. *I have to go. Our new friends need my full attention, and I need to pass the word to Corporal Boske so she can prepare. Don't do anything hasty, okay?*

Who? Me? I would never cut into your act.

His quip made her smile, which it probably wouldn't hurt to allow the man coming her way to see. Her humanity and passivity would help speed this along.

She could've let Talbot warn Boske himself, since the armor had the com range to reach him, but this was her fight to coordinate. She needed to do so quickly, because time wasn't on her side and there were so many ways things could still go wrong in the next few minutes.

Boske, she said over the short-ranged com, *we have about ninety incoming horsemen. It sounds like they're not going to be hugging things out with this group or us. Work that into your plans and be ready to give me some cover if things go south. Things just got complicated.*

7

J ared thought about Kelsey's unfolding situation and considered sending the rest of the ready response team after her but rejected the idea. There was no way they could get to the area around the pinnaces in time to make any difference, and they might need them here. If his sister broke away from the first group and avoided the new people completely, she and the marines could make their stand in powered armor and not be in any significant danger.

He'd leave Talbot in charge of the tactical situation while he focused on the strategic. They now had two separate sets of players, and he needed to know as much about them as he could before they started shooting at his people or each other.

"Talbot, what do we know about the second force?" he asked the marine when he stepped out onto the ramp.

The sun was over the horizon, and the scent of the air seemed to be changing in a way he couldn't describe. As a Fleet officer, he'd never been one for camping, so nature was going to take some getting used to. He approved of the cool breeze coming in from the northwest, though. It somehow smelled of water.

The marine officer shared a virtual display with him. It showed a map of the general area, and part of the lower screen was taken up by video from one of their drones. It showed a large force of people on horses, moving quickly over open ground.

They had a determined look about them and were moving very fast. He also noticed that they didn't have extra horses like the first group had come with.

"My guess is that the second group is responding to the intrusion of the first," Talbot said. "You'll notice that they don't have any remounts. They know exactly how far they're going to go, and they don't expect to do a whole lot of riding after that. They're running toward a fight."

That didn't sound promising.

"What kind of scenarios are we looking at?" Jared finally asked. "Should we be getting everyone ready for a forced march?"

"We wouldn't get there in time to make any difference. Kelsey and her people have powered armor, and if they get caught in crossfire, they'll be able to take care of themselves. Even if somebody out there has advanced weaponry, our people are trained and ready to deal with them. They'll be fine.

"Our best plan of action is to position ourselves to deal with the fallout. Let's say the worst-case scenario happens and the two groups start fighting and catch our people in between them without us being able to determine who the good guys are. The marines will be able to put down any direct attacks. What we need to worry about are the political consequences.

"Or I should say, that's what *you* need to worry about. I'm setting my people up to make this building more defensible in case there are *other* groups out there coming to see what all the fuss is about."

Jared didn't like thinking that his sister was outside his ability to help, but she was more than capable of taking care of herself. She wasn't the same woman that had started out with him on the original expedition. She was tough, resourceful, and more than capable of shooting back at someone that wanted to make her a target.

Her doppelgänger could handle herself in a fight too, he suspected. Julia was tough, even if she didn't think so. What really concerned him was the fact that there might be more than one group making for the crash site. While he hadn't been on the ground when Kelsey crashed the pinnace, Jared was certain that she'd made *quite* a show coming in.

If it had been as visible as he suspected, anyone within a hundred kilometers or more might know about their presence. If that was the case, the wrecked pinnaces might become the center of attention for a large number of potentially hostile groups. That could lead to a brawl that he desperately wanted to avoid becoming part of.

"Is there any way we can minimize the chances that they're going to track us to this building?"

"I'm not sure how," the marine officer said. "We had a lot of people hiking through the tall grass to get here. That's going to leave the kind of trail that *anyone* can follow. Add in the marines in armor, and the arrow pointing directly at us is unmistakable. Since they know where we landed, they won't have any difficulty zeroing in on us."

So, anything they left here was likely going to be taken as loot. Perfect. They might as well have left it all at the pinnaces and tried to make better time.

Worse, even after they left this place, anyone that came across their trail would be able to track them down and attack them at will. He had to figure out if it was even possible for them to evade discovery by the locals. If not, this mission might be over long before they made it to the Imperial Palace.

"What about once we leave?" he asked slowly. "If we abandon everything except the absolute essentials, are we going to be able to get our people off the radar of any pursuers?"

"Possibly." His brother-in-law didn't sound optimistic. "The forest isn't that far away. Once we get there, there'll be a lot of undergrowth and overhead shielding that will help. There are things that we'll be able to do to disguise our tracks and to minimize our trail. Once we've done that, it might be possible to break contact with any pursuers, though I wouldn't count on things being that easy.

"A more likely scenario is that we can have the majority of our people go into the forest while some of us hang a little bit behind in order to dissuade anyone on our six. If we can show them that chasing us is a bad idea, they'll stop.

"Hell, if Kelsey makes a big enough impression on the people back at the pinnaces, they might not pursue us at all. It's going to depend on how things work out there."

"What can we do to support her?" Jared asked. "I doubt she's going to be challenged to the point that she needs to retreat, but that situation could turn into a bloodbath for the locals.

"Just the fact that there are two sets of unknowns coming in means there's almost certainly going to be a fight. If we add in other groups, there's going to be a war over the crashed pinnaces and anything they can salvage from them. How do we deal with that?"

"We're going to have to let Kelsey do what she does," Talbot said simply. "That boat has sailed."

Jared could almost hear the marine's mental shrug. He was right though. The best they could hope for was that Kelsey found them some friends. If they could turn one of the local groups into allies, that would make their mission a lot easier.

If they made nothing but enemies here, that was probably going to be a death sentence for them, the mission, and the human race. He'd just have to hope that Kelsey did all the right things because she was the one on the ground and she'd be making the calls.

He trusted her, but her track record was a bit daunting. She might succeed and *still* give him grey hair. And that was if everything worked out.

If not, well, things would really get ugly really soon.

* * *

JULIA CURSED under her breath as Kelsey passed on the warning about the new group. This was *just* what they hadn't needed. More incoming natives and what certainly looked to be a brewing fight.

With ninety potential hostiles inbound, it was a virtual certainty that they'd be fighting very shortly. The group inside their former camp was going to defend it against this new set of people, and her doppelgänger would be right in the middle of it.

The possibility that someone would shoot her out of hand with one of those arrows or stick a sword through her was *very* high. If they came to the conclusion that Kelsey was somehow connected with the people attacking them—maybe assuming she was a distraction—they'd do their level best to kill her.

Julia wasn't certain how her doppelgänger could talk her way out of that, but she hoped that she could.

Meanwhile, she and the marines had to deal with intercepting the incoming hostiles—if that's what they really were—while still keeping an eye on Kelsey. They didn't have the numbers for that, and they were going to have to improvise. Thankfully Corporal Boske seemed to be very competent.

The pink-haired marine called everyone on the short-ranged com channel and informed them that the situation had just gotten ugly. She passed along the details of the incoming force, which wasn't much. What they *did* know was that with ninety-odd hostiles incoming and thirty inside the camp, they were looking at worse than ten-to-one odds if all of the horsemen turned on them.

Even with powered armor that rendered them invulnerable to primitive weapons, there was going to be a lot happening.

The corporal turned to her. "What's your plan, Highness?"

Julia felt her eyes widen. "I'm not a good judge of military tactics, Corporal. You'd be better off making the decisions on how to deploy your troops than me."

"One learns by doing, Highness. The colonel told me to run anything past you, so that you can improve your education on combat-related matters, time permitting. How would you allocate our people to meet the incoming force and still provide cover for Colonel Bandar?"

Everyone knew that she wasn't a warrior, so why did they keep trying to turn her into one? It was damned irritating.

Rather than argue, Julia accessed the map of the crash site and looked for areas they could use to provide extra cover and concealment. There were some low hills scattered around the area, but most of them weren't close enough to provide effective covering fire for her doppelgänger.

The marine weapons could hit someone at quite a distance, but precision when you had someone you wanted to keep safe mixed with potentially hostile individuals was a more complicated matter.

She accessed the data that her doppelgänger had sent and saw which direction the new forces were approaching from. There were a couple of hills off in that direction that were fairly close to the camp. Those could provide concealment for a few marines without difficulty.

Also near that side of the encampment, there was a single rise that was close enough to allow for a sniper or two to keep the people inside the compound under observation and still be of use against the incoming force.

The beginnings of an idea started percolating, so she sent the map to the corporal with updates.

"These two hills can hold a couple of marines each, ready to respond once the larger force gets past them and closer to the camp. The smaller rise right here can hold some snipers that can keep an eye on Kelsey or the others as the situation requires.

"If the incoming troops pass between the hills like it seems they're going to, they'll be trapped between them and the camp if we decide to fight. With our superior armor and weapons, we should be able to use that constrained space to cause a lot of damage in a short amount of time."

The corporal nodded. "That's a solid plan, Highness, though I'd move the snipers out of the pinch zone. Also, those hills are close enough to the camp that the first group might send a lookout or two of their own, after they process that they might have more than the colonel for company. What do we do if individuals from inside the camp attack her?"

"Kelsey has to be our primary responsibility. If she's in any danger, then we need to neutralize those threats. She'll be able to communicate with us, so she can tell us what's happening inside the compound.

"If she thinks she's safe enough, then we can hold off unless there's an overtly hostile action to respond to. If someone looks like they're going to shoot a bow at her or stick a sword in her back, the snipers can take those individuals out. Otherwise, we need to leave what happens in the camp in her hands.

"The biggest unknown is going to be how the first group reacts when a force three times their size comes racing in on them. Once the second group arrives, we can be pretty sure that the fighting will start.

"These folks don't seem like they're going to be old friends. I hope that I'm wrong, but the second group isn't moving like they're expecting to join somebody for lunch."

Boske chuckled. "I think you've read that just right, Highness. Your basic plan is sound enough. What about our mobile units? We're going to have to get mixed up in the fighting to bring a conclusive end to the engagement. We've got nine people in armor, counting yourself.

"If we put four on the hills to be our backstop against this new force, put two on this rise to act as snipers, that leaves three of us: you, me, and one of the other marines.

"We're going to have to be the hammer that hits the anvil. Just shooting into a group of hostiles isn't going to be enough. You've got to be able to fight hand-to-hand and break their will, or you're not going to be as effective in stopping them as you'd like to be."

The corporal turned and stared out over the grasslands. "I know you don't like fighting, Highness, so I'm going to leave the choice up to you. Where in all of this mess do you want to be?

"Personally, I don't think you're the right person to be part of the blocking force on the two larger hills. You could act as one of the snipers on the closer hill, but I'm still not really sure that's what you're cut out for. Do you have the type of precise fire capability a sniper would need? Can you hit someone next to the colonel without hitting her? Could you even do that kind of thing? Killing at long range is a cold-blooded business."

Julia considered that and thought she could probably do it, but it would require her to allow her implants to control her actions while firing, something she was loath to do. And the corporal was right to doubt she had the mental fortitude to do something like that. Could she kill someone like that, without being in danger herself? She just didn't know.

After a few moments, she shook her head. "I think somebody else would be better suited to that task."

The corporal nodded. "Then you, me, and the remaining marine are going to be the mobile force. If the fighting kicks off like I expect, we're going to drive a wedge into the larger force to keep it back from the camp.

"We don't really know who the bad guys are, so we're going to lead this off using stunners. We may need to resort to heavier weaponry, but there's no need to lead off with indiscriminate killing. The snipers won't fire unless lethal force is called for.

"We've got the tools to take the second force down. If we set the stunners on wide aperture, even with mobile enemies on horses, we should be able to take out at least half their force before they get their act together. Then we have to go to tighter beams and hit targets that are farther away. Targets that are probably going to be trying to retreat.

"Horses are faster than we are, even in armor, though I'm not so sure when it comes to Raider armor. If somebody breaks free, do you think you could chase them down and stop them?"

"I'm pretty sure that I can catch up with a few of them when the horses start tiring," Julia said. "They can't keep up that kind of speed for very long, whereas I can do so in the armor without too much trouble.

"The problem is going to come in when they split off in multiple directions. When they do that—which they will—there's no way that I can catch up with everybody."

The corporal nodded. "We can only do what we can, Highness. Stick close and be ready to start stunning people when I give the order. And by the way, that was a pretty good battle plan. I think you're better at this than you give yourself credit for."

Julia watched the corporal marshaling her forces and dispatching them to the positions she wanted. She disagreed with the other woman's assessment of her, but it was hard to miss the fact that she'd worked out a plan that would effectively deal with this large a force.

She was going to have to think things over again. She'd never be a Marine Raider, but maybe she could play one on TV, as her doppelgänger said. Whatever that meant.

Meanwhile, they needed to be ready to fight. Kelsey's life depended on them. She wished the other woman luck in convincing the smaller group that she was friendly in the roughly twenty minutes that she had before all hell broke loose.

8

The two men held Kelsey at arrow point while they summoned others to search her for weapons. Which, of course, they found in plenty.

They seemed to know what the pistols were and treated them with due care, so that told her that these people were aware of how dangerous those kinds of things could be. Not a primitive people, just like she'd suspected.

There turned out to be unexpected danger when they took her swords. One of them drew a blade and was about to flick a finger across the edge when she held up her hand and drew a tense response from the people with the bows.

"I wouldn't do that if I were you," she said. "It's a *lot* sharper than it looks, and you could severely cut yourself without trying."

The sword blades had an almost monomolecular edge and could cut through just about anything, if used with enough force. If somebody applied too much pressure, they'd cut themselves to the bone or perhaps even lop off the tip of a finger entirely.

Since that wouldn't be productive for anyone, Kelsey preferred to keep her captors from maiming themselves on her weapons and developing a grudge or starting some kind of blood feud based on them not knowing how to treat her weapons.

The man she'd spoken to eyed her for a moment and then pulled his hand back from the weapon. He slid the sword back into the sheath and placed the harness with her other weapons. None of them had said anything to her, other than the calls for her to stop moving. They were obviously waiting for someone to come and take charge.

That someone else turned out to be an exceptionally tall, well-built woman with an extremely dark complexion. She'd have towered over even Angela, who at two meters, was very well-built herself. This woman was at least a head taller than *Persephone*'s commanding officer, and that meant that she towered over Kelsey by an obnoxious degree.

Like Angela, the new woman appeared to be a warrior. She wore armor, carried weapons, and her bare arms were roped with muscle. Her skin had some scars that certainly looked like they'd come from combat as well.

The armor that she wore was interesting, too. It was formed mostly of leather which looked as if it had been boiled and waxed to make it harder, but there were strips of metal woven into critical areas to provide extra protection while keeping the overall weight down. Based on some of the historical and entertainment vids that Kelsey had seen, she half expected to see chain mail used as part of the armor, but there didn't seem to be any.

The woman's helmet, which she had in the crook of her arm, was made wholly of boiled leather, though it might have had some type of metal insert that Kelsey couldn't see. The woman's belt held what certainly looked like a sheathed longsword. Based on the well-worn leather-wrapped hilt, the woman used it regularly.

The woman's night-dark face showed no expression, and there was no humor in her dark eyes. Her tight, close-cropped, curly black hair seemed well suited to fit inside her helmet. Physically, she was almost exactly the opposite of the short, blonde, long-haired princess with her pale skin.

"Who are you, and how many people have you brought with you?" the woman asked in a slightly accented version of Standard, her voice low and flat.

"My name is Kelsey Bandar," Kelsey said with what she hoped was an easy smile. "I'm not alone, you're right about that. I've brought some friends along just to make sure that this meeting doesn't go badly before we've had a chance to get to know one another. They're out there watching us, but they're not going to interfere unless they think that I'm in danger.

"Before you start thinking that they have to get within bow range, let me caution you that they have high-tech weapons like my pistols and that they'll use them if they feel that I'm in danger. I don't want to see any of your people hurt, and I'd rather not get into a fight with you either. I just want to know the same sorts of things you do. Who are you, and what are you doing here?"

The corners of the other woman's lips twitched upward slightly. "My name is Clarice Beauchamp, and I command this company. As one might gather from looking around us," she said, making a wide gesture with her free arm, "we are here to see what came from the sky yesterday. Are those ships yours?"

Kelsey considered lying but decided that that wouldn't suit their overall plans for very long. Honesty might get them more than deception.

"They are. We had an unfortunate series of accidents, and you also may have seen a large explosion up in orbit. That was the System Lord destroying our main ship before we came down in the pinnaces. Needless to say, I would've preferred a gentler landing, but circumstances being what they were, I suppose that I should be happy that no one was killed."

The woman's gaze went hard and cold. "You are Fleet, then. We have known your kind before. You are the scourge that carries out the will of the System Lords. Give me one reason why I shouldn't cut you down right now as a traitor to the human race?"

Kelsey felt herself tensing but forced her expression to stay calm and open. "Perhaps you missed the part about where the System Lord was trying to kill us. We're not here as its allies. We came from far away, hoping to free the people of Terra.

"Well, to be clear, freeing your people is a secondary goal. We came to retrieve something to fight the System Lords and bring down their rule. We want to free all of humanity."

The woman considered what she'd said but didn't seem convinced. "Pretty words, but they mean nothing. You have two choices, Kelsey Bandar. You may summon your people so that I may take them into custody, or you may send them away. I give you my word that I shall cut you down first if your people attack mine."

Kelsey shook her head. "Not going to happen. My people will never leave me in your custody, and they're not going to surrender. Unlike you, they possess plenty of firepower to make certain that I stay safe, so let me give you the same type of warning.

"I can either speak with you peacefully or you can allow me to walk away unharmed. Any other choice risks forcing them to use lethal force. I don't want to see you killed. Hell, I don't want to see any fighting at all.

"In fact, I'm here looking to make friends, and I can trade valuable information with you to make certain that you understand what that can mean."

The other woman's cold smile widened. "And what kind of information is that?"

"There's a force on horseback coming from that direction." Kelsey raised a hand just enough to point a finger in the direction that the attacking force was coming from. "They have about ninety people and no remounts. They're riding hard, and they should be here in about fifteen minutes or so. If you're planning on defending yourself against a force three times your size, perhaps now would be the time to forget about me and worry about them.

"Or better yet, convince me that I have the possibility of becoming friends with you, and my people will help defend your group. Otherwise they're going to stay neutral and let what happens happen. I'd rather not see your groups kill each other, but I don't know you and I don't know them. This is the one brief window of time that you have to convince me that I should help you.

"If I were you, I'd start talking."

* * *

TALBOT, Admiral Mertz, and Commander Roche stood around a tabletop simulation of the battlefield that was projected through their implants via their ocular augmentation. It was as if he were standing around a *real* table, only there was no hardware outside of what was in their heads.

It was strange, but it was damn convenient.

With the feed from the tactical drones, the display had representation for every single individual on the battlefield. Blue for friendlies and yellow for unknown. When the new group arrived, they'd be labeled in red, simply because the odds of them being ultimately hostile were much higher and Talbot had to differentiate between the two groups in some way.

It worried him that Kelsey was still mixed in with the yellow dots. If she didn't get clear soon, she was going to be entangled in the fighting. The worst-case scenario would be that both groups were hostile and she'd be fighting against one hundred and twenty enemies with just a handful of marines as backup.

Since she wasn't in armor—not even unpowered armor—she'd be vulnerable to attacks that the marines in powered armor could shrug off. It was also conceivable that those people had modern weaponry stashed in their gear and no one would know about it until they brought something into play. The same was true of the group that was approaching.

He hoped his marines could stand up to what they were about to face, but it was always possible things could spin out of control and all of his people—including Kelsey—could die in the next twenty minutes.

"What can we do to help?" Commander Roche asked, his voice a mixture of worry and frustration. "There's got to be something we can do."

"I sent the other half of the ready response team," Talbot said. "They're going to get there faster than the rest of my people could, but they're still going to arrive late to the party. If things go pear-shaped, Corporal Boske knows to regroup her people and retreat toward the incoming support.

"Once our people leave the area around the camp—if they can break contact and move at full speed—they'll join up with our other people in maybe half an hour, but I don't expect that to happen.

"If they get forced out, they're going to be in contact with the enemy, and breaking away is going to be impossible. Horses are faster than armored marines. They'll have to set up a defensible position and wait for relief. That could take as much as an hour. If the enemy actually has modern antiarmor weapons, this could be brutal."

Roche turned and stared at him, his eyes cold. "If something happens to Princess Kelsey—my Princess Kelsey—then we're going to have a real problem."

"If something happens to *Julia*, you can rest assured that the same is going to happen to *Kelsey* as well because she's not going to abandon her," the admiral said grimly. "She's not going to abandon *anyone*.

"And before you forget about it, both of them have Marine Raider augmentation. If things really go bad, as much as she'd hate to do it, Julia will give her combat controller the green light and it will clean house for her.

"She's in Raider armor, with Raider weapons, and has Raider augmentation. If anyone can survive this situation, it's her. The rest of the marines face worse odds. Kelsey, unarmored as she is, probably has the worst downside if things go bad, particularly since she'll be in the thick of things no matter how dangerous it is."

Roche rubbed his face tiredly. "Sorry. We've only been on Terra a single day. How can they have found us so fast?"

"We do the best we can, but we always seem to catch the bad breaks and have to fight our way through," Talbot said grimly. "Let's look on the bright side. The odds that both groups are going to be actively hostile to the marines are small.

"The most likely scenario is that the approaching group isn't going to open fire without talking first. There's going to be some kind of dialogue before there's shooting. Maybe the smaller group will surrender. We just don't know yet.

"The most likely situation is that the smaller group is made up of people that Kelsey can convince to be friendly. She has that way about her. Then our forces and theirs are going to be playing defense against the larger group.

"Unless somebody has antiarmor weapons, the only one of our people in any real danger is Kelsey. I know that Corporal Boske is going to do everything possible to shield her from all threats, even if that means sacrificing every marine in her unit. That's what she's trained to do, and that's what's going to happen if she has to make that choice. Let's hope it doesn't come to that."

"Does the drone system have audio capability?" Admiral Mertz asked. "Are we going to be able to hear what these people are shouting back and forth?"

Talbot shook his head. "They have audio, but it's not going to be good enough to pick up regular conversation, particularly in the middle of a battle. If somebody is shouting something that's meant to be heard at a distance, odds are good that the drones will pick it up. If they have to get close enough to hear something said in a normal tone, they're going to be in the open and the hostiles are going to see them.

"I'm assuming at this point that we want to keep the drones up in the air and not down where they can be detected. They're not armed, and we don't have an infinite supply of them."

After what felt like forever but was probably only a couple of minutes, the yellow dots around Kelsey began moving into what looked like a defensive perimeter from above. Kelsey stayed inside the group, near one specific dot. A couple of others were stationed nearby, obviously watching her from behind.

"Can we have one of the drones provide a visual of Kelsey and the people she's with?" the admiral asked. "It would be helpful if we could see who we're dealing with and pay attention to their body language. That's going to tell us a lot about how this situation is playing out."

Talbot singled out one of the drones flying over the camp and commandeered it with his command overrides. He focused the visual down on Kelsey and zoomed in closely enough to see her standing next to a tall black woman in primitive armor.

The pair of them were staring off in the direction that the hostiles would be coming from, and based on how they were standing, they weren't being actively hostile to one another. Though there were two guards stationed behind Kelsey with bows. If something went wrong, they could easily shoot his wife in the back.

Well, *easily* might not be the right word. They could certainly *try* to shoot her in the back, but he knew that Kelsey was plugged into the same drone network that he was and was undoubtedly watching carefully to see what the people around her were doing. If someone tried to ambush her from behind, she'd be all over them.

If she resorted to her full-powered augmentation to fight and escape, Talbot had no doubt that she had a very good chance of managing it. She was incredibly fast, well trained in hand-to-hand combat, and stronger than a dozen normal men. If push came to shove, his wife *would* escape.

But to do that, she'd have to *choose* to escape.

Knowing her, she was more likely to stand and fight beside people she saw as potential allies than run. That, more than anything, was likely to get her killed or severely wounded.

Commander Roche frowned. "What's she doing? If she's managed to convince these people to be friendly, shouldn't she be heading back out to join the marines and get into her armor?"

Jared shook his head. "That's not how Kelsey's mind works, Commander. Now that she's made up her mind that she's going to fight, she's going to stay beside their leader and fight. She's not going to take the time to retrieve her armor and make herself safer.

"You'll notice that she's not wearing her weapons, so they haven't decided to treat her as an ally at this point. Mark my words, once the fighting starts, she's going to retrieve those weapons from whoever's holding them—whether they're ready to hand them over or not—and be in the fighting before you can blink."

Roche shook his head. "She's insane. Worse, I think she's influencing *my* Kelsey. Or Julia, if you *insist*. She's been doing things recently that I think are unhinged. I just don't know what to believe anymore."

Talbot gave the man a wide grin. "When we have women like them in our lives, we have either the choice of accepting them as they are or having them forced down our throats. Gentlemen, I recommend that we just accept what's going to happen. Kelsey is smart and tough. She'll come through this intact. So will Julia."

Brave words aside, Talbot really hoped that his wife knew what she was doing this time. If she got into a fight with people capable of taking out marines in powered armor, one unlucky hit could obliterate her, and that would kill him too.

9

J ulia watched her doppelgänger through the drone feed and growled. The woman was just standing there like an *idiot*. Didn't she realize that the potentially hostile force was going to be on them in just a few minutes?

"What the hell is she doing?" she demanded of Corporal Boske over the command channel.

"It looks like she's making friends," the corporal said dryly. "Doesn't she just pick the damnedest times to do that?"

"I think using the term *friends* is perhaps a little early," Julia muttered. "It certainly seems like they're not going to give her weapons back, so maybe they're checking to see if she's telling them the truth about the incoming force. How far out are they?"

The corporal made a show of checking her implants by putting her fingers to the side of her head, no doubt implying that Julia could've done exactly the same thing herself.

That was annoying. Why couldn't people just answer her damned questions?

"It looks like they're about five minutes out at their current pace. I doubt that's going to hold, to be honest. If I were them, I'd send out scouts to make sure that the camp is clear, or to at least figure out where all of their potential targets are located.

"I'd also slow the main body down and spread them out a little bit. Those two hills they're coming up on would make for a great ambush site, as you well know, since you suggested using them for exactly that earlier."

Julia pinched the bridge of her nose and counted slowly to five. "Are you saying that they're going to send people up to make sure that the hills are clear? Did I just put a bunch of our people into danger?"

The corporal turned to face her. "Highness, when you're in command of a military action, *everything* you do puts *someone* in danger. Do I think that they're going to send people up on those hills? Yes, I do. Is that going to put our people in danger? Yes, it is.

"Now, the key is that they can't completely search those hillsides. As long as our people have found good hiding places, that's not going to be a serious problem. In fact, it's going to put them in a good position to ambush the enemy scouts, if that's what we decide to do.

"If worse comes to worst, their scouts are going to find our troops and the fighting starts right then. Our people won't be in any danger from people carrying primitive weapons. As Colonel Talbot told me privately, the real worry is that they may have advanced weapons capable of damaging our powered armor.

"If they've ever fought the Rebel Empire version of Imperial Marines before, then they'll have dealt with the type of armor that we have. It may have been a long time since they've had to face that kind of thing, so perhaps I'm worrying about nothing, but I'm not going to be taking unnecessary chances. If they engage, we come down on them like a hammer."

Julia split her attention between her doppelgänger and the approaching force. The people inside their old camp had spread out and formed a defensive perimeter, seemingly watching for danger.

A minute later, she grunted when the approaching forces sent riders toward the hills that she'd selected for the marines. Corporal Boske had been right, and now things were getting a lot more dangerous. It looked like a total of three riders were headed toward one of the hills, so she supposed it wasn't as bad as it could've been.

In fact, the larger force was slowing down and curving off to the left so that it would pass around both hills. That was probably to limit their exposure. It meant that the oncoming forces would circumvent both hills and come on the camp a little bit to the side of their previous path.

Coincidentally, the forces inside the camp had dispatched one of their number to go to the same hill. That was going to put forces from all three groups in the same place at about the same time. It would be interesting to see if everyone could avoid contact with everyone else.

Corporal Boske made an announcement over the general marine frequency. "It looks like we're about to make contact with the larger group. Everyone on the hills, keep your heads down and avoid being spotted for as long as you can. If we can hold out until the main force rounds the hill and engages the group at the camp, we might be able to keep ourselves hidden.

"Snipers, be ready to cover the colonel. If it looks like she's in danger of being attacked by the people around her, those two guards behind her are your primary responsibility. If the woman she's standing next to decides to make a move, I have no doubt the colonel can handle herself. Your job is to make sure that no one sticks a sword through the boss when she's not looking. Weapons free at your discretion."

With that, Boske closed the channel and turned to Julia. "This is where we get down to brass tacks, Highness. Once that larger force engages— which I have no doubt at this point that they're going to do—it's going to be our job to take them down a notch or two. Once we go rushing into their center, our people on the hills will pin them against the camp. That should leave only one direction for the larger force to escape.

"You're pretty fast with that Raider armor, so when we start moving, I want you to dash around the hills and be ready on their other flank. It's going to be your job to plug that last exit point. If they try to run, that's going to be the direction they go.

"Stun anybody that comes your way, no matter which side they're supposedly on. Under circumstances like these, it's best we figure out who's a friend and who's not when the shooting is over. Any questions?"

Even though her stomach was roiling, Julia nodded, slapped her helmet into place, and locked it down. "I'm ready."

And ready or not, she'd be acting in just a few minutes because there was no backing out now. It was showtime.

* * *

Jared was considering the impending fight at the crash site when a soft beep through his implants preceded a change on the virtual display. Actually, *changed* was the wrong word. It had expanded its perspective and now showed him a much larger area, including another set of scarlet dots that were crossing the map.

These were beyond the outer edge of the drone's range, which momentarily confused him. A closer inspection revealed that it wasn't the drones at the original campsite at all. These readings were coming from the drones accompanying the second half of the ready response team.

A swarm of additional red dots had entered the map behind the marines, who were sprinting toward Kelsey's position. He watched as the new arrivals seemingly turned in place and began racing away from the marines, heading directly toward the building where Jared and his people were hiding.

Cursing under his breath, Jared opened a link to Talbot and Roche. "We've got trouble. It looks like another force has found our trail and is trying to backtrack us. Based on how fast they're moving, I think they're probably on horses, which means that the ready response team isn't going to be able to help us."

Even before Talbot responded, Commander Roche raced up to the virtual table and stared down at it, his expression worried. "It looks like this force is almost as large as the one that's attacking the camp. How do these people have so many troops ready to fight?"

"Whatever the answer is to that, it won't be good," Jared assured him.

Talbot came on the channel. "I'm taking a look through the drones now. They're on horseback, and they look a lot like the other big group. While

I'm only guessing, I think that the two sets are probably part of the same organization, based on the style and details of their armor.

"The ready response team can back us up, but they're going to arrive after these people have a chance to attack. Even moving at full speed, I think it's going to probably take them twenty or thirty minutes past the arrival of the new people to get back, if we order them to turn around right now. They're almost directly between the camp and us. Bad luck, that, though if they'd been a little faster, we wouldn't even have any warning that these guys were coming."

"Princess Kelsey and the others have half the ready team already," Roche said. "We should bring the second half back to help us."

"I think you're right, Commander," Talbot said. "If the force they have isn't enough to stop the group at the camp, then we're not going to stand a chance if a group of similar size attacks us. We're short on rifles, even though most of the marines have pistols. We're also short on ammunition. We could really use the extra support."

Jared thought furiously, comparing the benefits of sending the marines on to help his sister versus bringing them back to protect the Fleet crewmen, scientists, and other marines.

It wasn't really a hard choice, though it made his stomach churn a little bit when he realized that there was only one viable option. He was going to have to bring them back because his force wasn't nearly as able to defend itself as Kelsey's.

"Have them turn around," he ordered. "We'll have to hope that we can take care of our problem before the ready response team arrives, but they should be able to settle things if we haven't."

"Order sent. Should I notify Kelsey that her reinforcements aren't coming? Or should I just tell Corporal Boske and have her keep that information to herself for now?"

That was a no-brainer as well. "She's focused on the negotiations. She doesn't need to be distracted by what we're doing. It's probably better if she doesn't know that we're under attack, so that she can focus on her own issues.

"Tell Boske to make sure that the information gets to her as soon as the fighting there is settled. It shouldn't take her and her marines long to repulse the initial attack and have some breathing room where she can pass on what's happening here."

Jared looked around the basement. There were two stairwells leading up to the main level, such as it was. Other than those and the ramp, there were no other ways in or out of the large basement.

"How are we going to handle this, Talbot?" he asked. "Are we going to keep our people inside the building, or are we going to move them outside and form a perimeter?"

Talbot chuckled darkly. "Kelsey made me watch a bunch of prespaceflight vids that involved mounted forces attacking stationary groups of people. They'll have a level of mobility that we can't match. If we put our people outside, they're going to hit us from every side.

"As things sit, the building is secure. I've got marines stationed at ground level, and they can shoot through the windows at the people racing around the building. The only access they're going to have directly to where we're hiding is through the ramp. I have marines there to hold the line and keep them out.

"If all the enemy has is primitive weapons, our unpowered armor is probably going to be enough. We'll likely take some casualties, but we'll win. If they have any hidden surprises, things could get ugly fast.

"Our best option is to hold them off as best we can until the ready response team gets back. I can handle the tactical details, but you're going to have to figure out what strategy you'd like me to implement. I'd recommend talking first and shooting second."

It wasn't as if Jared had a lot of options to choose from. "Set up the defensive perimeter like you said. I'll try to talk to them. If they start shooting, we're going to shoot back. I don't want to start a fight, but if they do, we'll end it."

"No dice," the marine officer said. "If they shoot the messenger, we can't afford to lose you, Admiral. I'll do the talking."

Jared's initial impulse was to argue, but he knew that Talbot was right. The marine officer could talk if the strangers were willing to negotiate. If all they wanted to do was fight, Talbot could handle that, too.

He really hoped they could deal with the people coming at them because he didn't want to distract Kelsey at this critical moment. She had enough on her plate as it was. She didn't need to be worrying about the rest of them. That, after all, was his job.

Well, if everything went to hell, at least he'd keep these new people from racing in to attack his sister while she was already engaged. Even the marines in powered armor she had with her might not be enough to save her if that happened.

Now he had to hope that he could pull this off without losing any of his people to the Terrans he'd hoped to save.

10

————

K elsey stood beside the warrior woman, trying not to let her impatience show. Beauchamp was waiting for word from the scout she'd sent out. As soon as the man arrived on the target hill, he was going to discover that the large force had circled around and was coming in from their left.

The larger force was also sending scouts onto the hills, so it was entirely possible that the man wouldn't report back at all. She didn't think the marines who were on the hill would allow that to happen, but it really depended on the situation. They'd keep to their concealment, but if the scout groups came face-to-face, she suspected that they'd stun everybody and wait to sort it out later.

And that was as it should be. The fewer deaths they had in this confrontation, the better the chances she could play friendly with both groups. Just because they were at odds with one another didn't necessarily mean that her people needed to be taking sides. If that didn't work out, she still hoped to have enough time to make an informed decision about who her allies would be.

A few minutes later, even as the main group was just about to come into view of the camp, the scout on the hill signaled. He was using a mirror to reflect the sunlight and reporting in via some kind of code.

It wasn't Morse, but Kelsey thought it was very similar. Maybe some type of encrypted form of code that could pass information in a similar manner. If each set of flashes represented a very limited set of words, then it was likely that they could pass messages quickly.

She vaguely remembered that the wet navies of prespaceflight Terra had done something similar. Ships would use lights to signal one another when radio transmissions wouldn't be advisable. They had short code groups that could transmit specific meanings from a limited playbook of options. Perhaps that's what this was.

She recorded everything and would study it when the space and time to do so presented itself. If nothing else, it would give Carl and the scientists something to argue about while they marched.

The larger force was roughly sixty seconds away from being visible at the camp when Beauchamp got confirmation of everything Kelsey had said. She could tell that's what had happened because the other woman began cursing in a low monotone.

She turned to Kelsey and glared at her as if this was somehow her fault. "It seems that you weren't lying after all. My scout has confirmed the rough numbers you gave and said that they are coming in from our left.

"As you indicated, they outnumber us three to one. With them this close, it's unlikely that we're going to be able to escape an engagement. While our horses are rested, they're right on top of us."

The woman smacked a fist against her armored thigh. "Dammit. I'd hoped to avoid meeting them at all. My warriors are good, but they're not good enough to win a fight at these odds."

"If I was convinced that we could be allies, I'd be willing to lend you a hand," Kelsey said quietly. "My people can tilt the balance in your favor. I just need you to be honest with me. Who are you people, and what are you doing here?"

The other woman chuckled sourly. "We don't exactly have time for that sort of thing, but I've already told you my name. We came to salvage what technology we could. We gather what we can from the ruined megacities, but the residents there always force us back out. We thought we could pick up something useful without having to fight for it this time.

"One of our enemies controls this area. We call them the horde. They're vehement foes of my people. They blame us for what happened to Terra, and I suppose when it comes right down to it, they're not exactly wrong."

Kelsey considered that. "Since we don't have much time left, what exactly did your people do to piss them off? How could you possibly be responsible for what happened on Terra so long ago?"

The other woman smiled grimly. "My ancestors were part of the general resistance against the System Lords here on Terra. Over the years, decades, and centuries, they increased the level of guerrilla warfare to the point to where the System Lords eventually had enough. They bombarded many of the cities and killed this world in everything except name about a century ago.

"The horde and other groups like them loathe and fear us because they consider us responsible for the deaths of so many people. I don't believe they cared for the System Lords any more than we did back then, but they chose to live as pampered prisoners rather than fight for their freedom. Now we're all the same, living in conditions that would have likely horrified our ancestors."

The woman made a gesture toward the pinnaces and the tents. "Our goals have not changed. We still hope to defeat the AIs, and we had hoped to recover useful military equipment, but that's not going to happen now."

Kelsey allowed her smile to widen. "I think that's something we can work with. At this point, we need to have a chance to sit down and talk this through. That's not going to happen with the horde trying to kill all of us."

The woman gave her a grim look. "You need to be warned. The horde has access to advanced weaponry. They won't tolerate an intrusion by what they consider forces of the AIs. They'll see you and your people as that, in case I wasn't clear enough.

"There have been incursions in the past, including people in incredibly powerful armor. The horde has weapons capable of killing them. I don't know whether they brought any of those with them or not, but if you're counting on technology protecting you from them, I suggest you disabuse yourself of that notion."

Momentarily horrified, Kelsey sent a quick message to Boske. *Corporal, the locals say the attacking group may have access to antiarmor weapons. I don't know what kind, or if they have any with them, but if they do, your people are in danger.*

Don't take any chances. Put them down as fast and hard as you possibly can and stay under cover if you can't. Do what you have to do to protect your people, and I'll see what I can do to get our potential allies clear of the firing zone.

Copy that, Boske said. *The enemy is just about to you. Good luck, Colonel.*

At that moment, a wide line of men on horseback crossed over a low rise and looked down on the camp. There were an awful lot of them. Ninety didn't sound like a large number, but seeing them arrayed like this made her heart quiver.

She'd expected them to talk, but one man in the middle of the line raised his spear and shouted something unintelligible. The rest of the men raised their own spears and shouted in return, then all of them charged forward, their spears lowered as they thundered toward the camp.

The attack was on.

* * *

TALBOT ALREADY HAD his people scattered around upstairs and on the ramp leading down to the basement, so it took no time at all to have them ready to defend the building. He watched the forces headed their way over the feed from the drones around the ready response team. The riders vanished briefly as they left the area under observation and then reappeared on the drone network surrounding the building a short while later.

Like the first group, the video feed showed that these were warriors mounted on horses. Men and women in armor, with primitive weapons, riding single mounts. No remounts with them at all, so they seemed to have only one task in mind: to fight.

It took a few minutes to have the drones zoom in as much as possible without revealing themselves, and he examined the riders carefully. All of them wore leather armor with strips of metal attached to critical locations.

They had hard faces, determined expressions, and their weapons looked well used. These were people that knew how to fight and considered it their business.

At the speed they were traveling, it only took them fifteen minutes to arrive in the vicinity of the building. They circled around it and passed on the other side, staying outside of easy bow shot, he would imagine. From their expressions, they were looking to see if the trail continued past the building.

They stopped perhaps five hundred meters away from the building and had a brief consultation before the group split into four parts. Each went around the building to cover a different cardinal compass point.

A minute later, one of the men wrapped a white cloth around the end of his spear, raised it high, and rode toward the building. He halted perhaps seventy-five meters away from the ramp. From his expression, he was content to wait there for someone to come to him.

Talbot walked up the ramp and started out toward the man on the horse. He was in his armor, of course, but had his helmet nestled in the crook of his arm.

His appearance caused the man to react. He must've pulled back slightly on his reins, because his horse danced a little bit.

The man's expression, which Talbot could clearly see with his ocular augmentation, went from passive to grim. He eyed Talbot for one long moment and then, without saying a single word, turned and rode back toward the group that he'd come from.

That wasn't good.

Talbot watched the man remove the cloth from his spear and put it into one of his saddlebags as he was having words with others in the group. There was lots of gesticulating and some elevated voices that were *almost* loud enough for him to understand.

After a few seconds of that, the group turned to stare at Talbot. Their expressions were just as grim as the man's had been. Since they didn't know him, it almost had to be the powered armor. He wasn't sure how that could make such a stark difference in their reaction, but these people had been suppressed by the System Lords.

Perhaps Rebel Empire marines had landed on Terra at some point. Perhaps even recently. Maybe they'd been involved in the fighting and these people had a long memory. If so, Talbot and his people were in for a fight, because these people didn't look like they were in a mood to negotiate anymore.

A single rider left the group and raced around the building. He stopped at each of the other groups and spoke for just a few moments before racing on to the next. A couple of minutes later, he'd returned to his original group, which then began spreading out in what was obviously an attack formation. They were going to make a run at the building.

Talbot didn't know how well the windows of the building would stand up to arrows, but they'd resisted the elements thus far. Only a few of them had shattered. His people would break as many as was required to defend themselves, but the people on the horses were going to be moving fast.

If he was any judge of how the battle would play out, they'd race in circles around the building, using their mobility to stay at a distance while they fired arrows toward his people inside the building. Since they knew the ramp was the most likely entrance, that would undoubtedly be their main target for breaching the defenses.

Talbot backed up to the ramp, clapped his helmet on, and opened a general channel. "All marines, be prepared to repel an assault. They're going to force an entry above ground, if they can't get in through the ramp. We have to hold them off until the ready response team gets back. Stick with stunners if they get close enough. Remember that horses are larger targets than people."

Kelsey wouldn't like that he'd targeted the animals, but she'd understand the tactical logic. She'd *still* tear a strip off him, but he had lives to protect.

He checked the drone feeds and decided that they had to keep the attackers occupied for between fifteen and twenty minutes to allow for the armored marines to return. This was going to be ugly, no doubt about that.

Talbot wished he could've talked the others out of an outright attack, but they hadn't to try. They'd chosen to fight, so the bleeding was on their heads.

He only hoped he and his marines could get this situation under control quickly, and that his wife was having a better time of it than he was.

11

Julia had only just made it behind the hills and was racing toward the other side of the pair when the larger group attacked. She could hear shouting as the invaders charged toward the camp.

That spurred her to run faster, which in turn caused her to trip over something and skid onto her face, before rolling over and stumbling back to her feet. She'd never practiced this kind of thing in armor, and she wasn't very graceful in the heavy suit, even with her artificial musculature. One more weakness.

The tenor of the budding battle changed almost immediately, and she knew that Corporal Boske and the others had revealed their presence and opened fire with their stunners. She couldn't see any of the blue bolts from where she was, but she wasn't sure that she would have anyway. At their wider aperture, the stunners didn't really fire bolts at all. More like fans of energy that only went a short distance before petering out into nothing.

As she was moving between the two hills, though still far away from the battle itself, she was able to jump up into the air and see over the rise enough to glimpse the mounted forces milling around in chaos, firing their bows at the marines. If that was the best they could do, the battle would be over fast.

She put on as much speed as she could and made it to the other side of the second hill just in time to have two men on horseback race over the rise directly for her. She pulled her stunner, raised it, and fired at them. The blue beam was still set to narrow aperture and only struck one of them a glancing blow. Or perhaps it missed him by a very small margin. She couldn't tell.

Seemingly, whatever it was wasn't enough to knock him out. He wavered in his saddle, but his trained reflexes seemed to pull him down, where he held onto his horse while his compatriot raised his spear and charged directly at her, screaming at the top of his lungs.

She tried to sweep the spear away before the man could strike her, but the surprising speed of his horse threw off her timing. The spear shattered against her armor, causing her no harm, but the horse running into her with its shoulder sent her flying. She landed in a heap, and the rider raced past her.

With a grunt, she rolled onto her stomach and fired her stunner at the retreating horseman, striking him squarely in the back. He spasmed and tumbled from the saddle.

She started to roll over onto her back and engage the remaining rider, but he'd been a lot quicker closing the distance than she'd thought possible and brought his horse's front hooves down directly on her back before she could move.

The impact was blunted by her armor, but not stopped completely. The incredible force of the blow drove the air from her lungs, and she gasped. Apparently being pinned between a huge animal and the ground was not the kind of place that even a Marine Raider in powered armor wanted to be.

With an effort of will, she rolled away from the animal and raised her hand to fire again, only to discover that she'd somehow lost her stunner. She jumped to her feet and scanned around for it, but it was lost somewhere in the tall grass. Just perfect.

The rider turned and tried to use his horse to ram her as he drew his sword and struck at her. She thought the sword was less of a threat than the horse, so she dodged to the side and exposed herself to the strike. Her raised arm deflected the blade, snapping the length of steel in two when he struck.

That seemed very disconcerting to the rider, and he stared at his broken weapon in shock for a few seconds that he didn't really have to waste.

She took advantage of his lack of focus and dragged him out of the saddle. Once he hit the ground, she carefully metered her strength to strike him with the lightest worthwhile blow she could manage. It was sufficient to knock the air out of his lungs and made her confident enough to strike him in the face. That knocked him out. And broke his nose, which she hadn't intended to do.

Off to her left about seventy-five meters away, three more horsemen raced out of the fighting and headed toward the wider grasslands. A loud explosion on the other side of the hill announced that her doppelgänger's warning had been spot-on. Some of these bastards had heavy weapons.

She turned her enhanced ocular implants up to maximum and looked around until she spotted her stunner lying in the grass by the output of its power pack in the ultraviolet range. It wasn't very bright, but it was distinctive at this short distance.

Julia snatched it up and considered how best to chase after these people. She could run faster than a normal person, but they were on horses. She wasn't that fast.

With a sigh she decided she was going to have to do this the hard way. She raced over to the horse standing near its fallen rider and vaulted up into his saddle—it was *definitely* a male—with more grace than she'd actually expected to have. Perhaps all of those riding lessons were finally paying off.

She'd never have been able to do such a thing without her augmentation, but she'd always been comfortable around horses. Such gentle creatures that always seemed to be such a pleasure to ride.

That experience was not replicated when she landed on *this* horse. She was able to quickly grab the saddle horn and stuff her feet into the stirrups, but the horse immediately spun in place and tried to bite her leg. Of course, her armored thigh was invulnerable to his teeth, but he didn't seem to care as he kept trying.

Julia grabbed the reins and pulled his head around. "Calm down, boy. I'm your rider now."

She wasn't certain whether or not he was going to pay attention to what she'd said. He was a trained warhorse, and he was probably bound in some way to the rider she'd taken out, so it was entirely possible that she was wasting her time.

To her shock and pleasure, he responded to the reins, and she quickly had him off in hot pursuit of the fleeing riders. Her armor was heavy, but she wasn't a large woman. She figured that even with her Raider armor, she probably weighed less than the man who'd been on the horse before.

With more assertiveness than she actually felt, she put her heels to the beast, and he responded by surging forward. Her experience with riding horses had been limited to a more sedate pace, and over even terrain. Here, she was racing at breakneck speed over grasslands that could conceal holes or irregularities that might send the horse and herself tumbling.

She'd probably survive that kind of thing, but the horse would be gravely injured or killed. She really didn't want that to happen, but she *had* to catch up with those warriors. If they spread the alarm, everyone might be screwed.

The warriors ahead of her were aware that she was coming. At least one of them had glanced over his shoulder and spotted her, shouting a warning to his fellows as she closed. She hoped they'd turn and fight, because that would've made her job a lot easier. As it was, they really couldn't hurt her, whereas, if she could get them into range, she'd stop them.

Unfortunately, it seemed that they were onto that particular trick and kept racing away as fast as they could. To her benefit, they didn't split up.

After a minute of hot pursuit, she was finally getting into the range where she might actually be able to start picking them off with her stunner. They stayed glued to their horses, obviously trying to keep her from getting a decent shot.

She could shoot the horses, but the idea nauseated her. She had no desire to injure an innocent animal. If she could do this *any* other way, she'd avoid shooting them.

The riders ahead of her crested a small rise and disappeared momentarily from view. When she raced over the top of it herself, she found that they'd set a trap for her.

Two of the riders were still racing away at full speed, but one of them had dismounted and pulled some kind of object from his saddlebags. She didn't really know much about weapons, but it was obviously a high-tech weapon, even if it looked cobbled together.

She was sure that her implants could tell her more about it, but she had no time to check them. The man was already kneeling on the ground, with his horse lying in front of him. The bastard was using it for cover as he fired at her.

There was a flash of light as something raced out of the tube and directly toward her. It was as bright as a star.

Julia did the only thing she could. She urged her horse to swerve as she launched herself into the air, using her legs to push off the horse and hoping she managed to pull her feet out of the stirrups.

She prayed that that would give her enough distance to avoid being struck by whatever that was, because the person who'd fired it seemed pretty confident that it would kill her.

The force of her jump was just enough to get her to clear the warhead. Even as her body arched, she saw it fly under her, missing her legs by no more than a handful of centimeters. Thankfully, it missed her horse, too. A detonation at this range might have killed her along with the beast.

It struck the rise that she'd just come over and exploded. The shockwave grabbed her out of the air and slammed her into the ground with more force than she dreamed possible in a nonlethal event.

For such a small device, it made a *huge* crater. If it had struck her, the weapon would've blown her armor apart and killed her instantly.

Julia figured all that out as she was tumbling to a stop. She'd lost her stunner again, but no longer cared. That son of a bitch had tried to kill her, so she was going to kill him back. She leapt to her feet.

Or rather, she *tried* to leap to her feet. What happened instead was that she staggered drunkenly upright, her sense of balance totally ruined by what had just happened.

The man who'd tried to kill her was busy reloading, and she realized that she had to stop him before he finished, or she'd be dead. With her body not functioning correctly, that really left her with only one choice. She hated having to do it. Hated, hated, *hated* it. But she did it anyway.

She activated the combat controller built into her implants and ceded her body to the machine in her head. It was like a switch had been thrown because her own personal balance issues no longer seemed to matter as the computer compensated for them and made things happen. Things she no longer had any control over.

Unfortunately for the warrior, the merciless computer in her head had no overriding desire to take him alive. Her hand darted down to where her flechette pistol was holstered, drew it cleanly, and fired a short burst right through the center of his chest.

His reinforced leather armor was worse than useless against this kind of attack. Not only did the flechettes penetrate the boiled hide, they blew chunks off of the protective metal, which then also plunged into his vulnerable flesh. He fell back, dropping the weapon he'd been trying to reload, dead before he hit the ground.

The computer turned her now merciless eyes toward the fleeing horsemen and immediately determined that she wasn't going to be able to catch up with them. They were outside her weapon's range, and by the time she gathered her horse and pursued, they'd be able to elude her. They had gotten away.

That wasn't what she'd wanted, but it wasn't exactly like she'd had a choice. They'd ambushed her with a weapon she really hadn't expected, even after hearing the explosion back at the main fight.

She deactivated the combat controller and shuddered in relief as she regained control of her body. Trembling, she found her horse, mounted him, and raced back toward the camp. She had to get there as quickly as possible. Every second counted now.

12

J ared made his way up one of the stairs and stood watching as the
marines looked out through the windows on the ground level. He
knew that he probably shouldn't be there, but as soon as Talbot had
gone outside, he'd been unable to resist the urge to see what was
happening for himself.

He probably should've worn his powered armor, even though he
couldn't use it very well, but doing so would've put the people below into an
even worse state of terror. If a commander showed fear—even though
armoring up wasn't based on fear in the middle of a battle—then they'd be
a lot more inclined to panic. He had to exude confidence.

The above-ground part of the building wasn't all that large when
compared to the underground area that held all the farming machinery.
Based on the debris left behind on this level—the remains of dividers
between small cubicles, desks, and ruined computer equipment—he
suspected that this had been the office area overseeing the vast agricultural
network the machines below had once served.

The marines had moved everything they could over to the exterior walls,
figuring that almost anything would be useful in stopping arrows. They'd
strategically broken out some of the windows, or used some that had already
been broken, based on the staining on the floors. The glass had to be pretty
tough to have survived this long, so he wondered what they'd broken the
panes with.

The marines had chosen to split their forces into four equal groups and
cover each of the outside walls. The center of the building contained offices
that were closed off from the rest of the large room, probably for
management. Not a very good way to provide leadership, but they hadn't
consulted him.

The marines didn't have enough people to cover every angle the enemy would come from, so they'd supplemented their numbers with any Fleet personnel that had training in the use of firearms. Even so, he wasn't certain they had enough weapons to go around.

Since some of the marines had had both rifles and pistols, they'd probably passed the pistols to the Fleet personnel, possibly their stunners, too. Ammunition and powerpacks were going to be a problem very soon. Based on what Talbot had told him, they really didn't have enough to be shooting indiscriminately.

They'd win this fight, of that he had no doubt, but this was only the first five kilometers of a fifteen-hundred-kilometer journey, during which they'd undoubtedly meet additional enemies.

They had to live as if the supplies they had now were all they were going to get. If they could salvage something along the way, that would be wonderful. If they couldn't, then pretty soon they'd be fighting with rocks.

He made his way over to Senior Lieutenant Chloe Laird. "Give me an update."

Laird turned to face him, her red hair damp with sweat. With no environmental controls, the building was already warming as the sun rose outside. It was also terribly humid inside the abandoned structure.

"It's not looking good, sir," she said. "They probably outnumber us three to one, if we're only counting fighting personnel. On the plus side, they're going to have to come at us through a fairly limited number of entrances. We should be able to use our rifles and pistols to good effect.

"If they come too close or lump up, we've got a few plasma grenades that will ruin somebody's day. We've also got a number of stunners we passed out to the Fleet personnel backing us up. They're going to start shooting first and hopefully take down a number of the attackers as they are closing in. We'll only resort to lethal force if we have no choice.

"Senior Sergeant Coulter has the other side of the building covered, and I'm keeping an eye on this side. Between the two of us, we've got a handle on things. You should go back down before the shooing starts, sir."

He ignored her pointed advice. "How easily are the arrows going to be able to penetrate the glass?"

The marine officer shrugged slightly. "The glass is tough, but a sharp strike from an arrow will probably crack a pane. A few hits like that and they'll come down. They're made to be strong against the elements, not against direct physical assault.

"I'd say that after a couple of minutes, we won't have glass in any of these frames. We've piled up a bunch of office furniture to use as cover, and that should work well enough against what they can throw at us.

"The problem is going to be when they get inside the building. They've got swords, and all we'll have are our marine knives. Admittedly, what we've got is a *lot* sharper, but they've got reach on us. Unpowered armor might save lives in some cases, but they've got to be well trained to work around armor with their weapons. If they get inside our guard, they're going to kill a whole bunch of people."

Her tone indicated the toll might include headstrong flag officers, but she politely left that as an implication rather than stating it out loud.

"Then we'll just have to make sure they don't get inside," he said grimly.

A loud series of shouts went up outside, and Jared turned his attention to look at what was going on in the early light. There were a lot of people racing around the building on horses at this point, so it looked as if the attack was underway.

"You'd best get back downstairs, sir," Laird said firmly. "The party is about to start."

Jared opened his mouth to decline, but a massive explosion on the other side of the building tossed him into Laird, sending both of them tumbling into the makeshift barricade beside them. The blast was powerful, so it took him a moment to blink himself back into focus and roll off the marine officer who was even then surging back to her feet.

"All marines, open fire," Coulter shouted from the other side of the building. "Aim for people with heavy weapons if you can spot them."

Jared could see at least half a dozen marines down near the blast site, though some were moving. The Fleet personnel that had been backing them up were in much worse shape. They hadn't been in body armor, and the blast had torn through them. He knew there had to be fatalities.

"Reinforce the area they just hit, Lieutenant," Jared said over his ringing ears. "If they try to push through there, they'll be able to get into the building."

"Don't teach your grandmother to suck eggs, sir," she said as she moved to direct her marines. "I'm already on it."

Marines from the other positions rushed to the area that had been struck and began firing out the windows at the riders. Jared didn't think it was going to do them any good because at the speed the horsemen were moving, the person with the heavy weapon was probably long gone. In fact, he was almost certainly going to strike from a different side of the building next.

Even though it was a stupid idea—and he knew it—Jared edged his way up to the glass and stared outside, looking for anyone carrying one of those weapons. Several arrows struck the glass in front of him, splintering the clear material until it fell away in a shower of small fragments. He shielded his face and eyes as the shards fell, but still managed to get some cuts that were going to sting later.

Once he could see again, he refocused his attention outside. All he saw was a bunch of screaming and shouting horsemen with bows. Then he saw one that had something that was different. A tube of some kind that he was aiming toward the building somewhere off to Jared's right.

"Incoming!" he shouted as he covered his ears with his hands.

An unbearably bright spark of light shot from the weapon and lanced into the building, hitting the corner off to Jared's right in another massive explosion. This not only killed or wounded more of his people, but it damaged the structural integrity of the building itself, and the roof came down in that corner.

Coughing from the dust that had washed over him, Jared crawled to the person nearest him. It was an enlisted Fleet crewman. A length of metal had gone all the way through her chest. She gasped twice, her hand twitching toward the debris that had impaled her, and then lay unmoving, her eyes focused on infinity.

Burning with anger, Jared crawled past her and found a marine with a similar shard of metal through his shoulder. It had pinned him to the barricade that they'd been using, and he was struggling to pull free.

"Stay still until someone can help you," Jared said calmly. "If you pull the metal out, you might bleed to death. Just leave it right where it is."

Jared reached down and grabbed the man's rifle. He then shrugged apologetically as he took the reloads from the man's belt. He looked for a place that he could shoot from while still being out of view of the attackers.

Once he was in place, he lined up on the first horseman that he saw and pulled the trigger. The flechette missed the man, flying somewhere behind him, Jared imagined. He was going to have to figure out how much to lead them.

He jinked the rifle to the left and fired again, this time achieving some success as the man wobbled sideways in his saddle but kept going.

Jared started looking for anyone with those strange weapons. They had to be his primary target. A few more hits like the last two would bring the entire building down on their heads, and that would be the death of them.

* * *

With everyone's attention focused on the charging horde, Kelsey stepped back to the man holding her weapons. "I think I'd best take those," she said, holding her hand out.

The man seemed to consider her words for a long moment before handing her weapons belt back to her.

She quickly strapped her pistols on before reaching for her sword harness. That was also quickly returned.

Now fully armed, Kelsey turned her attention to the battlefield and saw a wild melee. The force of horsemen had charged toward the camp where the defenders had drawn up to receive them, but halfway there, several armored marines had come out of hiding almost in the middle of them and began using stunners to take down riders and animals alike.

Set to wide beam, a stunner's range was short, but it could take out a number of targets for long enough to be quite useful in a battle like this. Unfortunately, at the speed the horsemen were traveling, there were going to be serious injuries and fatalities when they fell.

Just as the charge was breaking around the marines, an additional four marines charged down from the hills at the rear of the horde. It would be a minute before they'd be in range to use their stunners, but just the sight of them charging roiled the attacking forces, giving the local defenders an opportunity to push forward and engage on a more equal basis.

With a good portion of the enemy focusing on the marines, Beauchamp and her forces were able to decisively engage the troops directly to their front, and the melee was on. The people on horseback had spears and what amounted to cavalry sabers to strike down from their height at the people on the ground.

Kelsey had seen that sort of thing in a number of old Terran vids. The people on the ground had similar weapons and the reach to strike up as well. What surprised Kelsey the most was the fact that they seemed disinclined to strike at the horses.

Someone off to the side was taking single shots with a stunner on tight beam. It must've been one of the snipers that Corporal Boske had set out. With the way the marines were arranged, there was only one viable route to retreat, and Kelsey wondered how long it would be before the horde took it.

Or would they just choose to fight? If they had some of those antiarmor weapons, they might decide to push on. That was Kelsey's main concern and one of the reasons that she'd wanted to take the enemy down as quickly as possible.

With that in mind, she drew her stunner and one of her swords before racing into the fray. She picked a direction full of enemies and triggered her weapon on wide beam. Half a dozen men and horses dropped where they were.

Almost immediately, one of the horsemen tried to shoulder her aside with his horse as he sliced down with his saber. Kelsey raised her blade to deflect his, knocking it to the side and also severing the enemy blade completely. She fired the stunner and took him and his horse out before seeing what else the field had to offer her.

This was what they'd once called a "target rich environment." There were enemies *everywhere*. Thankfully, they were more worried about the armored marines than they were about Kelsey or the people in the camp, which was going to cost them.

While that might be safer for her, she quickly discovered that it wasn't safe for the marines. Out of the corner of her eye, she caught someone wielding a weapon that she wasn't familiar with.

One of the horsemen had pulled some kind of tube out of his saddlebags and was aiming it off the left. A glance indicated one of the armored marines was the target.

Kelsey immediately raced toward the man, knowing what was coming and doing everything she could to get to him before he fired. *Incoming heavy weapon!* She sent over her internal com, praying that the marine would dodge.

Even as she gave the warning, Kelsey flipped the focus on her stunner to narrow beam and fired, but the man's horse moved at the wrong moment, moving the warrior just enough for her to miss him.

A bright spark flew from the tube and struck the marine, who was already dodging. A massive explosion marked the spot, and pieces of armor and flesh rained down in a wide circle.

Anguish filled Kelsey for just a moment, before rage pushed it out. The rider turned just in time to see Kelsey as she launched herself into the air at him at a dead run, her sword slashing down at his head.

He raised his tubed weapon to deflect her blow, but the edge of her blade sliced through it and him, sending his body tumbling from the saddle in pieces.

All marines, they have antiarmor weapons, she said into her implant com. As if they didn't already know. *You are cleared and encouraged to use lethal force.*

Look out behind you, Highness! Boske shouted back.

Rather than look, Kelsey used her powerful leg muscles to spring to the side and spin in the air. A bright spark from another one of the antiarmor weapons flashed through the spot where she'd been just a moment before and struck one of the horsemen to her side right where his body met the animal he rode.

The massive explosion killed them both instantly and sent blood and bits of flesh over everyone close to the blast, including her. The blast smashed her out of the air, but she tagged her combat controller to get her back on her feet and attacking the riders closest to her. They'd all be blown out of their saddles and couldn't defend themselves. Too bad for them.

Once her body seemed to have shaken off the effects of the blast, she resumed direct control and waded back into the fight. She'd lost her stunner but didn't care. With blades in both hands, she became death incarnate, making even the hardened warriors she was fighting recoil from her.

Not that that would save them. Playtime was over.

13

Once the fighting had kicked off, Talbot hunkered down on the ramp with his marines and waited for the assault that he knew was coming. He suspected that he knew the enemy's plan, and he intended on giving them an ugly surprise when they tried it.

He expected them to try to distract him, and then have someone with one of the antiarmor weapons pop up over the lip of the ramp and fire down into the group of marines below. The door behind him was fairly heavy, but it wouldn't stand up to a significant explosion. If they breached the door, they'd be among the noncombatants before he could stop them.

That meant he had to be ready to act instantly. They couldn't have many of the damned things, and if he could take out the people wielding them, he'd be able to stop the attack cold.

The next few seconds proved his expectations dramatically wrong.

An above-ground explosion shook the building and sent clods of dirt raining down on him.

"Report," he said over the command channel, tensing and preparing for the attack he was sure was coming down the ramp.

"We just took a hit on one corner of the building," Chloe Laird said. "Unknown number of casualties. Coulter is handling that side."

"Find those bastards," Talbot said through clenched teeth. "Shoot any son of a bitch that looks like he has anything bigger than a bow and arrow. Hell, just start shooting all of them. At this point, they've initiated hostilities and we should just go ahead and clean house. The gloves are off. Weapons free and cleared for lethal force."

"Copy that."

Another explosion rocked the building, and Talbot cursed. At this rate, he wasn't going to be able to wait for the enemy. He was going to have to go out to them.

He almost started up the ramp but paused. Maybe that was part of their plan.

They'd seen him in armor and knew where he'd gone. They had to know how dangerous powered armor was, or they wouldn't be carrying weapons like that. What if the explosions were meant to draw him out?

Coming at the problem from that angle, the answer seemed obvious. They'd have somebody making a ruckus upstairs to bring him back up the ramp. That had to mean that there was someone out there waiting for him with one of those weapons. He'd probably just stopped himself from walking into an ambush.

So, if he wanted to get up top while keeping his skin intact, he needed to make certain that whoever was waiting for him wasn't going to be in a position to hurt him. To do that, he needed more intelligence about the layout of the enemy.

He tapped into the drone network and watched the enemy running around the building. There were a lot of them, and even though folks from upstairs had taken some down, their main force appeared to be intact.

The building itself was in worse shape. It looked like the two explosions had struck different corners of the building, and one of those had collapsed. That had to be bad for the marines and Fleet personnel inside. They'd come out of this with dead and injured friendlies, there was no getting around that.

He refocused his attention on the enemy. All of them were in motion except for one. That solitary dot was positioned inside the rough ring that marked where the enemy riders were circling.

The man had hidden himself behind a small rise in the ground— probably less than a third of a meter tall. He had a tube that just screamed antiarmor weapon aimed right toward the ramp. There was no sign of his horse.

With his newfound knowledge, Talbot had the drones scan the other riders, looking for any other antiarmor weapons. He found two more with the tubes. One was in the process of reloading his weapon with something from his saddlebags, while the other one was taking aim at the building as he rode around it.

His companions had moved clear of the area behind and in front of him to give him a clear shot. Moments later, a bright spark of light fired out of the tube and slammed into the building in an area that hadn't been struck by an explosive yet. More of the roof came down after the blast ripped the wall out.

The enemy riders hooted their approval and shook their bows in the air. That pissed Talbot off, and he decided it was time to end this farce once and for all.

He plucked one of the few plasma grenades they'd been able to recover from the pinnaces from his belt and pulled the pin. With the drones flying overhead, he knew *exactly* how far away the man in front of the ramp was. With a plasma grenade, all he needed to do was get close, and that little rise in the dirt wouldn't make any difference at all.

"Fire in the hole," he said over the general channel. "Duck and cover."

He cocked his arm back and engaged his combat computer. It double-checked his calculations, adjusted the angle of his throw and the strength he was going to use, and then lobbed the grenade out over the ramp for him. Through the drones, Talbot watched it arc cleanly through the air and land directly in front of the man, rolling to a stop almost underneath him.

The target attempted to scramble back. He might not have known what the grenade was, but he obviously thought it was bad news.

He was right.

The grenade went off in an unbearable burst of light that put dots into Talbot's vision, even down on the ramp with a helmet on. The shockwave struck the building, probably blowing out every window on this side of the structure. He hoped everyone had taken his warning seriously.

Another check of the drones revealed a fairly deep crater and no sign of the enemy or his weapon. They'd been atomized, along with a number of horsemen that were too close to the blast.

Even more were down, injured and screaming in pain. The wounded horses sounded like hurt kids, and that tore at his heart. The sound was going to torment his dreams for a while, but he hadn't had a choice.

"Chloe," Talbot said over the command channel. "The drones show two more bad guys with antiarmor weapons. I'll take out the first one as he comes around. I'm marking him as target A. Target B is your responsibility."

"Copy that."

Since he had complete drone coverage, Talbot wasn't worried that he'd lose the location and identity of the next man on his hit list. The building itself had shielded the horseman from the blast, and he was still coming around on his previous course, if a little more cautiously.

When the man cleared the building and raced into the area closest the ramp, Talbot ran up the incline and tore straight for him. The guy saw him coming and swung the antiarmor weapon around, but he was far too slow.

Before he'd even closed a portion of the distance, Talbot raised his rifle and fired a burst, cutting the man in half. He'd targeted well enough to miss the horse, so Kelsey would be pleased about that. That only left one threat to them now.

"Got him," Chloe said moments later. "He's down on the other side of the building, and our people have him covered. If anybody tries to go for the weapon, we'll take them out. If there are no more high-tech weapons, we should be able to turn this fight around."

Talbot sure as hell hoped so, because the butcher's bill was already going to be too high. Now that he'd seen these weapons in action, he was deathly afraid for his wife. He prayed to the gods that they'd watch over his impulsive woman and keep her from the fate that so many of his people here had just suffered.

* * *

KELSEY LAID into the attackers all around her, leaping as needed to come up to their level. After a few engagements, no one wanted to duel her. She was death on two feet.

The enemy forces didn't have any more of the antiarmor weapons. Without them, they had zero chance against her marines. In less than two minutes, they'd broken the will of the attacking force and sent them scattering.

With the marines using their stunners or lethal weaponry, not very many of the enemy had gotten away, but that didn't mean that everyone fighting them had been captured. The drones were able to tally each of the fleeing riders, so they knew that twenty-six of them had escaped.

When Julia arrived back at the camp, she'd passed word of the ones she'd taken out. Corporal Boske sent a couple of marines to retrieve them and tasked others with helping Beauchamp's forces gather the horses. They'd accumulated quite a few, which might be useful in the upcoming journey.

If, of course, the other woman didn't just take them. Kelsey and Beauchamp still had some things to figure out.

Most of the prisoners were unconscious and laid out in a long row. Others had been taken awake but wounded in one way or another. Those were shackled and seated in a rough circle, with armed guards around them. The last group were the dead, who were also laid out in a line.

Only the one marine had died in the fighting. His name had been Thomas Reed. Kelsey knew virtually nothing about the man, as he hadn't been part of *Athena*'s original complement.

As for the defenders, they'd had half a dozen killed and maybe twice that many wounded. Their leader still moved among them, assessing the damage and preparing her people to move.

While Kelsey watched the woman, Corporal Boske stepped up to her side, her helmet off and resting in the crook of her arm.

"There was nothing you could've done, Colonel," she said softly. "Even if we'd attacked them before they'd arrived at the camp, they'd have still pressed forward. These weren't the kind of people that just broke and ran."

Kelsey didn't know about that, but she wasn't going to argue with the woman. If there was one hard lesson that she'd learned over the last few years, it was that second-guessing yourself was a path that led to misery. You did the best you could with the information that you had at the time and dealt with the consequences. Which was what she needed to do now.

"We need to bury him," Kelsey said tiredly. "We're not going to be able to take him with us."

The other woman delicately cleared her throat. "Colonel, he was struck by high explosives that utterly destroyed him. It would take a long time to find all of the pieces, and that would be one of the grisliest jobs I could imagine. I found part of one boot with his big toe. That might be the largest part of him left in one piece.

"Perhaps that's sacrilegious of me, but I have no desire to dig through the dirt and find bits and pieces of a friend. Let him lie here where he died."

Kelsey grunted and nodded. "You're probably right. Have you kept Jared informed about what's happened?"

The other woman nodded. "Yes, but I haven't kept *you* informed of what was happening *there*. They're engaged with a similar size group right now. Our reinforcements turned around and are almost back to the building."

Kelsey spun on the corporal. "Why didn't you tell me as soon as we'd finished fighting? Get everyone gathered up. We move out in three minutes."

"Colonel, take a breath. By the time we get there, the fighting will be over. Your husband is *more* than capable of defending that building, and from what I've heard, he's taken steps to eliminate the antiarmor weapons. They took some casualties, but the fight has already swung in their favor.

"You have a job here that you need to finish. If we don't find allies, we're all going to die. We've offended this horde, and now we need to know what they're going to do about it. We need to find out if we're even going to be able to start the journey toward the Imperial Palace, or if we're going to be digging in somewhere for a last stand.

"Friends would help us a lot right about now, and we can't let this opportunity pass. You've made a connection with this woman. It's time for you to do what you do best: make friends."

Kelsey felt the corner of her mouth twitch up. "Is that what I do best? I thought it was breaking things and killing bad guys. They certainly seem to think so."

She gestured toward the prisoners, many of whom were staring at her with expressions of terror on their faces. She'd made a strong impression, it seemed.

The other woman seemed to consider her for a moment and then shrugged. "I've always considered that more of a hobby for you. Right now, your ability to make a connection with these people is what's going to get us out of the trap we're in.

"If there's a way to get to the Imperial Palace, to know what threats are between here and there, and come up with a plan to help us to dodge them, she and her people might be our best source of information about them."

Kelsey considered that for a long moment before nodding. She took a deep breath and looked over at where the others were gathering. The marines were still patrolling, but Julia had stepped over to, and was talking with, Clarice Beauchamp.

Interesting. Kelsey hadn't considered that possibility, and she wondered what the other woman was going to tell the warrior. Was Julia a better diplomat than she was? Now might be the time to find out.

"You're right, Corporal. Gather as many of the loose horses as you can. Since we did most of the heavy fighting, I'm going to press our claim to them. If Talbot can capture those around the building, we might have enough for everyone. That would cut our travel time down significantly.

"Meanwhile, I should probably head over and see what my doppelgänger is telling our new friends. We wouldn't want her to give away the farm, would we?"

14

J ared kept firing until the enemy finally broke and raced off in numerous directions, undoubtedly to regroup at a safe distance. He had no idea how many of the horsemen they'd killed or stunned, but he thought they might have gotten more than half.

They stayed on guard in case the enemy returned for another run at them, but after about ten minutes, Talbot told everyone to stand down.

Jared stood and shook the debris and dust off of himself. They hadn't had any more ceiling collapses, but a lot of the material had drifted down onto the combatants during the fighting.

He wanted to assist in pulling survivors from the rubble, or treating the moaning and screaming wounded, but he knew that he had to pay attention to the overall picture first. He'd find out what the butcher's bill was soon enough.

Commander Roche was waiting when he got downstairs. He'd been in charge of the non-combatants, even though he wasn't technically in their version of Fleet at all. Jared had made an exception for the grave circumstances they'd found themselves in. He'd had Sean Meyer heading the armed Fleet personnel to defend the room if the enemy breached it.

"What's going on?" Roche asked quietly once he'd come down the stairs. "I can see from the drone network that the enemy has broken off, but did we win?"

"We survived," Jared replied as he found a brush on one of the walls and started getting the worst of the debris off of his marine fatigues. He'd just finished when Talbot came down the ramp with his helmet off.

The larger man headed directly over to him. "We've driven them off, Admiral, and the building is secure. Chloe is still working on rescuing the trapped personnel and tallying our casualties. We've got a number of injured that are going to start coming down fairly quickly. Commodore Stone is waiting to be receiving them."

The other man's eyes narrowed. "Is that dust all over you, sir? Were you upstairs?"

"Of course I was. I wasn't about to let them fight without me. I'm my sister's brother."

Talbot chuckled. "I suppose that I shouldn't have expected anything else. In any case, the fighting is wrapped up at the landing camp as well. We lost one marine there to one of the antiarmor weapons.

"I'll have Chloe gather our dead so that we can bury them. There are a lot of enemy bodies as well, so we'll create a separate grave for them. We've got a few prisoners, but not as many as you'd think. Apparently falling off of a horse racing at full speed doesn't do well for your chances of ultimate survival.

"What we do have is plenty of armor and weapons suitable for use under primitive conditions. A lot of bows and arrows, a lot of swords, some spears, and some leather armor that we can probably use for a number of our people.

"The marines have their unpowered armor, so they won't need that, but the Fleet personnel and scientists could probably do with a little bit of extra protection, when push comes to shove again."

"Are we going to interrogate the prisoners?" Roche asked. "Maybe they can tell us what we're up against. Maybe they can tell us why those people felt the need to kill us."

Jared nodded. That kind of information would be good to know. If they were going to have to fight people like this all the way to the Imperial Palace, they needed to have a better idea of what they'd done to offend them. Had it just been their presence? Or had it been something murkier?

"What about the horses?" Jared asked. "How many did we capture? Do any of us know how to ride them?"

The marine's eyes unfocused for a moment as he checked something through his implants. "It looks like we've captured roughly forty. We'll probably pick up a few more as we finish sweeping the area, but I'll bet we get no more than fifty. Kelsey's group also captured a number of horses, though it's uncertain whether they'll get to keep them or not. The other group might object.

"I'm hopeful that she can make a deal with them. At some point, the enemy is going to come looking for payback. They don't know exactly who we are, but they know where to find us. I'd imagine it's going to be a significant force with as many heavy weapons as they can gather. Since we won't have powered armor when they come back, we need to be gone without leaving an easy trail for them to follow."

"How do we do that?" Roche asked, throwing up his hands. "No matter what we do, we're going to leave a trail a kilometer wide. Even if we figure out how to ride the horses and take off for the forest, they'll still be able to follow our tracks right to us. Nothing we do is going to get us clear of their response."

Jared nodded. "There's something to what you're saying. We'd best hope that Kelsey can make friends with these new people. If they're already involved in a war with our new enemies, throwing in a few more people behind their protective walls isn't going to hurt them. We can probably trade equipment for our safety, if we can trust them."

He scratched his chin and looked up at the ceiling. "I want everybody ready to travel within the hour. Have Doctor Stone consult with me about who's too injured to move and what we can do to move them anyway. We can't leave anyone behind, so she's going to have to figure out how to make this work.

"Let's hope that Kelsey makes us some new friends. We really need a few right about now."

* * *

JULIA FOUND herself amused as Clarice Beauchamp studied her closely. The other woman was undoubtedly confused at how the woman she'd been speaking with earlier had suddenly gotten into armor. Or perhaps even why she'd bothered to do so after the fighting was already over.

"I'm not the woman you think I am," she said with a bland smile. "That's my twin sister."

While that wasn't *technically* true, giving the woman the impression that she and her doppelgänger were twins by birth rather than variants of one another from different dimensions was *a lot* easier than trying to explain the whole story to someone that she imagined either wouldn't believe her or didn't need to know the truth.

"Sisters?" the other woman said slowly. "I see. What's your name?"

"I'm Julia. Now that the fight is over, what are you going to do next?"

"We'll gather what equipment we can quickly salvage and then depart. We thank you for your intervention, but the horde will not allow this invasion to pass. If we're still within their reach by dusk tomorrow, they'll do their absolute best to kill every single one of us. They don't take intrusions to their territory lightly."

Julia gestured toward the tents. "Everything that we couldn't carry with us is in those. Take whatever you like. It's not something that we're going to be able to carry with us."

Though that was possibly inaccurate, if they got their hands on some horses. Other supplies were inside the pinnaces, so they could play this by ear if they got their hands on enough mounts.

She looked out at where the other group's people were busy capturing the loose horses. "As we shared in the fighting, I believe it's also customary that we share in the spoils. While we don't want any of the equipment, we would find it useful to have extra mounts. Do you have any objection to us taking the horses that were orphaned in the battle?"

The other woman seemed to consider that for a moment and then slowly nodded. "Horses are easy enough to come by. They roam free, and we can capture and train those we need or raise them in our own corrals. These are *warhorses*, however, and they may be somewhat dangerous for your people, particularly new riders. If I were you, I'd definitely wear at least leg armor before trying to ride them."

The other woman was undoubtedly referring to the more primitive armor that was being salvaged from the dead. Those that had been shot with modern weapons had most of their armor chewed up, but perhaps the leggings could be salvaged. Or it would be a case of mixing and matching to find what worked. In any case, that grisly task belonged to someone else.

She did some quick calculations. Based on the number of people they had back at the building, minus the casualties, and the number of horses that Colonel Talbot said that he'd recovered, added to what she was getting here, they still didn't have enough to give everyone a mount of their own. They did have enough to put two people per horse, with some left over for the experienced riders. That would have to do.

At that moment, Kelsey stepped up and joined the conversation. "Julia."

"Kelsey," she responded with a wry smile. "I've been talking with our new friend and arranging for us to take possession of whatever horses can be captured. We'll also take all the armor that we can salvage. In exchange, they can have everything in the tents."

"That sounds like a good deal," Kelsey agreed. "I'll also open up the pinnaces so that they can look inside and determine if there's anything they'd like to take with them. Though, we have some supplies there that we could carry on horses, so we get first pick of that.

"The horde will eventually manage to breach them. If there's anything that you feel worthy of salvage, Miss Beauchamp, it's yours. We'll never be using these craft again."

The other woman smiled slightly. "That's quite generous of you. I believe there are likely several things that we would like to salvage. We can carry them on our remounts as we retreat. And my rank is captain. These men and women are my company: Beauchamp's Bastards."

That was… quite the name.

Beauchamp then stared at the two women. "I find myself quite curious as to the story behind your arrival here. It saddens me that I'm not going to hear the end of it. Perhaps there is further business we can conduct."

Julia hadn't ever heard a better opening than that. The other woman obviously wanted to make a deal that might involve getting them to safety, and at this point, they certainly needed a place to go.

"As it happens, we're not going to be able to get away from the horde unless we have some local assistance. I suggest that we accompany you to a location that is convenient and safe."

"We've got other people about five kilometers from here," Kelsey interjected. "They'll be moving within the next hour. At least the ones that have horses.

"They were attacked as well and recovered about fifty horses. With the ones we have here, that should be enough for almost everyone to ride doubled up, but they won't know how to do so very well."

"Let me be clear. They won't know how to ride *at all*. Is it going to be possible for us to still get out of the horde's territory in time to keep them from catching us?"

Beauchamp nodded. "My people have an outpost a day's ride from here. My company was dispatched from there to salvage what we could from the crash. If your people are prepared to travel, and aren't too slow, we should be able to reach the walls of the outpost by dusk tomorrow. If it was just my people, we'd be able to make it much sooner, but that should be enough time for your people. Barely.

"The horde will know roughly where we're headed, but right now they don't know that we've thrashed their forces. They'll find out about the battles just before dark. They'll respond with every warrior they have close at hand. For such a large force, they're not going to want to travel while it's dark.

"They'll set out first thing in the morning, bringing remounts to pursue us with all the speed they can manage. It's going to be close, but I believe that we can make it to our outpost before they do. Once we get behind its walls, you'll be under our protection while we negotiate further agreements."

"And the horde isn't going to try to burn your city to the ground?" Julia asked.

"They're welcome to try," the other woman said grimly. "It has fixed emplacements of advanced weapons capable of killing any who come too close. If they could've destroyed that outpost before now, they would've already done so.

"This incident is going to anger them greatly, but I don't believe it will change the balance of power all that much. In fact, the loss of the warriors they've had today will blunt them to a degree. They'll still hate us, they'll still want to kill us, but they won't be able to do anything serious about it for now."

Kelsey raised an eyebrow and gave her a slight nod. "I can provide whatever you want quickly, but in exchange, I'd like some of your remounts. That trade-off will allow us to make better time and still let my people all ride. The building where they're at is almost directly back in the direction you came from, so we won't lose much time going for them."

Beauchamp considered that before slowly nodding. "I have some things that would make that agreement worthwhile. Let's gather everything we want and get ready to move out. We will await your riders and then return for the rest of your people. Let's not waste daylight."

15

K elsey watched Julia as she gave lessons to the marines about how to ride horses. She shook her head at the sight of the otherwise competent marines falling off horses and tried not to smirk.

Her amusement temporarily satisfied, she turned her attention back to where Captain Beauchamp's people were quickly sorting through the equipment in the tents and deciding what they could take and what they'd have to leave behind for the horde.

They obviously wanted to take *everything*, but circumstances weren't going to allow that. The horde would be here sometime tomorrow. If they wanted something other than what they'd asked Kelsey to find for them from the pinnaces or the camp, they'd need to take it with them today.

She'd consulted with Talbot and Jared as soon as she'd been able to, and some of them were on their way to the camp even now. Once they arrived, they'd pack what they could and then head back for the rest.

With the horses, it would be possible to take their powered armor with them, though it would have to be packed away. That would be *extremely* helpful. Still, with all of the antiarmor weapons that the horde seemed to have, they were far from a panacea.

They'd have to be extremely careful about how they fought the locals because they didn't have that many marines and they were all her friends. She didn't want to lose a single one of them. They'd gotten lucky in their first fight. Damned lucky.

With their improved ability to carry supplies, she'd selected a lot of extra food from inside the pinnaces. The extra rations would drastically improve their ability to move quickly, at least for now. If they had to stop and hunt, enemies might catch them.

With horses, that equation changed. If they could parlay the other gear into more horses and some assistance, they might be able to get to the Imperial Palace in a couple of months rather than half a year.

Captain Beauchamp interrupted her introspection when she stepped up beside her. "My people have selected what we're going to take from the tents. We should be loaded in the next twenty minutes. Are you going to be ready?"

Kelsey nodded. "We've already gathered some extra food. We don't have those oversized cargo bags that you do, so we're doing the best we can to get it all loaded. It's nice to have more supplies, but it's a little unwieldy right now."

The other woman pursed her lips and nodded. "Traveling long distances can be challenging. It's all a balance between taking everything you need while not carrying too much. Larger saddlebags and using dedicated pack animals would improve your speed. Looking at your people, I'm not certain that you're going to notice much of a difference right now. Forgive me for saying so, but they are terrible riders."

Kelsey was forced to agree. "Thankfully, they're getting a good bit of education from my sister, and they'll manage to figure it out. None of them are stupid. They're going to be slow in the beginning, especially doubled up, but I believe that we can get them moving at a decent pace.

"If we can get your people to assist us in poking them to change behaviors that they shouldn't be doing, I think that will speed us up even more. Riding along and telling someone don't do that, do this, and showing them an example. Like I said, they're bright. They'll figure it out."

"Having spoken to both your sister and you, I have to say that you're an odd pair," the other woman said. "I've met twins before, and they often have relatively different personalities. I suppose it comes from wanting to make one's self different from someone that looks just like themselves.

"The two of you seem inseparably close. You use a lot of the same turns of phrase, your opinions on things are often very similar, and it's eerie how difficult it is to tell the difference between the two of you. Even with twins, one can usually tell which is which with a little time.

"With you two, I'm never certain. Each of you has peculiar quirks that I'm starting to pick up on, but you also have some that are identical. That's unusual."

Kelsey grinned. "Let's just say that we spent a lot of time together when we were younger, and our experiences only really diverged when we were adults. You'll find that Julia and I can be reliably the same in a lot of ways, and then you'll run into a landmine where our opinions are completely different."

"A landmine? As in bombs planted in the ground? Thankfully, I've never run into any of those, though I have read about some in the texts put together by our ancestors during the guerrilla wars."

Kelsey really wanted to ask more about that. That history hadn't been in any of the data banks, either for the Old Empire or even the Rebel Empire. The AIs had perpetuated the myth that Terra was still a civilized world, never allowing word that they'd bombed it a century or more ago to get out.

Learning how they'd fought the AIs and been successful enough that the computers had written them off would be fascinating. There were probably hundreds of tales of derring-do that she could use to distract the people making those idiotic vids about her on Pentagar. If she could get them interested in the siege of Terra, then she could have her life back.

"I'd really like to learn more about that," she said. "It sounds fascinating. Maybe once I have us ready to move out, we can talk more. With our people about to arrive, I need to get the last of the food packed so that it won't take too long to get everyone out of here."

"I'll leave you to it, then," the other woman said, shooting her an oddly casual salute with two fingers to her forehead before rejoining her people.

Kelsey took the next several minutes to make sure that the marines knew that they needed to wrap things up. She didn't want to delay their departure any longer than necessary. By the time they reached the outpost, every minute might count.

She'd heard about the aftermath of Jared's battle. The horde had managed to damage the building where they'd been hiding, killed six people, and wounded fourteen others. Thankfully, the wounds were within Lily Stone's capabilities, and everyone could still ride.

Talbot hadn't directly said so, but she suspected that Jared had been involved in the fighting, and part of her approved. Her brother was a little too restrained when it came to personal combat. Put him on the bridge of a warship and the man would fight like nobody's business, but slap a gun in his hands and he became reticent. A good commander needed to learn how to fight on the ground, in the air, and in space.

She didn't consider herself a leader in that mold, but she was working on it. He, on the other hand, was a genius when it came to fighting spaceships. If she could expand his capabilities with ground fighting, he'd be one of those people that could do anything up to and including commanding marines in action.

Her thoughts were interrupted when Corporal Boske stepped up. "We're done, Colonel. We've bagged everything we can, and the marines have stripped off their armor. Everything is packed away, and our people are ready to travel.

"Captain Beauchamp's people will help us guide the extra horses, since even once the rest of our people get here, we don't have the skills to make it work. They should be here in ten minutes, and we can move out.

"Do we have any idea how we're going to handle this on the way back to the building? Watching my people attempt to ride horses is a comedy of errors. I can only imagine what the Fleet personnel and scientists are going to look like. Can you imagine Carl Owlet trying to ride?"

Kelsey could, and the vision made her laugh. "We'll figure it out. Mount up. Let's join Beauchamp's Bastards and get the hell out of here as soon as Jared and the others get here."

16

Talbot struggled to stay in the saddle while simultaneously glaring at Carl, who rode easily beside him, moving as if he'd been riding horses for years. "How the hell do you know how to ride a horse? Better yet, how did you make friends with that mean bastard you're on?"

Carl gave him an insulted glance. "Buttercup isn't mean, he's just misunderstood."

"Buttercup?" Talbot asked incredulously, feeling his eyebrows rise toward his hairline. "I'm pretty sure that horse is a dude. And a major hardcase, based on the marine he almost stomped after he threw him. The bastard is vindictive."

"The name is kind of an inside joke," Carl said with a grin. "I'll wager Kelsey gets it right off. My mother sent me to a camp when I was a kid because I had difficulty socializing. It was a nice break from all of the tutoring and studying, so I didn't mind too much, even if it meant I had to deal with other people. The instructors said I had a real talent for riding, they taught me all the tricks they knew, and I soaked it up. Up until we went on the expedition, I still rode every chance that I got.

"As for Buttercup, he and I have come to an agreement. I'm not sure what kind of relationship he had with his previous rider, but I showed him who's boss. The trick is making sure that you're the master of the situation and that the horse can't smell your fear. Frankly, it's better not to be afraid at all."

He raised an eyebrow Talbot. "You're not afraid, are you, Talbot? You look kind of nervous to me."

Talbot scowled at the insult. The fact that it was somewhat true was just an added irritant. The big beast he was riding seemed determined to test him at every opportunity and had already tossed him off twice.

These horses had to be trained to obey commands, but only a few of them knew what did what. Worse, everyone was ham-handed with the reins, and that just seemed to make the beasts cranky. There was nothing like having a horse take off into a gallop when you least expected it, leaving you hanging on for dear life.

At least Carl had been able to help them. He'd gone from person to person, giving them what instruction he could to help them at least stay in the saddle. If they were going to make it back to the camp and then move out with the experienced riders, they were going to have to know at least a little about how to keep up.

Having most of them doubled up wasn't helping. Nothing to be done about it though. They only had so many horses, and they couldn't leave anyone behind.

From what Kelsey had said, the woman leading the force at the camp was going to task some of her people to help teach them what they needed to know, so that they could get to the outpost before the horde caught up with them.

Based on what he could see of their performance so far, his people were going to need all the help they could get.

No matter how this worked out, it was terrifying to think that they had to count on these unruly creatures to make it to safety. He wasn't sure that any amount of instruction was going to do them any good over the short term. They were lucky that no one had been injured falling off the horses. Yet.

He glanced over at where Doctor Stone was overseeing the wounded. All of them could ride, though none of them was one hundred percent. Grisham, the worst of the wounded, had his left arm bound tightly to his chest.

They'd selected what seemed to be the most pliable of the warhorses for the wounded and put someone solid behind them. That seemed to be working out so far, as the animals looked as if they were sensing their riders' injuries and going a little easy.

And, Carl had a few extra people to help show them the ropes. Elise and Olivia knew how to ride, though the warhorses were more than a bit challenging for even them.

Kelsey and Julia also knew how to ride, so technically they had five experienced riders, but that wasn't nearly enough for over a hundred people. He'd gratefully accepted the strangers' help getting them to the outpost because he didn't want to see any more of his people die.

Just having to bury the six that had already fallen burned his soul. Kelsey hadn't been able to do anything with the marine that had been killed at the camp. Some tasks were just too hard to do under these conditions.

If they survived, Talbot had sworn to see them properly interred at the Spire on Avalon. If any of them made it off this cursed world.

Even as he was thinking that, they came over a low rise and he saw the camp spread out below them. There was a beehive of activity still taking place, and he also noted the lines of dead and the captured prisoners still huddled together under guard.

None of the prisoners at the building had seemed inclined to speak, so they'd cut them loose, on foot, and with no weapons or armor. They'd undoubtedly rejoin their friends within a couple of days and that would mean they'd fight them again, but they couldn't exactly take the captives with them.

Kelsey must've noted their approach because she rode out to meet them. As she got closer, she angled over toward Talbot and soon matched his slow pace, grinning at him.

"So, how do you enjoying riding?" she asked cheerfully.

"Don't you start with me," he warned. "My ass is already hurting like a bitch."

"Don't worry about it," Carl said smugly. "By nightfall, it'll be completely numb. And tomorrow? Oh, you are going to be in such pain."

Talbot narrowed his eyes at his friend and considered spooking his horse, but the little bastard would probably maintain control of the beast and then smirk at him.

How that scientist boy could smirk. It was so unfair.

He forced his attention back to his wife. "How are things here? Are you ready to go?"

Kelsey nodded. "Everything's packed. We've loaded up every horse we could catch and have all the food we could gather already loaded. We should be ready to go inside fifteen minutes, and then we'll head back for the rest.

"The stunned horses should be awake by the time we get there. The ones here are already up. It must be because they have more mass than a person. Take a break while we get the last details right. You're going to need more of those than we can give you by the time this ride is over."

Her smile had faded as she'd spoken, and he knew she was speaking nothing but the truth. The next few days were going to be hell.

* * *

JULIA RODE between Scott and Mertz. Unlike the two of them, she had experience in the saddle and sat easily. Since none of the marines, Fleet personnel, or scientists, except Carl Owlet, had any experience on horseback, she'd chosen one of the more recalcitrant beasts. She had the strength to control him and the skill to not need it.

Her doppelgänger had chosen a relatively docile beast—or as close to it as a warhorse got—for Mertz. Even so, his mount had already tried to bite his leg several times and had successfully thrown him once. Scott's horse had done even worse, having thrown him and then tried to stomp him.

She turned her head and looked back over the trail of horses scattered out behind them. They'd made their way back to the building and picked up the horses that had been stunned and the last of their people. Most people were doubled up, but they all had rides. Now they just had to get to the outpost alive.

Clarice Beauchamp's people were spread out along the line of riders, trying to keep anyone from being injured or run over by the horses they were forced to ride. Olivia West, Elise Orison, Carl Owlet, and her doppelgänger were helping, but the group was a sad, straggly sight.

The local riders were also responsible for maintaining the security of the march as they tried to keep the group's speed up. They'd been on the trail for a couple of hours now and had taken more breaks than she was comfortable with. If they were going to beat the horde to the outpost, they were going to have to pick up the pace.

"My ass is killing me," Scott complained. "Please tell me this gets easier."

She nodded, but her smile was anything but reassuring. "It gets easier, but not until it gets a *lot* worse. You're going to be really sore tonight, and tomorrow is going to be agony."

"It doesn't matter how bad we feel, we're going to have to do better," Mertz said.

Jared, she mentally corrected herself. He was not the Bastard, and she needed to get out of the behavior of referring to him by his last name. Either she needed to attach a title to it, to increase the respect that she was presenting—even in her head—or use his first name.

If she'd housed any remaining doubts over what kind of person he was, the stories of how he'd fought with his people to protect the building against the horde had put that notion firmly to rest.

The Mertz from her universe was not selfless. He'd have stayed downstairs and let others do the fighting for him. He wouldn't have risked his skin to save those under his command.

"Let me tell you how it's going to go," she said. "Right now, you're feeling sore. It's because you're not sitting properly. That means that every time the horse moves, rather than moving with him, you're slamming into the saddle. You're also abusing muscles that you've never had to use like this before. If you want to have a smoother ride, you need to learn the right seat and use it for an extended period.

"That's not going to happen today, and it's not going to happen tomorrow, but it *is* going to happen, if we live long enough. Focus on not fighting the horse. If we have to ride all the way to the Imperial Palace, you're going to be accomplished horsemen by the time we get there. You just need to live that long."

Scott grimaced but nodded. "Living in pain is better than dying. We'll manage. Do you think we're going to get to the outpost ahead of the horde?"

She shrugged. "I have no idea. We don't really know how far away it is, and we don't know where the horde is going to come from. Or if they'll come after us at all. They may stop at the camp and decide that we're just not worth the trouble."

Jared laughed cynically at that. "Oh, I think they'll come after us. We've used advanced weaponry, and we came down on ships from the sky. They've got a bug up their butts about that, it seems.

"The prisoners we captured wouldn't talk very much, but just the presence of Talbot in armor was enough for them to try to kill everybody in the building. They associate us with the System Lords, and they tried to kill every last one of us. Seeing the pinnaces is going to provoke an extremely hostile response from them.

"They'll use whatever force they can scrape together to bog us down until an even larger force arrives with more heavy weapons, I'll wager. If they bring enough heavy weapons, they'll feel comfortable dealing with us. As Kelsey is so fond of saying, 'ten men with clubs can beat a man with a flechette pistol, if they're prepared to bleed.'

"It's going to be a race. If we can get to the outpost before they can catch up with us, we're probably going to survive for a little while longer. If we don't, we're going to be making a last stand tomorrow."

Julia turned in her saddle to look back down the line of riders again. Based on her experience, they'd pick up some basic skills in the next couple of hours. Not enough to be comfortable and not enough to avoid pain, but enough to increase the pace. With lives at stake, people were going to grit their teeth and ride through whatever troubles they came across.

One of the riders caught her eye. Carl Owlet was moving up the line of scientists, giving them advice. The way that he sat his horse spoke of years of experience in the saddle. She was surprised to see that and pleased. He was a man of many talents and surprising depths. The more she found out about him, the more interested in him she became.

Again, she wasn't going to encroach on Angela Ellis's territory. The man was her husband, and he was safe from any interest that she might have. But that wasn't going to stop her from spending a good amount of time with him and learning what she could about him.

In her universe, his doppelgänger would be very similar, though less experienced. Just like the Kelsey in this universe, the man she was looking at had been put through the fire. He'd come out the other side forged in a different way than her doppelgänger or herself, but he was still a warrior scholar.

The man back in her universe would probably be a bookish nerd—a word she'd picked up from Carl, ironically—who wouldn't realize what he was capable of. That was fine by her because she didn't necessarily need a warrior at her side, but she still knew that he'd react well under pressure and that he had a backbone.

That was *really* important. All too many people in the nobility ended up being self-centered, spineless jerks. Seeing that this young man was none of the above made him an excellent candidate for her consort.

While she wouldn't know for certain until she got back home, she thought Ethan would like him. Eventually. He'd be shocked at her choice, of course, but he always had been. Not that she'd ever had an active dating life, but Ethan wouldn't guess a mousy scientist would interest her.

She didn't know what was going to happen in her universe, but the odds were high that the AIs were going to arrive at Avalon before she returned home. When they did, they'd force the New Terran Empire to surrender.

Her job, when she returned—if she couldn't stop the AIs with the override—would be to work behind the scenes with whatever forces she could pull together to free them. If she could get people like Carl Owlet to help her, to understand all the technology that they were being given, then the Empire might have a chance.

Right now, he was just a student. He wouldn't stand out on anybody's scanners as a threat. That meant he wouldn't be locked away—or killed—like Ethan would. Like she would. He'd still be free and approachable.

Much like the people of Terra had formed a guerrilla movement, that was what she was probably going to have to do when she returned home. If she could bring enough information and technology with her, Carl Owlet would be a very potent ally in a fight like that.

She turned and looked ahead of them. "If you gentlemen are ready, I think it's time we picked up the pace a notch. We need to get to a good camping ground by dark, and I'd like to make it as far away from the first camp as possible."

With that, she used her heels and a flick of her reins to move her horse into a canter. Groans sounded behind her as the two Fleet officers followed suit.

17

By the time they'd stopped riding for the day, Jared's legs and thighs were solid bands of pain, while his rear felt like lead. He'd needed help getting down from the saddle and could barely walk. It only took a single glance around their campsite to see that everyone else without training on horse riding was in just as bad a shape. Or worse.

"Everyone listen up," Kelsey said, waving her arms in the growing dusk. "You need to walk it off. I understand that everything hurts, and I have bad news. It's going to get worse if you don't move around. Walk the campsite, do some stretching exercises, and work those muscles as much as you can. We'll get something together for dinner, and then you're going to have to get as much sleep as you can, because we'll be up before dawn and doing this all over again."

Her announcement was greeted with loud groans, and Jared felt like adding his own to the chorus, but long training as a Fleet officer had taught him that that wasn't wise.

"You heard Her Highness," he said in his best command voice. "We're going to have a long ride tomorrow, and we'll have people that want to kill us right on our tails. I suggest you loosen up as much as you can, because there's not going to be nearly as many breaks tomorrow. Colonel Talbot and Commodore Meyer, take charge of everyone."

His people, with the exception of the scientists, knew better than to groan back at their commanding officer. Kelsey, though, was more like everybody's little sister, even though everyone knew what a badass she was. They'd give her a little back talk, but not him.

The place they'd stopped at looked like every other piece of the grassland that he'd seen this far, except perhaps just a little bit higher in elevation than the surrounding terrain. Beauchamp had had her people gather the horses into a picket off to the side of the camping area.

She had some of her people digging fire pits. Not just places to keep the flames from catching anything on fire, but deep holes so that the light wouldn't go out to the sides. No riders in the distance would see them. Thankfully, there were enough scrawny trees scattered around to provide firewood.

Based on what he'd seen last night, it wouldn't be getting very cold tonight. They were in the middle of the summer season, so the temperatures would be moderate. That had meant that riding during the day had been a hot, sweaty affair though. Jared desperately needed a shower that he knew he wasn't getting anytime soon. The marine fatigues had materials built into them that kept the smell down, but there were limits to what even that could do.

While he was trying to work the worst of the pain out of his legs and back, Elise stepped up beside him, looking as if she'd just had a refreshing and enjoyable day out riding. He tried not to glare at her, but from her expression of amusement, he'd failed.

"I think I hate you," he said matter-of-factly.

She laughed and pulled him into a hug. Then, after a moment, she pushed him back, her nose crinkling in distaste. "You stink."

"Thanks for that," he said dryly. "You're no spring shower either. You don't just smell like sweat. You smell like horse. Then again, I suspect I do, as well. Neither one of us is going to be able to fix that for a while, so you're just going to have to get used to it."

She grinned at him, showing that she wasn't hurt by his commentary. "After a day on the trail, everyone needs a shower. On this planet, I suspect our noses are going to go numb as to how bad we smell after a while, which will be a blessing."

His wife stepped close to him again, tilted his head down, and kissed him. "We'll just have to get used to it. Call it your warrior smell or something."

Their moment of closeness was interrupted when someone softly cleared their throat beside them. He turned his head and found a smiling Kelsey standing beside him, with Beauchamp at her side.

"I'm sorry to interrupt your moment, but we've got some things to discuss," his sister said. "It's time for us to get to know one another. We can't ride in the dark and, even though we need to get some rest, we need to take the time to introduce ourselves.

"Captain Clarice Beauchamp, this is Admiral Jared Mertz of the New Terran Empire Fleet and his wife Crown Princess Elise Orison of the Kingdom of Pentagar. Jared is my brother, though the family tree is somewhat... convoluted. The man who raised me was his father."

Jared repressed a smile. The part his sister was leaving out was that Emperor Karl Bandar hadn't actually been Kelsey's biological father, though he was Jared's. Kelsey's mother had been somewhat... free with her favors.

He extended his hand to Beauchamp. When she took it, her grip was firm and professional.

"It's a pleasure to meet you, Captain. Thank you very much for helping us get out from under the heels of the horde."

The woman smiled slightly. "I'm not exactly certain what an admiral is, but your sister has explained to me that you don't belong to the same organization that works for the artificial intelligences. If you're fighting them, then it serves the interests of my people to help you."

"What we're going to do now is make certain that's true. You could've lied in order to get my assistance. And if you cannot convince me of your honesty, then I believe the officials of my government are going to have some very ugly questions for you."

The woman turned and gestured toward one of the fires. "My people are preparing enough food for everyone. It's not the best tasting, but trail rations rarely are. We'll eat and then we'll talk."

Jared considered putting the discussion off until Sean and Talbot were done but decided that this needed to be settled as soon as possible. He and Kelsey would be the best choices to state their case. The others would probably arrive before the story was done.

He rubbed his backside. "That sounds good, though if you'll forgive me, I think I'll stand for a bit. I've done a little bit too much sitting today."

* * *

KELSEY STAYED CLOSE to the two as they walked over to the fire. She wasn't surprised when they arrived and found her doppelgänger already seated on the ground and sipping something out of a metal cup. The other woman made an expression that said she didn't particularly care for what she was drinking, but she didn't stop consuming it.

"Julia, how are you feeling?" Kelsey asked. "And what have you got there? Something good?"

The other woman waved her cup around slightly. "It's been a while since I've ridden, but it came back to me just fine. This coffee, on the other hand, I don't think I'd use the word 'good' in reference to it. It's hot, has caffeine, and is hitting the spot, but it's *far* from good."

Even as her doppelgänger was saying that, Elise walked out of the growing darkness with a cup of her own. "Oh, it's not that bad. If all you're used to is something from the palace, then it's pretty rough. If compared to army coffee, it's better than average."

Kelsey raised an eyebrow. "What would you know about army coffee, and how do I get some?"

The Pentagaran noblewoman grinned at her. "I just took a small detour to the next fire over, where I could smell it brewing. I'm surprised that you didn't figure out where it was before you got here with that enhanced nose of yours.

"As for getting around, part of my father's legacy revolves around that kind of thing. As you know, he believes in getting out among the people and did so when he was younger. I took full advantage of that when I was growing up, and I've been to all sorts of places and sat down with a number of people that a woman of my social status probably shouldn't have been associated with, strictly speaking. It's all been very illuminating."

That made Kelsey a little bit jealous because she'd been somewhat closeted as a child. It wasn't that her father had blocked her from going places, it was that her position insulated her from the same kind of people that Elise had been able to visit.

Before she could say anything further, Olivia came out of the darkness with two cups of coffee and handed one of them to Kelsey. "Here you go. Like your sister-in-law said, it's not awful."

Kelsey accepted the hot metal cup from the other woman and took a sip. The coffee was black, unsweetened, and *exceptionally* strong. The bitter flavor threatened to overwhelm her for a moment until the wash of caffeine smoothed things out.

After a few moments, Kelsey nodded slowly. "This works. Olivia, would you do me the favor of getting Jared a cup? I'd imagine that he could use one right about now."

The other woman nodded and headed back toward the other fire.

Kelsey settled down near Jared and listened as her brother explained their people's history. He was starting back at the beginning, where Lucian fled Terra for Avalon while Emperor Marcus led the final fight against the AIs. Or the rebels, as they'd called them back then, simply because the Old Empire had had no idea what they were really facing.

By the time he'd finished his story and gotten to the point where they were fighting against the AIs in the modern age, all of the other leaders of their group had arrived. Each of them had found the coffee and sat. One of Beauchamp's people had brought food around, and they'd eaten while Jared continued telling the story.

Beauchamp might've only expected a brief introduction, but she didn't stop the story. Telling it took a couple of hours, even without questions. By the time her brother had finished, full night had fallen long ago, and the glory of the stars dominated the sky above them.

To Kelsey's shock, the wildlife around them was deafening. The insects, which had been loud during the day, *really* opened up at night. There were also other animal calls in the darkness, but she couldn't put any names to them. She had no experience with anything like that. It was amazing.

Beauchamp sat silent for a long while after Jared had finished speaking. She asked no questions, and she didn't act as if she either believed him or doubted his words. When she finally did speak, her tone held no hint of judgment.

"If it were up to me, I'd be inclined to believe you," she said quietly while staring into the fire. "I'll warn you that others will not be as accepting as I. When we arrive at the outpost, you'll have an opportunity to tell your story. The leaders there will have many questions.

"I also have things that I want to know, but it's not the right time for me to inquire. Tomorrow is going to be a brutal day of riding for all of you, as well as difficult for myself and my people, eking out every single bit of speed that you can give. We will be brutal taskmasters.

"Honestly, I think that we'll make it to the outpost before the horde catches up with us, but they could surprise me. We're going to have to be ready to fight if they try to block us from reaching safety.

"To do that, everyone is going to need all the rest they can get. I suggest you retire for the evening and be ready to rise in just a few hours. We'll ride as soon as we can make out the ground around us. Focus on your survival and worry about the political implications of your arrival once you're safe, relatively speaking."

The woman smiled grimly. "After all, there'll always be time to hang you later if we don't like what you have to say. Tomorrow could be a day of great danger for you, but don't believe for one moment that you're any safer at the outpost, unless you can convince our leaders there of your honesty. If you work for the artificial intelligences, they'll find out and they *will* kill you.

"And if it's true, I'll help them do it."

With that, the woman rose and walked off into the darkness, leaving them alone near the fire, which had burned down to coals over the hours.

Rather than wait for someone to say something, Kelsey stood and extended her hand to Talbot. Together, they walked off toward where they would sleep.

The other woman was right. Their survival depended on convincing their potential allies that they shared their goals. She had a few ideas about how that might best be done, but it was a toss of the dice. They had to be convincing, because if they failed to win friends and allies, they'd all die.

Worse, everyone on Terra would eventually die as well. And if the AIs were willing to do that to Terra, how long before they decided that humanity in general needed to perish?

Convincing them to help her would be the most important task that Kelsey had ever faced. One her Raider augmentation couldn't help her with. One where it might be a strong negative influence on the discussions, in fact. Beauchamp had seen her fight without armor. That *would* come up, and she'd have to explain how she could do what she did.

That was a lot of pressure, but she'd make it work. She had to.

18

The next morning, Talbot woke feeling a lot better than he'd expected to. His medical nanites had done yeoman's work while he'd slept. The pain and soreness that he'd been feeling was mostly gone.

Kelsey was up and seemed to have no ill effects at all, which annoyed him all over again. She made up for it by hunting him down some coffee. He needed it.

He wasn't looking forward to another day in the saddle, much less the more difficult ride he expected them to make today, but at least he wasn't suffering debilitating pain.

A quick check revealed that he was doing better than the regular marines because his Raider nanites were doing a much better job of caring for him. The artificial muscles woven throughout his real ones were also taking off quite a bit of the stress.

The regular marines, Fleet personnel, and scientists also had nanites, but theirs weren't as capable as his. Each of them had been hit harder than him, his wife, and her doppelgänger.

That said, they were doing better than Beauchamp's people had expected them to. He could tell by the natives' expressions and whispered conversations that they expected everyone to be almost bedridden. Instead, they were up and doing what they needed to.

Beauchamp cut off their discussion with a loud whistle, and everyone settled down to eat some rations and get ready for a day of hard riding.

Talbot tried the local version of pre-prepared food and wasn't surprised to see that it was just as unappetizing as the marine version. Well, that hardly mattered. They need the calories. He ate his share and then ate some more.

Watching Kelsey eat everything in sight had always amused him, but now that he was also a Marine Raider, his appetite dwarfed hers. Now it was her turn to be bemused by how much food he could put away. Luckily, he'd packed a *lot* of ration bars for just this situation.

That didn't stop him from devouring everything Beauchamp's people had to offer. Never look a gift horse in the mouth. That new saying was completely appropriate for this situation, he decided, having seen the beasts up close and personal.

By the time they'd finished eating, the sun was coloring the horizon. It would've been helpful if the moon was showing more light, but it would've also put them in danger since someone could see them at longer distances. On balance, it was probably better that only a sliver of its silvery gray surface was lit.

Talbot wished his marines could help, but their "assistance" would undoubtedly be more of a hindrance than a help, so they stood by, stroking their horses' necks, talking to them, and trying to get them used to their presence.

The Fleet personnel and scientists put on the captured armor, while his people put on the marine unpowered armor. They also had the primitive weapons that they'd captured, but they weren't worrying about that right now. No one had the time to even learn how to safely handle the swords. When the call came to mount up, they did so, and the column moved out.

The next four hours were brutal. As much work as their nanites had done, their bodies weren't ready for the stress of riding as hard as they did. Unlike the first day, this time they only stopped twice during the morning, and those only briefly. Not even really enough time to recover any feeling in their legs and butts before they were in the saddle again and on the move.

He spent his time conferring with Scala, Chloe, and Boske about the overall layout of their troops and the terrain that they were coming up on. With the drones overhead, they had a good view out to about five kilometers. He might've been able to push that a little bit, but he didn't want to lose any of the devices. They were irreplaceable at this point.

That didn't mean that he wasn't willing to risk the occasional one by sending it out on a recon mission out to ten kilometers. He mainly did that going forward, but he also sent out recon missions to the sides and to their rear.

Over the morning, they hadn't seen anything worthy of note. Nothing but animals and long dormant desolation. This borderland between whoever Beauchamp served and the horde wasn't well traveled. There were no roads and very few trails.

They broke for lunch, if it could be called that, and ate quickly. They didn't bother with a fire because speed was more important.

It was late afternoon when he spotted the outpost coming up in the visual from one of his drones. The device was about at the limit of its ten-kilometer range when it spotted the structure growing out of the ground ahead of them.

When Beauchamp had used the word outpost, he'd thought of something fairly small and fortified. That was not exactly what he was seeing now. The structure ahead of them was a walled city. Maybe a small one, but definitely a population center that had thousands of people living in it. Perhaps tens of thousands.

The construction was a mixture of wood and stone, natural elements rather than plascrete. Based on the height of the walls, and the vigilant guards observing land around them, the locals weren't taking their safety for granted.

There were also reinforced positions on the walls that spoke to him of heavy weapons emplacements. He was willing to wager that something high-tech and powerful lurked inside those well-protected locations, though he wouldn't know for sure unless he had a chance to look at them more closely once they were inside the outpost, should their hosts prove willing to show them to him.

He was about to pass that information on to the admiral when one of their drones reported an anomaly. Off to the left-hand side of their column, it had spotted another band of riders. This group was about twice their size and looked all too familiar. It was a horde war band.

He used his implants to do some calculations based on their direction of travel and speed, comparing it with their own. The horde would probably intercept them just short of the outpost. If that happened, this wasn't going to end well.

"Heads up," he said over the command channel and passed along the readings from the drones so that everyone would know the situation. That earned curses as his friends realized they weren't going to get out of this unscathed.

While the higher-ups considered the situation, he called for Corporal Boske to join him. When she had done so, he spoke with her in a low tone.

"You're going to command the ready response team. If we can keep that group off the main column until the admiral and Kelsey can reach the outpost, I'll call that a win."

The pink-haired noncom nodded. "You can count on us, sir. We'll keep them off your necks."

"I know you will. Good luck."

What he actually knew is that he just ordered his subordinate to lead what could all too easily turn into a suicide mission. If they got bogged down in the fighting, even with their technological superiority, they'd be exterminated to the last man and woman.

Of course, since he was going to be personally leading the rear guard, he might find trouble of his own that would keep him from getting to the outpost.

He wasn't going to tell Kelsey that. She'd try to come up with a different plan when they really didn't have any other options.

While Boske was gathering her people, he called Chloe over a private com channel. "Chloe, I'm going to do what we can to keep the horde off your back. I need you to keep Kelsey and the admiral safe while we do it. Work with Howard to make sure. Adrian will be with me."

His officer didn't have to be told what that meant. "You got it, Colonel. Nobody's getting through me or my people."

"Excellent. We're leaving in a couple of minutes. Good luck."

He'd already marked the spots on the map where he'd make his stand, if he had to. Right now, he'd settle for grouping most of his marines on that side of the column. The drones told him the other side was clear out to the ten-kilometer mark. Depending on how well Boske did, he'd make the decision on whether or not to set up a blocking force.

Talbot let his eyes wander up to the front of the column where Kelsey was riding beside the admiral. They were discussing the information he'd sent them, and she wasn't looking back toward him. She was a warrior, but she wasn't as experienced as he was yet. She hadn't realized at a glance what the situation was going to require. When she did, she was going to be pissed.

Well, he'd hope that things were well underway before she caught on. If someone was going to die today, it would be him and his people, not his wife or the admiral. He didn't want that to happen, but if that's the way things fell, he'd rather she live. If those two died, humanity likely died with them.

* * *

Julia was still tied into the marine net and heard Talbot's instructions to Corporal Boske. A glance at her doppelgänger showed that the other woman was not aware of what her husband was doing. After a moment's consideration, she decided that was probably for the best.

The hazy outlines of Talbot's plan were already beginning to take shape in the mental battle space that the marines were constructing. She could see exactly how they planned to split off the ready reaction team to meet the incoming hostiles. The remaining marines would defend the column from somewhere closer, making a blocking force if required.

If her doppelgänger realized that her husband was preparing to put himself in harm's way so that she could escape, she had no doubt that the woman would lose her mind.

Oh, she was much more of a warrior than Julia was, but she wasn't going to let her husband sacrifice himself for her. Oh no. She'd make certain that she stood beside him until the bloody end. She wouldn't leave him behind to die when she would live.

Her eyes slid over to Scott Roche. While they weren't in the least romantically entangled, he'd have the same type of reaction if it were her in danger. That was going to be awkward because she'd already decided that her assistance might make the difference between the ready response team being able to break away from the incoming horsemen and being bogged down in a fatal encounter.

They already knew that the horde had heavy weaponry that was capable of taking out powered armor. If they were going to stop the horsemen, they needed a way to do that where they didn't expose themselves or get bogged down, allowing the horde to cut them off from escape.

With her mind made up, she nudged her horse over closer to Scott. "I want you to coordinate with Admiral Mertz and Kelsey. You've been doing a good job of keeping an eye on the scientists, and I want to see that continue. We can't afford to lose any of them on the final rush to the outpost."

He nodded. "I'm on it, Highness." With that, he rode forward to join that part of the column.

With her friend distracted, Julia took the opportunity to edge farther away from the main column so that she was trailing behind Corporal Boske and her subordinates tasked with stopping the horde from cutting them off from safety.

The marines never glanced back at her. They were focused on the task ahead of them, and they had their implant maps to tag everyone who was going. Julia took the opportunity to utilize the overrides that she had built into her implants to add herself to the ready response team listing as a member.

Her ability to do that would probably shock Jared Mertz. After all, he'd recommended to the emperor and the senate in this universe that she be declared unfit to be heir as a way to make certain that someone they didn't trust didn't have authority she wasn't supposed to have.

The problem with that was that now that they were reunited with her doppelgänger, they'd had to find a way to have their cake and eat it too. A turn of phrase she heartily approved of, since she loved cake.

They'd secretly re-enabled Princess Kelsey's authority without telling Julia. She'd already been checking for that because she'd expected that's what they'd do. They'd added some code that Carl Owlet had created to make a perfunctory effort at keeping her out, but it was easily subverted.

At least that's what Austin Darrah had told her when she'd asked him to bypass it. He hadn't even needed to get someone more skilled than himself at programming to make it happen. The system just wasn't designed to keep someone with the right access codes out.

As her codes were exactly as valid as her doppelgänger's, the kludge was never going to work. She'd just needed someone to subvert their hack without letting them know that they'd done so.

She had no intention of abusing her authority as heir to the throne, but when push came to shove, she'd do what she needed to do to be certain that this mission succeeded. It only took a little earnest conversation to convince Austin of that, and now she was able to do what needed to be done.

Someone had to get out of here with the override. Only victory in this universe would see the device get back to hers. If her participation in this fight made it more likely that Scott would eventually return to her universe with the key to victory, then it would be worth it, even if she didn't make it.

She'd taken an opportunity last night to go through the heavy weapons that the marines had brought along for their armor. The last fight hadn't involved the use of them because the marines hadn't expected to run into anything dangerous to them. This time they were carrying weapons capable of knocking pinnaces out of the sky or destroying entrenched positions. *Modern* entrenched positions.

While she was no expert at the use of something like that, she'd taken the opportunity to pilfer one of the spare weapon systems, packing it away with her armor. Now she'd be able to assist in this battle in a way that she hadn't before.

There'd be no stunners this time. They'd hit the enemy as fast and hard as they could. Their only real hope of doing so and getting away was to catch them before they knew they were in danger and exterminate them. And that's what she intended to do.

19

J ared tried his best to split his attention between the interface accessing
the drone feeds and riding his horse. As an inexperienced rider, that
wasn't exactly easy. In fact, every time he thought he had the hang of
it, a change in his horse's gait distracted him.

The marines in the ready response team were moving off to intercept
the incoming riders while Talbot sent Major Scala and more of the marines
on a course that put them between the column and the hostiles. They'd only
dismount if the ready response team wasn't able to delay the horde forces.

The distance between the column and the outpost was shrinking as they
rode toward it, but it was a race to see if they reached the walls before the
horde caught up with them. A race that he wasn't certain they were going
to win.

Out of habit, he performed a check of where his senior people were and
what they were up to. A good leader trusted his subordinates to take care of
the mission at hand, but as he was ultimately responsible for what
happened, it paid to make sure that everything was actually getting done the
way it needed to be.

Talbot had the majority of his marines in hand, Scott Roche was taking
care of the scientists, Sean Meyer was overseeing the Fleet personnel, Olivia
and Elise were safely tucked away in the middle of the column, and Kelsey
was furiously studying whatever she was looking at through her implants as
she rode next to him.

The one person he didn't immediately spot was Julia. Kelsey's
doppelgänger was nowhere in sight.

He double-checked what he could see of the personnel through his
implants. Marine officers and sergeants had the ability to track of all their
personnel, their condition, and other salient facts about them at a glance.

He normally didn't access that type of information, but he did know it existed.

It took him longer than it would've taken Talbot to scan down the list of people in the column, but he reached the end without finding Julia. That wasn't good.

He expanded the view and finally found her tagging along behind the ready response team.

He cursed under his breath. He could order her to return to the column, but he knew that was useless. Just like his sister, the woman never changed her mind when she made it up. If she thought something needed doing, she'd do it and damn the consequences.

"What's wrong?" Kelsey asked, sparing him a glance.

"Your double attached herself to the ready response team. It looks like she's on her way out to fight the horde."

Kelsey said something distinctly unladylike. She'd obviously been hanging around Talbot and the marines for far too long.

"It's too late to stop her now," she growled. "She's got Raider implants and her armor, so she'll be as safe as anyone. Her presence might actually help them accomplish their mission, which I'm sure is exactly what she had in mind. I can't say she's wrong, even if I do want to strangle her."

"Pot, meet kettle."

His sister barked out a short laugh. "I suppose that's true enough. The question is, would slamming these bastards hard enough make our lives easier? Instead of just sending the ready response team to ambush them, maybe we should divert most of the marines to hit them head-on and crush them."

"They've probably got a lot more of those antiarmor weapons," he argued. "They didn't come all this way looking to just fight. They intend to catch us and kill us before we reach the outpost."

"Then they're going about it all wrong," she said bluntly. "Even though they've got more warriors, they've got to know that we're going to punch their lights out. There is literally no chance that that force is going to catch up with the main column."

"I realize that it looks that way, but if we delay them any amount of time at all, the column will make it to the outpost. They're screwed when it comes to keeping us from getting there if that's their plan."

Jared frowned. He wasn't experienced with fighting on the ground, but if he put this into the same frame of reference as a space battle, he could see what she was saying.

Thinking about it that way brought another, uglier thought to mind. If this was a fight he was orchestrating, that attacking force wouldn't be the only one on the board. There'd be others waiting for that obvious group to drive them into an ambush. Ships with their drives down, hiding in plain sight, and waiting for his ships to waltz right into the kill zone.

"Then they're a distraction," he said grimly. "They're herding us into an ambush. There's another force somewhere in front of us waiting to spring a trap. Maybe that's being paranoid, but we have to plan for the worst and hope we're wrong."

Kelsey's eyes widened as she understood what he was saying. "I've got to tell Beauchamp. Get Talbot to get his people on the move. I want them in front of the column right now. We need to have the drones looking more closely at the ground we're going to be traveling over. Damn but that's clever."

With that, his sister raced off in the direction of Captain Beauchamp.

Jared opened a channel to Talbot and passed word of what he suspected to the marine officer. The other man cursed, oddly enough using the *exact* turn of phrase that his wife had used earlier. Maybe that wasn't so odd, now that he thought about it.

"We've sent all the armor to meet the incoming force," Talbot said. "Do you think that's what they wanted?"

"I'd count on it. They have to know that we have the means to see them even when others on this world don't. We've proven it to them in ambushing them at the camp. A canny leader will deduce that.

"Now they've put a large force out there so that we'd respond, so of course we're going to use the strongest force we have available. They probably have other weapons at their disposal that will be just as surprising as the antiarmor weapons. We're not going to know what until we engage them. We also won't know anything about the group I suspect is ahead of us until we find them."

With the tall grass that covered much of the area between them and the outpost, Jared suspected that the intruders were concealing themselves somewhere in relatively plain sight.

The marine drones had the capability of detecting things infrared and ultraviolet, so it shouldn't be difficult to switch them over and locate any hidden groups. They wouldn't have had time to dig a deep enough hole to conceal their presence. In this fallen world, they probably didn't have much need to do that either.

Even though he knew Talbot was undoubtedly thinking along those lines, he added his suspicions.

"I've been thinking about that too," Talbot said. "I've got a couple of drones running through the area ahead of us looking for locations they could be using. Once I find them, if they're there, I'll start putting together a tactical response.

"I've already searched the area closest to us, and it looks clean. I'd imagine they're another two or three kilometers in front of us, if they're out there at all. They have to allow space and time for us to be spooked by their diversionary force.

"In fact, they may not be directly in front of us. They may expect us to change course based on contact with their diversionary force. We don't have enough drones to search all around us for a great distance, but we should be able to provide enough coverage to locate where our problem is going to be before we run over them."

"Keep me informed," Jared said. "If you need to act without direct orders, consider the word given. Do what you think best to defend us. Kelsey is talking with Captain Beauchamp right now, so her people will be in the loop. I'll join her right now to pass along any information you get because I doubt Kelsey will stay in the column when the fighting is imminent."

The other man laughed. "I suppose not. Well, we'll do what we need to do. You'll make it to the outpost."

"Good luck, Colonel. Mertz out."

Jared killed the channel. The unspoken part of what Talbot had just said was that the people in the column might make it to the outpost, but the marines engaging the enemy would take losses. Losses they could ill afford.

Jared considered donning his powered armor but decided he already had enough problems riding. Besides, if the horde did ambush them, the men and woman in the armor would be their primary targets during the initial attack. Best not to paint a bull's-eye on his back when he couldn't react like Kelsey. Her augmentation might give her a chance to survive something like that, but he had no such edge.

He put his negative thoughts out of his mind. There was nothing he could do to minimize what was coming, other than trust the marines to do their jobs. Now he needed to focus on doing his.

* * *

KELSEY LAID out the situation for Captain Beauchamp. The other woman wasted no time asking how she knew, instead ordering her people into action. Some of her men went out to bolster the scouting forces ahead of them with orders to spread farther out in front of the column.

Unfortunately, the only way that those scouts would likely get information back is when they were ambushed and some of the number killed. Those were brave men and women, Kelsey knew. Very much like the marines.

Almost as soon as Beauchamp finished doing that, Jared rode awkwardly up and told them what he'd told Talbot to do. The news wasn't pleasing to Kelsey, because she could read between the lines. Talbot was going to put himself and his people between them and whatever danger was out there waiting. She wasn't going to let him do it alone.

Jared could apparently sense where her thoughts were going, because he gave her a stern look and shook his head without her saying a word. "You're critical to this mission, Kelsey. Talbot and the marines can handle the fighting. You need to stay here with the rest of us. We've already got Julia off helping them."

She immediately balked with a firm shake of her head. "I can do more if I make sure we don't get ambushed at all. It's all fine and good that Julia is doing her part, but I need to do mine. The farther away from the column we can keep the fighting, the less chance that any of the civilians get hurt."

"You're looking at this all wrong," he said. "We have the marines to do the fighting for us, just as they should. This is one of those times where you have to stand back and direct what's going on. Talbot is controlling them in the field, and we need you to be our leader."

"You're our leader."

"No, I'm not. I'm the military commander of this mission. You represent the Imperial Throne. Neither of us can afford to die. We need those codes in your head once we get to the palace."

She scowled. "That's playing dirty. Julia has the same codes. She's obviously found a way to make them work, so you should be happy you have a spare."

He shot a look toward Beauchamp, who was focused on directing her subordinates. When he spoke again, he pitched his voice low.

"Even though she's been with me for months, I don't trust her to the same degree that I trust you. She has her own agenda, and I'm smart enough to realize that. Right now, it aligns with what we're doing. What happens when her people would benefit more from working against us?

"Even leaving that aside, you're my sister. I'm not going to lose you fighting out there when it isn't critical to our survival. I'm the senior military officer, and it's my job to declare who does fighting and where. This is one of those times where you have to obey orders, Colonel."

Her scowl deepened, and she felt her teeth clenching. Dammit. As much as she wanted to argue, she knew that she had to support the separation of civilian power from the military. If they were fighting, it really *was* his call, and she had to acknowledge that. She could overrule him when it came to policy, but not strategy and tactics.

This was one of the flaws of being both an ambassador plenipotentiary and the senior officer in the marines. Sometimes she had to follow orders, and other times she had to give them. Sadly, this wasn't one of the latter.

She pulled her horse around to his other side with an easy tug of the reins. Pitching her voice low, she gave in to the inevitable.

"Fine, but I'm going to get into my armor. If those bastards get anywhere close to us, I'm going to smash them into little bitty pieces."

He smiled a little and shook his head. "I'm not ever going to change who you are. All I can do is remind you of what we need to save, the human race. I understand that you want to go out and fight, but your survival is just as critical as mine. We're both going to have to make some sacrifices."

While she didn't disagree, she worried that the sacrifices would be paid for in blood. If the horde came close to the column, she wouldn't hesitate to do her absolute best to pound them into the ground like a tent stake, but she had to bow to reality. He was right, as much as it galled her.

It looked as if it was going to be up to her husband and her doppelgänger to settle this unpleasantness. She hoped they were up to the task, because they'd only get one shot at it. If they failed to stop the horde and reach the outpost, this mission was over and so were they.

20

The ready response team was more than halfway to the oncoming enemy force by the time Corporal Boske figured out that Julia was tagging along. To say that she was less than pleased would've been something of an understatement.

The woman slowed and made her way directly toward the off-center path that Julia had been following, making no effort to conceal her intentions. She planted herself directly in Julia's path, planted her fists on her hips, and glared at the princess.

At least that's what Julia assumed the other woman was doing. Boske's helmet was opaque, so she'd just have to take the glare on faith. Julia had armored up when the marines had, so Boske was just as in the dark about her own expression.

"Dammit, Highness," the marine noncom sent over a private channel. "What the hell do you think you're doing?"

Julia slowed to a stop in front of the other woman, doing her absolute best to convey nonchalance with her posture. To avoid giving the other woman an advantage, she kept her armor's ability to project her face onto the outside of her helmet turned off as well.

"I'm making certain these marines have the best chance they can get at surviving this encounter," she said firmly. "We both know those horsemen are going to have a lot of the antiarmor weapons. The more firepower you have, the better the chances are that you'll take them out before they kill our marines."

"Those marines are *my* responsibility, Highness. Don't you think that your unexpected presence would make their survival *less* likely? If you just pop up with no warning in the middle of a fight, someone is likely to shoot you or get shot at because *you* surprised them. You need to go back to the column."

"Not going to happen," Julia said firmly. "I brought along enough heavy weaponry to do my part. You don't have enough people in powered armor to be picky. Let's do both of us a favor and not waste time that we don't really have. I'm going to be part of this fight. You might as well make use of me, because I'm going to be there whether you like it or not."

The other woman spent a full ten seconds cursing but caved to the inevitable. "Fine, but you do this *my* way. I give the orders, and you follow them to the letter. We don't have time to argue about who's in charge, so it's going to be me. If you can't handle that, I'll have my marines hold you down, strip that armor off of you, and make you run your little ass right back to the column. Am I clear?"

Julia's initial reaction was to tell the woman that she'd like to see her try. That, however, wouldn't be very helpful—particularly if she carried out her threat—so she decided to be cooperative.

She wondered if the marine would be so bold while talking to the Kelsey from this universe. Probably not.

"We'll do it your way, Corporal," Julia said. "How can Big Bertha help?"

With that, she tapped the large weapon that she'd commandeered for use with her armor. She'd picked up the name from one of the other marines when he was explaining how it worked to her, but she wasn't precisely sure where the phrase came from. It sounded mildly insulting, but the marine didn't seem to take it that way, so she wasn't sure.

What she did know was that the weapon was more than capable of doing its part in the upcoming fighting. It was a plasma rifle built for powered armor. In the scheme of things, it wasn't that large, but had an outsized ability to damage people, equipment, and the landscape.

They didn't have a lot of ammunition left for it, but they needed something that could take out a large group of riders before they could scatter. Which, based on their previous behavior, was exactly what they'd do. Then they'd keep shooting at the marines until they killed them all before heading on to attack the column.

"How many shots do you have for that thing?" Boske asked.

"Six. It was all I could find. Most of the ammunition didn't survive the crash."

Boske nodded. It was hard to see while she was in armor, but the slow tilt of her head gave Julia the clue.

"I'd rather keep that weapon in reserve, but I understand the need to take out as many people at once as we can. I'm authorizing you to fire *two* shots. That's it. We need to save the rest of the ammunition for later because we might desperately need the ability to use plasma at some point, and if we use all of the ammunition too quickly, we could be screwed."

"What if they get past us?" Julia asked. "They're going to catch our people out in the open. We've got to use whatever firepower we have to take them down while we can."

The noncom raised her hand slightly. "I don't have time to argue with you. You're authorized to fire *two* rounds, and if you see a large grouping of personnel after that, you may fire *one* more, but I don't expect that to happen. Right now, they're clumped together because they don't think we know they're coming. As soon as they realize they've been discovered, they're going to scatter.

"Frankly, I'm not even sure that you'll get that second shot off before they've separated enough to render the plasma blast zone too small to make a dent in their numbers. All we can hope to do is to take out as many of them as we can and try to get them to engage us.

"If they decide that they're going to ride on, nothing we can do can stop them. We just have to make ourselves the target they want to take out. Otherwise, Colonel Talbot and the rest of the marines are going to have to deal with them, and that'll mean a higher number of casualties that I'd rather avoid."

That was what Julia hoped to avoid, too. The horde wouldn't have sent such a large force against a group protected by high-tech armor if they didn't think they could handle the problem. That meant they had some kind of surprise hidden up their sleeves. One that she was certain that no one would like.

They'd have to adapt and overcome. They really didn't have much of a choice.

* * *

TALBOT HAD to admit that the attackers had hidden themselves well. If he hadn't had access to drones with infrared and ultraviolet capability, he would've missed their hiding places in the grass.

It seemed that they'd dug shallow holes and then dragged mats of woven grass across themselves. The cover perfectly matched the grass around them, which impressed him a great deal.

However they'd gotten themselves into position, they'd done so without disturbing the living grass enough for him to notice. In fact, he'd wager that they'd done well enough to fool even Captain Beauchamp and her people.

"So how do we go about this?" Adrian Scala asked from where he lay beside Talbot. The two of them were a short distance in advance of the column, peering through the tall grass at the crest of the hill they were on. The smell of the earth and grass felt like it was helping conceal them, too.

"I think the best way to get this started is to drive them out of hiding before we engage," Talbot said in a low voice. "We have a pretty decent idea of how many people we're looking at, based on the infrared signature, but I'd rather see them running around so I can be sure. Besides, we won't be able to see what kind of weaponry they have unless they're out and about. I wonder what they did with their horses?"

There were no horses anywhere within the tactical drones' range. If he had to guess, Talbot would wager that the horde had brought extra people to lead the horses away. Off to the right of their hiding place, set way back from where the column could see it from the ground, there was evidence that a large number of horses had recently been there, so the ambushers must've ridden in from off to the side of the known path, allowed the riders to dismount, and then had the horses led away.

No doubt the people with the spare horses were waiting somewhere in the distance, likely ready to come in once the ambush was sprung. Just one more thing for him to keep an eye on, but one with a potential upside. They could always use more horses, either for trade or for their own use. They still had fifteen hundred kilometers or so to travel, and extra horses would make that journey easier.

"So how do you want to spring the ambush?" Scala asked.

Talbot grinned. "We use our technology to our advantage. We have the drones start buzzing their position, out of reach of their hand-to-hand weaponry, and see if that gets them to come out and do something ill-considered.

"The drones will be inside bow range, and potentially even a thrown spear, but I'd wager the odds of a hit are low. The drones will be moving quickly and using at least a little bit of jinking to keep from being an easy target, so we won't get very many hits."

Scala nodded. "Okay, let's say that works, we spring the trap, and everyone comes running out. They have other forces in the area that they might be able to signal. If we get bogged down in a heavy fight, and more forces come in to pin us in place, a lot of people are going to die."

Talbot nodded grimly. "You got that right. So, we make sure we deal with these guys quickly. Most of the marines are back at the column, but with the flechette rifles our people here have, we should be able to take care of most of them. We'll have the drone coverage up, and if we see other attackers coming in, we'll modify the plan on the fly to deal with them. No matter how we play this, it's going to be quick and ugly."

He looked across what he could see of the plain and felt sad that such a beautiful area was being used for such a bloody purpose. Under other circumstances, he could imagine these fields filled with crops tended to by large machines, like the ones they'd found in the building.

This place had once been the breadbasket of Terra. Maybe at some point in the future it would be again, but until then, it was going to have a little bit of blood soaked into the ground.

He opened a communication channel back to Carl Owlet, who had a number of people controlling the drones for the marines, so that the fighters could be focused on what they needed to do.

"Carl, execute plan bravo."

"Copy that," his young friend said. "We've got some drones coming in from a couple of different angles and we'll buzz them as close to the ground as we can, then circle around and come in from other directions. With the pattern we're working up, it's going to seem like a lot more drones than we actually have. We've also arranged a little surprise for them that I think will probably help get them out into the open."

His friend's words filled him with a little bit of dread. "What are you planning? This isn't going to cause any big explosions, is it?"

Carl laughed. "Nothing like that. We took some of the smoke grenades that your people recovered from the crashed pinnaces, and we've attached them to the drones. Once the bad guys start moving around, we'll drop smoke into the middle of them to confuse their situation even more. That shouldn't obscure them from your advanced optics."

Talbot thought about that for a moment and then nodded. "That sounds like a good idea. Make it happen."

He switched channels to the general marine frequency. "Squad Charlie, this is Talbot. As soon as the drones come onto the scene and flush our ambushers, you are cleared to take them down. Make sure you hit your targets but be sparing with the ammunition. We need to take all of these people down as quickly as possible, but we don't have many reloads.

"We're going to drop smoke into the middle of them, so don't get excited about anyone you can't clearly see. Wait for your targets. Use the drone feeds to figure out who's going where and keep engaging them.

"Squad Delta, circle around and be ready to keep them from getting away. Once we lay enough firepower into them, they're going to make a break for it, and there are other fighters from the horde out there. We've got to be ready to interdict them."

Even as he finished speaking, the drones flew in from seemingly every direction and began buzzing over the target area. For a moment there was no response, and then large swaths of grass flipped over.

Screaming men and women came boiling out from under the mats and charged toward where the column would be, only to find Talbot and his marines on the hill between them.

There were more dismounted horsemen than he'd expected. At a guess, he was looking at over a hundred people. Maybe as many as a hundred and fifty. His ability to count was disrupted when the drones began dropping smoke into the middle of the charging enemies.

That disturbed them a lot. The smooth charge of the armed men and women was quickly turned into a chaotic rush, as people were both charging forward to fight while others ran away from what they thought was deadly danger.

Talbot didn't notice any of the antiarmor weapons, but visibility was crap. He had to assume that they had them until he knew for sure they didn't.

"All marines," he said in a flat tone. "Open fire."

Every marine with him on the low rise opened fire, sending flechettes into the screaming confusion below them. With that kind of firepower, it wouldn't take long to mow down the fighters they were facing.

"Enemy contact!" Chloe Laird shouted over the command frequency. "There's a second group just off to the side of the column popping out of concealment. Holy hell, there has to be two hundred people there. We're engaged. We're *heavily* engaged and need backup ASAP."

"Hold them as best you can," Talbot said as he stood. "Adrian, stop these bastards here while I go back and help the column."

"Got you covered, boss."

Talbot took off at a run, using his powered armor to build speed. This was an unmitigated disaster. With that many bad guys, the column was going to be overrun no matter what they did. The chances of keeping them off the civilians and unarmed Fleet personnel were effectively zero.

Talbot hoped the admiral had a good plan, because he didn't know of anything that he could do that was going to change the outcome now. All he could do was fight. With any luck, he'd make it back to Kelsey, so that they could stand back-to-back when the horde rolled over them.

21

J ared was watching the ambush play out over his implants when disaster struck. He heard shouts of alarm off to his right and turned in the saddle to find a lot of fresh enemies coming out from under grass mats barely fifty meters away from the column.

The new attackers were leading off with bows and arrows, shooting at Captain Beauchamp's warriors. They also paid particular attention to anyone with a rifle.

The marines quickly turned their flechette rifles—those that had any—onto the attackers. Captain Beauchamp's mounted forces charged toward the intruders, drawing weapons as they moved. There was a lot of yelling, screaming, and whooping in the air.

Jared turned his attention to the noncombatants and started ordering them to the other side of the column. He had to get armed warriors between the ambushers and the people that couldn't defend themselves.

He saw Kelsey racing toward the attackers, her powered armor making her leaps seem effortless. She had both of her swords out and seemed prepared to go in swinging. He wasn't sure it was going to be enough, considering how many people the horde had coming in.

This group looked at least as large as what Talbot had reported ahead of them, and they also had the mounted column that the ready response team was attempting to deal with. If that group also managed to disengage and get to the column in fighting order, he and his people were in *extremely* dire straits.

"How the hell did we miss these people?" Elise asked as she moved closer to him. She had a small flechette pistol in her hand, but she was obviously not confident that it was going to be enough.

Neither was he, though he drew his own weapon.

"I don't know," he said grimly. "Maybe we'll have time to figure it out after we've dealt with them. We've got to form everybody into a circle so that we can protect the group from every angle."

He sent out orders to that effect over the implant coms, and his people coalesced into a ball with all of their weapons pointing outward.

The situation had changed so quickly. They'd gone from almost being to the outpost to being caught in a deadly ambush just a few kilometers away from supposed safety.

He wanted to think that they were going to come out of this okay, but the situation seemed too ugly for that. It didn't seem as if they were going to have an opportunity to get this situation sorted out in their favor. Their enemy had been far cleverer than he'd imagined possible.

A number of them had already begun firing antiarmor weapons at Kelsey, but she seemed to be everywhere. She dodged left and then right, allowing the explosives to fly past her as she waded into the enemy. Her blades flashed out, severing arms, heads, weapons, and anything else that got in her way.

A crashing off to his left brought his attention around as Talbot came thundering out of the grass, barely pausing as he rushed toward the fighting in his powered armor.

He wasn't as lucky as his wife. One of the antiarmor weapons smashed into the ground right in front of him, exploding in a bright flash and sending the marine tumbling through the air to slam into the ground hard. A number of the enemy cheered his fall and rushed toward him.

"Kelsey," he said over the command channel. "Talbot is down off to your left."

His sister whirled in place, cutting a man down to clear the way for her to jump forward. With her powered armor, she was able to achieve an impressive height and came down on another warrior, crushing him in place as she sprinted toward her husband. She planted her feet near him and diced anyone that came close.

Jared felt a very bad feeling. As the enemy was massing to overwhelm Captain Beauchamp's forces, they'd split off a good chunk to face Kelsey as well. Several of them were already bringing antiarmor weapons to bear.

This was not going to end well.

* * *

KELSEY DREW her neural disruptor with her off hand and began shooting the men holding antiarmor weapons. The bolts sent them spasming to the ground, dead before they fell. She couldn't hit them all, unfortunately and at least one person managed to fire before he went down. Thankfully, his aim was somewhat off, but that was no reprieve.

The warhead flew past her and impacted in the middle of the column with terrible effect. It sent Fleet personnel and civilians flying in every direction, dead or wounded. Mostly dead.

Captain Beauchamp's people were also heavily engaged with the ambushers, but the odds were stacked against them.

To add insult to injury, that's when Major Scala called on the general com channel with word that while the ambushers had lost a lot of people, they'd split around the marines and were making their way toward the column. The marines were in pursuit, but the enemy had left a force to slow them down. They weren't going to be able to keep the horde warriors from reaching the column.

Perfect.

She didn't have a chance to check Talbot, but her implants told her that he was still alive. He wasn't even terribly injured. The impact had just knocked him out. The problem was that she couldn't move him while still defending their position. She was stuck by his side or she'd have to abandon him, something that she would never do.

A quick check of the drones revealed that the force coming in from the ambush site was going to hit the circle of Fleet personnel and civilians, and they were going to do it hard. She sent a quick warning to Jared and focused her attention on using her weapons to the best of their ability.

She'd sheathed her swords even as she was running for Talbot and had a flechette pistol in one hand and a neural disruptor in the other. Both were taking a toll on the enemy, but the power supply for the neural disruptor and the magazine for the flechette pistol weren't infinite. She'd have to put one weapon away to reload the other.

Even though she was cutting down swaths of the enemy, they didn't seem inclined to retreat. The deaths of their fellows only pushed them to charge her harder. It was almost as if they were suicidal.

Even as she was being forced to choose which weapon to reload, she saw something else happening back where the ambushers had concealed themselves. Several of them were dragging a large device out of the pit where they'd been hiding.

She didn't recognize what it was, but it had to be something bad.

Choosing her flechette pistol, she smashed one of the attackers out of her way with her other hand and emptied the small magazine at the enemy working on the machine. She took them down, but unfortunately, she didn't kill them all. One managed to crawl his way back up to his knees and continued doing something to the machine.

Kelsey fired her neural disruptor. Too bad he was out of range.

The top of the machine opened, and a metallic ball shot into the sky. She had no idea what it was and no time to figure it out because when it reached about fifty meters in height, it glowed as brightly as the sun and the world around her went dark.

* * *

JULIA HAD CIRCLED AROUND JUST like Corporal Boske had instructed her to and found a good hiding place in the tall grass. She'd opened fire on command with the plasma rifle, sending the two unbearably bright spots of coherent light flashing into the middle of the column of enemy horsemen, where they'd detonated with tremendous explosions.

The blasts not only threw horses and people in every direction, it had incinerated those closest to the point of impact. Much like Boske had anticipated, the horsemen had immediately split apart and began fleeing in multiple directions.

Julia fired the third authorized blast from the plasma rifle at the man who seemed to be in charge and took out him and the half a dozen riders still too close to avoid destruction.

Her three shots had started a fire that would likely rage out of control in the flat grassland. Luckily, the wind wasn't blowing in their direction, or toward the outpost. It would end up being a crisis somewhere, but it wasn't something she could worry about now.

With that, she backed away from the fighting, as ordered. She raced around to the left, using a slight rise in the ground to hide her movements from the enemy. Her new course took her to a seasonal stream bed and toward a low hill that the water had cut into the base of.

When she was right beside it, she leapt as far onto it as she could and caught herself at the top of the incline. That sounded impressive, but it wasn't much of a hill. She'd only cleared a dozen meters over the base of jumbled rock.

When she was on the top of the rise, the additional height gave her the perspective to see where all of the horsemen were. She settled down into a good hiding spot and started calling off the locations to Boske.

She'd barely gotten started when a bright flash off to her left seemed to slam against her with psychic force. It didn't move her body, but it still knocked her out.

An indeterminate amount of time later, she blinked as consciousness returned. She was immersed in complete darkness. What the hell had that been? She tried to get her mind to work, but her thoughts were as slow as molasses.

She tried rolling over, but her armor refused to cooperate. Thankfully, she had the internal musculature to force it.

Only her artificial muscles weren't working either. She pushed, but nothing happened. She felt as weak as a kitten.

A quick check showed that her implants were offline. She'd never experienced that before. The armor wasn't transmitting any visuals to her implants, or her implants weren't receiving them.

Based on the evidence in front of her, she thought both of those things might be true. Somehow the enemy had managed to disrupt not only her armor, but her implants and her Raider augmentation.

Her armor was made so that it could be opened manually, so she reached up and found the manual releases for the helmet. They weren't made to be easy to manipulate, because no one wanted an enemy to get their armor open while they were inside it.

Still, Kelsey had trained her hard on knowing that part about her armor. The woman seemed to know *everything* about Marine Raider this and Marine Raider that. In this case, Julia was happy that she hadn't argued.

It took a minute of fumbling around to finally get the helmet to come free. The fresh air slammed into her face, cooling her immediately. She had no idea how long she'd been out, but the sun was still shining brightly down on her face.

The view showed her she had another problem. Her artificial eye wasn't working. The only vision she had was through her natural eye.

She needed to get out of her armor and figure out why her implants and hardware weren't working. She closed her eyes and tried everything that she could to access her implants. No dice.

Was there any way to force them to reset? That wasn't something she'd ever needed to know. Her implants were always on. They'd never turned themselves off before. She hadn't even suspected they *could* be turned off.

After having a lot of conversations with Ralph Halstead on board the destroyer, she knew that almost every piece of equipment had some type of reset. One could never count out having some type of critical error freeze everything in place.

There'd be something that would allow her to restart her implants. At least that's what she hoped. As much as she loathed the things, she absolutely needed them right now. Their enemies were all over them, and if she couldn't get herself back in motion, a lot of people were going to die.

While she kept thinking about that, she managed to roll herself over. Having her helmet off made that a little easier because she could see what she was doing. It took a supreme effort of will and force to get herself onto her stomach, but she managed.

Once she was there, she brought her hands to her torso and found the covers that went over the manual releases. Like the helmet, they weren't easy to manipulate, but she managed to remember what needed to be done.

With a loud click, all the latches that held the various pieces of her armor together disengaged. They were mechanical and so allowed the torso to split apart in the back where she'd normally get inside.

Arching her back, she forced the panels apart and extracted herself from her dead armor. Finally, she sat on the ground, covered in sweat, and looking at the armor beside her.

What the hell happened? What had that flash been?

Probably some type of electromagnetic pulse or something. Whatever it had been, it had obviously been designed to work against Imperial technology that was hardened to stop that kind of thing.

Julia spent another ten minutes attempting to manipulate her implants and Raider augmentation but was unable to get *anything* to work. There had to be a way, but she didn't know what it was.

Out of options, she rose to her feet and stared out over the plain where she'd been looking earlier. Before the blast, she'd been tracking a number of horses and riders. They were all gone now. However long she'd been out, it had been enough for them to leave.

If everyone in the party had had their implants affected this badly, it was a disaster. It meant that the horde had won. There was no way that Captain Beauchamp's people could have held them all off.

And considering how bloodthirsty they'd seemed, her heart was filled with dread at what she'd find when she got back to the column.

Clumsy and lacking the strength that she'd subconsciously begun relying on, Julia made her way down the hill and onto the plain. It was going to take her at least half an hour to get back to Boske.

She wasn't even wearing her marine fatigues or boots. Those were still in her saddlebags. She'd put them there when she'd gotten into the armor. All she was wearing was a skinsuit.

Her feet were going to be torn to pieces walking on the rough ground if she hurried at all. It might take her two hours to get back to the column, and that would certainly be too late to help, unless she could find her horse.

She prayed that everyone was still alive, but deep down she knew that was unlikely. She dreaded what she was going to find when she got there.

Resolute in spite of what she knew was coming, Julia began walking back toward where she'd last seen Boske. If the marines were still alive, maybe the group of them could still make a difference. Somehow.

22

Talbot woke groggy and disoriented. He immediately realized that he was riding, but the last thing he remembered doing was fighting. He blinked dazedly down at his hands, which had failed to move when he'd tried to raise them to his face. Someone had bound them tightly to the saddle horn.

His feet were similarly secured to the stirrups, when meant that any attempt to dismount would end with him being dragged by the horse. As he wasn't a skilled rider, he'd be an idiot to even *try* to get his feet free before his hands.

It would be child's play to use his Raider augmentation to break the rope securing his wrists, but he looked around to see what their situation was first.

A relatively small group of prisoners were being moved on horseback. There were dozens of enemy warriors around them, a number with bows out and arrows already nocked. Any precipitous action on his part would result in immediate bloodshed.

It felt like he couldn't completely wake up, and he shook his head trying to clear it. That's when he noticed that his implants weren't responding to his mental calls. They were offline.

His blood ran cold. He'd never heard of anything like that before.

Surreptitiously, he tried to flex his augmented muscles and found that his enhanced strength was also gone. He didn't know if that was because his implants were offline or if there was some kind of damage to the augmentation itself. He wasn't precisely certain what happened.

The last thing he remembered was being thrown into the air by the explosion of an antiarmor warhead right at his feet. His armor must've saved him, but it was nowhere to be seen now. Someone had stripped it off, and he was only dressed in his skinsuit, not even having any shoes on his feet.

Giving up on the idea of an immediate escape, he focused on what he could see. He needed to know what the situation was so that he could create a plan of action.

His captors seemed content to allow him to look around, so long as he didn't make any move they didn't care for. Talbot craned his head around and finally got an accurate count of just how many of their people were with him.

There were thirteen horses being led in the center of a group of about four or five times as many armed and armored enemies. None of the prisoners wore armor—either Imperial or local. All of them were stripped down to their uniforms, if they had them, or their skinsuits if they'd been in powered armor.

Talbot was relieved to see that his wife was at the front of the group. She was unconscious, but she was bound upright in the saddle just like the rest of them.

He knew it wasn't Julia, because he'd taken the precaution of memorizing their hairstyles. They were almost identical in appearance, but not indistinguishable, if one paid close attention to the details.

He also could see Admiral Mertz and Commodore Meyer directly behind his wife. A quick check ahead of him revealed Commodore Stone, Commander Cannon—the assistant tactical officer from *Athena*—and Chloe Laird.

A glance behind him showed Captain Beauchamp, Elise Orison, Olivia West, Austin Darrah, Ralph Halstead, and Carl Owlet. Only Beauchamp was semiconscious. From the blood and bruising on her face, she'd been brutally beaten.

Thirteen prisoners out of just over a hundred marines, Fleet personnel, and civilians. Whatever had happened, they'd lost the fight. The horde wouldn't have all of the senior people if that weren't the case. It worried him that none of the marines under his command and none of the regular Fleet personnel were present.

Were they being kept in separate caravans to prevent an uprising? He wished he knew for sure, but without his implants, he couldn't see anyone's status, contact the drone network, or even assess his own condition.

The next person to start moving was Admiral Mertz. His head came up abruptly and he also had weapons aimed in his direction, but since he wasn't enhanced, he wasn't going to try to break his bonds.

The other man blinked owlishly around himself before he turned in the saddle and his eyes locked on Talbot. They were separated by a couple of horses, and Talbot wasn't certain that their captors would be pleased with them talking to one another.

He wished he could open a com channel with the admiral and tell him to stay where he was, because they were in exceptionally dangerous circumstances right now.

The admiral was bolder than he, because he used his heels to urge his mount to slow. Their captors watched him but didn't interfere. Perhaps they thought that the display of weaponry was enough.

After all, wasn't it? They'd won the fight. No one here was in a position to resist them. If the prisoners made any kind of move, they'd be slaughtered. Without reins, they couldn't even really control the horses they were bound to. Not that they had the skills to do so, in most cases.

Admiral Mertz finally made it up beside him. "What's going on? My implants aren't responding."

Talbot shrugged slightly. "I was unconscious when whatever it was happened, so I'm not really sure."

"It must've been that big weapon they fired up into the sky," the admiral said quietly. "I think it was some kind of EMP device. Maybe one tailored to operate against Imperial equipment."

"My implants are offline. Maybe burned out. The last thing I remember was that weapon going off. It must've knocked everyone with implants out. We're in deep trouble."

"I'd say that's something of an understatement," Talbot said with a grunt. "Do we have any idea where everyone else is? I find it peculiar that the people here are mostly what I'd call our senior staff. There are a couple that are a little lower in the hierarchy, like Commander Cannon or Chloe Laird, and the science types, but everyone else is what I'd say is a major player. How did they get all of us gathered in one place? Hell, how did they get me out of my armor?"

The admiral shrugged. "I don't know, but I think we're about to find out."

He gestured with his chin toward where Captain Beauchamp was edging in their direction. It looked as if she were awake enough to talk. She looked like hell. Whatever she had to say, it wasn't going to be good.

* * *

Making her way across the grasslands barefoot and half blind wasn't anything close to easy, but Julia managed to get back to where she left the marines. It took her a while to circle around the fire that her plasma shots had started. What she found when she got there was devastating.

Whatever had taken her down had also taken out the ready response team. Each of them lay where they'd fallen. Or at least where their armor had fallen.

Someone had removed their helmets and then slit their throats.

Julia went from person to person until she found Corporal Boske. The woman lay on her back, her eyes closed and her expression peaceful. She'd probably never even felt the cold kiss of death, which Julia supposed was a blessing.

She stumbled a few feet away and threw up as she sobbed. She'd known these people. She'd fought beside them. Now they were gone.

Julia wiped the tears from her face, found a canteen to wash out her mouth, and gathered what weapons she could find. The final tally was half a dozen marine knives, flechette rifles made for the armor, a couple of flechette pistols, and a couple of stunners.

None of the advanced weapons worked. They were just as dead as the plasma rifle that she'd left on the hill. That flash had to have been some kind of extremely powerful electromagnetic pulse.

That left her with the marine knives. Very old school, but they didn't require any power source at all, other than her muscles. Not her strongest asset, but they'd have to do.

There were a couple of ration bars and a pair of maintenance slippers that someone had kept in one of the suits of armor. They weren't very tough, but they'd slip over her bare feet and give her *some* protection as she made her way back to the column.

Julia took a small bag from another set of armor and stuffed the food that she'd recovered inside with the knives in their sheaths. Her skinsuit had no place to strap on a knife, so she carried the final one in her hand, still sheathed because she wasn't an idiot.

She'd use it if push came to shove, but without her augmentation, any kind of confrontation was going to be heavily one-sided against her. Her very best option was not to be noticed at all.

With a final look at her dead comrades, Julia set out toward the column.

It took hours to get back into the general area where the column had been. She found it because a little bit of smoke smudged the clear sky in that direction. The smoke from the fire she'd started was a pall off to the side. Someone was burning something ahead of her.

Or maybe cooking something. If so, they were charring it badly because the smell of burnt meat was overpowering.

Julia moved as carefully and cautiously as she could. Where possible, she used grass where others had gone before her. It was helpful that she'd found the area that the invaders had come through because the grass there made less noise as she passed. She had no ability to do any kind of stealth, so every noise she made sent her heart bounding into her throat.

She arrived at what was obviously some type of hastily dug concealment pit with mats of grass that had been thrown aside to allow ambushers to attack the column. She didn't know how the ambushers had known where the column was going to be, but they'd done damned well at placing them. The column was only about fifty meters away.

Rather, what was left of it.

Dead bodies lay everywhere. Based on the few people she saw moving through the carnage, the horde had won. It looked as if they'd killed *everyone*.

Taking slow, deep breaths to calm herself, she ducked into one of the pits and started counting the enemies that she could see, trying to figure out what they were doing.

There were seven people searching for things to load onto pack horses. All the horses that had come with the column were either gone or being held ready to leave. The people she was observing were perhaps making a final pass to gather anything that they considered worthwhile.

One of the men, a tall, powerfully built fellow with his dark hair drawn back into a ponytail, shouted at the others to mount up and get moving. They obeyed his orders quickly, finding their mounts and climbing aboard. They quickly tethered the cargo animals to them and moved out.

That just left the one man who waited patiently for them to leave. She wondered what he was doing. Why hadn't he left with his friends?

The answer came when he seemed satisfied that they were gone and he moved over to a different area, bent down, and uncovered something.

When he rose, Julia recognized what she was looking at. Those were Kelsey's swords. The ones made of the same material as the marine knives. The ones that could cut through just about anything. It looked as if the man intended to claim them for himself and didn't want any of the others to know that he'd done so.

He had a horse nearby and started heading toward it. Julia knew that if she wanted to get a ride out of this place and not be completely unarmed, she needed those swords and that horse.

She dropped the bag with her food and spare knives, rose quietly to her feet, and moved forward as quickly as she could, hoping that he wouldn't hear her coming. She unsheathed the marine knife she'd kept and made the best speed she could toward his back.

Sadly, she wasn't good enough.

When Julia was about ten meters away, he whirled in place and spotted her. Before she could rush him, he dropped Kelsey's swords, bent his knees, and grabbed a spear off the ground.

"Well, well, well," he said with a grin as he hefted the probably more familiar weapon. "It seems we have one final survivor. You're pretty. Perhaps I'll save killing you until I've had some fun."

With that, he stepped toward her, his weapon held ready to attack or defend. It gave him a lot more reach than she had. He could stab her or use the blunt end to beat her.

This wasn't looking good at all.

ll it took was one look at Clarice Beauchamp's face for Jared to know that their situation was grim. She sagged in the saddle, her face badly bruised and swollen. Her hands and legs were tied like his own. If they hadn't been, she might've fallen off her horse.

"Tell me," he said quietly.

"We fought as well as we could, but there were too many of them," she said, her voice slurred. "We couldn't stop them. Once they deployed whatever that weapon was, all of your people collapsed. It was just my warriors against many times our number when the enemy finally coalesced around us. I tried to get riders free to go for help, but the horde killed them all.

"The raid leaders questioned my surviving people and myself closely, since we were the only ones awake. They asked who the most important of your people were. I had no choice but to tell them. I enhanced the roles of a few of your people to save more of them. It was all I could do."

Jared felt his throat constrict. "What happened to the rest?"

"Dead," Beauchamp said softly, her head falling forward. "They killed them all, your unconscious people and my own survivors both. We few are all that is left."

The news was like a kick to his groin. He was responsible for those people, and he'd led them to their deaths.

"What about Julia?" he asked when he could finally make himself speak again. "Or the marines that went with her."

The local shrugged. "I don't know. None of them were brought back, so I assume that whoever they were fighting killed them where they fell. I saw some of the people take your sister and her husband out of their armor, so they knew how to remove it. Nothing would've stopped them from getting to the people that went hunting them."

"I don't see Commander Roche," Jared said. "Didn't you give them his name as well?"

She shook her head. "He was killed in the fighting. I saw him go down with two arrows to the chest."

In a way, Jared hoped that Julia was dead. He knew that if she wasn't, the death of her friend would break her.

"What happens now?" Talbot asked. "Where are they taking us? What are they going to do to us?"

Again, Beauchamp shrugged. "Nothing good. They're taking us to their capital city. It sits on the outskirts of one of the ruined megacities. They're going to torture us, put us on trial, and then execute us.

"They'll do their best to extract what information they can from us first. That's where the torture will come in. They'll want to know everything they can about you, what you can do, and where you came from. For me, they're going to want to know everything I can tell them about my people's defenses. They'll want to know how to destroy us utterly.

"That's why they've got our arms and legs tied, to make certain that we can't somehow kill ourselves. The strapping held you in the saddle while you were unconscious, but they're not going to remove it until we stop for the evening, and then they'll secure us again once we've taken care of our necessary business. They'll take no chances with us being able to get away or take our own lives."

The news made Jared feel hollow inside. Not only had he failed his people, everyone he cared about was going to die in the most horrible manner imaginable. He had failed the Empire utterly.

"Where's everybody else?" Talbot asked. "There have to have been a lot more of them than this."

"Gathering everything that we salvaged and chasing down all the horses that got away," she said. "They're also burning their dead. They'll leave ours where they fell.

"No doubt there are groups of pack animals somewhere around us. That will have the majority of their forces acting as guards because they don't want anyone to take all their new toys. They'll also have people back at your camp breaking into your crashed ships and securing everything for their own use."

"That had to be some kind of EMP weapon," Talbot said slowly. "My implants are offline, and so is my augmentation. I'm not sure if it's fried or if it simply needs to be reset in some fashion. I had a manual that explained how it all worked, but it was stored in my implant memory. Maybe Kelsey knows more. I'm a little worried that she hasn't woken up yet."

"One of the invaders took special pleasure in making sure that she was unconscious once they removed her from her armor," Beauchamp said. "He kicked her in the head several times. She was still alive, obviously, or they wouldn't have strapped her to the horse, but she may be gravely injured.

"I was warned that we can talk amongst ourselves when we wake but that we are not allowed to approach anyone that is unconscious. I know you want to check on her, but we're going to have to wait and see if she wakes up on her own. If you try to violate their rules, they'll hurt you badly. They only need a few of you alive to talk.

"I hesitate to mention this, but gelding is a favorite torture of theirs, so I would be *very* careful not to get on their bad side any more than you already are."

"We have to assume that Julia and the other marines were killed after the bomb went off," Jared said, wanting to go to his sister in spite of the risk, but not daring. "The only people that could help us are right here. I doubt that any of your people will be coming for us. Is that right?"

Captain Beauchamp nodded. "They'll find the bodies left on the field once all the fighters are gone, but they're not going to send anyone after us. The horde is too strong. The only help that we can count on now is right here, so we're as good as dead."

* * *

JULIA FROZE IN PLACE. Without her augmentation, she didn't have a chance against a trained warrior. His spear had reach on her knife, and she didn't have even a third of his strength without her artificial musculature. She had no speed advantage, and she couldn't even turn her combat over to the implants in her head. She was outclassed in every way imaginable.

There was no way she could win this fight.

He'd obviously come to the same conclusion, because his grin only widened as he advanced toward her. He casually twitched his spear with nimble fingers so that she couldn't be sure from which way a jab or strike might come from. His movements definitely left the impression of a predator playing with its food.

"I'm not certain how the outriders missed you, but I'm glad they did," he said with a dark chuckle. "You're a luscious piece of fruit just waiting to be plucked and savored. What secrets do you know? How does one as pretty as you serve the monsters in the sky? The ones who killed our world."

His playful tone had vanished by the time he'd finished his little speech, replaced by a cold sneer. Obviously, he didn't like the Rebel Empire any more than she did. Perhaps Julia could use that to her advantage.

Though she didn't drop her knife, she raised her empty hand. "I don't serve those monsters. None of us do. We're fighting them, trying to stop them. There's been a terrible misunderstanding."

The man laughed without the slightest bit of humor. "I'd say so, because you should never have come here. Your kind is not welcome. You might not think you serve those things, but you do. They have things in your heads that control your every move. We know.

"Don't worry, we'll make sure and cut it out so that they don't ever have the chance to do that again. We might even let you live once we've finished, if you're *very* cooperative.

"I hope that you yield completely, because you'd make an excellent addition to my household as a comfort slave. You don't look like the kind that would survive as a drudge, so if I were you, I'd start learning how to please me right now."

Yeah, that wasn't going to happen. She might as well die right here and now. She'd never give herself over to someone like this. Better to bleed out than to be a sex slave. Or worse.

She was just about to throw herself at him and take her chances when a cry from just off to her right captured both their attentions.

Staggering up out of the grass, Scott Roche rushed toward the man, a flechette pistol in his hand. "Die!" he screamed as he raised the weapon.

Julia knew damned well that the pistol had to have been fried. There was no way it was going to work as anything better than a rock.

Deep down, her attacker had to have realized the same thing, but his trained reactions betrayed him. No warrior would allow a charging enemy to get to him with a weapon that he knew was deadly, even if subconsciously he knew the weapon was useless.

With one smooth motion, her attacker turned to face Scott and met his charge with the tip of his spear. The primitive weapon easily knocked the flechette pistol away before plunging through her friend's chest.

"No!" she screamed as she charged forward. She held the knife in her hand low and used her short stature to come in at a lower angle than the man might expect.

He immediately tugged on the spear and made to turn toward her. Unfortunately for him, Scott had his hands wrapped tightly around the spear and wasn't letting go. The man's weapon was hopelessly tangled and couldn't possibly stop her charge.

The warrior released his spear and drew his sword, using that motion to slash it toward her head, but she was already rolling on the ground at his feet.

She came up blade first, and the wickedly sharp knife cut through his armor and flesh both, opening him from groin to sternum.

The stench of blood and offal was almost a physical blow to her senses as she threw herself back from the fatally wounded man, watching for him to collapse in death.

Only he wasn't done yet. Holding his guts in with one hand, he staggered after her, seemingly determined to kill her before he fell.

If she could keep him at arm's length until his wound dragged him down, she'd survive. If he caught her, she was dead.

Even though her attention was fully on her attacker, she saw Scott Roche do the impossible out of the corner of her eye. He pulled the spear from his chest, turned it so that the point was facing toward her attacker, and hurled it with his remaining strength, even as he collapsed to his knees.

His aim was off, but the spear still struck the man in the back of his head with its shaft, once again distracting him at a critical moment. Julia took advantage of his distraction to race inside his sword's reach until the two of them were almost touching.

He grabbed her with his free hand, yanking her hair back painfully, but it didn't stop her from plunging her knife through his chin and into his brain. Hot blood spattered across her face as he quivered. Moments later, he collapsed and she let him go.

Certain that the man was dead, Julia raced to Scott's side just in time to catch him as he slumped. A quick look showed her that he had two arrows buried in his chest, as well as the horrific wound that the spear had caused. Without modern medical facilities, her friend was dying.

Already he was coughing blood and had trouble breathing. She wasn't sure how he'd survived as long as he had.

"You shouldn't have," she whispered as she stroked his upturned face.

"It's my duty... and privilege... to trade my life... for yours," he gasped out between coughing fits. "They took... Mertz and... the others... alive. Save them. Make them... save our people."

With a final gasp, he went still and stopped breathing. She sat with her dead friend's head in her lap and cried until she had no tears left inside her.

She wasn't a warrior, but she'd track the horde down and kill as many of them as she could. She'd save her new companions, no matter the price. Then she'd do whatever it took to save her people. Scott's sacrifice demanded no less.

The horde had chosen the wrong person to make an enemy of. She'd make them pay for what they'd done. Terra would run red with their blood. She swore it.

24

When Kelsey woke, her head hurt terribly, and her face felt almost as bad. A glance around revealed that her greatest fear had come true. Somehow, she'd been captured. There'd been some kind of weapon, she remembered foggily. She'd tried to stop them from setting it off but had failed.

It only took her a few moments to realize it must've been some type of electromagnetic pulse weapon. Her implants were offline, and her augmentation wasn't working either. That was patently obvious because her face still hurt. If her medical nanites had been functional, they'd have already taken care of the cuts and bruises, and her pharmacology unit would've stopped the pain.

A look around her revealed most of her friends scattered around her, but they were all prisoners. She didn't see Julia, which might be very good or very bad. There was also no sign of Commander Roche either. She hoped they were okay and had gotten away.

Everyone else seemed to be in just as bad a shape as she was, but they were all awake. She was obviously the last one to wake up, which was an unusual state of affairs for her. She felt as if someone had beaten her, and that might not be far from the truth.

With as many people as she'd killed, it was entirely possible that they'd taken out some of their wrath on her. It felt as if her ribs might be cracked, although that was impossible. The Graphene coating would've kept the bones from breaking, but she was certainly bruised in all the wrong places.

As soon as it was obvious that she was awake, her husband made his way up to her. Since his hands were tied to the saddle horn and his legs were secured to the stirrups, his pace was slow. The warriors guarding them seemed to be okay with him getting close to her, but had their bows prominently displayed. She was certain that if anyone made a break for it, they'd catch several arrows in their back and would be dead before they got outside bow range.

Hell, the horsemen probably could ride faster than any of them under the circumstances. They might just cut them down with swords. She and her friends were helpless to resist at this point.

"It's bad, isn't it?" she asked Talbot when he got beside her.

He nodded grimly. "I'm not going to hide this from you. That EMP weapon took everyone with implants out. The horde then overwhelmed Captain Beauchamp's people, started figuring out who the important people left alive were, and executed everyone else. We're all that's left."

His words were like a sledgehammer to her gut. She almost whimpered in the pain of knowing that so many of the people she was responsible for had died. All because they'd inserted themselves into someone else's business.

"We should've just kept going," she said softly. "We should've ignored the group heading toward where the pinnaces were and run. We stuck our noses where they didn't need to be, and now they've chopped them off for us. Where are we going now?"

Her husband took a deep breath and let it out slowly. "From what I understand, Captain Beauchamp seems to think that they're taking us to their capital city. It's built next to one of the ruined megacities.

"Once we get there, they're going to torture us for whatever information we have and then execute us. Apparently, this isn't something that even cooperation is going to change. Unless we figure out how to get away, we're going to be put through some of the most horrific things you can imagine and then they're going to burn us alive. That's their form of execution, just in case you need extra motivation to come up with a brilliant escape plan."

Kelsey's stomach roiled. She *had* to figure out a way out of this. She was a damned Marine Raider and the Crown Princess of the New Terran Empire. There was no way in hell that she'd let these barbarians kill her and her friends.

She looked around at the guards shepherding them. "It looks like we've got about fifty guards. We're tied up, but they have to stop sometime. We need to at least try and escape. Even if we fail, what's the worst that can happen? We get a clean death in battle. That's a hell of a lot better than torture and immolation."

Kelsey looked up at where the sun sat in the sky and tried to guess the time. It wasn't easy without her implants, but it seemed like evening. They probably only had another hour before the sun set.

She had no doubts that the guards would keep them tied up for as long as they could, but they had to cut them loose to use the bathroom and eat, if they wanted to get them back to their city so that they could be questioned.

Kelsey knew that they'd be under heavy guard, but surely they could do *something*. Maybe not tonight. Maybe it would be tomorrow night. She had to figure out what the horde's patterns were before she could find a way to subvert them.

"Are we sure that Julia and Scott are dead?" she asked.

"Scott is," he said. "Captain Beauchamp saw him with a couple of arrows in his chest. I'm sorry, Kelsey, but he's gone. As for Julia, she was off with the ready response team. None of them were seen or heard from again, so I can't imagine that any of them escaped."

His words infuriated her. How could they have misjudged the situation so badly? How could *she* have misjudged the situation so badly?

She cast a glance over at where Jared was talking with Captain Beauchamp. Since none of the woman's people were with her, the horde had butchered her entire command.

What would they do if they escaped? There had to be more horsemen scattered around than those she could currently see. These people were doing things that she didn't know about, and that put every plan that she came up with at risk.

If they broke out of this camp, they'd have to somehow evade the other horsemen, figure out how to get clear of this entire area, and still make the fifteen-hundred-kilometer journey to the Imperial Palace. All by themselves with no advanced gear or even basic supplies. On foot while evading horsemen who would no doubt be determined to capture and kill them all.

Simple, right?

The thought of all that made her frown. The EMP had probably fried the Imperial Scepter. It was the physical key to get into the vaults. They also didn't have possession of it anymore. Could they even access the Imperial Vault without it?

There was probably a way in without it, but they didn't have their implants, so how could she activate computers to try to bypass the security system?

The odds stacked against them seemed overwhelming. They had no outside help, and even if they managed to resist the people holding them captive, they could expect extermination in the ensuing fight.

Maybe one or two of them could get away from this, if the rest gave up all hope of escape and fought, but that was probably wishful thinking.

It certainly seemed as if everything they'd fought so hard to accomplish was for nothing. The artificial intelligences would win. They'd eventually bring the Omega Plague back to Terra and exterminate every living being on the planet, which she supposed was a kind of pyric revenge on the horde, but that wouldn't help the New Terran Empire.

Humanity's best hope of beating the AIs was lost, and she had no idea how they could possibly survive, much less win.

* * *

IT TOOK every bit of her strength, but Julia managed to drag Scott's body to where the horde had been burning their dead. It broke her heart to heave him onto the smoldering flames in the hastily dug pit, but she did it. She wasn't going to leave him out for the animals to eat. He'd been her friend and loyal supporter for years, and he deserved the final care she now showed him.

The stench of burning flesh made her stomach heave, and she threw up as soon as she'd accomplished the task and staggered away from the hellish scene. Then she sat on the ground and wept.

When she finally regained control over herself, she set about searching the remaining dead for clothes she could wear. Her skinsuit wasn't going to be helpful in what she needed to do. Her pack horse was gone. Probably taken by the raiders as a matter of course, so none of her own belongings were available.

She gathered some marine uniforms and some boots that she could use with several layers of socks to take up the extra space her small feet would leave, but that wouldn't do for the first part of what she needed to do. She had to blend in, and that meant she needed local clothes, armor, and weapons.

It took a while, but she managed to find one of the warriors who was almost as small as she was. The man was thin and wiry, and it looked as if he'd specialized in the bow.

In fact, his weapon was exquisite. Its polished wood looked strong and its bowstring was taut, but that hardly began to tell the story of this weapon.

Its surface was polished from use, and the wood almost glowed under the protective coating that the man had applied often to keep it pristine. The length of the short bow was etched with all kinds of detailed patterns. They were very similar to something that she'd seen in the library on the destroyer. Something called Celtic knotwork. It was simply gorgeous.

The weapon was obviously made to be used from horseback because of its short length. That had the added benefit of reducing the pull on the string to the point where she could use it. The arrows the man carried were a bit thicker than she was used to shooting in her youth, and the heads had wide, razor-sharp blades of metal that would cause great wounds, likely killing the targets quickly.

The challenge would come when she needed to use it. With only one eye, her aim would be put to the ultimate test. Thankfully, she still had her dominant eye, so it wouldn't be impossible.

Julia stripped the man before dressing in his clothes, which was a disgusting and gross thing that she wished she didn't have to do. Then she put his armor on over them. At least she was able to keep her skinsuit on underneath everything, so it felt like a layer of mental insulation from wearing a dead man's things.

The man had died of a neck wound, so even though his armor was stained in blood, it wasn't damaged in a way that would stand out to anyone that saw her. At least until they got close enough to see her clearly. Or smell her. Ugh.

She took a few minutes to wash off the blood with water salvaged from the dead. She'd need to take enough to survive on, and some food as well, when she departed. One more thing added to her mental checklist.

That done, she pulled the man's sword from its sheath, once she had it belted on. It was almost as much a work of art as his bow. The blade was made of brightly polished steel. The wavy marks of folded metal were vaguely familiar to her. Something called Damascus? That sounded right.

Her brother had an interest in knives and had raved on about this kind of weapon, telling his very disinterested sister all about it in excruciating detail. It had bored her to tears, but she was now grateful that she had any frame of reference at all.

The man also had a pair of long daggers of the same metal. Based on the mark at the base of the blades, the weapons were probably forged by the same smith.

She took them all. They were no use to the dead man, but they might make the difference between her life or death. She hoped the dead man would have approved.

Not that she had a lick of skill with either weapon. Their excellence wouldn't save her if she fumbled when she had to use them.

Julia moved back to the horde raider that she'd killed and recovered Kelsey's swords. She'd strap them to the horse and use them if push came to shove. They might make up for some of her lack of training. No matter how good other blades were, one strike from a hull metal blade with an almost monomolecular edge would shear it off.

Kelsey would want them back whenever she caught up with her. That was fine. The other woman would be far deadlier with them. In the meanwhile, she'd use them.

Once she had all her newly acquired weapons in place, she gathered every bit of food and water she could find. Running out of either while trying to cross the plains would be a recipe for death, and she had no idea how many people she was going to be chasing.

She also found a plasma grenade on a dead marine. It was Major Scala, she thought, though with the damage to his face, it was hard to say.

The weapon might not work, but she took it anyway.

All that done, she mounted the captured warhorse and turned him in the direction that the horde had ridden away in. He was surprisingly willing to have her as a rider. The other man must've been a jerk to him, too.

The tracks were already diverging as she left the scene of the battle, so she suspected that the horde warriors might've split apart to cover more ground. She'd know for sure once she got closer to them.

Her best bet for survival would be to avoid contact altogether until she'd caught up with them. If she could skirt the groups ahead of her, she could figure out where the prisoners were, and perhaps find a way to release them.

She was their ace in the hole, a gambling reference she actually understood. Without the horde expecting any survivors, they'd be focused on their prisoners. With any luck at all, she'd make them deeply regret that oversight.

Julia put her heels to the horse's flanks and set off in pursuit of the others. It was time to try and snatch victory from the jaws of defeat.

25

By the time they'd stopped for the evening, Talbot was exhausted and sore all over again. His lack of riding skills was magnified by the fact that he couldn't even move around on his saddle. His captors also didn't appear to be the kind of people that liked to give breaks, so his ass was a mixture of lead and pain. Much worse now that his medical nanites were down.

Four warriors came to untie him, two holding swords, while a third covered him with a bow from a different angle. The fourth person used a knife to cut the rope binding his legs and hands before gesturing for him to dismount.

Talbot barely managed to get off the horse without falling over.

His captors almost dragged him over to a moderately secluded place and allowed him to use the bathroom. One of them poured water over his hands and handed him a small sliver of soap to clean up.

The lack of toilet paper was somewhat disturbing, but they had a coarse cloth that they dropped into a bag when he'd finished his business. Then they bound his hands tightly behind his back again.

The rest of the marauders were setting up camp and guarding the remainder of the prisoners. All of the horses were picketed off to the left, several fire pits were being dug, and people were gathering wood from the scraggly trees around the area.

One of the marauders sat in a folding chair, watching Talbot. She was dressed in armor like the rest, her helmet set off to the side of her chair next to her sheathed sword.

His captors dragged him before her, forced him to his knees, and stepped back. He didn't look, but he was certain they were all covering him with weapons as the woman examined him.

"So, you are one of those that serve the sky machines," she said, her voice low and melodic. Her tone was one of cold fury.

"No," Talbot said firmly. "We're not. We were fighting them when we came to Terra. They destroyed our ship in orbit. We're no allies of the machines."

The woman threw her head back and laughed mockingly. "If only you knew how many people just like you said the exact same thing, or so the histories say. But that all changed when we put them to the question. The *truth* came out then.

"I don't know why you've come back to Terra after so long, but you'll meet the same fate as your predecessors. First, though, you're going to tell us everything that you know about what the computers intend."

"I don't suppose there's anything I could say that would change your mind?" Talbot asked sadly.

"No. I've determined that you're most likely the leader of this particular expedition. You seem to be the strongest warrior, and you were captured inside forbidden armor. That makes you someone that knows much about what the machines intend.

"My associates at the capital are going to ask you many questions. It would go easier on you if you cooperated. In that spirit, I'll give you the opportunity to save your people some pain. Why are you here, why did you bring those ships from the sky, and why did you crash them so that you couldn't leave again?"

Talbot snorted mirthlessly. "The crash was unintentional. The last ship failed right before landing. If things had gone according to plan, we'd have gotten to the ground without the machines—or you—knowing that we were here at all."

The woman made a face that showed she didn't believe a word he'd just said. "You tell a fanciful tale, but it will not save you in the end. Do you know how the horde questions recalcitrant prisoners? Would you like a demonstration?"

Talbot's stomach clenched at that, but he stood firm. Well, knelt firm. "No."

The woman chuckled darkly. "Understandable, though I still think you deserve to know what awaits you. Observe the fire off to our left."

One of the warriors there held up an iron bar whose handle was thickly wrapped in leather. He stuck one end in the fire and grinned at them.

Talbot's skin grew cold. That didn't look good at all.

"We use hot pokers to convince you to tell us what we want to know," the woman said conversationally. "Even the bravest warriors break after a while. It doesn't matter how long you lie to us, eventually you'll tell us what we want to know, or you'll die screaming under the question. Frankly, either one of those outcomes is satisfying.

"It's our tradition, if you will, to start with those who are not warriors to convince the warriors to speak. You'd be surprised how many strong men and women break when seeing those they're supposed to protect being tortured. Though I have a different idea.

"Perhaps I'll start with the blonde that caused us so much trouble. We found her in armor standing over you, so I think she cares for you. How much do you care for her? Will you save her from that fate? Or will you watch her scream until she dies?"

It took every bit of Talbot's will to keep his expression blank. He wanted to snarl, leap to his feet, and attack the woman, but he couldn't do that. They'd know for sure how important Kelsey was to him then. Not that they didn't already know.

The woman sat there letting the silence drag on as the sun touched the horizon behind her. She seemed content to stay that way until the sun had completely set, then she rose to her feet and stepped over to Talbot.

She leaned close and smiled darkly. "I will take great pleasure in conducting the questioning once we return to the city," she said in a low, throaty voice. "I will start with the woman, and then I'll move on to the weakest among you. You won't feel the heat of the poker until all of your friends are dead, warrior. Will you break when you see those under your care screaming in agony?"

Talbot tried to headbutt the woman, but she hopped back and laughed as her men began beating him. With his hands tied behind his back, he was helpless to resist as they pummeled him into unconsciousness.

* * *

Julia rode in the direction that the horde had taken when they'd left the area. She had no idea how many people were ahead of her, or even which subgroup contained people she was looking for. And she was going to have to look through subgroups, because the horde force had definitely split into different parties.

Unsure of how to proceed, she stopped for a moment to consider her options. She had no skill in tracking, and each of the subgroups left what looked to her like identical sets of prints. While she had a lot of riding experience, telling different sets of hoofprints apart was something she wasn't knowledgeable at.

Yet, if she was going to find her friends, she was going to have to locate the appropriate group and follow them. She was going to have one chance at this, and she needed to make certain she did the very smartest things she could. This wasn't the time to go running off killing people. She had to think this through and act cautiously.

The answer, when it finally came to her, seemed blindingly obvious in retrospect. The cargo horses were heavily laden, and thus their prints were deep. Those who were riding regular mounts without that kind of load tended to move faster than the cargo horses, so their strides were longer. She found one group of tracks that had relatively light hoofprints, yet the distance between prints was short, as though the horses were moving slowly.

While that certainly didn't mean that she'd found the group with her friends, this at least gave her a logical starting point.

It was impossible for her to judge just how many riders there were, but the interior group had a few different sets of markings on their shoes. These were obviously beaten metal, and there were some differences in the shaping and texture on them. That led her to believe that there were at least six people in the center of this group, though there might be twice that many. Again, she had no way of knowing for certain.

The surrounding group seemed significantly larger than many of the other sets of tracks she'd found. To her mind, that meant that it was far more likely that this was a prisoner convoy. That meant she was likely following the people that she most wanted to find.

Julia got back on her horse and started after the group. She rode cautiously, because she wasn't sure if they'd leave someone riding behind as an early-warning system. If it was her, that's what she'd do.

Still, there'd been the one man left behind to go over the site of the battle. That meant they'd expect at least one person to follow along behind them. Since she was dressed in similar armor and riding one of their horses, it was likely that they'd initially believe she was him.

If someone came too close though, the game would be up. She probably didn't look exactly like their comrades and didn't know enough about them to spot what she might have wrong on the armor and such. She also didn't know their idioms, so any kind of conversation would likely give her away.

The worst thing that could happen was if a group of horsemen approached her. If any of them stayed at a distance with bows trained on her, she was screwed. If there were only two people close in, she might be able to cut one down by surprise and then deal with the other one, but even that was chancy.

She didn't have her Marine Raider augmentation to help her win this fight, so stealth was a much better option than fighting. She had Kelsey's swords, but those would be a one-trick pony. She might kill a single warrior by surprise and *might* even beat a second. Three? She'd be a dead woman.

To her relief, she didn't see anyone as she traveled. She didn't rush, but she didn't dawdle either. She had some distance to make up. They'd have to stop for the night, and that would give her a chance to see if she was after the right group.

If so, and if she could get to them while the camp was quiet, it was possible that she could free one of the warriors. Her search of the battle site hadn't shown any of the senior people, so if she could find Kelsey or Talbot, that would be ideal.

One of the advantages that she had was skill with a bow. Nothing like the one she'd captured, but she'd grown to love shooting the bow while growing up and still had a modicum of skill with one. If she had to use a weapon, she'd be much more comfortable using her new ranged weapon.

If she could get to Kelsey and back her up with a bow, perhaps the woman's husband could take the other sword, and the two of them could cut the rest free.

It was almost dark when she finally spotted something promising. There were wisps of smoke rising from just over a small rise ahead of her. That probably meant that there was a campsite somewhere on the other side.

If so, they probably had watchers out. They wouldn't want to be surprised in the middle of the night. She had to approach carefully and cautiously, so as not to alert them to her presence.

Julia hobbled her horse behind another small rise so that no observers would see him. She'd have to sneak up on foot once the sun had fully set.

They wouldn't have night vision goggles, so they wouldn't be able to see her coming, so long as she didn't make a lot of noise or do something that caused them to spot her. These guards would probably think they were in a relatively safe place.

After all, they'd killed the group that they'd been after, she thought bitterly They were on their way home all safe and sound.

In actuality, the best time to move would be sometime early in the morning, but she needed to scout. Insertion and extraction would take time. She had to assume that this was the wrong group, simply because if she assumed it was the right one and made a mistake, then she was screwed.

She found a good place to wait and spent the next several hours trying to think about what she needed to do. She ate and drank from her supplies but didn't dare take a nap because she was afraid that her exhaustion would overwhelm her.

Without her augmentation, Julia's body wasn't nearly as resilient, and without her implants, her mind was already clouded with fatigue. It was like she'd been before the Pale Ones forced the change on her and she was having trouble readjusting.

When she finally decided that she'd waited as long as she needed to, she made one final check to be certain that nothing on her armor would make noise. She then circled around to approach the campsite from a different angle.

If she were the guards, she'd be watching along their backtrack, so her best angle of insertion would be from somewhere off to the side of that. This was a plain, so there was high grass and scrub brush that she could use for cover, but she had to move slowly because she didn't dare cause any motion or noise that would attract their attention.

That meant getting into position to see what was inside the camp took far longer than she expected. Luckily for her, she'd approached near where they were keeping the horses. So long as she didn't spook them, their soft movements and noise would cover hers. With that in mind, she kept enough space so that they didn't react to her.

It only took a few minutes to figure out that she was in the right place. There were a few banked fires that had enemy soldiers sleeping around them. It was hard to tell in the darkness, but she thought there were perhaps forty people sleeping there.

Some distance away from the fires, sleeping in the chill air, were the people that she was looking for. Their captors had their arms and legs tied, and they were under guard. Two men with bows stood watching from a safe distance, each on opposite sides of the group. She almost missed the second one in the dark, but he coughed and drew her attention to where he was standing near a scrub tree.

His presence made her stop and look around more closely. She couldn't afford to miss any other guards in the dark. Even one left alive would raise the alarm.

If her guess was accurate, there were probably between six and eight other people scattered around the camp acting as sentries, and the two she'd seen keeping watch over the horses. She wasn't certain how she would deal with them, but the glimmering of a plan started working its way into her brain.

It was dangerous, but if she could pull it off, they might all be able to slip away before the people around them even realized they were gone.

If stealth failed, she always had plan B, which was risky because of the EMP. She'd recovered that one plasma grenade. If it was dead like all the rest of the Imperial equipment, then using it would be futile and stupid.

But those were primitive devices with little or no electronics. Basically, you pulled the retaining pin, threw the grenade, and it blew up. It should still work. Theoretically.

If the plasma grenade went off, she'd kill at least two thirds of the enemy. At the very least, that would slake some of her bloodlust and reduce the fighting to a manageable level. She hoped.

Still, her preference was to let Kelsey make that decision. To do that, she had to take care of the guards and get to her.

Well, there was no time like the present.

She held her bow with an arrow comfortably nocked against the string in one hand while she had a marine knife in the other, carefully hidden behind her thigh. She strolled directly up to the first guard. They were going to see her coming, no matter what she did, so her best defense was to look exactly like the rest of them.

Perhaps she could pretend to be their relief for that one critical moment. Dealing with the other guard was still going to be problematic, but she'd have to trust in her own skills and hope for the best.

As it happened, the guard she was approaching had his back directly toward her. She actually managed to get right at his back without him being aware that she was even there. She was pretty sure that his partner across the fire had seen her approach, but he hadn't had any reason to be alarmed.

That was about to change.

She jammed the knife into the back of the first guard's skull as soon as she was within arm's reach. The blade entered with an audible—though soft—crunch, and the guard fell like a puppet whose strings had been cut.

Not giving the other guard a chance to react, Julia brought up her bow, drew the arrow back, and fired at his head. She was already grabbing for another arrow and getting ready to fire the next shot, because she was certain the first one wasn't going to be enough. No one was that lucky.

Except that today she was.

The arrow struck the man right in the eye, and he collapsed without a word. His fall was almost as noiseless as his partner's.

Julia slowly turned in a circle, her bow ready to fire, making sure that no one else was responding to what she'd just done. Miraculously, it seemed like her insane plan was working. No one seemed aware of what had just happened.

She had to act quickly, since time was not on her side. None of the prisoners had woken up during the attack. They were probably exhausted from everything they'd been through, and now things were about to get a *lot* more hectic.

Julia retrieved the marine knife from the skull of the dead guard and wiped it clean on his shirtsleeve. Then she stepped quietly through the prisoners until she was standing next to her doppelgänger. Julia bent over and placed a hand across the woman's mouth.

Kelsey's eyes flew open, but with her hands and feet tied, she was unable to do anything. It only took a moment for those eyes so like hers to narrow, then the other woman nodded.

Julia removed her hand and spoke very quietly in Kelsey's ear. "I've killed the two guards watching over you, and I'm going to cut your hands loose."

Cutting through the ropes with the marine knife was easy. The most difficult part was making certain that she didn't accidentally cut Kelsey's hand off. She repeated the work on the woman's legs.

Once the ropes were gone, Kelsey rubbed her wrists and feet, probably to help restore more circulation, and then rose.

Julia turned so that Kelsey could see her swords strapped low on her back. She hadn't dared wear them where the silhouette could've been seen. That might have given her away.

Kelsey slowly drew one of the swords from Julia's back. "Give Talbot the other one," her doppelgänger said softly into her ear. "Then we need to get everybody else cut loose and get out of here."

Julia handed the plasma grenade to her. "I have no idea if this will work, but I figured I'd bring it along."

Julia repeated the process with Talbot, and he was just as quick on the uptake. Once she'd freed him, he rose to his feet and took the second sword.

The two of them went from person to person, quietly waking them up and cutting them free while Julia kept watch, her eyes scanning for sentries or waking enemies near the fires.

Clarice Beauchamp retrieved the weapons from the two dead guards. She'd be best trained in the use of them, so that would be helpful. She'd also take one of the bows, and Olivia or Elise could take the second.

Once the entire group was awake, Kelsey gestured toward where the horses were being kept. "If we can get the horses saddled and get going before they realize that we've escaped, we might actually get away."

Of course, that's when someone near the fire stood, saw what they were doing, and started screaming that the prisoners were escaping.

Well, so much for the easy way.

26

Kelsey reacted instantly, pulling the pin on the plasma grenade and hurling it toward the fire. While she didn't have her usual Marine Raider enhanced strength, her normal muscles had gotten stronger with use, and the grenade made it the full distance without any trouble.

Her aim was true, and it landed almost in the middle of the group of scrambling enemies, rolling to a stop just at the lip of one of the pits. It sat there for one extended heartbeat even as Kelsey was turning her back to the impending explosion.

"Fire in the hole!" she shouted. "Cover your eyes!"

She hoped to God that the grenade worked because otherwise no one would be looking at the enemy as they came to kill them.

The grenade's explosion made it sound as if the world had ended. It was only then that she realized that her augmentation was no longer protecting her hearing. Her ears rang, and she felt as if she'd been kicked in the back as she staggered forward, almost falling.

She'd been a little too close to the explosion, she decided. But if it was bad for her, it was going to be *really* bad for the enemy.

Kelsey turned and saw that while the grenade hadn't killed everyone, it had certainly maimed most of the survivors. No one was standing, and those that weren't dead looked as if they were seriously injured. Hell, many of them were on *fire*.

The grass all over the camp was also on fire, and she expected that was going to mean a big blaze since no one was in a position to control it. The smell was already spooking the horses, she was sure. Like the explosion hadn't.

Even though that took care of almost everyone in their general vicinity, it had certainly attracted the attention of the camp sentries. She didn't know how many of them there were going to be, but she'd have to be an idiot to think that those warriors wouldn't be rushing toward them even now.

"To the horses," she shouted over the ringing in her ears. "Anyone with a weapon—particularly a bow—shoot at anything that moves."

Julia ran beside her. "Based on what I saw, there's probably six or eight sentries out there. Two more near the horses. They'll be ready for us."

"You've got a bow. Help cover us."

"Good idea, Princess Obvious."

Kelsey smiled a little as she watched Captain Beauchamp hand the final bow to Olivia. She found a place near the back of the group as they made for the horses. The sentries would be coming from every direction.

They had a real chance of getting away, but only if they broke contact completely. Any pursuers would find a way to signal other groups to come after them. She had to make sure that nobody survived this fight.

Julia and Captain Beauchamp engaged the guards ahead of them before Kelsey saw anyone. She had no idea how effective their fire was in the dark and confusion, but she hoped they were good. Otherwise, someone was going to die.

Two guards came running in from the left, and Olivia brought her bow up and snapped a shot off at one of them. He grunted and went down, but it didn't look like he was completely out of the fight.

Kelsey ran forward, even as the second guard fired an arrow at her. She managed to successfully throw herself to the side enough for him to miss.

She'd do a lot better if she still had her Marine Raider augmentation, but in this case, even a few centimeters were enough for the arrow to fly harmlessly past her with an audible "thwap."

Olivia hadn't been idle. She'd already drawn another arrow from her quiver and fired it at the second guard. Her aim was true, and the arrow caught him squarely in the chest, dropping him on the spot.

She could hear Talbot and Captain Beauchamp fighting somebody on the other side of their small group as they continued toward the horses, but she couldn't spare them any attention. The wounded guard had thrown aside his bow and drawn his sword. He wanted to fight it out man to woman.

Kelsey wasn't obliging. She let Olivia shoot him in the stomach. He went down writhing and groaning.

Unfortunately, her focus on those two had allowed a third to slip close without her seeing him. The man seemingly appeared out of nowhere with a sword in hand, already swinging at her.

Kelsey's reflexes were exceptionally good, even without her Marine Raider augmentation. She'd also been practicing the Art for quite a while now, and that included weapons. She blocked the attack at the last moment.

She'd intentionally used the flat of her blade so as not to cause the piece of steel flying toward her to snap off and continue on its merry way. That would be almost as bad as not blocking it at all. Her hull metal blade was more than strong enough to take a hit on the side.

The unexpected blocking of his blade put the man off-balance enough for Kelsey to swing around and take his leg. In one stroke—even with her reduced strength—the blade's edge was more than sufficient to cut through his leg, armor and all. He went down screaming as blood gushed from his gory wound.

Looking around as she stepped away from the writhing man, Kelsey saw no further signs of guards, so she risked a glance at where Talbot and Captain Beauchamp were fighting. Talbot was using her other sword and engaging two foes while Captain Beauchamp fired arrows at several more that were threatening the group.

Kelsey raced toward them as Olivia turned her attention to the new threats.

Talbot was a lot stronger than she was, and even though his use of the sword wasn't as good as hers, he managed to hold his own while the archers dealt with the more distant threats.

She intervened and quickly killed one of his attackers. Talbot followed up with an immediate strike on his man that decapitated him.

With that, the fight was over.

There might still be a guard or two out there, so they stayed watchful, but the other members of their party were able to secure the horses they needed and scatter the rest.

Captain Beauchamp searched out the wounded enemies that were still alive and finished them off. That might've seemed cruel because they were technically prisoners at this point, but the wounded were so gravely injured that there was no chance that they'd be able to do anything for them. What medical supplies they had were gone, lost somewhere in the gear that had been stolen from them.

More disturbing, Julia was going through the main camp doing the same thing, her face cold and merciless. Kelsey didn't know if that was because of experiences she'd had as a Pale One or simply the loss of Scott Roche and so many others, but the woman never hesitated as she strode from body to body, her expression blank and her eyes cold, making sure they were truly dead or ending their suffering with firm thrusts of her captured sword.

Kelsey took a deep breath and regretted it. The mixture of burning grass, spilled blood, and cooked flesh was nauseating.

She turned her back on the carnage and considered what they needed to do next. They had to figure out exactly where the scepter was if they were going to retrieve it. They simply couldn't complete their mission without it.

Unfortunately, not knowing which group had the damned thing, the only place they could be certain they'd find it was the city where all of these bastards were going.

That was going to mean going deeper into enemy territory. Not exactly a plan for guaranteed survival. Still, what choice did they have?

She'd talk it over with Jared and see what his opinion was, but her thought was they were going to have to follow the enemy right straight into their lair.

* * *

NOT KNOWING how long they had, Jared made certain they gathered as much food, water, weapons, and other supplies as they could find before they fled the area. It was still dark, so they weren't going to be traveling fast, but the plasma grenade blast would've been a big, bright neon sign to everyone within line of sight that something terrible had happened.

There were probably scouts from various groups of horde riders already on their way to figure out what had happened. He and his people need to be long gone before they arrived.

Beauchamp helped get everything secured to the horses, since the majority of their personnel weren't skilled riders and none of them really knew the esoteric secrets of packing lots of gear on the beasts. If somebody came across them and they had to make a run for it, that would not be the time to find out that their packs were going to come undone.

They also gathered up any armor they could find that might fit somebody in their party. Most of the people had been killed in the explosion of the plasma grenade or had caught fire from the effects of it. Their armor was a bit more resistant to that sort of thing, but it would still look totally scorched if anyone examined it closely. They'd have to make do with what they could find.

He wasn't looking forward to riding in the dark, but it beat the hell out of being on his way toward torture and execution. Right now, he still couldn't tear his mind away from how many of his people had been killed.

When the EMP weapon had knocked them all out, it had made them completely vulnerable and the horde had executed virtually all of them. It was so inconceivable that he still couldn't get his mind wrapped around it.

Beauchamp was in the same position. Her people had fought to the end, but they'd been greatly outnumbered, and all of them had been killed or executed except for her. Now here they were, a small group trying to figure out what they were going to need to do to survive in the middle of enemy territory.

After the fighting, Julia had disappeared for a short while and then returned with her horse. They all immediately mounted up and set out, moving slowly in the darkness.

As the group rode, he pulled the people he needed as close together as they could get and went over the situation with them. When he was finished, he looked at Clarice Beauchamp.

"What are the chances that we can get back to your outpost without the horde hunting us down?"

The woman shook her head. "They're going to be swarming the general area come morning. We need to be gone by then. If we turn around and go back, we're going to discover that they've sent parties back to stop us. We just don't have the numbers to fight off an attack.

"Besides, that group you sent off with your sister-in-law started a grass fire, like the one that your sister started tonight. The first one is between us and the outpost, and the second will cut off some of the enemy coming to search for us, which is a good thing. There's no easy way to get past either of them. I'm afraid that the only way open to us is forward."

Jared grunted, not really surprised to hear that. "They're going to know that we're loose. They'll do a search around the campsite, and they won't find our bodies. Worse, they're going to find the people we killed and know it was us. We can assume that means they're going to be hard on our tails once they figure out what happened."

Beauchamp smiled. "There's a reason that we scattered the horses back in the direction of the outpost. That's going to make them initially think we fled in that direction. If we're lucky, the morning winds will push the fire across our path and hide which direction we actually went.

"We can't count on that, but we're going to get a little bit of time because of their uncertainty. I suggest we use it wisely. If we can change into armor and clothing that the horde wear, they won't realize that we're not another search party unless they close with us."

He was still thinking about that when Carl Owlet spoke. "The Imperial scepter is somewhere out there, and it's being taken toward our original destination. If we're going to get into the Imperial Vault, we have to have it."

"Is it any use now?" Jared asked. "The EMP probably junked it, just like everything else electronic, including the implants."

The young scientist smiled. "It has safety measures built into it to prevent it from frying. If I can get my hands on it and access to some tools to get into its interior, I can probably reset it. Also, our implants have a reset, too, although it's going to be a *lot* more difficult to get to. They were designed so that they would resist EMPs of almost unimaginable strength, but being so close to that huge weapon overloaded ours.

"I'm afraid this is going to require Doctor Stone's help. She's going to have to make an incision to get to our implant nodes—a specific one—and then I can apply a specific frequency of power to it. I'm afraid that it's not something that's going to be simple, because as we all know, the implants are inside our skulls. But if we can get our hands on her medical gear—the stuff that wasn't ruined by the EMP—it's not out of the question."

Jared thought about that and shuddered a little. Brain surgery in the wilds of Terra with no implants to guide their way would be hard. If they couldn't find Doctor Stone's surgical kit, it would be impossible, and they'd have to make do without their implants.

Lily confirmed that fear when she shook her head. "We have to find my spare medical kit—the one I left at the pinnaces—if we're to have any chance of doing that. I don't dare open up anybody's skull without it. Admiral, we need to recover that as badly as we do the Imperial Scepter.

Hell, anything at all that we can get back is going to increase our chances of success. We need to do what we can to make that happen."

Jared rubbed his face as his horse moved forward in the darkness. "So, what you're saying is that we're going to have to sneak into an enemy city right under their noses, find where they've stashed all of the gear they're taken from us, all without them raising the alarm? Then we'll need to get out of the city and somehow escape what is probably the seat of their power. That doesn't sound difficult at all."

Difficult or not, they really didn't have a choice. If they were going to succeed in their mission, they had to have the scepter. They'd find a way to sneak into the horde city without raising the alarm, steal what they needed, and then somehow escape again without being noticed.

And that was only the first step. From what he knew, the horde city was actually farther away from the Imperial Palace than the campsite where they'd crashed the pinnaces.

They had no advanced weaponry, were down to just over a dozen people, and Terra was a hostile world that seemed determined to kill them. He just didn't know if they could make it.

Still, he wasn't going to give up. This wasn't his kind of fight, but he was going to make it work. The New Terran Empire was counting on them, and he wouldn't let them down.

No matter the cost, they'd do what needed to be done. And that started with getting into the horde city without being captured.

27

After five days of riding, Julia was exhausted. They'd traveled mostly by night, terrified that one of the horde search groups would catch them. To help mitigate that, they'd chosen not to head toward the horde city directly.

Instead, they'd slipped away from the direct line between Captain Beauchamp's outpost and the city, looping far off to one side and only turning toward the latter two nights ago.

The first day she'd been terrified that the horde would come down on them, but they didn't see a single rider. Beauchamp seemed to believe that the direction they'd taken might have fooled them. She believed that there were so many riders out there, that their tracks were being confused with the rest of the search groups.

It probably helped that the grass fire Kelsey had started had cut a huge slash behind them and the smoke filled half the sky. That had to be distracting. They'd caught a break that none of them had had any reason to expect.

Beauchamp had worked with her to make some modifications to her armor that she'd said would make it blend in more seamlessly with the horde, should they be spotted. Julia didn't really understand the significance of the changes, as they all seemed cosmetic, but anything that kept her from blowing their cover was a good thing.

As she worked, Beauchamp had told her stories about the man who'd once worn the armor that was now hers. He'd been a practical joker, but fierce in battle. A loyal friend that would trade his life for his comrades without a moment's hesitation.

A truth the local knew firsthand as he'd done exactly that during the fight, saving her life at the cost of his own.

She couldn't understand how the other woman was just calmly talking about her man. She seemed reflective and at peace. Not unhurt, but not as if she'd just lost so many people she'd known and commanded.

Julia was a wreck in comparison. The pain of losing Scott squeezed Julia's heart tight in her chest. She couldn't stop replaying the last fight over and over again in her mind. What could she have done differently? What actions would've allowed them both to have survived?

Her brain knew that he'd already been dying and nothing she'd done would've changed that, but her heart still wailed at her failure to save him. His death would always lie heavy on her soul, a stain that she would never fully wash away.

Though she intended to try. The blood of their enemies would make for a satisfying start. If it would ease her pain, she'd bathe in it.

They'd entered a light forest early yesterday, which had slowed them down, but also served to conceal them from any pursuers. That gave her hope that they might finally be in the clear from the most immediate threats.

She certainly hoped so, because as tired as she was, the rest of them were infinitely more exhausted. None of them were trained riders except for Kelsey, Elise, Olivia, Carl, and herself. Oh, and Beauchamp. So almost half of their number. Yet the other half desperately needed some rest. They also needed to plan.

By the best of Beauchamp's estimates, the horde city was just over twenty kilometers away. The other woman thought that they'd start seeing the tallest of the buildings in the megacity in the morning, if they found a suitably clearing.

"Why not just live in the megacity?" she asked Beauchamp as they drank water and ate cold rations in the chill dawn the next morning. "If they're going to build their city right next to it, why not just go ahead and take the extra step to move into the larger accommodations? I understand that they wouldn't have power, but something could probably still be done to make it work."

"The ruined megacities have their own inhabitants," the local woman said. "To journey into one is to risk being captured by those people, and they're significantly more paranoid of outsiders than the rest of us, which is saying something. They don't want contact with others. In fact, they'll use force to drive others out of the megacities. Those that they don't kill outright.

"Yet the megacities are such rich sources of salvage that other groups can't help but go into them. They don't go in unarmed or in small numbers, though. It doesn't take long for the inhabitants to start shadowing them. No one else could possibly know a megacity like its inhabitants. So, such excursions are brief and heavily armed. Those that aren't are never heard from again."

Well, didn't that just sound peachy?

It was probably best that they didn't make any plans to go into the megacity, then. There really wasn't any reason to do so, but knowing their luck, something would come up and force them to retreat there.

That might be negative thinking, but they had to plan for the worst-case scenarios. If their raid inside the horde city went off without a hitch, they could ride away. If it didn't, they were going to need a handy place to retreat to because the horde city would become an anthill of people searching for them. They had to do everything in their power to avoid being recaptured because nobody wanted to be tortured and then burned to death.

If that meant retreating into the megacity and hoping that they could evade the inhabitants long enough to find a way to escape again, that's what they needed to plan for.

Going inside the megacity would likely be the worst of all worlds. None of the technology would work, and the inhabitants would be hostile. They'd know every square centimeter of the city they lived in, and it would be impossible to find where they lived without capturing some of them, which would enrage the rest.

Based on what she'd heard, it sounded as if anyone captured there was dealt with harshly. Perhaps as harshly as the horde dealt with their prisoners. Though it was possible that the captured invaders were kept alive as labor, or worse, it would be best to consider how the horde treated their prisoners.

Though, to be fair, she wasn't sure that held for run-of-the-mill captives. Those might just be enslaved. Which, on reflection, might be a worse fate than even a painful death.

This could easily be a "from the frying pan into the fire" sort of moment. Yet another catchy phrase that Kelsey had shared with her. Considering that the form of execution the horde favored was immolation, it had an ironically grim meaning as well.

Julia took a few moments to look over the rest of the party, many of whom were still asleep. They'd travel again today and make it close to the horde city by dark. Tomorrow, they'd have to figure out how they were going to sneak inside the damned place.

One thing was for sure, the horde would never expect them to come wandering right up to their seat of power looking to sneak in. That kind of behavior was insane.

She wasn't exactly happy that that's what they had to do either. They'd have to observe the horde city before they could make any decision about how to get inside it. Once they did get inside, they'd have to find out where all their gear was being kept, which she was sure would be under heavy guard. Then they'd need to get access to it without the horde knowing, and finally slip away unseen.

At any point, they could make a critical mistake and their goose was cooked. Yet *another* catchy phrase with a double meaning from her doppelgänger that involved fire. She was just a font of gruesome sayings.

Julia sighed. It was no use complaining. Their situation was what it was. She really hoped they could get Doctor Stone's medical supplies—maybe even the spare medical kit that had been left at the pinnaces—because she'd love to have her augmentation back online. That would make escaping the city at least possible.

If they could scrounge up their gear and find a place inside the city to hide while they recovered, then they could come up with a plan to escape completely. Perhaps once they'd left horde territory, the rest of the trip would be easier.

That overly optimistic thought made her mentally laugh. It was almost guaranteed that the trip was going to get harder with every single step.

Thankfully, figuring all this out wasn't her problem. She could give Kelsey and Mertz—Jared—advice and opinion, but in the end, those decisions rested with them.

As she chewed the last of her meal, she wondered what they'd decide to do. Would it be a straightforward plan that she'd never have considered, or would it be some kind of crazy mission that was bound to get them all killed?

Knowing her doppelgänger, Julia was betting on the latter.

Well, it was time to get the rest of them up and start that planning. They had some more riding to do and then someone would have to scout the city. Probably Talbot, since marines had that skill set.

It was crunch time, and everything needed to go just right, or they'd all be dead, just like Scott and the rest.

* * *

THE NEXT MORNING, ten minutes after her husband had left to scout the area toward the horde city, Kelsey forced herself to stop worrying about him and what he might find on his search. She couldn't afford the distraction. They needed to have a plan of action once they found a way into the city.

Which they would, one way or another.

The information that Talbot brought back would certainly help them figure out the details of what needed to be done, but they'd need to have a plan already firmly in mind before then. They were only going to get one chance at this.

Their newest hideaway in the woods was well concealed, and they'd stashed the horses in a thicket where they'd likely not be discovered. Kelsey was well aware of how much noise a horse made as it went about its life, but these seemed preternaturally quiet. It had to be part of their warhorse training.

If they hadn't been quiet, they'd have had to stash the horses much farther away from themselves and hope that no one came along to discover them.

With only a dozen of her friends left alive, she felt empty inside. She couldn't stop thinking about all the people she'd known or was responsible for that the horde had killed. So many people.

Yet here they were, about to give the horde another chance to kill them.

Worse, this wasn't for revenge. It was only to get their equipment back before trying to slip away undiscovered.

A big part of her wanted to see these bastards bleed. To make them pay for all the pain and suffering they'd caused. But revenge wasn't something that they could afford to dish out right now. The cruel sons of bitches were going to get away with everything they'd done while she and her friends fought the AIs to save humanity, including their sorry butts.

"Once we get inside the city, we'll need to get under cover quickly," Beauchamp said. "Every interaction we have with one of them is an opportunity for them to figure out that we don't belong. It will only take one person sounding the alarm for us all to die.

"One thing going for us is that we're going to look like warriors from inside their own society, so I'm hopeful that we can make our way deeper into the city without the regular populace disturbing us. The horde has a terrible reputation about how it treats its people—almost as bad as they treat everyone else—so the average man or woman on the street is unlikely to interact with a horde warrior, much less a dozen of them."

Jared nodded his head slowly at that. "I'd imagine they have a seat of government of some kind. Probably a palace. Right?" At her nod, he continued. "They're going to have people in charge that want to see everything that's been captured. That means everything being brought in on pack horses will be taken to some kind of central repository to be sorted and identified.

"That location is going to be heavily guarded, and we're going to have to get inside without raising the alarm, take what we need, and then get away without them being any the wiser. If anyone has any ideas about how to make that happen, I'm all ears."

Before anyone could respond, the sound of horses riding sounded in the distance. The noise was faint, but it was clear that they had visitors. Thankfully, they didn't have a fire burning or anything else that might give away their position.

Kelsey rose from where she was sitting, picked up her bow from where she'd set it beside her, and headed for the trees in the direction the noise had come from. If they were going to have to fight, she was going to be ready.

Of course, if they had to fight, they were all dead anyway. They couldn't allow a single person to get away with word of where they were. Even missing people would raise the alarm sooner or later. Any sign at all that something unusual was happening would give them away eventually.

She made her way through the trees using a path that she'd discovered early this morning. It brought her to the exterior strip of this stretch of forest and allowed her to observe what was going on out on the plain.

About two hundred meters away, a group of horsemen rode along the edge of the forest. At her rough count, there seemed to be about three dozen riders and about twice that many pack horses.

One of the pieces of equipment strapped on the outside of one of the packs was a computer that the science team had brought with them. It looked as if she'd spotted one of the groups that had ambushed them heading back to the city.

The good news was that they weren't in immediate danger, so she relaxed a little. Once they'd safely passed, she wormed her way back to the clearing and told the others what she'd seen.

"We might have made a mistake in sending Talbot off alone," she ventured while they digested her words. "We're a little exposed out here. It might make more sense to follow along behind him.

"All we're abandoning are the horses, and they can pull themselves free because I made certain the knots in their reins would give way with any kind of determined tugging. If something happened to us, I didn't want them to starve to death."

"We're going to need the horses to escape the area," Beauchamp said. "We can't afford to have them discovered while we're gone. Still, I agree with you doing that."

"With any luck at all, we'll be in and out of the city before they have a chance to be discovered. If we lose the horses, that hurts our chances of survival. If we get captured, we're dead."

"Neither of those options is very appealing," Jared said. "Do you think we should just head down the path after him? He's not going to be expecting us, and we really don't want to surprise him."

"We also don't want to be spotted out here," Kelsey countered. "We're committed to this, Jared. We need to follow him so that we can take advantage of whatever he finds. Honestly, we should never have let him go alone. Time is not on our side."

Her brother sighed and rubbed his face. "You're probably right. Let's pack our gear and make it look as if no one was ever here. We'll follow along behind Talbot and see what we can find. Hopefully, he won't run into any trouble and we can make contact without any fuss.

"If we miss one another, we'll need to leave a note here telling him that we decided to follow him. Put it under some stones in a pattern so that he'll know it wasn't here when he left."

Kelsey hoped her husband wouldn't run into anyone, that they'd get close to the city and find some way to make this damned plan work. This was a make-or-break moment. They had to get the scepter and get away again, and the clock was ticking.

28

Talbot moved slowly through the forest, keeping an eye out for any sign that the horde had been there before him. Any path leading toward the city was likely to be either observed or possibly trapped. He absolutely didn't want to be a victim of something he could've spotted long before he chanced upon it.

He was approaching both the horde city and the ruined megacity, as they were seated next to one other and both perpendicular to his position. The ruined megacity was significantly larger and taller. Even in its present condition, many of the buildings still stretched an unimaginable height into the sky, and he caught glimpses of the towers through the closely set trees and the leafy canopy.

The horde city was significantly more primitive, though much newer in construction. If he had to make a guess, it was probably only fifty or sixty years old. It would've been constructed after the AIs had crushed Terra. No one would have been comfortable building a city so close to the dead megacity if some time hadn't passed to make them feel safe in doing so.

The occasional clearing allowed him an unobstructed view of the megacity, and he was hoping for a better look at the horde city, if he could find a hill with a view. It irritated him that he'd once had access to drone video of the two cities, but it was now locked away in his implants. His personal memory of the details wasn't good enough to plan with.

Relying on his implants had made him sloppy, and he vowed that future Marine Raider training would include more working without implants. Basic skills needed to be maintained, even if new recruits thought they no longer needed them. This situation had *thoroughly* proven that.

There were animal paths crisscrossing the underbrush, so those were what he mainly followed. That brought risks, but it was significantly more difficult to move through the foliage without using them.

Not being familiar with the normal sounds of the forest life, every movement of leaves or snap of twigs on the ground made him freeze. He saw a few small creatures with bushy tails. Some of them chittered indignantly at him.

Once, he saw a larger four-legged creature, but it was obviously an herbivore, even with the magnificent rack of horns on its head. It stared regally at him for a few seconds once he tried to move, and then bounded off with far more grace and beauty than he'd expected.

He'd thought travel through the forests would be easy. Wrong. The travel time projections for getting to the Imperial Vault would need to be extended. Rather than speeding their journey, the horses might slow them even further. At this point, six to eight months might be optimistic.

He continued on his way, focused on the area around the trails as he moved. If he were the enemy, this kind of chokepoint was where he'd put any traps or observation points. That meant he had to go slowly and be exceptionally careful.

They'd discussed this before he'd left the temporary camp, and he'd decided that his look around would take as long as needed to make sure this was done right. If that meant he stayed overnight, he'd prepared the rest for that option as well.

Talbot found his first sign of other humans maybe two kilometers from the horde city. There was a small blind set up away from the path, but within view. It was almost a pillbox set into the side of the hill, made of logs covered over with dirt and foliage.

He probably wouldn't have spotted it, if it'd been well maintained. Whoever was in charge of making certain that it wasn't visible hadn't kept the plants atop it alive, so the dead growth tipped him off.

Perhaps it was only occasionally manned. If the horde didn't have a full-time force working in the forest, then they'd rotate between observation blinds similar to this throughout the area around their city.

Its presence told him something important. The horde expected people to try to sneak up on the city. That meant that there was going to be more difficulty getting in than they'd hoped for.

Or perhaps the observation posts were to keep people from leaving. From his point of view, it was difficult to tell. They knew virtually nothing about the horde, other than their murderous intent. Maybe they had slaves. Or something worse that he couldn't imagine at the moment.

To satisfy his curiosity, Talbot headed closer to the blind.

He moved cautiously, trying to stay away from the path so that he wouldn't be easy to spot as he moved through the undergrowth. Since it had been a damned long time since he'd trained at moving through the wilderness, he certainly hoped nobody was inside the damned thing, because there was no way they could miss hearing him coming.

He really wished that the marines had taught more ground operations of a covert sort during his training. There'd been a couple of exercises and classes over the years, but whatever he learned in them was long out of practice. He made more mental notes to adjust the as yet theoretical Marine Raider training that he was supposed to be helping formulate.

When he got close to the observation post, he could see the door leading into the back of it. No one had bothered trying to disguise the thing from the rear.

He wondered what made this particular path more viable for travelers than the other animal trails that he'd seen. It didn't look any larger than the others. Perhaps it was because it moved more directly toward the city. Or perhaps they were all monitored at some point.

The door leading into the bunker was manually operated and didn't seem to have a lock. He considered the possibility that it was protected by some kind of alarm but dismissed that.

While it was obvious that the horde had some of the means to generate power and construct high-technology items—as demonstrated by the EMP weapons and the antiarmor rockets—he doubted very seriously that they used such technology for anything as pedestrian as an alarm system so far from their city.

Looking inside was going to be a risk, but only a small one that might pay dividends down the road. He tested the handle and found it unlocked, just as he'd suspected. He opened the door and looked in, his hand on the hilt of Kelsey's borrowed sword.

It was dark inside, but he could make out the general details from light filtering through the observation slit on the far side of the structure. As he'd suspected, there was no power, no lights, and no indication that this post had been occupied anytime recently.

In fact, based on the debris that had been deposited inside the small, low structure—likely by bad weather—it had probably been at least a couple of weeks since the last time anyone had been inside it. Maybe a month. Assuming, of course, that they cleaned up after themselves.

There were two chairs and a slender shelf built into the wall beneath the observation slit. It was likely that the observers were stationed here during times that the horde suspected there would be unauthorized travelers moving around the city.

The slits weren't useful for firing bows—being laid out horizontally rather than vertically—so he suspected anyone stationed here was meant to simply observe and warn someone else about what they saw via a runner or some other low-tech method. As there were no signs of any kind of communication device, that would be the only way they could do it.

He was still thinking about how the horde would carry out those tasks when he heard the sound of a branch snapping somewhere outside the observation post. It was probably an animal, but he needed to be on his guard. If somebody spotted him now, they were all in very deep trouble.

Moving as quietly as he could, Talbot exited the observation post and eased the door closed behind him. The slight squeaks that the hinges had made when he'd opened the door the first time now sounded like screams in his ears. He certainly hoped that if that was someone out there, they wouldn't hear it.

Talbot eyed the surrounding forest and tried to judge which direction the noise had come from. There was a path—though it wasn't well-defined —leading away from the observation post and deeper into the forest. It sounded as if something or someone was coming down it.

He needed to get out of there and do it now.

Even as he started moving, he saw some of the branches farther up the path move and caught the outline of a human form. No, two human forms.

The horde had finally sent people to watch the trail, and he was directly in their way. He was moments from discovery.

* * *

No matter how quiet he tried to be, Jared felt as if he'd stepped on every single twig and brushed against every branch as he'd moved. Each noise sounded incredibly loud in his ears, though he knew most of them were too soft to carry. Most of them.

He tried to emulate Captain Beauchamp, but he'd never capture her grace and skill at moving through the forest like a ghost. For someone who he'd only ever seen ride a horse, she had a lot of grace at moving through the forest.

None of the rest of them did, that was for sure. Each and every one of his people seemed unable to miss anything that made noise, and the animals around them quickly went silent as they passed. If any trained woodsmen were lurking out there, they'd immediately know something was wrong. He just hoped they didn't figure out exactly what the silence meant while he and his people were still here.

Even as he was thinking that, Beauchamp froze and held up a hand to halt the rest of them. Everyone else shambled to a stop, though their eyes were all darting around, looking for what had caught her attention.

She took two steps back and placed her lips directly next to Jared's ear. "There's someone up ahead. It might be Talbot, but I'm seeing some kind of movement on the side of the hill. There's too much underbrush in the way for me to get a clear look, but the man I see seems to be about the right size for him. I'm not sure what he's doing, but it feels like he's hiding from something. If so, we should do the same."

Taking a risk, Jared stepped forward until he could see what she'd seen. It took him almost ten seconds to spot the man on the side of the hill. He was crouched behind what could have been a low wooden wall, so there was some kind of structure up there.

Beauchamp was right. It was impossible to tell exactly who it was without getting a little closer, but Jared's years with the marine made him feel certain that it was Talbot.

"It's him," he said softly back to Beauchamp. "What's he doing?"

"Hiding," she said with more than a hint of tension in her soft voice. "There's someone else up there."

Jared motioned for Kelsey and Lieutenant Laird to join them. In a low tone, he explained what was happening in front and above them.

"Chloe, I want you to take point on this," he said when he'd finished. "Kelsey will assist you because she's got the best hand-to-hand skills of any of us. I'd put her as the lead, but you have better tactical training than she does. Sorry, Kelsey."

His sister shrugged slightly. "It's all going to come out in the wash. If there's trouble up there, both of us are going to be involved. Talbot has one of my swords, so if he has to come out swinging, he's going to be effective. With his training in the Art, he has a good grasp of melee combat with a blade and his body.

"The key here is that we can't let anyone report our presence. We not only need to ambush the people he's looking at, but we need to make sure that even someone who gets away is taken out before they get back to the city."

"I think that's where Captain Beauchamp and Julia come in," Chloe said, brushing her tangled red hair out of her eyes. "We need to let them take the other side of that building Talbot is behind. They're both experienced with bows, as are you, and they'll be able to pick off people that are fleeing at a distance.

"But even that isn't going to be enough. If we start chasing someone through the forest, they're going to lose us unless we stay on their heels. Bows are going to be useless beyond a fairly short range in this environment. This is going to be blade work."

"Yes, it is," Jared said grimly. "Once you engage, we'll come up behind Talbot and provide a backdrop behind him with extra bodies. None of us are trained for this kind of fighting, but we've all got swords and marine knives. If we have to help with the fight, we'll do it. We'll just hope it doesn't come to that."

At his nod, Kelsey, Chloe, Julia, and Captain Beauchamp moved out. The rest of them stayed where they were for the moment, because they didn't want to risk making any noise until the fighting started. They'd make their way up the hill as quickly as possible once things got rolling and come in behind Talbot.

With any luck at all, they'd be able to silence whatever patrol Talbot had spotted. That was only a short-term solution, though. Someone would eventually miss those people.

At this point, they were committed to making this crazy plan work. Even if killing the patrol set off a search for them, it wouldn't happen immediately.

But the clock *was* ticking. It was time to make the magic happen.

29

K elsey followed Chloe Laird up the hill. They both moved slowly because neither one of them was skilled at woodcraft. They couldn't afford to make any loud noise because that would alert whatever group Talbot had spotted to their presence. If that happened, whoever they were, they'd have too great a chance of warning the city that they had intruders.

By the time they'd reached the top of the slope, at least some of the people up there had moved into the structure. Her husband had slipped around to the closer side of the low building but hadn't noticed her presence yet. His attention was focused on the back of the structure.

She didn't know if that meant there was no one else outside but decided to take the most pessimistic view. They'd assume there were more people in the woods and that it was *her* responsibility to take them out.

As she was edging onto the area above the slope, Talbot sheathed his sword, drew his marine knife, and darted inside the structure. There was a muffled shout and the clang of steel on steel. Well, hull metal on steel, which was pretty close to the same.

With the attack in progress, Kelsey immediately discarded stealth and raced toward the forest behind the structure, her bow up and ready to engage targets of opportunity. Laird had a captured sword and was standing beside her side, scanning the forest for threats.

Farther across the hill, Kelsey caught a glimpse of blonde hair and spotted Julia and Beauchamp, who were both using their bows to seek out potential targets. She ignored them and continued to scan for any enemies.

She didn't see any.

With a gesture, she sent Chloe deeper into the forest to see if she could spot anything. Beauchamp was moving forward to do the same thing.

Kelsey watched their backs, ready to fire her bow or race after them, but she also kept an eye on the structure. The sounds of combat had already ceased, so she certainly hoped her husband was victorious.

She really *should* check just to make sure.

Keeping the majority of her attention focused on Laird, Kelsey edged closer to the door leading into the strange, low structure. "Talbot, tell me you're okay," she said, pitching her voice low enough to carry inside, but softly enough not to warn everyone in the general vicinity.

"I'm fine," he answered with a hint of a growl. "I got a cut on my arm, but it's not serious. Both of the people I spotted are down in here."

Kelsey considered passing that information along to Laird but decided against it. They should treat this as if Talbot had missed some of the enemy. Instead of fretting about it, she kept watch while she waited for Talbot to come out.

He stepped out of the short building a few moments later. He had his right vambrace off and was using a piece of cloth to wipe at a bleeding cut about five centimeters long on the back of his forearm. He was right. It didn't look too bad, so the armor there had mostly stopped the blow. The gash would need stitches but didn't seem immediately dangerous.

She half snorted at how her conception of what made for a serious injury had changed over the years. This kind of cut would've freaked younger her out. Now? Losing a finger *might* qualify as a moderate injury.

"Tell me what you've got," she said, keeping her eyes on the woods. "We spotted you from down below, so we have no idea what's going on up here."

"Two warriors came up the path from deeper into the forest. This observation post seems like it's only manned intermittently and isn't very well maintained. The plants on top are dead, so its camouflage is gone. They may've been coming to repair that rather than actually performing observational duties.

"At this point, it hardly matters. Now that I've killed them, somebody is going to be asking questions about them soon enough, and then they'll start looking for them."

He frowned toward her. "Aren't you supposed to be back at the camp waiting for me? Did something happen? Is everyone else okay?"

"We had a group of riders come past, likely heading toward the city. It made us feel a little exposed, so we left the horses tethered where they were and followed you in. Our window of opportunity is closing faster than we'd have liked. We need to get inside the city, get what we need, and be gone before they start looking for us in earnest. Once that happens, getting clear of the area is going to be a lot harder."

He grimaced at her words. "It's going to be hard no matter what we do. Those bastards will be all over us. I haven't gotten close enough to the city to see much yet, but I'm sure it's well guarded. I'll bet that it has a wall and plenty of roving patrols to make sure that nobody gets in or out without being challenged. These people strike me as the kind that don't want their 'citizens' wandering off, if you know what I mean."

"Yeah, I get that impression too," she admitted.

This wasn't the time or place to rush things, but the situation had been out of their control from the moment they'd landed. They just hadn't known it. Now they did.

Laird and Beauchamp came out of the woods with their weapons lowered, shaking their heads. Julia joined them as they converged on the observation post.

"There's no sign of anybody else out there," Beauchamp said. "It doesn't look as if that path is well traveled. Sending two people out into the woods like this isn't really a patrol. These men must've had some kind of task that they were performing."

Talbot nodded. "I've got some ideas on that, but it doesn't really matter what they were doing. Whoever sent them is going to be wondering why they don't come back once it gets dark. We're going to have to get rid of the bodies and clean this site up so that no one can tell anyone has been here.

"The goal of this is to leave them wondering exactly what happened. If we could arrange for an animal to eat them, that would be great, but we can't count on that. We're going to have to stash them somewhere and hope they remain undetected for a couple of days."

The local woman shook her head. "No matter what we do with them, crows and buzzards will feast upon their corpses, and that means that they'll be visible circling over this area. Anybody with half a brain will follow the carrion birds to see what they're eating once the missing people are remarked upon.

"This definitely shortens our timetable. We're going to have to get into the city tonight, if we can. By tomorrow, there will be search parties all through these woods and it will not take them long to find the bodies, since we have no tools to bury them. We'd be better off expecting the horde to seal the area sometime tomorrow. If we can get in tonight, find what we need, and then get back out before dawn, that would be best."

"We'll just have to make this work," Kelsey said glumly. "Chloe, make sure that everyone gets up here safely. We'll move the bodies into the woods and hope that buys us a day. Then we'll follow the path and see where it leads."

The clock was running out far faster than Kelsey had hoped, but their goals hadn't changed. The chances of failure were huge now, but they'd make it work. They had to.

* * *

JULIA FOLLOWED Captain Beauchamp as she made her way along the path that the two dead men had been traveling. The two of them were scouting ahead to see where it led while the rest of the party took care of the bodies.

They didn't have a lot of water to clean up the blood that Talbot had spilled, so she wasn't sure how well they'd do, but that was someone else's problem.

Beauchamp moved slowly, taking deliberate steps, and making certain that her feet didn't land on anything that was going to make noise. Julia tried to follow her example, though with less success. A *lot* less success.

The forest around them was filled with unidentifiable noises, and she felt her eyes darting back and forth, always concerned that what she was hearing meant more men coming to attack them. None materialized, however.

It took them half an hour to make their way to a hill that gave them a decent look at the horde city. Shorter than the abandoned megacity beside it by a significant margin, it was still somewhat larger than she'd expected.

Definitely low tech, but with high walls made of stone and wood, and patrolled by what looked like a strong force of armored warriors. Outside the walls in the cleared area between it and the forest, groups of horses rode along the perimeter of the city, either to keep intruders out or to make certain that the populace stayed inside. She wasn't sure which.

There were fortified enclosures along the wall that she suspected held weapons, based on the way they could be opened outward. That might mean low tech weapons, but Julia suspected there were advanced technology killing devices behind the covers. Hopefully, they wouldn't find out the hard way.

The two of them found a place to crouch behind the ever-present underbrush and observe the operations around the city without being visible themselves. Beauchamp was obviously watching what was going on with the guard patrols, but Julia found her attention focused on the dead megacity.

It was an amazing thing. She'd seen the implant tour of Imperial City from the destroyer's library as part of her preparation for this mission. The abandoned megacity seemed very much like it. Innumerable buildings reached impossibly high into the sky, and it dwarfed the collection of primitive structures beside it.

The megacity, whatever its name had been, wasn't as big as Imperial City, but it was far larger than anything on Avalon by many orders of magnitude. She could only imagine what her home world would look like when they'd advanced to that point. If they survived the oncoming war with the Rebel Empire.

"Getting inside isn't going to be easy," Beauchamp finally said. "They've got a lot of guards on the walls, and those roving patrols are going to be a real pain in the ass to get by. You can bet they've got observers watching everything from those towers spaced along the walls, too. I'm not sure how we're going to slip in."

Even as they watched, a group of pack horses accompanied by warriors was approaching the massive gate set into the intimidating wall. They couldn't hear anything being said from this far away, of course, but whatever exchange there was, it was brief. The pack horses and riders were passed into the city with barely a glance.

"Maybe we need to find one of the groups with some of our salvaged gear, kill them, and go in disguised as them," Julia said thoughtfully.

"They're expecting those kinds of groups and aren't checking for identification. People tend to see what they expect to see, after all. The guards at the gates can't possibly know everyone."

"There is some risk in doing that," Beauchamp said after considering the idea for a minute. "Though I will admit that I like the audacity of it. If we try an ambush, we can't let even a single person get away. If they do, they'll spread the alarm, and the hunt will be on. This close to the city, they'll find us in short order."

Julia nodded. "As I see it, we don't have a lot of options. Whatever we're going to do, we need to do it quickly. Any type of stealthy insertion is going to take time to set up, and even more to execute. We need to be inside the city today. It seems to me like the most direct path to success is walking in right under their noses.

"Besides, they're going to take the cargo right to where we want to go. That means we'll be able to find what we need much more quickly. If we have to search for where they're holding it, we might never find it in time. If we're expected, they'll let us right in."

The warrior sighed. "We're going to have to convince your compatriots of that, but I think you're probably right. If we can get our hands on a group of pack horses, we can probably bluff our way in. Getting back out is going to be a lot more difficult, but perhaps not impossible. Now all we have to do is find a group that we can eliminate."

Julia heard a noise coming from off to the side of the area they were hiding in. It wasn't coming from the path they'd taken to get there. She strained to see what was making it but couldn't see anything through the trees.

She picked a handy tree whose species she couldn't identify and climbed up as far as she could get. She'd become a much better climber over the last few years. She credited all the exploration that she'd done inside the ships she'd been on. The maintenance tubes had lots of ladders, and navigating those translated well into climbing trees, so long as she made sure that the branches weren't going to break under her weight.

The climb gave her a view of the area just on the other side of the strip of forest they were in. Crossing through that open space were two dozen horses packed high with gear, shepherded along by six riders.

That seemed like a small number of people to be escorting something as valuable as that, but it suited her purposes better than what she'd been expecting. As Kelsey had once said—with a phrase that was oddly appropriate for this situation—"never look a gift horse in the mouth."

Whatever *that* meant.

The group she was watching would have to go around to the right-hand side of the woods to get into the cleared zone around the city. That would take them an hour or so at their current pace.

If she could convince Mertz and Kelsey that they could take this group out without making too much noise, they could then use the pack horses as cover to get inside the city. This might be their best chance to make something happen.

Unfortunately, they wouldn't have time to retrieve their horses. That meant some of them would have to stay outside the city. That might actually be a plus, because the noncombatants could go back to the horses they'd stashed and have everything ready for them to retreat once the deed was done.

Or to get away when their last stand made the horde go nuts.

"We need to get back to the group," Julia said once she'd climbed back down, her hand still resting on the rough bark of the tree. "I think I see an opportunity coming our way. If we take advantage of it, we might just be able to get inside the city undetected and get what we need."

Of course, if they screwed up any part of this, they wouldn't get another chance to try again. This was going to be one of those things where they had to succeed on the first try. Like skydiving.

Talk about an incentive to do one's best.

There was always the chance that someone in the city would realize that they didn't belong. Every word they said, every gesture they made, was an opportunity for someone to figure out that they were outsiders. If that happened, they were all dead.

In a lot of ways, she was facing something very close to what she'd faced with the mad computer on Erorsi. If the horde got their hands on her, they'd torture her just as badly—or possibly even worse—than the AIs' damned electronic henchman that had implanted the damned augmentation into her without anesthesia.

And unlike in the machine, the horde would then set her on *fire*. While the end would be relatively quick, it would be horrific beyond measure.

She'd do *anything* to make certain that didn't happen. They all would.

As rough as this first leg of the journey had been, how difficult was it going to be when they got closer to the Imperial Vault? Or even partway there?

This mission was just like one of the adventures she'd read when she was a kid. As her father had told her, adventure was something very bad happening to someone else, very far away, or a long, long time ago. Even so, she'd always wanted to go on an adventure.

Her younger self was an idiot.

"We need to get back to the rest," she finally said. "We've got a lot of work to do if we want to capitalize on this, and we'll need every second to make sure we don't screw it up."

With that, the two of them headed back to where the rest were going to be as they followed along the path behind them. She'd seen a decent ambush spot while up in the tree. All she had to do was convince the others to back her play.

30
_____

J ared listened to Julia's plan, but started shaking his head before she was halfway done explaining it.

"That's too risky," he said when she'd finished. "_Anything_ can go wrong, and then we'd be totally screwed. First of all, if even one person escapes the ambush you propose, we're dead. Second, if the gate guards don't recognize someone in the party, they might have us right there. If that's the case, we'd never get away, and once again, we're dead."

He took a deep breath and continued. "Third, after we get into the city —if we're that lucky—then any interaction at all will be dangerous. The chances of us being discovered go up dramatically with every word we speak or gesture we make."

"It doesn't matter," Julia said firmly. "Within a day—perhaps two at most—this entire area is going to be swarming with people looking for us. We have to plan on that happening sometime tomorrow, or we'd be crazy. That means we've got to get inside the city today, and preferably get out before dawn with what we need.

"If you can come up with another plan that accomplishes that, I'd be happy to hear it. Unfortunately, I don't think you're going to. The city is heavily guarded and well patrolled. We're not going to sneak inside without someone seeing us. That means we have to go in under their eyes. I think my plan is probably the best option to do that."

At that point, Kelsey stepped in and put her hand on his shoulder. "She's right. This situation requires bold action, and she's come up with a viable plan. Perhaps the only one possible at this point."

Talbot sighed and nodded. "We don't really have any choice, Admiral. We need to get inside that city today, and if they lock everything up at night, that means we're limited to just a couple of hours to make the magic happen. We have to go for it."

"Just give me a second to think about this," Jared said tiredly, rubbing his eyes with his right thumb and forefinger.

As much as he wanted to reject this crazy plan out of hand, he knew that they were right. They'd run out of time and options. They had to have the Imperial Scepter, and they really needed Lily's spare surgical kit to reactivate their implants and augmentation.

Everything else they could do without, but those two things would make or break their chances of making it to the Imperial Vault and then getting inside it.

He was going to have to go with Julia's plan. He had no choice.

It worried him because he knew that the slightest miscalculation or bit of bad luck would see them dead in minutes—if they were lucky. Hell, even success might still mean that most of them died before the rest got away. This was easily the grimmest situation he'd ever been in, and that called for taking an insane risk for even a slim chance to get away.

He tilted his head back for a moment and stared up toward the hidden sky. The intertwined branches overhead formed a green canopy that mostly blocked the sun from getting through, except in dappled shadows. How he wished he had time to enjoy the scents, sounds and sights of nature, but he didn't.

Putting the almost wistful thought from his mind, he looked at Julia intently. "Tell me where the ambush has to take place. We need to get there as quickly as possible, because we'll need every second to improve our chances of taking them down. Do you have any ideas on how to most effectively do that?"

Julia crouched down and brushed the dead leaves and branches away from a small area, leaving a spot of open ground. She picked up one of the sticks and began drawing on the earth with it.

"This is the outline of the forest as I saw it from up in the tree. This 'X' is where the enemy was. They were coming around this section of the woods to get to the cleared zone around the city. Do you see this indentation in the forest right here?"

Jared nodded when she looked up. "You think they're going to go inside there? That would be odd."

She shook her head. "No, but if we put some of our archers on the far side of this gap, they'll be hidden in the woods right next to where the enemy is going to pass. If we spring a trap at the right moment, I think that there's a better than fifty percent chance they'll dodge into this cul-de-sac and be trapped inside.

"What I'm recommending is that we put our archers here to take out the outermost riders while we have a couple of our own troops move to block them from going forward. They only have six riders in total. If we can take out half their number at one go, and they also see a blocking force in front of them, they're going to try to get away.

"We'll post archers at the back in the first section of forest that they've already passed as well, so that if anyone tries to reverse course, they can take them out.

"It makes me sad to say this, but horses are easier to hit than human beings. We can take our initial shots directly at the people, but they're armored and our best chance of stopping anyone from getting away is to remove any possibility that they can outrun us. We don't have the horses with us, so we have to target their mounts. I'm sorry.

"Also, with only six riders, we can only take that many people inside. Our horses are too far away to be of help. They'd spot people on pack horses right away and think that was too odd to pass unremarked. These people know horses and riding.

"We'll already be taking a risk just having any of us that can't ride along. We can't chance it. The ones we leave behind can head back to our camp and wait for signs of our success or failure."

"This situation just keeps getting worse and worse," Kelsey grumbled. "I get the possibility of hurting or killing the horses. I don't have to like it, but I get it. If that's what we have to do to survive, that's what we have to do. We should get moving."

Jared watched his sister stalk back down the path. He was no happier than she that they might have to kill innocent animals, but he understood the stakes just as well as she did. The horses were combatants in their own way, at least while the enemy was on their backs.

They'd do whatever they had to do. Far too many people were counting on them for them to cut any corners. There's be time for regrets later.

* * *

TALBOT CROUCHED JUST inside the tree line and waited. He couldn't hear the approaching horses yet, but he suspected that they were close. It wouldn't be long before they were fighting. He and Chloe were going to be the non-ranged response force in front of the group. The admiral and Commodore Meyer were doing the same thing on Kelsey's side of the opening.

Kelsey had given Jared her other sword, so if they had to fight, they'd have that one advantage. They had to keep the riders from getting past them at all costs. Her swords gave them an edge—if one could forgive the pun—that the enemy wouldn't expect and couldn't counter.

He'd made certain that the admiral knew about the dangers of directly blocking a sword swing. Kelsey's weapons would shear off the other blade in a heartbeat, and it would just continue on flying toward him.

That reminded him of his arm wound, though that wasn't how the injury had occurred. His arm still throbbed where the enemy's dagger had cut him earlier. They had no medical supplies, so he'd washed it out as well as he could, wrapped it in cloth, and then put his vambrace back over it.

Lily was worried about him getting an infection. Without his medical nanites or access to his pharmacology unit, that was a very real possibility. One that could render him unfit to fight in short order, or even kill him. If it got that bad, they'd have to take his lower arm off without any anesthesia, probably using one of Kelsey's swords.

Kelsey hadn't figured out that she needed to be worried about that, and he had no intention of telling her. They'd either have access to the medical supplies soon, or they'd be dead. Losing his arm to amputation because it was infected was the least of his worries. He had to focus on the moment.

Looking out into the area that the small caravan would be passing through, he could see how Julia's plan might play out in a perfect world. While this wasn't a chokepoint by any means, their enemy's options would be severely limited during the attack. The enemy would be pinned between the forest he was hiding in, the forest a hundred meters away on the opposite side of the open area, and the forest on the other side of the cul-de-sac, with only three paths to ride away in.

It was possible they'd manage to ride around Chloe and himself, and make a break for the city, but Captain Beauchamp, Elise, and Olivia would do their very best to make sure they didn't get past them in the front with their bows.

The horde fighter's second most dangerous option was retreating back the direction they'd come. If they did try to reverse course, Kelsey and Julia were back there with bows to make certain they didn't get anywhere, with the admiral and Commodore Meyer backing them up with swords.

That left any survivors of the initial attack the option of fleeing directly into the cul-de-sac. That's where the majority of their people were waiting. They had the swords that they'd captured, though they weren't skilled in the use of them. Still, quantity had a quality all its own.

There were six riders with this group, so with any luck, their initial shots would take out at least two. The follow-up arrows might take out another one. That would leave three figuring out which direction to flee.

If they tried to go past Talbot and Chloe, the archers would take a toll on them. He didn't think the enemy riders had a great chance of making it past three skilled shooters. If they retreated, that was going to be more problematic. The admiral and Commodore Meyer had no skill with swords to stop them if they directly engaged.

Commander Cannon was in charge of the force inside the cul-de-sac. The redheaded tactical officer had basic hand-to-hand skills, as did most Fleet officers. Hopefully she and her team wouldn't have to deal with more than one or two riders, while the main fighting team raced in to cork the bottle behind the enemy.

Well, this was either going to work out or it wasn't. Worrying wasn't going to change the outcome.

Talbot glanced over at Chloe and found her watching him.

He raised an eyebrow. "What?"

"I'm just trying to figure out how you do it," she said softly. "It seems like disaster after disaster is falling on top of us, and you're handling every blow like it's no big thing. How do you stay so calm?"

He chuckled. "It's getting to me too, but I've got more experience at keeping my worries buried. It's all my time as a noncommissioned officer, I suspect. Officers could run around with their hair on fire, but the noncoms had to be steady."

She smiled slightly and shook her head. "They frown on officers running around with their hair on fire because it's bad for morale. At least that's what they said at the academy. I think most of us do okay, but you're a rock. No matter what happens, you're there doing your part to make things work out.

"I've learned a lot by watching you. If I survive this little adventure, I think I'm going to be a better officer because of it."

"I think you're a fine officer as it is, Chloe. It wouldn't surprise me at all if you get bumped to major once we get off Terra. Hope you're ready to command a company."

She blanched a little at his words. "I'm not ready to command a company. I think I need more seasoning."

"This may surprise you, but you're getting that seasoning right now. There's an old saying, 'good judgment comes from experience, and experience comes from poor judgment.'

"While I haven't seen you exercise any poor judgment, you've certainly seen *everything* that can go wrong, and that's almost the same thing. Most officers never consider how bad things can get until they're in over their heads.

"After this mission, you're going to be thinking about all the curveballs that life and combat can throw at you. That's where success lies in our line of work. Preparing for all the possibilities, good and bad. If you've considered the good breaks, you can capitalize on them. If you've gnawed over the unpleasant surprises, then you can try to mitigate them."

"I've been thinking about that, actually," she said. "We're about to get into one of the most important fights we've been in since we landed on this damned planet. There are so many things that could play out badly, even though this is only a small action. If even one person gets away, we're screwed."

He reached over and put a hand on her shoulder. "Planning out the things that can go wrong doesn't mean we let them paralyze us. Sometimes you just have to trust that the dice are going to come up in your favor. If they don't, well, to mix metaphors, you'll just have to play the cards you've been dealt."

"You really need to work on your motivational speaking, Colonel."

Before he could respond, he heard the sound of horses approaching in the distance. It was time. They'd either stop the enemy in their tracks and move on to the next phase of their crazy plan, or they'd blow it and go from the frying pan into the fire.

He watched and waited until the caravan came into view. What he saw was like a blow to the side of his head. There were more riders than Julia had indicated. At least a dozen, possibly a few more.

That was going to make carrying off this ambush significantly harder. The chances of some of his friends being killed in the process also went up significantly.

Well, he'd just told Chloe that one had to learn to roll with the punches, and he'd been worried that this sounded a little too easy. There wasn't much they could do to improve their odds, so they'd just have to fight harder.

This was all Kelsey's show now. As soon as she gave the word, they'd kick this party off and hope for the best.

31

Kelsey watched the horses as they began riding past and felt her heart sink. There were more people than Julia had said there would be. At least double the number, in fact. The one group her doppelgänger had seen must've met up with a second group. Now, with their numbers bolstered, taking them all out went from challenging to seemingly impossible.

That sucked, but there was nothing she could do about it now. They were going to have to carry off the attack just like they'd planned, because there was no way to make any changes to it.

She waited until the group had ridden past her hiding place and then kicked off the party by shooting one of the trailing riders in the back. The woman she'd targeted screeched and fell off her horse to writhe on the ground, her arms futilely reaching for the length of wood that had plunged into her back, which was just out of reach.

Julia had been waiting for that and fired moments after she did. Her arrow struck one of the men on the far side of the caravan, taking him in the torso. He didn't fall off his horse, but he didn't look like he was in very good shape either.

The three archers positioned with the forward group opened fire, taking down two of the riders directly ahead of the caravan, potentially killing them both. The third shot must've missed because Kelsey saw no sign of anyone else being inconvenienced by an unexpected impalement.

Even as Talbot and Chloe were running out in front of the group, Jared and Sean were doing the same on her end. Jared had her blade, so he was going to take the brunt of the hand-to-hand fighting. Her worry now was that there were too many enemies to stop them from retreating back past her. She had to make it her mission to stop that from happening.

"Target anybody running back our direction," she told Julia. "If they're not running, shoot anybody that goes for a bow."

Julia's answer was to fire another arrow even as Kelsey was tracking her next target. The other woman's shot flew right past one of the warriors as he jinked his horse to the side. Unfortunately for the other team, there was a second man right behind the first, and that rider caught the arrow in the throat. He pitched backwards off his horse and fell to the ground, lying there unmoving.

Kelsey's next shot caught one of the trailing riders as they turned to retreat. The arrow struck the man in his chest but must not have penetrated very far. Though he staggered in the saddle, the experienced horseman kept moving forward. She had to rush her third shot, but it did catch him in the side before he could get past her.

While he didn't fall out of the saddle, the way he was sagging to the side led her to believe that he was dead or critically injured. They'd have to catch up with his horse before it got too far, assuming they won this fight.

The archers up front had been just as busy as she was, so all three of them were peppering the vanguard of the caravan with shots. Kelsey had no time to count how many people went down, but it was at least two more.

Several of the riders raced toward Talbot and Laird, even as two more turned and bolted toward Jared and Sean. With the speed of their horses, they were on her friends before Kelsey could fire again.

Sean proved unable to strike at the man racing toward him. It was obvious that he meant to strike the horse, but the rider was very well trained. His mount seemed to leap to the side, and in a flash, he was past the officer, striking down with his sword as he passed. Thankfully, Sean blocked the strike even though it knocked his sword out of his hand.

As the escapee blazed past their blocking force, Julia fired an arrow into the man's back.

Or rather, she tried to. He dodged, not even seeing the first one until it flew past him, but her follow-up shot struck him in the spine, and he fell off his horse.

The one that attacked Jared found out immediately that that was a bad idea. Jared had paid attention to Talbot's instructions about her sword and so he struck from the side at the descending blade, seemingly aiming to break it off just above the hilt.

His aim was off, and he ended up taking the man's hand instead.

Well, that worked, too.

The pure shock on the man's face at what had happened to him didn't slow him down from trying to escape, though he was having to use his knees to control his mount as he tried to staunch the flow of blood from his severed limb.

That slowed him down quite a bit and made him an easier target. Kelsey's next shot took him in the side, and over he went.

Up front, Talbot and Laird had done their part to stop anyone from getting past, and the three archers had put down everyone on that side.

Kelsey saw that their side was doing just as well, with a couple of people on the ground wounded, and two wounded men that had ridden out of sight around the curve of the forest.

She raced out of concealment and leapt on the nearest horse that she could catch. It gave her some grief, but she firmly put him in his place. All those years of riding were paying off now as she was able to get the recalcitrant beast headed after the people that had retreated.

As she came around the bend in the forest, she saw that one rider had fallen off his horse and his mount stood nearby, looking nervously toward Kelsey.

The second mount was standing a little further away, but Kelsey couldn't see any sign of his rider. It was possible the other man had fallen off his horse as well, and that his body was hidden by the grass, but she wasn't going to assume that was the case. This could be some kind of ambush.

A quick glance up the open area between the tree lines showed no sign of the man running, so if he wasn't lying in the grass somewhere ahead of her, he was in the woods somewhere to her left. The trees on her right were too far away for even an unwounded man to make it to them in the time that he'd been out of her sight.

Since the man in the open was between her and the second horse, she dismounted, drew the local sword she'd appropriated, and approached him carefully. He was still breathing but was only twitching sporadically. He tried for a knife at his belt, but she planted her boot on his wrist to stop him.

Kelsey considered finishing him but wasn't sure she had that in her. She'd hunted men down and killed them, but the idea of killing someone she'd already defeated turned her stomach. She settled for kicking the knife a short distance away and stepped clear of the dying man.

That's when the man hidden in the grass nearby chose to strike. He seemingly rose out of the ground less than a dozen meters away and rushed toward her. He had his long blade out and was already slashing it toward her head.

He was *huge*, taller than Talbot and much more muscular. He outweighed Kelsey by more than three to one. Without her Marine Raider augmentation, he was significantly stronger than she was too, and he was also a trained warrior. The scars on his face proved that.

His first slash, though powerful, was a little high. He was probably used to fighting people that were significantly bigger than her. For once, her short stature was working in her favor.

Kelsey managed to duck and used her blade to nudge his over her head with a loud clang of metal on metal. That put her near the man.

Seeing an opportunity that likely wouldn't come again, she jumped inside the arc of his blade, drew the marine knife from her belt, and plunged it through the armor on the side of his torso. The armor was thick and scarred from other blows, but it didn't even slow the almost monomolecular point of the hull metal blade.

The wound didn't stop the man from jerking back and pulling the knife's grip right out of her hand. He brought his blade back around, and it smashed into hers hard enough to knock it out of her grip. It went flying somewhere off into the grass on her left.

Suddenly disarmed and knowing that she didn't have time to search for her weapon, she went on the attack. If she'd just had her body and no skills, she'd be dead in the next five seconds. Thankfully, the Art gave her something to work with.

Lacking any strength to go along with the moves she was going to execute, she wouldn't be able to do any throws or body checks. She was going to have to bring him down to her level as quickly and efficiently as possible without any of that.

Even as he was drawing back to strike at her again, she lashed out and connected with his right knee. There was an audible pop, and the man's leg gave way. He didn't fall, but he staggered to the side like a drunken sailor.

Following up quickly, Kelsey ran two steps forward and launched herself into the air. His blade was already in motion, coming to strike at her—low this time—and she used her armored forearm to slap it away as it slid beneath her flying body.

She planted both her feet right in his face. The impact was sufficient to send him crashing to the ground with blood spraying from his nose and mouth. Momentarily stunned, he seemed unable to figure out how to move for just a few critical seconds.

Kelsey hit the ground a bit off-balance, but continued her roll forward, grabbed the knife still protruding from his side, and plunged it back into his throat.

Even mortally wounded, he tried to hit her with his sword one last time. She was far too close for the edge to hit her with any force but ducked close to him just in case.

The pommel of the weapon struck her leather helmet hard enough to throw her to the side with her head ringing, but there was no follow-up. The man gurgled, writhed beside her, and died.

Kelsey stood, her legs momentarily unsteady. Her face was covered in blood, but it wasn't hers. The foul iron stench made her want to throw up, but she managed to control her stomach.

That was of course the moment the man she'd spared stuck his recovered knife into her left calf.

The sharp, bright pain made her yelp as she hopped away from him. He lay there unmoving, his hate-filled eyes already starting to cloud over.

She knelt and looked at the wound. The puncture wasn't bad. The knife had probably only penetrated a couple of centimeters. Not enough to cause her more than inconvenience. It was bleeding freely, but there was no bright-red arterial blood. She'd live.

This damned fight reminded her far too much of the battle at the Imperial Retreat where she'd stalked and killed the assassins associated with her dead brother. It had been just as brutal and bloody. Thank God that her experience there had hardened her for what was happening now.

Kelsey staggered toward where her sword had fallen. She didn't have time for weakness. The fight might still need her.

Even as she searched for it, she made a mental note to practice fighting with her augmentation turned off. She'd been very lucky this time. The next fight might kill her.

A moment later, she had her sword in hand, had mounted her horse, and galloped back toward the fight.

Which was over by the time she came back into sight. Talbot and Laird had almost made it to the bend of the open area closest her, and Julia—now mounted—was also headed her way.

Kelsey slowed and made a gesture for the others to slow down. No need to rush now.

Their reserve force had come out of the cul-de-sac, and it seemed that all of the enemy was accounted for. After making sure no one else seemed badly wounded, she made her way over to Talbot and Laird. His torso was liberally coated in blood, though his posture didn't speak to any serious wounds.

"Are you hurt?" her husband asked with a note of worry.

She shook her head. "I was just a little too close to someone having the worst day of their life. Did we get them all? Are you hurt? Is anyone else?"

"All the enemy is down, and no riders bolted, other than the two you chased. We're okay. Did you get the two you were after?"

"I finished them off," she answered grimly. "We're going to have to hide the bodies, though thankfully we won't have to worry about them being discovered until tomorrow. It's already late in the day, and the horde warriors won't have time to become concerned about any birds, if they see them at all."

He nodded. "The archers took care of most of the ones here, but there were a couple that were still alive. They weren't going to survive, so Captain Beauchamp finished them. It makes me sick to my stomach having to do something like that."

She pulled him into a hug. "Harsh times call for harsh measures. It's not like we killed them out of hand. They fell in battle, and she made certain they didn't suffer. After what they did to the rest of our people, I don't have much sympathy for them."

He shook his head slowly. "Just because they're monsters doesn't give us a right to be monsters as well. I agree that she did exactly what needed to be done and that it was a mercy. We just have to be careful that we don't become hardened to this kind of thing. I'm a little worried about Julia on that front."

She looked over at her doppelgänger. She'd joined the captain in killing the wounded back at the campsite where she'd rescued them, and she'd been cold-blooded and methodical about it. Not cruel, but still something to watch. If they survived the day.

Talbot gave her one final squeeze and then stepped back. "Let's move the bodies into the cul-de-sac. We'll load them onto their horses and dump them a couple of dozen meters inside the forest. Hopefully no one will discover them before we make our escape."

Relocating the bodies was going to be a grisly task, but Kelsey threw herself into her work. Talbot was right that they couldn't afford to become monsters, but she wasn't going to lose much sleep about the indignities and unfairness of cutting down bastards like these. These men and women had chosen to butcher her unconscious people. They more than deserved what happened to them.

It looked like all of the pack horses were gathered in a clump—almost twice the number Julia had originally reported, which matched well with the idea two groups had merged. A couple of their people made sure that they didn't run off. As soon as they'd taken care of the bodies and washed the blood off their new mounts—and themselves—they'd see about getting into the city.

Ready or not, it was time to confront the enemy in their lair.

32

J ared felt naked as he rode out into the cleared area around the horde city. They were now in plain sight of both the guards on the walls of the ominous place and the mounted patrols that circled it. They were now fully committed to this crazy plan because there would be no backing out.

Even though he was near the front of the caravan, he wouldn't be doing the talking. He'd leave that to Beauchamp. She understood more about the horde than he did. She'd at least heard them speaking before and knew how to get the inflections right.

While everybody still spoke Standard, pronunciation of certain words had changed over time here on Terra. And on Avalon, too. The linguistic drift might kill them if someone got suspicious.

As a group, they'd discussed what they'd do if their ruse was discovered. As grim as it sounded, everyone had the means to make certain that they weren't captured. They all had knives that they could use on themselves.

None of them wanted to commit suicide, but if the other option was torture and immolation, he'd slit his own throat without a second's hesitation. The next few minutes were going to determine if that was necessary.

If their journey ended here, the New Terran Empire was doomed. Humanity itself was probably doomed. The AIs might have been satisfied with ruling over humanity before, but their development of the Omega Plague told him that they were now prepared to start eliminating their creators.

Beauchamp had gone over some basic ground rules of their behavior for this meeting. No one was to speak except her, unless directly spoken to. Even then, they were to keep their responses as brief and basic as possible.

Not that the woman expected the guards to question everyone. Based on what Julia and Beauchamp had seen, conversation was minimal. After all, what kind of idiot would try to sneak into the city right under their very noses.

His heart was pounding as the group approached the gate. None of the guards stationed in front of it or on the walls above seemed overly concerned at their approach.

Nor should they. A dozen people—even if they'd been trained warriors —would pose no threat to the city.

One of the guards standing in front of the gate stepped forward as they approached and raised his spear into the air, point first. "Hold. What news of the escaped prisoners?"

"We haven't seen them," Beauchamp said with a grimace. "If we had, you'd see them strung out behind us. Someone else will catch them. They won't get away."

The guard grinned at that. "True enough. Pass."

Jared was starting to breathe a silent sigh of relief when that same guard narrowed his eyes and once again raised his spear.

"Hold." He was looking directly at Kelsey. "Take off your helmet."

Jared tensed. This was it.

The man looked her up and down once she'd removed her head cover, revealing the bruised and battered face she'd gotten when she'd been captured. He eyed her suspiciously for a moment, and then he smiled.

"How can a little thing like you be a warrior? Did you steal Daddy's armor, little girl? Maybe you need a real man like me to show you how to use that sword and not get beaten up like that."

His companions rumbled with laughter, and he visibly preened a little.

Kelsey slowly smiled in a way that made Jared's blood run cold.

She edged her horse closer to the man and leaned over toward him. "That assumes you could even find the sheath with that short sword of yours. You look a little... clumsy."

"Oh, my mistake. That's just a dagger with a dull edge. So, is that what this is? You're looking for a real woman to sharpen that thing for you because your whetstone has grown worn from overuse and you think I have a firmer stroke than you? I hear that comes with age, old man."

There was a brief moment of stunned silence before the guard's companions roared in laughter. Many of them had doubled over, unable to contain their mirth.

The man's face flushed a deep red as he scowled. "You have a saucy mouth, girl. Do you just use it to talk? Did you mouth off to the wrong man and he beat you like a drum?"

Kelsey gave him a disdainful sniff as she turned her horse to return to the formation. Her horse's tail flipped almost dismissively.

"I set him on fire, so I think I came out ahead in the end. Shall I climb down so that we can compare blades? I promise not to look disappointed when you come up... short. After all, I'm sure it's cute for its size."

The guards roared again, and the man's flush deepened even further.

"I'll give you this, woman, you've got a quick tongue," he ground out. "Get inside before I'm tempted to teach you some manners," the guard said as he gestured with his spear for them to proceed. "And don't be surprised if one day I make you call my name with that sassy mouth."

"Keep dreaming, big man," Kelsey said with a toothy grin as she rode past him. "Keep dreaming."

The exchange had made Jared feel as if he was having a heart attack. Once they'd crossed through the gate and into the city itself, he motioned for Kelsey to ride up beside him. That was easier than trying to redirect his horse to meet hers.

"*Have you lost your mind?*" he demanded quietly as she fitted her helmet back on. "You deliberately provoked him."

The corner of his sister's mouth quirked up. "Once he'd singled me out, I didn't have a choice. It would've been out of place for a warrior to take that kind of challenge without responding. Yes, I upped the provocation by mocking him that way, but trust me when I say that I had to. Anyone who has spent any time around the marines would know that."

"She's right," Beauchamp said from his other side as they rode through the city, the sound of the shod hooves loud on the cobblestones beneath them. "I'm glad she reacted the way she did because no woman of the blade would allow that kind of talk about her without striking back. Not all combat is physical. Her silence would've raised their suspicion."

She grinned at Kelsey. "And that was well said. I'll have to remember that when I next need to put an uppity man in his place."

Jared wanted to rub his face but that would've seemed out of place, so he just allowed himself a single sigh. Instead of responding, he looked at the buildings they were passing.

Most were made of wood, though some stone was used in their construction. They all looked primitive, but not because of the materials they'd used. He'd seen the Imperial Lodge where Kelsey had stayed for a while on Avalon once they'd put down Ethan's regicidal insurrection. It was wood and stone but built by true craftsmen. These buildings were... sloppy.

He wondered if they'd built the structures themselves or used slave labor. There was no telling, and honestly, he didn't even want to know at this point. Some things were best not thought about.

A much more pressing concern was where they were going. Wandering the streets would not serve their purposes. In fact, if they didn't figure out where they needed to be very soon, someone was going to get suspicious, of that he was certain.

At the moment, they were on a wide street that led deeper into the city. The smaller, packed dirt alleys that led away from the cobblestones were narrow and seemed to only serve the areas just off the boulevard. That wouldn't be where they were keeping anything valuable.

For the moment, he thought they were safe heading directly into the city. The powerful lived in the centers of such places, and that would be where these caravans were heading. The trick was going to be finding the right building, and then fooling whoever guarded it into thinking that he and his people had the right to go in.

Jared looked up at the sun with a hand shading his eyes and estimated that they had an hour and a half before dark. He had no idea what the city guards would do at that point, but he was willing to bet that everything would be locked down for the night. This seemed like the kind of place where they didn't like the idea of random people wandering around in the dark.

At this pace, moving through the timid crowd that hurried to get out of their way, he estimated that they'd arrive at the city center in twenty or thirty minutes. If it took much longer than that to figure out their ultimate destination, they were going to end up fighting in the middle of a hostile populace with nowhere to go.

Jared gritted his teeth and gently used his heels to urge his horse to go just a little faster. He had to be careful because he didn't want it breaking into a gallop, and he still wasn't that good at controlling it, but every second counted. They had to get to the right place and get under cover, and they needed to do it right now.

* * *

Julia guided her horse along the cobblestone street almost on autopilot as she watched the crowd move around them. And it *was* definitely moving around them. The people looked terrified of her party, and that told her all she needed to know about how the horde treated its own people. The bastards that ran the horde were brutal.

She wished she had the ability to overthrow their regime but knew that that wasn't in the cards. They'd be lucky to get out of the city with their skins intact. Her thirst for their blood wouldn't be slaked today.

The crowd parted around them, rushing to be as far away from the horses as possible, and allowed the group deeper into the city at a fairly decent pace. Once they'd left the gate, the quality of the buildings began slowly improving. The rough wooden structures were replaced by stone, even though that was still just as slipshod as the buildings behind them.

With every block they traveled, the quality of the construction continued to improve until they were finally in an area that looked somewhat prosperous. The crowds had changed here as well. While they still had a fearful aspect to them, they didn't seem to be completely terrified of her party.

This section of the city had a lot of shops, and the people around them were either conducting business or making things. The scents of hot metal, burning wood, and odd chemical smells seemed to dominate the air. Maybe this was where the horde merchant or service classes lived and worked.

Interestingly, there were carts here that were being used to move goods of some kind. They weren't being pulled by horses, she noticed. Everything was human powered. That had to impede the ability to move large quantities of goods, so there had to be some kind of societal reason for it. Maybe the horses were reserved for the higher classes.

As they rode, they passed other warriors on horses. There were also some that patrolled on foot, but those seemed to be of a lower class than the ones on horses. It looked as if there were strata in the warrior class. She filed that information away as potentially useful.

On the other side of the merchant quarter, they entered a portion of the city that seemed to be much more finely designed and constructed. The streets were of higher quality, the cobblestones fitted more tightly together and easier to ride on. There were even horse-drawn carriages that moved people from place to place on their unknowable business.

The carriages were of very fine construction. The play of dark and light woods used, as well as the intricate carvings and bright painted surfaces, spoke of wealth. The drivers seated atop them dressed in bright clothes that seemed oddly designed to Julia. There had to be some kind of ceremonial aspect to that, as all of them dressed in a similar manner.

The buildings they traveled between were imposingly tall and extremely well-built. Where wood was used, it was planed down to flat surfaces, sanded to smoothness, and then painted in bright colors. If there was stone —which most buildings here used stone in parts of their construction—it was shaped and smoothed to be aesthetically pleasing as well.

Definitely a high-class neighborhood.

She was still admiring some of the houses—though in many cases the word "house" seemed trivial when used for the buildings in question—when she saw another group of horsemen approaching them from directly ahead.

There were warriors, but there were also pack animals. The packs were noticeably empty.

This group looked like the same kind of caravan that they were pretending to be. Perhaps these people had already been to the repository of the stolen gear. If so, she and her companions were definitely headed in the right direction.

She hoped the others passed by without trying to converse but wasn't shocked when one of the horsemen edged over and changed direction to ride directly beside her. He was examining her armor, and he had a slight frown on his face.

"Your armor is very well constructed, but it's made for a man," he said, his frown deepening. "Why don't you have one more fitted to your form?"

That sounded like a personal question, but she wasn't sure she should challenge him like Kelsey had the guard. That had been *insane*. She should probably just answer the question.

Sadly, it was one that she hadn't been prepared to answer. She'd hadn't considered that there might be different styles of armor for men and women.

There had to be, she belatedly realized. While she wasn't well-endowed, other women were. Lieutenant Laird, for example had a generous bosom. So did Commander Cannon. Their armor—which they'd probably salvaged from dead women—must have a more expansive chest segment to allow for that, so they could be protected yet comfortable.

She'd gotten hers from a small man because her options at the time had been limited but hadn't realized there was a difference in construction for gender. Now she might have gotten them all killed because of her ignorance.

For a couple of seconds, her brain ran in every direction searching for *anything* that she could say that would make sense and seem innocent. Then the perfect answer struck her. In fact, it was so perfect that she had to resist the urge to smile.

She shrugged her shoulders at the man. "These are my brother's hand-me-downs. You know how it is, the first son always gets the good stuff. I suppose I'm lucky to have this. One day—maybe soon now—I'll buy my own gear."

At her words, the man slowly nodded. "I hadn't realized that happened across gender lines, but I've done the same thing for my younger brothers."

He examined her torso closely, likely trying to imagine how small-breasted she had to be to fit into such tight confines. There was nothing sexual in his gaze, just cold-eyed professional curiosity.

She was glad the warrior couldn't see the weapons she'd taken from the dead man whose armor she wore. The fine steel blades were safely in their scabbards, and her bow was on her back. Those were definitely not hand-me-downs.

Julia turned slightly in the saddle so that her torso obscured the bow a little better. It's exquisite artistry might catch the man's attention.

He started to say something else, but someone from his own group shouted at him to hurry up. The man shot an irked glare back at his group but did pull away and start after them.

"Once you drop off your cargo, do me the honor of joining me at the Tavern of the Elk. I'm there most evenings. I'd like to learn more about you, and I believe I can recommend an armorer that can help you."

His tone indicated that he was giving her an instruction rather than requesting she do as he asked. He was someone with natural authority. She wondered who he was in this society.

Without waiting for a response from her, the man hurried after his fellows, leaving Julia and her party blissfully alone.

She wondered if her armor implied that she was of a lesser social standing than him or if he was a higher-ranking member of whatever they called their horsemen. If something on the armor indicated rank, she didn't know what it was.

Thankfully, she had no intention of ever seeing the man again, so it wouldn't matter. Whether he had been hitting on her or giving her an order that he expected her to obey, he was going to be sorely disappointed when she not only didn't show but turned out to be one of the people that had escaped their clutches.

That complication dealt with, she focused on where they were going. They just had to find the holding place for all the captured gear and deal with whoever was guarding it. Somehow. And they had to do it fast.

33

Talbot grew more antsy the closer they got to the center of the city. The number of guards around them had been steadily increasing over the last few minutes, and it now seemed as if they were everywhere. They outnumbered the civilians in their now opulent clothing by a significant amount. That meant they dwarfed his party's numbers.

Off in the distance, a larger structure rose above the buildings around it. He'd seen pictures in books on various planets of the Old Terran Empire. Kelsey loved reading about that kind of thing and always had a few printed up from the ship's library in their quarters. What he was looking at was a castle.

Most of those structures in the Old Empire were recreations of what had existed on Terra back in the prespaceflight days, but the building in front of him, though similarly constructed, had a brooding, brutal look about it. It wasn't just for show. It was a working edifice meant to stand off a determined attack. It looked strong enough to even survive some advanced weapons.

Though his party was still making its way through the crowds, he noticed that the civilians were less inclined to hurry out of their way. These more affluent people believed that they had the right-of-way, and that implied a level of power in their stratum of the social fabric of the horde. These were movers and shakers in their society.

Or at least they thought they were.

It was hard to believe that these people had been an industrialized, advanced civilization only a century ago. They looked as if they belonged in the Middle Ages, of which Kelsey had also read a few books. The clothing styles were strange, but none of them would've known anything different during their lifetimes.

It was interesting. Even on Avalon, when the AIs had used their EMP weapons and destroyed all advanced technology, his people had never devolved into this kind of primitive society. They'd remained one civilization, under the rule of Emperor Lucien. They'd kept the manners and education that they could and pulled themselves back out into space. It had taken a while, but they hadn't lost their identity as a people.

To him, it certainly seemed as if the people of Terra had abandoned their identity in favor of this more primitive and warlike mode of living. He wondered if that was because the AIs were still above their heads and ready to blast any civilization that became too advanced with their kinetic weapons.

In the end, he finally decided that that might be a mystery that he'd never solve.

He was still thinking about that when he noticed another emptied caravan coming around the corner ahead of them. The warriors surrounded the empty pack horses and pulled them down the street back in the direction that Talbot and his people had just come from.

Talbot inclined his head toward them as they passed, and one of the warriors in the group did the same. No words were exchanged, which was just fine by Talbot. He'd rather not risk saying the wrong thing, and frankly, he just wasn't as bold as Kelsey or Julia. Those two leapt in where angels feared to tread.

He urged his horse to move faster and made a hand gesture to the admiral that they'd be changing course. The other man nodded.

Once he'd made his way around the corner, Talbot saw what he was sure was their ultimate destination. The building in question was squat and made of thick stone blocks. He wasn't certain what its original purpose had been, but it was now surrounded by guards that were keeping even the entitled populace of the horde city at bay with stern looks and occasional shoves.

The latter was greeted with cries of outrage, but the guards seem unimpressed. A few were forced to show a few inches of blade to send the most pompous scurrying away.

To Talbot, that told a tale. These powerful people were not used to being treated so cavalierly. That meant that whatever was going on here was new. Otherwise, everyone would already be aware of how defensive the guards would be. That made this place the most likely repository of their stolen gear.

As their horses approached the building, one of the guards on foot walked out and held up a hand. This man was older than many of the guards that Talbot had seen so far, his hair iron gray and his beard only containing a few strands of black. His face had two wide scars that went from his hairline on the left side of his face down close to his chin. Both wounds were red and ropey.

"Hold, there," the man said gruffly. "You must wait until the current group finishes unloading before you can enter."

Talbot nodded and contented himself with edging closer to the admiral after the guard had returned to his companions.

"With the number of guards around this place, I don't think we're going to be able to fight our way out," he said softly. "Whatever we do inside, we're going to have to come back out looking as if everything was normal. That might be a little bit difficult if we have to kill a bunch of guards in there."

The other man smiled sourly. "It's not as if we have a choice. I doubt very seriously that Lily could get Kelsey's Raider augmentation back online in just a couple of minutes, even if we found her surgical kit. We'd still never get out of the city alive.

"Our only chance of success is to find the scepter and the supplies that we absolutely must have, stash them in our saddlebags, and then just walk out just like every other group that we've passed. Unfortunately, there *will* be guards inside to keep people from doing *exactly* what we plan on doing. Count on it."

Talbot pursed his lips. "Maybe not so many. The people that we're pretending to be have already been trusted to bring everything in that they've captured. I think the mounted warriors are a different, higher caste than the foot soldiers. Maybe even nobility. That might give us the break we need.

"We have to get a jump on the next part of the plan and secure the inside of this building while we conduct our search. I doubt very seriously that the guards on duty are going to allow us to look for what we need.

"Once we do, we're going to have to figure out how we get out of the city before they discover what we've done. I think we can get out of the general area before someone comes along and starts screaming, but that's not going to get us out of the city.

"We'll have to get over the wall and past the mounted patrols outside. Once we do, where do we go from there? If we make a break for open country, you can bet they'll have riders running us down before we get even an hour away."

Jared looked over toward where the towers of the megacity rose in the distance, dark and empty. "I think the answer is sitting right in front of us. If we can get outside the city walls, we're going to have to make a break for the megacity. Even with all the bad things we've heard about places like that, at least it offers us a chance of survival."

Talbot had already come to that same conclusion. It wasn't a happy idea, but no matter what they did, there was going to be a bad outcome. At this particular moment, he'd be happy if they survived to see the sunrise.

Before he could say anything more, another caravan of warriors and packhorses began coming out of the building through the opened doors.

This was it. They'd have one chance to carry this off, and if they failed, each and every one of them would die fighting or at their own hands to avoid capture. The only avenue to survival was success, and he was going to do everything within his power to make sure that his wife and the admiral got away, even if it cost him his own life.

* * *

JARED EXAMINED everything he could as covertly as possible as they entered the squat building. The exterior walls were significantly thicker than he'd expected, and he'd been expecting them to be thick indeed.

It looked as if the stone blocks used to construct the outer shell were at least a meter thick, and the wall was made up of them stacked four deep. The passage through the wall was about two meters wide. He'd think of it as the foyer, though the term seemed off in the context.

He couldn't imagine what they were defending against in this primitive environment. Lesser walls would stop most basic attacks, but nothing would stop a kinetic projectile from orbit.

Well, it didn't matter. What was important now was making note of every guard he could while trying to determine the best method to conduct this operation.

Once they were through the narrow foyer, they came into a larger room with the ceiling supported by pillars of stone even thicker than the blocks that made up the walls. The room seemed to take up the entirety of the building. Lighting inside was provided by a number of smoking torches that cast a flickering yellow glow over everything.

Their smell wasn't as acrid as he'd have expected. It was actually somewhat pleasant. It made him wonder what they used for an accelerant.

A glance upward showed that the smoke went out through narrow vents in the ceiling. From the amount of soot up there, no one had bothered cleaning inside the room for quite some time.

Half a dozen guards were stationed along the walls at equidistant locations. They weren't the most interesting contents of the room, however. It looked as if a lot of his people's gear had already been brought in and stored. Piles of everything imaginable were stacked high in every open portion of the floor except for that directly in front of the large, reinforced wooden doors they'd just passed through, the cramped foyer, and the area where the horses now stood.

Searching through those piles to find what they'd need was going to be a huge pain in the ass, and there was absolutely no way they could accomplish that while still under the watchful eyes of the guards.

Even if they took the guards out of play, there was no telling how long it would take to find the Imperial Scepter, much less Lily Stone's spare medical kit or the requisite supplies for even simple brain surgery.

Interestingly, the center of the room was taken up by what looked like a huge, ornate altar of some kind. The flat surface was made of stone that had been smoothed flat by whatever artisans had created it. The side panels were carved with intricate designs that he couldn't make out from this distance, but they looked ceremonial.

The purpose of the altar was unimportant. It was a mystery they didn't have time to solve.

Jared looked over his shoulder and saw a huge wooden beam leaning against the wall in the foyer nearest the doors giving access to the interior of the building. That probably meant the doors could be barred from the inside. That might be useful, if things went downhill.

He wasn't certain how they could possibly get what they needed and still escape. With the doors open, the exterior guards would certainly hear the sounds of combat. And with no means of silently disabling the interior guards, he wasn't sure they could even find what they needed, much less escape. It seemed like an impossible task.

Captain Beauchamp edged up beside him and casually dismounted. "Do you see the stone cover at the center of the room?" she asked quietly.

He nodded as he got off his own horse. "It's some kind of altar, isn't it?"

The woman shook her head. "It's a protective cover. I believe this is the treasure house for the horde. That cover probably leads to stairs going deep underground to where they keep their most revered and valued artifacts."

Jared thought about that and felt his eyes narrow. "Do you think that they dug out the area beneath here specifically for that, or would they have used something that was already present? With the megacity adjacent to this city, there are probably old tunnels down there."

"Almost certainly the latter. If I were a betting woman, I'd suspect that they walled off an old tunnel and are using part of it for their own purposes. It wouldn't be accessible to anyone above ground, and not even the people living inside the megacity would be able to break down a formidable barrier."

Jared smiled. "Then I think that I have a plan. You're not going to like it. Hell, *I* don't like it, but it's the only chance I see for us to succeed. If I'm right, we can get away clean. If not, well, we're totally screwed."

34

K elsey tried to make sense of the piles of equipment and supplies
that surrounded them but couldn't. It seemed like there was no
rhyme or reason about how anything was placed inside the room.
It was just unloaded wherever happened to be convenient for the person
placing it there. That was going to make searching through the mess much
more difficult.

She stepped over and joined Jared as he eyed the guards around the
room. "We need to have our noncombatants start unloading, or they're
going to get suspicious," she said softly. "I can't tell where anything is in this
place. It looks like they brought a bunch of stuff from the crashed pinnaces
as well as what we were carrying with us. Sadly, we don't know if we're the
last caravan, so some of the stuff we're looking for may not even be here."

"That's true," he agreed. "It's even possible that something like the
scepter was taken to their palace rather than being brought here. That
seems like the kind of thing a ruler would be interested in."

"Maybe it's just me, but it also seems odd that they'd have their treasure
vault outside their castle. That's what Captain Beauchamp thinks that
formation in the center of the room is, an access to an underground
treasure vault in a walled-off tunnel from the ruined megacity. Well, I think
it's in a section of tunnel. At least I hope it is."

She shrugged slightly. "If that's what it is, they must have some reason to
do it, because no one would just put their stuff out in the open without a
good reason. How are we going to do this?"

As the noncombatants started unloading the horses, Jared covertly
directed her attention back toward the doors they'd come through. "See that
bar? I'm pretty sure that locks the outer doors from the inside.

"It's thick, so it'll hold until they can bring something significant to break it down. The doors are heavy and braced with metal as well. I'd imagine that's because they'd rather not have somebody stealing all their stuff.

"Commander Cannon, Sean, Carl, and I will get the doors closed and the bar in place. Austin and Ralph can back us up and help with the bar if it's heavier than it looks."

He turned slightly to face the interior of the room. "That leaves Julia, Captain Beauchamp, Talbot, Chloe, Elise, Olivia, and yourself to deal with the guards. You got enough ranged firepower that you should be able to take them out before they know what's going on. Lily will be on standby to help anybody that's injured. Did I miss anyone?"

She shook her head. "No, that's everybody. I'll brief my team on what they'll be doing. You take your group."

Kelsey casually walked to each of the designated fighters and told them in short, quiet sentences exactly what she wanted them to do. Each was assigned a specific guard to target with their ranged weapon, if they had one. Talbot had one of her swords, so he should be able to deal with the last one with a few strokes.

With five people wielding bows, they should be able to eliminate the half dozen guards before anyone was hurt. The initial shots would be a complete and utter surprise, so the targets wouldn't be dodging.

She was much more concerned about Jared and his people getting the door closed and locked. It looked stout, but she was certain that the horde had the means to get in. She'd seen plenty of old Terran vids where doors like that were cracked open with battering rams.

Of more concern was what they'd do once the plan was in motion. If the strange stone structure in the center of the room did lead downstairs, would they be able to get out of this supposed treasure room? If not, then they shouldn't attack at all.

Yet she already knew that they didn't really have a choice. This would be their one and only chance to try to recover what they needed and get away, if they could. If the vault was in one of the old tunnels that once had served the megacity, they might even succeed.

Jared was probably right. There had to be hundreds of tunnels running around beneath the ground this close to the place. Maybe thousands. It was very easy to dig deep and place things underground when you had high technology. The towering structures of the megacity were testament to the skills of the builders, and so were the less visible aspects of the old place.

Once she and her people were in position, Kelsey kept an eye on Jared as he and his team stopped unpacking the remaining horses and moved as casually as they could toward the reinforced doors. The guards seemed somewhat confused by their actions but didn't do anything more than glance at one another.

The one thing she and her people couldn't do ahead of time was draw or prepare their weapons. That kind of thing would spark a response. They'd have to draw fast and make their first shots count.

The moment that Jared made a gesture to his people and they rushed the doors, Kelsey drew her bow from across her shoulder in one smooth movement, her free hand already grasping an arrow from her quiver and bringing it up to the string.

The guard she'd selected for herself seemed stunned and was slow to react. Her shot took him in the center of the chest. Though his armor did an admirable job of stopping much of the force, at this range the arrow still won. Just to be certain, she fired another one into him even as he fell.

Not everybody had been as lucky with their initial shots, but their follow-up arrows were keeping the guards busy even as the enemy drew their weapons and shouted in alarm.

Talbot was rushing his target. She was tempted to fire an arrow at the guard in front of him, but that might be a mistake. She'd have to let her husband fight his own fight. Instead, she shifted her aim to one of the remaining guards and helped bring him down quickly instead.

None of the guards were able to reach her team, except for the one fighting Talbot. That man discovered how outclassed he was after two blows from her man. One of them took the guard's arm off at the wrist, and the other struck off his head. God, but that was a bloody spectacle.

With all the guards down, she turned and rushed toward the doors.

Jared and his people had them closed and were holding them tight while someone—or more likely several someones—pushed hard on the other side. The tech team was struggling to get the massive bar into the metal holders that secured the doors from opening, but it seemed a little heavy for them.

Without her augmentation, she wasn't exactly made for the task, but she figured that every little bit would help. Together, they managed to get the massive bar into place with a loud "thunk."

Everyone stepped back from the door and eyed it warily as the people outside continued slamming against it and shouting. The heavy wooden planks didn't even quiver.

"That should hold until they bring in something significant to break it down," Jared said in a tense rush. "Everyone split up and go through the piles. We need to find the Imperial Scepter, Doctor Stone's spare medical kit, Carl Owlet's tools, any equipment Carl could find from the pinnaces that hadn't been burned out by the EMP, and anything else small enough to carry with us while we're moving fast, but that might help us get to the Imperial Vault.

"Throw anything that we don't need into the foyer leading toward the doors. That might keep them from getting in for just a little bit longer."

Kelsey raced around the other side of the room and started digging through a pile. She was too far away from the foyer to throw anything into the tunnel, but Ralph Halstead was at her side, grabbing everything that she tossed away and racing back toward the tunnel to dump it.

A glance at the rest of the room showed that others were emulating his example so that the searchers weren't slowed by having to also help barricade the doors. That was smart. If they could get some large, heavy items directly behind the doors, that would help wedge them shut, even if they did bring in a battering ram. The horde troops would have to completely demolish everything.

Captain Beauchamp was recovering the arrows they'd shot. She'd done that every time they'd been able to after fighting. Kelsey approved, because once they were out, they were left to fight at close range.

"We should take the biggest things and put them directly behind the doors at the hinges," Kelsey shouted. Anything that gained them a few more minutes was worth doing.

In fact, the stone slabs covering what they hoped led to a vault below might be more massive than anything that had been brought from the pinnaces.

"Ralph, come with me," she said. "I want to check something out."

The stone edifice in the center of the room was even larger than it had looked from the entryway. It was at least three meters long and a meter and a half wide. It stood about waist high for a normal person, so chest high for her.

The top was unadorned, but the sides were heavily engraved with scenes of what looked like battle. A closer inspection revealed horsemen fighting against what certainly looked like Rebel Empire marines in powered armor.

Interesting, but she didn't have time to examine it.

The top slab seemed to be unattached to the sides, so she pushed on it. There was the sound of stone grinding on stone as it shifted maybe a centimeter to the side. It was *heavy*. The slab was as thick as her fist and seemed to weigh a ton. Which might be the literal truth. Getting it to the foyer was going to be a monumental task.

She turned to face everyone else in the room. "Stop what you're doing and come help me get this stone slab into the foyer. We're going to lay it on the floor directly in front of the doors. It can be on top of whatever you've already put there."

With a dozen people helping move the slab, it wasn't impossible. Sliding it off where it had rested was a serious chore, but they finally had the thing off, revealing a dark pit below with steps leading down where the torchlight couldn't reach.

The fact that they could move it still didn't mean that it was easy. Everyone grunted and strained as they carried it toward the doors. Once they arrived, they discovered a problem. The opening in the stone wall was too narrow to get it in longways.

They settled for placing it at an angle, with one corner jammed into the door on the right-hand side, its adjacent corner right against the stone wall to that side, and the corner on the other end of the long side, braced against one of the massive stone blocks making up the left wall.

Jared grinned at her. "That's going to make it a *lot* harder for them to get those doors open. Let's see if the sides of that structure come off. A few more pieces like this, and we might just be able to keep them from getting in at all without demolishing the side of the building."

The stone slabs on the side of the covered structure above the stairs were attached to the floor, except for one of the shorter ones at what would be the foot of the structure. It was removable so that people could use the stairs revealed below the structure.

The steps leading down were wide and somewhat shallow. They wouldn't be easy to speed along. It was pitch-black below, but Kelsey could see that they went down a short distance and then began turning to the right.

That would be useful if they had to form a defense going downward. Frankly, that was probably why the turn had been designed into them. She'd seen something about this in a vid. Any archers going down the stairs would have their dominant hands obstructed by the wall to the right, so they'd have to expose themselves to fire. Any archers defending from below would have their dominant hands free and clear to fire up at their opponents and could use the inner stone wall as cover.

Of course, any lefties were going to get an advantage going down and be obstructed in defending. None of their archers were left-handed, so it wasn't going to inhibit them.

As several of the others carried the removable block of stone away and tossed it into the entryway, the remainder of them put their effort into pulling down the still-standing stone slabs that made up the sides.

While they *were* secured, they weren't that secure. Jared quickly ordered the slabs taken into the entryway and placed on top of the first slab, alternating the directions they were wedged. The smaller sections were placed on top of them.

"That was a great idea," he said as he wiped his brow. "Everyone not searching, take the castoffs into the entrance and throw them on top of everything else. I want to get that foyer packed so full of debris that nothing is going to be able to move, even with a ram smashing into the doors. Anything that gains us time is worth it.

"Julia and Talbot, head down the steps and see what we're dealing with. Get torches from the walls up here to light your way. Ralph, follow them down and be ready to be a courier to get us information or warning of what's down there."

Kelsey quickly returned to the pile she'd been working on. Even though her brother seemed to think they had plenty of time, she wasn't so sure. The sooner they could finish, the sooner they'd be out of there.

She only prayed that they could find the things that they needed and escape with their lives.

If the scepter wasn't here, then all of this was for nothing. If the spare medical kit Lily had left at the pinnaces wasn't here, they'd never get their implants back online. The same went for Carl finding the tools that he needed. Those items were absolutely critical to their success and survival.

With a sigh, she gave herself over to the task at hand. They were committed, and the next few minutes were going to show if the gamble had been worth it or not.

35

Julia followed behind Talbot as he descended the spiral staircase. He had Kelsey's sword out and was being wary of anyone coming up from below, not that she thought they needed to be that concerned about that. After all, the entrance to the crypt—because that's just what this might be—had been sealed up tight and under guard. She doubted very seriously that anyone was down there.

Anyone alive, that was. This still might be a crypt. Hell, it might end up their crypt if things went badly.

She followed behind the large man with her bow out and an arrow nocked. She stayed as far to the left as she could so that she'd have as much range as possible, but with the relatively tight turnings of the stairs, that still wasn't very far. If enemies rushed up from below, she'd have time for one shot before they engaged her doppelgänger's husband.

As they were wielding their weapons, Ralph Halstead was holding three torches up high as he followed behind them. Their flickering flames cast more than enough light to see what was ahead, but the distortion in the illumination levels made her twitch every time she thought she'd seen something.

Julia tried to guess at how deep they'd come, but it wasn't easy. In fact, it was impossible. She'd started out counting steps but had lost track somewhere along the way and given up.

Then she'd started trying to estimate how many full revolutions they'd made, but that led to the same outcome because she wasn't sure what direction was what. In any case, whatever was below them was a long, long way down.

"I think I see something," Talbot said a few minutes later.

Julia could see that he was right. The stairs had terminated into a flat space that was void of steps. Perhaps it was the bottom or maybe only a landing. She couldn't tell.

As they reached the flat area, she saw that it did in fact lead out of an alcove into a much larger space. This was no landing. This was the bottom of the stairs and their destination.

The torchlight didn't extend very far, but it was more than enough to see that they were in the remains of one of the old tunnels that must've serviced the megacity. It had been greatly enlarged and the ancient flooring covered with paved stone that had been polished smooth, but the wall immediately next to them was made out of plascrete and still had a number of pipes and cables running along its length.

It also had a holder for a torch crudely mounted to it. A glance to the right showed a similar holder mounted to rough-hewn stone that had to have been added later. It looked much like the blocks that made up the building above, but these were much smaller.

If they'd needed to be brought in from the surface, they'd have had to come down the stairs, so that made sense. Stacked neatly next to the arch was a pile of unlit torches, a wedge of metal, and a rock. The last two things made no sense to her, but they had to serve some purpose, even if it was obscure.

"It looks like this started out as a tunnel," Talbot said, mirroring her guess, as he stepped into the large room. "Somebody went to a lot of trouble to dig it out, though."

The area closest them was empty, but out where the light was fading, she could see vague shapes in the darkness. Gray on black. That probably wasn't an accurate assessment of the colors involved, but in the low light at the edge of the torches' illumination, it was hard to tell. Nothing sparkly, so probably no gold, silver, or gems.

Whenever she thought of vaults, that's what she'd always imagined: a room stacked high with wealth in physical form. This didn't seem to be that stereotypical.

"Should I stay with you?" Halstead asked uncertainly.

"For a little bit, yes," she said. "I want to get at least a basic description of what we're seeing before you go back up to report. I'd also like to make sure there's not anything hiding down here before I put my bow away. Put one of the torches into the holder by the arch and light another one for yourself."

Once he'd done so, she and Talbot advanced side by side with Halstead right behind them until the shapes in front of them resolved into something that they could identify.

Wooden crates stood piled high enough that they rose at least four times Talbot's height. The wood was roughhewn, so she didn't think they were very old. At least not in the scheme of things on Terra.

Talbot stopped next to one stack and leaned over to examine the crates more closely. "I wonder what's in them."

"Something important enough to be this well protected," she said as she eyed the stack to make sure it looked stable. The last thing they needed was to be crushed by someone else's neglect. "There has to be some way of identifying what's in them. Are there any markings?"

He walked around the side of the stack in front of them and grunted slightly. "Yeah. There's a number carved into each crate. That must mean something to whoever put them here, but it's not going to help us determine anything about them. If we want to know what's inside, we'll have to open them up."

"We don't have any tools, and we certainly don't have the time," she said as she turned toward Halstead. "Give us two of the torches and head back up to report."

He handed them the torches as soon as they'd put their weapons away and retreated to the stairs, his bright torch dimming until it was just a glowing spot in the darkness, near the other torch positioned there. Then it vanished as he entered the stairwell, and they were alone deep under the surface of Terra.

"Should we split up?" she asked. "It looks like we've got a lot of ground to cover if we're going to discover what's down here, and probably very little time to do it. If there's an exit that we can force to get out into the tunnel itself, we need to know about it before they break down the doors upstairs."

The marine officer nodded. "Yes, but let's keep an eye out for each other's torches and make sure that we know where the other is. If one of us runs into trouble, we need to be sure that the other will come running when we shout."

She raised an eyebrow. "Do you really think we're going to run into trouble down here? I don't see how anything could live in the dark."

"Our entire stay on Terra has been filled with things that we never expected. Let's just be cautious and make sure we don't find another one."

The man had a point.

"I'll take the right, you take the left," she said. With that, she headed off to see what she could find.

If everything was in crates, it was going to be a pretty boring search, but if she found an exit into the tunnel itself, that would be worthwhile.

Her side of the cavern was the one that had the wall blocking off access to the megacity. If there was an exit leading to it, it would be here. She knew it faced the megacity because it had been blocked off here as soon as the people digging down had found the tunnel. That showed the horde's concern about the inhabitants of the megacity.

Talbot would be looking at the side of the cavern where the tunnel led away from the megacity. They couldn't discount there being a door on that side, too. Or no door on any side. They might have to make their own.

While a lot of the things she was seeing as she walked were stashed in crates, not everything was completely obscured from view. As she advanced into the darkness, her eyes searching all around her, she spotted an area with tables holding what looked like chests on top of them.

Curious, she made her way over and examined one. The was made of polished wood that glowed yellow in the torchlight. It had a built-in lock, but she had the perfect lock pick for something like this.

She inserted the point of her marine knife between the lid and the body, using the palm of her hand to drive it in. Once it was wedged deep, she wiggled the blade through the locking mechanism itself. It took a little bit of strength to cut the metal, but not as much as it would have if her knife hadn't had an almost monomolecular edge.

When she lifted the lid, she was greeted with the pile of gold, silver, and jewels she'd been musing about earlier. Everything sparkled and gleamed. Too bad stuff like this had absolutely no value to them right now.

She did stuff a handful into her pocket. If they lived, they would make for memorable souvenirs.

Closing the chest, she moved on to explore more of the room. The chamber was ridiculously large for being just a treasure room. If the horde had wanted something like that, they could've just left the tunnel intact and blocked off both ends.

As she walked, the scope of the area became clearer, just based on the echoes from her footsteps. This place was massive. What all did they have in here?

That really wasn't something that she needed an answer to, she decided. Time was wasting.

She turned and made her way back to the area nearest the stairs. The stone blocks that filled in what had been the tunnel were perhaps as tall as her head and three times that wide. There was no telling how deep they were laid, but they had to weigh far more than even a pair of people could lift unassisted.

And they would be thick, of that she had no doubt. There was absolutely no way the horde would place a flimsy barrier between themselves and the megacity. Not if the people inside the damned place were as bloodthirsty as Beauchamp believed.

Walking up and down the length of the wall, she found no openings. That was exasperating and potentially deadly, but not really a surprise. They'd have to dig out the stones and make their own tunnel through whatever they found.

"Julia," Talbot's voice echoed from deeper inside the chamber. "I've found something interesting."

She turned and trotted deeper into the chamber toward where she thought his voice had come from. Spotting his torch in the darkness, she shifted course. He was at least a couple of hundred meters away. Her estimates of the size of this place kept growing.

The chamber was large enough to sit at least partially under the castle she'd seen in the way in. There didn't seem to be any stairs on that side of the chamber—because surely they'd have sent guards down by now—which was decidedly odd. Shouldn't the ruling class *want* handy access to their goodies?

Julia started to ask what he'd found as she approached but found herself jerking to a halt just before she reached him. Piled deeply on the floor beyond him were the remains of a number of suits of marine powered armor.

And by remains, she meant what was left over after the wearers had been killed with those damned antiarmor weapons. Everything was shredded and in pieces.

"Well, I guess the stories about them dealing with the Rebel Empire before were true," she said as she stepped up beside Talbot. "This is certainly gruesome. I hope they at least took the bodies out before they left the armor here."

"I'm not smelling anything," Talbot said as he turned toward her. "If they'd left any human remains inside this pile, it would stink to high heaven. Maybe not so much after a period of years, but who wants to smell up their treasure room? What did you find?"

"Oh, the usual. Gold, silver, precious stones, that kind of thing. I also examined the wall blocking off the original tunnel leading to the megacity. I can't tell how thick the blockage is, but there's no door and those stones are stout.

"Not as big as the ones in the building upstairs, but they're going to be a problem. I'm betting it's also packed full of dirt and debris from excavating this chamber, too. After all, why carry it up those stairs if you can just pack the tunnel in? There's probably two sets of stone barriers with fill between."

"Good fences make for good neighbors," the man said with a wry smile. "Yet another Kelsey saying that I don't really understand. I found the other tunnel exit, and it looks exactly like you described.

"I'd say the horde was paranoid about letting anybody into their treasure room, and by extension, into the city above. I looked on the far wall, but there are no stairs leading up. There's only one entrance, and it isn't leading to their castle.

"I also found an amazing number of crates. I'm not sure what they're storing down here, but it's like a huge warehouse. Why build something like this underground just to store your stuff?"

"It has to be something that they don't want anyone else to get their hands on. Obviously not something they access very often, either. This whole 'treasure room' vibe makes me suspect that we're looking at salvaged materials from the megacities.

"Old technology that maybe doesn't work anymore but was worth socking away. Hell, maybe some of it *does* work. There's no telling, unless we look inside every single crate."

The marine officer raised his torch a little higher and looked around. "This chamber has to be at least four hundred meters across. Probably a couple of hundred meters from the tunnel blockage on your end to the tunnel blockage on my end. Looking up, the ceiling is at least forty meters high. That's a *lot* of room to store salvaged material. Why keep it down here?"

"Probably because they're terrified to use most of it," she said grimly.

"That also explains why it's buried so deeply. They don't want the AI to drop a kinetic strike on them for being naughty."

"This is like storing seeds for future use," Talbot said after a few moments. "This is what might grow Terra back into a technological world, if the AIs ever go away."

"You mean if we ever manage to defeat them," she corrected. "They're not going away on their own. We're going to have to stomp them and do it hard. And to do that, we've got to figure a way out of the trap we've gotten ourselves into.

"We're going to have to bust down the stone wall leading toward the megacity and dig out whatever is behind it before the horde forces their way into the building above and kills us all."

"No pressure," Talbot said dryly. "It's possible that somewhere in this pile of armor is a weapon that could breach the wall. That's not exactly going to help us dig it out, but it's a start. Somewhere in all these crates are probably a number of things that would help, if we only knew where anything was."

"The horde has an index somewhere," Julia said as she looked around. "We just have to find it. Let's start looking."

36

Jared was beginning to despair. They'd been searching the piles of captured gear for what felt like hours—but had to only have been twenty or thirty minutes—without success in finding the primary gear they needed, though they had found some useful items.

The guards had stopped beating on the outer door after about five minutes. At this point, he was certain they were busy searching for something sturdy enough to bash their way in and making sure the higher-ups knew what was happening. The question was, how long would it take them to build a ram or bring one here?

In the meantime, his people had piled a truly impressive amount of random gear into the foyer. It was almost full of stuff. Even if the horde managed to break the doors apart, it was going to take them precious time to dig everything out.

Unless they just decided to use a few of those antiarmor weapons. Those would be more than powerful enough to destroy the thick wooden doors and blow a good amount of the material they were blocking the foyer with back into his people like a giant shotgun.

He was going to have to hope that they weren't *that* desperate to get at them. After all, based on what Ralph had told him, they weren't going to be leaving the vault below anytime soon. With any luck, the horde would want to keep their building intact and use a less powerful means of gaining entry.

"I found it!" Kelsey said, triumphantly raising the Imperial Scepter above her head.

Jared had to be careful walking over to her because she was knee-deep in scattered supplies that might cause him to lose his footing or twist an ankle, which was something he desperately wanted to avoid.

"Do we have any way of knowing if it's operational?" he asked.

Kelsey turned toward Carl as the young man cautiously made his way to them. She handed it over without a word.

The scientist had found a few of his tools and was able to remove a hidden access plate and plug a cable into one of the ports thus revealed. The device he held showed something on its screen, and Carl frowned.

"I believe the main memory is intact, but the EMP must've shorted out something in the control circuits. I can *probably* fix it, if I can find the parts and tools I need somewhere in this mess."

"Then that's the priority," Jared said, raising his voice. "I want everyone looking for whatever tools and parts Carl tells you he needs, as well as any medical supplies or equipment for Commodore Stone."

Even though they'd already been searching quickly, his words spurred everyone to even more feverish action. They were going through what remained of their piles at a rapid pace and throwing whatever they didn't need or couldn't use toward the foyer. Most of it didn't make it, but at this point, that hardly mattered. The end was in sight.

Unfortunately for them, that was when someone chose to knock on the doors. Hard.

A loud, echoing boom seemed to shake the room as something massive slammed against the reinforced wooden doors. It sounded as though someone had finally found the ram they were looking for. Now it was only a matter of time until they broke the doors apart and the horde began tearing at the debris blocking them from getting in. His people needed to wrap this up as soon as possible.

"Lucy, I'm home," Kelsey muttered, to his momentary befuddlement. Sometimes, he figured that he'd never understand her.

Jared walked over to Lily, who was busy tearing open a pack that she'd taken off of one of the pack horses they'd brought with them as part of their cover. She dumped it out as he spoke.

"Do you have what you need to get at our implants?" he asked.

She shook her head and kept pawing through the pile. "I found some basic medical supplies, but not my spare kit. At this point, I'd have to crack your skull open with a rock to get to your implants."

"Hard pass. Is there anything that we've come across that you could use as a substitute surgical instrument?"

She paused long enough to shoot him a stare that told him that he was being an idiot. "Absolutely not. I *could* use a marine knife to cut open your scalp, but while it would cut through your skull quite easily, I'd be far too likely to cut into your brain and ruin your entire day. To get into your skull *safely*, I need the right tools.

"And even if I do manage to find them, I don't know if Carl has the necessary equipment to reboot the damned things. You know that old saying, that 'this isn't brain surgery'? Well this *is* brain surgery. I have to find my spare medical kit."

He understood. He really did. But that didn't change the fact that they were running out of time.

"If you can't find it in the next couple of minutes, we're going to have to leave without it," he said firmly. "As sturdy as those doors are, they won't last long. Once they're gone, the horde will have plenty of willing hands to pull out the junk that we've thrown in there. Find something that will do the job, or you *will* be using a marine knife."

That seen to, he made his way over to Carl, who was once again searching frantically through the scattered gear in the corner of the room. Like Lily, he barely glanced up as Jared stopped near him.

"No," the scientist said before being asked. "I haven't found my kit yet. I found a lot of other tools and equipment that *might* be useful, and I've tossed them into one of the packs, but I need to find a very specific kind of equipment to generate the correct pulse to reset our implants."

"Then I'm going to give you the same speech I gave Lily," Jared said. "You've got a couple of minutes, and then we've got to get down the stairs. Grab whatever you can and, if it might work, take it."

"Got it," his young friend said. "On the plus side, I did find both the FTL com and the small rings that Omega gave us. The com is burned out, but I can potentially rebuild it, if we can salvage the right kind of basic equipment. The quantum entanglement module isn't subject to being ruined by an EMP."

"What about the rings?" Jared asked.

Carl shrugged. "It's alien tech, so who knows? Until we have a power supply capable of feeding it, we can't test it. I packed both of them away for later examination, just in case."

Even as Carl finished speaking, Lily shouted behind him. "I found the spare medical kit!"

Jared turned toward Ralph. "Go carry her stuff. All noncombatants, it's time for you to head downstairs. Carl, find something that's going to work. Kelsey, Captain Beauchamp, Elise, and Olivia, meet me by the horses."

Once the four women had gathered, he made a gesture toward all the horses crowded into that side of the room. They were watching the humans who seemed to have gone nuts with wary expressions.

"I've got a crazy idea," Jared said, "but I don't know if it will work. Could we take the horses partway down the stairs with us? It would be a serious pain in the ass for the horde to have to get past them, either dead or alive."

Beauchamp looked skeptical. "Horses are intelligent creatures. They're not going to want to go into a dark hole."

Kelsey was rubbing her chin. "We might be able to make it work, if we can fashion hoods to put over their heads. Or anything that would cover their eyes. If they can't see where they're going, the odds are much better that they'll cooperate. I wouldn't count on the warhorses for this, though. We need to stick to the pack beasts. They're a bit more placid."

The local woman considered that for a moment and slowly nodded. "That might work. Let's see what we can get together in the next few minutes. If we can use some of the ropes to help take the horses down with us as a group, we can perhaps drive a few stakes of some kind into the wall to keep them from continuing down or backing up when we reach the midpoint in our descent."

"Make the magic happen," he told them and headed back over to Carl.

"Time's up. Tell me you've got something."

"Maybe," his young friend said, holding up an unidentifiable piece of equipment. "I *might* be able to tinker with this enough to produce the output we need, but it's going to be chancy. Our implants are embedded in our brains. If I screw this up, it could fry them and us. It wouldn't even take that much of a charge."

"We've run out of time, so we'll just have to hope for the best," Jared said, clapping the young man on the shoulder. "It's time to make our way down and hope the hole in the ground doesn't end up being our grave."

* * *

TALBOT WIPED the sweat off his face with one arm as he stared at the remains of the powered armor and what the troops had been carrying. The antiarmor weapons had done a real number on everything. No suit was intact or even close to operational.

Even if any had been, the Rebel Empire believed in locking their marines down, so none of the armor could've been activated without the appropriate codes, or the built-in self-destruct charges would've detonated.

Carl could've probably done something about that, if he'd had his implants active, but he didn't. Well, if wishes were horses, they'd all be neck deep in horse crap, as Kelsey liked to say.

What *had* survived intact was a plasma rifle suitable for powered armor. It would be locked, but Carl had gotten into the guts of similar weapons and overridden the codes before. These wouldn't be nearly as troublesome as the armor's self-destruct lockouts.

With his augmentation offline and no armor, this monster could very easily injure him if he fired it. That said, it definitely had the raw power to blow a hole in the obstruction. If, that is, they could find any of the pellets of tritium it needed for ammunition.

As he was considering his options, Julia walked up out of the darkness. In her free hand, she held a leather-bound book.

"What's that?" he asked.

"It seems to be an inventory book," she said as she sat on the floor and opened it. "It lists what each of the crates has in it, though unfortunately, since it's written by non-technological people, some of the descriptions are rather obtuse. They don't know what many of the things do, so they've made guesses at what the locations they were found in might have been for."

He squatted and added his torchlight to hers before examining the page she was looking at. It listed crate numbers with odd designations like "red metal room" and "dark mirror room." She was right, none of that was very helpful.

"Well, I suppose it beats a kick in the head," he admitted. "By any chance do you see anything that references invaders or marines or fighting?"

"Not so far, but let's flip through and see if anything looks interesting."

He watched as she flipped the pages and read the neat script as quickly as possible. They were out of time, and he really didn't hold out any hope that they'd find anything useful.

Then she stopped and poked a finger at a line on the page. "Look at this. 'Monster Invasion.' What do you think it means?"

Talbot felt his heart beat faster. "Maybe a lot. We have to find the crate listed here and get access to it to be sure. This isn't really an inventory. It seems like it's more of a map to take us to the areas in question, if you know what I mean. Let's go find this one."

"You're in luck," she said as she stood. "I think I've figured out how the numbers are patterned. If I'm right, this crate is somewhere over there." She pointed off into the darkness toward a distant pile of crates.

She hefted the book, he grabbed the massive plasma rifle, and they started toward the crates.

"Can you use that?" she asked as she eyed the huge weapon.

"Not without ammunition. That's what I'm hoping to find."

"Too bad I left the pellets Corporal Boske made me save back on the grassland with the dead plasma rifle," she said through gritted teeth. "It was exactly this model, and I'd really like to have it here to blow some of these horde asses up."

The cold rage in her tone reminded Talbot of some of Kelsey's worst moments. The times when she wanted to kill people that had hurt her or her friends.

He'd known Boske as well as a senior officer could, but Julia had worked with the woman. Learned from her. And, apparently befriended her before the woman had been murdered, along with so many others.

She wanted payback, just like he did, but this wasn't the time, so he said nothing to encourage or discourage her. She had to work through her own feelings on this in her own way.

They arrived at the stack of crates and began looking for the numbers at ground level. The crates above them would be out of view, so he hoped they got lucky.

He didn't, but he did find a number close to what he'd been looking for and called Julia over. "I think it might be further up this stack. Do you think you can climb it safely and look?"

Without answering, she jumped up on the crate and began pulling herself up.

"Found it," she said once she reached the top of the pile near the ceiling. "How do I get into it?"

Before he could answer, Talbot heard a shout off in the distance and turned to face the stairs. Their companions were pouring out, torches raised high, so that meant that they'd run out of time.

37

Julia watched as her new friends and associates flooded into the treasure room. What the hell were they going to do now? They hadn't managed to find anything to break down the wall. This was going to end *very* badly if they didn't find ammunition for the plasma rifle.

She pushed against the crate, but it didn't even move. It was damned heavy, and she had no leverage. It was going to take some kind of assistance for her—for all of them—to get this crate to slide off the end of the stack.

"I need some help over here," she shouted to the main group. "If you have some rope, that would be awesome."

About two-thirds of their party rushed over to join them at the stack of crates, mostly looking around wide-eyed at everything around them.

Carl Owlet held up a coil of rope. "Got you covered."

His words made her smile. Of course he did. The man always seemed to have what they needed.

"Throw the end up to her," Talbot said. "Julia, run it around the crate and let the end of the rope fall down where we can get at it again. We'll center it as well as we can, and then you can hold it until we get a little tension on it. We'll spread ourselves out and pull until the crate slides off. What I'm looking for won't be damaged if the container smashes to pieces."

It took three tries for them to get the rope to her, but it was easy enough to run it down the other side of the stack until she had the middle of the rough hemp in her hands. She then held it near the top of the crate as the others spread out on either side and tugged it tight.

She was very careful not to get her fingers caught between the rope and the crate. Even with graphene-coated bones, that wouldn't end well.

They sounded off together and started tugging on the rope. The crate shifted a little, and that gave her more space to put her feet on top of the crate below it. She put her shoulder into the one they wanted to fall, and she gave it all she had.

Unfortunately for her, the next tug didn't move the crate at all. Instead, the stack began teetering forward, obviously unbalanced by their actions.

Not relishing the idea of a fall to the floor, Julia leapt for the stack directly behind her, even as the stack of crates she'd been standing on went over, eliciting shouts from everyone below.

She slammed into the side of the second crate from the top of the next stack and barely managed to get her fingers onto one of the boards long enough for her feet to find purchase. That was good. A fall from this height might have seriously injured or killed her.

From the continuing sounds behind her, the falling crates had struck another stack and sent it falling over as well. As the noises continued, Julia became convinced that this was not going to stop with just a few stacks.

A glance over her shoulder showed that she'd been right. Spreading out away from her, piles of crates were being struck by other falling piles and knocked over. She only prayed that nothing came back around to knock *her* stack down while she was still on it.

It took a full minute for the chaos to stop. In the darkness, she couldn't tell exactly how far the devastation had spread, but whoever was in charge of inventorying these boxes was going to be *seriously* pissed.

"Are you okay up there?" Talbot called from below.

"I think so," she said as she edged along the side of the stack until she had a better grip. "Is everybody okay?"

"We're good. Come down and help us look for the plasma rifle's ammunition."

By the time she'd carefully made her way to the stone floor, everyone was digging through the wreckage. There was all manner of salvaged materials scattered around, and it looked as if the crate they had been eyeing had broken apart, but at least its contents were on top of the rest. Mostly.

She threw herself into searching through the items along with everyone else. It looked like a lot of basic military equipment, but there were no weapons. Mostly it was what might be found at a campsite.

After digging for a couple of minutes, she found a single box labeled "tritium pellets, large." It was exactly the same size box as she'd had during the ambush for her plasma rifle.

She held it up over her head. "Talbot!"

He waded to her side and took the box from her, opening it quickly. Inside, three pellets just like she'd used were carefully set in cavities in the shock-absorbing foam. It looked as if there had once been half a dozen— just like in her original box—but the other three slots were empty.

"Jackpot!" Talbot said. "This is *exactly* what I needed. Everybody, break off your search and let's join the rest by the stairs."

Getting down off the huge pile of debris wasn't nearly as easy as she'd hoped, but they all managed it without injury. As a group, they quickly rejoined the rest of their party.

Everyone left at the stairs was crowded around the opening with their bows out. They obviously anticipated an attack from above. As they got there, Kelsey turned to face them and grinned at the sight of the huge plasma rifle.

"Now we're talking! You have any ammo for that thing?"

Talbot held up the box with the plasma rifle ammunition. "Three shots. I sure as hell hope it's enough. What's the situation upstairs?"

Kelsey grimaced. "Just as bad as you'd imagine. They were just breaking the door apart as we came down. It's going to take them a couple of minutes to clear the stone slabs and other junk we left in the foyer, but not that long. As soon as they get people through, I'm sure they'll send them right down.

"We brought the pack horses down about halfway and tethered them. Now they're sitting in the dark, and I'm sure they're not going to be very cooperative about moving anywhere without the hoods we used to calm them. Still, once the horde gets past them, we're going to be fighting down here."

"Then we should get the hell out of here," Julia said firmly. "Like right now."

Just how right she was. A terrible screaming began coming from up the stairs, followed by the shouts of men. The horde was in the stairs, and they were killing the horses. They'd be here in just a few minutes. It was crunch time.

"Carl, I sure hope you have the tools to remove the lockout on this weapon," Kelsey said grimly. "No pressure or anything, but I need this working right now."

* * *

THANKFULLY, Carl did have the tools he needed and quickly had the plasma rifle opened up and reenabled. He closed it back up and looked at Kelsey. "You're green."

Kelsey pulled the torch out of the holder beside the stairwell and dropped it in the center of the barrier that she needed to shoot. She then led the entire group back into the cavern until she had a clearance of about a hundred and fifty meters. Safe distance for the explosion of the plasma was going to be a relative thing, but she hoped that would be enough.

If things went badly, they'd bring the roof down. At least that would probably be quicker than the end the horde had planned for them.

She took the ammunition from Julia and gestured for her husband to hand over the weapon. "Give it up, sport. I've got a lot more experience firing that sort of thing than you do. We've got to get the placement of the blast absolutely right, or we're screwed."

He raised an eyebrow and shook his head slightly. "You *do* remember how much of a kick that thing has, don't you? Even with your augmentation online, firing that without a suit to back it up would knock you on your ass. If you fire it now, you might seriously injure yourself. Let me handle it."

"We're not going to get a second chance at this," she said firmly. "It doesn't matter if I get hurt so long as everyone gets away. Besides, I have a plan for that, and you're absolutely going to love it. Now, give."

With a sigh, Talbot handed her the plasma rifle, which she struggled to hold upright until she got it up onto her shoulder. She aimed it back in the direction of the wall she needed to blast.

"Somebody said we had two exits from this chamber," she said as she removed the magazine and handed it to Talbot to load with pellets. "How sure are we that the one next to the stairwell is the right one? We absolutely can't afford to waste ammunition opening up the wrong side of the chamber."

"It only makes sense," Julia said. "They dug the stairs down from the surface and broke into the tunnel right there. They'd want to seal it up as quickly as possible to keep any enemies from getting to them. That means they'd have sealed off the side leading toward the megacity before they dug much of the cavern out.

"They probably filled in after the first barrier with rubble they accumulated as they excavated and finally capped it off with more stone on this side, but they certainly didn't dig down to the tunnel and then expand the cavern before closing off the end nearest the megacity."

"I sure hope you're right," Kelsey said grimly. "If not, we're screwed."

She gestured for everyone to get behind her. The plasma weapon didn't have a back blast, so they weren't in danger of being incinerated. From their point of view, the danger was going to be purely kinetic. When Talbot said the weapon had a kick, he wasn't joking.

"I want everyone to get behind me and be prepared to help absorb the recoil. For such a little bit of ammunition, this thing generates one hell of a kick. With everybody working together, we can minimize how much impact it has on me. Set your torches off to the side. We don't want to set ourselves on fire."

Everyone crowded close behind her and formed a kind of human barrier to try to hold her up and resist being thrown back when she triggered the weapon. At this range, she could see the torch she'd dropped clearly. Her aiming point became the spot just above it. She centered on that and waited.

After a few seconds, Talbot nudged her. "Are you going to shoot that thing? I thought you said we were out of time."

"Wait for it."

Time seemed to drag, and then she heard the sounds of men at the bottom of the stairs. The horde had arrived.

Kelsey smiled coldly as she saw the first of them come into sight with a sword drawn. Right next to the wall she was aiming at.

"Say hello to my little friend," she murmured as she triggered the plasma rifle.

The impact of the discharge sent her slamming back into everyone else. It hurt like hell and her shoulder felt bruised, but the speck of intense brightness flew straight and true into the wall where she'd aimed it before detonating.

The savage brightness overwhelmed her vision, leaving spots in her eyes that she had to blink away. Her low-light vision was gone, and she couldn't tell what had happened at the impact site.

What she could sense was the sound of falling stone and the lack of screams. She'd killed whoever had been stupid enough to come to the bottom of the stairs.

Hell, she'd probably collapsed the stairway at its base and killed most of the people that the horde had sent down.

"I need a scout," she said. "Somebody go make sure I hit the tunnel blockage squarely. Toss another torch down on this side of the cavity so that I can see it, and then come back. I need to know if I have to adjust my aim."

Chloe Laird ran in the direction of the blast and returned a minute later without her torch.

"You were spot-on," the marine officer said. "The plasma detonation took out the stone wall and a good bit of the debris on the other side. The tunnel is still clogged with melted junk, so I'm hoping this next shot will clear it out.

"The ceiling of the cavity seems to have been fused, so it *might* hold up under all of this. The second shot will be taking a chance, but it's not exactly like we have a lot of choice in the matter. On another positive note, it looks like you collapsed the stairway, so we won't be getting any more uninvited guests while we work."

Kelsey nodded. "Perfect. Everyone, brace me again."

The second shot hurt even worse than the first but cleared out even more of the tunnel and revealed stone blocks on the other side. The bottom of the cavity was now rough and deeper than she liked, and also *very* hot, but their boots would allow them a little bit of time to examine the final wall, if they'd cleared the debris all the way to it.

"I don't think we're going to need that third shot," Talbot said after he'd ventured in and returned. "Part of the far wall is ruptured, and I could see into the tunnel beyond. It's clear over there. Given a couple of minutes, we can clear enough space to get through."

"How long is it going to take for them to dig out the stairway and start after us?" Jared asked.

"They're not going to be chasing us this way," Kelsey said firmly. "As soon as we've got everybody inside the tunnel and safely away, I'm going to go use the last plasma charge to bring the ceiling of the cavern down."

"You have to be on *this* side to do that," Talbot argued. "You might bring it down on your head."

"That's a chance I'm willing to take," she said. "Let's get that wall broken out and get everyone on the other side. We'll want to set up a defensive perimeter, just in case all of this noise brings somebody from the megacity to investigate."

Over her husband's objections, Kelsey got him and the rest moving through the blown-out cavity her plasma rifle had created. The stone under their feet was hot enough to put the scent of burning leather into the air and to heat the soles of her feet to an uncomfortable degree. Still, it was bearable.

Even if it hadn't been, that wouldn't have changed anything. They *had* to get through there.

As Talbot had said, the far wall was partially breached, and she could see the original tunnel in the darkness beyond. The hole in the stacked stones wasn't that big, and that section of the wall around it looked dangerously unstable.

That didn't mean it was impossible to get through, though. The stones were large and wide, obviously meant to be hard to get through or move. On this side of the original blockage, they were stacked five deep. That meant it would take them hours of sweaty labor to clear enough space to walk through.

Thankfully, the part of the wall that had blown out was near the roof of the tunnel and was big enough for even Talbot to wiggle through. They took the time to push the more precarious of the stones over, where they fell on the ones that already littered the tunnel with a crash.

The rope Carl had found allowed them to lower their party down to the rock-strewn floor one at a time. Each person took care in the rubble not to twist an ankle.

Once they had everyone on the other side, they started clearing the floor nearest the breach. When Kelsey had to run through here in a few minutes, the last thing she'd have time for was dealing with unsteady footing after she cleared the wall.

When they'd finally cleared that section of the floor, Kelsey made a shooing gesture with her hands. "I want you to get as far down the tunnel as you can in the next few minutes. I'll use the floor in the cavern to brace the weapon and then haul ass after you as soon as I pull the trigger.

"We have no idea if the collapse of the cavern is even in the cards, but if it does come down, it might bring the tunnel with it, so I don't want anyone nearby. Understood?"

Talbot gave her a tight hug before hoisting her up to the hole in the wall. Once on the other side, she made her way back to the cavern and stared around at the huge cavern.

The best odds of bringing the ceiling down were to hit it in the center of the ceiling. There was no support at any point along the interior of the cavern, so that would be its weakest point.

With a final sigh, she tossed her final torch into the tunnel. It was going to have to provide her with light while she ran for her life.

She braced the weapon on the floor just outside the radius of the first impact crater, where the surface was smooth enough to provide steady resistance, and aimed the bore of the weapon at the ceiling in what she judged was the center of the cavern.

Kelsey took a deep breath and squeezed the trigger.

As soon as the plasma rifle recoiled against the stone and skidded past her into the cavity, she threw herself after it and raced after it toward the undamaged tunnel beyond the breach.

Kelsey didn't see the plasma hit, but the bright flash of the detonation lit her way forward like a strobe going off. Then she heard rumbling from behind her. The cavern ceiling was coming down.

Kelsey dug her feet in and dove through the breached section of the final wall, hitting the floor of the original tunnel hard, rolling, and coming to her feet, still running for her very life.

Even as she ran, she heard the sound of the tunnel behind her cracking and collapsing. She *might* have overdone it. The whole thing might come down on their heads.

Ahead of her, she saw that the others had come to the same conclusion as they turned to run farther up the corridor. Unencumbered as she was, she made up a little bit of the distance between them before the tunnel behind her finally gave way completely and collapsed.

Imminent death was an excellent motivator.

A wave of choking dust engulfed her, making her cover her face and slow down as she coughed. The ceiling above her seemed solid enough, so she hoped they'd gotten clear of the collapse zone.

Weary, she walked forward until she'd rejoined the others. Everyone was coated with dust, but they were all grinning at her.

"You did it!" Talbot said as he snatched her up in a hug. A hug that was soon joined by all the rest.

"*We* did it," she corrected. "That should keep the horde from following us. The danger behind us is over. We're probably going to have trouble when we try to leave the megacity, because I'm sure that I've just stirred the horde up like a nest of bees. They'll be looking for where we're going to come up for air."

"And we're going to have to be careful of running into anyone in the megacity," Jared said solemnly as they all broke apart. "With everything that Captain Beauchamp said, I think that they're just as unfriendly as the horde. In this case, the enemy of our enemy is *not* our friend."

"One life-threatening disaster at a time, please," Kelsey said as she tried to wipe her face with her hands, succeeding only in smearing dirt and grit all over her exposed skin. "Let's deal with tomorrow's problems tomorrow. Right now, we need to find a place to hide and recover. It's been a *long* day, and we've still got a lot to do.

"Once we get ourselves situated, we'll let Lily and Carl do their magic and see if we can get our implants back online. Then we have to figure out what we're going to do to get out of the megacity, while avoiding its inhabitants, and also dodging the horde once we do.

"Then we still got fifteen hundred kilometers to go before we get to the Imperial Palace and find out who or what might be living inside it. Piece of cake, right?"

All of them stared at her for a few seconds and then started laughing. She grinned and joined them. At this point, that's all they could do. This mission had gone bad early, and nothing had worked out the way they'd expected, but they'd made it this far.

Whatever it took for them to survive and get what they'd come all this way for, they'd do. The AIs would not win today or in the future. They'd overcome any obstacle in their path on the way to victory. They had to.

With the battle finally done, they turned as a group and began trudging down the old tunnel toward the megacity and their next challenge.

EPILOGUE

L eader Mordechai stood on the balcony and stared out from the top of the sacred tower toward the horde city. This structure was the tallest in Frankfort and had an excellent view of the primitive city that had been built next to it after the Fall.

He normally didn't walk up the stairs because the building towered over the megacity and five hundred flights of stairs were hard on a man his age, but he'd needed to see this for himself.

There seemed to be a lot of excitement in the horde city. Smoke rose from its center in a huge column, and it looked as if the palace had collapsed into a large hole in the ground. The savage warriors that ruled that place with an iron fist were milling around like ants disturbed in their mound.

At first, he'd thought that whatever had occurred had been an act of nature, but as soon as the horde started sending out armed patrols into the growing dusk, he knew that there was something more afoot.

Some of his people had reported loud noises deep underground at around the same time. He wasn't certain what was happening, but he needed to find out. The survival of his people might depend on it.

At the soft tread of boots behind him, he turned to see his son Jebediah approaching. To his amusement, the young man seemed more winded by his climb than Mordechai himself had been.

"What news?" he asked his panting, sweating son.

"There are intruders below Frankfort," Jebediah said in a gravelly voice. "One of the blocked tunnels appears to have collapsed, but only after allowing a dozen or so people through. One of our scouts used an old lookout post to observe their passage. Shall I have our warriors trap and kill them?"

Mordechai considered that for a moment before shaking his head. "Not yet. I find my curiosity aroused. From the horde activity, I'm prepared to grant that they might not be friends of the barbarians. Their story might prove interesting."

He smiled at that last, but only for a brief moment. "If they were at that depth, it would take more than even lost weapons from the Empire to cause such a collapse. Who were these people, and how did they cause such devastation?

"Are they intruders sent by the computers above?" he asked rhetorically. "It's been many years since we've had such an incursion, but if this is the beginning of a new one, we need to know. Use all force necessary to subdue them but give them an opportunity to surrender first."

"And if they resist?"

"Kill as many of them as you need to break them," he said bluntly. "Take no undue risks. My curiosity does not require our blood to be spilled to satisfy it. Find a good ambush point and make certain that they have no chance to sense your presence before you strike."

After his son had departed, Mordechai stepped back out onto the balcony and looked over the ruined megacity that he ruled. The shadows of the approaching sunset were far below him, and the red light of the sun cast an almost bloody shade across his city.

He'd been born after the computers had crushed Terra under their heels, but he still remembered the stories his grandfather had told of the time before the Fall. The things he spoke of sounded magical, but impossible. If he hadn't had Frankfort itself as proof that such technology had once existed, he'd never have believed the tall tales.

Seeing the world from up here never failed to move his heart. Both from the beauty of nature, and the destruction and loss that he could see from this very spot. Also the sheer savagery that those beyond Frankfort exhibited on a daily basis.

Would the events of today send the cruel warriors into his city? Part of him hoped so. Their dead from any such excursion would remind them of their place in this world. Their fear of his people kept his charges safe.

Mordechai sighed and turned to start his long walk back down to the warrens underneath Frankfort. He needed to focus on the strangers and the danger that they brought to his people.

They would make the choice between survival and bloody death. One way or the other, he and his people would deal with them as tradition demanded. Even if they surrendered, they would never leave this place.

Whoever they were, their adventures were assuredly over.

VICTORY ON TERRA

BOOK TWELVE

Kelsey Bandar and Jared Mertz must retrieve the electronic override buried under the ruins of the old Imperial Palace to win the war against the AIs. Oh, and get off the planet in spite of the murderous warships orbiting the destroyed world.

How hard could that be?

Imprisoned in a dead megacity and surrounded by howling savages thirsty for their blood, they must triumph or die. And if they die, humanity dies with them.

1

———————

Kelsey Bandar sat in the gritty, ancient tunnel, perched on a plascrete ledge just at the edge of the torch light deep beneath the horde city they'd just escaped from. The crash from the adrenalin high made her feel ready to collapse.

Dust still filled the air, and her eyes stung from the grit. The air was stale yet somehow managed to smell like something mechanical was burning off in the distance. It made her taste burnt toast.

That same dust had gotten under the primitive armor she wore and into her clothes. She itched all over. Parts of her felt like they were being rubbed by fine-grained sandpaper. It was like all the worst parts of making love on the beach without any of the awesome aspects.

Tired and sore, she scrubbed her face with both hands, trying to bring herself fully back to wakefulness. That probably ground more dirt into her pores and made her look like she'd been buried alive. Which, on reflection, wasn't that far from the truth.

Her hair had to be a nightmare. God, she needed a bath. No, two.

She ached from the efforts of the last few minutes. She hadn't broken anything—which was a good thing, since her medical nanites and the rest of her Marine Raider augmentation were still offline due to the EMP blast almost a week ago—but it felt as if several people had enthusiastically beaten her for hours.

After their flight from the vault where the horde had kept their scavenged Imperial technology, she'd used a plasma rifle built for marine powered armor to blow a massive hole through the stone walls that they'd used to plug an old tunnel leading to the ruined megacity they'd built their capital next to.

She'd fired a lot of plasma weapons over the last few years, so even without her enhanced strength, her graphene-coated bones and reinforced joints had taken the beating while she'd placed her shots just where they'd needed to go. It was her flesh that had paid the price in bruises and strained muscles.

Her ears, no longer protected by her augmentation, rang from firing the huge weapon. It was an annoying "squeee" that never seemed to go away and sometimes made it hard to understand what the others were saying. She hoped it wasn't permanent. That would totally suck.

Even if it was something that she had to live with, it had been worth it.

Two shots had utterly vaporized the barrier that the horde had put up to keep the inhabitants of the ruined megacity from sneaking under their walls. That had left her with a single shot left to fire into the vault's ceiling.

It had quite literally brought the roof down, fully sealing the area behind them. There could be no retreat now. The only path out of this mess was forward.

And going forward meant that they had to make their way underneath the ruined megacity once called Frankfort. She had no idea what they were going to find there, but based on the evident fear that the horde had about entering the old structures, it wasn't abandoned. There had to be people living there, and they would likely take her party's intrusion poorly.

Jared had brought down all of the people on board his destroyer before the AI had destroyed her. That had been more than two hundred people. When she added in the scientists and marines that she'd brought from *Persephone*, that number had grown to almost three hundred.

The electromagnetic pulse weapon that the horde had deployed had taken them all down when it had crashed their implants. The bastards had then slaughtered just about everyone. They were down to fourteen people.

Her mind still couldn't grasp the scale of their loss. It wounded her deeply that she'd failed so many people. It didn't matter that they'd had no idea the horde had that kind of weapon before they'd used it. All of those people were still dead.

The sorrow she felt was mixed with hot rage at the people who'd casually butchered so many innocent people. She hoped she'd killed a lot of their warriors in the fight they'd just finished, but it wasn't enough.

It would never be enough. Given a chance to exterminate them, she'd do so in an instant and deal with the trauma that caused her later. It wouldn't be the first time, though she'd hoped to never be in that mental place ever again.

Clarice Beauchamp, the warrior in charge of the first group of locals that they'd met, had lost all thirty of her warriors. Together, the survivors had made their way to the horde city, because retreat was impossible. The fires that they'd started during the fighting had cut them off, and they absolutely had to have some of the tools they'd lost to retrieve the override from the Imperial Palace.

Kelsey opened one of the survival rations that she'd recovered from the storage room where the horde had been sorting their captured gear. With what they'd found there, they probably had enough food for a week.

Whether that would be enough to escape the ruined megacity remained to be seen.

She ate slowly, looking around the hollow-eyed group. Each of them had been devastated in their own way, and this was the first chance they'd had to take a breath since the final fight had begun.

Hell, this was the first real break they'd had since they'd landed on this damned planet.

Talbot was off scouting with Clarice Beauchamp. That left Senior Lieutenant Chloe Laird and Commander Kaitlinn Cannon managing security over the makeshift camp in the tunnel.

Huddled in a small circle around a couple of the torches that they'd propped up for light and heat were the remaining people in their group: Jared Mertz, Carl Owlet, Elise Orison, Olivia West, Commodore Sean Meyer, Austin Darrah, Ralph Halstead, Doctor Lily Stone, and herself.

And, of course, her doppelgänger, Julia, a version of herself from another reality. That was still a little hard to accept, but the woman was growing on her.

They were all ragged and worn because of everything they'd been through over the last few days. Not only the fighting, but the mad searching through the debris that the horde had scavenged while looking for any tools that could help them turn their implants back on.

Doctor Stone had found her spare medical kit, so she could get to the implants now. Then the struggle would be for Carl to convert a piece of equipment that he'd found to generate the exact frequency and charge needed to initiate a reboot of their implants.

Honestly, that was one of the first things they needed to do. Without her Marine Raider augmentation, she wasn't able to protect them. A lot of people had died because of her arrogance in thinking that their technology would keep them safe, but without her augmentation, they were working at an extreme disadvantage.

They needed to get their implants back online as quickly as possible, without rushing things to the point that they killed someone. And that process needed to start now.

She rose to her feet, futilely tried to dust her hands off for the umpteenth time, and walked over to Lily. "You said that you'd recovered enough of your medical kit to perform the surgery. Is that something we could do here?"

Lily shuddered. "I can theoretically sterilize the surgical zone, but this is an *incredibly* dirty area. The chances of something getting into someone's head—even with all of the precautions I can take—is greater than zero. If that happens and we can't get their implants back online so that their medical nanites restart, they could get an infection of the brain, and that would be fatal.

"Even if I perform the surgery successfully, the real work is going to be for Carl. If his modifications to the equipment generating the charge are flawed, it could fry the wiring in the brain and kill someone outright.

"All told, I suspect that working with this jury-rigged technology is going to put the first person at significant risk. Perhaps as much as a thirty percent chance of death or cerebral injury. And that's on top of the infection risk if the reboot fails."

"That's too high," Jared said, his voice echoing off the plascrete walls around them. "What can we do to bring it down?"

The doctor shook her head. "Absolutely nothing. I doubt that we're going to find a functional surgical center anytime soon, and at least Carl knows the equipment that he's modifying.

"If we find other equipment that could be used, it's going to be in questionable condition, and that would make the risk go up. As high as the chances of a negative outcome are, they're still probably the best we're going to get. The positive in this is that once we can assess the process, the risk goes way down for subsequent patients."

Before her brother could respond, Kelsey squatted down in front of the doctor. "I'm willing to risk those odds. If we don't get my augmentation back online, the chances that someone is going to kill us all will rise exponentially.

"You can bet that there are dangerous people in this city. People that had to have heard those explosions. Our time is running out."

Jared looked skeptical. "We're deep underground. They might've heard something, and they might even know that it came from the direction of the horde city, but they're not going to be able to know precisely which tunnel it took place in.

"Hell, the tunnel leading to the horde vault has been sealed off for a long time. This isn't going to be the first place they think of, if they even think that the explosion affects them at all. They may just end up believing that the horde did it to themselves."

"We can't take that chance," Kelsey said with a shake of her head. "We have to assume that the residents of Frankfort are going to come looking for intruders and that they're going to find us shortly.

"The question is, are they going to find us in a condition to resist or take us prisoner like the horde did? With their reputation, are we willing to chance that they won't torture and execute us like those bastards up there intended to do?"

Those were the million-credit questions.

Jared shook his head slightly. "Even with your augmentation, that's still not a guaranteed defense against attack. Yes, you've got all those unarmed-combat skills, but how far is that going to get us?

"We have no advanced weaponry. What if they do? This deep underneath the city, if they still have some kind of power generation, they may have functional Imperial weapons.

"The horde has to have something like that, or they couldn't have made the EMP weapon. If the people here bring something like that to bear, swords and bows are going to be useless."

They stared at one another for a few moments before she nodded. "There's something to what you're saying, but I think you're missing the bigger point. Our best bet is to negotiate passage if we run into the inhabitants. I believe that we have a better chance of doing that if we can prove our story of coming from the sky above, and my augmentation gives us a better chance of making that happen.

"I understand there's a risk, but it's one that I'm willing to take. When you get right down to it, this is relatively mild when compared to some of the chances I've taken over the years."

"One of these days, the odds are going to catch up with you," her brother said with a sigh. "I'd rather not have that happen today, Kelsey."

She smiled slightly. "Me either, but beggars can't be choosers. A thirty percent chance of death right now is better odds than a hundred percent if we're caught with our pants down around our ankles again. We've got to take the chance. I know it, and so do you."

"Talbot's not going to be happy about this."

"No, I'd imagine not."

Jared grimaced. "Do it."

* * *

CARL OWLET WATCHED NERVOUSLY as Doctor Stone made her first incision into Kelsey's skull. The small woman was unconscious due to the somatic stimulator attached to her forehead, which kept her in a state of sleep much more profound than any kind of anesthesia would have done.

He wasn't a big fan of the blood the incision caused, which Olivia West was wiping away with a sterile wipe, but this was far from the first surgery he'd witnessed. He'd worked with the doctor when they'd installed the new communications module in the princess's torso.

At least that had been with a full medical team in attendance and in a real operating theater. Doing this kind of thing in a filthy tunnel on a mostly dead world made him shudder.

Ever since they'd discovered the dead fleet crewmen aboard *Courageous* all those years ago, he'd seen a lot of implants inside skulls. It was still very much a gruesome sight but a familiar one.

After a few minutes of deft work, Doctor Stone had a small area behind Kelsey's right ear shaved, cut open, and a small section of bone removed. That exposed the node he needed access to inside his friend's skull.

He still wasn't exactly sure how the electromagnetic pulse had been strong enough to knock everything offline. That was supposed to be impossible.

Obviously not.

Unfortunately, that fact introduced a level of uncertainty into the procedure.

Would this reset even work? Was the equipment in their heads so damaged that it wasn't going to come back online no matter what they did? Honestly, there was no way of knowing if he'd be able to make this work or fail miserably.

To make it work, he needed to use a piece of modified equipment to generate a charge on a specific frequency and with an extremely low amperage—a range of power output that the gear he'd recovered and modified had never been designed to generate quite so precisely.

As Doctor Stone had prepped for the surgery, Carl had made the needed modifications to his equipment. To the best of his knowledge, this was going to work, but it was still a gamble.

He had no way of measuring the output. If his modifications didn't do what they needed to do, there was the possibility that he'd fry Kelsey's brain and kill her.

Lily turned to him. "Over to you, Carl. What can I do to help?"

Taking a deep breath, Carl held up the probe that he'd use to trigger the charge. "I'm going to need you to immobilize her head. In fact, if we can get everyone else to grab onto her and keep her from moving at all, that would be best.

"I know that the somatic stimulator isn't supposed to allow her brain to send any commands to move her body, but once I trigger her implants to reset, there's the potential that her augmentation will move her body without any input from her. Potentially at full strength.

"Even that should be okay, so long as she doesn't move her head toward me. I'll pull back as fast as I can, but if she moves too quickly, she could impale her brain directly on my probe. That would be really, *really* bad."

The rest of them grabbed onto Kelsey. Four of them had her head wedged as well as they could with their legs and hands. That was going to be as good as he could get.

If this worked, she'd be able to hold the next patient steady while he worked with absolute certainty that they wouldn't be able to yank their head around until he was clear. This was going to be the most dangerous operation of the group.

He inserted the curved tip of the probe into her brain tissue. He was moving directly adjacent to the implant node with a very thin tip, so it shouldn't have any adverse effect on her, but it still made him feel exceptionally nervous.

The location where he had to apply the charge was on the far side of the node, something that was easy to do in a modern medical facility but incredibly difficult with makeshift equipment down at the bottom of an ancient tunnel under a destroyed city.

Once he felt that he had the probe tip where it needed to go, he took one last deep breath. "I'm about to trigger the charge. I'll give you a count down from three and hit the button on zero. As soon as I deliver the charge, I'm going to retract the probe and get clear. Again, it's possible that she could seize with the full strength of her augmentation, so don't let her grab you. As soon as I'm clear, get well back."

If she got ahold of anyone at full strength, there would undoubtedly be broken bones and other serious injuries, so he hoped to avoid that. If his actions killed his friend, he wasn't sure he could ever get past that.

He took a deep breath and put his finger on the button that would send the charge. He made sure the tip of the probe was in contact with the implant node and looked around at the group one last time.

"Three... two... one... zero."

With the last word, he sent the charge into her implants and extracted the probe as quickly and carefully as he could. That took less than a second, and everyone else pulled back from Kelsey as he finished.

The only reaction he saw to what he'd done was her eyes twitching. Even that motion ceased a moment later. It looked like the somatic stimulator had kept her under.

She was still breathing, so she was alive. They wouldn't know the condition of her brain or her implants until she was brought out, though.

He sat back on his heels and watched Doctor Stone clean the exposed area, put the small sliver of bone back in place, and begin sealing it into place with surgical glue. Once that was done, the doctor used a portable regenerator to close the skin over the wound.

"We've done the best we can," Lily said a few minutes later. "I'm going to wake her up."

Carl watched closely as the doctor turned off the somatic stimulator and put it aside. After a few moments, Kelsey's eyes fluttered open, and she took a deep breath.

"How are you feeling, Kelsey?" Lily asked softly.

The blonde woman frowned up at the doctor. "Who's Kelsey? And who are you?"

2

J ared's heart leapt into his throat. He'd been an idiot to let this happen. He should've told her no.

God, how were they going to fix this? Then his eyes narrowed as Kelsey started chuckling.

"You should see your faces," Kelsey said with a smirk.

"That's not funny!" Jared snapped. "You scared the hell out of us."

His sister grinned as she slowly sat up with the assistance of Doctor Stone. "Blame Talbot. I think his sense of humor is rubbing off on me."

She stared up at the ceiling and blinked. "My implants are back online. My augmentation is coming up too. It's going to take a minute for me to do a complete diagnostic and make sure that everything is working, but this is a good start. A *really* good start."

Jared walked over to the ancient plascrete wall. His heart was still racing from the prank his sister had played on them. He wasn't going to snap at her, even though he wanted to tear a long, bloody strip off her.

"I'm sorry," she said, her voice contrite. "I probably shouldn't have done that."

He rested his forehead against the cold stone and sighed. "It's not really that big of a thing, I suppose. I'm sure that I'll be laughing about this in a couple of months if we make it out of here."

Jared walked back over to the group. "I'll agree that Talbot has really been a bad influence on your sense of humor, though. Are you going to try this on him when he comes back? If so, I don't think he's going to take it nearly as well as we did."

She sighed. "No, he wouldn't. It was a bad idea, and I'm very sorry that I made anybody worry. If it's any consolation, my implants are fully back online, and my augmentation is as well. Error checking is complete, and it looks as if there are no ill effects. My medical nanites are back in business."

His sister stood slowly, as if she were still cautious of how her body was going to react. "It feels weird having everything back online. It's interesting how deeply I'd become used to the changes. I've been fully enhanced for several years now and never had to deal with normal human strength or the lack of all the augmentation. Now that it's been gone for a few days, it feels weird coming back."

Lily put a hand on Kelsey's shoulder. "You're going to want to take it easy for a couple of hours and let yourself get reacquainted with your augmentation. Right now, we're not in a life-and-death situation, so there's no need to push the envelope."

The doctor turned her attention to Jared. "Since Talbot is keeping watch, I suggest we do Julia next. Everyone else's augmentation is significantly less intrusive than theirs, so I'm not nearly as worried about possible side effects. Based on how long it took to get Kelsey done, I'm anticipating that I can have all of us back in operating order in a couple of hours."

"If we have that long," he said. "We took a chance doing this, because the inhabitants of the megacity could come looking for us at any time. Let's focus on doing as many people as we can, starting with the most critical. Julia next, then Talbot as soon as he gets here."

Kelsey stretched and then took a moment to put her sword harness back over her shoulders and grabbed her bow and quiver of arrows. "It should only take me a couple of minutes to get him headed your way. I'll stay at the guard post and keep an eye on things while you work on him."

Without waiting for a response, she took off at a jog. In moments, she was lost in the darkness of the tunnel. Only after she'd left did Jared realize that she hadn't taken a torch with her.

"How can she see in the dark?" he asked. "Doesn't she need at least some light to amplify?"

Carl shook his head. "Her ocular augmentation is capable of seeing in both infrared and ultraviolet. It's also capable of using a weak scanner signal to generate input for her to see even in something like this. She's not going to get colors, and it's not going to work well at any kind of a distance, but she'll be able to move around without tripping over anything. Marine Raiders are pretty damn capable."

Jared supposed they were. He'd seen his sister in action numerous times and still hadn't delved into the full nature of her augmentation.

It had taken her years to get past her resentment about what had been done to her. Now, she'd learned to take it in stride but still didn't talk about it much.

Lily went to work on Julia while he was thinking. Based on how long it had taken to get Kelsey operational again, it was likely that Talbot would be back just after they finished with his sister from another universe.

There might even be time to activate one other person's implants before the marine made his way back to the group. Since he was in charge, he vowed that was going to be him. He needed every advantage to figure out how they were going to get out of this mess.

* * *

TALBOT STOOD in the darkness at the center of the tunnel, facing in the direction of the city of Frankfort. Or where it would be if they weren't a hundred meters under it.

The torchlight only went out a short distance, and then everything was lost in the gloom, so he really wasn't sure what lay beyond what they'd already explored.

The tunnel had several offshoots, small chambers that contained equipment that he wasn't familiar with that at some point in the distant past had once served the dead city above them.

Perhaps it was for power distribution. He suspected that any kind of long-distance power transmission would need boosting so as not to degrade, but only somebody like Carl could actually determine what the junk had once been used for.

Clarice Beauchamp stood near him, her hand resting on the bow that she held wedged against her boot. How she'd be able to shoot anything in the utter darkness was beyond him. Still, her presence made him feel better. The only weapon he had was a sword that he wasn't that great using.

Yes, sword work was part of what his wife had taught him of the Art, the martial form used by the Marine Raiders for thousands of years. That didn't mean that he was any good at it yet. He wouldn't cut off his own arms or legs, but a skilled swordsman would still have him at a significant disadvantage.

It was his augmentation that would've made the real difference in a fight like that. Without it, he was a rank novice. In fact, he suspected that Beauchamp could beat him handily with the sword on her hip. His larger size would do nothing to offset her skill with the blade and her lifetime of training.

He wondered what tips she might be able to offer him and his wife for enhancing their training with weapons. He'd have to look into it if they survived the next few days.

"How far underneath the city do you think we'll be able to go before they know we're here?" he asked softly, worried about how far his voice would carry.

"I suspect that they already know we're here," she responded matter-of-factly. "They'll have heard the explosion. It's possible that they could've felt the vibration of our attack on the wall down here. They may not be precisely certain where it came from, but they're going to be looking around to make certain that they don't have unwelcome guests."

She turned toward Talbot and raised an eyebrow. "What do you plan to do when they find us?"

He shrugged slightly. "I suppose that depends on how they engage us. If they attack, we'll defend ourselves. If they want to talk, we'll talk. If it's something in between, we'll have to see what happens."

"Hey, you two," Kelsey said as she stepped out of the dark behind them. "Lily wants you, Talbot. You should both go back, I think. I have this covered."

His wife wasn't carrying a torch, so either she'd staggered through the dark, or her augmentation was back online. She'd taken the risk of the surgery.

Of course she had.

He turned to face her. "I assume your implants and augmentation are back online."

"I'm good, though I should probably be taking it easy today," she said. "The circumstances aren't going to cooperate, I'm sure.

"I could overhear you talking from a little way back. You're right to be worried about how the inhabitants are going to react to us. That's why we need to get your augmentation online as well.

"Julia should be done by the time you get there, so send her back to join me. Even relatively untrained, she'll help keep any incursion at bay while you guys prepare."

"Are you sure you're going to be okay alone?" he asked, putting a hand on her shoulder. "You just had brain surgery."

She smiled, pulled him into a hug, and kissed him on the lips. "I'm fine. Time is probably going to be short, so you need to get moving. Get your ass back there and make it happen."

He grinned at his wife and grabbed one of the torches. "Try not to have all the fun while I'm gone."

With that, he took off back toward where the rest were waiting at a jog with Clarice Beauchamp at his heels. Kelsey was right in that the clock was ticking. When it reached zero, things would get ugly.

With Julia's implants back online, she and Kelsey could hold here if the weapons arrayed against them were primitive and the number of enemies low enough. She certainly hoped so, because they were only going to get one shot at surviving what came next.

3

J ulia blinked as consciousness returned. It felt as if she'd only gone to sleep a moment ago. She tried to sit up, but Doctor Stone put a hand on her shoulder.

"Just give it a second," the other woman said. "Everything went fine, but I want to give you time to gather yourself back together."

That made her frown slightly. Her double hadn't required any extra time to get herself together. Why was she getting a little extra cushion where Kelsey hadn't?

"What's going on?" she asked. "What happened?"

"Your implant hardware reacted a little bit more than Kelsey's did. You thrashed around a little, and I want to make sure that everything has settled down before you try to get up."

Julia blinked a little at that and then looked at the faces around her. Everybody seemed to be okay, so she must not have hurt anyone, but Carl Owlet had a slight bruise on his cheek. Had she struck him? Or perhaps just knocked him back to the ground while he attempted to hold her down?

"Did I hurt anyone?" she asked quietly.

"It's just a bruise," Carl said. "I rolled and took up most of the impact. Nobody has anything serious, so don't worry about it."

Julia closed her eyes. "I'm sorry about that."

She had no desire to harm anyone, but specifically, she *really* didn't want to hurt the scientist. Though she hadn't developed feelings for him—he was a married man after all—she was fond of him and intended to seek out his duplicate in her universe once she'd returned there. It was growing more likely by the day that his doppelgänger would be her consort if things played out the way she hoped.

After a few more beats, she sat up and began examining her implants and augmentation. As much as she loathed the things, she needed them. Especially now. They'd all need them in the weeks and months ahead if they were to survive this horrible planet.

Her implants were back online, and her augmentation indicated that it was functional as well. She could once again fight if forced to. She wasn't trained like her doppelgänger or Talbot, but she'd do what needed to be done.

She'd also do whatever she could to bring death and destruction to the horde for killing Scott Roche. They'd slaughtered him even as he'd saved her life after the big battle. His sacrifice would not go unavenged.

The rage sparked by her memory made her clench her fists. She wasn't a violent person, but for them, she'd make an exception. She'd see them all dead if she could arrange it.

Julia blinked away the red that had formed in her vision and sighed slightly. As much as she wanted to make the horde pay, the smart move would be to escape the area entirely. They had to get away so that they could get the override from the vaults underneath the Imperial Palace. Then they had to escape Terra, rejoin *Persephone*, and get out of the system.

She waved the others away and got to her feet. If there was another glitch, she didn't want to be responsible for harming anyone. Her balance was decent enough to get her to her feet.

"I'll go replace Talbot," she said. "Everything seems to be working the way it's supposed to. Since we're working with makeshift equipment and we'll be running into things he'll have to help fix, I suggest you bring Carl's implants online soon. That can only help us as we go forward."

"Are you feeling okay?" Mertz asked, his tone concerned.

It shamed her a little when she found herself again questioning his sincerity, even though she knew better. This version of Jared Mertz wasn't the Bastard from her universe, but she still couldn't get past how much he looked and sounded like the man who'd killed her father.

That made perfect sense, since the two were identical in a physical sense. She'd seen how willing this version of Jared Mertz was to make sacrifices for his people, how much the loss of every single one of them tore at his soul.

She knew he wasn't a monster, but that didn't make it any easier for her to treat him differently. The habits of a lifetime were hard to overcome in just a few months. She was trying, but she wasn't certain that she'd ever fully succeed.

"I'm fine," she said curtly. "Now stop wasting time. We don't know how much of it we have left."

Without allowing time for him to respond, she took off down the tunnel at a slow jog. That would allow her time to become accustomed to her augmentation again. Her balance felt odd, and she knew that it would adjust itself.

Sadly, her artificial eye was still dead. That was irritating, but she'd work with the partial blindness. It had been far more bewildering when she'd lost her real eye, so this was a lot less disorienting.

The dark tunnel suddenly became lit as her ocular augmentation in her natural eye began peering into it. Everything was shades of grey and somewhat indistinct. Not because of distance, but from imprecision in the data she was getting back from her surroundings. Her implants were compensating for the gaps in data by extrapolating everything she saw. It was kind of eerie.

She'd have thought that after so many years, the thought of those machines inside her head would stop bothering her, but the violation never got any easier to live with. It was like rape, only worse. Counseling helped, but she still had a long way to go.

Somehow, her doppelgänger had adjusted and embraced what had happened to her. Julia thought that was most likely because the other woman hadn't fallen completely under the domination of the implants in her head. She hadn't become a Pale One. Her Jared Mertz had rescued her before that horrible fate had befallen her.

She supposed that there was nothing like being an unwilling passenger in your own body as it fought for its life against others, killing and maiming, to twist one's soul like it had done her.

Those thoughts consumed her until she passed Talbot and Beauchamp on their way back to the others. The man gave her a cheery wave but said nothing.

Her doppelgänger had fallen in love with the man and married him. Personally, she didn't see the attraction. Their tastes had somehow varied quite a bit over the last few years. Julia didn't want a warrior in her life, not like that. Someone like Carl Owlet would suit her tastes much better.

She finally saw her doppelgänger ahead, slowed, and made sure that the other woman was aware that she was coming. Kelsey had the honed reflexes of a trained warrior, and Julia absolutely did not want to trigger any kind of surprise in the woman.

Kelsey turned to face her as she came to a stop. "How are you feeling?"

Julia shrugged. "I'm torn. I hate the implants and augmentation, but we need them to survive this mess. It feels like I'm addicted to them, like they're some kind of drug. That's really hard for me to take."

"I'd tell you that it gets easier with time, but I'm not sure that's exactly right. It does get easier to deal with the hardware but not the kind of baggage that yours have brought along for the ride. I didn't suffer like you did, so it's easier for me to accept what they've done to me. How they've changed me.

"I know I've said this before, but I'm sorry about what the AIs did to you. It was a horrible, horrible thing, and it makes me feel guilty that I avoided the worst of it and that you didn't."

Somehow, the other woman always knew the right thing to say. It was like she could see into Julia's soul. She supposed that was literally true.

"What do we do now?" Julia asked, putting the uncomfortable conversation behind her.

"You have a decision to make," an unfamiliar voice said from farther up the tunnel.

In the blink of an eye, Julia had her bow in her hand and an arrow aimed up the tunnel. But there was no one to shoot. No one showed up in her enhanced vision.

Kelsey also had a bow out and took a step forward. "Who's there? Show yourself."

There was the rumble of stone grinding against stone. It came from far closer than Julia would've expected.

Barely twenty meters in front of them, part of the wall slid back from the tunnel and then to the side. From the opening stepped a man dressed in armor similar to that worn by the horde but not identical. His had bits of chain mail woven into it.

He was a young man, large, fit, and strong looking. His face was impassive as it considered them.

"My name is Jebediah, and you are trespassers in the city of Frankfort," he said coolly. "I call upon you to surrender. Do so or perish."

* * *

KELSEY OBSERVED the man for a moment and then turned her auditory augmentation up to the highest setting that it could go to. Now with the wall open, she could hear the breathing of others behind it. That noise would've been too soft for her to hear with the plug closed.

That was a clever hiding place, one where they could safely observe the tunnel. It was just her bad luck that Talbot and Beauchamp stopped almost directly in front of it.

She only had a few moments to make a decision, and that choice was going to dictate how they proceeded. If she rejected the man's offer to surrender, they would be committed to a fight to the death against an unknown number of people. People that apparently knew exactly where they were.

On the other hand, if she surrendered, then they'd once again be prisoners of people that might very well want to torture information out of them and then execute them. Maybe they wouldn't use immolation like the horde, but death was still death.

Was there a third option? There was no way to go back, even if they could get past the horde. The tunnel had been thoroughly and utterly collapsed behind them. They were trapped against a place with no exits.

Or maybe they weren't. There was always the possibility that even while this man was talking to her, others were waiting behind similar hidden doors and observing the rest of her party. If she rejected their offer, they might come swarming out and kill everyone in sight.

With a sigh, she set her bow on the ground slowly. "We surrender. I'm going to have to tell the rest so that they don't resist, but I'm not going to fight you."

For a moment, she thought Julia wasn't going to follow her lead, but the other woman closed her eyes and then set her bow on the ground as well, raising her hands above her head.

"You have chosen wisely," the man said. He gestured, and men came boiling out of the hiding place behind the wall. There were dozens of them.

Even with her augmentation, though she could have taken them in a straight-up fight, it was entirely possible that they could've maimed or even killed her in the fighting. Primitive weapons didn't necessarily mean that they weren't a threat.

The men quickly and efficiently stripped her of all her weapons and then bound her hands behind her back. It amused her that she could snap those bonds with just a moment's effort, but that was something that she wasn't going to reveal to them unless she had to. If things went badly, she still wanted that ace up her sleeve so that they could escape, given the opportunity.

Julia raised an eyebrow at her and submitted as well. She said nothing openly but sent a message through her implants.

Are you really going to surrender to them?

I don't see that we have any choice. If they've got another group waiting back where the rest are, they could kill everyone. I'm not going to take that chance. I've talked my way out of worse situations, and until we know that these people aren't as brutal as the horde, we're going to give them the benefit of the doubt.

Her doppelgänger made a slight shrug to indicate that she would follow along.

Once she was thoroughly trussed up, Jebediah stepped over and scrutinized her. "You wear horde armor, but you're not of the horde. Where do you come from?"

"A planet far from here," she said, looking up at the large man. "You wouldn't know the name of it. It wasn't very well known even before the rebellion. What are your intentions toward us?"

"I'll take you to my father. He rules this city and will make the ultimate decision about your fate, but the fact that you have surrendered means that you will not be executed. Allow me to congratulate you on your cool thinking and wise decision-making skills."

"Save your congratulations until I find out whether or not this really ends up being a good decision or not," she said grimly. "I might just have thrown us out of the frying pan into the fire."

The man inclined his head slightly. "My father finds himself curious as to your story and how you managed to cause so much damage to the horde city. If you tell a good tale, he'll likely show you some mercy."

"You mean he might let us go?"

The man shook his head. "No intruder is ever allowed to leave Frankfort. Yet there are different levels of duty that you may be required to serve, and your cooperation and storytelling skills may influence my father in making that decision. Consider that well before you speak too harshly to him. Or me.

"Now, take me to your companions. So long as they also surrender peacefully, no one needs to be harmed today."

Kelsey allowed the man to take her arm and guide her back down the tunnel toward where the rest were waiting. Even though she had an extended-range com built into her augmentation, only Carl had a matching set. She wouldn't be able to warn the others about what was coming.

Hopefully, Jared would see the logic in what she was doing and stop the rest from putting up a fight. If they didn't have cool heads, there might still be a slaughter today. If need be, she'd snap her bonds and fight with everything she had, but she was praying that cooler heads prevailed.

4

Carl felt nervous. Doctor Stone had insisted that she go through surgery after Talbot, and that meant that someone with very skilled hands had to perform the work.

That meant it had to be him. His scientific duties often required him to do extremely delicate work, and while he'd never performed surgery, he felt confident that the techniques he used would carry across well.

At least he certainly hoped so.

Once the doctor was out, he very carefully removed the sliver of bone from her skull and set it onto a sterile pad. He then reset her implants before using surgical glue to put the sliver of bone back into place and seal it up. Once that was done, he ran the regenerator over the incision until it looked well healed. He then removed the somatic stimulator, and her eyes opened.

"How are you feeling?" he asked softly.

"Good," she said. "My implants are online, and I can even interface with my medical equipment. Excellent work, Doctor Owlet. Congratulations on your first major surgery.

"Swap places. You're next, so show me one last time how the equipment generates the charge."

"I'll stick with my PhD, thanks," he said dryly. "I prefer less blood and brains when working."

He lay down and went to sleep as soon as she fitted the somatic stimulator. It only seemed like a moment later when his eyes blinked open.

Rather than say anything, he quickly checked his implants and found them operational once more. That was an incredible relief because he'd grown used to the things over the years and had so much research and information archived inside them.

The additions that he'd made to his hardware also allowed him to work on Imperial equipment much more easily than would be possible without them.

There was a message waiting for him, marked as extremely urgent. It was from Kelsey. She'd sent it seconds after his implants had come back to life.

She'd had to have been continuously checking to see if he was receiving to do that, and that probably meant it wasn't good news. He played the message.

Julia and I were ambushed, and I decided the best course of action was to surrender. It's the city residents. We're coming down the tunnel, but I'm slow-walking them. Get all the surgeries done that you can because they'll almost certainly confiscate the equipment. Tell Jared we need to surrender without resisting.

"We have a problem," he said even as he acknowledged the message. "Kelsey and Julia have been captured by the residents and are on their way back. She's moving slowly but says we have to surrender once they arrive. She said that if we can't get everyone's implants online before they get here, they're almost certainly going to confiscate our equipment."

The doctor abruptly gestured for Admiral Mertz to lie down. "Time permitting, we'll move on to Lieutenant Laird and the remaining two of the three amigos next."

The three amigos were himself, Ralph Halstead, and Austin Darrah. Together, the three of them had overlapping scientific, computer, and technological skills that could potentially work miracles on any equipment that they found.

Carl wished that they could get everybody's implants back online, but with time working against them, there was only so much they could do.

Once Admiral Mertz was done, they moved on to Lieutenant Laird and got her back online. While she didn't have Raider augmentation, she was a trained marine, and that would undoubtedly prove useful going forward.

Ralph Halstead and Austin Darrah were next and quickly done. That left four people remaining: Commodore Meyer, Commander Cannon, Elise Orison, and Olivia West.

"No one make any hasty movement," Kelsey said from up the tunnel. "If you have a weapon in your hand, put it aside. Stand still and raise your hands over your heads."

Carl raised his hands. Since he had no weapons worth mentioning, he left them in the sheaths. No doubt the enemy would strip them from him.

A few moments later, a group of men pushed Kelsey into the torchlight. When they ascertained that no one was holding a weapon, they came forward in pairs and bound everyone's hands behind their backs. Once that was done, they stripped away every single weapon that they possessed.

Once again, they were prisoners. Hopefully, these new people wouldn't be as bad as the horde. He supposed he'd find out. It wasn't exactly as if they had a choice in the matter.

* * *

As Talbot surrendered, he took a good look at their captors. They were dressed like the horde fighters but didn't seem inclined to cause casual pain like the plain's dwellers.

His questioning at the hands of the crazy woman at the camp where Julia had rescued them came to mind. She'd had her men beat him and threatened to use a hot iron to brand him while telling him how she'd torture and kill everyone while he watched. She'd taken great pleasure in telling him so.

These people didn't seem to have the same worldview, and that was better than nothing.

There was no sign that they had any higher technology on them. No flechette pistols, no plasma weapons, and no stunners. They were seemingly just as primitive as the horde or Captain Beauchamp's people.

Once his hands were bound behind him, he allowed them to herd him together with the rest. He did manage to work his way over to his wife. He looked at the man standing next to her.

"She's my wife. May I speak to her?"

The man considered his words and then nodded. "Speak loudly enough that I may overhear. I have no interest in your personal business. My only concern is to make certain that you are not attempting to escape."

If he'd wanted to speak in a way that they couldn't hear, he'd have used his implants. He didn't have her long-range com, but his internal unit was good for a dozen meters without amplification.

This conversation was as much for their captors' benefit as it was for his own. If they were going to survive this, they needed their captors to see them as people. People that had something to offer when the time came and weren't the kind of threat that they needed to do anything strenuous to restrain.

"Are you okay?" he asked.

"They offered me a chance to surrender before they presented themselves, so I didn't overreact," she said. "Not that I suspect they would've taken me as much of a threat in any case."

"That's only because they don't know you as well as I do," he said with a slight smile.

Having said that, he didn't try to maintain his appearance of humor. Their situation was still grave, even if he didn't think it was immediately dangerous.

The man in charge had them bound together by a single rope and led them down the tunnel. Some of the others picked up all of the gear that he and his people had transported so far and brought it behind them. No doubt some of it would cause raised eyebrows and prompt pointed questions.

Operational technology would have to be scarce in a place like this. Still, living with even nonfunctional technology all around would make it obvious to them what kind of things he and his friends had in their packs.

He started to say something else to Kelsey, but she shook her head. "Just let it be, Talbot. We'll find out soon enough what they've got to say. I'm tired. It seems like we've been running for days. Maybe once they lock us up, I can take a nice long nap."

He had to admit that sounded good. The last week had involved a lot of hard riding and very little sleep. If they had a chance to eat and rest, that would be helpful.

The group moved along in silence for a while, and then he saw the opening in the wall ahead of them. He had no idea how he'd missed seeing something like that. It was inside the range of the torches that he'd leaned against the walls.

He eyed the door as they went through it and into the unknown portion behind the tunnel wall. Someone had gone to a lot of trouble to make a segment of wall on tracks that fit very tightly into the hole like a plug in a bottle. There must've been a seam, but without his enhanced ocular augmentation, he'd missed it.

That was sloppy and annoying. If Talbot had been writing his own efficiency reports, he'd ding himself for it hard.

Behind the fake wall was a series of tunnels that led away from the one they'd been traveling down. Unlike the abandoned one leading toward the horde city, this one showed signs of traffic. The dust on the floor had been disturbed numerous times, so it was probably an observation post where the city inhabitants kept an eye on the tunnel leading toward the horde.

Even though the larger tunnel had been plugged for decades or even centuries, it seemed that they still worried that the horde would try to sneak into the city through it. Considering how ugly the rulers of the horde and their warriors were, Talbot couldn't blame them.

Do you really think you can sweet-talk them? he asked Kelsey over their implants.

I'm not sure. No matter how we play this, they have the cards to trump us right now. We need to know more about them before we can make any decisions about how much to say or whether we need to fight or not.

Talbot grunted slightly in response. Everything she'd said made sense, but he hated being under someone else's control. These people might be just as monstrous as the horde but in a completely different way.

He supposed it didn't matter. Kelsey was the one calling the shots, and Admiral Mertz would back her up. So would he, for that matter. At this point, they were prisoners, so it didn't hurt hearing what their captors had to say. If nothing else, they might learn a little bit about what was happening in the area.

It was disconcerting realizing that they might never get to the Imperial Palace or access the vaults below it. Or if they did, it would either be with the help of the people now holding them prisoner or over their objections.

They reached a set of stairs and started upward. No matter what happened, they'd have their answers soon enough, he supposed. He might as well be patient and see if they got some good news for a change.

The thought of good luck almost made him chuckle. That wasn't their way. He'd just have to see what flavor of bad luck came their way. Then they'd figure out a way to overcome it.

5

J ared used the time that it took to climb the many stairs to figure out exactly how he was going to approach this situation. He had no idea how the locals were going to question them yet, but he knew the general approach that he intended to take. Everyone on this world hated the AIs. They hated the things that had destroyed their civilization.

If he could turn that hatred around so that these people became his allies rather than his enemies, that would be the best outcome. It would have to be done delicately, but he could at least start the conversation. The horde had doubted their story, according to what Talbot had said. Doubt was probably a mild word for what the horde had actually felt, honestly.

Now they'd have a chance to reframe the conversation, and he didn't want to waste it. Whatever he said, he had to make the most of this one opportunity.

While he had no augmentation like Kelsey, Talbot, and Julia, climbing the stairs didn't tire him as much as he'd expected. All of the riding had toughened his legs. If they got away from the city, he imagined that they'd all be tougher by the time they reached the Imperial Palace.

The stairs eventually let out into a large room that seemed to occupy the center of one of the buildings. Based on the height above their surroundings, Jared believed they were near the top of the building. There were large windows all around with what had likely once been a stunning view of Frankfort. Even in its ruined state, the city still commanded his attention.

He'd never been to a city like this before, but the recording of the building in Imperial City gave him a frame of reference. Even so, this structure had a way to go to reach even half that height.

The room was set out much like the throne room back on Avalon. This was where the ruler of the city received visitors or passed judgments. Based on what he'd heard about these people, he'd wager they didn't get many visitors, so this was where they conducted their internal pomp and circumstance.

The large room was devoid of decoration. The view of the ruined megacity seemed to be all the splendor these people needed. Contrary to his expectations, the room was spotless. No dirt or dust lay anywhere, and the glass was so clean that it sparkled.

He could see how they'd clean the inside, but getting to the outside of a building this high had to be terribly dangerous. Why risk someone's life just to clean the glass for this one room?

Jared turned his attention to the spot where the guards were taking them. There was no throne, only a large dais that held a table, behind which a single man sat. He was older, with a lined face and hair almost entirely white. He wasn't dressed overly formally, and the clothes he wore didn't seem ceremonial.

The man also didn't have anything on his head. No crown or circlet. No decoration of any kind from what Jared could see. Whatever his authority, he didn't feel the need for regalia to emphasize it.

In addition to the man, dozens of others stood along the circumference of the room. Men and women watched suspiciously as Jared and his people were led to the center of the room and stopped directly in front of the table.

Their captors lined them up so that they were all equally distant from the table. Then they stood behind them while the older man leaned forward and steepled his fingers as his eyes roved over each of them. He finally settled on Jared, and his eyes narrowed.

"I must admit that I have many questions as to how you came to be inside my city, but I think I will start my questioning with a simple and straightforward request. Do not lie to me. Whatever happens next is entirely within my discretion. Honesty and full disclosure will serve you best. Which of you is the leader of this group?"

"I am," Jared said before Kelsey could open her mouth. If things went badly, he wanted to make certain that she was as shielded as possible from the consequences. The more he could keep her to the shadows and not have her suspected of having more capability than she did, the better their options if they had to try something dangerous.

The man nodded slightly. "So I had believed. You may call me Leader Mordechai. Who are you?"

Jared thought about it for a moment and then took a single step forward. The guards didn't react. It seemed that so long as he didn't do anything rash, he had a little freedom of action.

"My name is Jared Mertz, and my title is Admiral. Before we get started with the discussion of who I serve, I want to make it absolutely and perfectly clear that I do not serve the computers that rule the Empire now. My people and I are here to overthrow them."

If his words threw the man off, it wasn't apparent at a glance. The older man simply stared at him, saying nothing.

"An interesting assertion," the man finally allowed. "And one wrought with danger for you. You claimed to have come from another world, according to my son. Considering the amount of damage that was dealt to the horde city, I'm certainly willing to entertain that statement.

"However, it's much more likely that you serve the computers and that you're here on some nefarious task. If so, your escape from the horde city will not save you. To work with the computers is death. Our penalties are perhaps not as draconian as those of the horde, but you can rest assured that they're just as final."

The man leaned forward, his expression severe. "I suggest that you measure your next words very carefully, Admiral Mertz. The story you tell will set the stage for what comes next."

Jared knew that he was taking a horrible risk. He could've made up some kind of story and maybe spared their lives, but then they'd be prisoners here, unable to complete their mission.

Yes, they might be able to escape later, but he'd rather find allies in this task, much like Clarice Beauchamp. In fact, she might be able to assist him in telling his tale.

He glanced toward the woman but decided this wasn't the right time to bring her into the conversation. He led off with his own story.

"About a week ago, the AI—the artificial intelligence—destroyed my ship, and our small craft crashed into the surface of this world. Perhaps your people saw something of that?"

The man nodded. "Our sentries did see a streak of fire coming from the heavens. You claim that was you arriving?"

"Yes. We came to Terra to retrieve something from the Imperial Palace that will help us overthrow the AIs. Our world was founded before the fall of the Empire, but crown prince Lucian retreated there during the final battles of the rebellion.

"He led us in recovering and gave us a message that brought us back to Terra five centuries later. The computers don't know that we exist. We're just too small for them to be aware of yet. But they *are* learning.

"As soon as we landed on Terra, we were caught up in the local fighting. It seemed that several groups were intent on retrieving the pinnaces that we came down to the surface in. They were too damaged to fly, but there were a lot of supplies in them."

He gestured toward Clarice. "Captain Beauchamp and her group of fighters arrived first. My oldest sister convinced her—at least preliminarily —that we were telling the truth. Enough so that her people were escorting us back to their outpost for further questioning when the horde overwhelmed us.

"They killed hundreds of my people and all of Captain Beauchamp's soldiers. Altogether, we had almost three hundred people, and those of us that stand before you are all that remain."

The man leaned back in his chair, slightly considering the group with a sweep of his eyes. "Captain Beauchamp, my people are at least somewhat familiar with yours. Your people have no love for the computers or the humans they control, yet you helped these strangers. Why?"

Beauchamp cleared her throat. "While it remained for my leaders to vet the truth of what they said, there was something about them that convinced me that they were telling me the truth. His people fought hard to save my people when we were outnumbered three to one in an initial skirmish. They revealed lost technology in a way that only an idiot would.

"I have to assume that they weren't trying to conceal their advantages because they had no idea what the consequences of revealing it were. That convinced me personally that they were telling the truth."

Jared couldn't argue with the logic of what the woman had said. What they were doing sounded insane. The people of Terra killed the servants of the AIs. He was taking a terrible risk in telling the truth, but he didn't think that he had a choice. Lies weren't going to help them now.

Mordechai considered him for a few moments and then shrugged. "I'm obviously going to have to consider your words most carefully. This isn't the time to make rash decisions."

The man that had overseen their capture stepped up behind Mordechai and whispered in his ear. The older man listened and frowned slightly.

"My son tells me that you were doing something to your people. You were cutting into their heads? Explain."

Jared had hoped that Kelsey had delayed them long enough so that none of the locals saw them reactivating the implants. That hope was obviously dashed.

"When we were fighting the horde, they used a weapon against us," Jared said. "We have equipment inside of our bodies that allow us to interface with computers and perform other work as well as store information. We were resetting that equipment so that it worked again."

"And how many of your people have these devices inside of you?" Mordechai asked.

"All of us, though some have not had theirs reactivated. The implants are similar to what the rebels used to turn humanity, but ours are protected against that sort of thing. Since the enemy uses them, we must use them as well to equal the fight."

"I see," the older man said. "Step over here so that I may see what you're talking about."

With a mental shrug, Jared stepped forward and pulled his hair slightly back, revealing the small shaved area behind his ear. With Doctor Stone's work with the portable regenerator, the scar there was probably barely noticeable.

The man probed it with his finger. "And this was done today? It looks as if it has healed for weeks."

"We have a device that is capable of speeding healing. If you'd like to see the process, I'd be more than happy to have our doctor demonstrate it for you. If you have injured, she might be able to treat them for you as well."

"You said that you had restored this machinery for most of you. Who remains yet to be done?"

Jared pointed at Sean, Commander Cannon, Elise, and Olivia.

"At this point, it won't hurt to allow you to finish the process, and it may provide me with information that helps me make a better decision about your fate. Proceed."

It took a couple of minutes for Lily and Carl to get the equipment that they needed from the guards, but once they did, it was a relatively quick and straightforward task to perform the reactivation surgery on each of the four that hadn't already received it.

In turn, each person went to sleep, had their implants reset, and then woke up—all under the close observation of Jebediah and his guards, as well as Leader Mordechai.

When the process was complete, the older man shook his head. "I've heard stories about some of the old technology and how it could do such miraculous things. Even seeing it with my own eyes, it's difficult to believe. What do these implants do for you?"

"That's a long story," Jared said. "One I'm certainly willing to tell, but my people and I have been running hard for a week and have suffered great losses. Is it possible that we could get something to eat and perhaps rest so that I can give you my best effort?"

Mordechai nodded to his son. "Take them to an appropriate place and guard them well. See that they are brought food, water, and allowed to bathe."

The younger man nodded and then started the guards herding everyone toward the stairs. They hadn't taken more than fifteen steps when there was a bright flash of light from outside the building. It was blinding enough to capture everyone's attention, and all turned toward it curiously.

"Kinetic strike!" Kelsey shouted. "Everybody down now! Cover your heads and faces!"

Jared had just thrown himself to the floor and covered his head with his arms and hands when the windows blew in. However durable they were meant to be, they weren't up to the task of stopping the shock wave.

The AI had finally decided to act. If Jared was right, it had just destroyed the two crashed pinnaces. The only positive to the situation was that the camp had probably been swarming with horde warriors. Maybe the AI would think it had killed them there.

Yeah, as if they were ever that lucky.

6

J ulia felt shattered glass lash across her primitive armor. If she hadn't
been protected, she was very much afraid that she might've been
seriously injured. She certainly hoped that no one else in the city was
going to be badly hurt but knew that outcome was extremely unlikely.

After a few moments, the air grew still, and the cries of the frightened
and injured could be heard more clearly. She raised her head and looked
around the room to find utter devastation.

All of the glass in the walls had blown out—on all four sides of the
building—shattered by the shock wave from the kinetic strike. No single
pane was in one piece. Many of the people closest to the strike had been
killed or gravely injured.

Thankfully, the majority of the injuries elsewhere in the room would be
less severe. That didn't reduce the gravity of the situation, but it did make
the number of wounded people they were dealing with significantly lower
than it could've been.

Julia leapt to her feet and raced to the area nearest the kinetic strike. Off
in the distance, she could see a cloud of debris boiling into the sky. There
was no longer any bright light, but it looked like a massive bomb had
gone off.

In fact, one had.

When someone struck the ground with a tungsten rod weighing
hundreds of kilograms moving at orbital velocity, it was more than enough
to create the equivalent of a nuclear explosion.

She focused her attention on the people moaning around her. She had
no medical training at all, but she could see that many of them were beyond
help.

Before she could decide what needed to be done, Doctor Stone was standing beside her. The woman didn't seem disturbed by the amount of blood and death, though Julia knew that probably wasn't true. She just had better training to wall it away.

Stone started pointing at various people. "Get these folks over into the center of the room. Someone sweep an area clear of glass. I'll need my medical equipment set out for me. Carl, get it laid out."

The doctor turned to Julia. "Be as careful as you can, but get them there as quickly as possible."

Even as Julia was picking up the first person, a woman with her arm missing below the elbow, Kelsey and Talbot were there helping get others. With her augmented strength, lifting a single human being and carrying them carefully to where they needed to be was no strain at all.

Others were assisting even though they didn't have Marine Raider strength. Even their captors were following instructions and moving people as indicated.

Julia had very little time to see exactly what Doctor Stone was doing, but the woman had a small circle of observers as she used her equipment to staunch bleeding and save lives. Leader Mordechai, his son Jebediah, and several others were observing her actions, getting themselves bloody while helping as directed.

The guards had reformed and were watching the exits, so there would be no escape. There might have been a few minutes during the chaos that her party could have gotten out of the room, but no one had run. They'd stayed to help.

She certainly hoped that made a difference in how the locals treated them.

Once she'd finished moving the most seriously injured, she walked over to stand beside Jebediah as people that looked like healers had arrived to take his and his father's places.

"There will be other injured," she said. "You need to bring them here so that Doctor Stone can take care of the most seriously wounded. Or take her to where you're working on them, probably."

The large man considered her, his expression blank. "I don't know that we can trust you. My father seems inclined to allow you an opportunity to earn that trust, but I find myself doubting your story."

Before she could respond, Mordechai arrived and put his hand on Jebediah's shoulder. "My son is my chief of security. It's his job to be skeptical of everything that he sees or hears. I shall not gainsay him in this matter, but I will allow you to prove your willingness to help.

"We already have people scouring the city, looking for injured. It's going to take quite some time to get everyone to a central, protected location, but it will be done. Meanwhile, I find myself with more questions. First, what is your name?"

Julia considered telling him the truth, that she was Kelsey Bandar, but decided that no matter how honest they were being, some things wouldn't be believed. The fact that she was Kelsey's duplicate from another universe was a little bit outside the scope of the story they were telling. It would be far better to stick with the story of being twins.

"I'm Julia Bandar. You've undoubtedly seen that my older sister and I are twins. She's also the more experienced of the two of us."

It was galling to have to admit that her doppelgänger was more experienced, but it was something that she couldn't argue with. Kelsey had the air of someone who'd done far more than Julia had. Experience had left its mark on her.

The older man nodded. "Twins are not that unusual, but neither are they commonplace. You and your sister seem to have significantly more strength than I would have expected of someone of your... slight build. Explain that to me."

Well, that was going to be a lengthy explanation and one that had the potential to see them all in very deep trouble. No matter what Julia said, she was going to have to be truthful yet circumspect.

"A few years ago, I was captured by forces under the control of the AIs. I had none of the implants that Admiral Mertz has spoken of before then. Also, everything that was done to me was done against my will and at extreme personal cost."

The man's eyes dwelt on hers for long seconds before he nodded. "I can see the shadows of the pain in your eyes. For the moment, let's say that I believe everything that you've told me. How does that explain the great strength that you've shown today?"

"I've just watched you pick up person after person, some of them weighing almost twice what you do. You showed no signs that this even inconvenienced you. How is that possible?"

Julia gestured toward her head. "All of us have computer enhancements inside our brains. They've been modified so that we cannot be taken over by the computers, but the hardware is similar.

"Without a frame of reference, it's difficult to explain precisely what it does. Let's just say that it allows us to process information significantly faster than we were able to do before and in much more comprehensive detail. It also allows us to interface with technology that was built by the Old Empire.

"Unlike most of us, because I was captured by the enemy and transformed, I have significantly greater physical augmentation than you would believe, I think. So do my sister and her husband. None of the rest has anything like this. It's not common.

"One of the benefits of this change is that I have artificial muscles woven through my biological ones. They grant me significantly more strength than you'd believe possible.

"Picking up the injured and moving them is just one example. I can also run faster and jump higher than anyone you've ever seen. As difficult as it is to believe, the equipment inside my body was designed to turn someone into one of the premier warriors of the Old Empire."

Mordechai pursed his lips. "We've heard tales of such. Fantastic warriors that had abilities far beyond those of us with normal bodies. Marine Raiders, they were called. Is this what you speak of?"

Julia nodded. "Yes. I never received any training to be anything like that, but that's the kind of hardware that's inside my body. It seems that when the AIs rebelled against the Empire, they took whatever civilians they could catch and forced them to become horrific fighting machines. They used the Marine Raider template to manage that."

She thought about it for a moment and then asked a question of her own. "If you don't mind my asking, what have you heard about the Marine Raiders? How is that possible when they all must've died out centuries ago?"

The man waved his hand dismissively. "That's a long story. We're going to have plenty of time to get to know one another, and I'll share it with you at some point. I appreciate your candor, and in exchange, I will warn you not to attempt to escape.

"Do not mistake the goodwill you have earned for clemency. While I'm forming an opinion of you and your people, I'm not yet swayed. Take things slowly, because rushing might mean unfortunate things happening to you and your friends."

That wasn't the news that Julia had wanted to hear, but it beat being told they were being turned into slaves without a hearing. Even having told him her secret, that didn't mean that he fully understood the scope of what a Marine Raider could do. That organization had been *very* secretive about its capabilities and methods.

"What happened to the horde city when we escaped?" she asked. "I seem to get the impression that there was a significant disruption of some kind. Those people killed hundreds of our comrades. I hope we caused them some pain in return."

"You lost friends," Jebediah said, his voice low. "I can hear your rage, though you try to hide it. Allow me to compliment you on the quality of your enemies. The horde is a blight upon the face of Terra. Come with me."

He led her to the far side of the room and gestured for her to look out. They could only get so close because the wind raging outside the building was a real danger. A fall from this height would kill her just as surely as being at the site of the kinetic strike.

Below her, she could see other buildings that had suffered from the blast wave. Off to her right, she could see the wall of the horde city and its makeshift buildings. It seemed to have taken some damage from the kinetic strike as well, but the most noticeable difference was the *large* pit in the center of the city.

Where the palace had once stood, there was now devastation. It looked as if the cavern that Kelsey had collapsed had drawn it in. The death toll was probably hideous.

The thought made her smile coldly.

"It couldn't have happened to nicer people," she murmured. "You're right about me hating them. They killed one of my closest friends. If I could slit all their throats, I'd do it. My sister wouldn't understand, but I'm thirsty for their blood."

Jebediah turned his head and examined her closely before nodding slowly. "That's the first thing one of you has said that I don't doubt at all. The horde is filled with those willing to torture and kill. The fact that they live so close to Frankfort sickens me. If we had the forces to do so, I would drive them from this place."

He gestured with his chin for her to turn back. "It's time for you to return to your fellows. We will take you to a place where you may rest and recover from your arduous fight. Your doctor will be returned to you unharmed as soon as she has finished her work. You have my word."

Julia had to admit that she could use the rest. Without her augmentation, she was exhausted. Now with it activated, she was feeling refreshed but famished.

"I don't suppose we could ask for some food. It galls me to say, but I eat like a horse, and I'm starving."

The large man smiled slightly. "I will see that each of you is given as much to eat as you desire. The quality is perhaps not as fine as you're used to, but I assure you it is filling and will sate your hunger."

"That's all a girl can ask for."

While they hadn't escaped the trouble all around them, she had to leave tomorrow's problems for tomorrow. None of them had died, so this would have to be chalked up as a win. Once they'd had some sleep, perhaps they'd be able to talk their way into better accommodations or convince their captors that they might be able to work together to further their mutual ends.

She wouldn't be doing the talking when it came to that, but she was confident that Mertz and Kelsey could sway the old man given enough time. He seemed relatively reasonable, all things considered.

It would have to do.

She joined the others and allowed the guards to lead her away.

7

Once the prisoners had been taken away, and the situation seemed to be in hand, Mordechai returned to his office under the city. As he walked, he considered his new prisoners and the events that had impacted his city today.

As spies went, these people were—at best—incompetent. Not only had they failed to sneak into the area they were supposed to observe, they'd gotten into several large-scale fights with the horde and been massacred.

Then, to escape the horde, they'd used Imperial weapons and destroyed the horde palace, along with the treasure vault underneath the city. He had no idea how many of the ruling class there had been killed, but the number must be significant.

The horde was still roiling and trying to establish new leadership. That seemed to be a bloody process. With any luck, the most powerful factions would be bled dry, and the horde would be crippled for decades to come.

While decisive, that blow apparently hadn't been the goal of the group that he'd captured. All they'd been trying to do was recover some of their equipment and escape. So what did they do next? They'd walked right into his trap. Not only that, they'd also surrendered immediately.

They then proceeded to tell him all of their deepest secrets. The woman he'd spoken to had to have suspected that the type of implanted hardware she was speaking of was an automatic death sentence. Yet she made no effort to conceal… anything.

As crazy as it sounded, he believed them. He wasn't certain what their real goals were, because they hadn't been very specific, but even the destruction of their vessels by the AI lent credence to their words.

If the AI was trying to slip people into the local population, it could've come up with a far better plan than what he was seeing. No. Whoever they were, whatever they were hoping to accomplish, they didn't work for the AI.

Minutes after he'd arrived in his spartan office, a knock brought him out of his reverie. Jebediah stepped through the door and took a seat without being asked. One of the prerogatives of being his son.

"I believe them," Jebediah said without preamble.

Mordechai raised an eyebrow. It was his son's job to be suspicious of *everything*. He was the one always spouting conspiracy theories and plots that had to be foiled. He saw shadows lurking just around every corner.

And, sometimes, they were even there.

Such a statement from a professional paranoiac was… notable.

He leaned forward and smiled slightly. "Did one of them perhaps slip you a drink spiked with some type of drug? Surely this cannot be my Jebediah, the man who trusts nothing and no one."

His son's face flushed red. "I understand that I'm not usually so gullible, but after having spoken with Julia, I don't think that they mean us harm. As insane as their story sounds, I believe that it's true. They've come to Terra on some type of mission to harm the computers.

"We'll need to question them more deeply to find out for certain that they aren't pulling the wool over our eyes, but at this point, I doubt that they're working in the best interests of the machines."

"I'm inclined to agree," Mordechai said. "This is not a group of warriors. Those most enhanced to do the fighting seem ill suited to do so."

The two of them discussed everything that they'd seen and heard. Mordechai focused on the story of Julia, the woman captured by merciless computers and forcibly implanted with their hardware.

It was an interesting tale. If only three of the people that they'd caught had full combat enhancements, the twins made no sense. If the intent was to fool someone into thinking that they were harmless, it made for poor policy to immediately reveal your capabilities at the first crisis, particularly when you weren't actually attacking anyone.

He had mentioned the Marine Raiders to her, and she'd known what he was talking about. His information about them came down through stories. A group of Marine Raiders had once been stationed here in Frankfort. After the rebels struck the Empire down, the Raiders had acted as guerrilla warriors to cause harm to the invaders.

Sadly, they didn't last for more than a few decades. One day, they went out on a mission and never returned. Undoubtedly, they'd been slain somewhere in a desperate fight.

His grandmother had told him many stories about those men. Some of the incredible feats they'd been capable of and some of the modifications that had been done to their bodies to make them the premier warriors of the Empire.

He could hardly envision a woman as small as Julia being capable of that type of mayhem. Or her sister, for that matter. Frankly, the one called

Kelsey seemed to be the more forward of the two. If one of them had the enhancements of a Marine Raider, it would be Kelsey.

Julia made no sense. She asserted that she wasn't a warrior, and Mordechai was more than comfortable in accepting that as truth.

"I want you to get to know these people better," he told Jebediah. "I don't know if I fully believe their story, but I've heard enough to allow them the opportunity to try and convince me further."

He smiled a little shrewdly. "They seem to have a mixture of people. Their doctor obviously has true Imperial medical skills. Some of their people seem like they are technicians or mechanics of some kind. Show them some of the malfunctioning equipment and see if they can assist in restoring it. That way, we learn something about both them and the old technology."

Jebediah nodded. "I'll see to it. What of their leader?"

"Leave him to me. As one leader to another, we shall speak. You focus on the twins. If they're deceiving us in any way, your suspicious nature will be our tripwire. While we may hope that they tell the truth, it's wiser to plan for finding out that this is all some kind of trick."

"If it's a trick, they're going to wish they'd never tried it," Jebediah said grimly.

* * *

KELSEY SLEPT FITFULLY and woke groggy. Now that her implants were reactivated, her need for sleep had been reduced, but her body was confused. She didn't blame it. Her head felt like it was stuffed full of cobwebs.

The "cells" that they'd been placed in were of significantly better quality and spaciousness than she'd expected. Over the years, she'd been locked up in a wide variety of locales, and this one certainly didn't rank near the bottom of that list.

That wasn't to say that they were free to roam about. They weren't. They'd been taken deep underground and placed in a series of rooms behind some substantial doors. She wasn't sure what the original purpose of this area had been, but it was more than sufficient to keep them penned in.

She had no doubt that she could force one of the doors. But it was only the first of several. They'd hear her, and then she'd walk into a lot of trouble. Common sense told her that they were taking her capabilities seriously and that she just needed to wait.

At least the area had a bathing room with large containers of water and what looked like a gas heater with some kind of vent to take away the fumes. It had been a *long* time since she'd cleaned up, and she'd been too tired last night to take advantage of the situation.

She considered waking Talbot up and having him join her, but that would probably lead to other things, and that wasn't going to be happening in such a public location. The tub was in a small side room blocked off by a curtain made of some type of woven material. Everyone could hear what happened in there, and anyone could walk in at any time.

There was a second room further up in the suite where a primitive toilet was secreted behind a similar curtain. That kept the smell down to a manageable level, but she imagined it was going to have to be emptied regularly to keep the rooms from smelling like a pigsty.

When she had the tub full of hot water, she found what passed for soap and began stripping off her clothes. She'd gotten about halfway through that when the curtain slid aside, and Julia stepped into the room.

The other woman froze and then started to back out, but Kelsey gestured for her to come forward, not bothering to hide her body from the other woman. "I haven't got anything that you haven't quite literally seen many times before. The tub is big enough for both of us, so let's not waste the water."

The other woman stood there, her eyes wide, for a moment. "How can you be okay with getting naked in front of *everybody*?"

Kelsey chuckled. "When you have no choice but to armor up in front of marines, you pick up their habits. They don't segregate by biology, so you lose your body modesty pretty fast. Once you get used to it, it's not so bad. Nobody is staring at you. They've got their own things to be doing. And even if someone does take a peek, what harm is there?"

She finished stripping off her clothes and slid into the hot water. It felt *wonderful*.

While her doppelgänger continued to struggle with the idea of taking her clothes off in front of her, she started lathering up. Perhaps it would help the other woman if she couldn't see anything.

Julia sighed, turned her back, and started stripping off her clothes. Even though the other woman had been through a full sequence of regeneration, Kelsey knew Julia had been chewed up pretty hard. There were no scars now, no real injuries, other than the artificial eye. Lily Stone knew her business.

Then it occurred to her that from the way that Julia was moving, she had a blind side. Her mechanical eye hadn't been reparable, at least in the short time they'd had with tools.

She made a mental note to have Carl do something about that if he could. That might not be possible, but she owed it to the other woman to try.

Moments later, Julia was in the tub, and Kelsey handed her the soap. The other woman took it gratefully and began lathering up.

"I saw you talking with Jebediah while we were helping the injured," Kelsey said. "He was listening to what you were saying, and I think you might've formed a connection with him. Tell me about it."

Her doppelgänger shrugged. "There's not much to say. He asked me how I could be so strong, and I explained how the computer had captured me and forcibly implanted the Marine Raider augmentation inside me.

"He said they already knew what Marine Raiders were, just based on tales told by the older generations. Since you and Talbot were busy showing off your own strength, I told him that you were the other members of our team that had augmentation. I stuck with the story that we were twins simply because it's a lot easier to understand than the truth."

"That works," Kelsey said as she started washing off. "You were looking out the other side of the building toward the horde city. What did you see?"

"It looked like there was fighting taking place, and Jebediah said that there was some type of power struggle to replace the leadership, so maybe they won't be looking for us for a while."

Kelsey smiled at that. She hated the horde as much as anyone, but she knew that Julia loathed them. There was a kind of bloodlust in her that Kelsey had never developed. It was somewhat worrying, but in this case, she thought it was understandable. Perhaps even laudable.

"What do you think the best course of action is that we can take to make friends with these people?" Kelsey asked as she began lathering her hair.

Julia shrugged and followed suit. "Be honest. The truth will serve us better than some story. Other than the fact that I'm you from another universe, the truth is the best story that we can tell."

"Then that's what we'll do," Kelsey said right before she ducked her head under the surface of the water.

Once her hair was thoroughly rinsed out, she climbed out of the tub, grabbed a rough towel from where they were stacked nearby, and wrapped it around her hair. In consideration of her doppelgänger's body modesty issues, she turned her back as she dried off with another towel. Then she dressed once more.

They'd have to see about getting their clothes washed. Hers smelled, and she felt dirty again almost immediately. Now that she'd cleaned up, she could smell her stink in the cloth. Perhaps they could get some clothes from their captors. She'd have to ask.

By the time she was done, Julia was out of the tub and drying off with her back turned.

Once they were both ready, Kelsey gestured toward the curtain. "Let's wake Jared and Talbot. They can clean up, and then we'll go see what our captors have to say. The sooner we start forming bonds with these people, the sooner we can be on our way to the Imperial Palace. And the sooner we can get off this damned planet."

8

J ared sat up when Kelsey woke him, rubbing his eyes. The bed that
he'd slept in wasn't anything to scream about by Imperial standards,
but it beat the hell out of the ground. The past week had certainly
taught him that.

Even with the thin cushions that they'd recovered from the horde,
sleeping on the ground was brutally hard on one's body, particularly when
their medical nanites were disabled.

He gratefully took advantage of the hot water to bathe and was
exceptionally pleased when Elise joined him. That made the bath take a
little more time than it should have, but they didn't hog it for unduly long, as
hanky-panky was out of the question. While rank had its privileges, he
didn't want to be standing between the rest and being clean for longer than
he had to.

Even though Kelsey had been urging them to get ready and go out and
meet their captors as soon as possible, Jared insisted that everyone get a
chance to bathe first. He didn't know exactly what his plans were going to
be, but he didn't want to be rushed into them.

Lily still hadn't returned. He wasn't shocked at that. With the sheer scale
of the carnage, it had to be like fighting the tide. He'd ask about her and
check in on her as well if he could.

His sister was smart enough to realize that she couldn't argue with him
on this subject just yet, so she sat beside her doppelgänger while the last of
them took baths, discussing the general parameters of their imprisonment.

They also talked about how the AI now knew about their presence and
undoubtedly suspected that they'd failed to deliver the Omega Plague that it
thought would eliminate humanity on Terra.

That was going to have long-term consequences, but he wasn't sure what they would be or when they would occur. It had taken years and a lot of money to secretly develop the virus. Lord Oscar Fielding—the man that had created the deadly pathogen—had claimed that he'd destroyed the actual research and tampered with the recipe that he'd given the AIs because he had no desire to see such a weapon spread beyond Terra.

Jared wasn't willing to give Fielding much credit, but he believed the man had no desire to die with the rest of humanity. That hadn't stopped the bastard from growing enough of the Omega Plague to kill the remaining population on Terra.

Once the rest of his people had bathed and dressed, he let Kelsey make her pitch.

"I think that we should form a small delegation to meet with Leader Mordechai," she said, moving her gaze evenly around the group. "Julia, Jared, Sean, and I would be a good start. We need to convince him of our sincerity about fighting the AIs. If we can do that, there's every chance that he'll not only let us go but provide us with valuable intelligence to help us get to the Imperial Palace."

Jared immediately shook his head. "I agree in principle, but I think you've picked the wrong people. They've seen how heavily modified you and Julia are. They're going to be distrustful of you and what you have to say. Admittedly, the rest of us are modified as well—except for Clarice—but I think that's going to give us a better chance to have an open and honest discussion.

"I think Elise and Olivia would be a better choice. They have the most experience as leaders in our group. I understand that you're not exactly lacking in that area, Kelsey, but I think you should focus your attention on Jebediah.

"He's going to be suspicious of everything we do, and I think you and Julia can help allay his fears. Sean and I could round out the delegation."

He looked around the rest of the group, and his eyes settled on Carl. "And that brings me to you, Carl. I think you, Ralph, and Austin would be an excellent delegation to see if any of the equipment in Frankfort can be repaired. I understand that you don't have much in the way of tools, but there must be a lot of things lying around inside this megacity that the inhabitants don't understand anymore. I'll bet you can rig up something to make their lives a little easier."

He paused for a moment to let all that sink in before continuing. When no one argued, he went on.

"The remainder of you get what rest you can and be prepared to assist any of the teams that need an extra hand or two. Our captors are exceptionally suspicious of us, and we're only going to get one chance to make a first impression."

"I agree with everything you've said, but I want to make one change," Kelsey said. "Julia has formed something of a bond with Jebediah. What you're saying about her talking to him makes absolute sense. But I'm the leader of the political side of this conversation, and I'm going to be going with you, Elise, and Olivia. Sean can help Julia. I think he'd bond well with Jebediah."

Jared considered that and slowly nodded. Her change wasn't that drastic, and he could live with her modification.

"Then we have a plan. Everyone be on your best behavior, and try not to get us all killed."

* * *

TALBOT DECIDED to include himself in the group that was going to see Jebediah. If, of course, the man was willing to let them out of their cells long enough to talk with him. Julia was the one leading the effort to have a conversation with him. They'd finally decided that Commodore Meyer, Commander Cannon, and himself should come along for the meeting.

Their captors had decided on an interesting way of providing security for them without endangering too many of their people. The rooms where they were being kept were isolated in a hallway with multiple heavy doors that one had to go through. Just outside the first set of doors was a pair of guards. This grouping was duplicated in each and every set of doors so that none of them could be taken out without the rest being aware of the attack.

Julia spoke briefly with the guards, and they passed the word to the next set of guards that she wanted to speak with Jebediah. Twenty minutes later, the man himself arrived to hear what she had to say.

"If you don't mind, I'd like to have a private conversation with you and a few of my people," she said. "We talked yesterday, but I feel as if we could expand on that and let you know more about ourselves and what we're trying to do."

The large man considered her for several seconds and then nodded. "My father is still uncertain whether we should believe what you've told us. Because of that, I'm inclined to agree.

"None of the other groups that we've captured have gotten this level of access, so you should feel honored that you're getting a chance to at least try to convince us that we should let you go. I want to caution you that that possibility is still unlikely, but it's not completely off the table at this point."

He gestured for her to follow him. "As you are probably ignorant of our way of life here in Frankfort, I feel as if I should give you a tour to show you what kind of society we have. Even though those who intrude here are not allowed to leave, we don't do anything like what the horde does to its prisoners."

Jebediah led them out of their prison suite, and fresh guards fell in all around them, staying at a distance to keep an eye on them without being in what they perceived to be danger themselves.

Talbot knew that they were underestimating the capabilities of Julia and himself. If they genuinely wanted to, the pair could reach the guards and disable them.

Since the guards weren't using projectile weapons, they risked getting cut in that fight, but there was no real doubt that they could disarm or kill all of the guards in just a few seconds with their bare hands.

Not that they'd ever dream of doing that. They already had one large group of bloodthirsty warriors itching to torture them before setting them on fire. Having a second group on the warpath would be suicide.

No, convincing these people that they could be decent allies was a much smarter play. Not that it would be easy, he suspected.

Rather than going up, Jebediah led them to a broad set of stairs that descended even farther under the city. Before they'd come down to join Admiral Mertz, he and Kelsey had wondered how far underground a megacity might have extended before the AIs suppressed all civilization on Terra. He suspected it was very deep indeed.

He doubted that would protect from something like a kinetic strike, but the illusion of security allowed people to live what life they could with some joy, so perhaps it was worth it.

Talbot's guess was proven correct when they continued on for quite some time. So deep, in fact, that they had to switch stairwells to continue down. With his implants back online, he could tell pretty well how far down they'd come. The level they exited on wasn't the lowest that the stairs could reach.

"I see that the stairs keep going down," Talbot said, giving in to his curiosity. "Is there more below us, or are we near the bottom?"

The large man smiled back at him. "Frankfort wasn't the largest megacity, but it was fully developed. We aren't in the lowest reaches of the underground tunnels. Those go so far down that the air is tainted, and no one can venture there. The explored portions that we've reached go down at least as far as we've already come."

That was a long way down, Talbot had to admit. Depending on what was down there, the air could have been tainted with any number of things once life support failed. It might be a naturally occurring gas coming through cracks in the walls. Methane perhaps. Or it could be some industrial chemical from work being done deep underground that had leaked out of its storage containers after the power went out.

Going everywhere with torches provided its own form of air pollution. The smoke made Talbot's nose itch and occasionally made him cough. The ceilings were coated with soot from generations of people that had used torches to light their way.

It was also possible that the use of so many torches had depleted the oxygen deep below. Not a pretty way to go.

Thankfully, that wasn't his problem.

"If you don't mind my asking, without any power, how is it that the air down here is still any good?" Julia asked. "After all this time, the air should be bad, shouldn't it?"

Their captor gave her a slight smile and a nod. "There's some truth to what you say, but we're in the right place for me to give you an example of why that situation isn't occurring."

With that, he stopped at a large double doorway with two guards posted outside it. The two men opened the doors for the party. Talbot stopped in his tracks as soon as he made it inside.

The large room in front of them certainly appeared to have formerly been used for life support. The massive air circulation machines were an obvious clue to that. Their original intent must've been to pull air from the surface and move it around the underground portions of the city.

A large wooden structure had been built around the circulators, and about forty people were sitting on what looked like exercise equipment, peddling gears set at the level of their feet. He wasn't sure what they were supposed to be doing, but it obviously served a purpose.

Julia scrunched up her face in disapproval. "Those people are peddling to drive gears inside the equipment, probably to rotate fans and pull fresh air down into this area, right?"

Jebediah gave her an approving glance and nodded. "The process also circulates the air to areas that we use on this level and above. The people you see driving the air equipment are primarily citizens of the city, but some of them are prisoners. They don't work any longer hours than our own people do. If you want to steal from us, then you can deal with the consequences."

He gave them all a stern look. "Unless you can convince us that you can grant us some benefit that outweighs the crimes you have committed against us by intruding into our privacy, work like this is the fate that awaits you. I suggest that you be convincing. My father is not one to take intrusion lightly, and neither am I."

Julia smiled at the man and nodded. "I think that we can come to some kind of arrangement once we convince you of our sincerity. Is there a place where we can sit down and have a frank discussion?"

The large man gestured for them to continue on into the industrial space. "There is a conference room attached to the offices just across this room. I believe it will suit our needs."

Talbot saw the doors to which the man gestured and started walking that way. He really hoped that Julia was better at talking her way through problems than Kelsey was. Fighting wasn't going to save them this time. They had to solve their problems with reason.

Not that his wife was unreasonable, just impulsive. For his love, far too many problems looked like nails, so her solution ended up being a hammer.

Or, as could be said after she'd made him watch an old entertainment vid called *The Fifth Element*, she negotiated like Korben Dallas.

The vid had proven far more humorous than she'd intended, and for entirely different reasons. Talbot had taken great pleasure in pointing out all the similarities between her and Dallas.

Her sudden consternation seemed genuine, so she probably hadn't even considered that aspect of the vid. His high point of the evening was telling her she was a pint-sized Bruce Willis.

After that, they'd watched *Die Hard*, which had proven his assertion decisively, much to his wife's annoyance.

Unable to help himself, Talbot grinned at the large man and Julia as they came in behind him. This should be... interesting.

9

Kelsey walked up the stairs slowly, since not everyone had her stamina for climbing what seemed like an endless number of steps. Now that her Marine Raider augmentation was back online, she could do this all day. And she meant that quite literally.

Her artificial muscles took up the majority of the strain, while her medical nanites kept her biological muscles working at peak efficiency. As long as she wasn't pushing things, everyday activities like this could be continued until she ran out of steam and had to eat.

The same wasn't true of Jared, Elise, Olivia, or Clarice Beauchamp. Hell, it wasn't even true of the guards that were trying to look tough as they escorted the prisoners up to meet their leader.

Their captors tried to put on a good show, but Kelsey could tell they were exhausted by the time they reached the tip of the spire high above the dead megacity.

With her implants active again, she could keep track of little details, like how many levels they'd passed and how high off the ground they were, but after a certain point, that just became a matter of keeping score.

Yes, this building was significantly smaller than the one that had dominated Imperial City, but it still rose more than three hundred levels from the surface and had a dominating view of the landscape around them.

When the guards escorted them into the single large room that filled the spire of the building, she could tell at a glance that it was once a restaurant of some kind. Many of the tables were still stacked by what was obviously a door to the kitchen.

Interestingly, the kitchen was situated in the center of the room right next to the stairwell and defunct lifts. The exterior of the room was one large circle with a panoramic view of Frankfort. Even from the center of the room, it was breathtaking.

The windows here had suffered just as severely as in the large room they'd been in yesterday. All the glass was gone. The gusts felt even stronger than in the level below, and Kelsey could strongly smell wood burning. That probably came from the horde city.

It was also chilly, even now during the summer. She imagined that this kind of wind would kill in the winter.

Someone had obviously taken the time to sweep the debris off the floor and to break out the rough shards that had remained in the frames. They'd also rigged up a makeshift rail along the outer edge of the room to keep anyone from getting too close to a lethal fall.

The winds might just snatch the unwary off their feet and send them out into the void. That included her, so she'd be cautious and keep an eye on her friends.

Seemingly unconcerned about all of that, Leader Mordechai stood beside the railing, gazing out at the horde city. From her current vantage point, she could see a good number of smoke plumes, so the blazes were severe.

At their arrival, Mordechai half turned and gestured for them to join him. They all did so, moving carefully.

"Thank you for taking the time to meet with us, Leader Mordechai," she said as she stepped up beside him, grasped the rail firmly, and got a better view of the horde capital.

The fires were worse than she'd expected. At a guess, maybe a fifth of the city had already been consumed by flames and was now just a smoldering pile of rubble. The active fires seemed to be burning out of control amongst the poorer sections of the city, where most of the construction was of wood.

Even the buildings made of a mixture of wood and stone seemed to be suffering. Whatever they had for a fire brigade was obviously overwhelmed and unable to deal with the scale of devastation they were experiencing.

Under other circumstances, she'd have felt sorry for those killed or rendered homeless by the flames. She didn't, though. Those people had killed almost three hundred of her people and their allies.

While specific individuals below might be innocent of wrongdoing, collateral damage was a sad fact of war, and that's what this was. She'd used the weapons she'd had at hand to escape their captivity before they could torture and murder her and her friends.

No, she had no sympathy for them at all.

"While my knees don't appreciate the climb to get here, I don't begrudge you your meeting," the older man said. "I realize that I could've done so in my offices below, but I do so love the view from up here. It's also good exercise to climb those stairs every day and overlook the city of my ancestors.

"I mean that quite literally, by the way. I can trace my lineage back to the Imperial mayor that ruled Frankfort at the time the computers crushed Terra a century ago. Even before then, our family controlled the city in the name of the emperor for generations, though I couldn't tell you precisely how many."

He turned and gazed toward her, his expression serious. "Like those that have come before me, I take my responsibilities to this city and its people very seriously. The rule until this time has been that any who dare intrude are never allowed to leave.

"Another rule is that those who work for the computers are to be executed. I must determine if you fall into that latter category. I will tell you now that I'm of two minds on the matter. Yet I will not rush to a decision. I will give you a chance to convince me of your honesty and expand upon why you've come to Terra.

"If I decide that you're telling the truth and that it serves our interests in assisting you, I'll not only allow you to depart in peace, but I'll do what I can to assist you in your task.

"That doesn't mean that it will be easy to convince me. My son and I have discussed this, and we believe that the only way to determine your mettle is to put you under pressure.

"So there will be some tasks that we want you to complete. Tasks that only someone with your evident technological skills could manage. They will not be easy, and they may yet prove impossible. Yet how you proceed with them will tell us much about you. I suppose you could consider them quests, just like in the old stories."

Part of her was excited to hear this, but the cost of failure could be drastic, so she was wary of being too pleased. "What kind of work are we talking about?"

"It's my understanding that you have three individuals with high technological skills. Is this correct?"

Kelsey nodded. "We have one man who is a specialist with hardware, another who is a specialist with software and computers, and a third who is brilliant at making breakthroughs in all of the above and more.

"I have to warn you though, we don't have a lot of tools with us. Only what we could recover before we had to flee the horde city. I'm not certain what you have in mind, but without the correct equipment, it might be impossible."

Mordechai smiled thinly. "We shall see. I will send guards to summon your remaining people to a meeting that Jebediah is already holding underneath the city. It's best if I gather you all together before I tell you what I have in mind. My apologies, but that will be quite far under the city, so you have more exercise ahead."

Kelsey almost smiled at how her companions' expressions fell. Now, after having climbed all those stairs, they'd have to go right back down and then even deeper under the city. She wondered if that was some kind of test as well.

"Whatever your tasks, we'll do the best we can," she said with all the assurance she could muster. "You have my word on that."

They really would give it their best effort. This was the one chance they had to leave Frankfort peacefully. If they failed, they'd have to fight their way out against a foe that knew the ground a lot better than they did. She'd like to avoid that if at all possible.

* * *

CARL SAT in the large room with his associates. He'd known Ralph Halstead since Kelsey had captured the man and his parents during an operation inside the Rebel Empire. Unlike the man's aunt, Ralph had passed the test given to him by Fiona, the newly constructed AI they had aboard *Persephone*.

He'd been working with his aunt, spying inside an Imperial research facility that Kelsey had raided. Carl had to admit that running into someone else stealing from the Rebel Empire while they'd been doing the same thing had been unexpected. Circumstances had demanded that they take Ralph, his aunt, and her husband with them when they left.

They'd turned Ralph's aunt and uncle over to the resistance. Not that he expected that they would deal harshly with them. They'd only been engaged in industrial espionage against the Rebel Empire, something the rebellion probably approved of.

But those people were better positioned to keep an eye on the aunt. She was wily. If it was worth money, she'd try to sell it, so maybe mercenary was a better word.

Ralph, on the other hand, had jumped at the chance to go with Kelsey and the rest on their mission to Terra. He'd passed multiple loyalty tests since then and was seemingly becoming well integrated with the science teams.

Carl was glad he'd survived the horde massacre. There'd been an inordinate number of research personnel on the mission because they'd expected to explore the Imperial Palace. All of them were now dead. It tore at his heart. Deep down, he wanted some payback, but he just wasn't sure how he could manage to get any.

In any case, Ralph was a hacker. While Carl could claim to know a lot about computers and programming, he was wise enough to admit that Ralph was his master in that arena. His friend had grown up inside the Rebel Empire and had learned from masters in the field at cracking and hacking into Imperial technology via software. Then he'd practiced that art for most of his life.

That put him almost completely at odds with Carl's other new friend, Austin Darrah. Unlike the lowly born Ralph, Austin had been a member of what the Rebel Empire called the higher orders. Their version of the nobility. His family meant something inside the upper strata of the Rebel Empire.

Not that that had interested Austin in the slightest. He'd found himself drawn to understanding how mechanical items worked due to the influence of his uncle when he was young. Oscar Fielding had owned and controlled a shipyard supplying the Rebel Empire version of Fleet and various civilian interests.

Sadly for Austin, his expertise in working with virtually every kind of Imperial hardware meant that he'd been forced onto the mission that was supposed to deliver a lethal virus to Terra: the Omega Plague.

Even worse from Austin's perspective, his uncle was neck deep in the project. He'd not only overseen the teams that had developed the weapon, but he'd also been the one that had sicced the AIs into pressganging his nephew.

The older man sounded like a real ass to Carl. He was glad that he hadn't had to meet the bastard. It amused the hell out of them that Admiral Mertz had found a way to maroon Fielding without a good chunk of his money after the guy had double-crossed the AIs and tried to do the same to the admiral and his crew.

So Carl now had both a software expert and a master of hardware. Combined with his own flair for working with Imperial tech, he felt confident that the three of them could do just about anything when it came to Old Empire machinery.

And that was what probably brought them to this meeting. He'd expected their captors to keep them in the quarters assigned to them, but they'd been led deep under the ground beneath Frankfort.

The group that had gone with Julia had already had some kind of meeting with Jebediah, the son of the ruler of this ruined megacity. They had joined them.

Considering the hodgepodge of work that was being done with the air-handling system just outside this meeting room, Carl was confident that they'd be tasked with doing something to improve the efficiency of moving the air.

Not that the man was talking about the work that he wanted them to do just yet. He seemed to be waiting for something.

A minute later, Carl figured out what the holdup was when Kelsey, the admiral, and the rest of their people walked into the room. Everyone except Doctor Stone, who was likely still struggling to save lives.

Along with the last group came another bunch of guards and Leader Mordechai, the ruler of this city. It looked as if this was going to be it. Whatever was going to happen, they were going to find out about it now.

Part of him almost didn't want to know. It seemed like the last week had been filled with tragedy following disaster. Almost nothing had gone right for them. In fact, it was hard to imagine how things could've gone *worse*, other than them all dying in the process.

Once everyone was seated, Mordechai joined his son at the head of the table. The overhead panels were dead, so the room was lit with oil-filled lamps. Those had a peculiar smell that wasn't wholly unpleasant, but it certainly wasn't something Carl would have sought out.

"I'm sure you're wondering why I've brought you all together again," Mordechai said solemnly. "As I told Kelsey Bandar and Admiral Mertz, my mind is not yet made up about your sincerity and truthfulness. I've decided that a test is in order. Perhaps the first of several. I'm told that some of you have particular gifts with mechanical items and old technology."

As he said that, he looked right at Carl. Not sure what to do, Carl decided to respond directly. He rose to his feet and softly cleared his throat as he put his hands behind his back.

"Yes, sir. Two of my associates and I have the skills you're talking about. What kind of task did you have in mind? Something to improve the air handlers outside the room?"

"No. Something significantly more dangerous. Deep beneath the city, at levels that have not been accessed in almost a hundred years, lies the fusion plant that once powered Frankfort."

The older man smiled slightly when Carl blinked in surprise. "Oh yes, I know what a fusion plant is, at least in general terms. My father saw to my education when it came to Imperial technology and how the city used to work. The diaries kept by my ancestors have much information about what equipment worked and what didn't, as well as how such items could be maintained in a general sense.

"The fusion plant was shut down before the AI struck. The level of resistance against the computer's occupation had reached a plateau that the Imperial mayor felt would invite retaliation. So when the number of ships orbiting around Terra began to rise precipitously, she decided that lowering Frankfort on the list of potential targets would be wise."

His expression grew dark. "My great-grandmother was a brilliant woman. I knew her briefly as a child before she passed. According to the words she wrote in the leaders' diary, the fusion plant was shut down in good order, and they had even incorporated shielding to keep it from being detectable from above ground. What I want you to do is venture deep, deep under Frankfort and bring it back to life."

Carl grimaced. That wasn't going to be an easy task, particularly with only the equipment he had available. He couldn't trust that anything down there still worked. Imperial technology was very long-lived, but components failed, and a century was a long time.

Still, it wasn't exactly as if they had a choice in the matter. If he and his friends wanted to earn their freedom, he'd have to find a way to make this work.

"I'll do my best, but I can't promise success," Carl said. "I'm going to have to look at what's down there. Even getting to the fusion plant is going to be tricky, because the air is probably foul. I'm not exactly sure how we can protect ourselves."

The older man smiled thinly. "If it were easy, it wouldn't be a suitable quest. I'll grant you access to all of the equipment that we have. Perhaps something among it will allow you to construct some type of protection.

"But make no mistake: your success will reflect upon your compatriots. As will your failure, should success elude you. I would suggest that you do your absolute best."

Yeah. No pressure at all.

10

J ulia stared at their captor. "Are you crazy? The AI can sense that kind of thing. I don't care what kind of shielding you have. If you reactivate it, lights all over the city are going to come back on, and *somebody's* going to notice. Hell, *everybody* is going to notice! The least bad thing that will happen is that the horde is going to come looking for what's going on."

Mordechai nodded. "That's certainly a possibility, but I'm counting on your people being knowledgeable enough to disconnect all of the power lines into the city itself until you can figure out which ones can be energized safely. That is within your control, is it not, Mister Owlet?"

"If we can get the system operational, we can certainly isolate it," Carl agreed. "If it has shielding like you say, then it probably won't be detectible on the surface, much less in orbit. So long as there are no visible indications above ground that power is back on, no one should be any wiser.

"The problem is going to come in when you decided that you want something specific powered up. Even if the equipment is operational—which is not guaranteed—then you're going to run into the problem of there being other things on that circuit.

"There are far too many connections through the power linkages in the city to be certain of turning everything off if you want to energize power to the basement of this building, for example. It's just not going to be that easy.

"It will take a lot of work to be absolutely certain that everything on a line is disconnected. Then rechecking it, probably with a separate set of people to bring fresh eyes to the work. And, considering the risk, probably a third group. It'll be time consuming and dangerous."

"And that's only the beginning," Julia added, already thinking of other potential problems. "What about the danger down there? You're talking about going into an area where the atmosphere is going to be full of carbon dioxide and perhaps other chemicals that were released once the power went off.

"It's not exactly like you have access to vacuum suits, Carl. How do you intend to stay alive long enough to even reach the fusion plant? Putting that aside, let's say that you do. How are you going to be able to stay there long enough to do any work?"

"I have a few ideas on that," Carl admitted. "If we search the area around us on this level, I'll bet we find some emergency lockers that have air bottles. Many of them are still going to be charged, at least to a degree. We'll have to make certain the equipment still works, and it's going to be something of a gamble, but I think that problem can be solved.

"Once we get the fusion plant back online, I feel pretty confident that we can at least set up some of the life support down below to get the toxic elements cleaned out of the air. The scrubbers should still be intact, even after all this time. The components aren't meant to break down over time to the point that they degrade past their useful operational life."

Julia wasn't convinced, and she was pretty sure that her expression conveyed that. Not that her opinion was likely to deter the pigheaded scientist.

"I can't stop you from going, but I think it's too dangerous. Is it really worth the risk?"

Mordechai raised an eyebrow. "Is your potential freedom worth the risk? Because I can assure you that without completing this task, you will not leave this city.

"And before you start to think that your enhanced physical attributes are going to make a difference in that, we have areas that we can isolate the three of you that have that capability and be certain that you won't escape. I'd rather not do that, but if you choose to be recalcitrant, then I won't have a choice."

Julia threw up her hands. "Of course you do! You're making the active choice to force us to do this work in exchange for our freedom. We haven't done anything other than trespass on your property.

"We had no choice in where we went when we escaped the horde city. You have every option in how you react to our presence and in how you help or hinder us in our actions against the AI.

"If we do this, you let us go. No other little tasks you want us to do. Once and done. Then we're friends, not intruders."

Almost everyone around her was aghast at how she'd confronted Mordechai. It was a risk but one that needed to be taken. If they just did everything he said, they'd never be free of the old man. No, there had to be a line drawn in the sand.

If her words disturbed Leader Mordechai, he didn't show it. He only smiled at her response.

"I suppose it's good to have limits on one's behavior. Now that we've settled what the limits are on what we'll each tolerate, I suggest that we get back to the problem at hand. My city will only have this one opportunity to take a quantum leap toward getting its old technology functional again.

"You don't understand what it's like living next to the horde city. Those people are monsters in human form. If you think we're xenophobic, then you don't know them very well. We don't wantonly torture or kill.

"I needed to make clear to you that armed resistance would have severe repercussions so that you wouldn't feel the desire to try to use your greater strength to try and overpower us. Our two groups *can* work together to achieve something that neither alone could do. Perhaps you haven't considered the options thoroughly.

"If power can be restored to Frankfort, that means that power can be used to reenergize the old trains that once carried people and cargo from city to city. Traveling over the surface to escape the area is asking to be chased down and murdered by the horde. What if you could just climb aboard a train and take it all the way to your destination?

"I don't know for a fact that the tunnels lead directly to the Imperial Palace, but the old stories certainly talk about them reaching Imperial City. Even though that wondrous place no longer exists, I'd wager that coming out of the ground near Imperial City would put you within striking distance of the Imperial Palace. Wouldn't you agree?"

That was certainly something to think about. Julia raised an eyebrow at Carl, who shrugged. He wasn't saying that it could be done, but he wasn't rejecting the idea out of hand. That meant that it was a possibility that they could cut the trip that would've taken them half a year down to a day, or perhaps even a few hours. That would certainly be better than walking the entire distance and fighting whoever they interacted with.

Still, even if they *could* restore one of the trains to functionality, the tunnel might be blocked, or the train might run out of power partway. Would the air inside the tunnels be toxic? She had no idea.

But she supposed that it was worth examining in greater detail, and that meant that they had to have power in order to check out the systems on the trains themselves.

"I think we can probably stop throwing threats around at one another," Mertz said, cutting into the conversation. "You're right that that would help us greatly in our mission, so we're going to help you get your fusion plant back online, so long as it's not going to draw the attention of the AI.

"That's one thing we have to avoid at all costs, particularly now that it knows we're down here. That kinetic strike destroyed our pinnaces, but you can bet that it's examining the general area with whatever resources it can bring to bear. It's going to look at this city and at the horde city, too.

"If it thinks we're here, it might be inclined to drop another kinetic strike on Frankfort just to be sure. That would be the death of all of your people, and we've got to avoid that. Right now, it can't be sure. We've got to keep it that way."

Mordechai opened his mouth to respond, but the door opened abruptly. One of the guards stepped into the room and bowed slightly. "Leader

Mordechai, something is happening at the horde city. It looks like a number of their warriors are exiting their walls and heading toward Frankfort."

The older man stood. "It looks as if some of our options have just been taken off the table. The horde must believe that you have fled to our city. You've definitely kicked over the anthill, and now they seem determined to sting you. I will allow that the kinetic strike may have also played a role in uniting them.

"They will regret that decision quite soon, but even though they're monsters, they're canny fighters. The defense of Frankfort is going to be important. I ask that you contribute your three trained fighters to my forces.

"If you would like to use your enhancements to your benefit, now would be the time to do so. If we don't stop them, not only are you again at risk of death, but you can rest assured that they'll never let you escape the area and complete your mission."

Mertz nodded grimly. "Talbot, you and Lieutenant Laird will assist with the scouting and in any other way that the local forces request. You actually have full military training, so it makes more sense for you to be on the sharp end of the stick."

He turned toward Julia. "You have the ability, but no training. I'd prefer that you help Carl. His work is going to be important, and your augmentation could save him if something goes wrong."

Mertz turned toward Leader Mordechai. "Kelsey has skill with swords and her augmentation. She could directly join your defenses. I'd like to request that the three that will be fighting be returned their weapons.

"I understand that you're concerned about whether or not we're going to stay under your control, so I'm not asking that the rest of us be rearmed."

The older man nodded at once. "I agree. The remainder of you can stay down here. There are additional quarters available that we can station guards at, but the odds of the enemy incursion reaching this level are small.

"You can assist your technical people in preparing for their mission. If I understand what they need correctly, they'll want to search for specialized equipment that might be refurbished. We can send individuals to escort you, so your time will not be wasted."

Julia wasn't sure how she felt about being kept out of the fighting. She knew that she didn't have the skills that Kelsey had, and so part of her was grateful that she wouldn't be directly involved.

The other part of her was still filled with rage and wanted to kill as many of the horde warriors as possible. That part of her was severely disappointed.

It was difficult to balance those emotions, so she didn't even try. If the incursion was as strong as they'd indicated, she'd get her chance to spill the enemy's blood at some point. She'd never be able to kill enough of them to pay them back for what they'd done, but she sure hoped that she had the opportunity to try.

For now, she had to focus on helping Carl do what he needed to do to earn their freedom. No matter how dangerous and foolhardy that turned out to be.

* * *

WHEN THEIR CAPTORS returned his weapons, Talbot accepted them gratefully. He really wished that he had something more modern, considering that the horde just never seems to stop coming, but he'd take what he could get.

Arming them showed a promising level of trust. He hoped Kelsey and Admiral Mertz could transition that into something more solid once this little problem was dealt with.

Talbot had used "little problem" intentionally, minimizing what he knew was going to be a significant incursion. If the horde felt it necessary to enter a place like the abandoned megacity, there would be a lot of them. This place's reputation demanded they use as many warriors as they could lay hands on.

Talbot wondered what that meant for the power struggle inside the horde city. After Kelsey had destroyed their palace and probably killed most of their leadership, there'd been fires scattered throughout the city and signs of fighting. They'd seen that from the towers. That had probably meant different groups had been vying for control of the horde and literally killing off the competition.

The fact that the horde was now invading Frankfort meant they'd almost certainly settled that particular struggle. Someone was in charge now, and he had blood in his eye.

Talbot's group consisted of Chloe and two guards, a man and a woman. The man identified himself as Richard and the woman as Lydia. No last names were given. Based on how well the two worked together, he suspected they were a couple.

The four of them entered a ruined building that was maybe a quarter of the size of the large tower they'd been in before. It was still a significant structure, but it was nowhere near the league of the big boys.

What it did possess was an unobstructed view down a broad boulevard that had once been a major thoroughfare in the city. Talbot could imagine the wide gap filled with grav cars moving in regimented order through the sky between the buildings as people went about their daily lives or walked through the gardens that once filled the ground level.

That sort of thing was still relatively new on Avalon, but he'd seen recordings of Imperial City, and it was truly mind-boggling. Imperial City had once housed over a billion people. Frankfort was much smaller but still far more extensive than anything on Avalon.

The four of them went up the stairs and only stopped when they reached the fiftieth floor. They were maybe halfway to the top of the structure. The door to the stairwell led them into what had once been a wide corridor, but the walls had decayed, giving occasional glimpses into the rooms beyond.

Their guards led them to windows, where they could see down the boulevard. These, like many others in the city, had been shattered by the nearby kinetic strike. Thankfully, there'd been no rain since the event, so there were only the glass fragments on a dry floor to deal with. Slipping in this could be very bad.

A quick search found an ancient broom that they could use to clean the small area where they'd be lying low and watching for the enemy. Once all four of them were stretched out on the floor, Talbot glanced at Richard and Lydia.

"What are we expecting? We're going to have a decent view of them coming, but we're so high off the ground that we're not going to be useful against them."

"With only four of us, that's probably a good thing, don't you think?" Lydia asked. "All we're doing is gathering information. You may not have seen it, but there's a mechanical telephone back at the stairwell.

"Basically, it's run by batteries that we charge via solar power and capable of sending short-range transmissions down a hard line that we've run underground. When we do, the leadership will decide where our major forces will strike. We're their eyes."

"What we need to do is give our leaders some decent information," Richard said in agreement. "The horde usually sends about thirty or forty people when they want to scavenge. That's not a problem if we can ambush them in a worthwhile manner.

"Even so, horde warriors make terrible prisoners. Most of them would rather die fighting than surrender. Even those we do capture alive will do their damnedest to force us to kill them. Frankly, it's better for everyone if we just end them in an overwhelming ambush.

"This is going to be a very different kind of fight. They're coming in force, and that means there's going to be hundreds of them in any group. Maybe thousands. We have plans in place to deal with a full invasion, but we've never had to execute them. What did you people do to piss them off?"

Talbot shrugged slightly. "As part of our escape, we brought the roof down on their treasure vault, and their castle collapsed with it. So not only did they lose all the treasures they had stored down there, but they lost their honchos.

"Based on the look I got at the city earlier, they were having some kind of succession war. Now that they've settled it, they've obviously decided that we came here, and they want to get us. I'm kind of surprised that you haven't at least considered handing us over to them to make this problem go away."

The man gave him a shrug in return. "Leader Mordechai doesn't cooperate with intruders. Well, until your arrival, at least. He'll never give in to the horde, though."

"I see something," Chloe said. She'd kept her focus on the ground below.

Talbot used his optic augmentation to zoom into the area she was watching. There were indeed a bunch of warriors creeping through the open ground between trees and high grass that had grown up over the century since the AI had suppressed Terra.

It was hard to get a firm count when you couldn't see the enemy clearly, but he suspected he was looking at a minimum of forty people moving through the foliage. They'd just entered the boulevard and were quite a distance away. He passed that information on to their guards.

The two guards seemed impressed. From this range, they probably couldn't see the enemy at all, much less count them. He was surprised that Chloe had seen anything. She didn't have any ocular augmentation, so she must've had truly excellent vision.

He was about to say something along those lines when the movement at the end of the boulevard increased significantly. It seemed that those forty were scouting for a larger force, and soon the number of people moving through the foliage left little doubt that there were hundreds of horde warriors down there.

When they finally broke into sight, Talbot saw that none of them were mounted. These were infantry. They had bows out, swords at their hips, and were moving in a well-drilled formation. They looked as if they were expecting an ambush.

He supposed being evil bastards didn't mean they had to be incompetent or cowardly. Pity.

Talbot passed that information along, and Lydia excused herself to go report. He turned his attention to Richard.

"How are you going to handle that many people? Do you have a large enough force to attack something like that?"

The man smiled grimly. "Just because we've lost the old technology doesn't mean we're helpless. We have a few tricks up our sleeves that will hurt them.

"My concern is that this isn't their only incursion. If they're really coming in force, they'll have sent every warrior they could muster. Many of the people that became the horde were expelled from Frankfort because they weren't suitable to have as neighbors.

"They've long wished to regain what they believe we stole from them. We've been preparing for this day for many years. We won't lose this fight."

Talbot certainly hoped the man was right because if the city fell, they were in real trouble. They'd never escape overland now that they'd stirred the hornets' nest. Their only hope of survival was getting the fusion plant online and taking a train toward the water-filled crater where Imperial City once stood.

Based on the information he had in his implants, there would probably be a station within a hundred kilometers of the Imperial Palace if there wasn't a trunk line that would take them most of the way to their ultimate destination. Supplies had obviously needed to get to the palace, and not all of them would come in via grav car.

Of course, none of those plans would mean anything unless they survived this fight.

Talbot didn't know what the city's defense plans were, but he vowed to make sure they succeeded. With the capabilities that his Marine Raider implants and augmentation gave him in a fight like this, he might be able to make a real difference.

He only hoped that Kelsey would be okay in the brewing fight. If she fell, it would be like he'd been killed, too.

11

Jared opened a metal door set into the wall of the passage. Its faded markings identified it as containing emergency supplies. If it was like the others he'd seen today, it wouldn't have been disturbed in the last century.

They held basic medical kits, air bottles, face masks that covered the nose and mouth, and other emergency gear that might be required in an area where industrial equipment was in operation.

The priority for him was air, though he did take the medical supplies as well since he figured that Lily was going to need as much help as she could get once the fighting actually started.

She had a full kit, but if they had hundreds of casualties, that would use up the supplies they had on hand almost immediately. The Imperial medical establishment had made supplies that would last for decades, and even though these were far beyond their expiration dates, many of them were still useful to her.

The air bottles were more problematic. Some still claimed they had a full charge, but most had lost some or all of their contents over the intervening years. Probably one tenth of the ones that Jared had found had a full charge. Of the rest, maybe thirty percent had anywhere from twenty-five percent to seventy-five percent. The remainder were empty or only held a fraction of a charge.

They'd have to test the equipment to make sure that it worked before they relied on it to keep someone safe. If anyone could determine how functional this gear was, it was Carl and Austin. Between the two of them, they understood the mechanical side of Old Empire tech very well.

Jared had found a wheeled cart that he was using to hold his haul. It was just about full, so he turned back the way he'd come.

He hoped the others had found more bottles because even those that were rated as full would only last for fifteen to twenty minutes, and if multiple people were going to work down below, they'd need a lot of them.

Since there'd be four people going down—Carl, Austin, Ralph, and Julia —they'd need four times the air. Thankfully, Julia could haul quite a bit, though he doubted that she'd enjoy being the group's pack mule.

Carl and the others in the technical squad were busy testing bottles and masks when he arrived back in the air handler room. They were making notations on each cylinder with different colored markers. He noted that perhaps half of what had been brought back was simply thrown into a bin. Their lack of care with them meant that the discards weren't going to be useful.

"All right, I've got my first load," he said as he pushed his cart up to them and started unloading it. "How's it looking?"

Carl glanced over as he tossed another bottle into the disposal bin. "The gauges are unreliable. Basically, if it says its below fifty percent, it's probably useless. If it says that it's around seventy-five percent, it's probably going to have maybe ten minutes' worth of air. If it says it's full, fifteen minutes is all that we can count on.

"The gauges weren't designed for this type of long-term use, and they've failed in a linear fashion. At least that allows us to make some estimates by looking at the indicators."

Jared looked over the stack of supposedly full bottles. There weren't that many of them.

"How long are you expecting to need to be down there?"

Carl shrugged. "Until we get there, I can't make any guesses. If the shielding is actually in place, we may only need to service the reactor before bringing it online. I don't want to commit to that without seeing things, though.

"I think this first trip is going to be an exploratory one. We'll just make it down to where the fusion plant is, make an assessment, run diagnostics if possible, and then return to this level to work out a battle plan.

"There are a lot of air bottles being brought in, and in a city this size, I suspect we're going to have more than enough. It's just going to take time to gather them.

"Right now, you're only bringing in the ones closest to the air handler room. To get more, we're going to have to move farther out, and that's going to take additional time and effort."

Jared thought about that and nodded reluctantly. "I can shepherd the search for more air. How long until you've got enough for the four of you to start down and make an assessment?"

Carl considered that for a moment. "I think we'll have enough in about an hour. We won't really know until we see how far it is to the fusion plant and what the obstacles are. We're going into this with a decent margin for error. If we use forty percent and we're not at the target, we're going to turn around and start back up."

"That's a good idea," Jared said. "I want all of you to be *very* careful. Not only are you irreplaceable as friends, but you're also the only technical support we're going to have when we get to the Imperial Palace. You're doubly important, and I don't want you to take any unnecessary chances. If you run into trouble, abort the mission and come back up. I'll deal with our captors if it comes to that."

Carl looked over at the guards. "I sure hope you're right about that because they seem determined to get the fusion plant online."

Jared considered the armed men watching them and nodded. "They are, but diplomacy is the art of the possible. We have to give this everything we have because that's the simplest way to get us out of the city and on our way. If the fusion plant is functional, then we can start looking at the trains and make an assessment of how far they can get us. All I'm saying is to do the best you can and be careful."

With that, Jared grabbed his now-empty cart and started back to get some more supplies. He really did hope this plan worked, because the horde would never let them ride away. Their only chance of escape was underground.

If Carl failed to get the fusion plant online, they might very well be trapped here for the rest of their lives. However short a time that might be.

* * *

THE RALLY POINT for the defensive forces was a large room at the base of one of the massive towers toward the center of the city. Kelsey thought it might once have been an indoor sports arena, based on the movable stadium seating.

The gathering included more people than she'd expected. Her implants calculated that there were probably seven hundred and fifty defenders gathered in the vast space.

She had no idea what the population of the dead megacity was, but if this was their defensive force, then the overall population had to be lower than she'd anticipated. Of course, there could be other gatherings. She had no way of knowing.

As far as the armament that they had available, they had the usual primitive weaponry that was commonplace in these days without technology, but that wasn't all.

Arrayed against the rolled-back seating were tables holding a sampling of intriguing weapons. Some held what looked like grenades. Others held primitive firearms, similar to those used in the prespaceflight wars on Terra: pistols, short rifles, and long-barreled weapons. Even what might be simple rocket launchers. In all, a respectable arsenal.

Kelsey wished she had more time to examine them, but a short woman with gray hair motioned for everyone to gather around her. The woman didn't bother introducing herself, which made sense since everyone beside Kelsey probably knew who she was.

"We're going to go with defense plan Charlie," the woman said with no preamble. "We'll fan out to meet the incoming groups at the designated ambush zones for their path of advance. If we can push them back, fine. If not, we fall back and strike them again at the secondary locations."

The woman turned in a slow circle to examine everyone as they absorbed her words. There was far less murmuring than Kelsey had expected. These people knew what they were about. That boded well for them all.

"Our goal is to bleed them," the woman continued. "If we inflict enough casualties, they'll retreat. At least that's the theory. If it doesn't work out that way, we may end up fighting hand to hand. In that case, reducing their numbers is going to be critical because they'll outnumber us badly if we don't.

"I don't have to tell you how important this is. If we want to keep our families and friends safe, we have to stand between them and the horde. I expect everyone to give this everything they have. Group leaders, take command of your forces and fight like hell. Dismissed."

A thin man with fringes of reddish hair around the base of his bald skull gestured for Kelsey to join him. It looked like a hundred people or so were gathered under his metaphorical banner.

"My name is Charles Davis," he said to Kelsey. "I want you to stick near me while we do our thing. Leader Mordechai has indicated that we're to trust you with your weapons, but I want you to know that I'll have my eyes on you. If you try to betray us, we'll kill you. Do you understand?"

"I'm not going to betray you," Kelsey said firmly. "We want to make the horde pay just as badly as you do."

The man considered her for a moment and then nodded with seeming satisfaction. "Excellent. I understand that you're trained in the use of Imperial technology. None of what we have available is of that caliber, and it will have to be explained to you. Step over to the table so that I can show you what we'll be working with."

He picked up one of the grenades and showed it to her. "This metal ball contains explosives, and the shell becomes shrapnel. To use it, one pulls the pin and throws the grenade. The spoon is spring loaded and flies up when you release it, lighting the fuse.

"Once you pull the pin, Mister Grenade is no longer your friend. You'll have roughly seven seconds before it explodes. The lethal radius is about ten meters, so keep that in mind. Aim for clusters of the enemy, and avoid your allies. It's quite effective if one can throw it far enough."

He examined her critically. "I'm not certain this is an appropriate weapon for you. To get one on target requires pinpoint accuracy and a bit of upper-body strength if one doesn't want to be too close to the target."

She smiled toothily. "I'm a lot stronger than I look, and my aim is exceptional. Trust me when I say that I'll be better at getting those on target than many of your own people."

He didn't seem convinced but didn't argue. Instead, he set the grenade down and picked up one of the metal tubes Kelsey had decided were rocket launchers. With a tug, he extended the tube even farther and revealed that it was about a meter long at that point. Two small sights popped up along the top as well.

"This is an antipersonnel rocket. They're constructed much like the grenades, as far as the explosive goes, but each has a chemical charge that propels the payload to its target. Basically, you take the tube that you've extended, rotate it onto your shoulder, line your sights up with the target, and then squeeze down this trigger along the top surface. It requires firm pressure to depress and is a one-shot, throwaway model. Once it's done, it's done.

"You'll want to be certain that no friendlies are behind you, as the propellant will kill at close range and maim for a distance beyond that. Best to make sure by calling out 'backblast area clear' and waiting for a positive response unless you are absolutely certain that no one you care for is behind you."

He did something to the tube and collapsed it back down again. Once that was done, he set it on the table and picked up one of the primitive firearms. It definitely looked like something out of one of the World War II movies that she'd seen in vids.

"This is a chemically based firearm. They're based on something we found in a museum after Terra fell. Basically, when you pull the trigger, a striker pin sets off a small priming charge that is built into the bullet, which in turn ignites gunpowder inside the brass case. That pushes a lead slug coated with copper down the rifled barrel, which imparts rotation.

"It's a fairly significant weapon at short range and can penetrate horde armor. Each of us will be issued one of these and several magazines of ammunition. More ammunition will be provided by people that are keeping us supplied during the fighting.

"We have short rifles that can fire very quickly, firing until you release the trigger or the weapon is empty. We call them submachine guns. In tight spaces, they are quite lethal. Also, very loud. They use the same ammunition as the pistols.

"In fact, the magazines will fit in either weapon, though the submachine guns will empty a pistol magazine in a few moments. The submachine gun magazines will work for the pistols but make them somewhat unwieldy. The pistols require a trigger pull for each round fired.

"Finally, there are longer weapons, but they are hard to make and difficult to form in a way that makes them accurate. The few we have will go to our snipers. They'll help us disorganize the enemy and make it so that we can perhaps attack them without them using their full capabilities in turn."

He focused his full attention on her. "They have rockets of a sort that are much more powerful. They are designed to penetrate Imperial armor."

Kelsey felt her face close down. "We've encountered them, and I've lost friends to them. I'll make sure those bastards die first."

The man smiled for the first time. "That's a plan that I can get behind."

He issued her a submachine gun, a pistol belt, and ammo for both and returned her swords. She settled everything into place and stuck close to his side as he started gathering his people and heading out.

She didn't have the same bloody rage that Julia did, but she also had a score to settle with the horde. Killing their leadership wasn't enough. She intended to send them racing back to their city with their tails between their legs today.

Those she didn't manage to kill. They'd pay for what they did today. On the souls of her dead people, that she swore.

12

C arl hefted the makeshift harness that held his equipment, making the air bottles rattle in their mesh. He felt a little overloaded. Well, better that than dead.

The others were similarly arrayed. Ralph had more air than Austin, but that was only because the hacker didn't need to worry about having that much equipment. Everything he required was in his implants, and all he needed was the appropriate gear to be able to link in with whatever he was going to be accessing.

Austin carried a lot more equipment. If they needed to work on anything, it would require a separate tool. That meant that the rest would have to carry sufficient air for him.

Thankfully, Julia would be able to carry a hefty reserve because of her augmentation. The woman, though small, was heavily laden with air bottles and gear. Carl figured they had enough air to stay down there for a couple of hours before needing to return to the safer levels.

"Are you boys ready to go?" Julia asked, her voice tinged with impatience. "I'd rather get this underway now so that we can get back up here sooner. If there's trouble, I don't want to be caught down there."

Carl didn't disagree. The sooner they dealt with any problems with the fusion plant, the sooner they'd be able to get on with their real business. If the horde managed to overwhelm the defenders, he'd rather not be caught down where he couldn't even breathe without assistance either.

"Let's do this," he agreed.

From what Mordechai had told them, they'd need to go to the nearest stairwell leading down—which his son had already pointed out to them— and start the process of entering the lower levels. They'd need to switch stairs below, as this one didn't go deep enough.

As they grew closer to the target, there would be signs indicating where to exit the second set of stairs. The older man had no idea how far down that was, but the old stories had indicated that it was quite some distance.

Once the four of them had entered the stairwell and started down, Carl began checking the air quality. For the first dozen levels, it held at about the same as it was in the area where they'd been.

That changed once they reached a certain point, and the carbon dioxide began climbing fairly rapidly. The oxygen levels were also falling. Within a couple of levels, the air quality had become bad enough that Carl was glad they'd brought air with them.

They stopped at that point, slid their masks into place, and turned on their air before continuing down.

Once they reached the bottom of that first stairwell, they exited into the corridor. The lower ceilings made him nervous about the torches they had to use. Even those weren't providing enough light as they flickered badly in the bad air.

They were pretty deep at that point, and the air quality would have been lethal to an unprotected person. Even their medical nanites weren't going to be enough to clean out someone's blood at this point.

They followed the directions given to them and were quickly at another stairwell leading downward. This one had a sign indicating the level that the fusion plant was on. It was almost twice as deep as they'd already come. Whoever had decided to build it down there had made certain that it was well protected.

Every five minutes, they each checked the air remaining in their bottles, discarding any that were too low. Best not to take chances. It took them half an hour of slow moving to reach the designated level.

The air there was so bad that the torches were almost dead. Carl pulled out one of the few battery-powered flashlights they had and turned it on.

To his surprise, the stairwell continued down. There was stuff below this incredibly deep location. He'd had no idea of the complexity and scope of the underground support system that made it possible to live in such a large city.

They ran into their first roadblock about five minutes later. It was a security door that had a keypad on it to keep unauthorized personnel out. It was dead, but they had an actual, physical key that Leader Mordechai had provided to bypass it.

That was certainly something one didn't see every day.

Carl fitted the key into the lock. It stuck a little, but he finally got it to turn and heard a loud click as the lock opened. He pulled the door wide and looked into the dark corridor beyond. Once again, it looked like every other section down underneath the megacity: dark, somewhat dirty, and cold.

A sign on the wall indicated that they needed to take a specific set of turns to get to the fusion plant. This level, even though it was very deep beneath the city, was enormous. Most of it seemed dedicated to the maintenance of the fusion plant and the distribution of power generated by it.

He immediately noted that the support system wasn't intact. A lot of panels were open, and it looked as if specific power conduits had been either removed or jury-rigged in some fashion. It was going to take a *lot* of work to get the fusion plant back to providing power to the city like Mordechai wanted.

The next security door was going to be more difficult because it had been computer-controlled, but there was no power. It was built with a battery to support itself during a blackout, but that would've drained long ago.

They were going to have to use a little brute force and ignorance, as Kelsey said, when they reached it. For that, Julia would come in very handy, indeed. As would the axe that she'd recovered from a fire station they'd passed.

Only when they reached the security door, it was wedged open. Leader Mordechai had been confident that it had been secured.

Carl led the group through the door and deeper into the power generation center with a sense of growing dread. His premonition proved dead on when they reached the area housing the fusion plant itself.

It was gone.

"Isn't there supposed to be a fusion plant here?" Julia asked, frowning.

Carl played his light around the large room and began cursing. Since he'd worked closely with the marines for years, the range and scope of profanity had become quite extensive.

When he finally ran out of nasty things to say, he headed for the cabinets along the periphery of the room that would typically contain the spare parts and tools needed to work on the fusion plant. As he began checking them, it quickly became evident that they were empty as well.

"Someone stole it," Carl eventually said. "Either that, or it was never here to begin with. Maybe Leader Mordechai got it wrong. Perhaps his ancestors moved the fusion plant to a lower level to protect it better, and that's where they installed the shielding."

"I don't think so," Austin said from where he bent over the area the fusion plant had been removed from. "The amount of corrosion on these bolts isn't all that great. Even with the low oxygen levels, I'd expect to see more rust and tarnish. These are almost bright. If I had to guess, the fusion plant was probably removed no more than a couple of years ago. Perhaps as little as six months."

He looked over at the rest of them and shook his head. "It seems to me that Leader Mordechai and Frankfort have been robbed. And without the fusion plant, I'm not sure how we're going to get out of this city either. Even if they still let us go, how will we power a train?"

"Who the hell could've taken it?" Ralph asked. "And how did they get in past all the guards up there?"

Carl started to answer, but Julia beat him to it by pointing downward.

"If they couldn't get in from the surface and the train system wasn't functional, there has to be something down lower that provided them with access. They also had to have a means of surviving in this awful atmosphere.

"Not only that, they had enough people, equipment, and training to safely disassemble and remove the fusion plant. Whoever they were, they knew *exactly* what they were doing and how to do it. We need to figure out who they were and where they went."

* * *

JULIA CONSIDERED the situation and did an inventory of the air bottles she carried. They had used maybe thirty percent of what they'd brought with them. They had a little bit of time that they could spend looking around, but they didn't have the air to go hunting extensively for where the equipment had been taken.

Thankfully, the people that had stolen the fusion plant hadn't taken any effort to hide their tracks. A lot of the equipment they'd taken was cumbersome and had left obvious marks on the floor. The series of scratches and scrapes led deeper into this level rather than back the way they'd already come. That gave her a direction to go looking for answers.

"We've got enough air for a little bit of searching," she said as she headed off.

The others didn't seem convinced, but they didn't argue against her plan either. They were undoubtedly as curious as she was.

Following the scrapes and gouges in the floor quickly led them to what could only be a service lift. Based on the doors, it was large and probably had a very high capacity. That would've allowed the intruders to get the fusion plant—suitably broken down into sections—moved to a different level.

What she didn't understand was how it could've been used without any power.

She pressed the button to summon the lift, and to her surprise, it illuminated. A minute later, the doors opened, and a large lift car awaited them. One with operational overhead lighting that dispelled the gloom all around them.

It was downright spooky. All the scene needed was some intruding mist and disturbing background music.

"How is this working?" Carl demanded. "This isn't possible. It's not designed to have an internal power supply."

"Could another fusion plant be online?" Austin asked.

Carl shook his head. "Cities aren't designed like warships. They have one fusion plant. Two would be an unneeded expense. Maybe Imperial City or the Imperial Palace had more than one, but not a mid-sized city like Frankfort. The technology is too reliable to need a spare. If well maintained, there would never be a need to shut it down. They were built for continuous operation."

"Is there any way we can tell which level the lift went to?" Julia asked. "If we can get to that level, maybe we can find out exactly how they did what they did and where this power is coming from."

Without bothering to respond, Austin opened the panel beside the buttons inside the lift and began pulling equipment from one of his pouches. He quickly had a cable attached to the internal systems and was looking at the small screen in his hands.

"We're at the highest level this lift services. It looks as if it's made a lot of trips down to the very bottom level. And, by the way, that's *really* far down. I had no idea that the city went so deep. Hell, it may go down farther if there are other lifts or stairs."

"There's no real way to know unless we look," she said.

Carl shook his head. "No. What do we do if the lift stops working? If we get trapped down there, we're dead."

Without bothering to argue, Julia pressed the button for the lowest level. The lift doors slid shut, and it started down with them all inside.

Carl glared at her. "Have you lost your mind?"

"If the lift has made as many trips as you say, the odds of it breaking during this one trip are pretty damn low."

The other three didn't seem convinced, but it wasn't as if they had a choice at this point. Julia had committed them all now.

13

Talbot watched the advancing forces and was impressed with the numbers he saw. For such a primitive people, the horde fielded quite a few dismounted fighters. He supposed that shouldn't surprise him, as warlike as they were.

When they'd had the opportunity to walk through the horde city, they'd only seen a small area. There had been a lot of civilians, merchants, and other noncombatants, but the number of troops they'd passed had been relatively large. Most of them hadn't been mounted, and neither were the forces arrayed against them now.

He wondered if that meant that the mounted forces were scouring the plains around the two cities. Did that mean that a large group of mounted riders was fanning out to make sure that they didn't escape?

Probably.

The group below the tower in which he was perched seemed to have grown to around a thousand people. That was quite a force. If they had more than one group penetrating the city, this was going to be a tough fight for the locals to win.

When Lydia returned from passing on what they'd seen, he broached that subject with her. "Is there word on other forces? Are we looking at multiple groups with this many people, or is this it?"

The woman grimaced. "There are three groups. This seems to be the main one, but two others parallel it. Our best guess is that we're dealing with maybe three thousand unmounted warriors, with possible reinforcements coming in behind them."

Talbot raised an eyebrow. "And do you have the defensive forces to resist that?"

She shrugged. "We've never been invaded on this scale before. When the horde first formed, they were a much smaller group. In the last sixty years, as they built their city, they've enslaved many from other groups and now have a large number of young warriors.

"Can we fight them head to head? No. We're going to have to use all the advantages of being a defender and knowing the terrain grants us. Some traps and ambushes will reduce their numbers.

"We'll start that process here. Before the building lost most of its glass, we'd break out a window to use for our attack, which might have given us away beforehand. Now that the glass is gone, we can pick any vantage point that we want and reduce their leadership while forcing them to keep their heads down."

"What kind of weapons do you have that will be accurate at this range?" Chloe asked. "For a bow and arrow, it's going to be impossible to hit any particular individual. There are enough people down there that the odds of you hitting *someone* are fairly good, but we must be seven hundred meters up and a few hundred from their lead elements. Add another hundred or more to reach their leadership if we can even identify them at this range."

The woman grinned at Chloe and went to a nearby closet, opening it to reveal a long-barreled weapon. It didn't look like a flechette weapon. In fact, it bore a striking resemblance to weapons used in war vids that Kelsey had made him watch from the prespaceflight era.

"This is a sniper rifle," the woman said. "It uses a chemical propellant to fire slugs of copper-sheathed lead. With an appropriate aiming mechanism like this magnifier and some skills, you can hit a human target at this distance.

"Admittedly, firing from such a high angle makes targeting a problematic concept because the bullets travel in an arc. When they're fired, they rise, and then they fall as influenced by gravity. They're also subject to deviation caused by the wind, which at this height is something to consider.

"We have other primitive weapons at the ambush sites that are going to make them pay for every meter they push into the city. At some point, they're going to get tired of being killed and turn around. If we don't decisively engage them, they can't inflict the level of casualties they'd need to make us submit."

Talbot nodded. "That makes sense, but what if they settle in? If they take over a set of buildings, you'll be at a disadvantage pushing them back out. With those kinds of numbers, they'll be able to come in and keep reinforcing themselves. The disparity in forces is going to make it difficult to kick them back out again."

Richard shook his head. "With the forces and weaponry we've managed to put together, we can take any building from them. All the structures are connected to the underground levels, and if we can get access to them, we can strike into their midst even though they think they've secured all access.

"The Imperials were quite clever about figuring out unobtrusive ways to get services into their buildings. These people will probably not be able to defend any building they try to hold."

"If you say so," Talbot said with a shrug. He didn't bother masking the uncertainty in his voice. These people might know their city better than him, but he knew that pushing out a determined force that outnumbered you was a tricky business.

"So, when are you going to start using that sniper rifle?" Chloe asked.

"If I was confident of my aim, I might try now," Lydia said. "We've been authorized to engage them, but they're still too distant to accurately hit their leadership."

Talbot held out a hand. "This might be a situation where my Marine Raider augmentation can be useful. Let me take a look."

She considered him for a long moment and then handed the weapon over. "Okay, we'll give it a try. I don't think that you're going to be able to target single individuals at this distance, much less hit them at this angle, but it'll be interesting to watch you try."

Talbot cleared broken glass away from the area nearest a shattered window that had a decent view of the enemy and knelt. The window had once gone from floor to ceiling. Now the opening allowed him to aim down as much as he liked without exposing himself overmuch.

Not that he expected that the enemy was going to be able to effectively return fire. Even their antiarmor weapons weren't all that accurate at any range at all. Bows wouldn't have a chance of hitting him since the arrows couldn't get this high.

The weapon had a primitive scope attached to it. It was a long tube that held what looked like very small crosshairs inside and provided a significant magnification of the objects being viewed. Of course, even at this distance, the magnification was insufficient to provide any real detail.

"Can we take this off?" he asked. "I need to have a direct look at what I'm going to be shooting at. I hate to say it, but my augmented vision is better than what you're getting through this scope."

Richard looked at Lydia and then shrugged. "It will need to be sighted back in once you're done, but I'm willing to give this a try because I'd also like to see you in action. Hand it here."

Talbot passed it over to the man, who quickly removed the scope and handed the rifle back.

"It has five shots in the internal magazine," Lydia said. "Once you've fired them, hand it back to me, and I'll reload one time. I'm not willing to squander more than ten rounds. The ammunition is quite time-consuming and costly to make. They're worth killing the enemy leadership with but shouldn't be wasted."

Talbot grinned. "Oh, I think you'll be pleased with how well this is going to work. How do I tell which of them are leaders?"

He looked down the fixed sights as he aimed at the horde warriors, using his augmented vision to zoom in on them.

"All of the officers have colored stripes on their shoulders. If you see color there, you're looking at an officer. The lighter colors are lower ranks, and the darker ones are higher. A deep red is pretty much the best kind of target if you can find one."

Talbot swept the sights across the approaching enemies. Spotting a bit of red, he focused in on the man and saw that this one was dressed in armor that was of much higher quality than the people around him.

His first shot was going to be an educated guess, so he lined up with the man and made an estimate of where he thought the shot would go. He kept his focus reasonably wide so that he could tell where the bullet hit and squeezed the trigger so as not to jerk the weapon.

The kick against his shoulder was surprisingly sharp. Luckily, his augmentation made the recoil manageable.

His first shot went somewhere beyond the target and caused everyone below to duck a little, but they didn't scramble for cover as the weapon ejected a piece of brass off to the side. It seemed ready to fire again, so Talbot lined up his next shot more carefully and lowered his point of aim.

The recoil was much easier to deal with the second time. This shot also went long, but Talbot saw its impact point as a puff of dirt a bit to the side and behind the target. The combat computer in his head made a few calculations, and he lowered his weapon to match where he thought he needed to aim to hit the target in the chest. Then, for the third time, he fired the weapon.

Blood blossomed from the target's chest, and the man fell backward. Based on the way he lay, Talbot was pretty sure he was dead. Even if he wasn't, it hardly mattered. He was out of the fight.

"Got him," Talbot said. "Now, let's see if we can make these bastards pay a little bit more before we have to relocate."

* * *

The group that Kelsey was assigned to set out through the labyrinth of tunnels under the city. Their destination was the ground floor of a large building halfway across the city.

Once they arrived, she saw that it didn't have windows on the ground level. The bottom floor had been thoroughly cleaned out and turned into another marshaling area and defensive redoubt. One with some peculiar features.

The leader of Kelsey's attack group quickly arrayed their forces behind a ramp of dirt that went all the way to the ceiling. There were depressions that people could fire their weapons through, but the holes were small, only as wide as a person and less than half a meter from the ceiling.

Without waiting for permission, Kelsey scrambled up the embankment and took a look for herself. Someone had driven a lot of metal rods between the dirt and the wall to keep it from collapsing once the wall was breached, she noted.

Against the exterior wall at intervals, placed away from the openings the people would use, were explosive charges linked by wire. She suspected they were shaped charges, designed to send most of their force outward.

It was going to be interesting to see whether it worked like the defenders imagined or if the dirt collapsed under the shock wave. Dangerous but educational.

Satisfied, Kelsey climbed back down and made her way to where the man marshaling their forces was standing. "How far away is the enemy, and how much time do we have before you blow the walls?"

The man shrugged slightly. "The observers say we have about ten minutes before the first group arrives. We're attacking the rightmost of the three prongs.

"The plan is simple. We set off mines buried outside the building to disrupt them, blow the walls, cause as much havoc and death as we can, and then retreat back underground.

"I'll arm self-destruct charges underneath the floor here as soon as we're clear. They'll trigger them when they pursue us, and the explosions will kill many more of them as we make our way to the next fallback position and repeat the process."

Grateful that she knew what was happening next, Kelsey found a place behind the embankment and waited for the fight to start. She hoped the piled dirt really did manage to stop the blast.

Even if it did, it was going to be impressively loud. Many of the locals would suffer permanent hearing loss, even if they stuffed their fingers in their ears, as was likely. There was only so much human flesh could do to stop the shock wave.

She hunkered down against the hard-packed dirt and examined her weapons more closely. When the time came to use them, she needed to know how everything worked. Some practice would've been a lot better, but she'd just have to make do.

The submachine gun was definitely handmade rather than constructed off a machined template, but the gunsmith had had real skill. She ran her fingers across the smooth metal and decided that it was an impressive piece of work. She confirmed that the safety was engaged and that she knew how to quickly make it ready to fire.

She'd seen weapons like this in a number of the old vids, so she had some idea what was going to happen when she used it. It would obviously have a fair amount of recoil because the stock was made to deliver it to the shoulder. Each of the magazines was filled with brass cylinders that contained copper-sheathed lead slugs. Such pretty things for being so deadly.

It was similar—if far inferior in quality—to the Pirone Nitro Express 18 millimeter semi-automatic hunting rifle she'd used to kill the assassins that had come for her at the Imperial Retreat on Avalon. The bullets used by the submachine gun were also far weaker.

Still, the experience of using the massive weapon—which presently graced the wall in her quarters with Talbot aboard *Persephone*—gave her confidence that she could use these without any problem.

Unlike flechettes, these wouldn't cause massive damage due to their slow speed. She didn't think they'd be very good at penetrating armor either. Without testing, there was no way to be sure. She supposed she'd find out shortly.

The pistol was of a similar make, obviously a one-off by a professional. It was even more of a work of art than the submachine gun. She wished that she had the time and knowledge to disassemble both of them so that she could better understand how they worked.

Once she got off Terra, she'd double-check the databases on *Persephone* and see whether or not she could build weapons like this herself. They wouldn't be the most effective choice for combat, of course, but they'd make for interesting pieces to hang on her wall with the Pirone.

Or maybe she could take these with her when they left Frankfort.

The examination of her weapons successfully distracted her, so it only felt like a couple of minutes before the man in charge made a series of hand gestures, and everyone crouched lower, plugging their ears with their fingers.

Kelsey did the same, even though she knew that her auditory augmentation would protect her. Sometimes it was best to look like everyone else and not raise questions.

Once everyone was prepared, the man held up a hand with five fingers showing. Then he pulled his thumb in, showing only four. Three… two… one…

Kelsey squeezed her eyes tightly shut and hunched as low as she could right before a massive explosion shook the ground she lay upon. It felt like she was tossed up into the air, but when her eyes snapped open, it was only the ground having jumped, bouncing her a bit.

A second blast went off, and dust flew through the perforations in the dirt embankment. That would be the wall of the building being blown clear so that they could fire. Now sunlight was filtering through the airborne debris, and the people around her were scrambling up the incline with their weapons leading the way.

Kelsey did the same, settling in with her submachine gun. The street outside filled with horde soldiers. A lot of them were down, either wounded or dead. The ground had smoking craters where the bombs had gone off underneath their feet.

That didn't seem to deter the survivors, who were already turning their weapons toward the wall to face Kelsey and her companions. Many of them were armed with bows, and they began firing at once.

Thankfully, the blasts had affected their equilibrium, and their aim was crap.

Even as the enemy was acting, everyone around Kelsey opened fire. The din of the primitive weapons was almost as bad as the charges had been. Kelsey was glad that her hearing was adequately protected. She could only imagine what this must've been like for people without augmentation.

The weapon's stock slammed against her shoulder, and fire shot from the muzzle of her submachine gun. With so many soldiers in front of her, she could hardly miss as she swung her weapon back and forth, spraying the enemy with bullets.

In what felt like just a few seconds, the large magazine was empty. She hastily removed it and fumbled a replacement into place. When she squeezed the trigger again, nothing happened, and she realized she had to release the bolt to chamber the first round. She found the catch, and the weapon clattered a bit as the slide locked into place, and it was ready to fire again.

The death and destruction caused by these weapons, particularly at short range, were merely horrific. Again, it wasn't the same as using flechette weapons, but for something put together by a relatively primitive people, it was outright deadly.

Kelsey resumed firing even as the enemy charged her position. She immediately realized that there wasn't going to be enough time for the people around her to retreat in an orderly fashion. There were far too many enemies about to overrun them.

Somewhere behind them, the man ordered a retreat, but Kelsey already knew that they were going to end up fighting the horde inside the building. She fired for as long as she could and then slid back down the embankment only when she was forced to.

She was on steady footing when the first of the enemy warriors came through the opening above her. Apparently, the embankment wasn't as hard to climb as the defenders had hoped. Now the building was going to become an abattoir filled with blood and death.

Kelsey allowed her submachine gun to drop, held only by a strap around her neck, and drew her swords. In close quarters like these, they'd make far better weapons than her pistol. As soon as the first enemy slid down the slope in front of her, she leapt forward and struck.

Her hull metal blades easily cut through the warrior's sword and his body. With her enhanced strength driving the blow, it barely even slowed her momentum, and she was already striking at the next person coming down the embankment even as the first one fell.

With her strength restored and her preferred weapons in her hands, she was a whirling dervish of mayhem. The problem was that there were dozens of new fighters climbing over the embankment to face her every single second.

They were going to be overrun no matter what she did. They had to retreat as quickly as possible so that the man could arm the traps under the floors.

"Retreat!" Kelsey shouted. "Run while I cover you!"

The enemy was pressing the people around her heavily, and the line couldn't retreat, but those to the rear of the room were able to dash for safety. Those that were heavily engaged would have to back up step by step while holding the horde away from their retreating friends.

Kelsey never doubted that this was what she had to do. The only question now was whether she'd survive defending these people and escape herself.

14

Once he'd gathered more air bottles, Jared found himself at a little bit of a loss as to what he should do next. Everyone else was assisting an exhausted Lily in setting up a makeshift triage station so that she could use her advanced equipment and have semiknowledgeable hands to help her when the inevitable stream of wounded began coming in.

He'd decided to assist in that, but when he arrived, the guards redirected him to the upper-level tunnels. It only took him a couple of minutes to realize that his ever-present minders were taking him to the same building where they'd last met Leader Mordechai.

His legs were aching by the time he was halfway up, and he was out of breath. He made a mental note to exercise more and maybe even start working out with the marines once he got off this damned planet. Being a Fleet officer was just a little too sedentary.

Once he'd reached the very top of the building, he found Leader Mordechai standing fairly close to the makeshift rail, arms casually arrayed behind his back as he stared out over the city he ruled.

Jared could faintly hear the sounds of battle below. The pops of gunshots—he could thank Kelsey and her preflight Terra entertainment vid fetish for knowing what those were—that echoed between the buildings and through the cavernous canyons that made up the city. He was sure there was a lot of shouting and swordplay as well, but they were too high for that to be audible.

Without windows, the wind blew into the building, gusty and strong. It also howled as it went through various openings in the buildings around them, creating a kind of subliminal growl.

He stepped over to stand beside the old man. Two guards stood nearby, undoubtedly making sure that he didn't do anything untoward with their leader. The two guards that had accompanied Jared for the last few hours quickly joined them.

After Mordechai failed to say anything, Jared felt the need to fill the silence.

"I can hear that the fighting has started."

Mordechai nodded without looking over at him. "Indeed, it has. This is a day that I'd hoped would not come during my lifetime, but now that it has, we shall crush our enemies. Or, I suppose, die trying."

Having said that, he turned to face Jared. "Some of your people are involved in the fighting. Are you concerned about them?"

"Of course," Jared promptly responded. "Even one bit of bad luck might see them injured or killed. That's the risk that even the very best of them take, even with all of their advantages. Every time I lose someone like that, it hurts. I want to see them all come back safely."

Mordechai nodded and smiled grimly. "Your feelings do you credit. That's how a leader thinks. You've obviously commanded people for some time to have developed those instincts."

"It's not really a matter of how long I've been in command of others," Jared said with a grimace. "I've seen people with similar authority view them as game pieces to be expended where needed to gain some tactical advantage.

"My views on the subject are a lot more complicated. My people's lives are something to be hoarded and treasured. I hate having to send them into fights where I know that some of them will die, but circumstances force my hand on occasion. It hurts each and every time."

He took a deep breath and let it out slowly. "How's the fighting going? Have you got any word on how we're doing?"

The older man nodded. "It seems the enemy is more resistant to ambush than we'd hoped. I'd forgotten how deeply ingrained their ferocity was. The majority of the people that we're facing are young and have been trained since birth to fight for the horde. It's almost as if they don't care whether they live or die, so long as their teeth are in the throats of their enemies.

"One of our ambushes has already gone bad. I don't have many details at this point, but our people are withdrawing from the areas as quickly as they can while a rearguard holds the horde back. I'm afraid that's the group where your sister Kelsey is."

Jared could feel the other man eyeing him to see how he responded to that. All he could do was shake his head slightly. Of course Kelsey was involved with something like that. How could she *not* be?

"I'm not surprised. If there's a desperate fight to be had, she's going to be in the middle of it. The only thing that's going to work to her advantage is that, with her Marine Raider augmentation, she's more than a match for any group of people that wants to kill her. Give her half a chance, and she'll get out of there in one piece, even if she can't win the fight."

Mordechai seemed to consider that for a moment and then nodded.

"That matches well with the stories that I've heard about the Marine Raiders as I grew up. They were gone long before the computers crushed Terra, but the stories of their exploits were passed down through my family.

"Raiders were based here in Frankfort, though I'm certain they weren't the only group. They lived deep down underneath the city in places that none of the enemy collaborators would've been able to find them. My ancestors kept their secrets and hid them until the time came for them to take the fight to the enemy."

The older man wrapped his fingers around the railing and stared out over the city. "Those men and women fought against the invaders for decades. From what I understand, those were strange days.

"The troops that the rebels sent down at first seemed insane. They'd scream and shout, begging for death even as they carried out the will of their masters. Very few people saw how crazed they were because simply seeing them meant that you were either taken into their number or killed. They left very few alive and free in their wake.

"There were other collaborators who seemed completely normal. They came down and took over for the leaders that the Emperor and his people had put into place. That was later, though.

"My ancestors vanished into the population then, hidden by the very citizens of the city, much like the Marine Raiders. I suppose if the enemy had been quick enough—or Frankfort important enough—they would've been taken to join whatever madness was taking place elsewhere. A number of the citizens were taken away to fight for the enemy and never returned."

The older man rubbed his face tiredly and looked over at Jared. "The Marine Raiders fought, and—even though their abilities were legendary—they weren't sufficient to win the day. Within two decades after the fighting had started, they were gone. They went out on a mission and never returned.

"Our ancestors waited for them, hoping that at least some of them would make their way back, but they were never seen again. I'd imagine that they ran into a force they couldn't defeat and were trapped. They likely died in a final desperate fight for survival. One they lost."

The two of them stood in silence for several minutes, listening to the faint sounds of fighting below. Eventually, the older man looked over at Jared.

"I understand that happened all too often in the Empire after the rebels won. I've heard many stories about ships that fought similar battles. You indicated that your rank is admiral, so you've commanded ships. Perhaps a large number of them. Yet you come to the city with a dozen people and no fleet. How is that?"

Jared sighed. "It's a complicated story. The truth is that I'm new to flag rank. Only a few years ago, I was in command of just about the smallest kind of warship that could travel through the flip points.

"The rebels missed the planet we came from during the fighting. Rather, I should say that they never invaded. They used EMP weapons five hundred years ago, just like they did against Terra. They also destroyed our capital and spaceport with kinetic strikes like the one you saw here.

"It took us a long time to get back into space. Even once we did so, our ships were nothing compared to what the Old Empire had. The only thing we had going for us was that we were independent.

"I suppose that we were also blessed by the fact that Emperor Marcus sent his son Lucian to our world. The warships that came with him defeated the force that was sent to occupy us. They all died except for Lucian and some civilians that they rescued along the way. With the emperor's line unbroken, Lucian led us, driving us to get back what we'd lost."

"After that, we began exploring to see what had happened to the Old Empire. After all the stories passed down throughout the years, we were certain that it was dead. It turned out that we were wrong."

He stared out over the city for a minute, letting his mind roam back over all that had happened in the last few years. When he finally spoke again, his voice was firm.

"My expedition found a derelict ship, the battlecruiser *Courageous*. The crew was long dead, but the computers on board that ship gave us the true history of what had happened at the end of the Old Empire.

"Once we knew the stakes, we set out to finish what our ancestors had started. The true story of the AIs was lost to us because it had been kept secret by the emperors and only passed down to the heirs when they were old enough to understand. That proved to be a mistake.

"Boiled down, the last few years have had a lot of fighting and more than our share of adventures, but we've found a lot of ships that could be repaired. Those now form the nucleus of the fleet that protects what we call the New Terran Empire."

The older man nodded slightly. "I'm sure there's a lot more to that story, but I really don't have time to hear it. So, now you had a fleet whereas before you just commanded a small ship?"

"That's right," Jared agreed. "Promotions came rapidly after that. I suppose that's not so surprising since our original fleet was tiny. With so many more ships being brought into service, rapid promotions were unavoidable. My original crew and I had a lot more experience using this new technology than anyone else, so we got promoted faster and sooner than many of the others.

"Personally, I'm not certain that I was ready. It wouldn't have been something that I'd have chosen to do on my own, but needs must when the devil drives."

Mordechai gave him a curious look. "And why would you say that you weren't ready?"

"I suppose that would require me explaining a few other things. The emperor is my father, but I'm a bastard child. Everyone in Fleet has always either gone out of their way not to show any favoritism toward me at all or been actively hostile. It's been... challenging.

"Kelsey and Julia are his legitimate daughters. Needless to say, they weren't huge fans of mine to begin with, and in the case of Julia, I still have some more work to do to convince her that I really don't want to steal the Imperial Throne.

"Their older brother saw me as a threat, and that made my life very hard. Getting promoted to command a destroyer was hard enough. Imagining more for myself? I hadn't bothered. Basically, I thought that was as high as I'd ever go."

The older man gave him a tired smile. "I think you'll find the circumstances of your birth don't dictate how well you do in life, which I believe you already know. So, where is your fleet, Admiral?"

"I went on a short mission into enemy space to gather information and deliver a report. We reprogrammed a computer-controlled destroyer for the ruse. The goal in that was to keep them from looking in the area of space where we were operating.

"The fleet that I nominally command was following at a safe distance. Our intention was to come to Terra afterward as a group. Only once we arrived to deliver the report, the Rebel Empire commandeered the destroyer and sent it off to Terra via a different route.

"My fleet was unable to follow. Honestly, I'm not sure that they're going to be able to even get here. They might have been forced to turn back.

"We hid aboard the destroyer and overpowered the people they'd put aboard. Their original goal was to pick up a lethal virus to deploy here at Terra and kill everyone on the planet. We disposed of that, and it will hopefully take them quite some time to figure out what happened."

Mordechai's face paled. "If they tried such once, they'll try again. The next time, they might succeed. How can my people fight against something like that?"

"You can't," Jared said bluntly. "We've got to stop the AIs before they can make another attempt. The design for the virus was supposedly destroyed, so they're not going to just be able to cook up another batch. If my people and I can get what we need at the Imperial Palace and get back to the ship that brought Kelsey here, we'll have a decent chance of ending this war. That's why we need your help in getting out of here."

Mordechai didn't say anything for a long while. He gripped the railing with his hands tight enough to turn his knuckles white as he stared out over the city and listened to the faint sounds of fighting below. At long last, he turned and faced Jared.

"Trust doesn't come easy to my people, Admiral Mertz. We've been under the heel of the computer for a very long time. Yet your story is so implausible that I have to give it credit. Honestly, I believe that you're telling me the truth. What are you hoping to find at the Imperial Palace, and how can it help you win this war?"

Jared considered whether or not he should tell the truth. They were only going to have one shot of getting the override. If he screwed this up, they might never get out of Frankfort. In the end, he decided that the truth would serve him best.

"There are vaults underneath the palace. Inside of them is a device called an override. It's a piece of hardware that was designed to shut down the master AI. If we can get into the space station where this thing is, all we need to do is plug it in, and the war is over.

"We can order the AI to send out instructions to every unit that it controls, telling them to stand down. If we can get our hands on the override, then we only need to find a way to get back into space so that we can use my sister's ship to escape the Terra system."

"That sounds like a daunting task," Mordechai said with a grimace. "If you have no small ships to escape Terra with, how will you ever get off this planet? Even if you do, the computer waits above. How will you stop it from just destroying you?"

"I'm not exactly sure," Jared admitted with a shrug. "No matter what happens, it's going to be complicated. We're taking a risk, but we can't afford to just give up. Even if the odds are against us, we must succeed. If the AIs have decided that killing humanity on Terra is a good idea, how long before they decide to do it everywhere?"

"The idea of the computers exterminating humanity is even more shocking than them enslaving us. Frankly, it's terrifying.

"I know nothing of the worlds beyond Terra. Let me be honest. I know little about the areas of Terra distant from my own city. I'm not certain how much assistance I can be to you in this matter."

The man's expression firmed. "What I can say is that I'm not a man given to blind trust. Yet everything you've told me has rung true, and I'm an excellent judge of character. I've decided that I will do everything within my power to assist your people in getting to the Imperial Palace. The computers cannot be allowed to win this fight."

The man's words were a relief to Jared. This was the kind of breakthrough that he'd been hoping for. The only problem was that they had to win this fight before any of it mattered.

If they lost, the horde would occupy the ruined megacity and hunt them down. With them controlling the plains around the city, there could be no escape that didn't involve getting the fusion plant back online and using the train system to escape the area. They couldn't fight all of those mounted warriors.

Everything was resting on Carl. He really hoped the young man and his companions were making progress because they really needed some good news right now.

15

When the lift reached the bottom of the shaft and the doors opened, Carl saw that it let out into a long, dingy corridor lit by functional overhead lights. Proof that this area was powered. Somehow.

The scrapes that they'd followed into the lift were still visible, heading directly down the corridor. There were side corridors, but none of them were illuminated. For the moment, it made the most sense to track the quarry they'd come after.

Julia moved to the front of the group, seemingly ready to defend them if there was any trouble. Carl was more than confident that she could do so with her Marine Raider augmentation, even though she was unarmed. Anything that she had in her hands was a deadly weapon, including the heavy bag filled with air bottles that she now hefted.

The sight of the bag made him pause to check his equipment and to determine what the atmosphere around them was like. To his surprise, it was breathable. The carbon dioxide levels were only slightly elevated, and the oxygen was normal. Unlike the floors above them, life support was online down here.

"There's breathable air," he said as he took off his mask. "We need to conserve our air."

Julia didn't look convinced, and neither did the others.

"It's safe," he assured them. "I'll let Ralph carry the tester, and he can check as we go. I'll set it up so that the alarm will go off if the carbon dioxide levels start going up or the oxygen levels drop.

"Someone took the time to refurbish the life-support systems down here. More interestingly, they had the knowledge to do so. It takes a lot of know-how to disassemble a fusion plant without destroying it, and their work on the life-support system only confirms that whoever did this has training. Based on the fact that the power is still on, we can't assume that they're gone, so we need to be careful."

Julia seemed to consider that for a moment before nodding. "Stand still and let me listen. If anyone is working around here, I might be able to hear them with my enhanced hearing."

After about thirty seconds, she shook her head. "I can hear the air handlers, but that's about it. I honestly don't think that anyone else is down here. We're seeing what they left behind after they finished taking the fusion plant. I'll wager they left the lights on in case they needed to come back."

"Why would they do that?" Austin asked. "If they've got a power supply, why leave it here? Somebody might come down and find it. Like, for example, us."

Carl gestured around them. "This is a bubble of good air. Everything above us is lethally toxic. That's one hell of a barrier to people without technological know-how. The locals would never have made their way down here on their own.

"And only the fact that Julia is insane got us into that lift. Honestly, any sane human being would think that this level had the very worst atmosphere. It's only pure luck that it's not. Seriously, the chances of anyone actually finding this place were very low."

"So let's take advantage of the situation," Julia said as she started walking forward. "Let's find out what's down here."

Carl expected her to keep walking forward until she found whatever was at the end of the scrape marks, but she didn't. In fact, she stopped and looked inside the rooms as they passed. Each and every one of them was filled with unmarked boxes and what looked like salvaged equipment. Nothing belonging to the fusion plant from what he could see.

"Let's get a decent idea of what we're passing by," he insisted. "A few minutes isn't going to cost us anything."

The room that he selected seemed to be mostly filled with parts from a power distribution system, undoubtedly from somewhere above them. It looked like whoever was stripping the lower levels of the megacity had been thorough. They'd taken everything that wasn't nailed down.

Leader Mordechai was going to be seriously pissed when he found out. Thankfully, that wasn't something that he or his friends had screwed up. Hopefully the man wouldn't hold it against them.

After a few more rooms, Julia grew impatient and strode ahead, forcing the others to hurry to keep up. Carl didn't blame her. They were almost certainly going to find parts and equipment stripped from the megacity in all of these rooms. They'd have plenty of time later to do a more thorough inventory once they found the fusion plant.

Where the hell had these people taken it? Why disassemble it and then move it all the way down here? He supposed it would make sense if they intended to hide out at this lower level and make sure that no one came looking for them, but Julia hadn't heard anyone. Where had they gone?

Honestly, this wasn't making a whole lot of sense. There had to be some aspect of the situation that he just didn't get yet.

As they walked, he started wishing that they had a map of the lower levels. There was nothing in this corridor to give them a clue what they were headed toward. Admittedly, there were lots of plaques over the doors that had letters and numbers, but their meaning was obscure without an index. He supposed it was only meant to be helpful to maintenance teams.

Thankfully, they had the scrapes on the floor to follow. Tracking them to their ultimate destination took about twenty minutes.

When they finally reached the end of the corridor, he wasn't really all that surprised to find a maglev train platform. Just exactly the sort of thing that Leader Mordechai had promised that they could get working and use from one of the upper levels. This station must've been used for maintenance purposes.

He'd seen stations just like this on other worlds in the Rebel Empire. The trains could go down the tunnels at high speed, reaching their destinations in relatively short periods of time.

Unlike the more public stations that he'd seen before this, this one had none of the amenities one would expect to see when the general public would be using it. That only confirmed his guess that it was meant to serve the people that kept the city running.

The other thing of note was that there was no train sitting at the platform. There was also no fusion plant.

"This has to be where the power is coming from," Austin said. "Whoever energized the system to get here needed to keep this online so that they could be certain that they could come back for everything else they salvaged. The cost of keeping a limited portion of the life-support system online wasn't that much in the bigger picture."

"I don't see a train," Julia said. "Is there a way to summon one?"

"There's going to be some kind of control room where we could probably do that, but the question is whether or not we should," Carl said. "Rather than doing anything hasty, we should go back upstairs and report what we've found. There's going to be some fallout when Leader Mordechai hears what's happened. It wouldn't surprise me if he wants to come down and take a look at everything himself.

"Well, he might be a little old to make that trip, so he could send Jebediah instead. In any case, they don't seem like the kind of people that'll take this lying down. They're going to want their stuff back, and they're going to want to make somebody pay for taking it."

Julia shook her head. "They've already got the horde to deal with, so they're not going to go after another group of people while the fighting is still taking place."

Carl sure hoped that she was right, but he wasn't completely convinced. He only hoped that they could convince them that a technologically advanced group of people were probably armed with weapons that would stop them cold. A fight with people wielding flechette weapons would be a bloodbath.

It was probably a forlorn hope. There was going to be a reckoning at some point. Carl only hoped that he and his friends didn't get caught up in the middle of that particular fight, because it wasn't going to be pretty.

* * *

KELSEY FOUGHT for all she was worth, slashing with both swords at any horde warrior that came near her. She used her augmented muscles to jump into their midst from distances they didn't expect and killed with single strikes.

If the enemy's numbers hadn't been growing so rapidly because they were rushing the position, that might have made a difference. Unfortunately, for every person she cut down, three more climbed through the openings from the street.

They were being overwhelmed.

She dumped Panther into her system, letting the combat drugs take the rough edges off the world, seeming to slow everything happening around her. In actuality, her nerve and cognitive speed had been increased, giving her more time to assess and react to everything around her.

Kelsey wasn't a fan of how the drug made her feel—particularly when she came down from it—but in this kind of fight, it might just save her life.

She ducked under an enemy warrior's strike and jammed one of her swords into the man's torso. With her now free hand, she plucked a grenade off of the belt of one of the dead defenders at her feet, grabbed the metal ring in her teeth, and yanked it out.

She threw the grenade into the largest concentration of enemy nearby and retrieved her sword from the dying man's chest, slashing at a woman trying to cut her down from the side. She took off both the woman's hands in the same strike.

The explosion of the grenade shocked even her system, but the break in the enemy's attack was just what she needed.

Resuming her two-sword attack, she pushed the horde warriors back and allowed the remaining defenders a chance to retreat. Many of them had already died trying to hold the line, but a few of them managed to extract themselves.

With a break in the number of attackers around her, she quickly sheathed her swords and grabbed more grenades from the bodies of defenders. Keeping in mind the lethal radius, she began hurling the grenades into pockets of the enemy inside the building.

She knew that there was always the chance that she'd catch a piece of shrapnel, but that was a risk she was going to have to take. Combat wasn't safe. Everything was a calculated risk, and if she didn't take chances, they were probably all going to die.

The explosions killed many of their enemies and stunned everyone still in the room. Everyone except her.

Kelsey followed the rest of the defenders out of the room and turned to protect the retreat down the corridor. That came in the form of a large metal barrier that slammed down when the man leading the raid manipulated a lever beside the door.

The horde warriors immediately began pounding on it, but they wouldn't be able to break through before Kelsey and the rest escaped. This was the break they'd needed.

"Where do we go now?" Kelsey demanded. "Where did the rest go?"

The man, bleeding from a cut across his forehead, gestured down the corridor. "This takes us directly to the stairs. We go down three levels, and then we exit. There's a trap set up on the fourth level, so anyone going that far gets blown up."

Having said that, the man smiled cruelly. "There's also some bombs buried underneath the floor in the room behind us. As soon as we get out of the area, watchers in other buildings will set them off and kill as many of those trying to follow us as they can."

Kelsey nodded her approval. Working with the rest, she helped move the injured down the stairs and into the appropriate tunnels on level three. There was only a small group of defenders waiting to see if anyone else escaped, but it was enough to get everyone that needed a hand someone to lean on.

Once they were sure that no one else was coming, the defenders armed the booby traps, and everyone fled down the tunnel.

As they ran, Kelsey flushed her system of the Panther, and the world became duller as her senses seemed to slow. The world seemed so much drabber now.

Honestly, that was what she hated the most about Panther: having to let go of the almost god-like feelings it brought. The damned stuff was addictive.

Fifteen minutes later, they'd been through many twists and turns and even changed levels multiple times, so Kelsey knew that even if the enemy had come through the booby traps waiting to stop them, they'd never be able to track them in time to make a difference.

That wasn't to say it was impossible. A number of the people with her were injured, and they were leaving a blood trail that a determined enemy could follow.

When they finally gathered at the new location, the man in charge grimaced. "It looks like we've lost almost half our people. That wasn't what we were hoping for, but the enemy was more ferocious than we'd imagined possible. We're going to have to combine forces with another attack group because we just can't defeat a force this size by ourselves."

"Aren't they already engaged?" Kelsey asked.

The man shook his head. "None of the other ambushes have kicked off yet. This was the first group to arrive at a suitable location. I've heard your husband will soon be on his way to assist another such group. If you'd like to join them, I have no objection to having one of our people take you.

"I'm going to take the rest of our force and merge with another group. Our numbers might make a difference there. We might have failed to stop this particular force, but if we can exterminate the other two, that'll give us an advantage in pushing the remaining invaders back."

Kelsey considered turning down the offer, but if Talbot was about to get into a fight like this, she wanted to plant her back against his so that they could cover one another. She trusted her husband to stay alive, but in a melee like this, one inattentive moment could mean death.

"That sounds like a plan," she said grimly. "Let's be about our business."

16

———

By the time he'd run out of ammunition for the sniper rifle, Talbot had made quite an impression on the horde forces below them. After the first few kills, the enemy had realized that he was able to hit them effectively and sought better cover.

While he didn't manage to kill a lot of enemy officers, he convinced them to keep their heads down. That delay might prove useful for the defenders when it came to fighting off the other groups.

Richard and Lydia seemed *very* impressed at his accuracy.

"I can't imagine how having a machine in your head allows you to shoot so well, but I'm glad you're here," Richard said with a grin. "I wish we'd brought more ammunition. We've kept their heads down longer than I'd expected. That's going to help the ambush groups."

Talbot was pleased, but fighting from a distance wasn't his usual style. He didn't object to it in principle. After all, keeping the enemy from attacking friendly units was a positive thing. The longer they managed to keep the horde at bay, the better their eventual chances of winning this fight. Still, he'd rather be in the rough and tumble.

"Any word on the other ambushes?" he asked. "In particular, the group my wife is with."

The way the two locals glanced at one another made him uneasy. Something was wrong.

"Trot it out," he ordered firmly.

For a moment, it seemed as if they were going to keep him in the dark, but Richard finally sighed and nodded. "The ambush didn't go as planned. From what I've heard, they engaged the enemy, but the horde swarmed their position. They charged right into the ambush site.

"Your wife and the rest managed a fighting withdrawal, and she wasn't hurt, but it was a close thing. She's on her way to the same ambush site that we'll be moving to, although she's going to be down in the fighting zone, while we're going to provide long-range covering fire. I'm sorry that we didn't insist that she come with you."

Talbot laughed before he could stop himself. "You don't know my wife. No one can stop her once she's made up her mind. And don't mistake her small size for a lack of ferocity. If she wanted to, she could thrash me in a stand-up fight. She's had her augmentation for a lot longer than I have and can fight in ways that none of us can really imagine without having seen it. Just trust her to do what needs to be done."

Once they'd digested that, he continued. "So, now that we all know that I'm not going to rush off to save my retiring flower of a wife, what's the plan?"

"We're going to head down into the tunnels and move to an observation site across from the new ambush zone," Lydia said. "The setup is going to be very similar to the one your wife was just at. They'll be inside a building so that the horde can't see them and will attack them just like this last time.

"I've made arrangements to have access to more weapons at this location so that we can utilize your specific talents more effectively. The plan for the ambush is going to be modified so that the engagement time is shorter for the people on the ground. They're also going to use heavier firepower to kill more of the invaders and keep additional distance between the groups so that they can escape more readily.

"Our job will be to provide both a distraction and kill off as many of the enemy as possible before they can get into the building. We're going to be the people that make sure your wife and the rest can effectively disengage when they're ready to."

Talbot slowly nodded. "That sounds like a serviceable plan, but I'd have to see the specific layout before I can make any suggestions for improvement. If you have any explosives that can be thrown, I'm pretty accurate with those as well. In any case, whatever you've got, I can probably use it better than whoever you originally planned to fire it."

She smiled at his response. "I've already taken that into account. We're gathering everything we can think of to take advantage of your specific skills and abilities. Unlike this observation post, others are going to be adding their fire to yours at this new site, so your friend doesn't have to feel like a third wheel this time."

"Chloe is used to me hogging all the glory."

His subordinate punched him in the arm. Hard. "Don't listen to this guy. I want my turn. Big guns for the win!"

"Then we'd best be about it," Richard said. "We don't want to be late to the party."

In the end, it took them about twenty minutes to get into position in the new building, and Talbot was both impressed and satisfied with the arsenal they'd gathered. Not only were there sniper rifles, he now had access to primitive grenades and even some rocket launchers.

Those would be an ugly surprise for the horde warriors, though how he was going to fire them effectively remained a mystery. He'd seen weapons like them in use in some of the vids that Kelsey insisted that he watch from prespaceflight Terra. An era called World War II.

This kind of weapon funneled burning propellant out the rear of the tube, and the exhaust would be lethal. As he was inside a building, Talbot wasn't sure how he'd make that work.

He supposed that they wouldn't have brought the weapons if they didn't have a plan. He'd just have to wait for them to explain it to him.

Chloe took her share of the weapons and went to a different section of the building. She'd be providing support in much the same way he would, he was sure. She might not have Raider augmentation, but her implants and experience would be more than enough to make her lethal at this range.

The ambush hadn't kicked off yet, though Richard assured him that the horde was very close. The building across what was like a deep valley from the building he was in rose five stories from the ground before it had any windows. The lower levels appeared to be natural stone. It was beautiful and would make excellent shrapnel when it fragmented.

Like the rest of the city, many windows were shattered, though there was more intact glass than he'd expected. Perhaps that was because the lower levels were closer to the ground and better shielded by the buildings around them.

Lydia had explained how the ambush group would use explosive charges to knock holes in the wall so that their people could fire through them at the enemy. There were also explosives buried in the ground just in front of the ambush site to take out any of the invaders unlucky enough to be caught in the blast area.

Based on how the horde had reacted the last time, that wasn't going to be as effective as the defenders had hoped. The horde warriors would countercharge and get in among the ambushers as quickly as they possibly could. Engagement time might be minimal.

Well, then, he'd just have to make the most of the opportunity. His efforts might mean the difference between life and death for the ambushers, including his wife. He'd damned well do whatever it took to see this work, no matter how dangerous it was.

* * *

Julia and the rest had finally decided that they'd gathered all the information that they were going to get and made their way back to the lift. Once they'd affixed their air, they boarded and began the ride back up. It only took a couple of seconds for the atmospheric readout equipment to start announcing that the air had grown toxic.

Arriving safely on the level the fusion plant had been taken from, they walked to the other set of stairs and began the long trek back to the occupied levels. By the time they reached breathable atmosphere again, they'd used up about two-thirds of the air bottles they'd brought with them.

They found a group of guards waiting for them, and Julia asked to be taken to see Leader Mordechai. Thankfully, they didn't have to go to the stupid building where they'd visited him the last time. Even with her Marine Raider augmentation, she'd done a lot of climbing today and wasn't in the mood to do any more.

Instead, they met the man in the air handler room. Seated beside him was his son Jebediah.

The older man leaned forward expectantly. "We were beginning to worry. I hope you have good news. What is the condition of the fusion plant?"

"Missing," she said flatly. "Somebody stole it."

The two men across the table blinked at one another before Jebediah frowned at her, his voice a low rumble filled with disapproval. "What do you mean by that?"

"I mean that the fusion plant and all of it shielding aren't there anymore. Someone disassembled it, dragged the pieces to a maintenance lift, and took it down to the very lowest level.

"The lift still had power, so we took it down and discovered that they'd stripped the lower levels. They stashed a lot of equipment and parts in various rooms, but they took the fusion plant to a maglev train station on the lowest level.

"There weren't any trains present, so I have to assume that they just left the power on in case they wanted to come back and pick up more stuff. They also fixed the life-support systems on those lowest levels."

Everyone sat in silence for a full minute as they digested what she'd said.

Finally, Mordechai leaned forward. "How did they manage any of this?"

Julia shrugged. "Whoever they were, they obviously had some level of training with Imperial equipment. Disassembling a fusion plant isn't something that just anybody off the street is going to do, even on a world that hasn't lost access to technology. Someone knew exactly what they were doing."

"It looks like they took the fusion plant sometime between six months ago and a couple of years ago," Carl said. "The rooms on the lowest level are stuffed full of boxes and salvaged equipment. The places we checked had supplies and spare parts.

"It's obvious that they were systematically stripping as many levels of your city as they could. They wouldn't have just left the train system powered unless they intended to return for everything at some point."

Mordechai leaned back in his seat. "If this is true, it's extremely disturbing. Jebediah, I want you to accompany them back down and discover the truth of the situation for me.

"I want the rest of you to know that it's not that I doubt your word, but I want to hear that this terrible thing has happened from a source that I trust completely. Once my son has verified what you say—which I have no doubt that he'll do—then I'll decide what needs to be done next."

"We don't have enough air to take us all back down," Carl said with a shake of his head. "If you want the entire group to go, we'll have to gather some more before we start."

"Then don't take everyone," Mordechai said evenly. "It's not as if you're repairing anything at this point, so it seems that Julia could accompany my son."

"I'd like to go as well," Mertz said from the door behind Julia.

"Why?" Mordechai asked with one eyebrow raised.

"Because if that's the direction we're going to have to go, I want to see what it looks like for myself."

Mordechai considered Mertz's words for a few seconds and then nodded. "Very well. The three of you shall depart immediately if you have enough air to see you through."

Julia shot a questioning look at Carl.

The young man frowned slightly, thought for a few seconds, and then nodded slowly. "If Julia takes the partially filled bottles that we left here in the air handler room, that should be enough for the three of them to make the trip down and back, so long as they don't dawdle."

"Excellent," Mordechai said. "Then I won't delay you any longer."

Before they started down, Jebediah led Mertz and Julia to an area where they could eat. Once they'd done so and secured extra water for the journey, the three of them retraced the path to the stairs that led down.

Without any of the others to tell her when the air got bad, Julia relied on her olfactory augmentation to continuously sample the air quality and have her implants keep a running tally so that she could see what they were dealing with. When it became necessary, she told the others to don their masks.

She wasn't sure why she hadn't thought of using her built-in equipment the last time. Perhaps it was because she just wasn't used to using the implants and augmentation at all. She had to keep reminding herself that she was capable of doing a lot of things if she just thought about how she could use her equipment.

Once they reached the level the fusion plant had been taken from, Jebediah insisted that they spend some time examining the reactor room. After a few minutes, he grunted and slowly nodded his head.

"The evidence here fully backs up what you've said. I can see where a large machine was removed, and it's evident to me that it could not have been done just by the four of you in the short amount of time that you were gone.

"Also, the scratches on the metal plate where it rested have rusted. Trust me when I say that I have an excellent idea of how long it takes something to rust. Based on the level of corrosion, your guess of between six months and two years seems plausible.

"Now, let's go see what they've done below. I have to admit that I'm very interested in seeing this lift. None of the ones in the city above have been functional for a century, and I'm curious what the experience of traveling in one will be like."

Julia led the man to the lift and pressed the button. Since the lift car was on this level, the doors promptly slid open.

Jebediah stepped into the center of the lift and turned in a slow circle, examining everything under the artificial lights in the ceiling above his head.

"The light seems unnatural," he finally said. "Too steady, and it almost wavers in my vision. It's definitely not like sunlight or torchlight. I have to admit that this experience is somewhat disconcerting."

She grinned at him. "If you think that's disconcerting now, just wait until the lift car starts going down. You're going to feel a sense of motion. It's not going to be too bad, but you need to be aware in advance that it's going to happen. The trip will take a minute."

Once he'd nodded, she and Mertz piled into the lift behind him, and she pressed the button to take them to the lowest level. The doors slid shut, and down they went. No one said anything until they arrived at their destination.

When the doors slid open again, Jebediah stepped out and looked back into the lift. "That was an amazing experience," he admitted. "I can only imagine how much time and effort something like this would save me on my daily climb to the top of my father's building. I'm a fit man, but all those stairs wear on a person. I can't imagine how the old man does it every day."

Julia laughed. "That's just how old men are, vexing us young people. Come on. I'll show you a couple of the rooms where they stored some of the salvaged gear so that you can see what they've been up to."

She proceeded down the hall, opening doors and showing the two men all the boxed goods and salvaged equipment. Ten minutes later, they stood on the platform at the maglev station.

Jebediah put his hands on his hips and scowled. The overhead lights here were much brighter than in the lift or the hallway. Even he had to see that there was no way that they'd missed anything.

"Everything you said is true," he growled. "Someone has stolen from us. My father will not stand for that. I can assure you that he's going to make absolutely certain that whoever did this pays. Come, we must return to the surface."

They retraced their steps to the lift, and Julia pressed the button to take them back up.

Nothing happened.

Frowning, she pressed the button again. Still nothing. It illuminated when she pressed it but went dark as soon as she removed the pressure. Only the overhead lights indicated the lift still had power.

"That doesn't seem very promising," Mertz said.

What had started as a short jaunt was now a survival situation.

"It looks like we've got a lot of walking to do," she said, pressing the button to open the doors again and gesturing at the stairway door to the right. "It's a good thing you've gotten all that practice in, Jebediah. We're going to have to get through the toxic air in a hurry, so all that exercise is now going to save your life."

With her augmentation, she wasn't going to have any trouble making the trip. If anyone was going to slow them down, it was going to be Mertz. She hoped he could keep up because she wasn't looking forward to having to carry the man.

Yet if that was what it took, she'd do it. For whatever reason, Kelsey loved him, so Julia wouldn't leave Mertz behind.

As much as part of her really wanted to.

She sighed. Maybe one day she'd get used to him. Unlikely, but possible.

With that, she opened the stairwell door. The sooner started, the sooner done. At least so long as nothing else went wrong.

17

"**H**old up," Jared said. "We should salvage air bottles from this level before we try heading up, just to make sure we've got enough."

If they ran out of air, they'd die. There were dozens of levels above them with bad air, and that was only to the old fusion plant room. There were even more above that. They could breathe now. Best to gather what they could while they had time.

"Good idea," Julia said with a nod, though her tone was grudging.

They headed back toward the maglev station. Unfortunately for them, the first safety compartment they opened was empty. So was the second. And the third.

Whoever had stripped this level had taken *everything*. The missing air bottles were likely in one of the rooms around them. He couldn't imagine them being worth hauling off for these people.

Jared passed along his thoughts and then considered their options. If they spent the time looking for the air, they were extending their stay in the area that was subject to dangers that they might not understand.

Even if they decided to search for air in the extended stash, only pure luck would allow them to find it. Nothing was labeled, and the rooms were stacked deep, with almost everything small placed into boxes.

"I understand what you're saying," Jebediah said when Jared explained his thoughts. "Even so, we're not going to get another chance once we start back up. Let's at least look into every single room and see if we get lucky."

Giving in to the inevitable, Jared acquiesced. A quick search of all the rooms along the corridor leading to the maglev station didn't find anything that they could use. It was mostly salvaged equipment that wasn't labeled. None of the boxes had anything on them to identify their contents.

They were going to have to do this the hard way.

"We're going to have to make a try," Jared said grimly. "If we can get part way up into the area where the atmosphere is bad, we might be able to find some air bottles they didn't take. Or we could just do the smart thing and send Julia up with all of the ones we have and let her bring back help."

Jebediah shook his head. "I don't believe any of us should go off alone. There's no telling what she'll find on her way up. If there is some kind of trouble, she'd need someone to help pull her out of it."

Julia's eyes narrowed. "Not to be a pain in the ass, but that's a sexist comment. I can extract myself from any kind of trouble that you can, probably even better than you."

The large man raised his hands in a gesture of surrender. "Giving that impression was not my intention. I simply meant that any one of us can fall victim to a situation where two people would allow survival for both. What I said about you I hold equally true for myself or Admiral Mertz."

The prickly princess gave the man a long, hard look before she nodded curtly and opened the stairwell door. It was lit, which was good, though they had a hand light for when the air became too foul to allow for the torches.

They made it up five levels before the lights no longer worked. This must be the boundary for the power the thieves had linked into the city.

He turned the hand light on, and they made it two more levels before they had to switch to bottled air. Once they were safely protected, they resumed their trek and almost immediately ran into their first roadblock.

In this case, roadblock was the perfect word for the situation. The stairwell was closed off by a metal door with a mechanical lock.

It was probably intended to keep anyone from getting down into the lowest of maintenance levels, and it looked extremely sturdy. Without a key to open it, their options fell to brute force and ignorance, as Talbot was fond of saying.

Unfortunately for them, while Julia was fully augmented, her hands and feet were still made out of flesh. Beating on metal wasn't going to do her any good. She needed a tool with leverage to bring force to bear on the problem, but the door was smooth and looked like it would be hard to get through.

She shook her head. "If I had a knife, I might be able to make this work, but I'm not able to get enough leverage to pry it open. We're going to have to find another way."

"Before we go back down, let's spread out and see if there any air bottles on this level," Jared said. "Since the life-support system wasn't activated here, it's more likely that we'll find something."

Sadly for his optimism, the safety compartments on this level had been stripped as well. They were going to be trapped unless they found another way up or took a chance in the lift shaft.

The latter was a risk that he wasn't willing to take. The former was problematic because they hadn't seen any other stairwells servicing this section of the underground.

"I think our best bet is to find some kind of tool that will let me force my way through the door," Julia said. "It's also possible that we can find the air bottles that they scavenged."

"Without food or water, we're not going to be able to hold out for more than a few days, but they'll have noticed that we're missing by then," he said confidently. "They'll send Carl and the others to find us, and when they find that the lift isn't operational, he'll know what to do."

Jebediah scowled. "I don't like relying on others for my safety. Unfortunately, I don't see that we have much choice.

"I think you're correct that we can productively search through some of the boxes and other storage areas to find items that have been packed away. Perhaps we'll get lucky and find something to point us to where these people came from."

As the group started back down the stairs, Jared sent up a prayer that Carl and Mordechai would quickly realize that they were missing and send help. Unfortunately, with the fight going on above, it was all too likely that other events would be holding their attention.

For the time being, they were on their own.

Lost in his own thoughts, he almost missed the flash of something shiny on the stairs as they went back down. It was wedged into the corner of the stairs, and he'd only spotted it because he'd been worried about placing his feet incorrectly and had been looking down.

He picked it up and found himself holding a metal pin with an enameled image on one side. The image made both of his eyebrows rise. He'd seen it before. It was the emblem of the Marine Raiders.

* * *

WHILE CARL WAS WAITING for Julia, Admiral Mertz, and Jebediah to return from their trip down, he busied himself by securing more air bottles. That meant that he, Austin, and Ralph had to venture fairly far afield because they were becoming hard to find close to the air handler room.

Not being as rushed this time, he only selected the ones that read full. That allowed him to carry a fair number back for their use without being overburdened.

Even though the process was easy, it wasn't quick. By the time they'd returned with all the air bottles they could scavenge and had finished sorting them out, almost ninety minutes had passed.

Carl knew that Mordechai and the rest would be focused on the fighting, so he wasn't surprised to discover that there was only one guard in the air handler room. What did surprise him was that those that had gone below hadn't returned.

That was concerning. There was no reason they couldn't have made the trip down and gotten back by now.

"Something might have gone wrong," he told the others. "We need to go below and find them. Gather up your gear and split up the air bottles."

"Shouldn't we get extra help?" Austin asked uncertainly.

Carl shook his head. "These people are in a fight for survival, and they need every hand they can get. Search and rescue is going to be up to us. Come on."

Since they'd made the journey down once before, it didn't take them very long to get to the room where the fusion plant had once been located. Once there, they quickly made their way to the maintenance lift. When Carl pressed the button to summon the car, it lit but went dark as soon as he released the pressure. He tried again with the same result.

That wasn't good.

"They've either got the doors wedged open below, or it's broken," Austin said. "From up here, we can't really tell which. We're going to have to go down another way."

"We need to get these doors open," Carl ordered. "Look around and find something that we can use to pry them apart. Once we get it open, we'll start making an assessment about how safe it would be to go down the shaft."

The three of them spread out, searching for tools. Unfortunately, they found nothing of value. Whoever had taken the fusion plant had stripped the level. In the end, they had to venture much farther afield to find a locked maintenance room on a separate level.

Inside, they found a pry bar and a locker full of reinforced rope. They'd have to test it to be absolutely sure it was any good, and even then, Carl was going to braid the strands to provide added strength.

With the help of his companions, he wedged the prybar into the crack between the doors and they put their shoulders into it, forcing the doors open.

Being very careful with his footing, Carl looked down the shaft. He couldn't see the bottom, but that was no surprise. The shaft was lit, but the panels were somewhat dim and mounted far apart. If memory served, there were at least four dozen levels between him and the bottom of the shaft.

Definitely not the kind of thing one wanted to fall into.

There was a ladder on the inside of the shaft. It was made of metal and thus really couldn't be trusted. With the amount of time that had passed, it was sure to have weakened.

"Help me braid some of this rope together," he ordered. "I'll have you anchor me as I go down. Once this strand runs out, you'll need to tie more on. Can you do that?"

Austin nodded. "I can, but I don't think this is a good idea. There's a stairwell right there. All we have to do is go down and get them."

"If it was that easy, they'd have walked back up themselves," Carl retorted. "There's no way that something down there incapacitated all three of them. With the lift out of service, that means they can't get back up through normal means. We've got to go down through the shaft.

"But you're right that it's dangerous. I'll keep my hands on multiple rungs and try to use the ladder's sides as much as possible. You'll need to wrap your end around one of the supports up here. It might take several lengths of rope to get to the bottom, but we can do it.

"When I get down there, I'll find out what's going on and pass it back up by shouting. Then we'll figure out what we need to do to get them out."

"This is insane," Ralph grumbled. "We should just get help and go down once we're better prepared. They're going to be fine. The atmosphere is good down there."

"In a perfect world, that would be true. This world is far from perfect, and sometimes we've got to take chances. They're worth the risk."

Without giving them any more time to argue, Carl gestured for them to secure the rope. Only then did he gingerly climb onto the ladder.

Once he was fully situated, he started down slowly and carefully. He made it three steps before the rung he put his weight on snapped off and went clattering down the shaft. The experience left him partially hanging, but the rope held.

"I guess I put too much weight on that one," he said. "I'll be more careful."

After taking a few more deep breaths, Carl started down the shaft again.

18

T albot had to admit that he wasn't thrilled about being slid out from a broken window this high above the ground. Even though he understood how he'd be balanced on the long plank they'd showed him—which was supported by ropes run through pulleys mounted to the ceiling—it was still unnerving.

He'd also be dependent on others to pull him back inside once the fighting got rolling, or they simply ran out of rockets for him to fire and grenades for him to throw.

When he got right down to it, he was showing a lot of trust in these people, and that made him uncomfortable. They were his captors, after all.

Then again, he supposed they were trusting him as well. Their forces would be fighting down below, and he could cause a great deal of damage with the weapons they were providing if he had a mind to.

Of course, then they'd drop him off the building.

The five minutes that he'd been told it would take for the enemy to arrive at their location dragged out until it felt more like twenty, but that was because he refused to check his internal chronometer. Waiting for battle always seemed to take forever.

He spent the time examining the rocket launcher that he held on the plank in front of him. The device was a tube that could be extended by grasping both ends and pulling them apart. Small sights within would then pop up, allowing him to aim at the target. It was already extended.

It was going to be a lot like firing the sniper rifle, he suspected. The height from which he'd be firing the weapon would make the sights almost useless. They were designed for a weapon that had to struggle against gravity, and, in this case, it would be working with him. Sort of.

On flat terrain, a rocket would rise in trajectory after it had been fired and then drop back down into the appropriate location to impact the target. Firing from this greater height and at a downward angle, it would probably strike somewhere above where he was aiming. His first shot was going to be a test.

The second thing he'd be testing was how deadly the weapon really was. He had no idea what the lethal radius from the explosion would be, and he needed that information to allocate the weapons he had available. His allies didn't have an inexhaustible number of rockets, so he had to make each one count.

"The enemy is about to come into sight," Richard said from behind him. "It looks like they have scouts out front, so we're going to wait until they're in position before we run you out. Once we're sure they're all in the trap, we'll slide you out, and you can begin firing."

He nodded his agreement without speaking.

Now it didn't seem as if time were dragging at all. The horde warriors weren't dawdling.

As they began filtering into sight, Talbot wondered where they were going. Was there something further inside the city that they wanted to seize? How did they know what was waiting for them? What was their plan to locate and subdue the inhabitants?

Those were all very interesting questions that he'd have to figure out at some later point. Right now, he needed to make certain that they not only didn't get what they wanted but came to an unceremonious end.

"We're going to push you out in five… four… three," Lydia said softly.

Talbot steadied himself and prepared for the motion that he knew was coming. When it came, it was *very* smooth. They'd obviously practiced this technique many times.

He approved since that smoothness meant that he wasn't going to fall off the plank.

As soon as he was stable again, Talbot began scanning the enemy spread out below him. They weren't quite in position just yet, so he waited a couple of extra beats to allow them to get closer. He wanted them to be in place for the other ambushers to have the best effect when they sprang the trap.

A couple of the enemy warriors shouted when they saw his movement, but the crowd below didn't react by freezing. They kept moving. If anything, they sped up a little bit.

Satisfied that the enemy was in as good a position as they were going to get, Talbot rotated the rocket until he could see the enemy through the sights. He depressed the trigger on top of the rocket launcher, and it fired with a loud whoosh.

He closed his eyes tightly for two beats so that he wouldn't get any debris from the rocket motor in them. By the time he opened them again, the rocket had slammed into the ground below him.

It had struck maybe ten meters above where he'd intended. That wasn't too bad. Based on the number of bodies lying around it, the lethal radius was about fifteen meters, but it still hurt others out to about thirty.

He could work with that.

Rather than hand the now-useless rocket back, Talbot let it fall and reached back for the next rocket they'd already extended toward him in a holder on a piece of old pipe.

Even as he did so, he saw another rocket lance down from off to his right and strike in the middle of the crowded area below. A glance that way showed Chloe on a plank just like his, already reaching back for another rocket. She looked focused and was grinning coldly as she killed their enemies.

He approved.

This time he fired toward the back of the enemy column. He opened his eyes just in time to see the rocket strike. His aim was true, and he blew up what looked like a group of officers and their subordinates. That was going to affect the enemy's ability to control their troops.

By this point, a number of the enemy fighters below were firing bows toward his position. Some of them actually managed to strike the plank that he lay upon, but their arrows didn't penetrate the tough synthetic material.

He dropped the second empty tube and reached for the next. Right as he grabbed it, someone below fired off one of the antiarmor rockets they'd used in the big battle to kill his marines inside their powered armor.

The bright projectile missed him and struck the building somewhere far above. Richard and Lydia hauled the plank in just in time for him to avoid being hit by shattered glass and other debris. This was also something they'd obviously planned for.

Once the rain of deadly wreckage ended, they ran him back out again. The man who'd fired the rocket had killed himself—and those around him —with the rocket exhaust. Others a bit farther away writhed in pain from their burns. Talbot hoped any others that might be tempted to use one of those weapons would decide that it wasn't worth the price they'd pay.

Since no one else fired rockets at him, that seemed a safe bet.

One after another, Talbot fired the rockets handed to him into the forces below, targeting the front and rear of the column. He wanted to keep them pinned exactly where they were. If they managed to slide away, the ambush would be less effective.

Based on her targeting, Chloe was following his lead.

"Last rocket," Richard said, extending him the final one. "Hit them dead center."

Talbot obliged, shifting his aim to the packed center of the column. The enemy had congregated far too close to one another while trying to escape death at the rear and front of the column. This rocket would kill many dozens and injure far more.

Without the slightest bit of remorse, he triggered the rocket and sent it on its way. As soon as he assessed the damage that he'd just caused—which was significant—he looked back to see what came next.

They extended a box on another plank that was supported by a second rope and pulley to keep it balanced. Inside the box were dozens of grenades.

He never seen anything so primitive in person, but he was familiar with how they were supposed to work, based on old prespaceflight vids that Kelsey had made him watch. All he had to do was pull the pin and throw the grenade.

The timing of it really didn't matter. Talbot hoped they'd actually reach the ground before they went off, but he was sure that the defenders had already taken that into account.

In quick succession, he pulled the pins from the grenades and lobbed them in long arcs toward where he wanted them to fall. With the combat computer inside his implants calculating how far he could throw and what the wind conditions were, his aim was pretty good. His artificial muscles made throwing them easy, even from a prone position.

Since there were other explosions below, Chloe was again contributing to the mayhem. Her grenades landed closer to the building they were in since she didn't have the augmented muscles he did. Seeing that, he focused on more distant targets.

The grenades landed in clumps of surviving enemies, detonating a second or two after they struck the ground and bounced. Talbot emptied two boxes of grenades before Richard and Lydia pulled him back inside.

Talbot stood and stretched. That had felt good.

He was about to ask them what happened next when there was a loud explosion from down below. He leaned out the opening and saw that the ambushers had set off the mines under the ground and blown the wall they were hiding behind.

As the smoke started clearing, they opened fire on the enemy. Their guns were similar to those used in the old vids that Kelsey had made him watch, too. They might not be as effective as flechettes, but whatever they fired was certainly getting the job done at the ridiculously short range.

With all the death and destruction that he'd already dropped on them, the horde warriors were not in the mental place they needed to be to strike back, and that allowed the defenders to cut them down where they stood.

In less than five minutes, no one in the streets below moved. Most of the enemy were dead, but a number of them had fled. Since they'd scattered in just about every imaginable direction, it was going to be difficult for their commanders to get them back together again.

Unfortunately, Talbot was sure that many of them would run to the remaining column, and word would quickly get out about what had happened here. The defenders could try to reproduce this ambush, but he wasn't going to hold his breath that it would work.

They'd succeeded here, but the first ambush hadn't gone as planned. That group had mauled the city inhabitants. If all of the enemy survivors managed to get back together, this was still going to be a tough fight.

Talbot felt good about what he'd accomplished so far. Not just the fighting and killing, but the building of trust between these people and his own. That would help them get to where they needed to be once they'd kicked the horde out of the city.

* * *

Julia stared at the pin in Mertz's hand and felt her jaw drop. "Is that what I think it is?"

"If you think it's a Marine Raider insignia, then you're right," Mertz said. "What I want to know is how it got here."

She stood there with her hands on her hips, trying to imagine a set of circumstances in which someone would've lost something so rare and arcane down at the bottom of an abandoned megacity.

She failed.

"Leader Mordechai did say that the Marine Raiders were here back at the beginning of the Fall, but this pin doesn't look like it's been exposed that long," she finally ventured. "Could it really have been down here that long?"

Jebediah shook his head, eyeing the pin suspiciously. "Unlikely. Remember that for the first four hundred years, this area was in use. Someone would've found that pin before now if it had been down here since the last Marine Raider was in our city. It had to have been dropped after the power went out.

"I can see a little bit of corrosion, so I don't think it's been here for more than a few years. That means it belonged to the people that stole the fusion plant. Exactly how that's possible, I can't imagine."

"Well, we don't have to solve this mystery right now," Mertz said. "Our immediate objective hasn't changed. We've got to go back down and figure out what to do next. These air bottles are a finite resource that we can't afford to waste."

As they walked down the stairs, Julia tried to figure out how the pin could be connected with the people that had stolen the fusion plant. What was their relation to the Marine Raiders? Were they descendants of some survivors? Or had the Raiders formed some type of organization that had survived all this time?

In the end, she probably wasn't going to figure out the answer anytime soon.

They shut off their air as soon as they made it back to the area with functional life support. The walk down to the bottom of the stairs only took a couple of minutes, and no one said anything. Everyone seemed lost in thought. Like her, they were probably trying to figure out what this meant.

Once they'd reached the lowest level, she gestured at the rooms around them. "I think we need to find a place to sit down and have something to eat. I'm starving."

Before either of the others could respond, there was a loud metallic clang from inside the lift shaft. All three of them turned and stared at it as if it might suddenly come alive.

For a moment, she considered that that might be exactly what had happened. If it had started working again, perhaps that noise was the lift adjusting itself.

"That sounded like something fell onto the lift car," Mertz said. "We should take a look."

Julia pressed the button to open the doors and quickly located the small hatch built into the roof. "Lift me up, and I'll see what happened."

The two men lifted her up, and she opened the hatch. As soon as she had her torso into the darkness beyond, she spotted a short metal bar lying about half a meter from her.

That made her wary. If one had come loose, another could come flying out of the darkness with no warning whatsoever. If so, it could maim or kill her in a heartbeat.

"Is anyone up there?" she shouted.

For a few moments, only the echoes of her shout floated back. Then another voice called down.

"Julia? Are you okay?"

It was Carl Owlet. Damn, but the man was *resourceful*. It seemed as if every time they needed a solution, he was there to offer it.

"The lift stopped working, and the stairs are blocked by a door that I can't open. Other than being stuck down here, we're fine."

"You need to get out of the lift car. I've already broken off a couple of rungs and don't want to hurt you. I've got some equipment with me that I might be able to use to repair the lift, but even if I can't, I'll wager that my cutting tool can get through your door. One way or the other, we'll get you back up.

"Austin and Ralph are on the level where the fusion plant was, so if need be, they can bring more help or maybe use the rope we found to lift us out. Don't worry. The cavalry is here."

Julia dropped back down into the lift, and all three of them exited the car.

She raised an eyebrow at Mertz as soon as they were safely clear. "Is it just me, or does that man have a solution for every problem?"

"He's got an answer even when there *isn't* a problem," Mertz said with a grin. "I've seen him do miraculous things. He's young, but when he gets more seasoning, he's going to be even more formidable. Why do you ask?"

"I was just curious. If I run into someone like Carl later, it would be good to know how he ticks so that I can form an alliance with them."

She couched her language that way because explaining the truth wasn't something that Jebediah needed to hear.

Mertz nodded, seemingly understanding what she was trying to say. "That's sound thinking. If you can find someone like him, you're going to have an ally that will stand with you through thick and thin. One who's more than capable of achieving the goals you set out for him."

Interestingly, it sounded as if Mertz approved. That shocked her a little bit. She'd have expected him to try and wave her off. Instead, he seemed to be giving her the green light to try and form a relationship with her universe's version of Carl.

That gave her a lot to think about. Sadly, she still had a lot of time to work out a plan. They weren't getting out of Frankfort anytime soon.

19

With the experience of the previous fight behind her, Kelsey was in a much better position to effectively attack during the second ambush. The moment the wall came down, she was firing.

The slide on the submachine gun quickly locked back once it had fired every bullet in the magazine. She'd been practicing with those too, so she was faster swapping out the expended magazine for a new one.

The group in front of her was in massive disarray. Someone had been firing rockets into the horde warriors and dropping grenades on them from what Kelsey could see. That had given her and the other ambushers the opportunity they'd needed to completely decimate the forces arrayed against them. In just a few minutes, the battlefield was empty except for the dead and dying.

While the rest of the defenders were gruesomely sorting the dead from the injured and seeing if any of the latter could be saved, Kelsey found the leader of her new group and asked the question that was most prominent on her mind.

"Is my husband okay? His name is Talbot. If possible, I'd like to see him."

The short woman nodded. "He was involved in the ambush, or so I'm told. He fired rockets from the building across from us, so he was never in any real danger once the enemy decided that they couldn't fire rockets back at him. I think we can credit some of our success to his skill. He seems like a great warrior. Much like yourself."

That made Kelsey smile. "Oh, he is. Would it be possible for me to go see him now?"

The woman nodded her assent, and they quickly crossed the street to another building. Finding a clear path through the carnage was impossible, so she just held her breath and accepted that her shoes and pants would be bloody.

From there, they went up several floors and exited into what looked like a staging area for a sniper's nest. If the sniper used rifles, grenades, and rockets.

Talbot was there, along with Chloe Laird and some people she didn't recognize. As soon as he saw her, her husband headed her way, and she greeted him with a grin, her arms wide open.

"I hear you ran into a bit of trouble," he said after he'd squeezed her tight and pushed her back to arm's length. "You seem like you're okay."

She shrugged slightly. "The first ambush didn't account for how ferocious the bastards were. They came right in after us. We hurt them, but not badly enough to break them like you did. Good job, by the way. You really kicked their asses."

"Chloe and I did okay," he admitted with a grin. "That still leaves at least one column that hasn't been bloodied yet. You think they're going to react the same way as the group you ambushed, don't you?"

"If they can," she agreed with a nod. "I'd imagine that a lot of people got away from the two ambushes and will join them, so they'll know what's about to happen. It seems like we've made a good start, but I'm not sure if we can count on it happening again. It looks like you caught them completely unaware and blew the snot out of them. That was decisive."

One of the men standing nearby came up and nodded at her. "Our people executed the third ambush just a few minutes ago. Just as you suspected, it wasn't as effective as this one. Still, they achieve their purpose, and the enemy has begun retreating.

"I think that we're going to have to be satisfied with them going back to the camp they've established just inside Frankfort. They lost one ambush and got hurt in a couple of others, so maybe that's going to make them think twice about trying again today."

"What do we do now?" Talbot asked. "How can we be certain which direction they'll go next, and what do we do when they do it?"

The man shrugged slightly. "We have people watching them. Depending on the direction they head, we'll move forces into place to ambush them again. They haven't run into all of our traps yet, so we've still got a few surprises left.

"The biggest one is that we've got explosives planted underneath certain open areas between buildings. Substantially larger charges than we used here. They didn't hit any this time, but if we play our cards right the next time, we might be able to lure them into a trap they didn't see coming, even if they're wary. If we can, that'll be almost as effective as this attack was."

"How many people are we talking about?" Kelsey asked, giving the man her full attention.

"We know that they've left some reserves to hold their marshaling area, so counting that, they've got at least two thousand people that are still able to fight, probably more. I'd imagine the walking wounded will total another fifteen hundred or so."

Kelsey nodded slowly. "If they regroup, I think Talbot and I might be the best choices to lure them into a trap. It may not seem like it, but we can move *very* quickly when we want to. Given a good opportunity, I think we can draw them into one of the areas you're talking about and get that decisive victory we all need."

Talbot looked as if he wanted to argue, but instead, he shrugged. "What's the plan?"

Kelsey smiled coldly. "We can taunt them with the fact that we're the ones that blew up their castle and leaders. That'll get them all excited. This may be our one chance to decisively engage them in a killing field of our choice. We can't let this pass by."

The people around them looked at her as if she were crazy, and she couldn't blame them. The idea sounded insane.

Hell, it probably was.

It was risky, but they had to thoroughly thrash the horde if they wanted to get out of Frankfort. Not only because they needed the permission of the inhabitants to leave, but because it would be impossible to get away with an effective enemy still fighting all around them.

The horde had slaughtered her crewmates and friends. She wanted revenge, and with this plan, she could get it in a way that it served their purposes.

No matter how they played this, it was going to be dangerous. All kinds of things could still go wrong. Having several thousand enemies baying at one's heels would be hair-raising under the best of circumstances, but that was really the only option if they wanted to end this fight decisively.

"Someone needs to show us where the traps are," she said coldly. "We'll take care of the rest."

* * *

WITH ONLY A FEW ADDITIONAL MISHAPS, Carl managed to get down to the roof of the lift car alive and unharmed. That was something of a relief, considering that he must've snapped a dozen rungs on the way down and knocked yet another one completely free just before he'd reached the lift car.

He certainly hoped that he could get the lift working again because going back up on the ladder was far too dangerous. He untied the rope and left it hanging there. He shouted up the shaft, telling Ralph and Austin to stand by.

Getting through the hatch in the roof of the lift car wasn't a problem, and just a few moments later, he was standing in front of Admiral Mertz, Julia, and Jebediah. To his shock, Julia pulled him into a hug.

"It's *so* good to see you," she said. "We weren't sure that anyone was going to realize that we were gone so soon."

Her hug made him feel a little uncomfortable. He wasn't used to intimate contact with women in general, and he wasn't sure that his wife would approve in any case. In fact, he was pretty sure she wouldn't like it at all.

When Julia let him go, he stepped back self-consciously and smiled as he nodded. "As soon as we realized that you weren't back, we came looking for you. Austin and Ralph will head back up and start gathering a rescue party if they don't hear from us in another hour. Hopefully, we'll join them before then."

Having said that, he reentered the lift and quickly had the control panel open. He plugged his equipment in and ran a brief diagnostic. The problem immediately presented itself.

"It looks like the main control board shorted out. I'm not going to be able to repair this without the right components—which I can salvage from another lift and swap out, given half an hour at some point—so I'm afraid that we're going to have to use the stairs."

Admiral Mertz grunted. "That's not exactly the answer I was looking for, but I guess it doesn't surprise me. Do you have something that can unlock a security door?"

Carl nodded. "I've got something in my toolkit that will help me get through just about any mechanical lock. I've also got a cutter that I can use if I have to."

"Then I suppose we'd best be about it," the admiral said. "I'd rather not waste any more air than we have to."

The climb up only took a few minutes, so Carl was quickly looking at the security door in the stairwell. "It's probably meant to make sure that only maintenance personnel can get down here. This isn't something one can hack, so it's secure in a technological society in a way that an electronic lock isn't. Let's see what I can do."

He opened his toolkit and pulled out a set of lock picks that he'd recreated from a template he'd found in the ship's library aboard *Invincible*. As he'd told the admiral, he very rarely ran into something like this, but when he did, it was nice to have the correct tools for the job.

Thankfully, they didn't weigh very much, so having them in his kit didn't cost him much extra weight.

Sadly, his skill with the picks was relatively basic. He'd only run into a few mechanical locks to practice with. Thankfully, he had some instructional vids stored in his implants that he could access now that they'd been rebooted.

He watched several in quick succession as he fitted the lock picks into the mechanism. In the end, it took him far longer than he liked, but he finally felt the picks catch just the way he wanted and rotated his wrists, turning the lock with a loud click.

"Gotcha!" he exulted as he stood.

That earned him a hearty back slap from Jebediah, which sent him staggering forward. "Excellent work, young man. Now, let's go before we run out of air."

The rest of the climb was uneventful though tiring. By the time they reached the level where the fusion plant had been, they'd used about forty minutes of the time that Austin and Ralph had promised to wait.

The two were pleased to see them, and congratulations were exchanged all around. They pulled the rope up, closed the lift doors, and set course back the way they'd come. They made it back into breathable atmosphere with a healthy margin of air still left in the cache that he'd brought down.

If they were going to be here long, they couldn't count on continually scavenging air bottles to use. He was going to have to tap into the power on the bottom level and get the life-support systems working in the areas that they had to traverse.

Basically, that was the stairwell leading down, the level where the fusion plant had once been, and the second stairwell. Until then, they'd have to harvest more air to be able to get up and down as needed.

More importantly, he had to focus his attention on the maglev train so that they could figure out how to summon it. It might be their ticket out of the city, and he wasn't going to let it slip through his fingers.

"Any word on how the fighting is going?" Admiral Mertz asked.

Carl shook his head. "Nothing so far. I'm hoping that Kelsey and Talbot are okay, but knowing them, they're in the thick of it. I really wish that we'd been able to salvage some operational armor or weapons. Too bad there isn't a stock of weapons left over from when the Marine Raiders were here."

He frowned and turned toward Jebediah. "Didn't someone say that the Raiders went out on a mission and never came back? Surely they didn't take *everything* they had with them. They must've left some equipment behind. I still might be able to salvage something from it that would make a real difference in the fighting."

Jebediah nodded. "We've kept what they left behind secure. I've never been into the room itself, so I can't really tell you much about the contents."

"Could you take me there?"

The large man considered his request for a few moments and then nodded. "I'll let Admiral Mertz and Julia report the situation we found below to my father. While they do, I'll take you to the cache."

Carl wasn't certain that they'd find anything helpful, but it never hurt to try. Sometimes luck was good, sometimes it was bad, but if one didn't check, one never knew.

"Excellent," he said. "Let's get this show on the road."

20

———————

A pair of guards escorted Jared and Julia up into the tower to meet with Leader Mordechai. He wasn't in the wide-open upper floor but down in an interior room about halfway up the tower. Someone had cut away part of an inside wall to give him a view outside the building, but he was still sheltered from any of the weather that was now coming through the shattered windows.

The man himself was seated behind a large desk, doing what looked like *paperwork*. The concept of that seemed almost unimaginable to Jared. This was a post-apocalyptic society. They might've retained some of the knowledge that they'd had from before, but the idea of working with actual paper boggled him.

As soon as they entered the room, Mordechai set aside the pen he'd been using and steepled his fingers as he considered them.

"Where's Jebediah?" he asked, his eyebrow raised.

"He's taken Carl to show him something," Jared said. "He said that he'd be up as soon as he was done with that but that you could accept that he'd verified what we'd told you."

At those words, one of the guards who'd accompanied them on the trip up stepped forward. "I overheard him, Leader Mordechai. That's exactly what Jebediah said."

"Then that's good enough for me," the older man said. "Now comes the mystery of figuring out who took our heritage from us. A theft of that magnitude is unbelievable. The effort that would've been required and the sheer number of people it probably took takes my breath away. The fact that they carried this out right under our noses makes me angry. Do we have any idea how they might've done such a thing?"

Jared reached into his pouch and retrieved the pin he'd found, placing it on the desk. "We found this in the stairwell. It looks like whoever was down there only activated the life-support system for the lowest few levels. This was on the stairs above that safe layer. Do you recognize the emblem?"

The older man picked up and examined the pin, his eyes narrowing. "It looks vaguely familiar, but I can't say that I know how I know it."

"It's the emblem of the Marine Raiders. My sister intends to use something very much like it once she has more of our marines fully transitioned.

"Jebediah said that based on the corrosion, he believed it had only been down there for a few years. Since it appears to be made out of conventional materials, I'm willing to accept that he knows better than I what its durability is. That means that somewhere on the maglev train system, there's a group of people that have some kind of association with the Marine Raiders."

The older man leaned back in his chair and shook his head. "That idea is ludicrous on its face. The Marine Raiders stationed here didn't last more than a few decades after the invasion."

"Could there have been other groups?" Julia asked. "Just because you only know of one doesn't mean that there weren't others. What if their descendants—or some kind of organization formed by them—came here to take the fusion plant?

"Obviously, whoever did this had a lot of technological know-how. Disassembling something as complex as a fusion plant isn't the kind of task that you're going to undertake without knowing how it works. So it's credible that an organization set up by people like that could still be in operation somewhere."

Mordechai sat there for almost a minute without speaking. Then he shrugged.

"The only answers we're going to find are those that we seek ourselves. Since there's a technological society out there somewhere, I think it would behoove both our groups to make some kind of effort in contacting them. The theft is long done, but it may be that my people can leverage the feelings of outrage that we have into some type of concessions from those people.

"For all I know, they may be worthy enough, even if they *are* thieves. It's not as if we've been using that fusion plant for the last hundred years. In any case, the next step must be finding them. At least that will be the case once we've won this fight against the horde."

"Speaking of the fighting, how is it going?" Jared asked. "Are my people okay? Have we managed to drive the horde out of your city?"

The man waggled his hand. "One of the ambushes didn't go so well. A number of our people were killed, and the horde was triumphant there. The second ambush went exceptionally well, and the enemy was decimated.

"I've only just received word that the third ambush fell somewhere in between the other two. We managed to inflict a lot of casualties, but the enemy withdrew in good order. Now all the survivors are retreating toward where they're keeping their reserves. I anticipate that once they regroup, they'll be back.

"Your people are well, though I must warn you that your sister and her husband have volunteered to lure the enemy into another trap. I can't imagine how, but they seem quite determined."

Jared chuckled darkly. "Kelsey's very stubborn. If anyone can make it work, it's her. While they're doing that, we should talk about what we're going to do next. Your son is escorting Carl to take a look at the hardware the Marine Raiders left behind when they vanished.

"It's possible that something will still be usable, even though it won't have power. It would be nice to face a technological society with weapons that might actually make them sit up and take notice."

Mordechai nodded. "While they're doing that, we should discuss what happens next. I've decided to release you, so as of this moment, you are no longer our prisoners but our guests.

"All of your weapons and belongings will be returned to you immediately. When it comes time for you to depart, we'll allow you to do so without any hindrance and give you what aid we can. It is my deepest hope that you will continue to assist us in the matter of the stolen fusion plant so that we can make contact with the thieves as well."

"I'm looking forward to that discussion," Jared said. "Almost as much as I am to lunch because I'm starving."

"Me, too," Julia said. "I'm so hungry that survival rations sound good right now."

Mordechai laughed as he rose from his seat. "Then let's go get something to eat."

* * *

TALBOT RAISED his head slightly and stared out over the area in front of the building they were hiding in. It was positioned much closer to the edge of Frankfort, so the buildings were shorter, and there was more space between them than there had been in the packed interior of the dead megacity.

The horde had taken advantage of that extra space to set up a fortified camp. His implants estimated that there were more than two thousand people inside it. That number was going to rise by at least another thousand as the survivors of the various ambushes trickled in.

He and Kelsey had discussed the matter and decided to wait until as many people as possible were present before they attempted to lure them into the trap. There was no use in leaving a fighting force worthy of the name behind to attack them again. If they could lure them all into an ambush, that would ensure that they achieved the maximum number of casualties.

Satisfied with what he'd seen and confident that none of the sentries had noticed his presence, Talbot stepped farther back into the gloom and found a place to sit next to Kelsey. The room had once been an office of some kind. The abandoned chairs allowed them to sit around a desk that was lit by the little sunlight that filtered in through the doorway.

Based on the ruined elegance of the furnishings, it must've once belonged to someone both wealthy and powerful. Now it smelled of mildew and prolonged neglect.

"I think we're going to have to wait at least another hour for the last of the survivors to make their way back," he said as he sat. "That'll give them a chance to report what happened and really piss the people in charge off. The angrier they are, the more likely they are to come after us."

She nodded and handed him a ration bar. "Then I suggest you eat and drink while you can. We aren't going to have a chance to rest once we start running for our lives. Even with our greater speed, we'll have to stay in sight, or they're going to stop chasing us."

He tore the wrapper off the bar and took a bite. Long practice allowed him to ignore the relatively terrible taste. The ration wasn't meant to be a gourmet meal. Rather, it was packed with nutrients and vitamins that were mandatory in a survival situation.

Still, couldn't someone have tried to make them taste less like sawdust?

"Do you really think that we're doing the right thing here?" he asked. "Getting thousands of people to chase us with murder in their eyes seems to be a pretty chancy thing."

She grinned. "If they catch us, we're screwed. So let that be your motivation to run just a little bit faster."

He grunted. That was the worst motivational speech he'd ever received. His wife really needed to work on that.

"Any word on the expedition to get the fusion plant back online?" he asked.

"I got a call from Carl a few minutes ago. The extended range of his updated implant communicator is handy. We definitely need to see about getting everyone else equipped with one as soon as possible.

"It turns out that somebody's been robbing Frankfort. They got down to the area where the fusion plant should have been, but it was gone. Someone had disassembled the whole thing and carried it off."

The news made him blink. "Seriously? How is that even possible? It's not as if you can disassemble a fusion plant without the technical know-how and have a useful device at the end.

"Even in the Old Empire, it took specialized skills to do that kind of thing. The man or woman on the street couldn't even follow detailed instructions to make that happen. Here and now? Impossible."

"Impossible or not, Carl says that's exactly what they did. Apparently, the theft only took place a couple of years ago, which only adds to the mystery.

"There's apparently a maglev train station on the lowest level of the city. Whoever they were, they used the power serving it and got the life-support system down there back online. They stripped an incredible amount of supplies and equipment from the lowest levels of the city. The ones that are blocked from access because of the bad air.

"I'd be willing to bet they turned on the life-support system all the way up to the level of the fusion plant for that. They got one of the lifts working and used it to transport everything they wanted down to the lowest level and probably took the most valuable things away via the train. Then they shut off life support—except for the lowest levels—and the bad air drifted its way back down, leaving no one the wiser."

Talbot shook his head. "Even hearing you say that, I still find it hard to believe. Still, if we've got an operational train station, that means Carl could probably find us a way to get to these people. Potential allies with technological know-how might be beneficial in our current circumstances."

"I agree. We'll see if Leader Mordechai is on board with that or just stays pissed off that somebody stole all of his stuff. He doesn't seem to be the kind of person to let go of a grudge, if you know what I mean."

The two of them sat chatting for the next half hour, with him making occasional trips to the window to look at the horde camp. By the end of that time, it was apparent that the survivors had begun arriving because the enemy camp was in turmoil.

Kelsey came over when he called her and nodded in satisfaction. "I think we've got enough people down there to be worthwhile. Why don't we go ahead and make a little trip up the street? We'll head back this way as soon as we get their attention. With any luck, we'll make them so angry that the whole lot of them gives chase.

"The nearest area that the defenders have buried explosives is about a kilometer away. It's along one of the main paths into the city, so it's a shame that the horde didn't choose that route when marching in. If they had, the defenders could've blown them up without having to fight."

"If wishes were horses, we'd all be hip deep in horse crap," he said philosophically. "Let's get this over with. I want to take care of these bastards once and for all so that we can get back to saving the Empire."

21

Carl followed Jebediah on a winding trip into the underground tunnels beneath Frankfort. The stash was obviously not centrally located. Thankfully, it didn't seem to be very far underneath the city itself. Otherwise, they'd have had to deal with the bad air again.

Not to say that the air they were breathing was of the highest quality, but it hadn't crossed the threshold of being noxious yet. The carbon dioxide levels were rising by the time they stopped, but it was still within what he'd call tolerable parameters.

Barely.

Rather than doing anything with the lock on the door in front of them, the large man reached up to the ceiling and pushed at a panel there. It rose slightly, and something shiny fell out. The large man grabbed for it but missed. It struck the ground with the distinctive sound of metal.

It was a key, probably like the one that the security door below had once required.

Jebediah picked it up, inserted it into the lock, and twisted. With a loud click, the door unlocked, and the large man pushed it open.

The interior of the room was just as dark as the rest of the megacity, but Carl could tell just from the torches that they carried that there was a significant amount of supplies within the room. The first things that grabbed his attention—commanded it, really—were the four suits of gray Marine Raider armor on stands against the far right-hand wall.

"Holy cow," he said reverently as he stepped into the room, automatically lowering his torch so that it didn't scorch the ceiling. "It looks as if these were put here in an operational state. If so, it may be possible to recharge the power cells and utilize them. That would have a huge impact on combat operations. You really should've said something about these before the fighting started."

"I've never been in this room before," Jebediah said. "I'm sure that my father had a rough idea of what was here, but I suspect that he hasn't been here more than a few times since he was a boy.

"In any case, we wouldn't have trusted you with such a thing before now. Even if we had, there was no power to charge them with nor charging facilities with which to do so."

Carl nodded and moved over to the armor. A quick check showed that the power cells were dead, as expected. He couldn't get any kind of status from the suits at all.

A quick visual inspection told him that, barring any fried electronics or otherwise faulty circuits, the armor looked as if it had been in operational condition when stored.

All of the suits were significantly larger than what would typically fit on Kelsey or Julia. Some of that could be adjusted. He'd done the customization on Kelsey's suit himself, so he was quite familiar with the process.

That didn't mean that it would be easy under the present circumstances. He'd had a ship full of the right equipment and spare parts to make the modifications before. These suits had almost certainly been adjusted for their last users, so there wouldn't be any need for them to have any of the more robust adjustment tools with them.

He'd do what he could.

Carl widened his search to the rest of the room. Placed nearby were cases holding flechette and plasma weapons sized for the armor.

Ammunition for each of them was stored adjacent to the weapons themselves. Each of the power packs was undoubtedly dead, but it should be a reasonably straightforward process to recharge them.

The smaller weapons used batteries inside the magazines themselves for their power. There were a lot of them, and it would take time to fully charge them all. Thankfully, there were a couple of racks made for just that purpose sitting nearby.

The problem was that everything was going to have to be carried down the stairs to the lowest level of the megacity. That would be backbreaking labor and require that Carl had enough air bottles to make it work unless he got the life-support system for the areas he needed to traverse back online. Getting the broken lift working again was also a priority.

If he could do those things, the process would be significantly easier, and it would take one big problem off of his shoulders. It would also allow others to work below without having to be trapped there.

The tricky part was going to be the fact that he couldn't just turn on life support for the entire lower section of the megacity. That might draw enough power to alert the people running it that someone was using their power, which might be enough for them to turn it off on them.

If any of their plans were to work, he had to avoid that outcome at all costs.

He returned his attention to the supplies around him. There were a lot of marine knives, as well as a collection of short swords like Kelsey's. Apparently, these people had had similar ideas to Ned Quincy.

Hell, for all Carl knew, they might literally have gotten the idea from the man. In such a small community, that certainly wasn't a big jump.

If he ever got back to *Persephone*, he'd have to devote some more attention to working on a new home for the AI. Ned's consciousness was currently in stasis inside jury-rigged hardware, but he had some ideas that might allow the strange being to finally have a place to call his own.

Ned had been created inside Kelsey's implants and had lived there his entire life as an artificial intelligence. That was awkward for both of them, so Ned had asked to be removed and archived until such time as a solution was put together.

It was risky. There was no guarantee that Ned would wake up again when his new home was ready. Still, it was a risk that the man had insisted they take.

Carl would do everything he could to make sure the AI survived, but he couldn't do that if they never got off of Terra. Which brought him back around to what he needed to do now.

There were three sets of blades just like Kelsey's, so that was going to make their lives a lot easier when it came to melee fighting. He knew that those who could use the weapons would be thrilled to have them.

He was about to turn away when he spotted another sword stashed behind the others. It wasn't a pair in shoulder harnesses but a single blade. Carl carefully picked up the scabbard and drew it.

The blade was made of the same hull metal as Kelsey's, so it would hold its monomolecular edge forever. Unlike her shorter blades, this one was long and had a gentle, elegant curve. It was very similar to the type of weapon that Clarice Beauchamp favored.

He immediately vowed to see that she got the weapon should they gain access to the cache. It was the least they could do for the woman who'd helped them survive this terrible planet.

Everything else in the room was crated supplies and weapons: handheld plasma grenades, regular explosives, and a wide variety of equipment that might prove useful in a guerrilla war. There were also selections of clothing and unpowered armor that would be useful as well.

Whoever had stocked the cache had done an extremely thorough job. With everything here, the Raiders could've continued fighting for a long time.

He wondered what had happened to them. Obviously, they hadn't taken their powered armor. It had probably been some type of scouting mission, and they'd been ambushed. Even Marine Raiders could be killed if one was willing to spill enough of their own blood to do it.

Having completed his circuit of the room, Carl returned to where Jebediah stood near the door.

"I think a fair bit of this could be useful," the scientist said. "The question is, what will you allow us to use?"

The large man smiled like a shark. "I'm quite certain that we can come to an agreement. You probably won't like the terms for some of the more potent items, but my father will be willing to deal.

"I can tell you now that the most significant thing on his mind—other than throwing the horde out of our city—is getting the fusion plant returned. That may be beyond the scope of what you'd been prepared to offer, but we each have something the other wants. You are perhaps in a better position to negotiate with the thieves, and we have all this equipment that might be critical to the ultimate success of your mission.

"You want it all. I can see that in your eyes. If your admiral is willing to negotiate, you can have it. My father is no fool. He knows that if there's a chance to destroy the artificial intelligences that wrecked the Empire, he must assist in whatever way he can, yet he has to serve our people as well.

"A balance must be struck. My guess? Convince the thieves to return the fusion plant and shielding, restore it to operation, and provide assistance in keeping it running, and you may have everything in this cache."

Carl nodded. "Then let me see if I can negotiate a down payment. If I were to manipulate the life-support system and power that's coming from the maglev system so that it was easy to get people down to those lower levels without having to breathe with air bottles, that would allow you to retrieve everything that was stored there.

"Right now, that's within my power. Everything I need to make that happen is in this room. You just have to give me access to it."

Jebediah nodded at once. "That sounds fair to me, but my father will need to agree. Having seen the vast amount of scavenged equipment already boxed below, I feel quite certain that he will approve of this interim agreement. Come. Let's go find out if I'm right."

* * *

KELSEY AND TALBOT made their way down into the tunnels again. Once there, they set off toward the enemy camp. The key was going to be getting close enough to be seen without being immediately engaged. It was going to be a delicate balancing act of enraging the enemy while not being killed by the rage they'd provoked.

Once they reached an area where she felt comfortable going back up for a good look, they crept up the stairs and peered out from the first floor of the new building. Off in the distance, she could see the edge of the camp and the sentries posted there.

She focused her ocular implants on the sentries and looked them over carefully. They were armed with swords and bows. Kelsey saw no signs of rockets or other advanced weaponry. Specialized groups deeper in the camp might have had them, though.

They might even have one of those EMP weapons, which would be a disaster, but she really doubted it. Those would only be useful against things like powered armor, from the enemy's point of view. They also had to be damned difficult to make. They wouldn't just waste them. They'd save them for some type of last-ditch defense against a large force that had high-technology weapons. Not against a dozen people.

At least that was what she told herself.

Talbot hunched down next to her, looking around the corner of the building. "How do you want to play this?"

"I think we should just step out into the open. They're going to see us right away and send someone to deal with us. That'll give us a chance to get them really riled up before we dodge back out of sight.

"It may take several attempts to draw them out completely. I've never done anything like this before, so I'm not really sure."

"Well, what's the worst that could go wrong?" he asked with a wry smile.

They stepped out of the building together, walked to the center of the open area, and turned toward the sentries. At this point, they were about two hundred meters away from the warriors.

The men on guard saw them and shouted for them to halt.

Kelsey laughed as loudly as she could for her audience. "You expect me to stand here and turn myself in after I blew up your leaders?" she shouted. "You've obviously lost your minds. And now that you've invaded this city, I've killed even more of you. You're powerless to stop me. You can't even *catch* me."

That started several of the men jogging in their direction.

She made a motion to Talbot, and they ducked around the corner of the building and back down into the tunnels again. By the time the guards arrived, she and Talbot were long gone. Their new hideout was in another building a short distance away.

With the maze of tunnels under the megacity, it was going to be hard for the horde to figure out where they'd gone. That would remain true unless the enemy flooded the tunnels, looking for them.

Once they looked back at the enemy camp, she saw that the sentries had returned to their post. It looked like they were arguing. There was a lot of gesticulating and finger pointing.

She allowed them time to summon some officers to deal with the situation. The higher the rage went into their command structure, the better.

They waited about half an hour for the enemy to settle down before she and Talbot confronted the camp from a different direction. This time, the warriors tried to race after them at once, and more people moved into place to back them up.

That was a heartening response. This might work after all. She was pissing them off, and they wanted to make her shut up. They wanted to kill her.

Time to make the pot boil over.

She and Talbot retreated to the building that they'd used as an observation post, grabbed the dozen rockets they'd brought with them, and moved to the next area she'd designated to confront the horde camp. This time, they didn't say anything at all after they'd revealed themselves.

Kelsey fired her rocket while Talbot did the same. The paired explosions blew up a lot of people and set the rest of the crowd that had gathered scattering in different directions.

It turned out one of the people in the crowd had a rocket of his own. He fired it back toward her and her husband. Sadly for him, it must've been difficult to aim because it missed by a wide margin.

Or perhaps it was just of a lower quality than the ones they were using, or he was a terrible shot. With the speed of the weapons, they could hardly have evaded if his aim had been good, but they could certainly make sure he didn't fire any more at them. Talbot fired a rocket that blew the bastard up, along with some of his closest friends.

The two of them raised their aim and began sending rockets into the main camp. The long arcs dropped the warheads into the larger concentrations of people gathered around the tents that the horde warriors had brought with them.

By the time they'd expended their supply of rockets, there was a general movement in the camp toward their position and a lot of shouting. Almost a roar, really.

Yup, they'd seriously pissed them off.

"Let's go," she said, turning to jog away from the disrupted camp.

Retreating from the area was a tricky proposition. They wanted to keep the enemy in sight to troll them but not let them get close enough to where they'd be a threat.

Unfortunately for them, the enemy had other plans.

To her dismay, Kelsey found out that the scouts the city had sent to observe the camp had failed to see about half a dozen horses. Worse, the concealed horsemen had circled around behind Talbot and her and were now blocking their escape.

Now she had to choose between facing the mob behind her and the mounted warriors ahead. That choice wasn't even particularly difficult.

She used the submachine gun she'd brought along to open fire at the horsemen as she charged forward. Several of the riders and their horses went down, but even more of them began pouring into the area ahead. The count was now up to a dozen.

Obviously, the scouts had missed significantly more horses than she'd imagined possible—or, more likely, the horsemen had arrived between the time the scouts had reported, and Kelsey and Talbot had taken up their position near the camp.

Arrows from the pursuers began falling around them, zipping past like angry bees. Kelsey turned on her heel and emptied her weapon at the warriors behind them, trying to make them pull back.

They ignored her fire and rushed forward, ignoring their own casualties. From the number of people that she could see, she might just have succeeded in emptying the camp. That was good if they could get to the ambush site. Not so good if they died right here.

"We're not going to be able to stop them," Talbot said as he switched magazines and continued firing at the horsemen. "What's the plan?"

"We go forward," she said. "Take one of my swords, and when the time is right, just start cutting a hole right through them."

They'd brought a lot of ammunition, but it took a surprisingly short time to empty the last of the magazines. When that happened, they let their guns fall onto their straps, and she drew her swords, handing one to Talbot.

Using their Marine Raider augmentation, they charged into the surviving horsemen, slashing and using their stronger muscles to leap farther than the enemy expected. To add to the chaos, the bowmen behind them didn't even slow their rate of fire, killing and wounding their comrades and horses with wild abandon as they tried to take her and Talbot down.

All she and her husband needed to do was get to the far side of the horsemen and haul ass. If any of the mounted warriors survived, she hoped the chaos would delay their pursuit.

That hope proved to be beyond reach, as the surviving horsemen turned to pursue them as soon as they broke through. Kelsey turned and charged them again, drawing her pistol and firing it with one hand as she prepared to use her sword with the other.

Talbot turned with her, covering her with his pistol. Those were meant to be last-ditch weapons, but she supposed it was all or nothing now.

Then the inevitable happened. An arrow struck Kelsey in the upper thigh. She grunted in pain and continued firing. Seconds later, the last of the horsemen was down.

The wound was deep and bleeding fast. Her medical nanites would handle that, and her pharmacology unit dumped painkillers into her system to allow her to keep moving. The wound wouldn't stop her, but it would slow her.

Under these circumstances, that would be deadly.

"I'm not going to be able to run with this," she said. "I have to get into the tunnels, and you're going to have to lead them on to the ambush. I'm sorry."

"Bull. Keep covering me."

With that, he tossed her over his shoulder and ran, dodging to try and avoid being peppered with arrows. She used her pistol to engage the enemy, but with all the bouncing around, her aim was crap. Luckily, with that many targets, a miss was difficult to achieve.

In a way, the situation was almost funny. Maybe she'd laugh about it someday.

If she survived.

22

———

"Holy crap," Julia muttered under her breath as she stared at all the equipment stashed around the room, her eyes wide. "You've hit the freaking jackhole, Carl!"

"Jackpot," he corrected absently as he moved a small crate and started searching another.

"Whatever. Neither one of those words means anything to me."

He turned to stare at her. "Kelsey routinely cleans everyone's clocks at cards and has more than passing familiarity with other forms of gambling. How can you not know what jackpot means?"

She frowned back at him. "Damned if I know. Where could she have learned all that stuff? You know? Never mind. Let's focus on what we have here."

The two of them were inside the room containing the Marine Raider cache, with only a single guard at the door. Not because they were under watch to make sure that they didn't escape but because their hosts wanted to make sure that nothing walked off from the stash without being properly accounted for.

They'd made a preliminary agreement to allow Carl the use of some of the gear to aid him in turning the life-support system in the lowest levels back on. The items that they were taking now were simply on loan to make that happen.

"None of it's powered," Carl said. "It's just been sitting here for five hundred years. Even the most cursory understanding of Imperial tech would tell someone that there's not any juice left.

"That said, if we can get some of this down to the maglev station, it won't be a problem to plug it in and start charging it. The magazines for the flechette pistols, for example, are virtually indestructible. In all the testing that I did with the magazines that we recovered from the battlecruiser *Courageous*, only a couple of them failed to charge. The Old Empire really knew how to build their stuff. We've probably got enough ammunition here for a small war, and if we can find half a dozen magazines that fail, I'll eat them."

"So, what do you want to do first?" she asked, smiling at his joke. "It seems like getting the life-support system down below up and running would be a big help. I know there's still a lot of air bottles scattered around the lower levels of the city, but we've been lucky thus far. Any of them could fail without warning because they were never designed for this kind of neglect. We need to start being more conservative. We're overdue for an accident."

The young scientist nodded. "Agreed. The thing is, I'm going to have to work inside that environment for at least a day. It's going to involve a lot of going from place to place and fixing things. I may even have to move equipment from one location to another. That's going to take a group of people—or someone very strong."

"So, me."

He nodded. "It also means that we need to adjust one of these suits of armor so that I can wear it. The suit reserves are still full, and we can easily swap out with some of the spares that are here in the cache when we run low on air.

"The suit will also provide me with enough strength to do some of the work. It's made to work with your augmented muscles, but it's got enough built-in enhancement to help carry out some of the tasks that need to be done."

He put his hands on his hips and stared at the racked armor. "The only problem is that we're going to have to get them down to the maglev platform so that they can be charged before we can do anything. That means carrying them down while wearing those dinky little air bottles."

"I can carry them down," Julia said. "I'll use up the air reserves faster, but hoisting both sets of armor over my shoulders and hauling them downstairs is going to be within my capability. Barely."

He didn't look convinced. "You might be able to handle all the weight, but that's a lot of bulk. Plus, it's going to be as unwieldy as hell. I think you should probably just take one at a time."

She ignored his suggestion and started unhooking one of the suits of armor. She hefted it for a moment and then tossed it over her shoulder. It *was* unwieldy but nothing that she couldn't handle.

Hell, if push came to shove, she could grab it by one leg and *drag* it down the stairs. It might scuff up the exterior, but this was powered armor. She could beat it with a club, and it would still be operational.

She grabbed a second set of armor off the rack and turned toward him. "I can handle it. How do we adjust one of these to fit me? I'm a little shorter than your average girl. Even you're going to have to shorten some segments to fit your height, mister 'I'm so average.'"

He grinned at that. "And there you were telling me just the other day how above average I was. You're lucky I don't tell my wife that you've been hitting on me."

She froze for just a moment and then grinned back at him. "I like the mouth you've got on you. You really can give as good as you get. And I'm not hitting on you. Your wife is safe, and so are you."

His eyes narrowed slightly, and she could see his lips pressing together a little as he considered her. "If you weren't hitting on me, then I can only imagine that this flirting means you're giving me a test drive to see whether or not you might like my doppelgänger."

Shocked at his unexpected insight, she considered lying, but the man was damned perceptive, and it really didn't matter. Why lie when the truth would serve her just fine?

"That's *exactly* what I'm thinking," she said honestly. "In my universe, Carl Owlet never left Avalon. He's still a graduate student there. Hell, he's probably a PhD by now. Angela has been serving in Talbot's place as my senior marine officer, so the two of you never met.

"Without the events that drew you together, there isn't going to be a relationship between the two of you. I don't feel like I'm stealing him from Angela, so yes, I'm giving you a test drive.

"I'm not the type to hit on another woman's man. Neither you nor Angela has anything to worry about on that account. But I do want to get to know you better because I think that your doppelgänger and I would be perfect for one another.

"I like you a lot, Carl, and I think I'd like him. You'd have to be the one to tell me if you think he'd feel the same. I suspect your relationship with Kelsey would be somewhat different if you'd never met. Tell me how he'd react to me slowly getting to know him and building a relationship. Could the two of us make something like that work?"

He shrugged. "I've been with Kelsey for so long that I see her more like a crazy sister than a woman, so I'm not sure that you should trust my feelings at this point. You're going to have to make the decision about what makes sense for you to do.

"What I *can* tell you is that he's not going to be comfortable around a princess. You're going to have to do a lot of work to become his friend before you try to become more. It's not exactly like he's got a lot of dating experience, and he's going to be intimidated. Think of him like a wild horse that you have to break to the saddle."

His face reddened when she grinned. "Maybe that wasn't the best analogy."

She laughed. "I think that has a lot of interesting possibilities for me to think about."

Then she sobered. "Someone like you could be the difference between life and death for the New Terran Empire in my universe. And, to be frank, someone like you would make an excellent consort for me.

"I'm not the warrior she is. I need someone like you, a scholar who's brilliant and has wide-ranging interests that appeal to me. I won't know until

I meet you there, but yes, I've made the decision that I'm going to be looking at your doppelgänger as soon as I get back to my universe and sneak onto Avalon.

"By now, it's going to be under AI control. If I can bring back enough information and technology, we can start a guerrilla war and fight our way back. That makes your doppelgänger perfect for me.

"And I really do like you. That's a huge bonus. If I had to forge a relationship for the good of the Empire, I'd do it. If it can bring me a companion that I *want* to spend time with and that I truly like, could I ask for anything more?"

Carl nodded slowly. "I can see it. I think my doppelgänger will find you appealing, but you're going to have to go slow, just like I said."

He considered her intensely for a few moments. "I'm not really supposed to say anything about this, but I think there's something we can do for you that will make a difference back in your universe. Avalon's going to be isolated because of its distance from the Rebel Empire, so even though they've only recently conquered it, the Rebel Empire won't have put as many ships there as they probably should.

"There are ways that we can help you deal with something like that. Technologies that we've built that might help protect Avalon against them. I'll have to talk to Admiral Mertz and Kelsey to be sure, but I think you can do it, particularly if you've got my doppelgänger on your side."

Her heart pounded harder in her chest. She really hoped he was right.

Knowing that she wasn't going to be able to pull any more information out of him until he'd spoken with the others, she hefted both sets of armor while he gathered the equipment that he was going to need. The two of them then headed down toward the lower levels.

* * *

JARED ACCOMPANIED Mordechai back to his office. The few hours they'd spent together over lunch had been very productive, but they hadn't done more than pass ideas back and forth.

The older man wanted his fusion plant back. He didn't know who'd stolen it, and neither did Jared, but that didn't matter. If Jared wanted the cache of Marine Raider equipment, they were going to have to figure out who'd taken it and get them to return it to Frankfort.

Jared *wanted* the Marine Raider equipment. Just the powered armor alone would be sufficient to get Kelsey, Julia, and Talbot fully combat capable. They'd once again be a force worthy of taking out almost any obstruction they came across.

The other weapons and supplies would make their job of getting off this planet easier, too. It wouldn't help them get back to *Persephone*, but that was a problem for another day.

Mordechai leaned back in his chair and gave Jared a long, considering look. "Your man says that he can get life support restored so that we can access the equipment and supplies on the lowest levels. I'm more than willing to trade some of the Marine Raider equipment for that accomplishment.

"As I've already passed along to the guard I've placed outside the room, I'm allowing him the use of the armor and whatever supplies he needs to complete his work. Once it's done, I'll make that trade permanent and give you some other equipment that will assist you in your mission of finding those that stole our fusion plant and making them return it.

"Once you've managed to convince them to do so, and the fusion plant is set up and operational, then all of the equipment and supplies inside the cache are yours. That's the deal that I'm willing to offer."

Jared knew he wasn't going to get a better offer.

"I accept. We'll do everything within our power to bring your fusion plant back and get it operational for you. I'm not sure we can convince them to provide maintenance, but if not, we can do what we can to train your people, though our time is short."

He didn't know how he'd convince the thieves to return the fusion plant, but they'd overcome difficult situations before. So long as he could find these others and learn more about them, there was a possibility that they could come to an arrangement.

If not, he might just have to steal the fusion plant back.

"Have you heard from Kelsey and Talbot?" he asked, changing the subject.

The older man nodded. "They managed to draw the enemy into chasing them. My scouts report that there has been some skirmishing along the way and that she was injured, but our people in the buildings fired enough shots into their pursuers to keep them back far enough for them to flee.

"At this moment, they're headed toward the trap. For the life of me, I can't imagine what she did to get all of those people chasing her. It seems like your sister has a gift for arousing the anger of her enemies."

Jared was worried about Kelsey's injury, but he knew how tough she was. Not only was she a Marine Raider—with all of the enhancements and augmentation that afforded her—but she was mentally tough. If she was still moving, then she wasn't very badly hurt.

At least that's what he told himself.

"How far away from the trap are they?"

"They'll be there within half an hour. It really depends on how direct a course they take. If the enemy forces them into diverting, then they might have to take a longer route. If the enemy starts slowing down, she's going to circle back and draw them into pursuit again.

"Even while they're doing that, our people are moving around the outskirts of the enemy so that they can surround them once they find themselves in our trap. No matter what happens, they're going to be too deep inside Frankfort to escape.

"They might have the numbers to beat us in a straight-up fight, but we have sufficient weaponry to make sure that we win in this environment. Killing many of them in this trap will save my people from unneeded injury or death. For that, I am indebted to you."

"What will you do once you beat them here?" Jared asked curiously. "They've got a lot of horsemen outside the city, and those can still be a problem."

The older man nodded. "Can we conquer their city? No. Can we set the rest of it on fire and drive them farther away? Yes. We'll use rockets and burn them out."

Even though doing something like that was hard to stomach, the tactician inside Jared understood why it needed to be done.

Changing subjects, Jared leaned forward and put his elbows on the arms of his chair. "Once Carl gets the life-support systems on the lowest levels operational, what comes next?"

"I think that depends on you," the old man said. "Are you prepared to begin your exploration farther up the tunnels? If you can summon the train that the thieves used, perhaps you can use it to find them.

"As for us, my people and I will move the supplies they've gathered below to somewhere less accessible should they come back. At any point, those who turned the power on can turn it back off again, so I don't want to lose this opportunity to recover what is ours."

"I hope you realize that you and these people might still be able to come to some type of agreement," Jared said. "They have enough technical know-how to completely disassemble and remove a fusion plant. They could help you rebuild this city.

"They also seem to be the type that can help salvage other parts of your city for reuse. If they've done this in other places, then they certainly have the experience. We won't really know until we get a chance to see who we're dealing with, but there's a potential partnership there if you can get past the fact that they stole from you.

"What I urge you to remember is that they may not have known there were still decent people in this city. They might have come the way they did to avoid the horde. If that's who they thought controlled Frankfort, it wasn't meant to be an insult to you or your people."

He licked his lips slightly. "Forgive me for saying so, but you and your people seem like the kind that might hold grudges. In this case, if you're looking for a true allegiance that might offer benefit to your people, perhaps you should allow them to prove themselves to you."

The other man chuckled. "We're not as bad as you seem to think we are, Admiral. Once you've made contact and we have an opportunity to speak with them, I feel confident that some type of arrangement will eventually be worked out.

"The only thing that I'm insisting you accomplish before that happens is to get them to return our fusion plant and shielding to us, restore it to the condition that it was in before they took it, and make it operational."

He held up a hand before Jared could respond. "I know that we don't have the skill to operate such a high-technology device. That's where the negotiation with the others will come in. I believe that we can come to an arrangement in which they provide the technological know-how to maintain the fusion plant and teach us to do so in exchange for services we can offer.

"Rest assured that I will not allow my pique at the way they've treated us to harm the long-term prospects of my people. Focus on these first steps, Admiral Mertz. If you're going to get to the Imperial Palace, you must find these people. I suggest that you hope that they're not as bad as you thought we were when we first met."

Jared repressed a shudder at that. "Let's hope not. We've already had enough things go wrong on this mission. Just once, I'd like to have something go right."

Mordechai gave him a lopsided smile. "Exactly how likely is that?"

"Damned unlikely," he muttered darkly. "Almost impossible, really."

Even as the other man chuckled, Jared wished he'd been joking. With their luck, they were still at least one big fight away from getting to the Imperial Palace. He could feel it deep in his bones.

23

Talbot raced forward with Kelsey over his shoulder, sprinting around corners and dodging to the other side of open areas to keep the enemy from getting a lock on them as they fled. He'd already spent the last twenty minutes running toward the trap and had been grateful that a couple of snipers along the way had fired shots that kept the screaming mass of horde warriors from *quite* catching up with them.

Not that he thought they'd be able to manage that for much longer. Once the enemy made a concerted effort to catch up, he'd have to put on a dash of speed, using his augmentation to open up the distance, and then the jig would be up.

Once they knew that he could've gotten away any time, they'd know this was a trap. The only thing making this trick possible was their unthinking rage. If they ever started using their brains, they'd quickly regroup and retreat to their camp.

They might even leave the city, and that would deny the locals the opportunity to end this conflict for the next couple of decades.

Using the map overlay function built into his implants, he knew they were only a couple of turns and one good dash away from the trap. He'd been unable to see that anything was buried under the ground when the locals had shown them the area, but considering how well they'd hidden the doors in their tunnels and their ambush sites behind solid walls, he had no doubt that the bombs were there.

As he rounded the final corner and entered the straightaway toward where the trap lay, a woman shouted down at him from one of the buildings. "Horsemen are circling around to stop you! Hurry up!"

He didn't bother responding, because the time had come to run. If they got pinned in the area with the bombs, the defenders probably wouldn't hesitate to trigger the explosives, even if he and Kelsey were right in the middle of them.

His only hope at this point was to get Kelsey past the area where the bombs were hidden and hope that the horde warriors kept coming. If they did, he could probably evade the horsemen.

That was a good plan—or at least he thought so, right up until the horsemen came around the corner just past the area where the explosives were planted. There must've been fifty of them, and there was no way that he and Kelsey were getting past them.

They couldn't retreat with all of the foot soldiers closing in behind them, but they weren't cut off completely just yet. If they really had to, they could run into one of the buildings and make their way into the tunnels.

If they did that, though, it wouldn't draw everybody possible into the kill zone. Talbot had to draw this out as long as he possibly could before they ran. If he didn't execute this flawlessly, they were completely and utterly screwed.

"So, you think you've got us?" he shouted at the horsemen. "You think this is all we have? We'll keep killing you until we drop."

Those were brave words that he hoped drew a lot of people toward them. Most people would've just stood off at bow range and opened fire.

A cruel enemy, on the other hand, would want to surround them so tightly that they couldn't help but see the fate that awaited them. Perhaps they'd even want to capture them alive so that they could be fed into the torture machine that the horde favored.

Personally, that was what he expected. The horde would lose people just to have the opportunity to torture him and Kelsey.

He turned slowly in place, his pistol in hand. Kelsey had hers ready as well, but he doubted they had more than a couple of magazines left between them. When compared to the number of people slowly filling the area, it wasn't going to be enough.

Not even close.

It was getting crowded between the buildings, with the enemy jockeying for position and packing themselves in tightly. No matter how this turned out, the explosives were going to take a deadly toll on the horde.

A large man, dressed in black armor, dismounted and took off his helmet. Talbot recognized him as the man that Julia had spoken to inside the horde city. He'd pegged the fellow as an officer of some kind.

Now that handsome face was contorted with rage. "You've killed the king, his family, and all the high nobles. We're going to take you back to the city and make you regret that. You're going to live for weeks as we take your bodies apart one piece at a time.

"Just when you think death is inescapable, we'll find a way to keep you alive for just a little bit longer. The agonies that you'll suffer will be unspeakable, and I'll savor each and every scream I tear from your throats."

Talbot simply grinned at the man. "Hard pass."

Without waiting for a response, he spun Kelsey off of his shoulder and hurled her through the shattered windows of the building beside them, easily getting her light form onto the third floor.

Even as the enemy charged toward him, Talbot took two quick steps forward, crouched, and levered his powerful muscles to leap after her. He almost didn't make it, but his hands just managed to grab the ledge outside where the window had once been on the same floor where Kelsey had landed.

She was there a second later, grabbing him by the wrists and yanking him into the building. What looked like a storm of arrows flew through the air where they'd just been, and his side ached with the impact of hitting the floor.

The two of them hobbled for the stairwell in the center of the building. If they didn't beat the horde down into the ground, the enemy would cut them off inside the building, and they'd die. Worse, the explosives that were about to go off might kill them too.

They barely made it fifteen meters into the building before the world went insane. The blast was unlike anything he'd ever felt before. It picked him up and slammed him through an interior wall.

Then it felt as if the building were coming apart. Talbot could hear the groaning of steel and other materials as they bent, and it sounded as if the upper floors were coming down.

Even as he was thinking that they were screwed and struggling to get to his feet, Kelsey put an arm around his waist and picked him up off the floor, obviously still favoring her injured leg but not letting it slow her down.

"Hang on!" she shouted.

Even as the building shook and parts of it started to fall, she raced to the far side of the building and jumped through the shattered window.

The impact was brutal, and the pain in his side exploded. It didn't feel like broken ribs, though. It felt worse.

Even as she dragged him to his feet, the building behind them began crumbling.

With a wall of debris racing up behind them, they ran into the building ahead of them and barely made it inside before a wash of debris slammed against the side of the building and brought the ceiling down on their heads.

Surprised that he wasn't dead, Talbot blinked and shifted the debris. It wasn't the building that had collapsed on them, only the panels set into the ceiling of this floor.

They staggered to their feet again and made their way deeper into the building until they found a stairwell that went down into the tunnels. Only once they were there did they even begin to start to feel safe.

"Let me take a look at that," Kelsey said as she turned to look at the broken-off arrows in his side.

He blinked at them stupidly, not even remembering having been shot. When had that happened? Maybe when he'd jumped for the first building? He didn't remember getting hit, but his adrenaline had been through the roof. Now he could tell that the painkillers in his pharmacology unit were keeping the agony at bay.

"We've got to keep going. Lily can take a look at me as soon as we get back, but we can't stay here. If the building comes down, it could still kill us. We'll run into some of the scouts in this area soon. They'll help us get to where we need to be."

Reluctantly Kelsey nodded her agreement, picked him up, and set off. They wouldn't be able to find out how effective the ambush had been until later, but he was pretty sure that they'd put paid to the majority of the invaders.

This fight was over.

* * *

CARL WAS glad that Julia was doing the heavy lifting by the time they'd reached the base of the final set of stairs. He couldn't imagine having had to carry both sets of armor down like she'd done. Even just his tools and the charging equipment had been almost too much.

Once they reached the platform at the maglev train station, he quickly found access to the power conduits. With the equipment that he'd brought, he knew that he'd be able to make a decent estimate of how much power was currently flowing and then guess at how much they could utilize for the life-support systems without alerting those on the other end.

Recharging the armor, weapon magazines, and power packs wasn't going to be that much of a draw. Nowhere in the league of keeping life support running for the area they'd need to allow unfettered access to this level.

As soon as he had the charging station spliced into the power circuits, he connected the cables to the armor where Julia had set both sets against the wall. He smiled in satisfaction when the power started to flow, and he was finally able to begin running self-diagnostics on them.

The batteries seemed intact and would probably hold a charge. Nothing negative leapt out about the armor in general, either. The suits appeared to be in decent condition. Carl crossed his fingers and hoped that continued to be the case as they drew more power.

He laid out the rest of his tools and began removing the parts of the armor that weren't required to be connected to the charger. Adjusting a suit for Julia was going to be difficult. She had the same slight frame as Kelsey did—obviously—and the only way that he'd been able to manage that the first time was because he'd had a lot more equipment at hand to customize things.

He'd make it work. It wouldn't be a perfect fit, but she'd be able to use the armor.

The work was somewhat mind numbing. When Carl looked up about half an hour later, he found himself alone. Julia must be scouting the area, he decided.

Now that they'd gotten access to the cache and he'd had an opportunity to charge some of the magazines, they were no longer unarmed. He swapped out the magazines that had now fully charged and inserted one of them into a flechette pistol, which he put into a hip holster. Another powerpack went into the stunner on his off side, situated in a cross-draw holster like Kelsey favored.

Completing the initial work on Julia's armor took about an hour. Making modifications to the set that he intended for his own use took maybe twenty minutes. Yay for being almost regular sized for a Marine Raider.

By the time he'd finished, the armor's power cells were at about sixty percent.

"How's it looking?" Julia asked from beside him.

He jumped a little and scowled at her. "Do you have to sneak around like that?"

She gave him an apologetic smile. "Sorry. I thought you'd heard me coming. I've been wandering around the platform, looking to see what I could find. It seems as if whoever was here cleaned everything out pretty thoroughly.

"I did find the operations center, though. It has a big map of what looks like the maglev tunnel network. Want to take a look?"

"Sure," he said as he stood. "This needs to finish charging anyway. Take a flechette pistol and stunner. Better safe than sorry."

Once she'd armed herself, she quickly led him through a door set into the wall behind one of the decorative columns. He hadn't seen it, and that was probably by design. On the maintenance level, they'd want to keep people from wandering where they weren't supposed to be.

Behind the door was a control room that wouldn't have been out of place aboard a warship. Lots of consoles, and as she'd said, a large map on the front wall. It only took a single glance to recognize that it had to be a map of the layout for the maglev train network, as she'd guessed.

He gave it his full attention, centering himself in the open area in front of it with his hands on his hips. Several incoming maglev lines fed into Frankfort.

There was a switching station maybe ten kilometers away that allowed for a single set of tunnels to feed into multiple outlets. The tunnels were bidirectional, with spare slots for the trains to use when workers were maintaining them.

Some of the incoming lines fed into the areas just under the city, but others would be for maintenance use, like the one down here. Others would be situated in the middle levels for the delivery of supplies and equipment. The uppermost levels would've been for passenger travel.

Since Frankfort was at the center of the map, that made it easy for him to see what lay in the direction of the Imperial Palace. The answer was, unfortunately, nothing.

There was a line leading directly to Imperial City, but the megalopolis had been utterly destroyed by the kinetic strikes a century ago. There was no telling how far away the maglev tunnels would be damaged, either.

The map was obviously meant to have lights where trains were located, but there were no brightly lit dots indicating active trains. Carl had no idea if that part of the system was broken or there really was no traffic. That would take some digging into the system to determine.

Interestingly, there was a substation short of Imperial City that looked like it might be a spur that had once served the Imperial Palace. There was no train line designated from there, but it didn't take a genius to figure out that there would be security concerns with having that data widely available.

The existence of a spur line was something of an assumption, but it had to be a valid one. They wouldn't cart all the supplies and people that needed to go to the Imperial Palace over land or through the air. Not only would there be too much traffic, but the security people would also want to control access, and a maglev spur would be perfect for that.

He gestured toward the wall as he turned to Julia. "It looks like we're going to be able to take one of the tunnels and get fairly close to the Imperial Palace. If I'm not mistaken, there's a spur station that will lead down a secure line directly to the palace."

"Okay," she said, eyeing the map. "So how are we going to figure out where the people who stole the fusion plant went? They could've come from just about anywhere, based on this map. We're supposed to be tracking them down, but we don't want to run into them without at least knowing a little more about who we're dealing with."

"I'll be able to figure that out in relatively short order. Once I'm plugged into the control system, I'll be able to see which train visited last and maybe even where it came from and went to. Since the power is on, that probably means the command-and-control network is active, so I might be able to call it directly back to us.

"If it comes from the direction we need to go, we'll have to deal with the thieves immediately. If it's coming from somewhere else, the admiral may decide that it's best to just avoid conflict for right now. This problem isn't one that we can afford to get bogged down in."

Julia shrugged, turning to look at the rest of the dim room. "That sounds good to me. I think I've seen as much fighting as I can stomach for the moment. How long is it going to be before the armor is fully charged?"

"It was at sixty percent when we came here, so it's probably over seventy percent now. Let's go find out."

Together, they made their way back to where he'd left the armor charging. He was pleased to note that both batteries were at seventy-five percent. That would be more than enough to get them suited up and complete the testing process. He could leave the cables plugged in to continue charging the armor while he did the final work of fitting Julia's set.

Reassembling Julia's armor only took a couple of minutes. He'd already shortened the arms and legs as much as he could, so he only had a few final adjustments left to make. It wouldn't be completely comfortable, but at least she'd be able to use it.

He plugged his testing equipment into her armor and was pleased to see that it had no major malfunctions. There were a couple of small parts and control circuits that needed replacement, but he had the spares available and would be able to quickly get them swapped out.

After ten minutes of doing exactly that, he pronounced her armor ready.

"I'll head back to the platform while you get yourself ready," he said as he started to turn away.

"That's not going to work," she said with a shake of her head. "I'm going to need someone to hold the armor while I get into it since we have no racks."

Carl blinked, unsure if that was the best idea. "I'm not sure I can do that without compromising your dignity. If I've got to position the armor, that means I have to see what I'm doing."

Sadly, they hadn't found any skinsuits in the Marine Raider cache and hadn't been willing to spend the time to open every single crate to locate them. The armor was meant to mold around a person wearing a skinsuit, but it would work almost as well on bare skin. Clothing would hinder the operation of the armor, cause chafing, and prohibit the use of the built-in plumbing.

"Your virtue is safe with me," she said dryly. "While I doubt that I'll ever be as comfortable stripping down in front of the universe in general as Kelsey, we're adults. You've seen her naked before, so you're not going to see anything you haven't quite literally seen before."

That was easy to say, but Carl knew it wasn't going to be that easy in practice. She might look exactly like Kelsey, but Julia was a different person. He felt embarrassed as she began stripping down, even though she'd turned her back. He averted his eyes as much as possible and held the armor up to block most of her form.

The armor wasn't light, so he wasn't going to be that adept at turning his head while moving the parts of it where they needed to be for her. He'd be draping it over her rather than allowing her to slip inside it.

Julia kept her back to him, and he only had to look at her once she started backing up. He aligned the armor and made sure it slipped over her slim form. He had to hold it still as she worked to get her plumbing connections in place and sealed up.

That made him feel really self-conscious. He could only imagine how awkward she felt.

"How does it feel?" he asked, relieved when the process was over and she was inside the armor a few minutes later.

"Kind of weird," she admitted. "I'm used to wearing a skinsuit. I'm sure that feeling will fade. Are you okay? You look a little red. The armor wasn't too heavy, was it?"

Carl flushed a little brighter as she smirked at him, showing that she knew it wasn't the weight of the armor that had gotten to him. "At least I'll get my revenge. If you'll hold up the other set of armor, I'll get myself ready."

He turned his back to her and quickly stripped off his clothes. He was feeling pretty good about not burning with embarrassment right up until she spoke.

"You've got a cute butt."

"That's harassment," he said with as much dignity as he could manage. "My face is up here."

She laughed. "Relax. I wasn't staring at your butt. Not really. Barely at all."

Carl sighed and backed up to where she held the armor out for him. He quickly attached the plumbing and slid his arms into the sleeves. Once he had the upper torso secure, he got the legs sealed up and verified that all the latches were secure.

He turned to face Julia and squatted, moving his body around as much as he could so that the armor would settle. It actually felt reasonably comfortable.

Mirroring his motions, Julia did the same. "It feels a little rough in places, but I think this will work. What do we do now?"

"Let's check the charge levels."

Both sets of armor were at more than ninety percent now. If he was being persnickety, he'd wait until they were fully charged, but this was definitely good enough. He disconnected the power cables and secured them nearby with the charging equipment.

"We'll go up floor by floor, and as I find the life-support system that feeds the stairwells, I'll get it turned on and do what checking and replacement of parts that I can," he said. "It should still be in pretty good shape, considering that they had this all operational just a couple of years ago. I'm guessing that it's going to take us probably two or three hours to get everything we need online.

"Once we get back up to the middle levels, I'll strip parts from another lift, and we can get this one working again. That'll add another half hour but make accessing this level much easier."

"So we'll allow three hours for the process," she agreed as she started back toward the stairs. "I suppose we'd best get started. The sooner we get this done, the sooner we can be on our way."

That was something that Carl could get behind. He grabbed the rest of his gear and quickly fell in behind her.

24

K elsey was *really* worried by the time she got Talbot to Lily. Marine Raiders were tough, but the arrows in his side were proving a challenge for his medical nanites to deal with, probably because they were stuck in something important.

Not that getting him there was easy with a broken-off arrow in her thigh. Thankfully, she'd quickly run into some of the defenders that had helped get them both to where Lily had set up shop.

Doctor Stone had been dealing with several injured people when they'd arrived, with Talbot barely conscious. The other woman immediately directed them to lay her husband down on an area of the floor where she could get at him.

She examined the arrows and the flesh they were broken off in with her scanner. "These are going to have to come out right now. Once I get them out, I can use the portable regenerator to give him a leg up, but he's in a bad way. Once the injury occurred, he really should've stopped moving. He's cut himself up pretty good."

"It wasn't as if we had the option of stopping," Kelsey said somewhat dryly. "Is he in any real danger?"

"If you'd waited another fifteen or twenty minutes to get here, it would've been chancier. His medical nanites are going to be able to boost his blood regeneration, but even with modern drugs, it's going to take time. I'll try to round up some donors, but I'm not certain how well that's going to be received by people here."

"Do you need any help?"

Lily shook her head. "Everyone gathered here knows a little bit about medicine and can assist me in doing the work. Jared stuck his head in a couple of minutes ago and said that he'd like to see you once you got back. Apparently, there's some good news that he wants to discuss with you."

That was nice to hear. It had been a long time since they'd had any good news.

Then Lily noticed the blood on her leg. "Is that yours?"

Before she could respond, Lily ran the scanner over her leg. "That needs to come out. Lay down over there and let one of my assistants get it so that you don't hurt yourself any more."

The woman who was waiting for her had an ugly looking set of pliers and a long, sharp knife. Thankfully, Kelsey could flood her system with painkillers.

That didn't make the extraction pain free, but it made it bearable. Thankfully, the arrow came out with a minimum of cutting to free the head. Once that was done, the woman sewed the wound closed, slapped a bandage over it, and moved on to the next patient.

That worked for her.

Kelsey rose and walked over to where Lily was just finishing with Talbot. The pain was manageable, and she could walk. That was a win in her book.

She knelt down beside Talbot and put her hand on his shoulder. His eyes fluttered open, and he looked up at her blearily.

"Lily says you're going to be fine, slacker," she said soothingly. "I've got to go see Jared. I'll be back to check on you soon as I can. Don't die on me."

The corners of his lips turned up slightly. "I promise I won't. Go find out what's going on. I'll be better by the time you get back. And find me something to eat. I'm starving."

Still worried about her husband, Kelsey headed out. She tagged up with one of the guards assigned to keep an eye on her, and he quickly escorted her to the air handler room, where it seemed that Leader Mordechai and some of his top people had gathered.

Kelsey walked into the room and stopped dead. Julia and Carl were there. More importantly, they were wearing Marine Raider powered armor, with their helmets off.

"What the *hell*?" she asked as she walked around the two of them. "Where did you find these?"

"It's a long story," Jared said as he gestured toward one of the seats. "Park it, and we'll get everybody caught up on the details."

He frowned at her. Rather, he frowned at Talbot's blood on her chest from where she'd hauled him out of the fight and at her leg.

"Is any of that your blood?"

"Some," she admitted. "I'm good now. Most of it is Talbot's, and Lilly says he's going to be okay. Eventually."

Never taking her eyes off her doppelgänger and her young friend, Kelsey sat. She'd thought she wouldn't see this kind of thing again until they got off Terra. She was utterly floored.

When they finished bringing her up to speed, she raised her hand slightly. "What about the attack? Did we drive the horde back, or are we still going to have to deal with some of them?"

Mordechai smiled widely. "The trap that you led them into was more successful than we'd imagined possible. There were survivors, of course, but not many. None of those escaped the city. The invasion is over.

"Considering that they must've lost between four and five thousand of their warriors in this incursion, I seriously doubt that they'll be back anytime soon. Their forces outside the city didn't suffer any losses other than the ones incurred when you destroyed their treasure room and palace and the fight for domination that caused, but they'd never had as many mounted warriors as foot soldiers. Considering how warlike they are in general, I don't believe they'll be back up to their normal fighting strength for at least a full generation or two.

"Since they had to execute so many of their surviving leaders to settle the rulership question, whoever runs them now is going to be consolidating power for some time. He'll have his mind on other things than trying to come after us."

The older man leaned back in his chair and considered Kelsey. "I've heard great things about how well you fought. Both you and your husband exhibited capabilities that I never would've expected possible. It appears my understanding of what a Marine Raider could do was incomplete and understated. Well done."

"There is something else that I need to tell you," Jared said solemnly. "When we were going up and down the stairs, I found this."

He opened the pouch at his belt and handed her a small metal pin. She took it from him and then almost dropped it as soon as she saw what was on its face: the emblem of the Marine Raiders.

She stared at him. "How is that possible? Has it been down there for five hundred years?"

"Doubtful. I think that whoever stole the fusion plant was wearing it, based on its condition. Maybe those people are descendants of Marine Raiders. Maybe their group was trained by the Raiders back in the day or perhaps simply inspired by them.

"Whoever they are, they still have technology and a connection to the Marine Raiders. We're going to have to find out who they are because, if we can get off this planet, they're probably going to play some part in getting us there."

Kelsey sat back and turned her mind inward, ignoring the rest of them for a minute. The news was shocking. She wasn't sure which of the possibilities could be the truth. Hell, they could *all* be true. Or it was something so strange that none of them could possibly guess the connection.

Coming back to herself, she focused on Carl. "Is there any way to use the maglev system to determine where these people came from and where they took the fusion plant?"

He shook his head. "The system was never designed to give a location for a train that's not currently in service, so our best bet is going to be reactivating it and then seeing where it comes from."

She gave him a raised eyebrow. "That's going to tell them that we're onto them. Is that what we really want to do?"

"Do we have a choice?" Jared asked. "Unless we want to walk a thousand kilometers through an unknown tunnel system with potentially toxic air, we're going to need that train. We might as well get it into our heads that we're going to be talking with them.

"We'll go in as prepared as we can, but we have to be ready to fight a technologically advanced group if things go badly. We'll do our best to make friends, but there's only so much we can do to cajole them into doing what we want."

Kelsey sighed. One more group that they might have to fight their way through to get what humanity needed. It felt like they'd either been on their way to Terra or down on the surface of this damned planet forever. She just wanted to be back in space and on her way to a new location with a new mission. This one felt like it would never end.

She turned her attention to Carl. "How soon are we going to be ready to do this?"

The young scientist smiled slightly. "I can go downstairs and call the train right now if that's what you want."

"I think we should rest up after the fight," Jared said. "We can gather all the equipment that we'll need, but tomorrow morning is soon enough."

Kelsey nodded. "A good night's sleep would do us all some good. If our history is anything to go by, we might not be getting any rest tomorrow."

She could hardly believe that they were almost ready to leave Frankfort and try to get to the Imperial Palace. Yes, they'd have to go through another group of people to get there, but this was just the kind of break that they'd been desperately needing since they'd arrived on Terra.

They had to make this work. They just had to.

* * *

JARED WAS UP EARLY the next morning and made his way down to the lowest level of the city. The air smelled significantly better on the journey than it had the last time, and he hadn't needed any air bottles.

Once there, he took a brief tour of the maglev control center and was impressed that so much of it still seemed operational. Carl was already going through what he could of the system. He'd plugged some of his gear into one of the consoles and now had the controls up and was trying to figure out how they worked.

Jared sat down next to him. "What have you found?"

"About what you'd expect," the young man said. "The system has had failures here and there, but it has enough redundancy that it can still do what we need it to. I've gotten the serial number of the train. It's been inactive for seven months.

"None of the other trains that used to use this system have been online for at least a century, so this one has to belong to the people that we're looking for. I can't tell you where it is, because it's not active at the moment, though.

"The system was never designed to pinpoint the location of an inactive train. Sadly, it can't even tell me the location where it last received a signal from it. Like I said, the original designers didn't think that was necessary. I mean, who steals a train?

"What I *can* do is send a signal to reactivate it and then summon it here. Once it starts moving, I'll be able to determine its location and where it's coming from immediately, because it's going to show up on the big board there.

"So long as it's on automatic control, I should be able to determine a lot of things about it. If there's anyone on board, they can cut me off pretty fast if they've got the knowledge to do it."

Carl quirked an eyebrow at him. "Did Kelsey ever make you watch any of those *Star Trek* vids? Particularly *The Wrath of Khan?*"

Jared shook his head slightly. "She's made me watch a lot of things, but I don't remember anything by that name. What's its significance?"

"In that vid, they have a situation where bad people stole one of their ships, so the good guys utilized their knowledge of its systems to lower its defenses remotely at a critical moment during a fight because nobody had bothered to change the codes their Fleet used.

"It's nothing like what we do with our ships since we don't allow other vessels to control them, but it's a lot like what happens with the maglev train system here. I'm utilizing the controls built into the system meant to redirect traffic. Those trains are designed to obey commands from authorized control systems unless that feature is turned off.

"I'll wager that since these folks seem to be the only ones using the system, they've never bothered changing the codes. If I'm right, their train will drive out right from under their noses before they can stop it. Once it's in motion, Ralph will hack it and change the control code to prevent them from calling it back."

"That sounds awfully complicated," Jared said with a scowl. "Once you gain control of the train, can you determine if anyone is on board?"

The young scientist shrugged slightly. "I can access the vid feeds from inside the control area on the train. If someone shows up there, I'll see them. I'm not going to be able to look into the passenger areas or where they keep cargo.

"The other feeds can be accessed from inside the train, but there was never any need for a general controller to be able to examine that information."

Carl leaned back in his seat, obviously thinking about it. "I suppose it's still possible, though. Once Ralph hacks the train, he can probably get access to the internal vid feeds. I'm not going to be able to say one way or the other until he gives it a shot."

"If we can get access to those interior vids, I want to make that happen."

"When are we planning to kick this off?" Carl asked.

He checked his internal chronometer. "They should have the last of the equipment that we'll be taking with us down here in about an hour. I think that would be an excellent time to make this happen.

"I spoke to Leader Mordechai this morning, and he said that he'd send troops with us if we wanted. While extra bodies might be good, I'm not sure that mixing the people that were our captors yesterday with the thieves that stole from them a few years ago is a great plan. I'd rather keep this first meeting as straightforward as we possibly can."

Carl chuckled at that. "You won't get any argument from me. What about Talbot? Is he going to be ready to travel?"

"Travel, yes. Fight, no. Lily says that he needs to rest a couple days before he tries to exert himself. I'm not going to argue with her.

"We're going to take all four sets of armor, which is why you had the other two brought down and charged them up this morning. Since we only have two Marine Raiders—counting Julia—you're going to be using the set that you've already fitted for yourself.

"The last one is going to Lieutenant Laird. As a trained marine, she's going to have an idea of what needs to happen if things break bad. She hasn't used Raider armor, but she has used the standard marine version. That'll give her a leg up."

"I'll get them fitted as soon as possible," Carl agreed. "Add another hour to your time estimate to cover it."

The scientist turned in his seat to face Jared. "Are you worried about this trip, sir? These people have technology, and they might be bad guys. If that's the case, they might overwhelm us, and we'll be screwed again."

"Sometimes you just have to do the best you can," Jared said as he clapped the other man on the shoulder and stood. "I'm going back upstairs to say our goodbyes. Be ready to start Operation Choo-Choo in two hours. We're probably only going to get one try at this, so I'd rather not have it all come down around our ears."

"Operation Choo-Choo?" Carl asked, amused. "That has to be a Kelsey thing."

"Got it in one. Now, back to work."

Jared smirked a little as he headed toward the door. Of course Kelsey had come up with the name. He had only the vaguest idea of how it connected to the maglev train, but she'd been insistent.

His expression grew more pensive once he was away from everyone else. He was less confident than he'd tried to sound. It was all too likely that they'd meet this next group and end up in another fight. One they might not be able to win.

They'd have to proceed as cautiously as they could and hope for the best because if they screwed this up, that was it for humanity. The human race might not die today, but it *would* die. And that was something he couldn't allow to happen.

25

Julia set the large pack next to the pile that she and Kelsey had already hauled to the maglev platform. Even with the lift now working, it had taken the two of them more than an hour to carry down the bags that Carl had packed for them.

Lieutenant Laird had stayed in the cache room and continued packing what their former captors would allow them to take while they moved it. Thank God they didn't have to carry everything down stairs the whole way.

Now that they'd repositioned everything on the platform, the rest of the folks going with them began sorting the contents so that everyone would have what they needed.

Carl had also come out of the control room and begun fitting armor to Chloe Laird, now that she'd arrived, and started fine-tuning Kelsey's armor.

Once she was done, Julia edged over to her. "Do you think we're going to make it?"

She had to ask because it seemed hard to imagine that they were going to get off this planet with the override. They'd been through so much and lost so many people that she was feeling really cynical about their chances at this point.

Kelsey gave her a sideways glance. "Don't fall into the trap of thinking that we're going to fail. We've got to have a positive outlook, even when things look darkest. That's how we triumph again and again, because we don't take no for an answer."

Julia considered that for a few seconds and then shrugged. "I guess that's one of the differences between us. I've failed so many times that I've just stopped believing that I can win. We're so far behind the eight ball—both here and back in my universe—that victory seems unimaginable at this point. The AIs hold all the cards."

Kelsey put her hands on Julia's shoulders. "You've got to remember that they don't know about you. They don't know about the people that we're training or the ships that we found for you.

"The knowledge of how things work here is going to give you a leg up there. By the time we're done getting the override and fighting the master AI at Twilight River, you'll know what you have to do.

"And you know that we'll help you do it. Maybe not us personally, because I doubt my father—our father—will allow Jared or myself to go to your universe, but we can send plenty of ships packed with advisors and helpers to guide you.

"Admittedly, it's going to be a challenge, but you can't go through life expecting everything to fail. At some point, if all you do is look forward to failure, you're going to give up. When that happens, victory is forever beyond your grasp. Don't fall into that trap. Imagine victory and then make it happen."

"You make it all sound so simple," Julia grumbled. "I know that it's not, and that's what makes me lose hope. We have so many balls in the air. All it takes is dropping one for the enemy to win. So many people that I love have already died. It's hard to believe I can redeem them."

Before Kelsey could respond, Carl waved the two of them over. Julia followed in her doppelgänger's footsteps.

"Kelsey, the armor is ready for you to put on and run through a test routine," Carl said. "It's not completely customized for you, but it's the best I can do with the generic equipment I've got on hand. If we ever get back to *Persephone*, I can have it completely customized inside an hour. The same goes for you, Julia. That's not going to be a problem."

"I'm sad that I had to leave my original armor here," Julia said with a shake of her head. "The black armor, I mean. It's odd how the color matters to me. I have no idea why it's different here, either. One of those little mysteries that we'll never know the answer to."

"It just goes to prove that when you're looking at the multiverse as a theory, there are going to be inexplicable differences between even the most similar realities," Carl said, visibly dropping into lecture mode. "Honestly, it wouldn't surprise me if there were universes out there that are exactly like either one of ours, with only things like the names of ships being different. Or perhaps even different people aboard, assigned to different positions. The combinations are literally infinite.

"I wouldn't get hung up on the details if I were you. When we get back to the ship, I can change the color for you. That's not really that complicated an issue. It'll take a little experimentation, but I can work it out in a couple of hours."

She nodded, but she wasn't sure that was what she really wanted. The black armor belonged to a different person. Even in the short time that she'd been in this universe, Julia had changed. Even thinking of herself by her assumed name was feeling more natural.

Honestly, it was like getting a fresh start. She could leave her mistakes and failures behind by merely changing her name. Julia would do better than Kelsey had in her universe.

Of that, she would make sure.

Julia nodded distractedly and looked around the platform. It seemed as if almost everyone was there and packing their gear. They'd only brought along things that they thought they could carry, as they knew that they might have to hike at some point.

There was only so much equipment that they could take that would help them in the long run, too. The immediate goal had to be getting from point A to point B and dealing with the people that they were going to negotiate with if that was even happening first.

The train would be great—if it actually arrived—but wasn't going to get them to the Imperial Palace. That was going to take some hiking, whether it be aboveground, where they'd have to potentially fight other people, or through the tunnels, where they needed supplies to allow them to see, breathe, and eat.

Weirdly, that made her think about the horses that they'd been forced to leave tethered outside the horde city. They'd left the reins in such a way that the horses could tug them loose, but she was confident that the horde had recaptured them by now.

Thankfully, those murderous bastards were actually the kind of people that cared for their animals. Still, she missed the ability to ride. What an odd, introspective thing it was to think about how horse riding brought her pleasure at a time like this.

While she was thinking about that, Mertz exited the control room and began waving for them to gather around.

"Everyone, it's time to get the last of your gear packed. Now that Carl has the armor fitted to our fighters, he's going to call the train. I'm not sure how long it's going to take to get here, so you need to begin getting yourselves in order. It might bring hostile guests right to our doorstep, and we'll want to give them a warm welcome."

Julia laughed at his joke as Kelsey stripped down and began putting her armor on. As usual, the woman paid no attention to who was standing around her, not even bothering to shield her privates by discreetly turning her body. It was as if public nudity no longer even registered for her.

That was another thing about the other woman that she'd never be able to comprehend. Her body consciousness wouldn't allow her to be so cavalier about strutting around naked in front of strangers. Or worse, platonic friends.

Just taking her clothes off in front of Carl earlier had pushed the limits of what she could imagine herself doing. Thankfully, he'd been a gentleman about the entire affair.

She really was going to have to have a conversation with Angela if they got to *Persephone*. She needed to reassure the woman and get her help understanding Carl as deeply as she could before the time came to seduce him in her universe.

The use of the word "seduce" made her pause. Her original intention had only been to lure the man in so that she could begin forming a partnership with him, but seduction had popped so easily into her mind.

There was definitely an attraction building in her mind, and that was something else she'd have to talk about with Angela. She needed to make sure the other woman knew that this version of Carl was off limits, and she knew it.

While Kelsey was getting ready, Julia went back into the control room. Carl was now sitting at one of the consoles, separated from the others, and working diligently with a virtual keyboard. She sat down next to him, causing him to glance over with a raised eyebrow.

"I want to apologize," she said quietly.

He frowned and gave her his full attention. "For what?"

"You're a married man, and I should have been more discreet when we fitted my armor. Maybe lying down on the floor and finding a way to wiggle into it. It was inappropriate to put a married man in the position where he had to look at another woman without her clothes on. It was disrespectful to you and to your wife."

He shook his head with a slight smile. "You did what needed doing, and I'm not disturbed by it. I can also assure you that Angela won't be bothered by it either. She's been a marine for a long time, and now she's a Marine Raider. That's just the way it is for them."

Julia let the air she'd been holding out slowly. "That's good to hear. I really didn't want Angela to beat me up. She's intimidating enough as a marine in my universe. As a Marine Raider, I can't imagine how scary she'd be."

Carl chuckled. "I doubt very seriously that she'd beat you up. If she were mad, she'd be much more likely to yell at you. Trust me when I say that it's going to be okay."

He went back to work, making sure that it was apparent to her that the matter was settled, so far as he was concerned. Without saying a word, she rose, stepped over to the nearest wall, and leaned against it.

She was lucky. He was a kind man who would make an excellent consort for her. She really hoped that she could get back home and meet him.

By the time she'd finished thinking that through, Mertz had walked over to Carl. "Do you really think you're going to be able to summon the train without any trouble? If so, it's time."

"Let's find out," Carl said.

* * *

CARL TOOK a deep breath and sent out the reactivation signal. Since he had the serial number for the train controller, that made it a simple matter to ping the entire network for it.

Almost immediately, a response came back that the train was in a powered-down configuration and had begun reactivating. The controller gave him an estimate of five minutes before it would be prepared to leave its current location.

That was actually pretty fast. It meant that all the systems on the train were operational. That five minutes would give the controller time to check all the propulsion and braking systems before the train began moving. If the people that had been using it were able to shut off that sequence in the next few minutes, they'd stop it from leaving their station.

Of course, they might also just choose to put people on board to confront whoever was stealing their train. If so, there were going to be people arriving on the platform that were pretty upset that they'd been taken for a ride.

Just as the counter on the timer struck five minutes, Carl saw a red dot appear on the main board. Unsurprisingly, it was flashing at what he suspected was the spur leading to the Imperial Palace.

Of course it was. Why wouldn't it be directly where they were going? It seemed perfectly fitting that the people who'd stolen the fusion plant from Frankfort had also holed up in the one place that they absolutely needed to be.

And if history was anything to go by, they wouldn't be friendly either.

What was mildly confusing to him was the fact that the blinking red dot wasn't moving. All it did was remain in one place and flash. He wasn't sure what that meant. If he'd read the files correctly, it should be green and moving.

He checked the readouts and brought up the camera inside the control area of the train itself. There was no one there, which was a relief. It meant that no one with the ability to control the train had gotten there in time to make a difference.

The controls indicated the train was in motion. That probably meant that the flashing red light indicated that it was on the spur and thus not able to be seen on the main map. A couple of minutes later, the dot turned to a solid green and began moving toward Frankfort.

"I've got it on the screen and moving," he said somewhat needlessly. Everyone else in the room had undoubtedly noticed it. "Ralph, can you see about hacking into its systems and linking into the vid system? The admiral wants to know if we've got passengers."

"On it," Ralph said as he began typing furiously on his virtual keyboard. "It doesn't look like this system is too complicated, and I've already managed to insert a couple of feelers that should give me a good idea what I'm looking at shortly."

Five seconds later, the young man grinned. "I'm in. One of my feelers found a back door that someone had designed into the system that I was able to activate. I'm bringing up the cameras in a rotating format. It'll be on the screen to our right."

As the images began flashing up onto the indicated screen, Carl's heart sank. Not only was the train occupied, but its passengers were also armed. They might not have gotten anyone capable of controlling the train aboard during that five-minute window, but there'd been armed fighters ready to move. That meant that there was going to be a confrontation as soon as the train arrived.

"Can you freeze some of those images and maybe enlarge them?" Kelsey asked. She stood next to the console in her new Raider armor, her helmet nestled into the crook of her arm.

Ralph shook his head. "I can freeze the feed, but enlarging the image will just reduce the resolution to the point where you can't see what you're looking for. That kind of nonsense is just a vid show trick. The real world doesn't work that way."

"Then do it," she said. "I might not be able to see all the details, but if what I'm looking for is there, I'll see it."

As soon as Ralph froze one of the images on the screen, she stepped closer to the big screen and stared up at the fighter. "Is it just me, or do they look like they have pins similar to the one that Jared found in the stairwell? It's right there on the lapel. And that sure looks like a uniform, doesn't it?"

Carl rose from his console and joined her in examining the man standing there. He was young and had the kind of close-cut hair that one might associate with the military. He looked just like the other dozen or so that had been standing in the same car.

"Ralph, you're the one running the vid feed," he said. "How many cars are we talking about and how many people? Do you see anyone that looks different than this guy?"

"They've got people in four of the cars," the young hacker said. "Roughly a dozen per car, so somewhere around fifty people. The men all look like him and are wearing that uniform, whatever it is. There are maybe a third that are female. The uniform is the same, but they have longer hair.

"They've got flechette rifles strapped over their shoulders, and I see flechette pistols in holsters on their hips. If we get into a fight with these people, we're going to have to be really careful, or we'll end up destroying the train."

Admiral Mertz joined them and peered up at the frozen image. "I think you're right, Kelsey. That sure does look like the same kind of pin, even though I can't make out the details at this resolution. The fact that there are so many of them, dressed in the same way, indicates this is probably an organization that the Raiders founded hundreds of years ago. Or maybe they inspired it. We'll have to find out when they get here."

He turned to face his sister. "Do you think you can use that mystique to your advantage when they arrive? If we can browbeat them, I'd much rather do that than fight. Ralph's right. If we start shooting, the train is going to be the first casualty."

Kelsey shrugged. "I can try. The only thing that I can't control is how they're going to respond. Maybe if they see some of us in armor, they'll realize that we're Marine Raiders. They won't know who has augmentation and who doesn't, so everyone needs to be armored up.

"Everyone that isn't in the control room needs to set up some of the weapons that we brought down to form a crossfire that we can use against them if they decide they're going to be hostile.

"I'd prefer stunners on wide beam. If I could be sure we'd get them all, I'd say ambush them. As it is, we'll probably have to talk first—if they'll let us—but I'll be damned if I give them a chance to kill one of us."

Admiral Mertz nodded and turned toward him. "Carl, how long until they arrive?"

He quickly walked back over to his console and brought up the data. "Judging by their current speed, it looks like they'll be here in about twenty-five minutes. If we're going to be in a fight, why don't we use some of the weapons that we've brought down to rig up a booby trap for them?"

Kelsey stepped over to him, her expression interested. "You've intrigued me, O designer of deadly weapons. What do you have in mind?"

"We've got all those explosives. We know *exactly* where the train is going to stop. Why don't we set up mines facing the cars where we know the enemy is going to be? Rather than hide them, we make them obvious.

"That way, when the doors open and they come out, they'll already be in the field of fire of weapons that they can't stop or control. We can tell them that we don't intend to set the mines off unless they start fighting, and maybe that'll calm things down until we can figure out what we're going to do."

Kelsey put on an impressed expression. "That's brilliant. We can stash people with rifles and stunners behind some of the columns to help cover them as well. If they realize that they're in a death trap, they might hesitate long enough for us to at least talk them down."

Without another word, Kelsey headed out, presumably to begin setting up the explosives.

"Good work, Carl," Admiral Mertz said. "Now, let's get everything locked down here. We don't want them shooting this place up and causing any of the systems here to do anything that they shouldn't."

"Yes, sir. I'll have everything ready."

Now all they had to do was wait until the thieves arrived. Then they'd find out whether or not they could stop them from fighting or if there was going to be a shootout that destroyed the train they so desperately needed to get to the Imperial Palace.

The Imperial Palace that, it seemed, was already occupied.

26

The next twenty minutes gave Kelsey an opportunity to work with Lieutenant Laird while setting up the explosives that they'd brought with them. Basically, these were antipersonnel mines that were designed around shaped charges that shot steel balls into the targets while leaving the area behind them *relatively* safe.

And even though the idea left her uncomfortable, she also assisted in planting explosive charges down under where the train would settle. Those were to destroy the train if the fighting became too difficult, and they had to end it quickly.

It would also mean that they'd be unable to use the train to get to the Imperial Palace, so she intended to avoid that outcome if at all possible.

If they could get past this first confrontation, she might be able to deescalate the situation and keep the other side from making any irreversible decisions. Once the killing started, she and her people would be forced to fight their way through to the Imperial Palace and capture it.

It would be far better if they could do this with words rather than weapons.

All of the noncombatants—plus Talbot—were in the control room. There was absolutely no need for them to be in danger. The walls were thin, but the control consoles would provide some cover if things went bad.

Jared, Sean, and several of the others with the skills to use flechette rifles were hidden behind some of the columns, ready to provide cover if needed. The only ones left visible on the platform were herself, Lieutenant Laird, Carl, and Julia.

Only she and Julia could use their armor effectively, but Chloe was a trained fighter and had used standard marine armor before. She'd do fine, Kelsey was sure.

Carl, on the other hand, was just there for show. He had orders that if the people on the train started shooting, he was to get his skinny little butt back into the control room and form the final line of defense in case she and the rest couldn't hold.

She resisted the urge to pace. Even though her nanites were working on her leg wound, it still ached and gave her occasional jolts of pain to remind her that she'd been hurt. Nothing that would stop her from doing what she needed to, but enough to make her aware of the injury.

Right on schedule, the maglev train pulled into the station and slowed to a halt just like Carl had programmed it to do. As soon as it settled to the ground, the doors slid open, and men and women began pouring out, their rifles up.

The train wasn't that big, all things considered. It consisted of an engine and four cars. The latter looked more like they were made for cargo because Kelsey couldn't see any seats inside. That made sense, considering that these people were using the train to strip nearby areas of equipment and supplies.

All told, Carl's count of fifty was pretty accurate. Her implants totaled the hostiles at fifty-one.

Each of the soldiers held an Imperial-made flechette rifle and had a flechette pistol in a holster on their belt. While Kelsey couldn't see behind their backs, there was a good chance that they carried stunners there. It was interesting that they'd decided to lead with lethal weaponry. Interesting and telling.

The people she'd positioned behind the columns would lead with stunners on wide beam, likely taking out most of the people on the platform if hostilities broke out. It spoke to how they'd rather not kill unless they had no choice.

The flechette rifles were a danger, but only if those people knew how to use them. Other than Kelsey, everyone had their helmets locked down, and their armor would be sufficient to stop a lot of the flechettes from penetrating.

Kelsey had her helmet off because she wanted to make the point that this didn't have to end like that. As the soldiers came out, their attention focused on her, probably because she was different.

"I'm sure you're all wondering why I've called you here," she said in a dry tone. "Before anyone gets too excited, let me suggest that you lower your weapons. If you start shooting, we're going to have to take you all down, and I'd prefer not to do that."

One of the women stepped forward, not lowering her weapon in the slightest. "Identify yourself. Why have you stolen our train?"

"Don't you think that's a little judgmental?" Kelsey asked, tilting her head slightly to the side. "After all, you used that train to steal a fusion plant from this city. Not only that, but I'm also sure that you took a lot of other things that were quite valuable as well.

"So, rather than call each other names, why don't we start with deescalating the situation before you make any more accusations?"

Before the other woman could speak, Kelsey gestured toward the antipersonnel mines arrayed in front of them. "Those mines will kill everyone on that side of the platform if you decide to open fire. Inside our armor, it's not going to hurt us at all. I really do suggest that you take this slowly because if you make a mistake right now, I'm going to be the only one left to regret it."

The woman eyed the antipersonnel mines and obviously considered ordering her people back into the train. Her thoughts seemed to pass across her face, and then, instead, she made a gesture for them to lower their weapons.

They didn't disarm themselves, but that was fine with Kelsey. She really didn't expect them to. All she wanted was for them to avoid making a lethal mistake.

"Who are you, and how do you know any of this?" the woman asked. "And how are you making the holy armor work?"

Kelsey blinked at that last. Holy armor? That seemed kind of… weird.

"My name is Kelsey Bandar, and I'm a Marine Raider."

The woman's expression went from cautious and suspicious to downright hostile. Her weapon came back up, and so did all the rest.

"Liar. Tell us the truth, or we'll kill you right now."

"Doesn't the fact that I'm working the armor count for something? What kind of proof would satisfy you?"

Before the other woman could speak, Julia stepped forward. Without waiting for the woman to say anything, her doppelgänger headed toward the front of the train and jumped down from the platform.

Then she bent low and lifted the front end of the train. That had to be a considerable strain on her and her armor, but she managed it.

"Does this count?" Julia asked through the speakers on the exterior of her armor. She then lowered the train back down and stared at the soldiers through her blank metal faceplate.

The troops arrayed on the platform stared at Julia, their weapons slowly sinking back down, and their faces struck with a mixture of shock and awe. The woman in command of these troops was seemingly unsure of how to respond.

Once Julia had jumped back up on the platform, making the feat look graceful in spite of her relative inexperience with the armor, the woman in charge of the troops swallowed visibly and gently laid her rifle on the ground.

"Everyone lay down your arms," she said.

All of the troops on the platform set their rifles down, unholstered their pistols, and set them on the ground as well. They then produced the stunners that Kelsey had suspected were there and set them next to the rest.

Once they'd done so, they stepped away from the weapons, even as the woman advanced on Kelsey.

"We deserve an explanation. Who are you really, and how are you related to the holy one?"

Kelsey shrugged slightly and then realized that the gesture wouldn't be visible through her armor. "I'm not sure who the holy one is, so you're going to have to explain it to me. What I said earlier was true. I'm a Marine Raider. I've come to gather what we need to free the Empire.

"The people of this city are angry that you stole their fusion plant, and we've agreed to discuss the matter with your leaders. We'd prefer to do so peacefully. How do we make that happen?"

The woman studied Kelsey for a long moment. "Just seeing you in that armor means that I need to bring you back to our base. Once I do, you can speak with our leaders, and they will make that decision.

"If you truly are a Marine Raider, then I don't believe you're going to have much difficulty in negotiating a solution. But you're going to have to explain everything to the god."

Kelsey frowned. "God? I still don't understand."

The woman smiled coolly. "It's quite simple. The god is a *real* Marine Raider, and I look forward to hearing how he responds to your tall tale."

* * *

JULIA WATCHED the exchange between Kelsey and the others with interest. When the conversation reached the point where the woman stated that their "god" was a Marine Raider, she laughed out loud. Thankfully, she'd shut off her external speakers, and no one could hear her.

That was ridiculous. Other than Kelsey and the people she'd begun enhancing, there were no Marine Raiders left in this Empire. They'd all died out long ago. These people were lying, even if she didn't understand what they had to gain by doing so.

The most likely explanation was that someone had tricked them. Though, Julia had to admit, whoever it was had gotten the train working and also managed to guide them through the process of disassembling the fusion plant safely. It had to be someone with a lot more knowledge than she'd expected anyone on Terra to have.

None of the Marine Raiders that had been on Terra back then could have possibly lived this long, and the ability to create them had fallen into the hands of the computers long ago.

There was obviously some kind of trickery underway. That meant the meeting with these people was going to be dangerous. After all, anyone with actual Marine Raider augmentation was a threat to the lie this person was telling.

She wondered how Kelsey was going to handle that. Was the woman going to realize that they were in danger when the trick was exposed? Her doppelgänger was really smart, and she was a lot more worldly than Julia, so she really hoped that was the case.

If the thoughts that were running through Julia's head had occurred to Kelsey, she wasn't letting it show on her face. She was busy asking the woman questions about their god and being deflected.

All the woman would say was that it wasn't her place to discuss the god. That if Kelsey wanted more information, she'd need to speak to her leaders.

The one positive aspect of this was that she'd said that she'd escort them there. It looked like the prospect of fighting it out here on the platform was over.

Kelsey stepped back from the soldiers and over to Julia. "What do you think we should do? They're basically inviting us back to their place, but it could be a trap."

"If it's not a trap, it's some kind of hoax," Julia said bluntly. "We both know that Marine Raiders don't live that long. Whoever they're referring to as their god is pulling the wool over their eyes."

She frowned. "And I don't even know where that saying came from, but it had to be something you said because it makes no sense."

Kelsey chuckled. "When you watch a lot of old vids, you pick up all kinds of obscure turns of phrase. I suggest that we only take a few of us when we go see them. That way, only some of us are at risk if the hammer comes down.

"If they really wanted to stop us from bringing the train here, they could've killed the power back at the Imperial Palace, and it would've stopped. They had plenty of time to do that, but they left it running. That means that whoever's in charge wants these people to come back and report. We've got to use that to our advantage."

She turned to face Julia more directly. "I'm going to suggest to Jared that only the four of us that can use the armor go. That way, they're not going to have an opportunity to take hostages without getting into a *real* fight. We'll leave the others here so that they can arrange a rescue if things go badly."

"And how are they going to get there?" Julia asked. "If these people aren't happy at seeing us and kill the power to the train, the Imperial Palace is still a thousand kilometers away. Not to mention that our potential rescuers won't have any armor to bring to the fight. This seems like a bad idea, Kelsey."

"Life isn't without risks," her doppelgänger said philosophically. "As my husband would tell you, I'm prone to taking more risks than the average person. If you want to stay here and reinforce the rescue team, I'll go along with that. I still think you should come with us, but the call is yours."

Julia sighed in exasperation. "How is it that you're so headstrong, and I'm not? I thought we were supposed to be the same person until a couple of years ago. Could you explain to me exactly how you're *so* different?"

"Just lucky, I guess," Kelsey said with a grin. "That doesn't change the question. Do you want to stay here or go with me?"

Julia slowly counted down from ten in her head to get the exasperation out of her voice. "I'll go with you, of course. If they're going to jump somebody, we've got to kick their asses."

Kelsey clapped her on the shoulder. "Now you're talking like a Marine Raider. Here's what we're going to do. We're going to step back into the other room and let Jared know what we're doing, and then we're going to let these people escort us to see their leaders.

"If the power gets cut, they're going to have to come and get us. Personally, I don't see that happening. These don't seem like the kind that shoot first and ask questions later like the horde.

"They're looking for answers and want to hear what we have to say. They may not give us what we want, but I believe that we can come to some type of arrangement if we work hard enough.

"More importantly, we have to come to some kind of understanding, or we won't get access to the Imperial Palace. We'll have to go through them one way or the other, and I'd much rather do that without shooting."

On that, Julia agreed. They didn't have the numbers to fight a large group because they'd lose, even with their access to Marine Raider armor and modern weapons.

Losing Scott was bad enough. Losing the rest would be unthinkable.

While Chloe and Carl kept an eye on their prisoners—or perhaps guests —she followed Kelsey in to speak with Mertz. The man listened to his sister's plan and then shook his head.

"If we separate ourselves, the chances of us being overwhelmed individually are too high. We've initiated contact, and now it's time for us to go see who the man behind the curtain is. Get everyone together, and we'll load them onto the train."

Julia sighed and hoped that they could carry this off. That they weren't jumping from the frying pan into the fire. Whatever that meant.

27

Jared eyed the soldiers in the train compartment behind them once the train had reversed course and headed back into the tunnel. The fact that the soldiers seemed willing to allow their higher-ups to deal with the problem didn't mean that they were safe to be around. No, it was far better to keep to themselves for the moment.

All of them were in good shape and ready for trouble except for Talbot. He lay on a small mattress that they'd salvaged from somewhere. He was still pale, and Lily didn't want him moving on his own for a day. They'd found a stretcher to move him in, which did nothing to improve the gruff man's temper.

He'd thought hard about leaving Talbot behind, but the Marine Raider had insisted that he needed to go. In the end, Jared had decided that he was right. They couldn't afford to leave anyone behind. Whatever happened now, it was going to happen to all of them.

One of the things he'd noticed right away was that none of the captured soldiers had implants. That made sense. Implant technology was something that the AIs had heavily restricted. These people might be technologically superior to the residents of Frankfort, but they had to deal with only having the equipment they had on hand.

By the time the AIs had suppressed Terra, they'd controlled all of the implant facilities on the planet and had undoubtedly yanked all of the equipment as soon as they were ready to start dropping kinetic strikes. Or simply made certain that none of it survived intact.

As the train went through the dark tunnel, occasionally passing through a pool of light cast by a functional illumination panel, he wondered what they were going to find when they reached the Imperial Palace. The story of there being a Marine Raider was incredible, if true.

He wasn't as cynical as Julia, so he wasn't discounting the idea out of hand. After all, what did they really know about the technology that went into creating the Marine Raiders? The specialized medical nanites they'd used were more advanced than those used by Fleet, but even the latter could significantly extend someone's life. Was it really so unbelievable that there might be a survivor of the original Marine Raider cadre here on Terra?

Still, he'd need to see proof of that to believe it.

If he was right, the soldiers were descendants of the original Marine Raiders left here on Terra or those closely associated with them. Someone had kept the power on at the Imperial Palace, and they still had access to technology.

The minutes dragged by slowly and seemed to go even slower the farther they traveled. Eventually, the maglev train reached the spur and curved into another tunnel. As Jared was looking out the window, he could see the one they'd departed from. It led toward Imperial City, which was nothing more than a water-filled crater now.

The thought of all that death horrified him. It also steeled his determination to overcome whatever situation they found at the Imperial Palace and get what they needed to destroy the AIs once and for all.

He couldn't believe how close they were to their destination. They'd been trying to get to the Imperial Palace for so long that he'd started thinking they'd never make it.

If the original plan had worked out, they'd have landed there with two pinnaces full of personnel. That would've almost certainly drawn a hostile response.

Even so, he'd had all the marines and their powered armor. They could've dealt with the problem, as he was willing to bet anything that these people no longer had access to something like that.

After another ten minutes, the train pulled into a station. Arrayed along the platform were about the same number of troops that he and his people had captured, their weapons pointed at the train. None were in powered armor, confirming his guess.

Obviously, there'd been some communication with his prisoners, and the defenders were ready to receive them. That was fine. He'd have expected nothing less.

"No matter what they say, we're not going to disarm," he said as he watched their prisoners leaving the other cars and streaming behind their armed comrades. That got a nod of agreement from the rest. They were done surrendering.

Taking the lead, Jared stepped out onto the platform. He'd considered carrying a flechette rifle but had decided against it. In the end, he'd settled for a flechette pistol on his hip and a stunner on his off side, in the style that Kelsey favored, a fashion that was fast becoming standard for both the marines and Fleet personnel on excursions.

If they ever made it back to Avalon, he'd recommend that Grand Admiral Yeats make that official.

Jared was dressed in a marine camouflage uniform that they'd recovered from the cache, as were the rest of his group that didn't have powered armor. He wore unpowered armor—as did they, except for Talbot.

Behind him, the four in Raider armor arrayed themselves. They were armed to the teeth with weapons suitable for use in the armor. If there was a fight, they'd end it decisively. His personal plan was to dive back into the train if shooting started.

"Halt and put down your weapons!" someone in the group of soldiers on the platform shouted at them.

Jared raised his hands slightly. "My name is Jared Mertz, and I'm an admiral with Fleet. Not the Fleet that crushed the Empire on behalf of the artificial intelligences but part of a group of survivors that managed to escape the original rebellion.

"We won't put our arms down. We've come to negotiate with the leaders here for the return of the fusion plant that you took from the city of Frankfort."

An older man, his hair more gray than black, pushed his way through the defenders. He eyed Jared and the four in powered armor critically. "You have a lot of nerve coming into our domain this way. You stole our train and assaulted our people."

"You stole the fusion plant from the city of Frankfort," Jared countered. "Do we really want to start arguing about who stole what? I'd have thought you'd be more interested in talking about the Marine Raiders at my back."

Jared gestured toward the four behind him. "We've heard that you also have a Marine Raider here. Perhaps ours should speak with yours and figure out between themselves what needs to happen."

The man started to say something but stopped and put a hand to his ear. Jared could see that there was an earbud, so he was in communication with someone else. Another indication of higher technology.

The man frowned deeply and said something under his voice. It looked as if he was arguing with whoever had spoken. Whoever that was, they seemed insistent. The man dropped his hand and glared at Jared.

"The god wishes to speak with one of your people. I have chosen that one." The man gestured toward Talbot, who had just been carried out on a stretcher.

"He's wounded. Pick someone else."

"I will not. The god gives you his word as a Marine Raider that your warrior will be returned to you unharmed and before any decision or action is taken."

Jared considered the unexpected twist of fate. There was a risk in letting them take Talbot, but it might be worth taking.

"I don't like them taking him off alone," Kelsey said through her outer speakers as she stepped up beside him. "I should go with them."

"The god insists that he come alone," the man in front of them said. "Is his word not good enough for you?"

The soldiers arrayed in front of them all stiffened slightly, and their weapons rose a little. A negative answer wouldn't be well received.

Jared held up a hand toward Kelsey. "Let's see how this plays out."

* * *

TALBOT WONDERED what he was going to find when the soldiers carrying his stretcher delivered him to his destination. Like the rest of them, he had no idea who was really pulling the strings behind the scenes here in the Imperial Palace.

Four of the soldiers carried his stretcher while another four walked around them with their flechette rifles at the ready. They'd taken his weapons, and he hadn't fussed. They were taking him to see somebody important to them, and he got their security concerns.

He had no idea how the maglev train platform was positioned inside the Imperial Palace, but the soldiers took him into an operational lift and descended several levels. He was grateful because going down stairs with him on a stretcher might've ended badly.

Lily had done as much as she could for him with the portable regenerator, but he was still weak. Even with his augmentation, the arrows had penetrated vital organs, and he was wary of tearing the wounds open again. Whatever happened next, he was going to do his best to keep the situation as drama free as he possibly could unless they gave him no choice.

When they exited the lift, the soldiers carried him along a wide corridor and stopped before two large doors that didn't look like they belonged there. They were made of carved wood, showing battle scenes.

In a way, they reminded him of some of the carvings that he'd seen in the horde city, though these seemed to involve people with advanced weaponry. He made sure to record them with his implants for later study.

Flanking the doors were two guards in white uniforms that were reminiscent of the white uniforms worn by the Imperial Guard back on Avalon. The two groups exchanged words before the men in white opened the large doors and allowed the men carrying Talbot to go inside. They stopped the other soldiers, though.

As soon as the men carrying his stretcher entered the room, Talbot felt his eyes adjusting. The illumination levels in this space were low. If he hadn't had ocular augmentation, he wasn't certain that he would've been able to see very far into the gloom. There were six more guards in white inside, arrayed against the walls, each with a flechette rifle in their hands.

In many ways, the large room was similar to the Imperial throne room back on Avalon. It was wide but also very long. With his enhanced sight, he could see that there were tapestries hung along the walls that showed battle scenes similar to those carved into the doors, though the gloom obscured the fine details.

Talbot turned his attention to where the men were carrying him. There was a long couch set up on a dais ahead of them. On it, a man lounged.

A horribly disfigured man.

As Talbot was brought closer, he could see that the man's face was terribly scarred, and he was missing his right eye. His salt-and-pepper hair and beard were crisscrossed with gray streaks that probably indicated scarring underneath.

The man lay on his side with his left arm resting across his midsection. His right arm was missing. There were no legs at the end of the couch, either. It looked as if the man were a triple amputee, and even the single limb that he had left was twisted, and the hand only had two fingers and a thumb.

The man gestured for the people carrying Talbot to set him down nearby. There were pillows scattered about, and the soldiers used them to prop Talbot up so that he could see the man on the couch.

Without speaking, the man gestured, and the soldiers retreated toward the doors. He waited until they'd exited the room completely before he spoke.

"When they told me that a group with people claiming to have Marine Raiders had arrived, I found that difficult to believe," the man said slowly, his voice sounding dry and unused.

Talbot gave the man a lopsided grin. "When I heard that you were a Marine Raider and a god, I found that hard to believe."

The corners of the man's mouth quirked upward slightly. "That unwarranted title is something of a cosmic joke since I'm incapable of doing much of anything for myself. I'm no god, but I *am* a Marine Raider. Can those people in powered armor prove they are?"

"Yep." Talbot reached out and grabbed one of the metal poles that were part of the stretcher that they'd carried him in on. He clenched his fist. With a loud groan, it bent and snapped off. He dropped it to the floor with a metallic clang.

For several seconds, there was nothing but silence in the room. Then the man blinked and shook his head. "That is *not* what I expected to see."

Talbot started to respond, but his implants pinged with an incoming communication request. Shocked, he accepted.

The man's expression became almost slack-jawed as he stared at Talbot. "Dear God, you have implants. Could it really be true?"

Of course I do, Talbot sent back through the implant connection. *I'm a Marine Raider.*

"I've got the full package," Talbot said aloud, terminating the implant connection. "Augmented muscles with graphene coating on the bones and reinforced joints, augmentation in my eyes, ears, nose, artificial muscles, and a full pharmacology unit. Like I said, I'm a Marine Raider. So, who are you?"

The man's smile became wry. "An anomaly. Before I answer that question, I want to hear you say that you don't serve the AIs."

Talbot shook his head. "We don't. In fact, we came here to get something to fight them with. Something that can kill the master AI."

The other man's eyes narrowed. "You're talking about Operation Imperium."

"I don't know what Operation Imperium is," Talbot said, shrugging one shoulder. "Our people were settled on a planet far from the center of the Empire. During the fighting, the rebels used EMP weapons, and we lost our technology, but we managed to keep them from actually putting people on the planet itself.

"We lost all knowledge of what had gone on here at Terra over the next five hundred years. We've been learning bits and pieces once we started exploring again. For the moment, the AIs don't know that we exist, though I suspect at this point they're starting to get a clue. What I do know is that the master AI is at Twilight River, and we've come for something in the vaults that can shut it down."

The man nodded. "Like I said, Operation Imperium. You're looking for the override."

Talbot blinked in shock. "You've heard of it?"

"Just like I know that Emperor Marcus sent Crown Prince Lucian to Avalon. Rather, Emperor Lucien, since he made him co-emperor before he led the AI's forces away from Terra. Avalon is the planet you're speaking about, right?"

Not sure how to interpret this turn of events, Talbot nodded wordlessly.

"Then I think we both have parts of the puzzle," the man said. "I wasn't joking when I said that I was an anomaly. Emperor Marcus ordered strike teams of Marine Raiders and regular marines to stay on Terra and fight a guerrilla war once invasion became imminent. This is going to be very difficult for you to believe, but I was one of those Marine Raiders."

Talbot felt his eyes narrow. "That's bull. Nobody lives that long."

The man's mouth quirked into a sardonic smile. "I've often wished that were true. I'm just too stubborn to commit suicide. My pharmacology unit has been out of pain medication for centuries now. At times, the agony is indescribable.

"Marine Raider nanites were brand new—less than twenty years—when I became a Raider. Before then, they had the same ones issued to the Fleet. No one had done any truly long-term studies on them at that point. Though, to be fair, I suppose long term is a tricky subject when talking about life spans in the Empire.

"It turns out that they do provide something at least approximating immortality. I don't think I've physically aged more than a decade in the last five centuries. Maybe less. I'm so chewed up that it's hard to tell."

Talbot struggled to understand what the man had said. That couldn't be true. The idea of someone living that long was ludicrous.

Nodding at his expression, the man continued. "I'm going to have some words with the ruling council. These people are all descendants of our original support teams. We made sure that we had plenty of technology hidden with them, and I've used it to keep them educated once the hammer came down about a hundred years ago.

"We've only been inside the Imperial Palace for about sixty years. It seemed like a good place to move to. Small and easy to defend, and very well shielded. Now, I think I really want to hear the story of how you became a Marine Raider."

Talbot chuckled darkly. "That's a *very* long story, and I'm not the right one to tell it. You're going to want to speak to my wife. She's a descendent of Lucian, and her father is the reigning emperor of what we call the New Terran Empire."

The man on the couch blinked, his eyes wide as he sat up as much as he could. "You brought the heir to the throne on a mission like this? Are you mad?"

That made Talbot laugh. "You'd need to meet her to understand. We don't *tell* her to do anything. She does what she wants, and we just try to keep up.

"I'm not going to tell her story for her, but she received Marine Raider augmentation before any of us. She certainly didn't come by her implants through any normal process, and quite frankly, she's wildly unsuited to be a Marine Raider just based on her size, but she's got the spirit. Oh, God, does she have the spirit."

The man considered him again, this time for almost a minute, without speaking. Then he reached over with his remaining hand and picked up what looked like a handheld radio.

"Bring more of them to me. Particularly the leadership of their group. Some of them can remain in the corridor with their weapons. Again, they are not to be attacked or harmed."

Without allowing time for anyone to respond, the man turned the radio off.

"You asked who I am. My name is Jake Peters, and I was in tactical command of the guerrilla forces in this area when Terra first came under attack. My rank, though I haven't needed to use it for a damned long time, was major. As I stated, I was a Marine Raider.

"I don't suppose that you have a doctor with you. I could really use a shot of pain medication."

28

Kelsey stared at the man on the couch, stunned. She was completely and utterly gobsmacked. She'd sat cross-legged on the floor, listening as he'd told his story. Hearing what had happened from someone who'd actually been there was surreal.

Reginald Bell, the single man they'd ever found who'd survived all that time, had done so only with the help of a stasis unit, a technology that wasn't rated for anything like the three centuries that it had kept him alive.

The former Fleet officer had been an ensign—a probationary tactical officer on the battlecruiser *Courageous*—during the rebellion. A man in his early twenties when he'd gotten his Fleet implants.

The ancient man lived almost two hundred and eighty years outside the stasis unit, which was an incredible achievement. It was undoubtedly also an outlier on the curve but showed what was at least possible with Fleet-grade medical nanites.

Jake Peters had lived through nearly twice that number of years, and though a physical wreck, he obviously still had many years yet to live.

Was he immortal? She sincerely doubted it, but there was an old quote she'd come across in her reading by an author named Arthur C. Clarke: "Any sufficiently advanced technology is indistinguishable from magic."

This certainly sounded like magic to her.

Jake Peters and his comrades had struggled over the years, but one by one, they'd been killed. To the best of his knowledge, none of the others had been alive twenty-five years after Terra fell.

He'd been gravely injured early in the fight, and though he'd been able to get civilian-grade artificial limbs through people that were associated with the resistance, he wasn't combat capable anymore. He'd had to retire to directing the fight from the shadows.

At some point over the intervening five hundred years, he'd somehow transitioned from being their leader to their god. He couldn't quite pin down when it had happened, but nothing he said seemed to change their minds.

Kelsey could see how that was possible. When someone didn't age, when they stayed the same as you grew old and died, generation after generation, at some point, you were going to decide that they were more than human.

Since the AIs had smashed Terra a hundred years ago, his civilian limbs had failed one by one until he'd been left crippled again. The lack of advanced medicine and the lack of people trained in its use left him trapped once again inside a scarred and pained body.

Jared, who'd been sitting next to her, nodded when the man finished. "That's a hard story. I'm sorry for all the pain and suffering that you've been through. It's downright amazing that you're still alive.

"We've met one other person who was born before the Fall. He was an ensign in Fleet and ended up in a stasis chamber as an old man. He wasn't awake for all that time, but at least he'd seen the Empire at its height before the rebellion."

"I suppose I'm not surprised," the scarred man said. "When you've got as many people as the Empire used to have, a few were going to figure out how to extend their lives that long. What terrifies me is that no one knew how effective the Marine Raider nanites were going to be.

"They were just advertised as a step up from what Fleet used. Well, maybe two steps. Like I said, they'd been in use in the Marine Raider community for a couple of decades when the rebellion started. There hadn't been time to do a truly long-term study, and people were only beginning to suspect how effective they might be.

"Even so, I'd have to say their guesses were wildly wrong. No one even dreamed that they'd grant someone a lifetime that lasted half a millennium. At this point, I'm terrified that other Raiders were captured during the rebellion, their implants overridden, and they've been alive this entire time. I can't imagine anything that horrible."

Considering that the AIs had disabled the medical nanites in the shock troops they'd forcibly upgraded, Kelsey suspected that the AIs *had* gotten their electronic hands on some and knew just how long-lived they might be. Based on that, it was likely that none of those people were still alive now.

The man took a deep breath and looked over at Kelsey. "I understand that you came into your augmentation through a nonstandard path. Your husband wouldn't give me any of the details. He said it was your story, and if you don't mind, I think I'd like to hear it."

Before she could say anything, Jared rose to his feet, making her look at him askance. He nodded to the man and turned to her.

"Before she starts, I should make a complete introduction. Major Peters, allow me to present my sister, Crown Princess Kelsey Bandar, heir to the Imperial Throne of the New Terran Empire. She's also Colonel Bandar of the Marine Raiders. Since she was the first and the most skilled of those upgraded, she gets to be in charge of them."

He turned to Julia. "This is her younger twin, Julia. She's also been upgraded, though her training is far from complete."

"Highnesses," the man said, inclining his head. "Forgive me for saying so, but it's a far step from having the equipment to being a Marine Raider."

"I *did* have training, Major," Kelsey said, rising to her feet. "It was a bizarre form of training, and one that I don't really expect you to believe offhand, but I'll lay it out for you anyway. Did my husband tell you which ship I came here in?"

Peters shook his head. "That never came up."

Kelsey nodded. "Until very recently, I was in command of the Marine Raider strike ship *Persephone*. We recovered her after the Fall. Her crew was dead, of course, but her commanding officer had taken the unusual step of leaving a message for those that came after him.

"You knew him, and I know that for a fact. His name was Ned Quincy, and even though I didn't know your last name, I knew *you* the moment I laid eyes on you because I've seen a memory of the two of you together.

"You weren't wearing rank tabs, so I didn't know your rank either. You were on some planet together, unloading and transferring gear between pinnaces. Ned called you Jake."

The man on the couch blinked. And then he blinked again before sitting up a little straighter. "How the hell could that even be possible?"

Kelsey tapped the side of her head. "He made a bunch of memory recordings of him doing all kinds of things. I'm not sure if he ever told anyone about it, but he had one of his tech people put some type of library program into his implants to coordinate the use of all those memory engrams of him doing various things.

"Ned said that he started doing it at the beginning of the rebellion to document everything that he and his people went through, so it's possible he told you about it."

"He did," Jake said slowly. "You talk about him as if he were still alive."

"Ned Quincy's body died, but his personality survived. When I pulled all those memory engrams into my own implants, a more advanced computer system worked on the library program he'd used to enhance its capabilities, and that somehow created a small-scale artificial intelligence that had his memories and personality.

"No one really understands how that's possible, and we have no way of replicating it without potentially making two Ned Quincys, which would be wrong. He's no longer inside my implants, but he lived there for over a year. He taught me everything I know about the Marine Raiders. Everything that he'd recorded, anyway.

"If he didn't know something, he studied it and made me learn it, too. All of that was integrated into my training, and he put me through what he called hell week as he tested me on *everything*. I doubt I got more than an hour of sleep a day, but I passed.

"So while I don't have the experience someone like you has, I *am* a Marine Raider. My husband has done the same thing, as has the person in command of *Persephone*, Major Angela Ellis. One by one, we're bringing the Marine Raider organization back to life.

"My sister isn't there yet, and I won't go into how she got her implants, but she's making progress."

If Kelsey had had her druthers, she'd have left Julia out of this, but people had seen her doppelgänger in Raider armor. She still wore her armor, minus her helmet. Better safe than sorry.

Carl, Chloe, and Julia were out in the hall, still fully armored up and armed. If something went wrong, they'd come busting in, weapons blazing.

Jake's expression remained blank. "That's an interesting story. I don't suppose you have any way of proving it."

She smiled slightly. "You know that Ned was a master of the Art, don't you?"

"He was one of the best," the man readily admitted. "He almost took the Raider competition one year. I've never personally met anyone better at that kind of thing."

"Then maybe I can demonstrate a little of what he taught me. You should be able to see his influence in my style. Will your guards object if I retrieve my swords?"

The white-uniformed guards—some kind of nod to either a priesthood, the old Imperial Guard, or perhaps both—had insisted that everyone in the room be disarmed before they entered the presence of their god.

Jake made a gesture, and an unhappy man in white went outside to retrieve her swords.

Once he'd returned with them, Kelsey strapped them on and stepped into a clear area a bit distant from the couch. They'd turned the lighting up so that everyone could clearly see one another, and there was no need to make the guards think she was about to slice and dice their god.

She went through a number of the fighting katas that she'd learned, using all of her Marine Raider augmentation and skill. Then she put some of her own work into it and proceeded to show how she could be a ferocious attacker or defender.

Once she'd finished and sheathed the swords, Jake nodded slowly. "It's hard to argue with the evidence of my own eye. I'll grant you that only someone very skilled in the Art and comfortable with their implants and augmentation could do that. I can also see something that reminds me of Ned.

"That said, I still find what you're telling me hard to believe. I knew Ned and commanded another strike ship back then. We were contemporaries. I can't imagine how you could even know that, but I'm willing to at least consider the possibility. Where is he now?"

"He's in computer storage aboard *Persephone*. One of our scientists extracted him from my implants. Now they're in the process of building an artificial body that will fool the program into believing that he's still inside Marine Raider implants.

"It's going to take a while to even understand the basics of what they need to do. Eventually, though, Ned is going to wake up again. He will live again."

Jake shook his head. "That's really hard to take just on someone's word."

"Let me give you some more evidence," Kelsey said. "I'm going to send you some files."

She initiated a connection to his implants and then sent him a lot of images and video files that she'd recorded aboard *Persephone*. Ones that were taken inside the bridge and other portions of the ship that wouldn't be known to anyone who hadn't been there. She also sent him the recording of the meeting between the man and Ned that she'd referenced.

He sighed and rubbed his face with his remaining hand. "I can't argue with any of that. That's me, and I remember the meeting well enough, though I hadn't recorded it. The layout of the planet and the uniform I was wearing are indisputable.

"There's also no way that you could've known the layout of *Persephone*. I've been aboard her, and that's exactly how she's laid out. I can even see some of the same scars and blemishes on the bulkheads of the bridge. They were there when I visited, so you must've been aboard that ship.

"If I grant that, I suppose I have to give you the rest of your story, as difficult as it is to believe."

He shook his head and chuckled. "I suppose it isn't any more preposterous than me being over five centuries old, so we'll just have to accept what the other is saying. You are a Marine Raider, and Ned—or some semblance of him—is still alive somewhere."

Kelsey stripped off the sheathed swords and handed them back to the guard. He quickly scurried away. She supposed he really didn't have any idea how dangerous she was with just her hands.

"Now that I'm unarmed again, there's something else that I'd like to discuss with you. In private."

Jake nodded and gestured for the guards to move back to the walls. They'd still be able to see everything that was going on but be unable to hear any normally pitched conversation.

Once they were out of earshot, Kelsey continued. "We need your help. We've come here for something that can beat the artificial intelligences."

"The override," Peters said with a nod. "I'm aware that it's down in the vault because that was part of my briefing. I have no way of getting in there, but I suppose you do. I can't claim that I have complete control over events that take place here in the Imperial Palace, but I'll do what I can to smooth that path for you.

"The leadership of the group that I once formed to support us has taken on a life of its own. They give me a lot of leeway in what I can order them to do, but I've run into some things that they've refused. They're decent people, but be cautious around them."

"Thank you," she said, smiling in gratitude. "We appreciate the help, though I'm still not sure how we're going to get off this planet and back to *Persephone*. Even if we manage that, we've still got to get out of the Terra system somehow."

"The Marine Raiders left a lot of caches of equipment and supplies," he said. "I know where you can find a couple of stealthed Marine Raider pinnaces."

That made her grin. "It just so happens that both Jared and I know how to fly. Maybe everything isn't lost after all. Why didn't you use one to get away from here?"

He shrugged. "Where would I go? The AIs had conquered the entire Empire. What use was it trying to get to another world?

"If they caught me, I'd have suffered an eternity of being a slave in my own body. I fought them and lost. Maybe you can win—and I'm more than willing to help you do it—but my time is past.

"When we moved to the Imperial Palace, we still had some older folk that could fly the pinnaces. They're stashed in the underground hangar, so you can probably get access to them. No promises on their condition, though."

"We'll make it work. Thank you."

"Don't thank me yet," he said in a low voice. "The leadership council isn't going to tolerate strangers like you here in the Imperial Palace for very long. At some point very soon, they're going to decide that it's time for you to go. You need to act fast if you intend to get what you need before then."

She smiled coldly. "Leave that to us."

29

An hour later, Carl was in the medical center that had once been reserved for the Imperial Family. It looked like it was still in pretty decent shape and seemed to have been well stocked.

The Imperial Palace had been abandoned before Terra had fallen, so no one had used this facility in more than five centuries. It looked as if the Rebel Empire had sent people to search it—as well as the rest of the Imperial Palace—to make certain that no one was hiding here, but they'd left it abandoned.

Doctor Stone was going through the medical gear piece by piece, and if anything needed to be repaired, he was right on hand to do the work. Like the room itself, most of it was in good shape, but he'd found the tools and replacement parts he needed if he had to do any serious work.

It was very similar to the repairs he'd had to do on the derelict battlecruiser *Courageous*. The Empire built to last, but everything had its limits.

Once everything was ready, they'd brought Kelsey, Talbot, and the crippled Raider into the room. Talbot went into one of the spare beds while everyone else focused their attention on Major Peters.

The man's guardians were not happy that he was leaving what they saw as his temple, but he'd made a fuss, and they'd allowed it. Now they stood next to the door, glowering at everyone with disapproving eyes.

Doctor Stone got the man up onto the exam table with Kelsey's assistance. Once she'd run the scanner across him several times, she pursed her lips.

"It looks like your physical injuries are relatively benign as far as such things go, though considering the amount of scarring and the loss of your limbs, I understand why it might not feel that way.

"The good news is that we'll be able to attach Marine Raider–grade artificial limbs if we ever get our hands on any. That wasn't a certainty, even though you'd been fitted for artificial limbs before. The ones I'm talking about are capable of delivering the same kind of strength that your augmented muscles used.

"The bad news is that we don't have anything like that here. In fact, there are no artificial limbs at all. I'm sure you already knew that because that would've been one of the first things you'd checked, but we looked again just to be sure."

Peters nodded slightly. "When we first arrived, I had them tear this place apart looking for any without luck."

Stone nodded. "Now that we've gotten that out of the way, we can get to something that's of more immediate importance to you. I'm going to tap into Kelsey's pharmacology unit and transfer half of her pain medication to you. You need that much more than she does right now."

Carl could see the man visibly relax. "That would be amazing, Doctor. This constant pain has been dragging on my soul."

"Between Kelsey and Talbot, we can bring you up to full on all your meds," she said. "Anything that they're low on afterward, we'll make up from our stocks on *Persephone*."

She lowered her voice, likely to make sure the guards didn't hear her. Carl could barely hear her.

"If we can talk you into going to *Persephone* with us, we've everything necessary to bring a Raider back to full capability, even after a major injury. I urge you to consider that option."

Peters pursed his lips, his eyes sliding toward the guards. "I'll have to think about it. I've been here so long that I'm not sure if I can leave. At this point, I doubt that these people would let me, even if I insisted."

"That's a problem for later then," Doctor Stone said loudly enough that the guards, who were becoming a bit concerned about the conversation that they couldn't overhear, visibly relaxed. "Kelsey, if you'd go ahead and lie down on your stomach on the adjacent exam table, I'll extract the drugs from your pharmacology unit and transfer them directly across to Major Peters. This would be easier from the front, but I can manage with just opening the back of your torso armor."

The process of moving the drugs from Kelsey to the crippled Marine Raider took about twenty minutes. When they were done, the man sighed and relaxed even further. "Man, you don't know how good this feels. I've dreamed of being pain free for *so* long."

"I've got a few more things to check, but you can go, Kelsey," Doctor Stone said. "And thank you for your help, Carl. I can get Talbot over here and hooked up without any assistance."

With them both being dismissed, Kelsey drew Carl out of the room and took them to another room, where Admiral Mertz was waiting. Two of the soldiers trailed along behind them, making sure that their hosts knew where they were at any time.

"We're going down to the vault," she said once they were inside the room and out of earshot of any of their watchers. "Everybody is busy keeping an eye on Peters, so it gives us a chance to slip away without a whole lot of attention being paid to us. We need to get the override before our hosts decide to kick us out."

"What are we going to do about the spies keeping an eye on us?" Carl asked.

Admiral Mertz smiled wickedly. "We're going to let them keep doing it. If my plan works the way I expect it to, they're not even going to be aware of what we're up to. While there's probably more than one way into the vaults, the information I got from the Imperial Scepter talks about a secret passage. We'll use that to give our watchdogs the slip.

"Since they're happier keeping an eye on us as a group, we'll all go to the Imperial Residence together. Once we get inside, we can use the secret passage while Clarice keeps up a conversation that makes the guards think that we're all inside. You'll note that they don't feel the need to keep an eye on us directly but are happy to guard the doors where we congregate. We'll use that to our advantage."

"Actually, we need to make another stop first," Kelsey said. "It's on the way."

She led them back toward the room where Major Peters had been kept. The guards fell in behind them as they walked.

To Carl's surprise, she went past that room and led them to an even more ornate set of doors, which were propped open. It was much larger than the place where Major Peters had been, and even though the doors were open, it smelled of disuse. The walls were covered in faded and threadbare tapestries, and a dais at the end held a golden throne.

The Imperial Throne.

Carl was awestruck. This was the place where Kelsey's ancestors had ruled over the Terran Empire for more than ten thousand years. He couldn't imagine how much history had taken place in this very room.

Kelsey led them to the back of the room, where she ducked behind the throne and through another doorway set in the rear wall. The guards remained in the main room, seemingly disinterested in following them.

The suite looked as if it had been used when dressing for state ceremonies. The racks were filled with the remains of formalwear. After five hundred years, everything was in terrible condition, but it didn't seem to have been disturbed.

Kelsey looked around for a few moments and then ducked through another door into what was obviously a private office. Carl immediately spotted a stand that looked like it was made for the Imperial Scepter.

Obviously thinking the same thing, Kelsey dug into her bag and pulled out the scepter, fitting it once more into the place that had been made for it.

"I bet that no one ever thought this thing would come back home," she said softly. "Life is strange sometimes."

She returned the scepter to her bag before circling the office and stopping at another stand, which held the remaining pieces of the Imperial Regalia. The Imperial Crown sat on a faded velvet pad, and underneath it was a thick, unadorned golden chain with heavy links.

"I bet my father would love to have these, and since we may never come this way again, I figured it was the right time to pick them up. I'd hoped they'd been left undisturbed. Sometimes the gods smile."

Carl considered that. She wasn't nearly as mortal as most. If Major Peters was anything to go by, she might live for a thousand years or more. Though, with all the fighting and other crazy stuff she did, that seemed unlikely.

Then another thought struck him. They'd given Kelsey's father Marine Raider medical nanites. He might be an older man, but he wasn't *that* old. He might still rule the New Terran Empire for a long, *long* time. How would that change society? Or would he choose to step down before then?

Once word got back to Avalon, it was going to set off a firestorm. Perhaps he should speak with everyone about keeping that little detail quiet for the time being.

As he'd pondered the implications of that, Kelsey had secured the regalia in her bag. Now she was looking at perhaps a dozen books on one of the shelves of a nearby bookshelf. He managed to see that the pages were filled with handwritten words when she opened one.

If he had to guess, those were probably Emperor Marcus's journals—historical treasures of incalculable value.

She closed the book and started stuffing them all into her bag. They'd fill it, and it would be damned heavy, but she was strong enough to handle it.

With that out of the way, the group returned to the throne room and continued on toward the Imperial Residence via another corridor accessed from the side of the chamber nearest the throne. Their bored escorts fell in behind them.

The hall was lined with oil paintings that depicted the emperors that had once ruled over the Terran Empire. Closest to the throne room was Emperor Marcus himself. It seemed as they went back toward the residence, they were going backward in time.

Carl made sure to pause at each long enough to get a high-resolution image through his implants. There were plaques below each painting that gave their names and the dates that they'd reigned.

He took particular interest in the first emperor as they arrived at the doors to the Imperial Residence. The plaque listed his name as Andrew Bandar, gave his regnal name as Andrew the First, and listed him as an admiral in the Fleet of the Terran Republic.

Carl knew little about the man. He'd overthrown the corrupt Terran Republic and formed the Terran Empire. There was probably one hell of a story there, but it was mostly lost in the sands of time.

He was a handsome man, young for his rank. Oddly, he bore a striking resemblance to Admiral Mertz. The two men could have been brothers if not separated by millennia.

While he'd been considering the painting, the rest had opened the doors to the residence and were moving inside. He hurried to join them before the guards could catch up.

Kelsey closed the doors in their faces, and everyone waited to see if they demanded entry. They didn't. It seemed they were content to wait outside. That was good. Otherwise, they'd have had to come up with another plan or do something irrevocable.

The common area in the Imperial Residence was a wonder. First, it was huge. Not as big as the throne room but far more palatial than anything he could ever imagine living in.

The deep carpet on the floor had likely once been white, though it was now so coated with dirt and dust that it was a dingy gray. Finely carved chairs, tables, and other pieces of ornate furniture sat scattered around the vast room.

What really took his breath away, though, was the extravagant centerpiece: a stone fountain almost ten meters across. It was filled with virulent green algae and smelled *awful*.

Above it was what had once been a waterfall. Natural stones piled one upon another going up three meters. Off to the right side, built of similar stones, a table projected directly out of the fountain. It was probably five meters long and bracketed by benches made of the same stone.

Kelsey turned toward them. "The table has the means of activating the secret entrance, which is under the fountain. It's going to require Jared's DNA to activate, but there's some kind of switch that needs to be turned on. Carl, can you find where this needs to happen and make sure that it's working?"

With a nod, Carl slid under the table. At the end directly opposite the fountain, there was a reader plate recessed into the underside of the table. He plugged a cable into it and brought up his diagnostic equipment on his tablet.

The reader had power but was switched off. It wanted verification of authority to reactivate.

"It needs your authentication, Kelsey," he said. "You can use your implants to connect with it, but you'll have to use my tablet as a bridge. Someone wanted to make absolutely sure that no one could get access to the hardware by accident. It has no implant-capable connectivity."

Moments later, his tablet showed the reader was active, so he unplugged his tablet and slid out from under the table.

"It should work now," he said as he put away his equipment. "Your DNA should activate it, Admiral."

Admiral Mertz placed his hand on the reader, and nothing happened.

30

———————

It took Jared holding his hand on the reader for five seconds before anything happened. Probably to prevent an inadvertent touch from activating it. His first indication of success was when there was a soft grinding sound from inside the fountain, and the water began draining away.

Relieved more than he could say, he watched the ugly green water mostly disappear before the stone bottom of the fountain sank into the floor. Once it had gone down about a hundred centimeters, it split into sections and retracted underneath the floor, revealing a set of stairs twisting tightly in a circle as they descended into the darkness.

It was very reminiscent of the stairs under the horde treasure building, and that gave him unexpected chills.

It looked as if the water had been intended to go into a reservoir of some kind, but the algae had clogged things up, and a fair amount of it showered onto the steps. They were now slick and treacherous looking. Everyone would have to be very careful when they went down them.

Jared turned to Clarice Beauchamp. "Keep up a running conversation with yourself. If the guards stick their heads in, make sure they can see you, and keep talking like we're in one of the other rooms. That might be enough."

"And if it's not?"

"Then you might have to use your new sword."

He'd taken her aside and given her the long blade from the Marine Raider cache before they'd left Frankfort. It wasn't worth what helping them had cost her, but it was what they had to give. Her people wouldn't accept high technology, but no matter how deadly and miraculous the sword was, it was just metal.

The warrior nodded and clasped her hand around the weapon's hilt. "They will not pass while I still live. You have my word. Good luck, Admiral."

Kelsey led the way down the stairs, moving slowly and keeping her hand on the rail. Her augmented vision would allow her to see what was in front of her more easily than he could.

That turned out to be unnecessary, as lights in the chamber below came on as soon as she started down. It turned out that the stairs only went down a dozen meters before they opened into a wide chamber directly underneath the common room in the Imperial Residence.

Once he'd made his way down, he saw that this room only had one exit, the short corridor that led directly to a lift. Jared walked over and pressed the call button. Moments later, the doors opened and revealed a lift car that could hold all of them. Barely.

Once they'd packed themselves inside, someone pressed the only button on the panel, the doors closed, and the lift descended. The trip took longer than he'd expected, but the doors opened again without any trouble.

Kelsey stepped out of the lift and into another short corridor that ended in what looked like a dead end, though there was a button prominently placed on the wall beside it. With a shrug, she pressed it, and the dead-end wall slid aside, revealing a larger corridor that led to the left and right.

He stuck his head out and saw that there was no button on the other side. In fact, it looked like this was a concealed door that no one would know was here.

"How do we keep it from closing?" he asked.

"I got a signal from the controller when I pressed the button," his sister said. "It wanted my authentication codes, and in return, it gave me permission to remotely control it from the other side. We're good on that front.

"The problem I see is that there was nothing on the map about this. Basically, it only told us to go to the Imperial Residence and use the secret passage. Which direction do we go?"

"Let's split up and go in opposite directions," he suggested. "We'll only go a hundred meters and then come back. Be watchful for any security devices. These are the Imperial Vaults, and there's no telling what's down here."

Jared found what he thought was the entrance to the vaults less than fifty meters down the right-hand side of the corridor, on the opposite wall from the secret lift. The large metal doors looked as if they would be sufficient to stop any kind of attack. There was a palm reader next to them.

A quick shout brought the rest of the team to his location, and Kelsey examined the reader for a moment before she quickly gestured for him to put his hand on it.

He did so, and it immediately prompted him to input an authentication code that he didn't have. Thankfully, he knew someone who did.

"It needs your codes, Kelsey."

She frowned. "I'm not getting any kind of prompt, so it must've just sent it to you because you were touching the reader. Let's try together."

Kelsey pulled off her gauntlet and placed a finger against the reader as he put his hand on it again. Once again, he was rejected, but for a different reason. Now it was complaining that there were too many sources of DNA.

"How can I touch the reader to get the signal without giving it my DNA?" Kelsey asked in a peeved tone. "I can't give you the codes, because my implants won't let me export them for obvious security reasons. What do we do?"

"Stick your hand out," Carl said. "I think I have something that might help."

The scientist dug into his tool bag and pulled out a small canister. He held it close to Kelsey's hand and sprayed a moderately thick gel into her palm. He then started rubbing it in.

"Give it a few seconds to dry," he said. "It'll act as a sealer and keep any DNA from coming across from your hand to the reader. Just to be safe, you might want to rub a finger across the admiral's skin before you use it so that it has his DNA."

Jared nodded. "We'll also be careful that it only looks like we're putting one hand onto the scanner. I'll keep my pinky a little bit up at the tip, and you can stick the end of yours just under it. Maybe if we do that, we can fool it."

"Let's hope this works," Kelsey said as they positioned their hands just above the reader and put them down together.

"I can sense it demanding the code," Kelsey said. "Sending it now."

A few moments later, the huge doors began retracting into the walls. The group around them erupted in cheers even as Jared stared. The doors were *significantly* thicker than he'd expected.

At a guess, they were about three meters thick and looked like they were made of hull metal. They were thicker than the armor on his superdreadnought.

Basically, if the entire vault was sheathed like this, it was invulnerable to anything short of orbital bombardment. It would even take a nuke placed right next to it and probably protect the vault's contents.

Thankfully, they'd made it inside.

"Let's see if we can find the override," he said. "Don't touch anything. I hate to be a worrywart, but it would be just like some paranoid security type to leave something tempting to set off a trap for the unwary. We don't want to be locked inside, because no one will be coming to rescue us."

"That's perhaps an exaggeration," Kelsey said. "I've interfaced with the palace systems and reenabled the communication systems. We can interface with them via our implants—even down here—and have them connect us with Talbot or Lily. I'm confident he could figure something out."

"Did you see that door?" he demanded. "I'm not willing to take chances, so everyone keep your hands to yourselves."

With that, he stepped into the vault, and the overhead lights came on.

* * *

JULIA STEPPED into the Imperial Vaults and was immediately overwhelmed by the scale of the place. As large as the Imperial throne room had been, this place was *far* more substantial.

And unlike the room above, this one was hardly empty. In fact, it looked like a warehouse. It was full of crates, all piled up to the ceiling a dozen meters overhead.

The air was dead, smelling of dust and age. No one had been here in a very long time.

"How are we going to find the override?" she asked grimly. "Are we going to have to start busting things open?"

The wreckage they'd made in the horde's treasure chamber was fresh in her mind. And as tightly packed as these crates were, she didn't think she'd have much luck knocking any stacks over.

Kelsey shook her head. "Emperor Marcus sent Lucian a full inventory of this place. He also told him exactly where we had to go to find the override. All we have to do is walk to the back of the room and pick it up."

That sounded suspiciously easy. Nothing they'd done thus far had been that simple, so she'd believe it when she saw it.

"What's in the rest of these crates?" she asked as they started into the stacks. "And why keep it all down here in an impenetrable vault?"

Kelsey shrugged. "I'd imagine this vault has been down here since they built the Imperial Palace. Whichever emperor was in charge at that point must've decided that this would be where the important stuff went. It's filled with gifts and offerings from various parts of the Empire, usually presented on the emperor's birthday.

"That kind of thing went on pretty much the entire time the Terran Empire existed. What we're looking at here is about ten thousand years' worth of gifts from any number of worlds to the reigning emperor of the day.

"That means that this room is filled with objects of incalculable cultural value, and probably every precious metal and stone known to humanity. Unimaginable works of art. But we're only interested in one thing though: the override."

They continued on in silence while Julia looked at the immense stacks of crates all around them and imagined the kinds of things that would be inside them. It was mind-boggling. All of this should be on display in a massive museum, not buried under a dead palace on a wrecked world.

If she were successful in overthrowing the AIs in her universe, she'd make certain to start building one. Humanity deserved to see its heritage.

Partway back, she discovered that not everything was in crates. Off to her left-hand side was a statue that had to be at least three meters tall. It was made of pale, polished stone and looked hand carved. It was exquisite.

She had no idea who the woman was supposed to be, but what little clothes she wore seemed unspeakably ancient. Why men felt the need to have art in which women were scantily dressed, partly—or fully—naked, or in provocative poses, she just didn't understand. It was one of the mysteries of life.

Just because she wanted to know who the woman was, she captured an image of the statue so that she could look it up later. If any records existed outside the list of contents that Mertz had, that was. She hoped so, as she'd rather find out on her own than ask him.

When they finally reached the rear of the massive room, Kelsey led them to a small crate. "This is the one in the picture that Emperor Marcus sent. He didn't say anything about any security protocol. Honestly, I don't know why anyone would bother. It's at the rear of a huge room in a small crate with no markings at all. Even diligent searchers would pass it right by."

"We should still be careful," Mertz said. "The last thing we want to do is to try and open it the wrong way and have it destroy the contents. That would be an utter disaster."

Carl stepped forward and ran a scanner across the exterior of the crate. "It's got no electronics in the box itself and no locking mechanism. Basically, it's just wood and conventional packing materials around something technological that's unpowered. We can open it up."

Kelsey reached forward and gently tugged the lid until it popped free. Nestled among packing materials was what looked like a small computer drive. It had some type of port where it could be plugged into another system, but it was totally unremarkable.

And utterly irreplaceable.

"So, this is the override that stops the master AI," she said slowly. "It looks so... normal."

"It *is* pretty normal," Carl said as he gingerly plucked the device out of the crate. "It's literally a basic drive meant to plug into the AI hardware and shut down the system or override anything that the controller wants. The only thing that makes it unique is the encrypted code that's bound to this one specific set of hardware.

"We won't be able to transfer the code to any other drive. It has to be this one. I'll have to take it apart and replace the power supply, but that should be simple enough."

"Why didn't they make more of them?" she demanded. "That might've helped humanity stop those monsters."

"They didn't realize that they needed them," he answered with a shrug. "No one in their right minds would have believed that an AI that didn't even have manipulators would be able to take over human beings to use as its toys. That's horror novel stuff.

"If the Singularity hadn't meddled, nothing like this could have occurred. Their agents had to have physically assisted the AI for those initial conversions. Only then would the AI have had a way to do more."

Mertz took the override from Carl and put it into his pocket. "Kelsey, you've got the inventory. Is there anything else here that we should take with us?"

Julia's doppelgänger shook her head. "Technically, *everything* here should be saved, but none of it's useful for our purposes now. We can come back once this is all over and take it to Avalon."

"Or move the seat of power here," Mertz said. "When the Rebel Empire falls, it might be best if we just relocate the government here. Terra is more centrally located for the Empire as a whole. Once we start rebuilding, it's not going to be convenient for the rulers of the Empire to be out on the rim like Avalon is."

Kelsey snorted. "I can't imagine my father would be happy about moving."

"He has time to get used to the idea. With those modified Marine Raider medical nanites in his system, he's going to be the emperor for a *very* long time."

Her doppelgänger shook her head. "It's a good thing that I'm not looking to inherit the throne anytime soon. Come on. I want to do something to the security system before we leave."

When they arrived back at the main doors, Kelsey stopped at a terminal just inside them. "Jared, press your palm here just like we did outside."

A few seconds later, she smiled. "Okay, Julia, press your palm to the door. I've got this gunk on my hands, so you'll be working with me to register our DNA. I'm adding us all to the security system. If something happens, I want to make sure that someone else can get back into this place."

Julia did so, and the system prompted her to set an access code. She used the one she had as the heir, and the system accepted it. She knew from checking that her authentication codes were exactly the same as Kelsey's, so they were both covered.

She made a mental note that she'd have to get samples of Mertz's DNA before she went home. With the right coating on her hand, she could fool the system just like Kelsey had. She wouldn't need to keep her Mertz alive once she caught him.

It took a couple of minutes for everyone to add their DNA to the security system. Once the process was done, Kelsey gestured back toward the concealed lift.

"It's time to get things in motion. We've gotten what we came for, and it's time to get off this planet. That means we have to get the FTL com online so that we can contact *Persephone*. Carl, that's your job.

"Once we know what's happening in the rest of the system, we can decide if we're going to take a shot at the AI in orbit. If we can get to it, we will. If we can't, we're going to have to just sneak away without being noticed.

"I don't like leaving Terra under the control of these murderous AIs, but it's not exactly like we have a battle fleet on hand to take it away." She paused and then smiled. "Actually, I suppose we do. We just don't know where it is right now."

Mertz nodded. "Let's get back to *Persephone*. We'll get in contact with

Marcus using the same trick that you used to signal us. There's no guarantee that he's going to recognize the attempted communication, but we have to try.

"We'll hope that he's a lot faster on the uptake than I was. If so, we'll arrange to meet them somewhere mutually convenient. Our next stop has to be Twilight River. It's time to end this war and free humanity."

With that, they started toward the secret door leading to the lift. The endgame was upon them.

31

Talbot had been asleep for over an hour when Lily woke him up. She'd been able to use the large regenerator at the Imperial Palace to fully heal his damaged organs, but he'd been exhausted by the time she'd finished.

He levered himself up from the bed he was resting on. "Thanks, Lilly."

She clapped a hand on his shoulder. "No problem, big man. That's my job. Try not to get banged up so much next time. Especially if I don't have anything to fix you with."

"I'll sure as hell try. Any word on the trip downstairs?"

He felt comfortable asking because there were no guards in the room with them. They were probably standing out in the hall, making sure that he and Lily didn't wander off. Peters was gone, so they'd undoubtedly taken him back to his hall.

"Kelsey called to let me know that everything went as planned. It seems that she's accessed the palace systems and reenabled them for our use. We're ready to exit stage left."

He frowned slightly. "What does *that* mean?"

Lily shrugged. "Ask your wife. Since we're ready to go, they think you need to have a conversation with Major Peters. We need to know for sure whether or not he's going to come with us.

"Everyone else is either providing a distraction for the guards by doing otherwise mundane tasks or is with Carl as he works on making contact with *Persephone*. The admiral said to tell you that he'd prefer if Peters came with us."

Talbot wasn't sure he could convince the man, though doing something to fully repair the horrific damage to his body might well do the trick. The only way to find out for sure was to try.

"I'm on it," he said as he stood.

Once he had his shoes on, he made his way out of the medical center, picking up an escort at the door, and headed toward the large room where they kept Peters. The man's guards in their white uniforms stopped him outside that room.

"What is your business with the god?" a short woman with dark hair asked imperiously.

"I want to continue the discussion that we started earlier," Talbot said, unperturbed. "There's nothing to be worried about. I'll be happy to leave my weapons here with you."

The woman seemed somewhat suspicious, but she allowed Talbot inside once he'd divested himself of his weapons.

Peters sat up a little bit straighter on his couch as Talbot approached, waving the guards out of earshot. "You're looking better."

"I'm feeling better," Talbot said as he sat on the edge of the dais. Even though he was fully healed, parts of him still felt a little tender.

"Did your friends pick up your package?" Peters asked.

Talbot nodded. "Without a hitch."

"So, what's your plan now?"

"I'd rather talk about *your* plans," Talbot countered. "We've got facilities board *Persephone* to mitigate all the damage that's been done to you. Do you want to be mobile again? Do you want to be able to use your Marine Raider augmentation at full power again?"

Peters considered Talbot for a few moments and then shrugged. "I'm not certain that my preferences really matter. Like I said, I'm not exactly in control of my own fate. I'm a figurehead.

"They tolerate me giving orders about some things, but then they go ahead and do what they want most of the time. The leadership council makes the decisions, and I'm sure that they won't allow me to leave, no matter what I say."

"But do you want to?" Talbot asked softly. "It just so happens that we're experts at breaking people out of places and getting around recalcitrant guards. If you want to leave, all you have to do is say the word."

The man sagged a little. "I don't want to see these people harmed, but I'll admit that I'm tired of being stuck here. The drugs you gave me will only last a decade or so. I don't know if I can go back to life with that kind of pain."

"It sounds as if you've already made up your mind, but you just haven't convinced yourself of that yet. You want to leave."

"I suppose I do. The question is, how are you to make that happen?"

Talbot rose to his feet and stepped over to the couch. Making sure that the suddenly hyperalert guards couldn't see his right side, he extracted the stunner he'd pocketed there and dropped it next to the crippled man's remaining hand. Peters promptly made it vanish under the blanket.

The guards really should've been a little less trusting of someone who came alone and volunteered to give up his weapons. Talbot stepped back without undue haste, creating enough space that the guards stopped advancing.

"You let us worry about the exit strategy," Talbot said. "I promise that we won't use any more force than necessary. If we can manage to get out with just stunners, that's what we'll do.

"But one way or the other, we'll get you out alive. If they want to use deadly force to stop you from leaving, then you're going to have to accept that we might have to use deadly force in response."

"I hope it doesn't come to that," Peters said with a sigh. "For all their flaws, these are decent people doing decent work."

"Speaking of decent work, we need to make sure that the fusion plant they took, as well as the shielding that would keep it from being detectable from orbit, is sent back to Frankfort. The people there would make excellent allies for your people.

"Terra is our past, but it's their future. You should let them build it back up together. To start the process, they'll have to return what was taken and get it set up so that it's operational. Can you convince them to do that?"

Peters shrugged slightly. "Possibly. I don't think it's actually being used. They're somewhat like packrats. They'll make a stink about it, but if I push things, they'll probably do it, especially if I make the point that these others would make decent allies. We don't have many of those since they insist on being hidden. I should probably start the process now.

"In any case, you've still got to check over the pinnaces to make sure that they're operational. It's been a long time since they've been up in the air, much less space. And if I were you, I wouldn't dawdle."

"I'll focus on that while you work your end," Talbot said. "We won't make any irrevocable decisions until we hear that you got your end in motion. The palace systems will allow you to connect with us via your implants. Let us know if something comes up and be ready to go at a moment's notice."

With that, Talbot made his way out and reclaimed his weapons. He sure hoped that Carl and the rest would be able to get the pinnaces operational. If they didn't get at least one working, they were stuck on Terra. All of their sacrifices would've been for nothing.

* * *

CARL LOOKED over the parts on his makeshift worktable and selected a few components that he knew he was going to need before even opening the FTL com. The device was extremely simple, as far as that sort of thing went, but it definitely needed the right parts to work correctly.

Thankfully, the bins here at the Imperial Palace were well shielded and had everything he could possibly need. He wished he could take it all with him because the stash would've proved damned useful.

Sadly, that wasn't to be.

Working slowly and carefully, he completely disassembled the FTL com, tested every component, and replaced any that failed or were questionable. It took almost an hour to get everything put back together again, but it passed its self-check when he connected it to a power supply and some jury-rigged speakers.

With more than a hint of trepidation, he initiated an audio call request to *Persephone*. Long seconds passed, and then a voice channel opened.

Since they were in the same system, it could be used at full speed rather than the Morse code setting that they'd had to use for longer-range communication. He could even have video if he'd bothered to attach the necessary peripherals, but he hadn't bothered. For this, voice was sufficient.

He cleared his throat. "*Persephone*, this is Carl Owlet calling. Are you receiving?"

"Carl, it's good to hear your voice," Fiona said a moment later. "We were all very worried about you after the AI destroyed your pinnaces. I'm assuming the fact you're speaking with me now means that you were not anywhere close to the target zone. Is everyone okay?"

It still amazed him how a computer could show such palpable emotion. Not a facsimile of feelings but actual emotions. The concern in Fiona's voice wasn't fake. The Old Empire scientists who'd created the AIs had made electronic life.

Well, and created the doom of humanity, of course.

He sighed. "We weren't there, but things haven't gone well. We were ambushed by armed locals, and only about a dozen of us are left. Admiral Mertz, Princess Kelsey, her doppelgänger, and most of the senior staff are still alive, but we've lost everyone else. I need to talk to Angela."

"I'm so sorry to hear that," the AI said with genuine sorrow. "I'm transferring your call now. We've also had some interesting experiences, and I'm sure that she will want to tell you what we've learned."

A few moments later, Major Angela Ellis, commander of *Persephone* and his wife, came onto the line.

"Are you okay?" she asked, her voice anxious. "Is everyone else okay?"

"I'm okay. There was an EMP that took out not only our equipment but our implants. It rendered us unconscious and left us at the mercy of people that wanted to kill us. Thankfully, Julia escaped and was able to help the survivors get away. Only the senior people are left."

"Oh, God," Angela asked, her voice a mixture of anguish and confusion. "Who's Julia?"

"Sorry. Julia is Kelsey's doppelgänger. Kelsey decided that it was too confusing having names like Kelsey One and Kelsey Two, so she made the other one rename herself Julia. If I understand correctly, that's the name of one of their cousins."

"Huh. I suppose that makes perfect sense. Where are you?"

"We're at the Imperial Palace, and we've recovered the override. We even have a line on a couple of Marine Raider pinnaces that may be flyable.

"If they're not, I'm not sure what we're going to do. That's really the only shot we have of getting back into space. What's the situation up there?"

"Let's just say that when the AI discovered that you were still alive, things got very busy up here. A lot of the ships that were scattered throughout the system made their way to Terra orbit.

"They're particularly tight around the orbital that we think the AI is on. If you had any ideas about sneaking onto it and attacking the AI, I suggest you forget that plan immediately."

Carl had pretty much expected that, so it was a relief not to have to worry about taking a dozen people to attack an AI on its own station. Still, that left the problem of getting off the planet.

"What about the rest of the system?" he asked. "Have you been able to get into contact with Marcus?"

"As a matter of fact, we have. They're having some difficulty getting to Terra from the direction they were forced to go, but they haven't been discovered yet. They've also had some command drama in the admiral's absence, but it seems like they have everything in order now.

"We've also found a far flip point that we can use to get out of the Terra system, but because of all the traffic in the system, we've done little more than make sure we can get through it. We're being *very* careful not to be detected."

"That's excellent news," Carl said with a smile. "Now all we have to do is get off Terra and slip through the net they've thrown around the planet."

"When do you think you'll have a status on your pinnaces?" his wife asked. "We can get *Persephone* into a decent position to pick you up and then slide back out of the area without being detected, but it really all depends on you."

"We should have information on that shortly. I've got a decent repository of parts here that I can use to repair any damage to the pinnaces' systems, but until I actually go through everything, I'm not going to know. Admiral Mertz is going to be in contact with you before we make the attempt, but I just wanted to hear your voice. I've missed you."

"I've missed you, too," she said softly. "I can't tell you how worried I've been. I'm so sorry that we lost so many friends and shipmates, but I'm ecstatic that you're still alive. Come home to me. I need to hold you in my arms and know that you're safe."

He smiled at the thought. "I'll be up as soon as I can. I've got to go now, but somebody will contact you shortly. I love you."

"I love you, too. Now go kick some ass."

He turned the FTL com off and leaned back in his chair, rubbing his face. Now all he had to do was get a couple of ancient Marine Raider pinnaces functioning again so that they could slip past every computer-controlled warship in the damned system, board *Persephone*, and sneak out of the heavily occupied system.

What could possibly go wrong?

32

Once Talbot convinced Peters to order the group holding him to give the fusion plant back to Frankfort, it didn't take long at all for them to summon Jared.

As he was escorted into the room, he noted that the group trended older. All of those arrayed against him wore stern expressions, as if they didn't want to talk to him at all. Maybe they didn't. Maybe they just wanted him and his people gone so that they could go back to their regular lives.

They were undoubtedly displeased that Jake Peters had given them the order. The major had indicated they were like pack rats, taking whatever they found and putting it securely away, just in case they might need it later.

Considering the world that they found themselves in, Jared couldn't blame them. That still didn't mean that he could let this slide. He'd made a deal with Leader Mordechai, and he intended to keep it.

Even knowing everything that he did, he was still amazed that they'd managed to disassemble and move the fusion plant at all. A task like that required skills and equipment that had to be in very short supply.

Yes, they had computers with full libraries at their beck and call, but some skills couldn't be mastered without actually doing them. Had they failed with fusion plants in other cities in order to build those skills? That was a bit frightening.

The woman at the center of the table leaned forward and glared at Jared. She hadn't bothered giving him her name, so that had to be a good clue about how this conversation was going to go.

"What you demand is unacceptable."

Jared shrugged. If she wanted to get right to the point, he'd accommodate her.

"What either of us wants is irrelevant, isn't it?" he asked in a tone that sounded more than a bit indifferent to his ear. "Didn't your god give you an order? How can you defy him? He *is* your god, right?"

"Of course he's our god," a man down the table to the left snapped. "Keep your unbeliever mouth shut."

The woman held up her hand and shot a disapproving look at the man who'd spoken. Then she returned her glare to Jared.

"The god does not direct our day-to-day operations. Everything we do is in service to him, but *we* make the final decisions."

Jared nodded slowly. "So you're frauds. You claim to serve your god, but you really serve yourselves. I guess I shouldn't be surprised. Tell me, how do you think your followers will feel if that information gets out?

"And before you decide that you need to do something drastic to prevent that, my people are already discussing what your god has said to anyone that will listen. This news will not be suppressed. You can either choose to obey your god and lose one of the spare fusion plants you've scavenged, or you can be found out for what you truly are."

He was taking a real risk by taking a hard line like this, but if he didn't, he was pretty sure they'd either stonewall or attack his group.

"You have no business telling us what we should or should not do or manipulating our followers," the woman said harshly. "You will gather your people and depart at once."

"Not until you redeem your god's word. Either you do that, or we're going to be a thorn in your side. If you want us gone with a minimum of fuss, you're going to have to give back that little bit of equipment that you took from Frankfort. Once you've done so, we'll leave at once."

His ultimatum led to an argument among the leadership council. Eventually, the woman made a gesture and ended the discussion.

"Very well. We will return it to the city from which it came. You may send some of your people to verify that it has arrived, been installed, and turned back on. Then, once the train returns here, you will leave. If you do not, you will be killed. Is that clear enough for you?"

"Yes," Jared said as he turned on his heel. "I think our business is completed."

With that, he walked out of the room without waiting for either their permission or acknowledgment. He'd made no friends, but he didn't have time to be coy. They needed to finalize their planning to get out of the Imperial Palace. They'd be buried in guards within minutes unless he missed his guess.

Jared found everyone gathered in the Imperial Residence. He walked into the main room, past the two guards even as he heard more booted feet coming up the corridor. That would be the extra guards he'd expected.

"I've gotten the FTL com working," Carl said as he closed the door. "*Persephone* is out there and ready to receive us. Angela has even managed to make contact with Marcus.

"The good news is that they're still safe. They said Terra's orbit is filled with enemy ships, and the orbital that the AI is on is now guarded even more closely than before. There's absolutely no way that we're going to be able to do anything to it."

Jared nodded. He'd expected something like that.

"Then it looks as if our goal is to just get off this planet and escape from the Terra system without being captured or killed," he said. "With the regular flip points so well guarded, that probably means we're going to have to find an undiscovered multi-flip point or far flip point."

"I should've mentioned that they found a far flip point," Carl said. "They've already tested it and said that it will get us out of the system."

"That's great news," Kelsey almost gushed. "We've got what we came for, and now we can finally get out of here."

"We do have one problem," Talbot said. "Jake Peters. We're going to have to figure out how to get him out without all of these cultists freaking out."

"I'm afraid that the people running this place aren't going to be cooperative," Jared said with a grunt. "They've agreed to send the fusion plant and shielding back to Frankfort, as well as reassemble it, so we'll have redeemed our word there. Honestly, it's in their own best interest, and I hope that they'll eventually see that.

"We need to send some of our number on the maglev train to make sure it really gets there and that they turn it on. Then we can go there ourselves and gather the cache. I understand that *Persephone* is well stocked, but we don't know what we're going to need in the future. That's a lot of Marine Raider equipment that we just can't afford to leave behind.

"Also, it's good to make certain that people follow through on their deals. When we come back—and we *will* come back eventually—we'll have established a baseline of cooperation with the people of Frankfort. They'll remember that we kept our word and know that we'll be good partners in reestablishing Terra."

He turned his attention to Kelsey. "We're going to have to figure out an extraction plan for Major Peters. We're going to have to breach those doors and get him out.

"Carl, your team needs to go over the pinnaces and make sure that they're ready to go. If we can't get one of them working, then we're not going to be able to get off this planet. I hate to put the pressure on you, but do whatever you have to do."

"We'll make it work," Carl said with a nod.

"I'll leave the details of the extraction to Talbot," Kelsey said. "I'll go with Carl and help them by preflighting the pinnaces. I'm the only one— other than yourself—that's trained as a pilot, so I'll need to make absolutely certain that one of them is functional by the time we're ready to go.

"A lot of what happens next really depends on the timing. We're going to have to put our best people where they need to be. Chloe can help Talbot. If they can't come up with a decent extraction plan, I'll eat one of the pinnaces."

Jared chuckled. "I'll bet. Okay, people, it's crunch time. We've gotten what we came for, and now it's time to get out of here. Let's go out there and make it happen."

* * *

KELSEY FOLLOWED CARL, Austin, and Ralph down to the level where all the vehicles were once kept underneath the Imperial Palace. As Jared had guessed, they'd picked up extra guards. Four disapproving young men armed with flechette rifles and pistols followed them.

The conspicuous absence of stunners was telling.

She had no idea how they were going to react once they realized that she and her friends intended to take the pinnaces. Probably not calmly.

When they arrived at the correct level, they found various atmospheric craft parked in neat lines in the hangar. All were covered by dust. Hulking over everything at the far end was a pair of Marine Raider pinnaces.

One of the young men raised a hand and stepped forward as they started to enter the hangar. "Halt. You're not authorized to examine our equipment any longer."

It seemed that the time for tiptoeing around the looming confrontation was over. She'd hoped that they wouldn't have to start trouble before the train had even left, but needs must.

"Carl, start giving the pinnaces a good check while I deal with our friends," she said softly. Then she turned to face the four men.

"I'm afraid that we really can't do that."

Without waiting for a response, she yanked her stunner from her off side and took them all down with a wide-beam shot even as they were starting to bring their weapons to bear on her. They'd been expecting an argument, not an attack. That momentary hesitation had cost them.

They all dropped like puppets with their strings cut. They'd be out for at least an hour.

"The clock is running, boys," Kelsey said, raising her voice. "Hustle."

She went to each of the unconscious guards and dragged them into the hangar and out of sight. If someone came looking to see what was going on down here, she didn't want them seeing that they'd already attacked their guards. That would just start the fighting early.

The next group, when it came, still wouldn't be expecting outright violence. She'd probably be able to handle them as well.

It was going to be the third group that was problematic.

Carl manipulated the controls to the ramp on one of the pinnaces, and it lowered smoothly to the floor. "Looks like the power still on. That's a good sign."

Instead of going up the ramp, he ducked underneath the pinnace. Moments later, he was back and nodding. "It's got a power cable running from the power grid. That's going to help."

Kelsey reached out with her implants even as the three men were going inside. Since the pinnace was online, that allowed her to do some remote checking.

It wasn't fully online, of course, but its automated systems responded to her link request and granted her access once she'd presented her codes. She brought the computer up and began running a self-diagnostic on the flight control systems.

To her utter shock, almost all of them passed. There were a couple of systems that were down, but they were running off their backups. She'd want to have Carl do a little bit of work on a couple of things, but if push came to shove, they'd be able to take off in it right now.

She turned her attention to the second one and repeated the process. Once again, the majority of its systems were functional, and those that weren't had backups. Somebody had been maintaining them. Maybe not for the last few decades, but they hadn't been abandoned for much longer than that.

Kelsey accessed the palace systems and send a message to Lily for her to send Clarice Beauchamp down to the hangar. She included directions to get there.

A few minutes later, the woman arrived with a pair of irritated guards at her heels. Without waiting for them to say anything, Kelsey used her stunner on narrow beam and took them down.

The warrior had her sword out and was looking for foes as soon as the bodies hit the floor. When she saw that nothing needed her immediate attention, she sheathed her new weapon and walked up to Kelsey.

"What's going on?" the warrior asked.

"They're about to throw us out. The pinnaces are functional, so we're going to break Major Peters out. They're about to send the fusion plant back to Frankfort, and I want you to go with it.

"By this time, I'm sure the people at Frankfort have guards on the platform to make sure that no one tries to sneak in and take anything else. What I'd like you to do is make certain that Leader Mordechai knows that we're going to be joining them very shortly. I'm sure they've got all kinds of weapons, and I'd rather not be shot down."

The woman nodded. "I'll go down to the train station and oversee the movement of the fusion plant. I look forward to seeing you again in Frankfort."

Kelsey extended her hand, and the two women locked forearms. "Me too. Thanks for everything."

Once the woman had departed, Kelsey returned to keeping watch while Carl and his boys made certain that the pinnaces were functional. The clock was definitely running, and she sincerely hoped that the train departed before everything came apart.

Her next call was to Jared. "Operation Johnny Bravo is in progress. I'm sending Clarice on the train, and we'll join her in Frankfort once we get out of here. Retrieving Major Peters is going to be the most challenging aspect of this, I suspect. It's a good thing that Talbot is on that."

"I'll make sure that everything on our end is in motion," her brother said. "Try not to kill anybody. Mertz out."

Kelsey turned and yelled up the nearest ramp. "Carl, I've tapped into the system and see a couple of things that I'd like you to work on. Remember that nothing you do can take any of the major systems offline, because we might have to leave on a moment's notice. Understood?"

"Copy that," he yelled back. "Send the information to my implants, and we'll get started. I'll send Austin over to the other pinnace. If we can get them both ready, great. If one of them fails, at least we'll have a backup. Ralph will take care of bypassing the lockouts on the hangar doors."

With everything in motion, Kelsey set herself into a good place to ambush anyone coming through the main doors. As soon as the people running this place figured out what was going on, they'd swarm them, and the fight would be on.

Her goal was to make certain that nobody figured out what they were doing in the hangar. The next steps of the operation were up to Jared and Talbot. If they got their jobs done, then the team would be gone within the next hour.

Things might be tight, and they might have to fight their way out, but she swore to herself that once they'd defeated the AIs, she'd be back. This place was her family's legacy going back ten thousand years, and she'd be damned if she'd leave it in the hands of jerks like this.

33

When Julia heard that they were about to send the fusion plant and shielding back to Frankfort with only Clarice Beauchamp to escort it, she approached Mertz. "I think you're making a mistake. Things might go badly here. You should send all the noncombatants back to the city."

Rather than arguing, he was silent for a few moments and then nodded. "You're probably right. Hoping that everybody can get to the pinnaces and out of here without being caught up in a fight is unrealistic.

"Right now, the people in charge don't know that we're planning to steal the pinnaces. They also don't know that we're going to take Major Peters with us. Either of those two things is going to start a fight that could get someone killed."

He grimaced slightly. "Actually, the fighting has *already* started. The guards with Kelsey, Carl, and the others down in the hangar tried to stop them from looking at the pinnaces, so she stunned them. The clock is ticking now.

"Take all the noncombatants with you and join Clarice on the train. Once you get to Frankfort, wait for us. With you going along in armor, there's very little chance that the soldiers these people send will be able to overcome you. They're unlikely to even try.

"I know this is going to introduce some complications into their relationship, but there's nothing we can do about that. Honestly, I still think that the people in the city will come out ahead. While they have technology, they're not exactly numerous."

He inclined his head toward her. "Good thinking, by the way."

Taking the compliment with an unexpected smile, Julia excused herself and gathered all the noncombatants except for Carl, Ralph, and Austin. Since they were working on the pinnaces, Kelsey would keep them safe.

By the time she'd gotten them to the maglev platform, the soldiers from the group holding the Imperial Palace had almost finished loading the fusion plant and its shielding. She wondered how Beauchamp was supposed to know that everything they needed was there.

The answer turned out to be Olivia West. She was overseeing the loading and apparently in communication with Carl via the systems inside the Imperial Palace to discuss what was supposed to be there. According to her, it looked like everything had been crated and labeled for future use, so it was a simple matter to go down a manifest in his mind to tell that everything they needed was there.

That might not mean much if some small, critical part were missing, but there was only so much that they could do. They wouldn't know if it was all functional until Carl got to Frankfort.

"I talked with Mertz, and he said that all the noncombatants are coming back on the train with us," she told Olivia. "They're going to meet us at Frankfort."

The other woman scowled. "Does that number include him? I realize that he's a pilot, but he's basically a noncombatant when you come to ground fighting. One of our leaders needs to go back on this train."

"They have two pinnaces and two pilots," Julia disagreed. "I understand that's putting all of our eggs in one basket—yet another Kelsey saying that I don't fully understand—but in this case, it's necessary."

She held up a hand when the other woman started to object. "We're on an *extremely* tight schedule, and arguing with him about this is only going to disrupt him at a critical juncture. Kelsey has already taken… steps that are going to cause us problems if we don't hurry."

Olivia sighed. "Great. We'll just have to hope for the best."

Twenty minutes later, the fusion plant and its shielding were loaded onto the train, and all the noncombatants had boarded, with Julia following behind the last of the soldiers. Since she was locked inside her armor and heavily armed, she doubted they were going to try anything, but she stayed on the lookout for trouble.

She linked her implants into the train and monitored all the cars as they left the station. Carl was in communication with her and verified that they'd made the turn heading for Frankfort.

I'm about to kill communications between the train and the palace, he told her. *I've already rigged the system so that they'll think it's still operational, but any attempt by the palace to call them is going to fail.*

And what if the people on the train try to call them?

Hopefully, with such a short trip, they won't try. Worst case, they'll attempt to send a message once they've arrived at the station to let the palace know that they've arrived. I've set up the com system here to forward incoming requests to me. I'll do my best to make sure they don't realize anything is going on, but you're going to have to keep your eyes open.

Thanks, Carl. Good luck.

You too, Julia.

After about ten minutes, she allowed herself to relax slightly. It seemed as if the scheme was going off just like they'd planned. That didn't stop her from keeping a close eye on everyone around her. If they made a move, she was going to be ready.

To her relief, they pulled into the station at Frankfort without anyone the wiser. She noted that the platform was filled with guards from the city. Standing at their center was Jebediah.

Everyone there had their primitive weapons raised when the doors opened, but she stepped out and changed her helmet to show her face through the holographic projectors.

"It's okay," she said. "We've got the fusion plant, and these people are here to make sure that it's installed."

Jebediah gestured toward his people, and they relaxed slightly, though she noted that they didn't really lower their weapons. They were worried about the people from the Imperial Palace, just like she was.

"So, who are they?" he asked her once the guards began unloading the crates. "And are you Julia or Kelsey?"

"Julia. And these are potential allies. Ones that we're going to piss off before this is done. Those of us that aren't here are in the process of stealing a couple of Marine Raider pinnaces that they had stashed at the Imperial Palace.

"That's what's going to get us to orbit. They're going to be seriously pissed about that. Admiral Mertz said to tell you that he's sorry."

Jebediah chuckled. "It seems like poetic justice to me. Don't worry. My father is an able negotiator. He'll blame you for everything, you won't be here to deny it, and we'll eventually find some common ground with these people.

"Once they finish unloading the equipment, I'll have someone take you up to the room where it once sat. We can oversee the installation together and await the arrival of your friends. I'll see that word is dispatched to our sentries above ground to make certain that no one thinks their arrival is that of an enemy.

"We'll also make certain that we don't let them in where the intruders can see them. No need to make them wonder how they suddenly and unexpectedly appeared."

He stood silent for a few minutes as the people from the Imperial Palace finished unloading the crates and started moving them laboriously to the lift. Some residents of Frankfort helped speed the process while others kept guard.

When the two of them finally stood alone on the platform, Jebediah turned to face her. "Will you or your people ever return? And by that, I mean once you've dealt with the computers."

She removed her helmet and shook out her damp hair. "Almost certainly. I don't know how long it will be, but I feel confident that my sister and Admiral Mertz will evict these people from the Imperial Palace. That's going to cause more problems, I'm sure, but it's our birthright."

Jebediah laughed again. "While we're willing to ally ourselves with these people, they represent the past, not the future. When the time comes, if you can take the Imperial Palace, do so with our blessing. Many places in the world could use advanced people like these. They will adapt.

"Now, let's go upstairs and watch this wondrous process. I can't wait to see our city once more providing for itself."

She walked beside the man as they headed toward the lift. Her thoughts weren't on the fusion plant, though. She was worried about Kelsey and the rest.

They had the hardest job at this point, and everything rested on them being able to get away cleanly. Julia hoped they had a little bit of luck on their side because if they didn't, things were going to get really, really ugly.

* * *

TALBOT LED CHLOE toward the room where the others kept Jake Peters. Four guards were walking behind them now, and he was beginning to suspect that gaining access to the Marine Raider was going to be difficult.

Nevertheless, they were going to get him out right now, or someone was going to bleed. Kelsey had already said that the pinnaces were ready to go, so all he had to do was get Peters, get to the hangar, and they'd be on their way.

There were several more guards outside the entryway to the area where Peters was kept, and they didn't look happy to see Talbot. One of them stepped forward and raised a hand. "The god has declined to see you. Leave."

"I think I'd like to hear that from the god," Talbot said easily.

He sent an implant message to Peters that the man immediately accepted.

We're being denied entrance.

They've doubled the guard inside, so I think they know something is going on.

We'll be inside in just a minute. We'll handle the guards outside. You take care of the ones in there.

He killed the connection, drew his stunner, and fired from his hip on wide beam. That took down all the guards in front of him but wasn't sufficient to penetrate the door. Behind him, Chloe whirled in place at the same time, taking out the guards trailing them. Moments later, they were the only ones awake in the hall.

It took them a couple of moments to figure out how to open the doors, and by the time they'd done so, they saw that Peters had taken care of his own guards with the stunner that Talbot had slipped him earlier.

The former Marine Raider looked down at the weapon and grinned lopsidedly at Talbot. "It's been a long time since I fought anybody and even longer since I've held an Imperial weapon in my hand. It kind of felt good."

"Keep watch while Chloe and I get everybody inside," he said. "As soon as we're done, we're getting the hell out of here."

The two of them quickly dragged all the guards inside the room and dumped them beside the main door. Then, with Chloe leading the way in her armor, he hefted Peters over his shoulder, and they headed toward the hangar.

They were definitely committed now. They either had to get to the hangar, or they'd never escape.

His hopes of avoiding trouble ended when a trio of guards came around the corner ahead of them and saw him carrying Peters. Two of them immediately charged while the last one ducked back out of sight, already screaming.

Chloe stunned the first two even as they were raising their weapons to fire, and then the three of them rushed down the stairs that they'd been headed toward.

They ran into a couple guards when they exited on the hangar level. Since they'd had their weapons out, it looked as if they'd run out of patience for Kelsey, too.

Talbot locked the door controls once they were inside the hangar. The locals would probably get through soon enough, but the doors were thick. That would hopefully delay them long enough to get the pinnaces out of the Imperial Palace and clear of its defenses.

He doubted very seriously that they'd fire any of the weapons designed to shoot aircraft down. That would garner the attention of the AI in orbit. Unless they were suicidal, as soon as the pinnaces were clear, they were safe.

Since the ramps to both pinnaces were lowered, and he could see that they were both under power, he just picked the closest one and raced inside it, gesturing for Chloe to get into the other.

It took him half a minute to secure Peters in one of the harnesses and race to the flight deck. Kelsey was seated in the pilot's seat, and it looked like she was in the final stages of getting ready to take off.

He dropped into the copilot's seat and strapped himself in. "Where's everybody else?"

"Jared's in the other pinnace. Carl, Austin, and Ralph are working to override the lock on the bay doors. Whoever was here last sealed it down pretty good. If they can't get the manual locks undone, we're screwed."

"Then let's hope they figure it out."

Looking through the viewports at the front of the pinnace, he saw the three working at a panel beside the large, blast-proof doors. They were hunched over and talking back and forth while Carl did something inside the panel.

Through the ramp that was still open, Talbot heard what sounded like a loud thumping somewhere behind them. The locals were trying to get into the hangar.

"I should probably take care of that," he said, starting to undo his restraints.

"Stay where you are," Kelsey said. "I think Carl just did it."

He looked forward and saw that Carl had turned and raised both of his thumbs toward the ceiling. The three of them raced back toward the pinnaces.

"I've used my codes to override the lockout," Kelsey said. "That should get the doors moving. Carl and the rest are headed for Jared's pinnace. Raise the ramp."

He did so remotely, and moments later, the large hatch at the end of the room began slowly rising. As soon as the ramp status went green, Kelsey lifted the pinnace off the deck and began edging toward the opening.

As soon as she could, Kelsey added a little bit more thrust and went under the door. Talbot saw that the exit led into a tunnel that was probably heavily shielded because no one really wanted their enemies to know what was going on underneath their homes.

A minute later, he saw another hatch in front of them that had already opened, and beyond that was sunlight fading into dusk. Kelsey brought them through the opening, and they rose into the air as she applied power and sent them racing over the darkening forest below them.

"Jared's out of the tunnel," she said. "I just sent the signal to lock the exit down again. As soon as we were through the first blast door, I closed it behind us. They won't be chasing us. Unless they're stupid, we're done here."

"Are you going to be able to use it to get back in?" he asked. "When we come back, we're going to need a way to get inside that facility. Being able to fly in right under their noses would be useful."

She shrugged. "We can hope, but we probably shouldn't count on it. There are other ways in, and they can't lock me out of the computer systems. I can undo any security measure they enact by fiat. But that's a problem for another day."

He settled back into his seat as she took the pinnace low over the ground, ducking in between hills and keeping them from rising too high. She wouldn't want to give the AI a chance to notice them. With their suspicions up, they'd be looking. Even with Marine Raider stealth technology, they didn't really want to take too many chances.

They had the override. Now all they had to do was get it safely past the AIs. And, of course, escape the Terra system itself.

He didn't try to fool himself. That was going to be tricky. Even with pinnaces like these, they couldn't just waltz right past the ships up there. They'd have to trust to luck to give them a break when the time came.

One way or the other, they were almost done on Terra.

34

Carl watched through the scanners as the pinnaces slowly glided over the ruined megacity of Frankfort. Kelsey and the admiral had landed shortly after escaping the Imperial Palace and waited for the moon to set and leave everything in complete darkness. They hadn't wanted to tempt fate by landing in the city while it was still possible someone would see them.

With the stealth material that the pinnaces were made out of, they should be safe from detection by the AI or the ships in orbit. If not, they'd hardly have time to know, because a kinetic strike would take them out before they had more than a few seconds' warning.

Since they didn't want to have the pinnaces visible from orbit after they landed, they'd needed a place large enough to get them under cover. They'd chosen a building that had once been some kind of sports arena.

They had no idea what the interior conditions would be like, but the plan was to fly through the partially collapsed roof and into the interior, gliding into an area that wouldn't be visible from above. They'd just have to hope that there wasn't another collapse while they were there.

Kelsey and the admiral brought their pinnaces in slowly and carefully, aligning them with the section of collapsed roof until they were just a few meters above the debris on the floor before gliding over to a relatively clear area near one of the remaining interior walls. There, they set down and deactivated everything once they'd dropped the ramps.

He led his people and Lieutenant Laird down the ramp, covering the area with one of the flechette rifles. There was no sign of movement, but the shadows seemed to twitch in every direction he looked.

Over at the other pinnace, Talbot came down the ramp holding the crippled Marine Raider with Kelsey right behind him. Carl heard Admiral Mertz joining him as well.

Carl couldn't believe that they'd retrieved the override and actually escaped the Imperial Palace. That was a *huge* victory.

"How are we going to find a way to an area that we're familiar with?" Carl asked as they gathered.

"The city has some major trunks laid out in a grid pattern," Kelsey said. "It won't be hard to get underground and find one of those. Then it's just a matter of letting them know that we're here without triggering some type of hostile response."

"We used to have a team stationed here in Frankfort," Peters said. "They lasted about twenty years. I suppose that might seem like a long time, but the resistance forces were supposed to operate for much longer and train the civilians to resist as well. We did that, but a couple of groups got ambitious and tried to do too much too soon.

"Back then, Frankfort was still just an average city, though occupied by the rebels. The AIs didn't show their ugly hand then, but somehow, they figured out what was going on all over Terra and began hunting the resistance teams.

"One by one, they fell out of contact until there were only a few of us left. My team got ambushed maybe five years after the group here in Frankfort vanished. The last operational group was gone within two years of that."

"I suppose no one will ever know what really happened to them," Talbot said. "Five hundred years is a long time, and over a hundred since the AIs brought the hammer down. I'm sure it was worse in a lot of places."

Carl nodded. "The core worlds were spared some of the most horrible things the AIs did. In some out-of-the-way places, they just dropped people into the Stone Age or blocked the supplies necessary for them to survive. On Avalon, we were lucky."

"Sometimes you make your own luck," Peters said. "It looks like that's what you've done. You should be proud of that."

Once they'd secured the pinnaces, they found their way down to the tunnels underneath the city and began making their way toward the still-occupied sections. It didn't take long at all for them to run into the inhabitants.

Thankfully, the locals had been warned that they were coming. Once everyone was sure that there wasn't going to be violence, the residents quickly escorted them down to the area where the fusion plant was being assembled.

Carl had Kelsey and Talbot hold his arms while he got out of his armor and dressed in clothes the locals scrounged up for him. The people from the palace almost certainly wouldn't recognize him since he'd had his helmet on most of the time he'd been there.

After making sure that his friends and compatriots would go somewhere else while he covertly watched the reassembly and reactivation of the fusion plant, he walked into the large room. As expected, none of the people from the Imperial Palace paid him the slightest bit of attention.

To the uninitiated, it was unbelievable that a fusion plant could be disassembled or reassembled in such a short time frame, but everything was modular. So long as it was done correctly and carefully, the process didn't have to take a long time.

Thankfully, the original mounts were still there in the plascrete floor. Basically, all the technicians had to do was drop the pieces where they needed to be, bolt them down, and add on the modules as they got to that part of the assembly.

Once it was fully assembled and the shielding was installed, the technicians began running tests. Carl made sure to be standing right there and going over everything remotely. They wouldn't know that he was looking over their proverbial shoulders, but he'd see everything.

While he was no expert, he'd had to learn a fair bit about fusion plants over the last several years, and he knew how to let the equipment guide the safety checks for him.

He expected at least a few things to be questionable, but the fusion plant had been shut down in good order and was undamaged. Everything started up just the way it was supposed to. All systems green.

They weren't putting out any power because the technicians had cut all the feeds going out to the rest of the city. It would've been stupid to bring the system online and then have it light up the city for the AI to see from orbit.

Once the work was fully completed, the guards from Frankfort escorted the technicians and fighters from the Imperial Palace to the lift and took them down. From there, they'd be put on the train and sent back to the Imperial Palace. When they arrived, they'd undoubtedly find the place in an uproar, but the deed was done.

Carl turned toward Jebediah once they'd departed. "We're going to need to know where you want power. The closer it is to the surface, the more likely you're going to do something that draws unwanted attention. I suggest you keep the lighting and power to this level and lower to reduce the risk."

The large man nodded. "That's what we were thinking as well. If we can make certain that only those areas and the maglev platform are isolated, that will allow us to operate the way we want.

"Once the others get back to the Imperial Palace, I feel certain that they'll cut power, so we need to spend the time to make certain that we get those areas connected and that nothing else is going to be affected."

"I'll be able to run power down to the area that they're currently energizing without any problems. It should only take a couple of minutes since it's already proven to be isolated. From there, it won't be hard to expand along the levels that we want one step at a time.

"I'll be able to show your people what needs to be done with the fusion plant reasonably quickly. The maintenance processes aren't all that complicated. They just have to be done on time and in a precise manner.

"I've got a lot of files on the operation and maintenance of this kind of equipment that I can upload to your computers now that you can use them. With the files in the fusion plant itself, those will help you keep it running. I'm hoping that the people from the Imperial Palace will come back and you can formalize arrangements with them. If not, I think you can learn what you need and manage."

Connecting just the areas that were now covered by power from the maglev platform was simple enough. Once he'd accomplished that, Carl brought the fusion plant up from standby to its minimal power production settings and verified that everything was working as designed.

When they finally cut the power, the output from this plant would be more than enough to make up for the loss. Since they hadn't died in a kinetic strike, the shielding was doing its job, too.

Because he was linked to the power system, he saw when the power along the maglev line cut out and knew that the train must've made its way all the way back to the Imperial Palace.

He made sure that power to the train systems remained unpowered and tagged the controls to sound an alarm if they powered up again. They'd know if the others were coming back, and they'd be ready for them if they did.

The process of turning the power on in the lower levels of the city was going to take hours, but it should be straightforward. It would easily be dawn by the time he was done, but then they'd finally be able to leave Terra and go back to the stars.

He was so ready for that.

* * *

As DAWN WAS BREAKING, Jared once again met with Mordechai in his high tower overlooking Frankfort. They stood there a while, just staring out over the ruined megacity without saying anything. Jared was content to let the man speak in his own time.

Eventually, Mordechai turned to face him. "You've done everything that you promised. The lower levels of the city are once again safe to travel, and we have power that we haven't had in a hundred years.

"With the power restored, Carl has shown us how to retrieve the information that we need from the computers that were dead. It's a good beginning. It will take us a long time to return to the level of knowledge that our forefathers had, but we will one day do so.

"Jebediah has turned all of the equipment that once belonged to the Marine Raiders over to your people. My people are even now carrying it to be loaded on your pinnaces."

"We hope to return one day and help you start rebuilding Terra," Jared said. "I wish we could leave someone with the kind of training that you need behind, but we can't afford to spare anyone. Take small steps, Leader Mordechai. Don't take chances with the AI. With any luck, it will be dead or under our control inside a year."

Mordechai cocked his head slightly to the side. "Do you truly believe it will be that easy? That it will only take such a short amount of time?"

"You've got a point," he admitted. "While it might be inside a year, it might be many years. Or it might never happen at all. The fight we're waging is going to be a hard one. We're the underdogs, and we know it.

"The system where the artificial intelligence was created and resides is going to be more strongly defended than anything we've faced thus far. I've got a fleet of warships that will help us, but even that might not be enough. To win this war, we're going to have to take a lot of chances. Chances that under other circumstances I might not take.

"Just like you, we'll have to do the best we can. If you don't hear from us again, I guess that will tell you what happened to us."

The older man stuck out his hand, and Jared took it.

"I wish you well, Admiral Mertz. You and your people have a chance to undo some of the most terrible wrongs that have ever been done to humanity. I hope that you can stop the evil that we caused and once again allow us to live free.

"If there's anything that my people or I can do or provide that would help in your task, you need only ask, and it shall be given to you."

"I appreciate the offer, but I think we have everything we need," Jared said with a smile. "Thank you, Mordechai, and good luck to you and your people."

An hour later, Jared was aboard the pinnace he was piloting, and the ramp was raised. Using short-range communications, he verified that Kelsey was also ready to take off. This was going to be one of the most nerve-racking parts of their escape from Terra. If anything was going to go to hell, now was when it would happen.

He'd had the others bring Major Peters onto the flight deck and strapped him into the copilot's seat beside him. Since he didn't have anyone to help control the pinnace, he might as well talk to their newest associate.

The disabled man looked a bit uncertain, so Jared spoke up. "Having second thoughts?"

Peters shook his head. "No. I want this more than anything, but I feel a little out of my depth. It's been a long time since I've done anything other than merely existing.

"I know that Doctor Stone says that she can get me fitted with artificial limbs and on the road to recovery, but that's a little frightening. I've spent so much time as a cripple that I'm not sure if I know how to be normal again."

Jared checked his console and then nodded. "You can't change the past. You'll never be the man you once were. What you can do is become the man you want to be."

The former Marine Raider nodded appreciatively. "That's deep, Admiral. I suppose with all the trouble that you've been through over the last few years, you've got some experience at coming out the other side now. I appreciate your insight.

"Once we get to Twilight River, how are we going to get into the system and onto the station where the AI is located?"

Jared shrugged slightly. "We'll have to figure that out once we've rendezvoused with my fleet. It may be that we have enough force to break through the inevitable blockade. Or, since the enemy doesn't know about multi-flip points or far flip points—which I'll have to explain to you later— we might be able to find a back door that lets us into the system with them none the wiser.

"Frankly, the latter option is my preferred method. If we can gain access without any of the defenders being aware that we're even there, we can smother the damned machine before it can raise the alarm."

"*Persephone Two*, this is *Persephone One*," Kelsey said over the short-range com. "I'm ready to lift. I'll take the lead as we head north. Once we're far enough out of the orbital coverage pattern, then we'll head straight up."

"I'll be right behind you," Jared responded. "Let's do this."

He brought his controls out of standby and lifted the pinnace off the ground, pivoting it in place slowly to follow Kelsey out into the sunlight.

Once again, they were taking a chance by leaving during the day, but the pinnaces were extremely hard to detect. Rather than wait for night, which wasn't much of an impedance to the AIs, he'd decided that he'd rather be gone.

It was time to end this chapter of their lives.

35

Kelsey took her pinnace northward with Jared close behind her, and Talbot sitting quietly beside her. As they traveled, the ruined cities and towns that they passed transitioned to an untamed wilderness. She crossed a small stretch of ocean and then onto the ice shelf beyond.

She knew roughly where Terra's axis was located, but she didn't need to be over it for this to work. In fact, it might be better if she wasn't so precise. That was the way machines thought.

Once she reached a frozen, isolated area that suited their needs, she double-checked to verify that her stealth systems were fully operational. Then she called Jared to make certain that he'd done the same, even though she knew that he already had. It was far better to be sure.

Only then did she lift the nose of her pinnace and begin rising from the surface of Terra.

Rather than rushing up to orbit, she lifted as slowly as she could while still maintaining good headway. She wasn't going to go fast enough to cause a disturbance in the atmosphere that might give them away.

Long minutes later, they finally exited the atmosphere and were in space. Kelsey didn't dare use active scanners, but her passives told the same story that Angela had passed on to them. The area around the equator, which held all of the orbitals around Terra and the AI, was packed with ships.

Quite a few more than there had been here when they'd arrived, in fact. Though her detection ability was limited on passive scanners, she thought that many of them were bigger than destroyers.

Thankfully, while the enemy had the planet encircled, their coverage at the poles only consisted of a few automated destroyers that were scattered fairly wide. They obviously didn't consider the chances of someone coming out this way very high.

Score one for her outguessing them. The AI was confident that it had destroyed their only means of transport. While it was covering its bases, it thought there was little chance unprotected humans could survive and escape from such an inhospitable place.

In fact, this would've been an excellent place to hide facilities meant to survive the invasion. She wondered if they were traveling over lost habitats deep under the ice where the descendants of the survivors even now lived out their lives.

The possibility couldn't be dismissed out of hand. Not for Terra or any other world. That was something to think about later.

"It looks like we've got a couple of destroyers that could be in position to detect us if we get unlucky," she told Jared over the short-range com. "I'll maneuver to avoid them as best I can. Once we get away from Terra, we should be able to rendezvous with *Persephone* without any issues."

"What do you think our chances are?" he asked, his voice quiet.

"Decent. That doesn't mean we can't have a run of bad luck, but I'm hopeful that we can pull this off. It would really suck to come this far only to have them spot us just as we're getting away."

"Don't jinx us. Positive thoughts only."

She took a deep breath and pushed her worries away. Slowly—ever so slowly—she edged between the destroyers that were farthest apart. The strength of the scanners searching for them rose toward the detection threshold with every second.

When she and Jared were as close to the destroyers as they were going to get, the scanner strength hovered just a few notches below disaster, but the automated vessels didn't react.

She only started breathing easily again once they'd left the blockade around Terra behind them and were in open space and headed for *Persephone*. Their passive scanners wouldn't be capable of picking the ship up as they approached, but she had no doubt *Persephone* would be right where she was supposed to be.

"I see her," Jared finally signaled. "Look off a bit to port and up."

She turned her eyes in the direction indicated. *Persephone* was only a dot at this range, but she was growing steadily larger.

Once her former command had come close, Kelsey lined up with one of the docking cradles. Ten seconds later, the pinnace made contact, and *Persephone* latched on. Kelsey watched as the controls locked everything down and saw the airlock seal go green.

Only then did she let out a ragged breath. "I can't believe that we made it," she muttered.

Talbot reached over and took her hand. "I knew you'd make this work. You always come through."

She laughed a bit shakily. "I had my doubts this time. This mission was worse than anything we've ever been through."

"Come on. Let's get out of this tin can."

Once everyone had exited both of the pinnaces, she headed straight for the bridge and found Angela seated in the command chair. The other woman rose and wrapped her arms around her.

"It's so good to have you back home," the big woman said. "I've been worried sick."

Kelsey squeezed her back. "We've got a lot of stories to tell, but first, we need to get out of here before someone spots us. How long is it going to take us to get to the flip point you found?"

"A while," Angela said as she sat back down. "That's why it's called a *far* flip point. Thankfully, it looks like the outer system is only intermittently patrolled. There are a couple of destroyers that might become problematic, but we won't know that's the case until we get a little farther out."

Kelsey gestured at the main screen in front of the bridge. "All those ships in orbit around Terra. We didn't see anything like them in the system when we arrived. Where did they come from?"

Angela's face scrunched into a frown. "The Alpha Centauri flip point was heavily guarded with both ships and stations. Almost all of them were shut down, and that's why we didn't spot them before you went to Terra.

"Once things started happening, the AI reactivated a bunch of the ships and brought them in. It also increased patrols in the system. It looks like you made them very nervous."

"Why would they have *that* flip point guarded?" Kelsey asked, feeling her brows knit. "Alpha Centauri is a cul-de-sac and not one with any habitable worlds. Why guard it?"

Angela shrugged. "It may be that's where the AI parked the inactive ships that it used during the rebellion. They won the fight, and they probably still had a lot of ships when they were done. They might've taken a lot of them to Alpha Centauri to make certain that no one could get to them, like the wrecks they put around Boxer Station. We don't really have a way to be sure."

"And we've got more pressing matters to attend to," Kelsey agreed. "That mystery is going to have to wait for another time. Right now, we need to get out of here and rendezvous with Jared's fleet."

Angela nodded. "We're already on our way. The nightmare is just about over. Why don't you and the rest go take a hot shower, get something to eat, and relax for a bit. Let me do the driving."

Kelsey was more than willing to do that, but she was worried that something could still go wrong. She wouldn't relax entirely until they'd left the Terra system behind.

* * *

An hour after they'd arrived aboard *Persephone*, Talbot was standing in the cramped medical center. Jake Peters was about to undergo the surgery to install Marine Raider–grade artificial limbs. He figured that he owed it to the man to be there.

He also needed to get Kelsey down here at some point to get her thigh regenerated, but figured that wouldn't happen until they'd made their escape from the Terra system.

Lily quickly had Peters on the table and had applied the somatic stimulator. With him fully asleep, her professional face quickly transitioned to one that looked concerned to Talbot.

"What's wrong?" he asked.

"Unlike replacing Julia's burned-out artificial eye—which went off without a hitch—this surgery is going to be difficult. These injuries have been scarred for a very long time. Longer than I would've imagined possible. They're going to be extremely resistant to regeneration, I suspect.

"I ran him through the regenerator back at the Imperial Palace, but I didn't have the time and equipment that I needed to go through and remove the worst of the scar tissue. Once that's done, I'm going to have to attach the artificial limbs in such a way that they're permanently bonded into place.

"I wasn't lying when I told Major Peters that I can do it, but I'll admit that it's going to be one of the more difficult surgeries that I've attempted. Success is not guaranteed."

She took a deep breath and stretched her back. "His recovery is going to be painful and difficult, too. He's going to have to go through retraining on a similar scale to what Kelsey needed after she was augmented.

"He's going to get frustrated and depressed, but he's still going to have to work his butt off if he expects to make a full recovery. That's where I'm hoping you'll come in. You know how hard it's going to be, and you can help him."

"I'll be there for him," Talbot assured her. "Better yet, Kelsey will be there. She'll shame him into doing the very best he can. After all, can you imagine a big, tough guy like this failing to perform when she's watching?"

Lily chuckled. "No, I suppose that's a pretty good motivator. It's worked for the entirety of human existence, so it'll probably work this time, too."

She took a deep breath and got to work.

As a marine, Talbot had seen more than his fair share of blood and injuries, but the process of opening a man up to get at badly scarred tissue had a kind of gruesome feel to it.

For whatever reason, the work she did on the man's ruined eye socket was the worst. Yes, Peters had had the eye removed after the injury, and a civilian-grade model installed. It had burned out when the AI had used the EMP weapons on Terra a hundred years ago.

That didn't mean that whoever had done the work had done the best job possible. It also didn't mean that someone that had lived as long as Peters had hadn't developed scar tissue where another person might not during an average—or even long—lifetime.

It felt like an hour had passed by the time she finished cleaning up the wound where his eye had once been. A check of his internal chronometer showed Talbot that it was less than half that.

No matter how uncertain Lily said she'd felt, that didn't slow her sure, quick motions as she did the work. Once she'd regenerated the tissue around his eye socket as much as she could, she carefully fitted an artificial replacement into the eye socket and began building the flesh back around it.

Talbot was always amazed at how well Imperial prosthetics could be made to replace something. They looked completely normal to the naked eye. He knew that based on the eye that Julia had. It had all the same abilities as her original Marine Raider augmentation. From what he understood, it even had a few extras.

The man's arm and legs took hours more for Lily to prepare the stumps and fit the prosthetics. Attaching the nerves was kind of gruesome, but Talbot accepted that was just part of doing business.

Then came the man's mangled hand. She cleaned the stumps of the missing fingers and attached prosthetic ones to replace what was lost. Then she opened the hand itself and reconstructed it to mitigate the damage done during the original injury.

Once that was complete, she began working on the other injuries he'd suffered. Some of that involved rebreaking bones that hadn't healed correctly and excising more scar tissue that had formed inside his torso.

It was a grueling, ugly task, but she eventually had him wheel Peters to the big regenerator next to the bulkhead and started it up.

She stretched her back before facing him. "I suspect I'm going to have to do some fine-tuning on just about everything, but I think I've made a good start. I've never dealt with long-term injuries like this before, so I'm going to reserve judgment until I have a better idea of what I'm dealing with, but his prognosis is good.

"I've also taken some tissue samples so that I can try to understand how his body is adapting to such an extended life span. It would be a lot better for us going forward if we really understood the process a lot better. I'm going to have to go over everything with the Imperial Physician, and I want to have the answers."

Talbot clapped a hand on her shoulder. "You did one hell of a job, Lily. I didn't think it was possible to put someone back together that way again. You're amazing."

"I just wish I was back aboard *Caduceus*," she said glumly. "I'd feel a lot better with more facilities and extra hands to help keep an eye on his recovery. If we can rendezvous with the fleet soon, I might take him over there to finish his recovery."

He watched her washing her hands, suspecting that she wasn't done talking. She confirmed that when she turned toward him, her face a mask of worry.

"Do you think we really have a chance at this? I know we've got the override, but defeating the AI in its lair seems so… daunting."

"We're going to beat this thing," he said. "We're going to take back the Empire. Don't doubt that for a second."

She nodded, likely not convinced by his projected confidence. "You should probably go check on your wife and Julia. You know, to make sure that they aren't getting into trouble."

"I'm not sure *anybody* could do that," he said with a chuckle. "But, I'll try."

With that, Talbot left the medical center and went in search of his wife. She'd want a report on what had happened with Peters, and he was finally ready to see this damned mission end.

36

————

Julia wandered the corridors of *Persephone* after Doctor Stone replaced her burned-out eye. This was a tiny ship. Significantly smaller than a destroyer. It also had a number of features that she didn't understand.

In particular, there was a room that had a series of large tubes going from floor to ceiling that had openings for large pods to be loaded in. She supposed they were escape pods, but why were they gathered in one place like this? She made a note to ask Kelsey about them once they were safely clear of danger.

At that point, she decided that she'd put off the inevitable for as long as she could and made her way to the bridge. Like the rest of the vessel, it was laid out differently than most Fleet ships. It was a much closer affair, with fewer seats, and it was arranged in such a way that everyone could see everyone else. It felt communal.

Angela was sitting in the center seat. Julia had to stop herself from rushing up to the woman and giving her a big hug because this wasn't *her* Angela. This was the Angela from Kelsey's universe.

While that woman was probably good friends with Kelsey, the two probably weren't as close as she and her Angela were. Though the relationship between her and her Angela had never been romantic, it was as close as Kelsey's relationship with Talbot otherwise.

Angela looked up at Julia and smiled as she rose to her feet. "You must be Julia. I've heard a lot about you, and I feel like I've known you forever. Of course, I feel the same way about Kelsey. Welcome aboard *Persephone*."

"It's good to meet you as well," Julia said. "In my universe, I've known you for years. You were the marine assigned to keep me safe, just like Talbot did for Kelsey, minus the kissing. We're friends, and it feels that way deep in my heart, so if I seem a bit too familiar, I apologize."

That brought a high-amperage smile to the tall woman's face, a grin that Julia remembered very fondly.

"You're not going to bother me with anything like that. Honestly, I hope that one of these days, I'll have an opportunity to visit your universe and meet myself. I think that would be an extraordinary sort of thing. If I might ask, why didn't your version of me come with you?"

"It's complicated, but you were needed there. Honestly, we really didn't expect this to be a long-term sort of thing, and I'd already brought Scott Roche with me."

Her face fell at the memory. "He didn't make it, and you're probably going to be very angry with me when I get back home, but the situation is what it is. Do you mind if we talk in a less public setting?"

Angela gestured toward the corridor that Julia had just come up through. "The wardroom is just this way. They'll call me if anything comes up that needs my attention."

Once they'd made their way to the small room, Angela closed the door and raised an eyebrow. "What can I help you with, Highness?"

Unsure of exactly what the best way to start was, Julia decided to just lay out the entire situation. "I've spent a good amount of time with your husband, and I've made the decision to pursue his doppelgänger in my universe and convince him to become my consort. If he's anything like your husband, he's just the kind of man that I need at my side to help save the Empire."

Angela blinked. "Of all the things you could've said, that's something I'd never have expected to hear. It doesn't surprise me, because Carl is a terrific man and a brilliant scientist, but I've never really pegged him as your type. Isn't he a little… geeky for you?"

"Kelsey and I aren't completely in sync," Julia said with a small shake of her head. "I'm a lot less prone to break things than she is. I think that she found the perfect man for her when she found Talbot, but somebody like that isn't for me. I believe that Carl might be.

"And with that in mind, I'd like to get your advice on how best to pursue him. Plus, I owe you an apology. Circumstances being what they were down on the surface, he had to help me get into my powered armor, and I think that as his wife, you probably should know that I was naked in front of him."

Regardless of what Carl had said, she expected Angela to be upset about that. It shocked her deeply when the big woman laughed and shook her head.

"Highness, I'm a Marine Raider and was a marine before that. I can't even count the number of people who've seen me naked. Also, I have no doubt that my husband was the perfect gentleman. So long as nothing improper happened—and I'm absolutely certain that nothing did—then you've got no reason to be worried about me.

"I'll be happy to tell you all about Carl and give you my best advice. Honestly, it took me a long time to understand the kind of person that he really is. If your version of Carl is anything like mine, you're going to need that information to plan your campaign, because this is not going to be something that happens overnight.

"Now, if that's all, we really should be getting back to the bridge. We're coming up on the area around the far flip point, and there's still a couple of distant patrol ships that we want to make sure don't cross our path before we leave the system."

Somewhat shocked at how easily the conversation had gone, Julia followed Angela back to the bridge and wasn't surprised to find Kelsey and Talbot already there.

Angela sat in the command seat just as one of the people around her looked up from his console. "One of the destroyers patrolling the outer system just changed course and is headed toward the area around the far flip point. It's going to pass within a fair distance of us."

"Can we change course enough to avoid them entirely?" Angela asked.

The man shook his head. "No, ma'am. We don't have enough time at this low rate of speed."

"Then let's hope that they don't see us. If they do, we might manage to blow the hell out of them, but that's going to clue the enemy in on the fact that we're out here. If they ever suspect anything like the far flip points or multi-flip points exist, I can't begin to tell you how screwed humanity is. That's our secret weapon, and we've got to keep news of them to ourselves."

At that moment, Mertz entered the bridge. From his expression, he'd overheard enough to realize the situation they were in. He stepped over to the command chair and put his hand on the seat back.

"It looks like the moment of truth is upon us," he said.

Kelsey clapped Mertz on the shoulder. "It's time to roll the dice. No snake eyes."

Julia shook her head. Where the hell did her doppelgänger keep coming up with all these strange sayings? She'd never understand her.

* * *

JARED STOOD BEHIND ANGELA, and between Kelsey and Julia as the Marine Raider strike ship slowly crept toward the far flip point. It was marked on the screen with a small blue dot.

The red dot approaching *Persephone* represented the Rebel Empire destroyer. Its course wasn't directly toward the flip point, and it was going to come closer to *Persephone* than the flip point itself, which made it a real hazard.

"Can we reduce our detection threshold?" Mertz asked. "What if we stop thrusting entirely and just drift?"

Angela considered that for a moment and then shook her head. "I would suggest, however, that we don't stop moving entirely. Maybe we can just give ourselves a little angular momentum and take ourselves as far away from the destroyer's course as we can.

"At the very least, that will keep us a bit further away from the detection threshold and reduce the time that we're in danger."

Without waiting to see if he agreed, Angela ordered the helmsman to make the course change, and the strike ship turned away from the flip point. Jared watched as the enemy destroyer kept coming closer and closer, waiting for the moment it turned toward them.

And thankfully, that moment never came.

They waited until the destroyer was out of detection range before they resumed their course toward the flip point. A little bit more than an hour later, they were safely there, and at a stop.

"I assume you've already sent a probe to the other side," he said. "What did you find?"

"It's not an occupied system," Angela said, turning to face him slightly. "It's not on any of the old trade routes, so the odds of any vessels detecting us there are low, particularly since we'll be appearing far outside the normal area where any ship would be.

"With any luck, we can wait there for the fleet to join us. It might take them a while to get to our location, but I think it's better if we wait for them than try to meet up somewhere else. We're isolated and need to play defense."

He couldn't argue with that. "Then that's what we'll do. Flip the ship, Major."

Angela gave the order, and moments later, the transition was complete. He waited for the passive scanners to report and relaxed when they said nothing was near them.

"I'm pulling data from the drone we left here," Angela said. "If anyone's been through, it'll have records. And we're good. No ships have transited this system since I put the probe here four days ago. If the system is used as a gateway from one place to another, it's not used very often."

Jared stretched his neck, feeling good for the first time in what felt like months. "Once we get the fleet to our location, our next step has to be Twilight River. We can't go in through the front door, but with our ability to use multi-flip points and far flip points, there's a decent chance that we can get in through the back door.

"It's going to be challenging to find the other end of an undetected flip point that leads to where we want to go, but we're going to have to spend the time doing just that. We can't count on using a hammer to break our way in."

"What if we can't find a way in?" Julia asked.

"Then we do it the hard way," he admitted. "We'd put the fleet through the flip point that we know leads to Twilight River and force our way through. I'm certain that it's heavily guarded, and if I were the AI, I'd do everything in my power to make sure that that system is invulnerable."

"Say we manage to sneak through a back door," Kelsey said. "You know the station is going to be surrounded by every ship they can stuff in there, just like Terra was. It's going to be impossible to get on board the station without being seen."

He smiled. "Getting on board the station is a Marine Raider job, so I'll leave that to you."

His sister grimaced. "At the moment, we've got three Marine Raiders and a few others that are partially ready. Oh, and one in the medical center. That's not exactly a Marine Raider strike force of old."

"We're not going to get to Twilight River today. We're not even going to get there next week. By the time we finally have a way in, months will have passed.

"Once we get everybody in the fleet together, I believe you can use *Caduceus* to get more of your people transitioned. Hell, there's a ton of marines in the fleet that would kill for an opportunity like this. Pick the very best among them, and you'll have your strike force.

"By the time we're ready, *Persephone* is going to be stuffed to the gills with Marine Raiders. We'll get your crew transitioned as quickly as we can as well, but the main thing is getting our fighting force prepared for the assault.

"We've got to get our people on board that station. All we've got are two Marine Raider pinnaces. If we stack people in armor aboard those, that means we can get almost a hundred and fifty people in regular marine armor. With the smaller Marine Raider version, maybe as many as a hundred and eighty. They're all we're going to have to make this work."

He looked around the bridge and at his friends. "Twilight River is coming, folks. This is a fight we can't afford to lose, and I want everyone's minds fully focused on winning it. When we get there, we're only going to get one chance at this. Let's make it count."

* * *

WANT to get updates from Terry about new books and other general nonsense going on in his life? He promises there will be cats. Go to TerryMixon.com/Mailing-List and sign up.

DID YOU ENJOY THIS BOOK? Please leave a review on Amazon. It only takes a minute to dash off a few words and that kind of thing helps Terry make a living as a writer and gets you new books faster.

WANT MORE BOOKS BY TERRY? Flip to the next page and grab one.

VISIT TERRY's Patreon page to find out how to get cool rewards and an early look at what he's working on at Patreon.com/TerryMixon.

ALSO BY TERRY MIXON

You can always find the most up to date listing of Terry's titles on his Amazon Author Page.

Note: the links below (ebook only, obviously) redirect you to my website where you can click a button to go to Amazon. This allows me to participate in Amazon's associates program and earn a little more. Sorry for any inconvenience.

ABOUT TERRY

#1 Bestselling Military Science Fiction author Terry Mixon served as a non-commissioned officer in the United States Army 101st Airborne Division. He later worked alongside the flight controllers in the Mission Control Center at the NASA Johnson Space Center supporting the Space Shuttle, the International Space Station, and other human spaceflight projects.

He now writes full time while living in Texas with his lovely wife and a pounce of cats.

TerryMixon.com

a amazon.com/author/terrymixon

f facebook.com/TerryLMixon

|● patreon.com/TerryMixon

BB bookbub.com/authors/terry-mixon

g goodreads.com/TerryMixon